Books by Amy Lane

available at iUniverse and amazon.com

The Little Goddess series

Vulnerable
Wounded
Bound
Rampant

Bitter Moon

Bitter Moon I: Triane's Son Ascending
Bitter Moon II: Triane's Son Reigning

Available at Dreamspinner.com and amazon.com

Keeping Promise Rock
If I Must (Dreamspinner Advent Calendar Only)
Curious (Anthology)

RAMPANT

The fourth book of the
Little Goddess series

Amy Lane

iUniverse, Inc.
New York Bloomington

Rampant
The fourth book of the Little Goddess series

Copyright © 2010 Amy Lane

This is a work of fiction. All of the characters, names, incidents,
organizations, and dialogue in this novel are either the products
of the author's imagination or are used fictitiously.

iUniverse books may be ordered through booksellers or by contacting:

iUniverse
1663 Liberty Drive
Bloomington, IN 47403
www.iuniverse.com
1-800-Authors (1-800-288-4677)

ISBN: 978-1-4502-0010-3 (pbk)
ISBN: 978-1-4502-0011-0 (ebk)

Printed in the United States of America

iUniverse rev. date: 1/6/2010

About *Jack & Teague & Katy*—

If you haven't read *Jack & Teague & Katy—A Green's Haven adventure,* well, you should. The book, posted as a series of novellas on my website at www.greenshill.com takes place between the action in **Bound** and the action in **Rampant,** and introduces us to Jack, Teague, and Katy, who figure fairly prominently in **Rampant.** The last Jack & Teague adventure will be available sometime in March (Goddess and finances willing) as part of the complete selection of novellas, which I plan to release in print. It will serve as sort of an epilogue to **Rampant** and to Jack, Teague, & Katy's own personal story as well.

In the meantime, don't forget to check out their story! If nothing else, it will help you understand why Teague gets his own chapters here, because otherwise, you're going to be *seriously* wondering what his damage is, and, more importantly, why Bracken and Cory have let his lover, Jack, live so long. In order to find their stories (because my website is not as user friendly as I might wish) do the following:

1. Go to www.greenshill.com
2. Click on Amy's Writings
3. On the side menu, choose one of these stories: "Yearning" (story one), "Waiting" (story two), "Reaching" (story three), or "Changing" (story four), or "Becoming" (story five) and then enjoy!
4. E-mail me at amylane@greenshill.com and tell me if you like my guys! I've got a soft spot for them myself, and I hope you feel the same:-)

How do I love these people? Let me count the ways…

I love Roxie for her support and her wisdom and her willingness to regard sex as a spectator sport for my sake. (I also love her for writing 'lol' in the margins of my rough draft.)

I love Needletart for her humor, her dedication, and her willingness to tell me to 'edit the slimy out of the sex' in spite of the fact that she's a little embarrassed to say things like that, much less read them. (I love her for writing 'lol' in the margins too!)

I love Eric for his intelligence and his willingness to read anything I send him, in spite of the fact that he really doesn't swing the same way my characters do.

I love Littlewitch because she is there for me all the goddamned time, and because just when I think I couldn't suck any worse, she screams "Write more, dammit! I need more!" over e-mail, and sure enough, I manage to do more and do more better.

I love Archer for giving Green a lovely face and drool-worthy body.

I love my blogbuddies (you all know who you are) and the people on amazon. com and the folks at KTT who will ALWAYS lend me a sympathetic ear, and who know how to make me feel like it's all worth it, all the time.

I love everybody who has e-mailed me to let me know *Rampant* is on their high priority list and that Jack and Teague really ARE a hot couple.

And I love my family, more than I can say, because they love me in spite of all this nonsense, and they put up with an enormous amount of shit so that mommy can live her dream.

CONTENTS

Character Lexicon

Characters introduced in *Vulnerable*

Cory—Corinne Carol-Anne Kirkpatrick op Crocken Green started this little adventure as a gas station clerk, and then she met Adrian, a vampire who loved her, and Green, who loved them both. She is now married to Green, Bracken, and Nicky, carries three of Adrian's marks and so leads his kiss of vampires, and is still trying to get that degree.

Green—Vernal Green, Lord of Leaves and Shadows: The leader of most of the supernatural peoples in Northern California, Green is not a warrior. Instead he leads and heals with sex and love, and people would die to protect him.

Bracken—The youngest full-blooded sidhe on the hill, Bracken was Adrian's lover and fell in love with Cory at first sight. He stepped away from her then, because Adrian loved her and they didn't share well, but upon Adrian's death he became her full-time lover.

Adrian—Adrian started life as the sexually abused cabin boy whom Green rescued on his way to America. Adrian became a vampire so he wouldn't age and leave Green alone, and even after he fell in love with Cory, he couldn't survive without his ties to Green.

Arturo—Arturo came from the jungles of South America to the new world in the '50's, trying to find an easier life. He found Green's hill instead, and instead of conquering, fell exquisitely in love (in a very heterosexual way) with a leader who would lead with compassion instead of violence.

Grace—A devoted family woman, Grace was dying of untreated breast cancer in Redding, when Adrian heard her yearning to see her family grow, with or without her. He granted her wish and made her a vampire, and Grace has come to love her Green's hill family even more intensely than she loved the mortal family she left.

Mitch—Mitch was Renny's first lover. Renny loved him since they were kids—when Mitchell was accidentally transformed into a were-kitty, Renny actually seduced him so he'd bite her and turn her too. Mitch was skittish and independent, and refused to accept Green's generosity and live in the hill, and

Renny's heart was so twined with his that she almost lost all of her humanity when he was one of Sezan's first victims.

Max—Max is the police officer who tried to 'save' Cory from Green's hill when she first met him. In the end, Green's hill saved him, and he ended up beguiled by a girl who was more cat than human.

Renny—Renny became a werecat to follow her first husband, Mitch, into the life. When Mitch was killed, Renny's cat personality became dominant and nearly feral. She's become more human since she and Max have become a couple and gotten married… but not by much.

Marcus—Marcus was a history teacher with a passion for snow skiing. He's got curly brown hair, big brown eyes, and a teacher's affection for Cory, who wants to document the world they've found themselves in now that he has fangs and a taste for blood.

Phillip—Phillip was a stockbroker with a passion for snow skiing. After Marcus found him buried in an avalanche and brought him over as a vampire, the two spent twenty years struggling with their sexuality and their boundless love for each other. What they finally decided upon was a relationship based on the sentiment, "I apparently can't live without you, asshole," and that seems to be working for them.

Sezan—Part sea-nymph, part-human, Sezan is what happens when someone is warped from conception on. He came to Nor Cal to torment and kill Adrian—but he had help.

Crispin—Crispin was the kiss leader of the Folsom Vampires, until Sezan arrived and brainwashed/drugged/threatened him to force Crispin into Sezan's own vendetta.

Crocken & Blissa—Bracken's parents, Crocken and Blissa are a study in opposites. Blissa is a flittery, sex-kitten of a four-foot pixie, and Crocken looks like an un-dusted pile of rocks. Together (and with a little bit of Green's magic to make everything fit the way it should) they managed to produce Bracken, whom they love to distraction.

Leah—Leah's little brother died and Leah descended into a spiral of sex, drugs, and self-destruction. Adrian saved her from all of that, but Leah's emotional make-up does not include any sort of monogamous relationship.

Still, she misses the stability of having a small, nuclear family, and has spent years trying to find a balance in the hill.

Characters introduced in *Wounded*

Nicky—Nicky is an Avian--a shapeshifter who turns into a bird. He met Cory while she was attending C.S.U. San Francisco immediately after Adrian's death, when he was working for Goshawk, the bad guy. Nicky accidentally bonded to Green and Cory in the course of saving Bracken's life, but because he was trying to atone for his assault on Cory at the time, Green and Cory took them into their family—and their bed.

Mario—Mario was an Avian who worked for Goshawk, the bad-guy in *Wounded* who convinced Nicky to mind-rape Cory on their first date. Mario's wife, Beth, was killed in an assault on Green's hill, and Green gave Mario back his will to live. Mario is mid-height, stocky, and very proud of his Mexican heritage.

La Mark—La Mark is another sweet-tempered Avian who had the misfortune to meet up with Goshawk while struggling with his identity. Unfortunately, La Mark's identity is not a comfortable one—a gay, black Avian is sort of doomed wherever he goes, isn't he? In spite of that, La Mark is a nice guy with a sense of humor and a blinding smile.

Andres—Andres is the leader of the San Francisco vampires. In *Wounded*, he allied his vampires with Cory's—and passed up on an opportunity to take both Cory and Bracken into his bed.

Orson—Orson is the leader of the San Francisco werewolves. He's not a particularly physical fighter, but he is an aggressive advocate for his people.

Mist—Green's old lover, Mist betrayed Green to Titania and Oberon. When Green escaped their faerie hill, Mist watched jealously as Green fought for a place of his own. Mist was responsible for sending Sezan Adrian's way—he couldn't stand that Green was happy, especially with someone Mist considered inferior.

Morana—Mist's lover at the time of *Wounded*. She's mostly just a smug, superior, elitist bitch who thought Green was a good lay. For that alone we despise her.

Goshawk—Goshawk was the leader of the Avians in San Francisco. He was working on world domination when he convinced Nicky to mind-rape Cory in order to get her most powerful memories to drive his power. Nicky was guilt-ridden, and turned against his former leader in order to help the girl he hurt.

Timmy & Danny—Timmy and Danny were two of the Avians who were set against Green's hill. They were captured instead, and given sanctuary. Like La Mark, Mario, and Nicky, they chose to stay at the hill instead of rejoining Goshawk's forces.

Titania & Oberon—The traditional leaders of the sidhe in England, Titania and Oberon's court was full of sexual excesses and cruelty. They held Green a prisoner in their famed Faerie Hill because nobody could provide sexual satisfaction like Green. Green hoarded his power though, and eventually snuck himself and his lime trees out of their garden and across the sea.

Characters introduced in *Bound*

Chloe—Grace's bitter, unpleasant daughter. Chloe had to have her memories of her vampire mother and of Green's hill wiped in *Bound* because she was not the kind of mortal Green allowed at the hill. (i.e., she was a REAL bitch.)

Gavin & Graeme—Chloe's sons, they *adored* Green's hill and completely accepted all of the strangeness within. Once a year they come back to the hill—Green has arranged a sham 'camp' to cover for their chance to visit with their grandmother and all the other people they have come to love.

Sweet—Sweet is one of the more promiscuous sidhe at the hill—but also one of the most pleasant. She's also one of the three sidhe who are known for being a healer.

Ellen Beth—Ellen Beth was brought to the hill when her lover was infected with some poisonous blood. Her lover died horribly, and Ellen Beth was turned over to Sweet for emotional healing. Sweet decided to keep her, and Ellen Beth has been happy to be kept.

Eric—Eric is a were-coyote with a sad past and a long ago history with Green, Bracken, and Adrian. He is content to live in Austin and run his own company, until he meets up with Green and Green introduces him to Nicky. Both of them realize that they have something in common—too low key for the intense emotions of the hill, they both make better secondary characters—except to each other, where they are the heroes of their own story.

Kyle—The lone survivor of the Folsom vampires, Kyle's beloved, a girl named Davy, was killed because she and Cory vaguely resembled each other—and because they were friends. Cory took Kyle into her kiss and forced him to want to live.

Hallow—Hallow is a sidhe, and a professor at Sacramento State University where Cory and the other students attend school. He is also—by Green's request—a counselor for the students themselves. Although Green usually counsels his own people, he felt that he was way too close to the situation as Cory's lover *and* her leader to be objective or effective, and thus his trust in Hallow.

Characters introduced in *Jack & Teague (&Katy)*

Jack—Jack is actually a nice, quiet young man. When his sister—who became a werewolf by choice—is killed, Jack asks Green for some answers to her world and the people who would kill her. Paired with Teague to be human liaisons to Green's hill and to go out and deal with violent and legal matters outside the hill, Jack fell utterly and irrevocably in love with his damaged, noble partner. When the two of them become werewolves (Jack by accident and Teague by choice) Jack's transition to the hill is marred by his realization that Teague really is the great man Jack has always believed—and that means that his loyalties can not ever be exclusively Jack's.

Teague—Teague was brutally abused as a child and inculcated in the same ideas of hate and prejudice that killed Jack's sister. One night while hunting a werewolf, he is injured while saving the life of a young man who looks very human—and Adrian pays him back by bringing him to Green. From that moment on, he is Green's devoted subject. When Jack is injured and Cory comforts him while waiting for the injury to heal, Teague's loyalty is transferred to the lady of the house, even while he pursues a relationship with Katy and Jack, whom he loves beyond reason.

Katy—Katy has loved Teague Sullivan since she was barely old enough to talk. When she found that fate had brought him to Green's hill too, she pursued him—and Jack—with a single-minded quest for happiness. Now that they're a family, she wants to be a part of Teague's adventures whenever she can be.

Lambent—Lambent joined the hill just before Jack and Teague were bitten. He had always been semi-independent of Titania and Oberon, but until he ended up on Green's Hill, he had no idea how much he'd valued his autonomy—or how much he hated the antique laws that governed sidhe behavior in the old country.

Characters we meet in *Rampant*

Tanya—a not-yet mated sylph

Sam—offspring of 'the other' and a human

Walter—a sweet, young, newly made vampire.

Rafael—the leader of the Redding vampires

Annette—Nicky's unpleasant ex-girlfriend

John & Terry—Nicky's parents

Creatures
Sidhe—*high elves—lots of powers, humanoid attributes and physical beauty*

Fey—*all of the underclasses of elves existing at Green's Hill—pixies, nixies, sprites, gnomes, sylphs, red-caps, trolls, fairies, etc. etc. etc.*

Weres—*shapechangers, they age at about 1/3-1/4 the speed of a human, have super-strength, super-speed, and whatever characteristics their chosen creature possesses. Were-creatures reproduce by biting humans. They probably can carry young of their own species, but interspecies mating is so prevalent at Green's Hill that no one knows for sure.*

Vampires—*the blood sucking undead—but in a nice way.*

Sylphs—*sex-less fey, they choose their gender when they choose their mates.*

Avians—the only shapechanger that's born and not made by another shapechanger. The Avians are bonded for life with the person/people involved in their first sexual experience. If this mate doesn't produce offspring within ten years, the Avian is doomed.

CORY

Buzzkilling

Getting bad news when you're suspended fifty feet above the ground is the definition of buzzkill.

Green and Bracken were below me, ready to catch—don't get me wrong, I'm not stupid. But there I was, holy-shit and cannyagimmehallelujia, I was *flying! Suspended* off the ground, hovering in the crystal-shard February blue, watching the fat-sheep clouds scudding much farther above me and shivering convulsively. Below me I could see big clumps of crocuses and pinks defiantly brightening Green's gardens. In the foothills they were rare, but in Green's hill, the rare was commonplace, and that crunchy sweet smell was teasing us with the promise of spring as I practiced my flying.

Last year, I'd been put in a position where being able to fly would have been ex*tremely* handy, but my lack of control had completely biffed *that* opportunity, so my husbands and I (no shit—we all had rings, Nicky too, who was a bird in his other skin and currently flying around my head annoying me with hawk-shrikes of encouragement) were out here, practicing my stuff. You never know when you might plummet hundreds of feet from a bad guy's nasty, slippery, dead-fleshed grasp, and a little initiative might make hitting bottom a lot more comfortable, right?

So there I was, arms spread like a psychotic bird (because Nicky wasn't psychotic enough for both of us he was so worried) and Green and Bracken just *freaking out* whenever my flight plan deviated and it looked as though they couldn't even hyperspeed it fast enough to catch me, and I was trying not to have too much fun.

I mean, it was sort of fun, even if it was cold enough to freeze the balls off a female Yeti (is that a Yetina? I have no idea...) but I was terrified, and I'm not that great at driving fast so what in the *fuck* made me think flying would be such a swell idea? Besides, my life was so intimately tied with the three men helping me that getting hurt or killed with what was, essentially, a training exercise, was absolutely un-risk-able. So I was having fun, but I was working *very* hard at being in control of myself, hovering, swooping, diving, and unintentionally scaring Bracken enough to make his sidhe-pale skin blanche almost green. (Green, on the other hand, was handling the panic well... the occasional frustrated 'beloved...' would waft up on a warning breeze, but mostly, he had faith that I wouldn't put myself in more danger than necessary.)

But I guess you can't help but buzz a little when you're, well, *buzzing,* so it was a definite distraction when Hallow, my professor-cum-shrink pulled up in a rather spiffy white Lexus, looking as though someone died.

Dammit, you don't look like someone died in my world unless the news is pretty fucking dire, right? I mean... people *do* die around us, all the time.

I came dropping out of the sky like lead shit from a helium duck.

Green and Bracken both screamed, "Fuck!" and then scrambled to find a place below me, but I beat them to it, putting a big, fat slice of power below me and sort of skimming off of it like one of those big bounce house slides. I whooped up for about ten feet at the end, and then set another cushion of will beneath me, coming to a rest about two feet off the ground on all fours, and then sinking slowly until I hit grass, like a Labrador on a punctured air bed.

Bracken collapsed next to me, his haggard face buried in his hands, his onyx-black hair in disarray around his perfect, inhumanly beautiful, triangular features.

When his eyes met mine, they were murky and dark, with hints of green, like a pond in shadow, but when he opened his mouth all of that murkiness disappeared.

"I cannot fucking do this. It scares the piss out of me every fucking time."

I sat back on my haunches and scooted into him, leaning my head on his shoulder. "At no time was the subject in real danger," I murmured, mimicking the dry voice of a TV documentary narrator. He grunted and jerked away, and I looked up to Green for help.

Green smiled and blew out an exasperated breath, shaking his hip-length butter-colored hair down his back. "Really, mate—after everything else we've done, you can't take a spin in the garden? Your mother let you do this when you were four."

No one could resist Green when he was determinedly good-natured, and Bracken was no exception. He looked up, the corners of his sour grimace quirking upwards, and shook his head. "It's a good thing I'm mortal, mate—I don't think I could take scares like that for a millennium."

And now *I* wanted to smack *him*. The big hoser had given his immortality up for me, because I was mortal, and he'd just rubbed salt in that wound. Typical, for Bracken.

I smacked the back of his head for real, and felt much better.

"Ou..." And then, also typical Bracken, he realized how badly he'd screwed up before he could get mad. By the time Hallow walked up, he was repeatedly smacking his forehead with the heel of his hand, and Nicky had landed in the open patch of green I'd fallen on and was rolling barefoot on the frost-melted grass.

I was about two breaths away from ripping into Nicky like a kid into a Christmas present for losing his *hand-made* woolen socks, when I remembered why I'd fallen out of the sky in the first place.

Hallow had the same preternaturally beautiful features as Green— triangular bone structure, over-large eyes (but his were blue), clean lines. Unlike my beloved though, Hallow's beauty had never moved me. I liked the guy, but that didn't keep me from spitting venom at him now.

"Who died?" I demanded, and for all his professorial dignity, Hallow managed to look sheepish.

"I'm so sorry about that—I do have bad news, but it's not that dire." He wore his hair long, like Green's, but his was plaited and pulled back from his aesthetic features. He was playing with the end of the braid.

So no one died. But someone was about to. "Cough it up, dammit!" I growled—I had been doing so well this time around—some of my other attempts had rewritten disaster movie scripts—and if he was going to drop in and make me just drop, well, he'd better have a damned good explanation.

Have you ever heard bad news that made your eyes glaze over and your brain black out? I understand it doesn't happen for REALLY bad things, like death or dismemberment or even cancer, but I knew a girl in high school who swore that it happened whenever her current boyfriend broke up with her. Apparently it made the next ten minutes after the break-up horribly awkward because she denied all knowledge of the preceding conversation.

When I came to, I was staring at Hallow with eyes that were dried by the wind and with a little bit of drool tracking the corner of my lips. The men were all staring at me as though I were a rabid bear, and I had to ask Hallow to repeat what he'd just said.

I swear to the Goddess I was listening the second time, and it still didn't make any sense.

"What do you mean, I'm not going to graduate?" This much had seeped in, but it was like getting cold maple syrup through the baked hardpan of a planetary desert.

Hallow grimaced uncomfortably—my sudden-onset-senility was worrisome to him, but since I'd been working my *ass* off for nearly the last four years to try to get my BA a.s.a.p., I had to admit that the 180 degree mind-fuck was leaving my cortex a little sore.

"You *will* graduate, Lady Cory…"

"Would you stop calling me that like it's going to calm me down?" I snapped, and he gritted his teeth and continued.

"It's just that you have too many units right now to graduate with a Bachelor's Degree."

I blinked slowly. "How in the fuck is that even possible?"

Hallow took another deep breath and waded in again. "You took so many units last year, that you have more than enough to graduate. But you don't have them in the right places. If you take the classes you need in the right places, you will have so many units, that you will have enough for two Bachelor's degrees. If you take the nine units of thesis work, you'll have enough for two Bachelors and a Master's Degree. Which I suggest you do. But it means that…"

"I don't graduate this year." Okay. I was finally starting to understand.

Hallow sighed and let out a whole lot of tension from his shoulders. "That's right, my Lady, you'll have to wait until next year."

Now two years ago I would have pitched a fit of cosmic proportions—six-zillion light years from here, some species that registered emotional sound through it's skin would have shuddered, turned brown, and said, "What in the fuck was that?"

But I was older now. I was more mature than that. I was the leader of my fucking people, and I did not pitch fits over bizarre twists of bureaucratic insanity, I simply… I just… Oh Jesus… I was going to be the first person in my family to ever graduate from college. I'd about worn my impending letters like some sort of badge of triumph over the ignominy of white-trash-dom that I'd been trying to shake my entire life.

"Uhm, Cory?" Bracken said gently, throwing himself under the bus of my potential meltdown. He was used to it. Our relationship had the passion of a sailor addicted to the sea—the storms were exhilarating and the smooth sailing was a thing of beauty, and he could weather the rolling thunder of my bitchiness like no other lover.

"Beloved?" Green asked, even more gently. Of the three of them, his sweetness, and the kind and even keel of his beautiful soul, could be the only things that would calm me down.

Nicky, my shape-shifting, accidental lover had no such finesse. "Well hell, Cory, what are you going to do?"

I turned to him and blinked rapidly, trying to slam this bit of unwelcome news into perspective. I mean shit, hadn't I just thought someone had died? I'd been prepared to deal with *death,* for crap's sake, couldn't I take a change in my goddamned plans?

I growled, grunted, and tried again from grinding teeth, finally finding my outlet.

"I am going to go knit."

And with that, I turned on my heel and stalked through Green's glorious gardens, blind to their loveliness, and pounded up the stairs to the landing, and then into the living room, leaving my three husbands wincing in sympathy behind me.

Renny, my best friend and part-time giant tabby cat has a built in radar as to whether or not I need a girl friend or a kitty when I'm upset.

She was curled up in a big, purring, tortoiseshell blob on the olive/turquoise/violet colored quilt at my feet, as I sat cross-legged on the gi-freaking-normous bed I shared with Bracken, knitting Nicky another goddamned pair of socks.

Nicky actually stuck his head in first, but I glared at him and he cringed when he saw the burgundy, brown, and lime-green yarn I was working with (always trendy for Nick!) and ducked right on back out. One of the things that made our poly-amorous marriage work was that Nicky had learned to recognize when I needed my man-friend with the nice body and comforting smell and when I needed one of my beloveds who could steady the world when it rocked beneath my feet.

I should have been ashamed that this was one of those times, but what the fuck. Sometimes even the Lady Cory, beloved to Lord Green and queen of the goddamned vampires could get stuck in a petty-shit-kicking funk about dumb-fucking bullshit that complicated her life, right?

Well, not for long.

Bracken stalked in after about a half an hour, so lost as to what to do for me that he was actually squinting in puzzlement.

"What are you making?" he demanded—and he was probably unaware of how arrogant he sounded. He was trying, honestly, to make conversation.

"Socks for Nicky," I replied mildly, and his frown deepened.

"Little fucker lost the last pair in trans," he said, and I nodded glumly. It happened sometimes—Nicky was an Avian, a bird shapeshifter, and they were the only species that actually didn't have to strip naked to shift. They carried their clothes and stuff on the oil in their feathers—except, when a bird is stressed or tired, that oil gets a little thin, and something has to go. I freaked Nicky out by almost plummeting to my death, and he lost his socks.

"You like Nicky," I reminded him. It had not always been so, but Bracken had finally accepted Nicky's accidental and unintentional place in my bed and my life. Still—it didn't hurt to remind Brack that Nicky had his place. Besides, there were things we could do with three people in a bed that you can't do with two, and Bracken was just bi enough—and had been raised with enough sexual diversity and privilege enough—to enjoy those things.

We were bound—if either of us took our pleasure outside our marriage or any of my pre-existing bindings (like, say, Green or Nicky)—the other one would die horribly. There is always a flip side to the passion of the Goddess' magic, and this was one of them. Marriage? Fabulous—but you'd better make good and damned sure that you were in it for the long haul. If I had been a sidhe instead of a human sorceress, Bracken and I would be locked inside this binding for a lot more than a mortal lifespan—not that either one of us would have minded then either, not even a little teeny bit, but, like I said, he'd been raised with some freedoms.

In the context of those freedoms, Nicky had gone from being a nuisance to a perk—even if he was only my perk. Bracken was bound to me and Nicky was bound to me, and the two of them had learned to tolerate each other, except in bed.

In bed, Bracken had taken to being my primary lover like sex was a competitive event. It was like a sweet lover's game, except the stakes seemed to be the increasingly colorful state of Green's once pristinely finished wood-paneled walls. My losses of control—even small ones--in bed, tended to change the state of the world around me. Sometimes it was cute—olive, turquoise and lavender paneling in the living room, for example.

Sometimes it was huge—Green and I, with our beloved vampire, Adrian, had completely reformed the crown of Green's hill, complete with trees doing erotic things with their trunks, if you can believe that bullshit. Bracken and I had created a hotel.

Sometimes it was terrifying. The things I had done upon Adrian's death were an object lesson of why power shouldn't be allowed to run rampant.

So Bracken strategized and Nicky accepted—and I treated their efforts with affection and passion and as practice sessions to control my body, my mind, and my magic.

No—I loved my husbands, all three of them, but no combination of us would ever be what Green and Adrian and I had been, and I knew better than to try.

Right now, Bracken was wishing that he didn't like Nicky quite so much, because it was much easier to use my lesser lover as a scapegoat than to figure out a way to comfort me. Not knowing how to comfort me was item # 2657 on the list of things that made Bracken cranky, and per usual, when he was cranky, he found some way to purge that emotion from his extremely passionate system.

"You never make me socks!" he accused, perfectly serious, and I fought the urge to laugh.

"You hate stuff on your feet!" I responded—it was true. All elves did. Even outside just now, in the chilly February, Bracken and Green had been barefoot. "Besides, I just finished your sweater for this year!" I fingered the gray wool on his arm. The yoke of the thing was a dark, masculine green and purple over a cream background. (My first venture into Fair Isle patternworking—I was very proud.)

"Well I wouldn't hate it if you made it!" he protested, a little panic in his voice—really bad shit happens to elves if they lie, and he was obviously hoping he really felt this way and wasn't just saying this to make me feel better. He brightened when the nausea and cramping didn't start and continued on, a little more confident. "But I wouldn't want them in…" Bracken wrinkled his nose and I held out my hands. Those colors. Enough said. "And they'd need to be strong. But not plain." He stroked the smooth fingering weight wool between my fingers. "And it needs texture…this is ordinary. If I'm going to wear something on my feet it needs to press your fingertips into my flesh."

I nodded, completely bemused, and unbidden, a pattern for Bracken's socks began to emerge in my head. "Man's colors, lots of texture, not plain…"

"And not feminine either," he emphasized, and I stifled the urge to chortle. From his square shoulders to his frequent glower, there was not an effete inch of Bracken's bisexual skin. I could make these things in pony-puke pink, and on Brack, it would be the next navy blue.

"Not a problem," I murmured dryly. "Bracken…love…you really don't have to…"

Bracken stood up and paced a little. If this was a death, a true tragedy, he'd know how to deal—he dealt very well with me when I was upset or unhappy, or feeling inadequate. But something like this—something that was frustrating, and (I admit it) self-inflicted—well, he was at a loss.

"Of course I want you to make me socks," he said softly, coming to a halt in front of me. An elegant hand with blunt, square fingers appeared under my chin and tilted my face so I would look at him. "You know I love the things you make for me."

"I meant," I murmured, feeling a helpless, foolish little smile steal across my face, "that you don't have to come with me for one more year."

He looked honestly surprised, and then he looked honestly pissed. "You think you're going there without me?" He backed up, eyes flashing, and I grimaced. Any little hint that I might *possibly* feel unworthy, and he acts like I stomped on his damned-near-prehensile big toe.

I laughed, shaking my head and wondering if now was the time in our relationship to stand up and soothe over that powerful, vast body with my own little hands. "I'm just saying that you don't have to live with my own personal fuck-up, okay?" I tried to smile winningly, and he was almost buying it, almost in my arms, when it suddenly occurred to him that now I was the one calming *him* down.

He shook his head and kissed me hard, literally leaning over Renny-the-cat's body to take my mouth with his until I whimpered just a little in surprise and arousal.

Renny reached out with a precisely extended claw and flexed those large crescents into Bracken's leg.

He jumped back and yelped and she gave a cat chuckle and settled down into her paws again. "What was that for?" he demanded and Renny, being the supreme bitch-kitty that she is, made a show of cleaning the pads of her front foot with a rough pink tongue.

"You almost squashed her, Brack!" I protested, much of my funk almost completely gone.

"I was just trying," he glared at Renny who continued cleaning undisturbed, "to tell you that I..." he shook his head sheepishly, "I like school. It's fun. Some of my favorite Cory moments come when we're working together like that."

My mouth quirked up and I wondered why my chest didn't explode. "And that you wanted socks," I added, wondering if he was going to back down on that.

"Absolutely," he said, and once again he looked surprised when he didn't double over and barf.

I leaned into him over Renny, and was about a half-a-heartbeat from kicking her out of my room, when a tiny sparkly pink creature popped into thin air about two inches from Bracken's face and started speaking in bumblebee or whatever. Sprites: the fey equivalent of the cell phone.

"Now?" Bracken asked reluctantly, and even I could interpret the emphatic little foot stomping that went with the little guy's (girl's?) sparking tinkle. Bracken scrubbed his face with both hands and nodded, and the sprite disappeared.

"It's Da," Bracken sighed. "Apparently they're having trouble stringing lights for the ceremony tonight, and they want..." He flushed.

"'*oi'anga*'," I supplied with a smile, and he nodded. I was having one hell of a time learning the language of the fey, but this word I had down cold. It meant 'the tall one'. Bracken's mother and father were lower fey—they were not only less humanoid looking than their gigantic offspring, they were also much smaller. Bracken got called into service as a walking ladder frequently. As my husband, he had also become a reluctant and baffled liaison between the lower fey and Green, the leader of the sidhe or high elves. Bracken had spent much of his seventy-seven years of life avoiding any responsibility that didn't get him laid—he'd been horrified to realize that being my lover made him a corner in our little triad of power, but he hadn't been able to leave his new status any more than he'd be able to leave me.

"As long as they remember you're my *due'alle* first," I muttered direly, and he grinned.

"I'll make it a priority to remind them, *due'ane,*" and I stopped him before he made an accompanying gesture.

"If you bow to me, you'll be best friends with your fist for a week," I warned, and he grinned unrepentantly and did a full fledged, head at his knees bow-with-a-flourish, and I was suddenly in my complete leather-stewing funk again, even as he dodged lightly out the door. (Sidhe always moved lightly—it didn't matter that he was over six-and-a-half feet tall. I couldn't move lightly when I was fifty feet in the air. Bastard.)

I sighed and scrambled over Renny's cat-chuckling body onto the other side of the bed, where I got on my knees and yanked out a big clear-white lexan. I scanned through the plastic lid, decided what I wanted wasn't in that one, and then yanked the other one out from under the bed.

Renny was suddenly a naked young woman kneeling next to me. She'd opened the first box and was sorting through the elbow-deep pile of lovely hand-dyed fiber within.

"Gees, Cory, it's a good thing you work at a yarn store, because you might run out of this shit and that would be a shame."

I looked at her sideways—her flyaway brown hair was sticking out all over her head like a lion's mane and her eyes were their usual dreamy, unfocused brown. "It would help," I said mildly, "if skeins wouldn't just walk out of the boxes sometimes when I thought they'd be where I left them.

Renny didn't have the grace to flush. "You have the best taste," she murmured, taking a blue-gray wool/tencel/cotton blend out and stroking it. Her bare shoulders did a sinuous little dance, and she reached into the box for the other five skeins, and it didn't take a genius in color theory to know she was planning a sweater for her husband, Max. Max had blue eyes and dark hair, and would probably look awesome in that yarn—I'd thought so when I'd recommended it to Renny when we were working, and she'd refused.

Bitch, I thought affectionately. It was like it was more fun to hunt and kill the little yarn cake herself, as long as it was under my bed.

"What are you making?" she asked, her yarn carefully hoarded against her bare breasts. It was funny how, in a place like Green's where everything was so very sexually charged, Renny (and hell, almost anybody—even Green and Bracken when they felt like it) could run around naked and inspire nothing but curiosity as to whether or not they were cold.

I pulled out a black, brown and red speckled yarn and eyed it with satisfaction. "Apparently I'm making a pair of socks that says 'I'm a big strong bundle of hypersensitive testosterone who can eat small animals raw for breakfast but who wouldn't mind touching another man's bare ass.'"

Renny smirked, and was opening her mouth to make a retort when the door opened again. There was only one other person who would open our door without knocking, and that was the one person Renny would leave the room for as a sign of respect. In a morphing flash of bare white skin and fluffy brown tortoiseshell fur, she streaked out of the room, leaving me to clean up. Bitch.

Unhurriedly I put the lids on the yarn boxes, leaving what she'd picked out for Max on top, even as I pushed the two boxes back under the bed. Then I tossed Bracken's ball of sock yarn on top of the bed and launched myself at my beloved Green with enough force to surprise him.

"I'm fine," I murmured, rubbing my face against his white linen shirt. "I'm fine, I'll live…don't worry about me."

Heaven was in Green's arms. They folded around me like I was a shattered bird, and his job was to put me back together again without disturbing a single hollow bone.

"I know you're fine, luv," he murmured into my hair. "You're stronger than letting something like this shake you—I just wanted to comfort you, that's all." He backed up and I smiled besottedly into his clean-lined, masculine and lovely face. His sidhe-pale skin was flushed and warm from an armload of little ol' me, and his green eyes were glowing for me alone. It had taken a long time for me to accept that he could love me with all of his heart—I took this moment to bask in that affection for a moment like a kitten in the sun.

Playfully he backed up and unbalanced us so we sprawled upon the bed, and I grinned up at him sunnily. He held his fingertips to my plain, mortal face and I leaned into his touch like lightning in a ball. I don't know what everyone else felt when he touched them—I imagined it was the difference between what a high school teacher feels for her students, and what she feels for her teenaged children. She may enjoy the company of all those others, but she would lay down in traffic and die for her own.

That was how my Green loved me.

My small, mortal body often felt as though it would peel back and split from the gigantic swelling of my soul when he touched me like this, tenderly and with passion. How could something as stupid as another year of school overwhelm me, when I was loved like this, by this man-god? It was impossible. Small things could be overcome.

"You may comfort me any time you want," I said softly, rubbing the curve of his pointed ear. He smiled and leaned into that touch—I think it was a sidhe-weakness, because Bracken liked it too.

When he lowered his head to kiss me, the tears I'd been ruthlessly squashing back trickled forward, and he stopped in the middle of my best kiss and wiped them away with his thumbs.

"See, luv, you are upset!" he chided and I shook my head. I wouldn't be upset, not when I had him, and Bracken, and Nicky.

"I'm happy," I told him gruffly. "I'm happy—I'm so happy that our disasters can be measured in headaches and not heartaches." And then all that mattered was his lips on mine, the taste of his tongue, his hands, warm and sweet, touching my stomach under my sweatshirt.

I sighed, sinking into him with the eagerness of an addict sinking into euphoria, and he rushed through my skin with my fix. My hands went to wriggle under his sweatshirt and jeans when he sighed and pulled away. I'd seen that expression in his eyes before, and this time I didn't need to wrack my brains to know why we had to stop.

"The ceremony..." I didn't need to finish the thought, and he nodded apologetically. Our recently appointed (shanghaied!) alpha werewolf and his chosen mates were being formally bound on the top of the hill tonight, in the Goddess Grove. Besides the fact that the entire hill would be there and it would be rude to be late, Green and I were sort of officiating.

"If it was our own shindig, luv..." he trailed off meaningfully, and I managed a grin. If it was our own shindig, we'd have our own quickie and make the world wait for us. But it was someone else's shindig, and not just any someone else—it was someone we'd come to care for, and someone who so often expected to be overlooked or abused. If it had been our celebration we might have been late and unapologetic. If it was a good friend's party, we might be late anyway, and they would understand.

But it wasn't ours and it wasn't anybody else's, it was Teague's. And while Jack and Katy would forgive us, we wouldn't do that to Teague for all the world.

"Goddess!" I groaned, throwing my head back against the mattress. "Are you sure he's back already?"

Green blinked at me. "Back from where? Where would he be going right before his wedding?"

I blinked back at him. I would have thought Teague had told him— sometimes I forgot that people treated me like I was exactly equal to Green.

I never knew what to do with that. Green was 1800 years old. I would be twenty-two in July.

"He went to see Lloyd and Spider," I told him now, hoping I hadn't done anything wrong. Teague had left early this morning—before the vampires went to sleep, actually. I didn't realize that he had slunk from his lovers' bed like a con-man from his virgin mark until Jack had come looking for him right before I went out to practice flying.

"Really?" Green asked, a quirk of private amusement on his lips. "I wonder what his tattoo will look like."

I shook my head—I had no idea, but I did know that it would be very private to the three of them. Since my little visit to Lloyd and Spider, Green had marked all of his people with an insignia—mostly through one big blast of magic that we had performed together with a whole lot of help. Anyone joining us—either as a were or a vampire or just a friendly human—came through their transition with the mark on their skin.

The werewolves were no exception--Teague's was on his right wrist, Katy's was on her ankle, and I had no idea where Jack's mark was. Whatever Teague was doing right now, it was something different, just for his lovers, and that was his business.

Green looked distant for a moment, and then he came back to me. "He's just hitting the driveway now. It really is time."

I covered my eyes with my hands. "Aw crap--Bracken was going to help me get ready!"

Bracken was good at that sort of thing—he had good taste, and I privately had to admit that he knew how to make me look like the Lady of Green's House when I often would have just blown off the occasion in jeans and a T-shirt. Yes, Bracken was good at picking out the clothes and the make-up and choosing the hairstyle, but looking at Green's grin now I remembered who bought the clothes and told the sprites to buy the make-up and suggested the hair-styles to the sprites who did them in the first place.

"You planned this!" I accused, not upset in the least. Green and I got so little uninterrupted time together that even having him help me get ready was a treat.

"I didn't, I swear!" he denied, holding up his hands and laughing. His playful grin faded though, and he gazed at me fondly. "But that doesn't mean I won't appreciate every second of it, if that's good with you."

Of course it wasn't a question. Green was in my arms and he loved me. It was all good with me.

GREEN

Master of Ceremonies

Green caught Cory's eye as she stood next to him, trying to look like being part of the 'officiating party' didn't chafe her like wet underwear. They were surveying the gathering in the winter twilight: high sidhe side by side with lower fey, side by side with were-folk (all of them in human skin), all of them showing only happiness and well wishes for the three mates about to be bound, as Cory and her lovers had been bound, in front of their people. It was what he had always believed was possible on his hill, and he was pleased.

Tonight, Cory was dressed in a cream colored, full-sleeved, full-skirted dress with an old-fashioned tabard that she had knit herself, although not for this occasion. (She had been speechlessly flattered when he pulled it out of the closet to go over the new dress.) Her hair was up in a complicated knot, accented with myriad tiny braids, and although she had complained that simplicity never hurt anyone, he'd been the one directing the sprites and she had finally conceded that yes, she did look a little more 'Lady Cory-like' with the delicate hairstyle. Besides, he'd told her dryly, with her riotous reddish-brownish-blondish hair, about a half-an-hour after the ceremony, the hairdo would be toast anyway.

Right now, she was casting reassuring glances and making soothing conversation with the fidgeting werewolves about to be publicly married on the hill. 'Public' bondings were as rare in the shapeshifting world as they were in the fey and the vampire world. The Goddess loved her children, but Her willingness to become other forms had led to a fickle and bizarre set of 'mating' rules for almost every species. Werewolf couples could, presumably, mate for life—but the werewolves often got along better as wolves than they did as humans, and so they chose not to. The fact that Jack and Katy had loved Teague long before any of them had become werewolves was probably what made this ceremony possible. The fact that the trio planned (eventually) to live off of Green's sexually charged hill and were hometown human to the core of their damaged and recovering psyches was probably what would make the bonding successful.

Teague, the new alpha, had an innate sense of what should be respected, and he had suggested having the ceremonies after the vampires awoke without being asked, and that was who they were waiting for. The dark-blonde, hazel-eyed, bandy-legged Irishman had passed up being short by a few bare inches, and now he stood nervously between his lovers. He stood more than half-a-foot shorter than Jack, his dark-haired, blue-eyed first beloved, and only a couple of inches taller than Katy, the determined young woman who had beguiled them both.

On this night, his palpable relief upon seeing Green and Cory more than made up for what they'd had to give up to be there on time.

"Glad you made it, brother," Teague muttered with his characteristic gruffness.

"You say that like you didn't just come skating in at the last fucking gasp," Jack muttered sourly, and Teague flushed.

"Gifts," he muttered, and Green looked sorrowfully at the terrible fear that surrounded the man's body like cotton-wool. Oh, if Green could give Teague any one thing for a wedding gift it would be the ability to believe he was truly loved, so the padding of fear that vibrated around his tightly muscled shoulders might never have to be resurrected.

"What?" Jack was saying blankly, as aware of that terror of rejection as Green.

"Gifts, Jack-ass. You needed gifts." Teague turned his head away then, and Katy and Jack met eyes, and then met hands—around Teague's taught, shivering body.

"You are our gift, you dumb motherfucker," Jack murmured, and then winced when Katy kicked him in the ankle.

"He's right about one thing," she said rolling her eyes. Katy was a pretty girl on most days, with dusky skin and blue-black hair, layer cut around a heart-shaped face. Tonight she was more than beautiful in a cream-colored wool dress with a dramatic blue shawl that Green knew for certain Cory had knitted for her, just for the occasion.

"You are our gift, Teague. Nothing else was necessary."

"Bullshit," he muttered back, but his chest seemed to grow with their touch, and in a moment he was the strong, brave man that Green had seen through years of abuse and self-hatred.

At that moment the last sword of sun was sheathed at its source and twilight dappled through the trees. Cory's body suddenly went on alert, and she turned her head with (had she known it) preternatural grace, as though listening to her favorite song from a radio in the house. There was a fluttering and lovely pale shadows, dressed in their best (and often most dramatic) clothing sprang from the dark of the grove.

The vampires arrived.

Cory snorted in private amusement. "You know they flew out the front door so they didn't have to lift the trap door, right?" she whispered into his ear.

Green chuckled. "But of course." Vampires—well *their* vampires anyway— loved to make an entrance. Odds were good they had all gotten ready before dawn broke, and then arranged themselves in a position least likely to rumple their clothes when they arose so they could arrive as close to the moment of darkness as possible. It worked: their entrance was spectacular.

In a moment there was a flicker of pale faces in the ambient light of the Goddess Grove, and the collective denizens of the hill let out a little sigh. The sprites rose gently into a halo of light-flickering color-spangled bodies, and every person, from the small, naked nixies in every color from dark blue to coffee brown and star-white, to the elegantly dressed, aloof and beautiful high sidhe, some much older than Green, regarded the three werewolves in the center of the grove with reverence and joy.

Teague's shoulders straightened, and he readied himself to pledge protection over the two people who protected his delicate and fragile heart, and Cory smiled at all of them reassuringly—she'd done this too. They would live through the ceremony and rejoice.

When the mass inhale of anticipation stopped and hovered for a moment, Green began to speak. He spoke simply and from the heart, and watching Cory's face in the twilight, he couldn't help but wonder what his beloved would make of the wedding vows.

Her heart was filled with unexpected poetry, as much as she still tried to hide it.

Jack began to speak, and then Katy, as they had planned, and Green's attention wandered a little to the very young, very mortal woman next to him.

She was completely enraptured by the proceedings, her eyes never leaving the lovers' faces and especially lingering on Teague. Both of them had a soft spot for Teague—he reminded them so much of Adrian, the vampire they had both loved beyond death. Watching Teague get the happy ending they had been denied was cathartic, somehow—and this wedding was important to both of them.

But there was something troubling her—something she would not vocalize, even to Green, and he was damned if he could figure out what it was.

He'd been proud of her this afternoon. She'd worked so damned hard for that human piece of paper, at one point sacrificing her health to do so—to have it pulled back from her, like a carrot on a string had been just too fucking cruel for words.

And his beloved had always had a temper.

They'd expected fireworks, all of them, and she'd given them socks. On the one hand, it had been a sign of maturity—and she'd been forced into maturity, like a lush cabbage rose into a daisy's box. To see that she had simply changed, become a tighter, more complex version of herself instead of simply a squashed one had been heartening.

The thought of her, squashing all of that passion, all of that temper, inside a box of her own devising, had been heartbreaking.

So he watched her now, her face open and joyful and happy, and wondered if maybe he wouldn't have been happier if she had lit the sky afire with her fury, instead of sat down and knit with tiny, angry stitches.

His attention was distracted by a sudden silence.

It was Teague's turn to speak.

The man looked decidedly uncomfortable. His skin was taut over his cheekbones, and a pulse throbbed at his temple. His eyes were wide and dark, and Green could smell his absolute terror of having his emotions out here in the open, for the world to see—the texture of his fear was thick and viscous.

"I don't have any good words," Teague muttered, stripping off his jacket. "I thought and I thought…I watched the two of you sleeping in the moonlight, and I wanted to cry, but I didn't have any fucking words." He looked beseechingly at Jack, the man at his back for nearly two years, and in his bed for scarcely three months. "You know me, Jacky—if I ain't being a smartass, I just ain't being." Now he moved towards the tie that he'd spent a week picking out, and in a moment it was over his head and discarded on the ground.

Jack opened his mouth to reassure Teague that it was all okay, but Teague cut him off, lost in the misery of being speechless for the one thing he wanted to articulate.

"So I don't have good words…but I've got…" His hands came up to the buttons of his white shirt. He looked over his shoulder at the bemused gathering, the expression on his face ripe with the misery of a private outpouring in a public occasion.

But not with indecision.

With an impatient rip that sent buttons spattering across the lawn (Cory had to duck to avoid catching one in the eye) Teague ripped off his dress shirt and the T-shirt underneath, and stood shivering and half-naked. The tattoo that completely covered his back was bright and eloquent as he couldn't be.

Three wolves played under a full and vibrant moon, framed by a border of oak and lime boughs. The little she-wolf had a black coat with whitish fringe, like Katy in her other form. The big, lanky beta-wolf had shaggy dark hair and blue eyes. The tightly muscled, intense alpha-wolf was between them, glaring from Teague's back, fierce and protective and angry at anyone who dared to intrude on the threesome.

The tattoo depicted a burning, intense, uncomfortable kind of love, the kind that spoke of death for an interloper, of the agonizing fear of separation.

Green blinked in surprise, and looked to his beloved to see what she thought, since she had been the first on the hill to mark herself for love.

There was an unholy sympathy in Cory's eyes, a fierce glee. She knew that angry, protective wolf. She *was* that wolf.

None of Green's concern about her almost passive acceptance of the day's disappointment vanished—in fact, he was suddenly very afraid of what she would do to the thing that *truly* touched her fury. He'd been there the one time that had happened, and she could barely live with the results. But that was not his focus for this evening.

Katy and Jack had found their voices, found their touches tentatively on Teague's back. Even through the magically healed (and permanent) ink they could see he was erupting in gooseflesh and shivering in the February mist.

"Jesus, Teague," Jacky murmured. "A simple 'I love you' would have done it!"

Katy leaned up and kissed his cheek soothingly. "It's beautiful, *mijo*—it says everything you wanted, I can see it. I love you too, *mi corazon*. Don't worry about words, no?"

Teague accepted her kiss, bumping noses with her playfully like the wolves they were. Then he glared miserably at Jack, who was bending over to fish the rumpled dress jacket out of the dew-shot grass. It was wet, and Jack shook his head and handed it to Green, shrugging out of his own jacket at the same time.

"I love you, asshole," Teague groused, not meeting anybody's eye.

"I love you too, you dumb motherfucker," Jack sighed, draping his jacket over Teague's shoulders, and the three of them stood, the perfect triad of gruff affection and true love, in front of their family and friends.

There was a burst of applause and cheering, and then, on Green's cue, a long, drawn out bow to the lovers as the ceremony closed itself.

Teague was so relieved that it was over that he didn't catch the droll look between Katy and Jack that indicated he'd cut about 15 minutes out of the ceremony they'd arranged. Green could tell that if they didn't know him better, they'd think he'd planned it that way.

CORY

The Trials of a Chess Playing Hamster

I like my husband's lover very much, but when I make the mistake of asking him about his job, he can glaze my eyes over in two seconds flat.

Apparently Nicky could follow him (which was good, since they managed to spend about one week a month in each other's company) and he was currently standing, his bleach-tipped, rust colored hair carefully gelled to fall carelessly around his face, and staring besottedly into Eric's eyes while his beloved—his *true* beloved it seemed—talked to me about the impact of Hurricane Gustav on gas prices. I'm guessing it was bad.

Nicky loved me, and managed to live with me in harmony that other three-quarters of the time, and he was not so besotted for Eric that he forgot about me. He fluffled his featherless neck and took Eric's hand in his, kissing the back of it tenderly. Eric was only a little taller than Nicky, with sandy hair, and he turned his gray eyes towards his lover with gentle attention.

"Uhm, Eric? Remember—I go to school with Cory. I know she looks interested, but she's got this built in 'queenie' thing that keeps her jaw from going slack. We should let her mingle and go dance."

I looked at him with a combination of gratitude and exasperation. "Way to blow my cover, bird boy—I've been practicing my 'Lady of Oz' bit for a year now, and you just showed Eric the self-involved bitch behind the curtain."

Eric laughed, and then, disconcertingly, gave me a little bow. "I don't need any incentive to dance with you, Nicky," he said with another tender smile, and together they headed for the open square of the Goddess Grove, where a band that consisted of two vampires and a were-puma (and wouldn't THAT be a great name for it!) were currently doing cover versions of old *Dire Straits* and *U2* songs.

The minute they were out of speaking distance, I felt Bracken's hands on my shoulders, and my entire body groaned with relief, as though I had been craving his touch on my skin.

Ah, Goddess, I had.

There is a club for the Goddess-get out in Auburn, and Nicky has taken me dancing there a couple of times. The first time ended in disaster, but the others…I discovered that there is something hypnotic and sexy about touching your lover to music, especially in a crowd of others doing the same.

I had never danced with Bracken.

Tonight, as the opening strains of *Desire* thundered over us, he wrapped his large hands around my thighs and literally lifted me up, until I was sitting in the cradle of his thighs, my toes barely touching the ground for balance.

Then he began to move, his swollen groin grinding into my back, his large hands on my hips and my stomach or thighs to hold me against him. I could feel his body heat through my dress and his harsh breath in my ear and along my neck as he taxed his strong body to hold me, to move me, to pound me to the beat. Suddenly the cool grove, warmed by Green's power just enough to make the night pleasant, became hot enough to make the sweat trickle down my back and between the crease of my legs.

My sex became hot enough to get wet everywhere.

Oh, Goddess…dancing with Bracken was like making love to music itself as it throbs between your legs, buzzes your spine and tingles your breasts. I turned my face towards him, catching glimpses of his profile through my tumbling hair. The long line of his chin, the full sensuality of his lips, even as they rubbed against my temple…all of it stopped my breath as I swam through the tides of Bracken's audio-sex.

Desi-i-i-re…

My head tilted back and my eyes closed and I both wanted the song to go on forever, building to it's ragged, thumping climax and I wanted to be suddenly alone, running my hands and my mouth along every portion of Bracken's skin I could possibly reach, until he thrust so deep inside me I could see the head of his prick reflected in the backs of my eyelids.

"Have you done your duty as hostess, *due'ane?*" he rasped in my ear.

I tried to think, but the music was rocketing to its conclusion and the hamster who usually powered my brain jumped his little wheel to get laid. What came out of my mouth was meant to be something like 'I don't know, I should check with Green'. What it actually sounded like was "Uuhhrrrrnnnngggg…" And that's all Bracken needed.

"Close your eyes," he whispered, and I listened to him. So help me Goddess, I listened to him. I was tired. My compulsion to do the right thing, to be the lady of the house in all ways was weakened, was dimmed by the disappointment of not graduating and made ridiculous by Teague's awkward, perfect, grandly beautiful declaration of love before Goddess and his family. I wanted Bracken, I wanted him naked, and I wanted him *now*.

Bracken's primary duty in Green's house was to keep me happy, and he gave me what I wanted.

Before the cymbals stopped shusshing, he had swept me into his arms and down the granite staircase, through the hallway and into our room. He didn't bother to turn on the lights, and I think only his sidhe-quick dexterity kept my dress from being destroyed as he worked the buttons in the back.

He didn't give his own clothes the same consideration, and he literally ripped his specially tailored shirt and slacks off his body. His pale skin was damp and slick, and his oversized erection stood rampant from his body.

I wanted him so badly I heard snarling, grunting sounds coming from my own throat, and my hands on his cock weren't gentle. The way he tangled his hands in my hair wasn't either, but I gloried in it, I gloried in *him* as I slid my lips down his smooth skin with its hard ridges of veins underneath. I couldn't make it to the base—it would have been madness to try—but I wrapped my fist around him and squeezed tightly, shuddering when he moaned because *I* did that to him, *I* brought out this frenzy in my *due'alle*, my lover who was my equal, the only lover bound exclusively to me.

He shuddered and spent just a little bit into my mouth and then he grunted and pulled my hair back. I went reluctantly, putting an insistent vacuum on his prick with my lips and letting him go with a loud, wet, *pop*. I'm sure my face was a mess of spit and pale lipstick, but Bracken kissed me as though he would devour me, his taste on my tongue and all.

His hands were so big they as spanned my ribs, covered my breasts, cradled my head, and finally parted my thighs. Before he buried his face between them and kissed my sex as passionately as he kissed my mouth, he grinned up at me, his teeth glinting in the darkness of our room.

"*Due'ane,*" he whispered wolfishly, and I gasped, because he'd moved his thumbs to part me too.

"*Due'alle,*" I replied, and then I stopped speaking words at all. There was something wild in me this night, something begging to be let off the leash of my hard-earned self-restraint and give Bracken everything he asked for as his tongue and fingers moved wickedly along the tender, nerve-screaming parts of my body.

But it wasn't until he slid up along my skin, slinking along my body with his perfectly shaped, perfectly smooth chest and ribcage that I was truly at risk of losing control of the monster of power growing in my chest. That didn't stop me from spreading my legs and welcoming him into my sex with a shriek and a small spill of orgasm, just from his cock in my body.

He was too large for me, had always been too large for me, and he pushed at me, battered at every pleasure place, battled for complete domination over my shaking, screaming sex. We were an uncomfortable fit, too tight, too painful, too intense for simple and sweet and tender, and our bodies moved in pounding rhythm, in terrible synchronicity, in painful bliss.

We were perfect, we were glory, we were cock and cunt and come and tender sweet and love, and my orgasm shredded my body, shredded my womb, annihilated my barriers of self and of power and set the blazing comet of magic that slept restlessly in my loins free upon the world.

"Aw shit…" I breathed, holding my skin over the power that was practically blistering the skin back from my face and hands. I had to control it—I had to. I had used this power to reform the crown of the hill, and it was full of people now. I couldn't set it loose among them.

"Fireworks," Bracken breathed, the blue veins popping under his sidhe-pale skin as he held back his own orgasm to help me battle with my body.

I hated fireworks—the smell and the sound terrified me.

"Flowers," I rasped, remembering the pinks and the daffodils on the lawn that morning, and with that I groaned and screamed, and Bracken covered my mouth with his and swallowed my total, utter shriek of completion and release.

My hands clenched and unclenched, blazed furiously blissful magic at the watercolor tinted ceiling.

Bracken groaned into my throat and threw back his head and roared as I wrapped my feet around his hips to pull him into my body and hold him there, shuddering.

He collapsed on me with a grunt and then rolled over, taking me with him.

"Goddess," I panted, lying my head on his ridged, washboard stomach, "that was so fucking close!"

"It happens," he panted back, "when we're close to people and fucking."

I tried not to laugh—I was horrified at myself—but it was our own personal word to play with, and we were, of course, the only two lovers on the planet to ever use it in every possible permutation.

I groaned and relaxed against him, not wanting to poison his testosterone exultation with my atomic-weight self-doubt. I kept my fears and my recrimination to myself, petting his perfect chest instead, taking casual swipes at the sweet, salty sweat on his nipples with my tongue. The sweat was not from the physical exertion, mind you, but from wanting me so badly he had no choice but to sweat.

Goddess—if that didn't turn a girl's head and turn her on at the same time, nothing would.

"I love you impossibly huge, you know that?" I asked, my eyes closing already with satiation and sleep. We wouldn't shower—not now. Not when there was the possibility we would do it again. The elves loved body fluids—especially sexual ones. You didn't wash yourself up after a moment like that one, you hoped you got to taste it again when the time was right.

"Is that anything close to English?" he laughed, the perfection of his playful smile and his rarely seen dimple in those harshly clean and handsome features catching my breath all over again.

"Let's pretend it is," I murmured to keep away tears. "I love you impossibly huge, tremendously large, gloriously fantastically ginormous."

He chortled, and then added, "You just love that my prick is impossibly huge," with understandable arrogance. I shook my head at him.

"I wouldn't care if it was completely humanly average," I told him soberly, enjoying the way he tilted his chin up and half-closed his eyes when his head was back on the floral sheeted pillows. I wondered if every couple since the dawn of time has had a conversation like this. *I'm too big, I'm not big enough, I hurt you, you couldn't feel me...* were these the male equivalent insecurities of *I'm too fat, I'm too plain, and I'm not worthy of all this glorious attention you shower on me like oxygen?* Maybe so, but that sameness didn't make the words and the reassurance any less vital to the heart-currents that flowed between us.

"I would love you just as huge, Bracken, if you were short and small, with a sunken chest and no chin to speak of." Of course I don't know if his arrogance and his protectiveness would have been in full force if it hadn't been for the reassurance of the sidhe beauty he had always possessed, but it didn't matter. It was the way he loved me that was the gift, not the package the gift came in.

And I had to admit, in Bracken's case, sometimes the package was a gift all by itself—but he had fed my body his life force when I'd been dying, and I had laid hands and healed him of mortal wounds. Nobody did that for an empty box.

"You love me 'huge', hah?" He grinned, and I grinned back at him, content beyond words, perched on top of his chest, my body humming and languorous.

"Huge?"

"Impossibly."

"Tremendous?" His grin lost its sharpness as his desire spiked, and he arched his hips and bumped me with his growing erection. Lucky sidhe to recover that quickly, lucky me to love him. I shimmied and wriggled down his body, until I engulfed him again, slick and hot from earlier. He arched his body off the bed and pulled me up and captured my mouth fully, slowly, in a kiss that engaged and parted, and again and again and again and he moved under me, holding my hips and pushing into me gently, in no particular hurry and with a repressed rapacious urgency.

It was slow and sweet this time, and I kept the fireworks to myself.

This time, when it was over we showered and fell immediately asleep, my head pillowed on his outstretched arm.

Adrian was gone. I could smell his soul on my flesh and feel his blood coating me like rain, and my power, the power he had helped me discover within myself was building.

It was building and building and the scream in my throat was blocked like a dam, with all of that pain and grief and fucking destruction ready to blow, and I was looking at the faces of the enemy, those who'd helped kill my beloved, the faces of the damned.

And instead of stranger's faces they were faces I loved. Renny. Max. Arturo. Bracken. Oh Goddess...oh Goddess oh goddess oh goddess oh goddess...

BRACKEN!!!!

And I was unleashed, loosed, out of control, unable to contain my passion, my power, my anger, my grief, and it was spilling, streaming, destroying, sizzling over the ground, over the doomed, over my lovers I hadn't had yet, and I could do nothing but open my mouth and shriek destruction over everything until the ground below my feet melted, and I plunged to hell gurgling in my own limitless hate...

I was suddenly conscious, sweating, managing—this time—to keep my whimpers to myself, and still partially immersed in the dream. I forced my subconscious to remember the real ending of that moment, to dream what was real, so I wouldn't keep seeing Bracken's dead, blistering, cooked face in the wake of my rampant murder.

Green's arms yanked me, ripped me out of my scream, tumbled me over a hill of razored rocks, screamed in my ear to stop, stop stop stop PLEASE BELOVED FOR THE LOVE OF GODDESS STOP!!!!!

Now I was wide-awake in the small hours of the night, instantly aware that sleep was irrevocably behind me. I reached out and touched Bracken's face, peaceful in the near absolute darkness of our room. He sighed and rolled into my hand, and I stroked a high, pretty cheekbone with my thumb. Bracken. I couldn't make myself touch his hair, which had been down to the backs of his knees until that dreadful night, and I was tired of burdening him and Green with the aftermath of this dream.

Some demons couldn't be kissed away. Some of them had the right to ride you, to rend the skin of your wellness with ragged, dirty nails.

I decided to go bleed somewhere else.

With a sigh, I carefully wiggled out of the uber-large bed and slid on a pair of pajama bottoms under Bracken's T-shirt. (I had to tie the T-shirt in the back or the neck would gape open and flash my miniscule boobs. It had taken me a year to figure that out—I have no idea why all the men thought I had a brain.)

Silently, I grabbed my knitting bag and the new sock yarn I'd picked out earlier and slunk out into the living room to think—or rather to not think. The thing worrying insistently at my chest wasn't ready to be let out yet, and I didn't want to force it.

The living room was a mess of pinks and daffodils, draped, wadded, and scattered limply over the floor, couch and various appliances. The pixies, nixies, sprites, brownies, fairies, and general smaller fey who would ordinarily be cleaning them up were laying drunkenly among them, stoned on the scent of flowers, beer (elfin magic), and sex that permeated the hill. It was like fey confetti on a grand scale, and after I moved a gentle heap of them to the long wooden coffee table and brushed the flowers off the couch I could look around appreciatively and laugh softly to myself.

Green's Hill hadn't been this messy since The Honeymoon (most of us referred to it in capital letters, since the power slips that kept rolling from my body that week not only redecorated the paneling but spawned a secondary baby boom among the same group of people currently littered around the floors in wanton abandon.)

Damn—for all the bad shit I could do with my power, it was nice to know I had enough good in me to make the fairies drunk.

One of the ones I had just moved suddenly sat up and yawned. She was a sprite with vaguely mouse-like features and a 'dress' of transparent pink silk over her little gray furry body, and I smiled at her, enchanted as always by the Green's tiniest kingdom. She smiled at me and stood with dignity. Out of nowhere, she opened her little mouth again and start singing *She Moved Through The Fair* with such sweetness and purity that the shattering of my heart could probably be heard throughout the hill. The song came to a pause, where normally a Gaelic chanting would fill the empty space, and the tiny creature crossed its eyes at me imperiously.

"I'm sorry," I told her courteously, "I don't know the words." I knew what they sounded like, actually, but I didn't know what they meant or even how they divided up into phonemes.

That apparently was not good enough, because she glared from her six-inch height and stomped her tiny foot.

I shrugged, and started to chant something that sounded like 'chessa-ma-boomb-bot-te-hey-yay-yay' and it must have been close because she closed her eyes and started to sing again, using my chanted refrain as a background. We continued to a conclusion, my part extending to her last sustained note, and then she bowed and collapsed, leaving me bemused in the now silent room, ready to start my knitting.

I cast on, and had worked a couple of rows of ribbing when I became aware of the wolf-shadow in human clothing in the dark of the hallway.

I looked up and caught Teague as he decided to slink into the kitchen. He flushed and turned around as though to leave me alone, and I smiled at him and tried to be natural. It was, after all, his home too (since the garage outside the hill proper was still being remodeled for the trio) and his wedding night. He ducked his head and looked up, longingly, at the plate of cookies on the counter, and I suppressed a sigh. Classic Teague.

"Take them, sweetie," I urged quietly, not missing the way he jumped. "They're white-chocolate macadamia nut--I think Grace made them specifically for you. She even stocked up on the chocolate milk."

I could see his flush from across the room, and he grabbed a handful of the cookies almost furtively and then a bottle of chocolate milk from the fridge. He took two steps, and almost as though remembering he was human, stopped and asked, "Want some?" from a full mouth.

Well—since he asked. "I'd love some," I told him, making to stand, "but don't let me keep you."

He shook his head and waved me off, grabbing the whole plate and another bottle of milk. Somehow, he managed to juggle the works over to where I sat, and I anticipated the plate by gently moving some more of those delicate, slumbering bodies from the coffee table.

"I heard you singing," he said on a swallow, and then crushed another cookie in his mouth, as though for cover. "You sound really good when you're not singing headbanger shit."

I flushed. The men were always trying to get me to sing in public. It had been touch and go as to whether or not I'd sing at the wedding tonight, but I'd managed to duck out. I hadn't wanted anything to distract from the people we were there for.

"Thank you," I murmured, taking a cookie, "but I think most of the credit goes to the sprite."

Teague's dark hazel eyes were suddenly very perceptive on my face. "Yes, Lady Cory, but your voice was pretty too."

I smiled and met his eyes, inclining my head and feeling dumb. "Again, thank you."

A silence fell over the wasted living room then, and I knit a few stitches, feeling surprisingly relaxed. Teague's head nodded, and for a moment I thought he was going to fall asleep on me.

"Teague, sweetheart," I prompted with a smile, "why don't you go to bed?"

His eyes fluttered and he flushed, and then he cast a look that was almost hunted over his shoulder towards the room that the three of them shared when they were staying with the family. "I'll keep you company for a bit," he said gruffly. "Here—let me go get a chess set."

Bracken had given Adrian a chess set—a really cool one, with different characters or special gemstone men and shit—every year for Christmas for fifty-five years running. Since Adrian's death, Green, Grace, and Arturo had continued the tradition by giving a set to Bracken. (Fortunately, after the first year when he got three sets, they all started going in on them together, or we'd be up to our eyeballs in pawns in another year or two.) Kyle, who had inherited Adrian's room, understood that the price of not having a roommate was that we had the right to run into his room and grab a set at will. Since Kyle was still mourning his beloved, there was no likelihood we'd see anything we'd rather not, but I suddenly wondered if we didn't need to make some shelves for the front room—I'd ask Green in the morning.

Now, I looked longingly at my knitting. Teague obviously had something he needed to pitch off his chest, and as Lady of the House, I was the one with his emotional catcher's mitt—I had been since the night I'd seen him in this very room, praying that Green would be able to save Jack's life.

"Sure, Teague," I said softly. "Get the *Harry Potter* one…" Teague winced, "Or whatever one strikes your fancy." I added dryly. Teague had a very finite list of pop-culture items that didn't offend his manhood. Apparently Harry Potter wasn't on it.

He was back in a moment, and I pulled out my basic patterned socks to work on while I was waiting for his move, and he set up while I knit. It didn't matter whether I knit or actually paid attention. I really sucked at chess, but so did Teague, so it was going to be a pretty fucked-up game.

"Why didn't you sing?" he asked, just as I was making my first move.

I practically pushed over my pawn in surprise at the sound. I had been wondering where the vampires were, and that had led invariably to a glimpse of a giant room and an impossibly big bed crawling with naked bodies and bared fangs. The heart of the darkling—I had never seen it myself, and the vampires were very careful to never talk about it in front of me. I flushed, both because of what I saw in my head through the vampires' (Marcus, I think) eyes and because the clattering of the pawn was absurdly loud.

"Why didn't I sing?" I repeated blankly. Wasn't I just singing?

"At the wedding," Teague enunciated, moving his pawn in response. "Why didn't you sing? Katy would have been honored."

I flushed—I hadn't known that. "I didn't want to make it all about me," I mumbled, embarrassed that I even had to say a thing like that.

But if anyone understood about self-effacement, it was Teague Sullivan. He grunted understanding and indicated the board for my move.

We played in silence for a moment—meaning, we both advanced our pawns out in an even line and tried to figure out some other way of fighting a battle besides straight on. It didn't come naturally to either of us.

Finally, I did something funky with my knight (I admired that bizarre combination of moves that a knight was allowed to make) and Teague was forced to contemplate his next move. I knit for a moment, watched him fight between boredom and sleep for a moment, and then I jumped into the breech.

"Why don't you want to go back into your room, Teague?"

He grunted, moved a pawn right into the way of my rook, and looked at me to move.

I took the pawn, and prompted, "Teague? Neither of us really likes chess."

"It hurt," he muttered.

"What did?" But I had the feeling I knew—and he wasn't talking about the tattoo.

"I was watching them sleep in the starlight and…" he shook his head and put his face in his hands. "I don't deserve them. Oh, Goddess, Lady Cory, the things I've done…"

His thoughts so closely paralleled my own that I wondered at the fates that had made him one of ours. "You were trying to be good, Teague," I told him, not wanting to get into my own personal shit when he so obviously needed me. "I've told you that, Green told you that. You had a shit life, and your shitty father told you the Goddess people were dangerous monsters, and you thought you were being as noble as God allowed you to be…"

"I killed innocent people!" Teague looked up at me in terror, as though all of the other times he'd told me this I had simply not heard him, and now, suddenly, I would recoil with disgust.

"Jesus, Teague—do you think you're the only one?" I asked, my own anxiety making my voice sharp enough to snap him out of it.

"It's not like *you're* a serial killer!" he snapped back in complete surprise, and I, who had been raised an only child, suddenly realized that this was how siblings fought.

"More like Columbine than Ted Bundy," I said, wondering if my voice was as cold as my face, "but yes, Teague, I've killed indiscriminately before."

Teague dropped the piece he was moving.

"Jesus—you're just a kid," he said in wonder, and now *I* was the one wondering if he would ever look at me with that same worship in his eyes. Well, I thought in embarrassment and irritation and sorrow, better he know me. He was the alpha of the werewolves, one of the people who sat the leader's table during banquet—better he know me for the flawed, mortal, dumbshit kid I really was.

I shrugged and tried to look like this wasn't the reason I had awakened in my lover's arms, terrified and soaked in fear-stink. "Hey, at least I can buy beer now," I said facetiously, but the joke fell flat and he regarded me soberly, those dark hazel eyes boring into me expectantly.

"This was supposed to be about you!" I protested uncomfortably. I could count on three fingers the number of times I'd been forced to tell this story. Even Hallow, for all his (formidable) patience hadn't been able to lure me into this discussion.

"And you told me you were a mass murderer to make me feel better," he returned with disturbing insight. "It's not going to make me feel better if you don't tell me the whole story."

"You're pretty fucking smart when it's someone else's emotions, aren't you?" I asked sourly, and Teague grinned, tossing the dropped chess piece back and forth between his hands. I hadn't seen his grin much, and it took me by surprise—it was probably this expression alone that had Jacky and Katy chasing his poor puzzled heart all over creation, because that 'fuck-me' grin was sooooo worth it.

"I'm not feeling sorry for myself right now, if that's what you mean," he returned mildly.

I shot him the bird, and found I felt good enough to continue.

"Did you like the flowers?" I asked him, musingly, pushing a piece on the board that I didn't particularly care about.

"Are we changing the subject?" he asked, frowning at the board. One of us was in a position to kick major ass, but we were both so damned bad at the game that we couldn't figure out who.

"I'm making an elegant lead in," I told him with dignity. "You've only seen the good shit I do with my power, you know? The flowers. The pretty walls. The pregnant sprites. The tattoo on your wrist—its all good shit."

He laughed a little, for reasons I didn't know. "Yeah it is."

A sudden onslaught of the bad things I've done with my power assaulted the back of my eyeballs like the slideshow of the damned. My body grew still, my heart grew still, and I was pretty sure the blood drained from my face again, leaving my chest and my cheeks icy. "Not all of it is good shit," I murmured, looking down at the chess piece in my hands.

"What did you do, Lady Cory?" There was a throbbing, a need to hear it, etched in Teague's voice, and I couldn't avoid it. Green had told me bad things about himself and Adrian too, but I had never truly appreciated my mortality until this moment, when I realized that I would have a finite number of years to live with this memory, as they did not. Even Adrian, who had died too young for a vampire, had carried a burden like this one in his heart for one hundred and fifty years.

"The night Adrian died…" I murmured, and suddenly I was lost in the tale.

"He flew into a silver net, wired for sound, and simply exploded, leaving Green and me coated in his blood like a warm rain." *I could see it on the skin of my arm when I closed my eyes. The gentle thick wet of it, the dislocation as I realized that the blood on my skin was all…was all… and then he blew through my soul like summer wind through a cotton dress… and…*

"I breathed in…" *Like a baby after a bad fall… just breathing and breathing and breathing…* "And Green killed the bad guys…" *And I was breathing and breathing and breathing…* "And then Green screamed at our people to move…" *breathing and breathing and breathing…* "And then I screamed." *The surprised faces looking at foes who were no longer there, turning slowly, bemusedly, towards me on the crest of the quarry, Green behind me, holding my arms, aiming me like a sexually powered atomic laser cannon gone mad…* "And as I screamed, I let loose all this power…this grief and this power in my chest…"

"And everybody in the way…" Teague prodded softly.

"Was vaporized." I nodded, relieved a little. I was getting better at the shortened version of the story, the clinical version, the agonizing poetry of it was closer to being locked in my own heart so that only I could see.

"So you see," I spoke into the lonely silence of the deserted room, "it could be worse. You at least thought you were doing good things, right? I was just…"

"Overwhelmed," Teague said softly, the compassion in his eyes hard to see.

"Out of control. A raging adolescent bitch with a humongulous rage-powered gun. A deranged fucking time-bomb with acne scars and a flat chest."

"A grieving woman wearing her lover's blood like her own skin," said Green from the hallway, and I couldn't hardly look at him.

My face softened, just hearing his voice. I had pulled my knees up protectively to my chest, and I muttered, "Yeah, well that too," to pink-and-black skull-and-crossbones on my pajama bottoms.

"Beloved…" he protested now, moving into the room, but I shook my head and met Teague's appalled, empathetic eyes.

"I've got a point here, Green, I really do." I swallowed and touched his hand which rested on my shoulder, then smiled greenly at Teague and soldiered on. "My point is that I melted Bracken's hair off that night—it used to be down to the backs of his knees, and it was up at his shoulder-blades the next morning. I almost killed Arturo, and Renny, and Max and…and Bracken's asleep in our bed, dreaming of me, and Arturo is my uncle and my father when I'm here. Renny's my best friend—I can't keep her out of my closet much less my life. And even Max forgave me. And if they forgave me for…" my gaze dropped and I clenched my hand convulsively in my working yarn, even as Green's hand tightened on my shoulder.

"For almost killing them," I finished, voice rough, "then Jacky and Katy—their forgiveness is done. It's accomplished. They don't…" I met his eyes again and he nodded, and maybe seeing how much this cost me helped him hear the words. "They don't give a pig's flying fuck about your past. They just want you warm and safe in their bed."

He stood up then, and to my horror, he sank to one knee in front of me, like a knight from a storybook, and from this position, he bowed.

"Oh Jesus… Teague…" I met Green's eyes, and he raised his eyebrows philosophically. "Don't," I finished weakly.

The bow deepened. "Why me?" he asked gruffly. "Why tell me?"

Green's hand tightened, and he wrapped his arms around my shoulders and said it before I could. "You are so much like him…" he started, his own voice rough.

Teague looked up. "Adrian?"

And my *ou'e'hm* and I both nodded.

"You already have your lovers, Teague, it's not about that," Green answered him, hopefully putting any doubts to rest on that score. "But you are fierce, and noble, and damaged, and we love you for living and being your best. We want nothing more than for you to be happy and whole."

Teague nodded, and rubbed his eyes on his shoulder.

"Goddess…Teague, would you get up?" I begged, and to my relief he did.

He came to the couch and kissed my temple and said, "I've already said this, but I'll say it again. I'll defend you to the death, Lady Cory. You won't ever have to be a big fucking laser cannon again." And then he bowed, and sweartogod, backed out of the room.

I sighed and sank into my beloved's arms. He was bare-chested, wearing nothing but a pair of jeans, and from experience I knew he'd be commando. Everybody wanted Green's blessing on a wedding night—the one time he'd ever managed to spend a wedding night with me had been when I was the bride.

"You didn't need to come out just for me," I murmured, finding solace in his bare skin and wildflower-and-earth smell anyway.

"When I can hear your heart weeping from two rooms away?" He asked, a familiar irritation in his voice. "Luv…" He shook his head and kissed my hair, and I tried to make his smooth, sidhe-pale skin my own. "How many times do I need to tell you…"

"My pain is yours, beloved. I know." Oh Goddess…he smelled so good, and his warmth was so lovely around my shoulders. Was this what it took to make him mine for just a night? Did I have to strip myself bare and bleed for a poor werewolf who had asked for comfort and gotten my lead-mercury emotional baggage instead?

"I was doing something," I defended weakly, taking my own solace and selfishly indulging in the pleasure that had been someone else's when I'd started my hellific little trip down nightmare lane. "It was a story that would help heal him," I finished, asking for approval I think. Green was so good at making people feel better. I was supposed to be his mate, his *ou'e'eir,* his 'queen' I guess. I had an 1800 year learning curve to make in a short mortal lifetime.

"I liked it when you were singing better," he said, and the warmth in his voice told me that I'd been doing okay.

"You heard that?" I asked, shyly pleased. Green and Bracken loved to hear me sing—I was glad that he'd heard something that would make him proud of me.

"Beloved," he murmured, a weariness showering from him like tiny petals from a mustard flower, "what will it take for you to let that moment go. To simply accept that it is you, and not to be angry that it was you?"

I sighed, and tilted my head back, holding up my arms so he could lift me into his because he so very much liked to carry me and I would be less of a burden in his arms than I would be bearing my own weight.

"I need to know it will never happen again," I said simply, feeling the heave and lift. "Not that way. Not that horribly," I murmured next to his chest, leaning my head on his shoulder and glorying in how close we were when he held me like this. "I'll do what I need to do to protect us, but I don't ever want to spin out of control like that again."

Green nodded into my hair. "Okay, luv. Okay…we'll see what we can do about that."

I laughed softly—I could laugh, from the safest place in the world.

"Come with me," he murmured. "We'll just lay together…we never have time to just lay together…"

Bracken would know where I was when he woke up—he always did, and it never bothered him. Green took me into his room, with its vast bed covered in dark green and burgundy and brown and its lightly varnished oak paneling (my magic never touched Green's room—maybe because it was sacred in my heart, just like Green) and its big hand carved bureau. There were no mirrors in Green's room, although the big bay window did look out at the canyon below us. The house itself was literally lodged in the middle of a hill in the Sierra Foothills, and beyond Green's environs you could find oak trees and pine trees and red dirt. Inside Green's hill was an English countryside, and inside Green's room was peace.

I lay there in his bed, my head on his pale shoulder, and played with his long, graceful fingers in the moonlight, staring at that view over the silvered canyon.

"How many nights," I wondered dreamily, "did you and Adrian do this?"

"Not enough, luv," he replied sadly, and I rolled over in his arms and took his beautiful, kind face in my hands and kissed him, devoured him, took him into my soul, and our bodies moved and heaved and shattered in the night and when he crested inside of me and I flew apart into starlight, I came back laughing softly through my tears, so happy to have him inside of me that there was no human expression for the joy.

When we woke up the next morning, the floors and the grounds above the hills were covered with mustard flowers and lupins in addition to the pinks and daffodils—and with the occasional ripe and tart lime in their midst, hidden like early Easter eggs and ready to be squeezed into the morning's orange juice for taste.

Bracken was curled up on my other side, and I was as content as mortal flesh could allow.

GREEN

Between Winter and Spring

Green and Arturo had been having breakfast together at the sturdy oak table in the kitchen for more years than Cory had been alive.

Arturo's first welcome to the hill had been some of Green's pixies and wood nymphs in his bed after a night of beautiful conversation and *very* good wine (for taste—alcohol didn't really affect the sidhe, but they did like the human richness of wine on occasion). The next morning, Green had been sitting at the table, doing his accounts (painstakingly by hand at the time) and eating oatmeal. He'd asked Arturo to join him, and then asked if Arturo was still bent on taking over Green's territory, which had been the reason he'd visited the hill in the first place.

Arturo had taken a bite of oatmeal (spiced with honey and nuts), noticed Green's spreadsheets out on the table with headings like 'clothes', 'grocery', and 'payoffs for authorities', as well as income reports for several (now several hundred) businesses that Green owned, and recalled his rather exceptional night.

"No," he'd replied thoughtfully, licking his spoon and going for another bite. "But I wouldn't mind helping you out, brother. Have you thought about killing the policemen instead of paying them off?"

Green had—but he'd decided against it, and in the ensuing conversation, a sixty year partnership had been born.

Arturo—being a South American fertility god from the outset—was not pansexual, as many of the creatures in Green's hill were, but that didn't stop him from loving Green with a purity of heart that transcended sex and bordered on friendly worship. Green could possibly do wrong, in Arturo's eyes, but Arturo would support him anyway simply because his heart was always looking for the way to do right. Arturo had witnessed over three-thousand years of petty human and sidhe behavior. Goodness for its own sake was not a thing to ever be taken lightly.

On this day, a bright, windy late March morning with more than its fair share of chill, the two sidhe sat together and opened mail, making various comments that were both practical and amusing, in the way of couples who have lived together for many years.

"Mmmm..." Arturo grunted, looking at the paper. "You see this thing, on the animal attacks?"

"Sugarpine?" Green frowned at a large manila envelope with his P.O. Box number in red sharpie. He didn't recognize the hand or the return address. "Yes—you think it's important?"

"Three people killed by a...a small cougar?" Arturo frowned. Wild cat attacks happened—but more often than not there were survivors. Lots of them. Wild cats could be vicious but for the most part, they didn't really like the taste of humans—and to kill all three?

Green looked at him, concerned. "Wasn't there another child in the family? Young?"

"A little girl, eight or nine," Arturo confirmed. "Something here brother..."

"Doesn't smell right," Green agreed. "Teague's coming back from a job this morning. Give him a day or two to spend with his family, then send him. If you send him during spring break, he may take Jacky and Katy with him."

Arturo grunted and rolled his eyes. "And he may leave them sleeping to go check it out on his own. I'm all for higher education but I'm not sure sending Jacky back to school was so good for Teague's lifespan."

Green blew out his cheeks and took another bit of Reeses Pieces. "Well, it wasn't guaranteed even when Jacky rode shotgun. You'd think he would realize..." Adrian. Green and Cory could both see Adrian in their damaged Alpha. They could see him no more clearly than when Teague went out on hunting runs and left Jack and Katy home in the name of 'protecting' his beloveds. Of course Jacky had proved he needed some more training in order to not be a danger to himself *and* Teague, but being left home was not making his temper easy on anybody at the hill either. Every time Green tried to bring the subject up, Teague nodded and absorbed the import of Green's words with sober eyes, and then went off on his next run alone. Cory had been busy with school, and she'd told Green that if she actually *tried* to have a conversation with the alpha, he ran away like a feral cat.

"What we need," Green said after a moment, "is a partner. Because he is right about one thing—Jacky and Katy aren't made for the runs. There was a reason I teamed him up with Jacky," Arturo never asked how Green knew a pairing like that would work out—Green just did, "but now... we need someone who's quick on his feet, preternatural..." Green took another bit of his cereal and mulled for a moment.

"Off limits sexually," Arturo said, and Green looked at him surprised.

"He'd no sooner move on another lover..."

"Than the moon start orbiting another planet—I know, brother," Arturo agreed. "But Jack and Katy..." were extremely possessive over their Teague. They would need the reassurance.

"Mmm...yes, I see. You're absolutely right." Suddenly Green brightened. "Mario!"

Arturo grinned broadly, his copper-lightning eyes crinkling at the corners and his silver capped teeth flashing in the sun. (Arturo was a little vain—but only a little. Unlike the European sidhe, he kept his raven-wing-black hair cut to his shoulders for convenience.)

"Dead straight!" He slapped the table.

Mario was one of the Avians who had once been aligned with Nicky against Green's people. He'd lost his mate in the fight, and Green had given him his will to live. The young man had appointed himself Cory's personal knight errant since, and had been going to school with the other students, but Green had detected a certain restlessness about him recently, and at Mario's request had put him in charge of building the Aerie—the home Mario and his people been living in, out on a vast property out in Camp Far West. They mated for life, and if they stayed in the hill, after a night like, say, Teague's wedding night, there would be a lot of Avians stuck in a relationship they hadn't ever foreseen. Until they mated on their own, it was really best to keep them away from the hill's seething sexuality, but that didn't mean that they didn't owe their allegiance—quite happily—to Green.

Mario was butch, hetero, and had absolutely no designs on poor Teague, who couldn't figure out what his spouses saw in him as it was.

Green nodded and grinned back, pleased with himself. "School breaks in a week—we'll send them before then," he decided. "But first we need to make sure Mario comes to dinner on Sunday—he's usually here, but it would be good to make it a solid."

Arturo stood and began talking about contacts at the campground and various theories as to what sort of problem it could be, and in the meantime, Green reached out his hand to open the manila envelope.

What he saw inside startled him enough to drop the envelope and scatter the contents across the crowded table.

Arturo, surprised, picked up the 8x10 photos—the images would have been blurry anyway, because they seemed to be still pictures taken from a video, but besides that...

"Man, we look like shit on film, don't we?" he breathed, panic coating his voice like salted butter.

"You weren't even there, brother," Green replied numbly. His hands shook, and he picked up the picture nearest him.

He remembered the day vividly—a funeral for a vampire's beloved, for his beloved's friend. There had been camera crews across the street—the young woman's family had been prominent—but when they hadn't been contacted then...Goddess, it was a year ago, wasn't it?

Well yes. Almost to the day.

Green looked at the photo again. Cory looked...well, like Cory did to humans. Squat and plain and ordinary. She was dressed in black, with a black raincoat that she probably didn't remember was in her closet, and she was scowling with both grief and purpose as they walked out of the church.

Renny was a little behind her, looking cat-like but still, only human, and Nicky was next to Renny—again, merely human. Shapeshifters have always been good on film. The vampires—there had been four of them including the grieving one—came out as dark mist, vaguely human shaped—ranged in logical, humanly spaced blurs around Cory.

Bracken and Green who had been at her sides, were not left with any human attribute at all.

"I could never understand why this happens," Green muttered, looking at the picture. He had been paired with Adrian as photography had emerged as an art form—he had, in his possession, some very nice oil miniatures of the two of them that he planned to share with Cory someday soon, now that the pain of losing their beloved was more manageable and she wouldn't cling to the trinket in grief.

But he'd only needed his photo taken once to know that cameras were not the Goddess folk's friends.

Arturo grunted in frustration. "I never could figure out why it's so different—you look like that...that character in that Tim Burton movie... except with an oval for a face!"

"Jack Skellington?" Green mused, not sure if he had enough play in him for outrage. "Well," he muttered, his mind still stumbling over the implications, "I guess that's an improvement over Bracken."

Arturo knew very well how serious this was, but he couldn't help smirking. "He looks like a gray scale version of that thing from the *Fantastic Four*..."

Green looked up, his humor finally catching up with him. "The Thing?" He asked dryly and Arturo met his eyes, a slow, real smile spreading between the two of them. Almost in tandem, they took a deep breath, squared their shoulders, and started to dig for the root of this particular problem.

"Is there a note with it?" Arturo asked, and Green shook his head no, then checked the back of the distorted pictures.

"Aha!" Green murmured, downplaying the gravity of the situation. His people on film—it was a dangerous moment in time, this. "*I know what you are.* That's original. Oh wait…" he scanned the rest of the red sharpie on the back of the photo which featured Cory the most clearly in the center of the shot. She was scowling, and he was swept with a terrible distaste that a mere mortal would see his beloved like this—he resented that someone would see her as plain, as squat, as ordinary. It was a violation of all he believed was true.

Still, he focused on the message. "*I know what you are. I know who you want to protect. Give me an exclusive or I tell the world about her.*"

The red sharpie blurred in Green's vision, expanded, distorted, filled his eyes, filled his mind, filled his chest with crimson rage. Dimly he became aware that Arturo had two hands on his shoulders and was ordering him to "Breathe, brother, in, out, repeat as needed, you hear me?"

Green looked at the crumpled photos wadded in his hand and pulled oxygen into his lungs and let it out on a snarl. Arturo nodded with him and when their anger had receded enough for reason, he said, "So, who you want should do the job?"

Green squinched his eyes closed and opened them in icy shock, Arturo bringing home to him the things he was and the things he was not. "We don't know this person, Arturo," he rasped, shaking off his second's comforting hands. "We don't know if he's good or evil or in a corner—or even if he's just blinded by purpose, or even if he's given the negatives to anybody else. He doesn't ask for money, remember? He just wants his precious 'story'. If that's true we can meet with him. We can reason with him…hell, if nothing else, we can wipe his bloody fucking slate clean and not have a body to hide. Bodies leave tracks—mind-fucked arse-fuckers just irritate their bosses."

Abruptly, Green stood up and started pacing. "We have a contact number, right?"

Arturo picked up the glossy photograph between his thumb and forefinger as though he were picking up something dead and nodded. "Yes, but I really think we should just kill this guy."

Green paused in his worry and his pacing to shoot Arturo a wry grin. In one form or another, they'd had this discussion before. "Let's see if we can do this with a mindfuck or a tumble in bed before we fuck him for real, shall we Arturo?"

Arturo shook his head in frustration. One of Green's great strengths and great weaknesses was that killing was always his last answer. Arturo had killed before and lived to regret it—but in the jungles of his homeland, where the gods had competed fiercely for their share of virgins, wine, and tribute, he had managed to live.

"Whatever you say, brother—but either way, we'll know who he is and how this is going to go down by the end of the week."

Green's grin widened again at his second's obvious reluctance, and he bent over the solid, light-oak kitchen table, cleaning up the offending pictures and looking to see if there was any more sweet cereal left for seconds. (There always was. Grace was very good at buying his favorite brands as well.)

"Either way, my friend," he said, taking a bite of cereal between clean-up efforts, "it's going to be a busy week."

Arturo rolled his eyes and then sat down to his own bowl of cereal. (When he wasn't eating oatmeal, he was partial to anything with marshmallows.) No matter what was for breakfast, it was obviously going to have to last them a while.

TEAGUE

Hawk and Wolf

Teague sure did like having Mario as a partner—now if he could only convince Jacky that the guy was straighter than a redneck's rifle, his life would be damn near perfect.

He hadn't been particularly excited when Green had suggested he partner off with someone else besides Jack. In fact, he'd flat out told Green "No!" But then Jack had suggested that maybe, since he was going to be on break soon, they should make the run out to Sugarpine together.

Teague had looked at the newspaper article with the wild animal attacks and dead family and said, "Can't. Green's got me a partner for when you're in school, and this needs to be handled now."

Jack had sulked, but he hadn't damaged any walls, doors, or furniture, and after the debacle after Thanksgiving, Teague was all for calling this one a win.

He'd loved being partnered up with Jack. Jacky could follow his thoughts, jolly him out of his dark moods, and read his cues in conversation like no one Teague had ever met. But Teague's need for those things in his job had stopped abruptly when he'd picked Jack up out of a pool of his own blood and made like a screaming hurricane for Green. Twice.

He'd figured that Jacky's need to follow him in the hunting life would have eased up once Teague had followed Jack into the werewolf life, and they had followed each other into bed. He'd really been hoping that binding to Katy would have made Jack see the joys of domestic bliss, and to some extent

- 40 -

it had—Jack had gone back to school, and he enjoyed helping Katy at the bakery and for the most part, all was well.

Which was great, because Jack may be up and around and whole and healthy, but Teague was pretty damned sure he'd never recover from seeing his friend, his lover, his goddamned other half, lying on the ground and bleeding. Twice. Yes, he knew that werewolves healed faster than humans and that the same wound today would barely faze Jacky as he scrambled up to kick some righteous ass—the question was, did Teague give a ripe shit?

The answer was, in order for Jacky to never be in that sort of danger again, Teague'd probably get along with Satan himself, if the fucker would let him play his own goddamned music in the car on the way to the run.

Seeing that he was willing to do all that, it was just as well and good that Mario liked *Nickleback, Linkin' Park,* and old *Metallica* almost as much as Teague, and that he seemed to be able to read Teague's mind too. The fact that brother had never looked at a man sideways--much less fucked him frontways or backways--should have set everybody's mind to rest, but everybody wasn't Jacky, who had a whiny, girlie possessive streak almost the size of his damned caretaker's heart.

Fortunately Katy was too level headed for that kind of shit, but since Katy had a couple of assets that Mario didn't, her place in Teague's life was relatively safe from that perspective. What Teague couldn't seem to convince Jacky of, was that it wouldn't matter—his heart was fragile, it could only take so much uncertainty. Offering it to Katy and Jack about met his lifetime quota of self-doubt, and he would, God and Goddess willing, not have to ever offer his heart on a silver platter for another fool blind-stupid enough to take it.

And of course it would help if his body would hurry up and mate already.

He was supposed to. After werewolves spent enough time in company with a chosen lover (or two) their bodies were *supposed* to stop responding to other people--forever, barring the death of one mate and the survival of another. The fact that Teague's body wasn't doing that—and fuck-it-all-to-hell, *he* didn't know why!—was driving jealous Jaqueline (as Teague had been calling him!) up the fucking wall.

Teague couldn't seem to explain that wood was wood—he certainly wasn't going to go out and club someone else over the groin with it. He didn't *want* anyone else, dammit, and what his body did when vampires fed off of him had nothing to do with where his heart was. It was bad enough that he hadn't been able to scare the two of *them* off—another lover, male or female, would 'bout kill him.

Which is what brought him on this winding, steep road with Mario in the seat next to him, both of them with windows down in the evening chill, scenting the wind with its promise of a good run in their other skins. Like Jack, Mario didn't need to talk much in the car, and what he did say was either funny or to the point, so right now they were silent and companionable. Teague could deal with a companion who didn't have a bone of drama in his Avian body.

Lake Sugarpine was a small recreational lake a good fifteen miles as the hawk flew from Green's hill. It was good for fishing if you weren't depending on your catch to eat, and good for swimming if you didn't mind the mountain chill, even in July. A lot of folks apparently didn't, because the campgrounds around the lake were pretty full in the on-season, and people who spent no time at all in the out-of-doors all year spent a week at the lake to track the dark red dirt into their homes in triumph of, for once, valuing some time outdoors over a homemaking disaster.

Late March was too early for campers—the unfortunate family who had been killed earlier in the month had been there with special permission from the owner of the private campground. Teague had left his cherished Mustang back at the apartment for Jack and Katy to use, so when he arrived he parked Green's SUV in the parking lot next to the murky green water. The egg-shaped lake was cold this moment just after sunset—he only had to look at the chilly emerald heart of it, rejecting the last few rays of sunlight, to get the shivers. Since he was stripping off his clothes and putting them on the front seat of the SUV, Mario shook his head in sympathy.

"Brother, I've got to tell you I feel for you skin-changing boys—nothing like going natural for the tourists, right?" Mario had a compact, muscular Latino body and could have given Arturo a run for his money in a masculine beauty pageant, complete with dimples and curly hair. The look in his brown eyes as Teague stripped had been devoid of even the slightest bit of speculation. Thank the Goddess. There was a certain relief in knowing the guy watching your back wasn't watching your ass.

Teague grinned at him fiercely. "Yeah, well, some of us are proud of our genes, and some of us just fold them on the car seat and get on with our lives." Mario chuckled and Teague gave an inward sigh. After a year and a half of sexual tension with the guy who had his back, Teague wistfully hoped Jacky would let him keep Mario. He was pretty sure the two of them might live—especially now that he had a Goddess-get edge.

He'd never paid attention to the moon before he started working for Green. Now that he'd been bitten by a werewolf—by request—he lived and died by the light of Her face. He looked into the sky and let the waxing crescent vibrate with his heartbeat at his temples, and he found a still, sweet place inside him. It was, curiously enough, a place devoid of lovers—there was no room in this place for anything but the demands that Teague usually bottled on principle. However, it was also devoid of pain. Just a perfectly round, silver space filled with the strength of Teague's heart. He loved this space—it was one of the few places besides Jack and Katy's arms where he'd ever found peace.

In a moment, he was on all fours, his muscles dancing to the moon's music and his own heartbeat, goose-stepping over his liquid bones in painful time.

And then he was a wolf, and he was free. Mario locked up the SUV, put the keys in the magnetic locker under the wheel-well, changed form and powered his way into the sky in short order. Teague stuck his wet black nose into the air and sniffed delicately, tasting the wind on his tongue behind his palette. His dark blonde fur prickled around his ruff and his back—there was something…alien in this particular wind-bouquet.

He gave a little yelp and went trotting off into the darkness, Mario keeping watch overhead.

Teague had been to Sugarpine many times before as a human—but never as a wolf. As a human, the sheer red shale hills that the road carved on its way down to the lake had simply been a part of the scenery—a place, he knew for certain that no enemies could hide.

As a wolf, he could smell the dimness of deep places in those hills, the damp musk of caves. He had been trotting in a focused direction, heading up from there for a place where the land became uneven enough to support caves for the bears and wildcats that were steadily being edged out by daring developers. He knew where the wild animals were—he was looking for something amiss with them.

Mario screeched above him and he whuffled in agreement.

Something was clearly amiss with the smell of the world.

What was that? He sniffed, and shook his head like he'd gotten thistles up his nose. No. Seriously. What *was* that? It was…there was something both right and wrong about that smell, like the garbage dumpster behind Denny's or something. Because, honestly, that dumpster shouldn't smell bad—it had good stuff in it, right? All the stuff that went into making food? What--a little bit of metal and some water and it had to smell worse than shit warmed over?

This smell was like that—like chocolate and tuna fish or ham and fabric softener. It *should* have been a good smell. In fact, it *should* have been two of them. But the two smells were so wrong together they were an abomination against every pore, fiber, muscle and capillary in Teague's husky, shaggy body.

Mario shrieked again, this time in panic, and Teague had one of those moments of clarity that had saved him as a child.

As a child, he'd developed an uncanny ability to know which direction the old man would be swinging. It was a damned good thing, too—more than once, Teague had woken up blinking and nauseous and beat-the-fuck-up, with the gut-level belief that if he'd zigged instead of zagged, he would have woken up dead. The strange clarity that controlled his actions during those times felt a lot like the peace he found in the moon when he changed.

And right now it was dreaming him through the darkness, to an even darker silhouette against the black of the hill in front of him, cut off from the light of the moon and the stars.

What *was* that?

Teague blinked, saw it move quicker than human, quicker than animal, turning a massive, shaggy head towards him with the fleetness of a robin, and that too was abomination.

That thing was between Teague and the car.

Mario shrieked again, furiously, and that clarity sailed Teague's body in a complete u-turn, and he bounded over the edge of the road and again over a massive log with all of the preternatural grace of one of the Goddess' chosen ones.

He was a werewolf. He could move pretty damned fast when he wanted to, and right now, his gut was telling him to run like a fucking bullet train through the wilderness.

Mario shrieked again and Teague heard a sound behind him that felt like the wrenching of metal asunder, the ripping of trees in half at their base, the shattering of the air above his head with destruction.

Teague hurtled with a terrible focus towards Green's house, towards his lovers and safety and life. He wished he could at least see what was riding his ass with the same uncanny speed that he was using to devour the woodland in his way.

What in the *fuck* was that thing?

CORY

What in the fuck is that thing?

Marcus and I were getting religious, sort of.

Marcus had been a history teacher before he was a vampire, and if you do it right, that sort of thing doesn't just 'go away', even when the blood runs thick and black with death. We both had an affinity for the old stories—the crushingly sad story of the first vampire, the story of the Avians and why they were different from the werewolves and why they were both different from every other were-creature in creation—basically, any of the stories of the Goddess folk that hadn't made it into Yeats or Arthur Rackham or the Brothers Grimm, we wanted to record.

We made a good team of it. For the most part, I'd always gotten along with my teachers, mostly because I sat in the back of the room, took in what they said and didn't make eye-contact. Marcus had been the sort of teacher who would have *forced* me to make eye-contact, I think, and once he got over his little crush on me, we worked well together. The crush had worried me at first—it's not as though my love life wasn't complicated, and Green, Nicky, Bracken and I have to work really hard to keep ourselves sane.

Of course, Bracken made it clear that he was always open to a third party, but I wasn't so sanguine about just letting another man into our bed --even Nicky got his own night most nights, unless it was a special occasion and all four of us were tumbling about like ducks in a whirlpool.

Marcus is a good-looking guy—don't get me wrong. He's a whole lot of Italian—dark hair, dark eyes, swarthy skin that still registered a blush (provided he had eaten recently). He's also a whole lot of taken, although his tempestuous relationship with his roommate/lover Phillip is notoriously open. Both of them had been completely het until death—but Marcus had brought Phillip over when he'd discovered Phillip's body under a shitload of snow up at Donner Pass, and that bond, coupled with the blood and flesh bonding that most new vampires endured had forged a relationship that neither of them wanted to leave, but nobody knew how to deal with.

Their taste in women was diametrically opposed: the fact that Phillip had never found me remotely attractive and Marcus had spent some time during the fall giving me a power zap through a simple handshake with the force of his crush was pretty much par for the course. Their taste in each other however, had been as constant as the storms on Mars for twenty years now (or so I've been told.)

So obviously it had been a relief when Marcus' blushing adoration eventually boiled down to a combination of the deference a good subject pays his liege (as embarrassing as that is) and the affection a really good teacher shows to a (slightly) gifted student. On this whole 'Goddess mythology' thing, we pretty much partnered up nicely.

I collected the stories from the older sidhe, and he helped me bring them to some semblance of order. Green would come up to our little sessions occasionally and help with things the other sidhe didn't remember, and sometimes he'd come up to look meaningfully at Marcus until Marcus got the hint and vamoosed. Then we'd sit in the moonlight, talking softly together about our day, waiting to see if Adrian would visit.

Our beloved visited rarely, usually when we missed him so acutely our pores bled from wanting him. We were always so grateful for that glimpse of him, the ghost with the autumn-sky eyes and the white-blonde hair. We tried so very very hard to miss him in secret, so we could cherish the time we spent with his memory given flesh of light and wind and moon. Adrian had been there, he told me, the night of the wedding—the date itself had been a painful anniversary for the two of us. He'd enjoyed watching my dance with Bracken very much, but unspoken in that sentence had been the awful fact that Adrian and I had never had the chance to dance

That's how it came to be that at dark-thirty a.m. on a fucking cold and clear morning, I was sitting in the Goddess grove with my laptop, working quietly with Marcus, discussing the offspring of the gods. If God created humans, and Goddess and the other (the chaotic one) created the sidhe, and Goddess and God's creatures created the shape-shifters, we wondered (or rather *me, I* was wondering) what happened if the other paired up with humans. After the vampire debacle, the Goddess declined to do it—she bore God's son and called it quits. The other, though… well, given the proclivities of the sidhe, he must have been one horny son of a bitch—what happened when he boffed Betty Cheerleader and had himself a rip-snortin' good time? Considering he is the 'other' precisely because he is chaos in god form, I'm reasonably sure he'd leave the rubbers in the desk drawer, but what then? I mean, I didn't think the little bastards popped out and screamed 'I'm the son of chaos! Change my diaper, bitch!' but other than that, why hadn't we heard of more little demon spawn, running around setting the nanny's hair on fire?

Marcus had choked on his own incisors when I'd asked him this question (verbatim), but then we started talking about it and here I was, nodding off as dawn thought nasty subversive thoughts about an hour away. All this discussion, and all we had to write about was, 'Well, what about an Incubus?'

We were about ready to give it up so this little day-dweller could go whine at Bracken and get laid, when Jacky hauled his ass up to the grove with Katy trotting behind him.

"Where in the fuck is he!" Jack snarled, and I blinked at him, keeping my temper and my bewilderment to myself.

"Which 'he' would you be referring to, Jack?" I asked pleasantly, although I had a pretty good idea. Jack only got unreasonably frightened for one 'he' that I knew of. "If you're asking about Green, he's downtown, doing business, and Bracken is off being *oi'anga* in the lower Goddess grove. Was that to whom you were referring?" Oooh—look at me being all proper and shit.

Something in my tone must have sliced pretty fine because Jack took a step back and then made a restrained bow in my direction. What in the fuck was it about these two men that responded to me like that?

"My apologies, Lady Cory," he said, both sincere and appalled at his own outburst. "Teague—he was supposed to go on a run with Mario…he told me he'd call as soon as they got out of the canyon…it should have been hours ago… we just got a call from the ranger who let them in, and the SUV is there but they're not."

And like that, my need for a title disappeared.

"Marcus?" I said, but what went from my mind to his, via our blood-link was a vision of every fucking vampire in the hill, spread out and flying towards Sugarpine.

"We're there," he responded crisply, placing the laptop on the marble bench and standing with that scary, stop-action vampire speed.

"Watch for Mario—he'll be in the air!" I ordered and like that, he launched, his black bomber jacket flapping in the considerable wind of his flight.

Jack blinked, surprised his concern seemed to be taken so seriously so quickly.

"Jesus, Jacky," I muttered, "didn't it occur to you to say something sooner? We could have been out searching an hour ago! You two need to go get the were-creatures—have them out on the green behind the hill and I'll be out to organize—the first person who sees Bracken and Nicky, tell them what we're doing and I'll meet you ba…"

Jacky and Katy were frozen, noses pointed in the air, the hair on their heads spiking up like a dog's ruff. Their eyes were so big I could see the moon in the whites as Jack let out a high-pitched whine.

"That's Teague!" he yelped, and just like that, I wasn't talking to a young man anymore, I was watching a humongulous gray wolf tear-ass down the hill dragging his clothes with him, with a smaller white-fringed, black wolf in his wake.

"*Fuck!*" I was wearing sneakers, which made the next part easy, and I started sprinting towards the cross-country track that Green had given me as a birthday/wedding present this last summer. I loved this trail, and knew it down to the last granite rock and sap-dripping tree. At least I hoped I did, because the ambient light left off at the crown of the hill, and suddenly I was hauling ass in the dark.

I'd tripped twice and gone sprawling on my face and then run into a couple of trees before Green snapped "*Beloved!*" in my head and I bounced off another tree and stopped.

Teague…

Will not live if you fall down the hill unconscious. You're a sorceress, dammit—make something glow.

Have I mentioned I'm not particularly bright sometimes?

Sorry Green. With that I opened my palm in front of me and forced some of my power through it. The glow—which I usually used to either destroy things or shield them—illuminated the path nicely, and with some prodding from Green in my head, I made it rise above me and to the fore, so I could trot down the path in full daylight. If I wasn't scraped all to hell with a bloody nose and what felt like a swollen eye (fucking trees) I probably would have been a little more triumphant as I got down to the lawn below the hill where everybody else was gathering. Green was an amused fulmination in my head, too, so my sheepishness was hard to keep to myself when I arrived.

"What in the fuck did you do?" Bracken asked as we gathered, and I rolled my eyes and shrugged.

"I went jogging in the dark—can we leave it alone?" Bracken's first instinct is to touch me—my blood pissed him off on several levels, the first being that if he did touch me, I bled more. Such was the life of a red-cap.

"Grace," I asked, pleased that I could speak to a vampire in person. Having the vampires I blooded able to talk in my head completely changed the meaning of the word 'psychobabble'. For the most part, I could tune them out, but in an emergency, I didn't really want to.

"What'ya need, sweet thing?" Grace: nearly six feet of lanky, red-headed mama-vampire. If it were not for Grace and her lover Arturo, odds were good I wouldn't have survived my first year in the preternatural world.

"Some of you have to stay back and get ready to catch," I gasped, and looked at Bracken. "And we need people on the ground to take out whatever is the problem, right?"

Bracken grinned wolfishly. His father's people were all built like granite quarries, scaled, speckled skin and all. They didn't get to fight much these days, and Bracken had been raised on stories of the red-caps fighting bravely in Scotland and Ireland, when the British got out of hand.

"Da' will be thrilled," he said with satisfaction, and, silly me, I didn't think to ask him what *he'd* be doing in the fight. "I'll go arrange them at the tree line."

In my head I asked if anybody could see Jack and Katy, and I got the affirmative—they were heading for the most northern path from Sugar Pine, and I wagered that wherever Teague was coming from, something had thrown him off track. I relayed this information to Bracken and he *blurred* into hyperspeed to go get his kin.

I didn't need to ask what Jack and Katy were heading for—the truth was, under the right circumstances, one wolf could hear another's bark from a distance of miles. The werewolves could hear their mate bark in either form. Whatever had happened to Teague, he had just run a very long ways over the course of the night, and he was headed here.

Suddenly there was a shout in my head from one of the vampires. Nicky was up there—I could see him through Marcus' eyes, and he was screeching at the tiny speck that was Mario, hauling giant bird ass over the pine trees that made up the higher elevations to our east.

Marcus swore, the wind tearing away his words, and the two birds dove down, taking my heart with them.

I stumbled, in my own body, and Bracken caught me, ignoring the flood of blood at my nose. Nicky and Mario emerged, their wings pumping, both their asses a few tail-feathers short. They evened out on a height and hovered there in the quickly diminishing distance, and as they held out their wings and caught a current, Marcus and the other vampires arrived and looked down.

The view down was complex with trees and brush, but I could make out the glimmer of a big blonde/brown wolf in the fore, running for all that he was worth, and behind him…

Abruptly I was myself, looking at Bracken in perplexity.

"Jesus," I muttered, "what is that thing?"

"What is what thing?" Bracken asked and I shrugged and tried to think. Teague needed help, and fast, because whatever that massive, hairy nightmare was behind him, he'd barely kept ahead. He had been moving with all his supernatural speed just to live.

Marcus! In his head I put an image of him, swooping out of the sky to scoop Teague out of the way and before I could even blink, he tried to comply.

I could barely keep my berth in his brain as he dodged tree branches and underbrush, coming from behind the thing, in its brown, shaggy vastness and flashed around it. In a heartbeat, a panicked, exhausted wolf was caught up in his arms…

And then the world spun on a crazy axis, the sky and the trees and the dark of the earth blurring together with nightmare glimpses of long teeth in a dark animal face. Marcus went tumbling up into the air like a deranged rubber ball, and Teague went flying across the forest to land, on his feet, running again, but this time he had a few feet of clearance.

I came to myself, looked at my beloved and swore. "We need fighters there, so we can clear Teague and trap that thing," I gasped, trying to think, dammit, think! I couldn't run through the fucking underbrush without killing myself and now I had to save Teague's life?

But Bracken had no doubts—he set me firmly on the ground and said, "I'll take care of it!" And then I went back to the vampires, asking them if they could harry that thing, slow it down, and give Teague a chance to break through the trees to safety.

I was, of course, planning to be safety, but Jack and Katy had other ideas.

This time, I shared head space with Kyle, who was closer to the center of the hill than Marcus, and when I looked down, I saw the two wolves running uncertainly in Teague's direction. They had no strategy, I thought in a panic. They were just *going to Teague* without thinking of how they were going to help him.

The idea of Jack and Katy facing that *thing* was enough to make me wet my pants. With a quick flash back from Marcus' eyes, I saw that Teague had heard them coming, and it was enough to make him stumble over a log. The thing was closing in with paws the size of soccer balls when Marcus dove down, hand extended, and grabbed a big chunk of (cold, matted) fur and then hurtled away, shaking the fur from his fingers as he went.

There was a terrifying howl as the thing stopped and reared, trying to get a hold of whatever attacked it, but Marcus was safely out of the way, and Teague had gained a few more steps through the hills. I barked an order into Marcus' head and then one into Kyle's and Raymond's, and Marcus hollered, "They're safe! Keep running!"

Kyle and Raymond dove down and scooped up two pissed-off werewolves and zoomed them back to me, depositing them on the grass wiggling and furious and out for my blood.

Jack quick-changed, shouting at me even as I tried to put myself back into the battle. When I ignored him and went back inside Marcus' head to gauge the time it would take for Teague to burst through the woods to the clear meadow surrounding the hill, he grabbed my shoulder and swung me around to face him.

"You bitch, we were trying to help..." his voice trailed off as I blinked my eyes at him, and I wondered if they had been glowing. Bracken told me they did that sometimes when I was vamp-surfing.

"Back the fuck off! I'm doing something," I snapped, without heat, still trying to establish that mind-link with Marcus. Something about my frantic, distracted air must have penetrated Jacky's panic, because he did take a step back, and I put my head back into the battle.

I heard a passing thought from Marcus, and looked toward my right, trying not to just let my jaw drop like an enchanted child as an entire contingent of fey warriors—most of them no taller than four feet or so, went marching double-time towards the edge of the hill. The foot soldiers of the fey were red-caps: they were built like forgotten corners of old quarries, granite skin, joints like stacked rocks, spiderwebs and all. Bracken's father was in the lead, and Brack himself was at the end, both of them carrying wicked looking spears with silver heads. I assumed Bracken's was ceremonial, because I may have mentioned, I'm not that bright, so I dismissed him from my mind (after an admiring glance in his jeans with no shirt, I'll admit) and had a sudden idea about how to get Teague the fuck out of there.

"We can do this..." I muttered, and I gave an urgent call to Green. In a gentle cloud of wildflowers, he was there in my head, like he always is when I need him, and then Marcus' lover, Phillip, hearing my side of the psychobabble gave an urgent shout for me to pick him.

Phillip, the perverse asshole, loved this part of my power, and well, hell, the dumbshit volunteered.

We had practiced this on occasion, since we'd been forced to do it in an emergency last year, and it demanded three things—my power, aimed with my will, a vampire who was a willing receptacle, and Green's power, acting like a plastic coating between live wires and skin. My power was sunshine, fueled by emotion, and we'd seen firsthand what it could do to vampires without some sort of buffer. Green got to be my buffer, and now he slid silkily in between Phillip's consciousness and my raw telekinesis. Together we shot a sunshine-shield around Teague as he burst into the clearing that marked Green's hill.

Phillip 'picked up' the bubble containing one very freaked-out, splayed-legged werewolf and 'threw' it towards me with enough force that I caught it midway, breaking off my connection with Phillip and taking Teague the rest of they way across the clearing. I managed to scream "Jacky, *catch!*" at the top of my lungs as I hurtled his beloved at him and dropped my shield.

Jack caught a wide-eyed, yelping Teague in both strong arms, wrapping them so tightly around his lover that I heard Teague yelp and snap, and then a fully human, "Jesus Christ, Jacky, you're gonna fuckin' break somethin'!" before I was back in the action, watching things from Marcus' eyes. (Phillip plopped limply out of the sky at the edge of the tree line, drunk on the power blast—Goddess love him, it's why he volunteered.)

"Holy Goddess, queen of cats!" I swore, and inside his brain I could hear Marcus swearing too. "What is that thing?"

It burst out of the trees, and was blurring towards us at a tremendous speed. Behind me I heard Jacky breathe, "Christ, Teague, you *outran* that thing?"

"He had my help, brother!" Mario panted, coming to a rest behind me in a flutter and drip of ravaged feathers and bleeding skin.

"Thanks for having my back," Teague added tersely, in what was, for him, an overabundance of emotion. Nicky landed next to me, partially naked and bleeding as well, and I fumbled for his hand, my attention completely on the giant, furry, lumbering form nearing the center of the clearing, and the red-caps coming to meet it.

Before the two forces could collide, I broke off my link with Marcus and screamed in effort and exultation as I slammed a shield in front of it, glowing a foot thick and solid with angry sunshine. That fucker caromed off my shield with a hollow, gut churning cathedral-bell ringing that had all of the were-animals (and there were a lot of them besides the ones on my little rise) rolling on the ground with their hands over their ears in agony. I shrieked and screamed and held out my free hand, spitting curses like that thing should have been spitting long, pointy teeth.

"Come on, mother-fucker, come on and dick with me!" WHAM!! It hit my shield again, and beside me Nicky fell to his knees as I pulled energy from him in an effort to stop this thing. "Ya wanna play, you colossal supernatural *prick!* Bring it, cocksucker, I'll fucking *murder* you…"

Nicky gave a little mewl next to me and I released his hand, jumping up and down in fury. "Attack *our* people? Come after *our* alpha-wolf? I'll fucking show you who's your fucking mama…"

Beloved? Green intruded politely, and I stilled, mid-bounce at the restraint in Green's tone.

Little busy here, Green. WHAM! It howled…oh, Goddess its howl practically peeled the skin off my eyeballs. I set my feet solidly on the ground, gritted my teeth and squared my shoulders.

Corinne Carol-Anne, came the sweet—but firm—reply, *our warriors haven't had a reason to fight in nearly fifty years—you wouldn't want to hog all the glory, would you?*

There was another reason he wanted me to stop—I could feel it in my buzzing bones—but he was right on this count too. The red-caps—now ringed around my shield, waiting impatiently for their turn—were singing some sort of blood song, with lots of 'hhhrrrrmmmms' 'ccchhhh'-sounds, and gnashing of teeth. I *liked* it!

"Are you ready guys!" I called, and the battle rage that roared from them actually covered the howls of fury from the creature inside the cage of light.

I dropped my shield and felt the rage-strength adrenaline flood out of me like blood from a wound. My body plonked to the ground like ice-cream in July, my eyes still fixed avidly on the battle.

It was like something out of the Lord of the Rings movie.

The red-caps formed a circle, like a giant mouth with gnashing teeth of savage spears, and then proceeded to advance and recede, chewing the enormous creature in the center. The were-creatures were in a loose layered circle around them. Giant tabby cats, giant feral cats, giant feral dogs, wolves, and the occasional selkie in horse form ranged in a ferocious furry rank around the general action. They were probably trying to be back-up but every time the thing opened it's mouth to howl, the were-people close to the damned animal abomination howled and rolled, some of them transforming in and out if the scream was particularly shrill or painful or the animal roar was especially long.

At least I thought it was an animal roar.

"No, seriously," I said to no one in particular, watching as a spear took the big hairy 'IT' in the side. The thing reared up, taking the spear and it's short, stocky spear-carrier with it. The red-cap got shaken off, spear and all, up and over the heads of his fellows, shrieking in what sounded like a berserker's laughter. 'IT' let out another eyeball-peeling howl, and turned around to bat at another soldier, who ducked, laughed, and caught 'IT' in the chest with his own weapon. As far as I could see, there was no blood, anywhere: not from the red-caps, because their skin really was like granite, and not from the enemy, because apparently, it didn't bleed.

"I'm totally fucking grave and sober, here. What the fuck *is* that thing?"

Behind me I heard Teague and Mario puff and then plop down in the grass, one of them on either side: my honor guard of exhausted were-creatures, still on alert.

"I have no idea, *mija*," Mario muttered, "but it is some serious fucking bad."

Teague growled, a residual of his other from. "Smelled like bear," he panted, tired from the adrenaline bleed. "Really fucking dead bear."

I spared a grin for both of them—you gotta love two guys who show the same devotion to the f-word that Brack and I do. Beside me Nicky groaned and struggled to sit up. His face was waxen, and I felt a terrible wave of guilt.

I reached out and threw a little will into my touch. "Sorry, Nick," I muttered. I'd totally drained him in my battle fury.

There was an azure spark between the skin of my hand and the skin of his elbow. Nicky made a sound like 'oolf' and shot up at a ninety degree angle to the ground. "Thanks! Wide awake now! Better than coffee!"

I gave him a weary grin and turned my attention avidly back to the fight. And blinked. And sat up straighter. And hopped to my feet. I was three steps into a full out run towards the battle itself when Nicky, Teague, and Mario caught me around the waist and hauled me back up the rise—I was shrieking in outrage the entire time.

"No. No. *No you asshole, don't you fucking dare!!!!*"

Bracken had entered the fray.

He was barefoot and bare-chested. His dark hair was a spiky mess over his head and his spear was twice the height and heft of the other weapons in the fray. His brawny chest was pale and sculpted in the pale moonlight, and, oh yeah, he was magnificent.

He threw his spear into the animal's flank and then ran towards it, out of the way of razored claws as he put a foot on the haft and sprang to the animal's back. With one hand in the bear's ruff he reached down and ripped the spear out, then raised it in both hands and heaved it down through the back of the thing's neck.

The thing sat up and howled and roared, obviously in agony—and obviously not going anywhere either.

"Oh Goddess," I moaned, trying to keep my insides from turning to water. The guys had thumped me down on my backside, and Nicky still had his arm firmly anchored around my shoulders. "Why didn't you let me get him?"

"He's a man, *mija*," Mario answered implacably. "He may be your man, but you and I both know he wouldn't feel like much of one if the rest of us got to party and he didn't."

I looked at Nicky, half-naked, bleeding and proud of it, and smiling softly from under the ends of his sweaty, rust-tipped hair. "Men are stupid," I said to him specifically, and he grinned without remorse.

"We're completely retarded," he agreed. "But remember—if you women didn't keep boinking us, we would have died out a long time ago."

I gave a little whimper and settled down resigned to watch Bracken risk his perfect sidhe body and then something else added to my tension. The vampires, Avians, and fey who could fly had formed their own eclectically weird circle above the action, sort of a warped version of theatre in the round, and they cheered (or shrieked) whenever a spear shot made it home or a swipe of turkey-platter sized paws missed its intended target. Just to make things even more interesting, Arturo fell out of that cheering circle of bloodlust and landed behind Bracken.

"Grace is seriously going to fuck that brother up," Mario said behind me, and I nodded. Nicky echoed the movement. With a little sigh, he leaned his head against my shoulder and I wrapped my arm around him. He scooted and half lay on me, comfortably, as we kept our eyes on the proceedings. There was a shout from the circle and the thing tried to roll. I gave a little shriek but then Arturo, Goddess love him, hoisted Bracken up under his arms and into the air. About twelve feet up, Bracken swung, Arturo released, and Bracken did a couple of incredibly graceful rolls in the air before hitting the ground with his hands and collapsing into another roll, well outside the circle of death.

I gave another whimper and put my face in my hands. "I don't think I can do this," I murmured, and Nicky rubbed my thigh reassuringly.

Wildflowers, a green and yellow smell, surrounded me, and Green's warm, long-fingered *real* hand rested on my shoulder.

"Llo luv," he murmured, and I smiled a little grimly and leaned into his touch. I looked up to meet his eyes and he gave a jerk of the head to the werewolves and Avians, all in various stages of undress around me on the hill. "I see you're surrounded by naked men!"

"Lucky you!" I teased, but we both knew my eyes hadn't left Bracken, shrieking and laughing like his father's brethren, throwing himself against the creature with the blunt, wrinkled snout and the nine-inch razored canines.

"Mmm…" Green plopped next to me and I leaned into him fully. He reached a hand in front of me and brushed back Nicky's rust colored hair. Nicky sighed, and I was pretty sure the wicked slash on his backside had knit together. Green moved again and wrapped his arm around my shoulders.

"I'm more interested in the woman in the sweats with blood crusting on her face."

"Wha? Awww..." I groaned. In the panic of the initial fight, I'd completely forgotten all of my hurts as I'd practically fallen off the hill to get to the meadow. Green turned my face reluctantly from Bracken and put both thumbs on either side of my nose. It was broken—I'd felt that nausea before—but not for long. I closed my eyes and felt the tingle of his healing, and then, completely disregarding the blood around my mouth he lowered his face to kiss me, and I responded to it, absorbing his sweetness and turning it into strength.

"Where were you?" I asked, when we surfaced, and now I saw him grimace.

"Business," he murmured, and he was obviously not lying, but there was something he wasn't telling me. Time enough, I thought wistfully. There would be time enough, I prayed, to be with my Green. "Nice job here, luv."

I nodded and turned unhappily back to the fight. The thing's howls of frustration and pain kept ricocheting against the hills and back, along with the slightly insane laughter of the gleeful red-cap army, and this added to the general battle roar, as well as Bracken's maniacal screams of triumph. My beloved had been riding the creature for a few minutes now, his arms locked around its neck as he turned the blunt, creased snout away from his brethren while allowing them to attack the invader that had gone after our own. The squat granite soldiers kept screaming *oi'anga!* with apparent worship, and I swallowed my terrible anxiety with a little more force.

"I don't think he's injured," I murmured casually, squinting in the dim light to see. I squinted some more, because the gray had just gotten a little lighter, and then I stood up cursing myself. I am not joking—how incredibly fucking stupid am I?

In my head I gave an urgent 'all-call' to the hovering vampires. *Dawn's a-coming, my children, time to get your asses inside!*

The general disappointment was obvious—they all wanted to see the end of this and I couldn't blame them. But I couldn't let them conflagrate either, so I got my best 'mom' voice going in my head until they reluctantly parted from the crowd of onlookers and flew efficiently (if dispiritedly) towards the house. Marcus, Phillip, and Grace came in for a landing in front of us before they went and I stood to go take report. Arturo came with them to (I assume) make-up with Grace.

"Seriously," I said as I got near them, "what in the fuck is that thing?"

All three of them shook their heads.

"I'd swear it was a bear, if it wasn't for the red eyes, Cory," Grace said, gnawing on her lower lip with her un-pointed teeth. It was one of the few gestures she had that was purely female, and Arturo dared her formidable wrath to come kiss the offended lip. She tried to glare at him but he just kissed the fight right out of her, and I looked miserably to where Bracken was, still riding the big hairy bad thing like a cowboy on a bronc.

"And I'd swear," said Teague, coming up to meet us, "that if it wasn't big and furry, it was a vampire."

We all looked at him, and Mario came up to verify. Jack came up to wrap his arms around Teague and eye me and Mario distrustfully, and Katy came up to roll her eyes her eyes at him.

"It moved like vampire," Mario nodded, ignoring their by-play. "When he was chasing Teague, here, he moved like one of you, but…not comfortable with it. He overshot sometimes and took a tumble. Like his animal brain just went on overload when he was running balls-out."

Teague nodded seriously. "It was the only reason the thing didn't eat me—that and Mario here—thanks again, brother. Jacky," Teague added, turning in his lover's grasp, "you'd best let me keep him if you want me to keep breathing."

Jack glared at Mario for a moment, and then tightened convulsively around Teague, as Katy moved up to add her two cents. I turned towards the vampires, figuring the wolves were having a family moment, and shooed the vampires along.

"Bed—everybody. I'll clue you in if anything happens before…" I stopped.

Oh shit. I looked at Bracken, still sitting on top of that thing in the increasingly ashy light. The vampires ignored my abrupt elsewhere-ness and took off in hyperspeed, and my panic started to churn in my chest like a runaway Mack truck down an 8% grade.

"Beloved?" Green called, catching my fear.

I blinked. "Sunrise," I said, looking at him with wide eyes. Together we looked at Bracken, and said "Sunrise!!!" in panicked unison.

The hills behind us started to tinge gold, and blinding sunshine touched the trees and the hovering fey and Avians and I screamed, *"Bracken!!!"* at the top of my lungs while my power was doing something more useful.

My fear and my power and Green's solid hand engulfing mine gave me the fuel to make a giant sunshine spatula, and scrape Bracken off that thing from the crotch up, like an egg from a pan. Bracken looked down at the widening gap between him and dead thing, surprised and then pissed off, but before he could start hollering at me from across the meadow, Green screamed in a voice I'd only heard him use once before. *My people, MOVE!*

The circle around the vampire bear immediately expanded, like debris from a supernova, as the first rays of dawn touched the coarse, matted, dead-thing fur.

And it burst into spectacular blue/white/orange flame, fueled by rancid fat around soulless bones, as the damned thing conflagrated with a roar that almost made the sidhe drop from the sky.

It took a second, maybe, a heartbeat, maybe two, and then there was nothing but a circle of burnt black ash about fifteen feet in diameter where the battle used to be, and a whole lot of red-caps, fey, and were-creatures scratching their heads as the light bulb went up over everyone's head.

Oh yeah—maybe we *really were* in danger.

I gasped out my last strength, dropped Bracken somewhat roughly about five feet from the edges of the big charred spot, and fell to the ground on general principle, flopping back into the frosty grass and shivering uncontrollably.

Green and Nicky were right with me.

"Nice catch, beloved," Green said, holding both our hands.

"Holy fucking shit, Green," I breathed, staring into the heartbreaking violet-blue of the spring morning. "That was close."

"Uhm, Lady Cory?" I looked behind me and up a long set of hairy shins and then even further up and then swore and closed my eyes. "Jesus, Jacky—would you put your shit away before you get that close! Personal boundaries, werewolf!"

Jack took a panicked step back and covered his crotch with his hand (which wasn't big enough—lucky Teague & Katy) and turned red—yes, even down to his hair-covered shins. "I just wanted to say I was sorry," he murmured. "You had Teague's best interest at heart...I..."

"You didn't trust us, Jacky," I sighed, still flat on my back and intent on getting lost in that spring sky. "I know you're mad because Teague left you behind on the run," I said wearily, "but you've got to trust that we have your back." I didn't look at him again, and there was a quiet murmur as Teague and Katy ushered him away. We'd talk later, but right now there was only one person I wanted to talk to besides Green and Nicky, and in a moment he was at my side, peering down at me from an even more improbable height than Jacky's.

At least he had jeans on.

"Thanks for that," Bracken said with a grimace, and I scowled unhappily up at him.

"I like those bits, beloved," I said, stroking the back of Green's hand and thinking that Bracken looked glorious from his amazing height, his sidhe beauty and shadow-colored eyes framed by the rapidly lightening blue.

Brack hunkered down, shortening the distance between us, and took my other hand. I let go of Green's hand, crooked my elbow and pulled, and he leveraged me up into his arms. "I'm rather fond of them myself," he murmured into my hair, and I nodded against his lower chest because, like Green, he was pretty damned tall and I was pretty damned short.

"Well you need to take better care of them," I shuddered, just breathing in his smell. Sidhe sweat was better than Irish Spring and Old Spice, and it did something warm and fuzzy to my stomach, just smelling him.

Green stood behind us and wrapped his arms around me from behind, resting his chin on my other shoulder, and then he opened an arm for Nicky to wiggle into, and we just stood there, wrapped in each other's arms, awkward and comfortable at the same time, relieved to find everyone in our odd little family still alive and well.

"Tomorrow," I muttered, muffled by all that love, "I'm going to rip you a new asshole and totally fuck you up." All of their bodies, keeping me warm, reminded me that I'd been lying in frosted grass, outside in the cold and unprotected portion of the hill for the dark, cold hours of the night, and a retroactive attack of the shivers hit me. The men tightened their ranks, and together we shuddered Bracken's near miss into the new morning.

"Looking forward to it," Bracken muttered back, and then there was a silence interrupted only by the brownies, pixies, and tiny hobgoblins, whistling as they wielded little spades and magic seeds, turning over and replanting the scorched earth the enemy left in its wake.

BRACKEN

Other things to fear

Cory told me once that she knew how close someone had been to death the night before by whose bed she was in and how many people were with her when she woke up. That was early—when Adrian was in her bed at night and Green was in her bed in the day. She woke up one evening after we'd almost lost her (too, too many evenings like that!) and found she was tangled up between Green and I, with Adrian hovering over her anxiously, waiting for her to open those fathomless brown eyes and reassure him that his undeath was worthwhile.

Even after our time together (more than a year of being married according to my people, nearly a year of being married according to her traditions), I haven't told her what an exquisite agony that moment had been. I wouldn't move on Adrian's girl, not then when he was hovering above us, watching us with love and trust I wouldn't ever betray. But I'd loved her since my first sight of her, glowering at the two of us from under too much make-up and ugly dyed hair. That moment in her bed was my first breathless moment with her, a moment rendered sunlight by the secret joy of touching her, of watching her sleep and knowing she would survive the attack from earlier that day.

Back when I thought Adrian would live forever, I thought it would be the most painful, lovely moment of my life.

This morning I awoke naked in a crowded bed with my beloved's mouth on my cock. Lovely, yes, but there was nothing painful about it.

We both knew the moment I was awake fully—there was no denying my body or its reaction. I groaned, tilted my head back without opening my eyes, and allowed her to show me that she loved me.

She grunted around me and the vibrations of her throat made me groan again—I needed to touch her. I reached out and caressed her bottom, which was up near my chest, groaning again when I realized her sex was slick and warm and used. I took her shudder and whimper as leave to continue petting her, stroking her, playing with her intimately, inside her body and outside, and then move up her thigh, between the crease of her buttock, inside…

"Auuughhhh…." I popped out of her mouth with a wet plop and she rested her head on my thigh. I was going to put my hand on the back of her head—remind her of what she had started—when I felt Green's hands moving towards her waist. I moved, and he lifted her up—so easy, in spite of the reassuring weight she'd put on in the last year—and with minimal fuss or positioning, straddled her body over mine, grasped my manhood and allowed her to slide over me.

Goddess…it felt so good my back came off the bed and I sat up, clutching her against me, moving, thrusting, treasuring every moan she made against my chest.

Green was busy again, and I leaned back, bringing her with me. She was slick with his spend and loose from my fingers and he slid into her backside with a satisfying push, his member thrusting against mine, separated by the thin, satiny membrane in her body. My eyes finally shot open and all of us groaned.

Her face was buried against my chest, but I could see Green, his brilliant butter-colored hair mussed and curtaining the three of us. A sunrise-peach flush of passion blotched along his fine neck and cheekbones. He was beautiful-- as beautiful as Cory in my arms, if not quite such a dragon in my blood.

There was a movement above my head on the pillow, and I moved my head to see Nicky, knees near my ear, waiting patiently for someone to notice him, to touch his pale, freckled skin, to love him in our rapture with each other.

His erection hovered near my mouth, red, throbbing, humanly sized but still lovely, a tiny clear drop of spend at his cleft, just from being in the same bed with us. As many times as the four of us had been in bed, tending to Cory, I had never touched him with more than the necessary friction for the two of us to service and be serviced by our beloved.

He was so patient, and she was wrapped up in Green and in me. A memory of the night before intruded; her, screaming at the enemy from the side of the hill while she drained Nicky, Green, and I weak because she thought it was her job to do it all.

Without warning, I stretched out my neck and took him into my mouth, gratified by his surprised "Unnnnnnngggghhhh…" and the way he fell limply forward, catching his weight on his elbows on the other side of my head.

Oooooohhhh… I had not had a man's cock in my mouth since Adrian's, and I had forgotten the taste, the texture, the fullness at the back of my throat.

I liked it very much. Not enough to regret my binding with Cory, but enough to appreciate it now.

Another sex sound—there were many of them from all of us, and they all aroused, enflamed, made a terrible fire out of the quiet warmth of the beginnings of our sex—but this one from Cory.

She was watching me with Nicky's cock in my throat.

We locked eyes then, every thrust from Green making her moan, making me moan as he dragged himself against me, seated and thrusting in the warmth of her, and Nicky began his own rhythm in my mouth.

I made a show of it, watching her mouth open and her eyes grow wider with desire. I allowed him to pop out of my mouth and slap my cheek and then sucked him back in, closing my eyes with the pleasure of it all.

Green leaned over, whispering in her ear—we could all hear him, but the whisper was the thing. The whisper rubbed her pleasure places, made her sounds deepen, grow higher pitched, frantic. The fact that he was whispering sex things, fantasies she wouldn't share because it would be asking too much, erotic ideas that we knew she loved but was still shy about voicing—only made the whisper more potent, and it started to affect us all.

Green's thrusts came faster, her groans became more frantic, and I had to squeeze against the blackness that threatened my eyes before my body exploded within her. I stopped playing with Nicky and took over—he no longer fucked my face, I fucked him with my mouth and enjoyed the helpless noises he made into the pillow in front of him. I moved my hand to his backside, letting one finger, then two go where it would.

Nicky screamed, spending into my mouth, and although I loved the bitter-salt-musk of it and could have swallowed it all, I let some of it drip out the corner. He flopped weakly into the pillows above my head, his member brushing my ear as he went, his stomach cradled around my head. I leaned up and with a helpful thrust from Green I could reach Cory for a kiss, and kiss me she did, tasting Nicky on my tongue, licking the spend from the corner of my mouth, from my chin, sucking on my neck for the last drop, and for me, that was the end.

At the pressure of her small teeth on my carotid I roared and Green bit her shoulder on his own cry and she shrieked and moaned and shuddered in the circle of our arms…

And released the sexual power that had been building in her loins, her womb, her heart, at our sensual assault, the sheer sexuality of it causing us all to twitch for a final burst of orgasm even as she did something secret and controlled with her sexual weapon.

We lay there, breathless, for several moments, before Nicky spoke.

"Thank you," he murmured to me with a rusty voice. His hand moved from his hip to my hair and I reached up and took his hand firmly, rubbing the back of his wrist with my thumb.

"Any time," I told him truthfully, and Cory looked up at me with gleaming eyes. I'd keep that promise for the expression on her face alone.

Green chuckled dryly and was the first to slide out of Coy, rolling to the side of us and peering up at her as she perched on my chest. "So, beloved," he asked, pushing her wild autumn hair from her face, "the walls seem to have remained the same color—what was it you just did?"

Usually she would have blushed and turned away, embarrassed by what her body did naturally when the lot of us touched together, but this time her face grew tense and somber. I knew that look—it was the look she'd worn last night as she was standing on the hill rise, being a general to our people.

"A perimeter warning," she said after a moment of putting words to it. "If anything we don't know crosses it, we'll hear something and see lights."

Nicky's snort of laughter echoed my own surprise. "I'm coming out my toes and you're setting security measures...Goddess, Cory—can't you just put up curtains?"

"I've already redone the curtains," she sniffed, smacking my chest a little when she saw that I was laughing too. "Twice."

Green's deep laughter resonated through the bed then, and he rolled towards his stomach, putting his face close to hers and forming a cocoon between the two of them on my chest. "I think you're brilliant, beloved," he murmured, nuzzling her temple, and she grinned at him, even as she rested her cheek near my nipple. Green lowered her head and I felt his cheek against me too as they kissed. He broke off the kiss and gave my nipple a quick nibble and suck before rolling off the bed.

"As lovely as this has been," he said with raised eyebrows towards us all, "I think it's time to wake up. We've got some planning to do."

"How about you and Cory go conquer the world," Nicky suggested cheekily, stroking my shoulder where he could reach it. "Bracken can stay here and give me another blow-job."

I rolled my eyes. "Are you planning to reciprocate, little man?" I asked archly, and Nicky gave a dreamy "Please, Goddess, yes!" that had Cory laughing a little too.

Still, she waited, unmoving, keeping me inside of her until Nicky slid off the bed and went to shower with Green.

Since she obviously was not going to rip me the promised 'new asshole', I assumed that this was the next best thing.

"You scared the hell out me last night," she said quietly, and I stroked her hair back from her face again. She leaned into my touch, still looking at me unhappily.

"Are you telling me not to fight?" I asked apprehensively, because there *would* be a fight then, but not between me and some bizarre vampire-bear thing.

She shook her head reluctantly. "No." A smile—also reluctant—twitched at her lips. "But it's a good thing Teague and Mario were there too—I don't think Nicky alone could have held me back last night. I didn't expect you to do that."

I blinked slowly. "The morning we met, I was holding a spear, beloved. Did you think it was decorative?"

She laughed ruefully. "I thought you were naked and sniffing my crotch. The spear was irrelevant."

"Apparently not," I said. My voice turned stubborn, and she gave me the serious consideration that made her so very necessary to so many of us.

"I've always thought of you as a warrior, Bracken Brine," she murmured. "But thinking it and seeing you in the middle of battle are two very different things. You and Green do all but lock me in a gilded cage. Forgive me if I'm not sanguine about you risking yourself, even when I understand that you need to do it."

'Sanguine'—it meant 'happy'. It also meant bloodthirsty, and it was a fancy word, the poetry of her heart.

"I'll be…"

"Fine," she finished for me. "I count on you being fine every day, you realize that? The moment you're not fine, my world falls apart and my strength fails me. We go on a job and you choke on your tongue if I so much as…get wet…"

"You were floating down a freezing river!" I protested. There had been very real danger.

"I got wet!" she laughed. "And I guess that's my point. Fine. You grab a spear and go attack the vampire bear and almost get your tender bits cooked to, well, tender bits… but you get to put up with me being just as fussy and over-protective as you are."

"But…" That wasn't fair! She was mortal and I was…well, I guess I was mortal now too—but by choice, not because I was as fragile as she was.

"The end," she said smugly, seeing me strangle on the complexity of my own thought.

I glared at her and she smiled and kissed me and I was reminded all over again of the touch of her lips on my body,.the warmth of her skin, the feel of her breath against my neck.

"We're going to miss Green and Nicky in the shower," she reminded me sweetly, and I was just happy enough from the morning's lovemaking to let that distract me.

The shower was…well, it was like the morning all over again, but quieter. Cory's power didn't escape her this time, but most of the time, we don't want it to. Our girl does a good job at keeping herself all contained, and as hard as it was to watch sometimes, we all knew that there was a reason she had to do it.

Breakfast was far less comfortable.

The werewolves met us—per Green's request—along with Arturo, Mario, Max, Renny, and an assortment of the upper and lower fey. Cory spoke for the vampires—of course—and for the most part, everybody was well represented.

Our people had been put in danger by a vampire bear. Who *makes* one of those things?

"Well," Cory said, pecking unhappily at her granola, "at least we know it's not one of ours."

It had taken her nearly a year, but she had managed to blood every vampire in Adrian's kiss, plus the three she'd helped pull over since Adrian's death. If one of our vampires had gone rogue, Cory would know.

"We went there to find what killed that family," Mario said thoughtfully. "Maybe whatever got them made the vampire-bear."

"Or most of them," Teague grunted, scowling at Jack as he got in the way of Teague and his food. Jack and Katy had both been almost amusingly over-protective of their mate as we sat in Green's living room and ate the food that had been left in the kitchen for us. Cory was used to being cosseted by now—she took the extra bacon Nicky put on her plate, she drank her milk as Green gave it to her, and generally, simply let us care for her in these small ways so she could fight the larger battles on her own.

When Teague first arrived, he wouldn't reach for a cookie that had been put forcibly in his hand and that he wanted with all his heart. He was better now, but still not happy about being fawned over—that didn't stop Jack and Katy from trying to break him in.

Cory chewed her bacon quickly and then frowned, as though wondering how she'd gotten bacon in the first place. "I'm going to get *fat*," she murmured to Nicky, and then rejoined the conversation. "Who was missing?" she asked curiously.

Teague, who had his own problems with his own mates, was frowning at the sausage biscuit Katy had just given him, and he and Cory met disgruntled eyes in perfect simpatico. "The little girl—eight or so. They didn't find her body—assumed it had been dragged off into the woods or something."

Cory chewed her lip and I brushed it with a thumb. She scrubbed her face and then looked at me and Green sideways. "There are just so many bad things that could mean," she murmured. She waved off more food from all of us and stood from her spot on the floor, gathering plates from anyone who was done. Teague tried to give her his, and she shook her head.

"I'm on their side, brother—it's a relief to have someone else here who needs to eat more than I do!"

We watched her then, moving quickly and efficiently to put the dishes in the sink and then one of my mother's friends—a pixie, blue from head to foot, including hair and skin—cleared her delicate little throat and fluttered over to take the dishes. Cory gave a grateful bow and returned to us, her body obviously not having worked through her dilemma.

"I don't want to think about it," she murmured eventually. "But there is something very rotten, and very hinky out there. I'm thinking we need to go out there—not a two-man recon, but a whole hunting party. Me, Brack, Nicky…"

"Me!" spoke up Mario—he had been missing 'honor guard' duty since he took this last semester off school.

Cory smiled at him and nodded, "Yes—you and Nicky and La Mark and maybe two more vampires to cover the sky…"

"And me," Teague insisted, and Cory's raised eyebrows suggested that Teague might not have the last word in his little family.

"No," Teague growled, pinning Jack and Katy with a gimlet, alpha-dog gaze. "Me. Not you. No arguments. No exceptions."

Katy didn't mind not charging into danger—she gave a human equivalent of rolling over on her back and offering up her stomach. Jack, who could be a pissy little bitch for a tallish human male, glared at Teague sideways, and Teague pinned him down with another glare. "Dangerous. I will not put you in this sort of danger."

Bark. Howl. Teague wins.

Cory shrugged. It was Teague's family. "Right, Teague, you're in…"

"And me!" Max protested. "Ouch, Renny, goddammit, you don't get to *do* that to me when I'm human!"

Renny had turned into a cat in the time it took for Max to volunteer, and was currently letting her beloved know how she felt about not being included with a splayed paw and extended claw.

"Oh Goddess," Cory swore, counting heads and frowning. "We can't have too many, we'll scare them away!"

"You're right, beloved," Green said mildly behind her. "We *can't* have too many."

Her eyes narrowed mutinously, and Green simply smiled in that kind, accepting way that made us all love him.

"I don't want us tripping over each other," she murmured.

"It's a big hunk of land, beloved," he murmured back. "You and Bracken might even get some alone time—wouldn't that be nice?"

Her lips curved up, but I recognized the melancholy behind the smile. She loved her alone time with me—but she so rarely got alone time with Green. Even I, who am normally a jealous asshole, had begun to try to negotiate some quiet moments between the two of them. There was a reason Arthur, Gwynyfar and Launcelot hadn't worked out, and it wasn't just that there were three of them.

"You could come with me," she murmured, but we all knew that couldn't happen. Green was needed on the hill—we were scrupulous about making sure the two of them were never gone at the same time, at least when there was any sort of danger.. Everything about our way of life—our secrecy, our unity, our power—it all depended on the survival of at least one of them. Of course, I thought, watching her mask her disappointment at what she must have known to be a doomed request, we all knew that none of us would survive another loss.

"Someday, when it's not a danger, I will," he murmured. "Besides, I have some business to take care of here."

She blinked—the word obviously plinked a sour string in her head. "Business?"

"Are you really going to take Teague without us?" Jack complained, and everybody—Teague and Katy included-- looked at him in exasperation.

"It's Teague's decision, Jack," Green said calmly, his eyes never stopping their intimate conversation with Cory's. "He's your leader as I am his, and you will abide by his wishes as I will abide by his judgment."

Cory's eyes remained locked with Green's. "However, that doesn't mean *you* can't ask Teague to come on the next run," she added to Jack, and then she blinked first.

Ou'e'hm. Her equal who was her leader. Green didn't want to elaborate, and no amount of intimacy between them would change it.

Green nodded—a thank you, I guess, that she didn't try to argue--and then spoke to the rest of us, but mostly to her.

"We're not done yet, beloved—you need to take a healing fey with you. You're not going out of my sight without someone who can stop your bleeding before Bracken touches you."

She wrinkled her nose and scanned the room. There were three full-blood sidhe whose specialty was healing—one was Green, the other was Sweet…

"Nope," murmured Sweet serenely, her lover's head on her lap. Ellen Beth had been a 'healing project' the year before, and although, like Green, Sweet could never be truly monogamous, Ellen Beth shared her room, shared her stories and her life. They were as close to being bonded as Sweet might ever possibly be.

"I hate the woods, Green—you know that!" The delicately featured little sidhe tinkled now, and Cory closed her eyes.

"Aw shit," she murmured, and a raw cockney voice spoke up from the back of the room—our newest import, and perhaps Cory's least favorite denizen of the hill.

"That's me, luv!" Lambent broke in cheekily, and she looked at Green in honest supplication. Lambent was a pain in the ass—sarcastic, sardonic, misogynistic and absolutely positive that he was always right.

"I'd rather bleed to death," she said loudly, not even bothering to turn around to him. To Green, since they were still having eyeball wars, she added, "Really?"

Green nodded, but he broke off eye-contact to pin the fire-elf to the back wall with both his gaze *and* his power. The elf was pushed three feet off the ground, his arms and legs spread-eagled in absolute helplessness.

"You are to obey her in all things, Lambent. She is the reason you're going, and *she* is my *ou'e'eir* and *she* is the one person here who can literally fry your ass for breakfast. If you give her too much grief to keep you, she has permission to do just that."

"Roight," Lambent replied, his rebellion clear in his tone—but he couldn't break the power bond that had him pinned, and the tattoo at his neck—the mark of Green and Cory's power that he had accepted with his free will—pulsed.

Cory raised her hand and squeezed, and then turned around to look at the flame-haired, ruddy complexioned elf as he turned a little bluer than was really healthy for his type of high sidhe.

"I'm not putting up with any of your shit, brother," she responded darkly, "You don't take a piss unless I say so. Is that absofuckinglutely clear?"

Apparently fire responded to cold force—I guess that's only elemental physics, isn't it? Lambent nodded, and Cory released him. He fell to one knee then, on his own, and bowed.

"My honor is yours, my Lady," he murmured, and for once, Cory didn't wince or grimace or roll her eyes.

She regarded the fire-elf soberly, saying, "I'll hold you to that, brother. Your power is very very dangerous in this part of the world. If you are not paying one-hundred percent attention, you could destroy everything we love in one incandescent tantrum. I don't want to be in charge of that, but if I have to, you're going to hear me."

Lambent looked up from his bow, a faint smile flickering on his lips. "Many men tell you they'd follow you to hell, luv?"

And now Cory *did* wrinkle her nose. "Why do you all *say* that?"

There was a sympathetic silence then. Even the men in the room who had never wanted her were all sworn to her—it was something she could never truly see.

Green broke the moment with a nod and a summation. "That's about three SUV's worth of people and gear. We'll make some calls and get you all let in there, since it's still off season, and start the lower fey packing for you today so you can leave tomorrow afternoon..."

"The vampires?" Teague asked, clearly confused.

"We've got a vamp mobile one of us can drive," Cory told him, "and if they don't want to sleep in it, they can fly in."

It was obviously a dismissal. Breakfast was over and we were all going back to our rooms to pack or to sleep (I planned to make sure that Cory did both) except when I looked to grab Cory's hand and take her back to our room, she was tracking Green with anxious eyes.

"What's wrong?" I asked, coming behind her and rocking her reassuringly against my body for a moment.

She touched my hands as they knotted under her breasts. "He's hiding something from me," she murmured.

I had to agree.

"What could be so bad that he'd hide it from me?"

There was only one answer to that.

"Something he's trying to protect you from," I murmured, and she nodded in my arms.

"And now I'm worried about *him*," she sighed, leaning against me. "Bracken?"

"Hmmm?"

"I don't want to be a grown-up anymore."

"I never wanted you to be one," I said truthfully. If I had my way, she would simply be one of the other lovely, dreamy creatures that floated ethereally in the apartments of the sidhe, like spidersilk in a soft breeze. But then, the woman I'd fallen in love with was more comfortable in my oversized T-shirts than she was in silk, and could order a hill to task with the authority of the general—and then blush when others bowed. The woman in my arms was a grown-up long before she'd been grown, and what mattered was that she was mine.

CORY

Queen of the fucking night

One of the things that I tried never to take for granted at the hill was the fact that there was a whole passel of little folks who liked to do all the stuff that drove me banana-shit. I never had to clean a toilet, mop the floor, do laundry, shop for my own make-up or clothes, cook if I didn't want to, or, in this case, pack.

The down side of this was that I never knew what was going in the car, either. I stood near the bottom of the stairs to the garage and watched a parade of brownies, pixies, and small trolls pack random and seemingly complicated things into the camper shells and the back of three SUV's and looked at Green in bewilderment.

"I don't know how to use any of this shit!" I said, squinting at what looked like a group-sized below-freezing-temperature rated tent.

"You won't have to," my beloved smiled. "You show up, they'll unload, it will be up when you get back from your first recon."

I blinked. The brownies tended to have gorilla-width shoulders and three, five, or seven arms, even if they *were* only two feet tall. "Where are they going to sit?"

Green laughed and shook out his butter colored hair. With a hint of proprietorship, I reached out and stroked it, waiting for his answer, but he just shook his head. "Beloved, your people will be anywhere you need them," he twinkled and I shook my head again, remembering the reason Bracken had sent me down in the first place.

"Uhm, Green—Bracken wants to know if the road down to, uh, Sugarpine has gotten any better."

Green turned from his supervision of the loading, an unlikely, graceful figure in the oil-scented echoing darkness of the underground garage. "And why would he want to know this, beloved?" he asked with a playful smile that I returned gamely.

"The...the uhm, general consensus seems to be that, well, maybe I might need some supernatural Dramamine or something, you know, on the road?"

Okay, that was an understatement so vast as to be a lie of cosmic proportions.

The truth was, that if I wasn't driving, I would be puking my guts out. Something about the way my body handled the balance between its human needs and its supernatural functions gave me a hair-trigger stomach—and it was never so apparent as when I was stressed about a job and we were on a windy road. I'd volunteered to drive, but that had been greeted with less enthusiasm than I had hoped. (Many of the men had turned pale and there had been several exclamations of 'No thanks, I choose *life!*') In the end, Bracken had suggested delicately that I might want to ask Green to put me under. (I believe his exact words had been, *Oh for the sweet love of my foot up your ass, would you go ask Green to knock you out? For me, goddammit, please?*)

And, well, here I was. All things considered, it felt a little like defeat.

Green could read me like I could read the plain sky for sunshine. He took my hands and kissed them, and grinned gently. "Beloved, admitting a limitation doesn't mean you've lost anything—you're no less our little warrior goddess when you're barfing from the bottom of your toes than a werewolf is when he ducks silvershot. It's a check on your power, that's all—it keeps you human."

I was close to letting him jolly out of my nasty mood of sour grapes, but I wasn't going to give in easily. "I thought I'd spent the last two years learning I was anything *but* human," I muttered, and he laughed, even white teeth showing, his head tilted back in that lovely openness and astonishing beauty that I would always associate with the clean-lined wonder that was my beloved.

"We're all human, Corinne Carol-Anne, even those of us with six arms or shaped like the root system of a drought-ridden tree." Nobody could resist Green's full-hearted kindness—especially not me.

"Really?" I asked, shyly. "Who's shaped like the tree root?"

Green's face lit up with pride, for me or for his kindred I'm not sure who for, but those up-tilted emerald eyes were practically glowing. "Come look," he murmured quietly, "they're very shy—they think you're beyond beautiful and they've served you since Adrian brought you to us, but they prefer to work for you in the shadows."

I blushed. I hoped I never stopped being grateful for the hill's little miracles. Green led me quietly to the front of one of the SUV's and we peered cautiously around a corner to watch the lower fey work.

I recognized the brownies and the gnomes, the smaller swamp trolls, the pixies, the nixies, the sprites—in spite of the fact that they numbered in the thousands, the ones who liked to serve Green the best were starting to distinguish themselves from the magical, tentacled, winged, whiskered, multi-hued lot of them.

Then I spotted the critters Green was talking about—literal walking tree-roots, barely clothed, with eyes and gnarled little faces in the thick top of what looked like root hairs. All of them—root hairs, individual root tendrils—were moving with prehensile intelligence, and it should've creeped me out, but it didn't.

"They're wonderful," I breathed, conscious of Green's warmth over my shoulder in the chill garage. His long yellow hair fell forward and draped over my shoulder, creating a veil between me and his shyest creatures. "What are they?" I whispered.

"Earth gnomes," he murmured. "Sort of the earth version of the grindleylow. They're one of the few creatures we have that doesn't really mind metal or oil—they do all the maintenance on the cars, you know."

I smiled and turned into his chest, hiding under that magical hair. He smelled like wildflowers and open meadows, and I think I loved spring in the foothills specifically because that was when the whole world smelled like my Green. "I didn't know," I replied shyly. When I looked up at him, his face was shadowed by his hair but behind him there appeared a halo of light.

"But I'd bet they don't get carsick," I added, remembering my original topic of conversation.

Green's mouth quirked and his hand came up, pushing my hair back from my face. The back of it was in a ponytail and he pulled the elastic out so he could run his fingers through it. "It's your body's way of reminding you that you can't do everything, luv," he murmured, closing his eyes as though the feel of my hair between his fingers was something to savor. He'd been doing that lately—touching me as though my touch was sacred to him, as though he were afraid of losing it. I didn't know how to pry, to yank open the lid on whatever it was he didn't want me to see.

"I don't want to do everything," I replied, still enjoying his care. "I just want to ride in the goddamned car while I'm awake!"

He laughed again, low, and bent down to nuzzle my temple. Just that easily, every cell in my body was on full sexual alert.

"Think of it like pregnancy, luv." His hands came up to my upper arms under my (okay, *his*) plain white T-shirt and he rubbed, the friction of his palms warming me and, well *warming* me at the same time. The ticklish place between my thighs that only Green could touch started to throb, my panties grew wet and then I actually realized what in the hell he said.

"Like *what?*"

He laughed, and I knew he could taste my flooded panties in the scent of my skin. "Like pregnancy—your body gets all sorts of pissed off at the miracles it's creating, but ninety-nine out of one-hundred women swear the results are worth it!"

I laughed and raised my face for a kiss, and his lips brushed mine to tease, to notch all of that 'goodbye sex' up a couple of degrees. "Well, we've got at least another year before we find out about *that* now don't we?" I sighed against his soft, sculpted lips. I raised my hands up to his ears, because Green loved that, and he pulled back for a moment, still leaning close enough to tangle me up in his warmth/scent/touch.

There was a reluctant expression on his face—a subject he hadn't wanted to open. "So soon, luv? You're so very young…"

I shook my head a little. "Yours first, then Bracken's, then Nicky's— Nicky only has nine years!" Nicky would wither and die—damn the Goddess anyway. I don't know what howling demon from the religious right had Her ear during her mating time with her favorite falcon, but Avians died if their mate didn't bear young within the first ten years of their mating. Since they also bond with the first person they have sex with, this means that there are a whole lot of gay Avians out at the Aerie waiting to see which couple would choose a three-way mate with the genderless sylphs who had volunteered to do a 'Big Brother' meets 'The Bachelor Couple' in the giant house. It was a risky experiment in preternatural dynamics—but it beat an automatic death sentence upon choosing a mate.

Green frowned, although his hands never did stop their lovely journey. Now they were spanning my waist under my T-shirt, and I shivered.

"It's not necessary to have my…"

"Shhh…" I didn't want to talk about it. Perhaps the only person who knew my plans was Nicky, and that's because I blurted them out to him after I came out of a coma. But I had loved Green first, after Adrian. Every good thing in my life—including Adrian—came to me because Green was seven kinds of wonderful, the magic of amazing, the pure, sweet water that sustained his children, allowed them to flourish, made them grow.

Giving him a child—our child—was the least I could do. Just once, Green deserved to come first.

But Bracken was a fiercely competitive second, and I wanted his child too.

"You're young, luv," Green protested, and I was not having this discussion here, not now, in the forced intimacy of the garage, in the secret dark and the warmth in the space between our bodies.

"I'll be less young when it happens," I murmured, and his lips turned up, but he didn't want to let it go.

"Your body hasn't completely recovered," he warned, and I shrugged self-consciously. After Adrian brought me home and started snacking regularly, I'd dropped a lot of weight quickly. Adrian died and I'd dropped even more, and then I'd been wounded and gotten sick and basically, I hadn't had a period in nearly two years.

"I'm gaining weight as fast as I can," I told him truthfully. Then I smiled with a wicked twist. "I know my boobs are bigger," I teased, and that teasing broke his last resistance. He bent over, his clean, masculine, triangular features beautiful even as his lips consumed mine and he began to blur in my sight. I closed my eyes and breathed him in and we kissed and we kissed, and then kissed again and then that pure sweet water turned to steam.

Green lifted me up with one arm and fumbled for the latch of the side door with the other hand. The latch snicked and my feet found the floor of the car. I couldn't stand up, and there were seat-rests and a height difference and for a moment I couldn't see how it would all work and then Green shucked my jeans even as he leaned into my neck and murmured two magic words, right into the hot spot that was nerve-wired into the shell-curve of my ear.

"Bend over."

Oooooooooohoooooooohoooooooohooooooooo...

My body was slick and hot and tight and wet. I came savagely with his first invasion, and then again as he pulled out, and then again as he thrust hard and deep and I screamed my orgasm into the car seat I was bent over, my knees on the floorboards, Green standing on the garage floor behind me.

He let me scream and thrust again, then leaned over and cupped my breasts under my bra, enjoying the spill of them (now that they were bigger) in his hands. I whimpered, gasped, screamed some more, and still he pounded, relentless, both of us a little high on the instant arousal. My body gave a huge convulsive shudder, bucking under his hands, and he groaned, deep and rumbly and bit my shoulder and then buried his face in the hair at my nape and came.

We stayed there for a moment, joined, his cheek nuzzling mine.

"Proud of yourself?" I asked archly, and I reveled in his chuckle.

"Proud of you. Always."

Perfect moment. A good life together is made up of such small, perfect moments, dotted together like an impressionist painting, us, together, nude and lean, beautiful in the clean lines of his grace.

It was good that we took that time together because no sooner had we fastened clothing and laughingly smoothed each other's hair than Arturo came striding across the garage to tell Green he had a phone call. There was something significant in the way Arturo looked at Green that said this was an urgent phone call and I was not to know about it.

Abruptly that wall of secrecy slammed between us—the button he had asked me kindly not to push.

Green took one look at my hurt, miserable face and gave Arturo the 'in a minute' nod, and bent over me again, that lovely yellow hair like a privacy screen for something not nearly as wonderful as what had just happened between us.

"Luv…"

"You're protecting me from something," I murmured, looking him straight in the eyes. I could have had a tantrum, or pouted or sulked off—I could have made him feel horrible, but how could you do that to someone who was trying to keep you happy?

"Yes," he murmured, as truthful with me as I was with him.

"Will you tell me?"

He looked away.

"Eventually?" I begged. *Please, Green, please. Please trust me with this if only because it's a burden in your heart.*

"I will tell you when you return," he murmured, and I could breathe again. "It's sticky, and…morally complex. I want to know everything we're dealing with before I lay it out for you."

We. He'd said 'we'.

I smiled, whole and real and honest. *'We'.*

"I'll hold you to that," I murmured, and then stood on my tiptoes and kissed him again. His whole incorruptible soul was in his return kiss, and then he slid gracefully out of my arms and to his mysterious phone call.

Two hours and a shower later (because the only bathing facility at the lake *was* the lake, and it was still fucking March and the elves might venture in because they were nature's children but I'd already done that once this winter and it *wasn't* happening again!) we were packed and ready to go. I checked my yarn bag, looking fretfully at the two extra balls of sock yarn in addition to the hat I was working on in self-striping wool—because you never know when your car is going to break down and you'll be stuck there for ten to thirty hours with no food, no water, and no toilet facilities but, by God, you'll have your yarn. I also made sure the gun was buried there under two of the ugliest balls of crappy worsted weight acrylic I ever hope to see, because hopefully all that cushiness would keep the harmful effects of the cold iron away from Bracken when the yarn bag bumped him—as it invariably did.

I was preparing to hop in to the middle row (because it was by the window but had easy access to the door for that fast break to the bathroom!) when Katy slipped away from Jack and Teague and came to talk to me.

I always felt a little intimidated by Katy—she was extraordinarily pretty, and she's got this air of 'lived through it' wisdom that makes me feel, frankly, like a green, dorky high school kid. But she had enjoyed working for Grace in the yarn store, and seemed genuinely flattered when we asked her if she wanted to run the bakery housed in the same building when it came up for sale. She had made quiet attempts to join us in the front room on occasions when Teague had been gone and she hadn't been able to take the were's little cottage without him.

Today, she looked pensive—unhappy about something, uncertain about unburdening herself. I tried my best smile on her and was a little dismayed when her eyes grew large and she took a step back. Shit—how bad could I look?

And then she sank to one knee on the fucking garage floor and I almost swallowed my tongue.

"Oh for sweet Goddess' sake, sweetheart, get up! No garage is that clean and those pants are white!" (See? White pants. I could think of a thousand reasons why my ass was never meant to be graced with white denim. Katy looked like a queen.)

"I'm sorry," she murmured, still on the floor. She took my hand when I extended it, but I was almost distraught that one other person had done the goddamned lady-of-the-fucking-house thing in front of me.

"Sorry for what?" I yelped. "Jesus—what is *with* that bowing thing?"

Katy laughed, low and charming, and shook her head. "I...we work together, you know? And you always seemed to know what you were doing, and you go to school, and you're like, hella smart, so hella smart—smarter than Jacky, and that's sayin' something—and I just thought..." Katy shrugged, and tried to make sense of this weirdness, and I wondered how long I would need to listen to her before I could speak with that awesome accent. Not even Arturo had that much South America in his voice, and he'd spent a couple of thousand of years there!

"I thought you were like, you know, Lady of the Manor—that you, you take Teague's service but you don't, like, appreciate him the way me and Jacky do. That just because you don't love him like us, that means you don't love him, right?"

"Right," I blinked, "I mean, you know, wrong." Hella smart? Really. If I was so goddamned smart, who in the hell broke her nose falling down a hill two nights ago?

Katy nodded. "I know. Wrong. I was wrong—you're smart and all...but you saved him. He been going out on runs witchu, and you have his back. You made him go with Mario because you have his back. I..." Katy started bouncing on her toes, and she was only about four inches taller than I was but it made me feel shorter when she did that.

"I don't go on no adventures. I don't carry no gun. I stay here, I'm the good little woman, I listen to Jacky bitch about not getting let to go on no adventures...but that don't mean I don't worry. Just because I'm not out there with him like you and your men, that doesn't mean I don't worry. I just want to say thank you, that's all. You take care of my man—not because you want him for your own, but because he's one of yours, right? That's probably the nicest thing anyone's ever done for me that wasn't Teague or Jacky, or, you know, Green."

What in the fuck was I supposed to do with this? I decided last year that I wasn't good with my own species—in fact, I pretty much sucked at dealing with them. It's why Renny and I got along so well—she was more cat than girl, and we dealt with each other just fine. But this was one of my people, and she wasn't taking orders or being 'shepherded into the fold', she was thanking me for...for...doing my job?

Awkward. Just fucking awkward.

"We take care of everybody, Katy," I said, wishing desperately for Green. "You included. I just...I wish you and Jacky would take Teague's word for it, you know?"

Katy managed to look sultry and sheepish at the same time. "It's not like that man talks too much, you know?"

I was forced to laugh. Teague and I communicated just fine—but that was because on some deep, cellular level, we both agreed that sometimes, words were overrated. The only difference was that I was supposedly good with them, and he believed that talking about his feelings was some sort of minimalist art. I could only be glad fate hadn't brought us together before we'd met our beloveds. Because we were so much alike, odds were, we would have ended up in bed together. And then we would have killed each other.

And then our ghosts would have gone out to wreak some *serious* shit upon the unsuspecting human race.

Yeah—every now and then I really did believe things happen for a reason.

"The vampires say more at dawn," I told Katy now, meaning it, and she laughed. It was a good laugh—low and earthy, and I was suddenly aware this woman could be my friend.

"This is true," she nodded. "So, why you not over there, kissing Green bye?"

I looked over and saw Nicky, shyly, blushing to his toes, kissing Green enthusiastically back, and I smiled. Nicky had never expected to love Green when they'd become accidentally bonded, but that didn't mean he didn't love him whole-heartedly now.

"He's coming to me," I said, flushing. "When he kisses me bye, I'm not waking up for a while, so it would be better if I'm sitting and belted."

I think I honestly shocked her.

"He's putting you under? Why for?"

Oh Goddess. I found I was blushing furiously. "I…I'm sort of a freakshow of spew on a winding road," I confessed, feeling useless. "It was this or Dramamine, but it seems like the longer I'm…I'm in this world, the less the human shit works on me. I tried to cure a headache with a Motrin at school one day and ended up puking blood for two days." It had scared the blue fuck out of Bracken, and not done much for Green and Nicky either. It was, in fact, the sole reason I'd agreed to bring Lambent, the jerk-off, because I didn't want them fretting over my dumb-assed human/supernatural translation difficulties.

"So Green gonna put you under? Who put you under on the way back?"

I shrugged. "Bracken, maybe, or Lambent. I'd ask one of the vampires, but…" I shrugged, because this just sounded like I was bragging.

"But what?" She was honestly intrigued.

"But I, you know, boss them around—I'm sort of their leader. Green doesn't think they can even spell me any more—not willingly." I shrugged again, wishing I hadn't felt compelled to spill all my weaknesses to this poor werewolf. "So I'll take Bracken and have Green cure the headache when we get home."

Katy was still flummoxed, although I don't know why it should surprise her. I was pretty much still a deeply fucked up college kid—with a super-charged-sexual-atomic-ray-gun and three vampire marks. Vomiting human fuel for ballast was par for the fucking course.

"You look all embarrassed and shit," Katy half-laughed. "Why it bother you so much? I mean, you go out with the men, you get to get all ninja-bitch and shit—why you worried 'bout one little glitch and all?"

I shrugged. "I just don't want to be a pain in their ass, that's all." Before she could respond or we could continue this damned conversation any more, I said, "Hey—Katy—you make sure you come into the common room when

Teague's gone, okay? Bring Jacky too—even after you guys move to the cottage." They still had a little bit of work to do in what used to be a barn/garage on the property. It had been a Christmas gift from Green, and Teague couldn't be careful enough remodeling it.

"I get why Teague wanted to live in the cottage and everything," I continued, "but when he's gone, you're both still ours. Grace is here, and Arturo, and Renny—Renny misses Max something fierce—and everybody. You don't need an invitation. It's your place too, 'kay?"

Katy smiled at me, and again, I felt grubby and unattractive—but this time, I felt like she probably didn't give a shit and just might like me anyway.

"You think Grace'll give me another one of those needle-point kit things? I liked the last two you give me," she asked shyly, and I grinned. I'd actually picked them out special for her.

"Go see Grace when you're at work tonight," I told her. "I'm sure she'd be happy to."

And then all my men came over, and we moved on to other things.

Green hopped into the car beside me, and I leaned my head against his arm, savoring his smell and his warmth and the love that he wore for me on his skin. He took my chin in his fingers and looked seriously into my eyes.

"No unnecessary chances, luv," he murmured.

"No unnecessary chances, Green," I affirmed.

"You'll let the others do their jobs, beloved?" Except it really wasn't a question.

"I'll let the others do their jobs," I answered solemnly.

"Even if it puts them in danger." The clean line between his brows was all scrunched up, and he put some serious warning into his voice. I reached up and eased that line with my thumb, and tried not to wince. I hated this part.

"Even if it puts them in danger," I muttered, but I rolled my eyes and shook my head and generally made my displeasure clear.

Green chuckled and kissed my temple. "Very good—now let me kiss you before I have you promising to play nice with the other sorceresses."

"I love you, Green," I told him, loving the way his eyes crinkled at the corners when he smiled like that, and the way the dimness of the car, dark blue and clean to the point of disturbing, disappeared behind the halo that was my sunlight lover, my beloved, my *o'ue'hm*.

"Love you too… sleep tight." And with that he kissed me and I slid into sleep like a swimmer slides into warm water.

GREEN

The Damage Done

Green didn't mind dealing with greedy men—greedy men could be manipulated, and he had money to spare. He didn't mind dealing with petty men, or corrupt men—he'd spent a hundred years as Oberon's captive wood-elf/whore—he'd seen enough corruption and enough pettiness to be able to manipulate those emotions in his sleep. (And fuck them in his sleep as well—nothing had been as boring as the sex in Oberon and Titania's famed damned cold faerie hill.) Pettiness was easily soothed by a willing body and corruption easily danced with hedonism, money, and some mental manipulation.

Hell, if nothing else, petty, greedy, corrupt men were easy vampire marks, and Green would have had no problem asking Cory to borrow one of her people do a complete brain-wipe in order to eliminate this problem.

So Green could deal with greed, pettiness, and corruption. He could even kill when the occasion called for it and the damage got out of hand.

Nolan Fields was not greedy, petty, or corrupt, and his damage had gotten out of hand long before those damning, surreal photos had ended up on Green's breakfast table.

"You'll give me more of the story?" Nolan had a raspy, whiny voice—the sort of thing that went with his receding hairline, weak chin, and penchant for white polyester button-up shirts. (Polyester… Green shuddered, just remembering his last meeting with the man. *Ugh…* did they even *make* those shirts anymore?)

"Within reason." Green managed to make his voice urbane and charming, when what he really wanted to do was spark into emerald lightning, zap through the phone lines and kill this motherfucker with a bald-faced sweep of the formidable power his people gave him to wield in his clenched fist.

"I want pictures—the last ones didn't come out!"

Of course they hadn't come out—Green had flashed supernatural power at the camera whenever it had gone off. If the damned device came onto the hill again, it would probably melt into a miniature pile of slag.

If only the sloppy, ugly little zealot would do the same.

"You were taking pictures of a place that can not be photographed—and you were taking them without my permission," Green told the man coldly. "I'd leave your camera at home tomorrow, if you want it to work again."

"Yes, Lord Green." The little man's voice was surprisingly meek. Of course it was—Green controlled the information, the truth, the *story*. Nolan Fields had literally bent over and waggled his bare ass in the air, thinking that's what it would take to lure Green into telling him the truth behind the creatures in the photographs.

Green had taken him up on his offer—but not because he'd wanted the (*ugh!!!*) sex, but because absolute contact made absolute control that much easier, and Green needed some measure of control. Nolan had more than one set of photos—and Nolan had an editor and friends and a safety deposit box, and Green needed a line on all of his safeguards before he wiped the man's slate clean.

"Is there anything else you want from me, Lord Green?" Nolan Fields was practically salivating in his willingness to satisfy what Green had heard him think of as 'unholy Satanic lust', and for a moment Green was tempted. One hundred years in Oberon's court, within fifty miles of the seething hells of an unrepentant British gentry—Oberon had learned of toys and restraints, of chains and clever devices that made pain a pleasure and pleasure painful, not just for the once but to wreak the perversion on the victim's psyche for the rest of his body's term to feel hunger.

It would serve his blackmailer right if Green twisted the man's desires into something that tormented him, but Green couldn't bring himself to do it.

Sex was sacred in his hill—consensual and sensual was and had always been the rule. What Green was doing was close enough to breaking his one cardinal rule—he wouldn't pervert his beliefs any further, not even in the name of petty revenge.

Green sighed. "All I want from you, my friend, is to not tell another soul about this conversation."

Before Green's first visit to Nolan's bland little house in the suburbs, his voice would have had no power over this little man. But now that Green had touched him—and touched him with power, whether or not the man knew it—Green could get him to do at least that much. But getting him to reclaim his negatives and destroy them?

That was going to take a little bit more… finesse. Definitely some finesse.

Green was usually great with finesse—it was his specialty—but the more time he had to spend with this obsessed reporter, the more he wished he were Bracken. Bracken would have clubbed the guy on the back of the head and made him bleed out. He would have regretted it, and chased his tail (or made Cory chase it for him!) as he stomped around in pissed-off boots to clean up the mess that would have left, but he would have felt a lot less… (Green shuddered) compromised.

"I won't tell a soul," Nolan toadied, and Green grunted goodbye into the phone and hung up.

"Brother, that man is bad news. You need to tell her about him, or this is going to bite you on the ass."

Green turned to face Arturo with his face still pinched from the call itself and nodded, feeling an unfamiliar surge of temper—but not aimed towards Arturo.

"If this next visit doesn't solve it, I will," he agreed, enjoying Arturo's surprised lift of the brows. Green gave a distracted grin and shrugged. "Well, what do you want from me, mate? She's stood by my side for nearly two years now—it feels wrong to have a secret from her, even when I'm trying to protect her."

"So why didn't you tell her straight off?" Arturo asked with a glance over his shoulder. Green was talking from the phone on the breakfast nook table—an old fashioned kind of phone with an actual cord. There were too many creatures in Green's Hill who could disappear or fly off with a portable hand unit, and after losing an embarrassing number of them, Green had finally gone back to the old fashioned kind. The one drawback was Green couldn't disappear into his room with the phone—and given the open nature of the hill, that wasn't usually a problem.

But folk were moving in and out today, trying to pack for the hastily planned camping trip, and Arturo didn't want Cory among them. It would be one thing if Green told her what he'd done himself—quite another if she found out by mistake.

Green scrubbed his face with his hands. "I miss the days when she was innocent," he murmured. "I love her more than ever, but…it would be nice to protect her from the worst of the nastiness in the world, you know?"

Arturo gaped. "Brother, you've been sending her out on runs all winter… and did you see her the other night?"

Green waved him off and met his second's eyes frankly. "Arturo, her ability to handle the supernatural world has never been in question—she's always been our weapon—I think she's learned to live with it." He paused, remembering that echoing conversation in the wee hours of a wedding celebration. "In fact," he murmured thoughtfully, "I think she has enough control now to be even more than that."

"Then…"

Green grimaced. "You know as well as I do that the one thing our Little Goddess has the most trouble with is the world she grew up in."

Arturo scowled, copper lightning shooting from his irritated eyes. "Fucking humans," he growled.

"It's not as fun as it sounds," Green replied with a completely straight face.

Arturo's eyes bugged, and Green had enough perspective to chuckle quietly as he turned back towards the garage to continue with the packing.

But it was hard, seeing her sitting in the SUV as meek as a child, trusting that he would do the right thing for her. She was his *ou'e'eir,* his equal, his beloved, the one person who could stand next to him and help him shoulder the responsibilities of leader, and who would love him through the decisions he would have to make.

If anybody would understand, it would be her.

She slanted him a look, one of her masking looks, trying to show him that giving her control over to him didn't bother her in the least when he knew that it did, and he shook his head.

She didn't need this extra thing, this extra problem in the human world. She was happy dealing with the supernatural, the dangerous, the paranormal. He would shoulder the burdens she was least comfortable with—anything to earn that implicit trust she gave him as she raised her face and waited for his kiss.

When she slumped forward into his arms he tucked a pillow behind her head and leaned her back, rubbing her cheek with his own. He backed out of the car and Bracken was there, waiting to get in and take over in the oddly satisfying tag-team they'd developed in the last year and a half.

"I'll take good care of her," Brack affirmed with a respectful nod of his head. Bracken had lived on the hill since birth—he had loved Green all his life, and things like that nod were not things Green took for granted.

"I count on it, brother," Green nodded back, and with a sigh got out of the way. He regretted it, he thought, watching his people pack for a journey without him. He regretted not being the one to go out and find the bad guys and kick some ass. He hadn't been great at it—mostly, in the early days, it had been Adrian and the other vampires who'd spilt the blood—but he had enjoyed it.

But now, watching Cory's organized, well-lubricated product of personal engineering kick into action, he realized once again that when it came to leading his people, he had always had another part to play.

CORY

Midnight in a Man's World

When I woke up, it was nearly dark, I was cold, and all the men were gathered outside of the SUV in front of the fire-pit.

Bracken was shaking me awake with what amounted to a sheepish expression on his rugged (for a sidhe, anyway), beautiful face.

"C'mon, Sleeping Beauty," he muttered. "We need you conscious."

"Don't I get a kiss?" I mumbled, and Bracken Brine, my stone-and-shadow beloved, my *due'alle*, actually snorted.

"You've been sleeping with your mouth open—here…" And he actually had the nerve to pop one of those godawful breath-freshener tapes in my mouth. While I was sputtering in outrage (now *very* awake—*Goddess* those things are strong!) he kissed me—hard and fast—and pulled away while I was still reeling from being breath-freshened into consciousness.

"What in the fuck do you want?" I asked, trying not to gape at him like a stoned turtle.

"We need you to start the fire," he muttered, not looking at me.

"What the hell is Lambent doing?" I asked, unhooking my seatbelt anyway. "That guy could probably piss on those logs and start something."

"Yes, luvie," said that unmistakable Brit-transplant voice from over in the dark muddle of men's silhouettes. "But since you told me I couldn't take a piss without your express permission, I thought I'd hold off on that."

I glared into the darkness and realized that even standing still, not releasing any power at all, the guy was a subtle ambience in the shadows. I shivered, abruptly freezing my ass off in one of those sudden, teeth-chattering waves that happens when you fall asleep near twilight.

"I could always catheterize you with broken glass and see what kind of fire you pissed then," I shot back through a tight, shuddering jaw. "Would you light the damned fire?"

"Are you sure I won't burn the forest down, luv?" he asked, still snarky, and my temper snapped and a giant fireball appeared over everybody's head and plummeted down into the log pile in the fire-pit.

I caught it, of course, and contained it, and it didn't land with so much as a puff of ash, but I had spoiled Lambent's fun and I knew it.

"Spoilsport," he muttered, and I'm sure he would have called me something worse, but Bracken was there, the need for the guy's blood throbbing under his fingers, and I don't think Lambent wanted to take any chances.

"Next time," I said sweetly, sticking my arms into the hooded zippered fleecy thing Bracken was holding out for me, "you'll light the fire when you have a chance, won't you?"

In the immediate orange glow of the pit I saw the flickery-thin, orange-haired elf stick his tongue out at me and I stuck my tongue out back. But that was the end—he gave a little bow, a small concession that I had won the battle of wills, and abruptly he was the loyal—and humble—elf he had been in Green's living room. Boundary pushing asshole—Goddess save me from five-hundred-year-old toddlers.

"Now children," Bracken murmured, but he was wrapping a wool scarf around my neck and putting a hat on my head (both made by Grace) and if he was going to baby me and Lambent was going to behave, I was perfectly happy to play nice with the other boys.

"He started it," I murmured, but that was the end. I looked around the campsite, noting that a number of tents had been put up on the flat spot reserved for them, and there was a supper laid out on the picnic table behind the guys.

"Did anyone bring a lamp?" I asked, and was met by seven blank stares. I shook my head. "Of course not," I muttered to myself, making a glow like I had the other night. I made sure it was a cold glow—not the heated mini-explosion I'd used to light the campfire—and fixed it to a tree in my mind. It would stay there and, well, glow, until I told it not to. "The only one here with crappy-human night-vision is the stupid ass human woman leading all the dumbshit men."

Renny meowed and bumped my hand with her head. I scratched her behind the ears as I went up to the table and rooted through the containers holding the remnants of a decent cold supper.

"You don't count unless you're human, puss," I told her truthfully, and she gave the cat version of a shrug and clawed my calf before sulking off to purr on Max's feet. I glared at Max and he shrugged in return and I threw together a sandwich and looked around some more.

We had camped in the upper loop above the lake, which was probably good because I would imagine the mosquitoes this time of year would really suck, in spite of the cold. Much of the shore by the lake itself was marshy and I imagined the water got warm enough to make more of the little bloodsucking bastards, so I was just as happy to be up top.

The land itself was pretty—the campgrounds were set on the slope of a large hill, so the flat-spot for the tents was mandatory—but the trees were tall pines, and as I stood and peered into the shadows past their silhouettes, I could see the last pewter shades of light glance off the small, mutant-eyeball-shaped lake. The air around me smelled like pine and damp red earth, growing grass and clean, rain-washed stones—in fact, smells that reminded me an awful lot of Bracken and Green—and I pulled in great gulps of it, because it centered me in my new place.

I turned back towards the men and moved to the campfire, munching on my sandwich thoughtfully, and in a moment there was the creak and grate of metal, as the specially designed trap door hidden in the floor of one of the SUV's opened up and the vampires spilled out. They flickered out into the twilight in sort of a dark counterpoint to Lambent's ambient light, and ranged themselves around the campfire, their eyes glowing red against the shadows.

"You guys going to eat?" I asked through a full mouth, and Marcus and Phillip chuckled deeply, while Kyle nodded with some enthusiasm. "Then someone better bring Renny a blanket!" I muttered, swallowing my roast beef and sourdough and looking around.

"No worries, *chica*," Mario volunteered cheerfully, and Nicky was moving towards Phillip with a playful waggle of eyebrows. I shrugged—feeding could be a sensual experience (shudder—oooh, it had been a *long* time since a vampire had fed from me) or it could be a friendly one. Friendly seemed to be the order of the day.

Max grunted and trotted off into the shadows with the others, and I fought the urge to goggle—friendly or not, I always had a fascination with that gentle 'snick' of the skin, and the pure look of blissful concentration as the vampires pulled blood from their food.

The look of pleasure on the food's face did something for me as well.

I gazed thoughtfully into the darkness, seeing only the shadowed forms of the men as one swooped and the other surrendered. Something about the helplessness of the food and the aggressiveness of the predator (and, let's face it, the unabashed slurping) made me remember that moment in bed with my lovers, and the look in Bracken's eyes as he'd taken Nicky's body into his mouth.

As though thinking it conjured Bracken, he was there, his arms around me, the very press of his body as intimate as his words.

"You liked that, didn't you?" he murmured.

I shuddered. "Stop it, you horny bastard," I tried to snap, but I ended up whispering the last part, and Bracken's shudders made me wetter than I was already. Then he leaned down and whispered in my ear—but it wasn't what I thought he'd say.

"Look at Teague," he murmured, and there wasn't a damned lascivious note in his voice.

I looked over to where the bandy-legged Irish were-wolf stood, and he was looking into the dark with sort of a baffled, fascinated look, and shifting his stance uncomfortably as he stood. Our poor little bi-sexual werewolf was fairly aroused, and suddenly a number of things about Jack and Katy's behavior clicked into place.

I looked sharply at over my shoulder at Bracken, his gorgeous face made ever darker and more brooding by the orange light from the fire.

"That's not supposed to happen," I muttered, and I felt Bracken's nod as his chin brushed my ear. When werewolves mated, that urge for anyone else was supposed to go away—unless a vampire was directly feeding from Teague, he should have been fascinated, but not aroused.

"Explains a lot," Bracken muttered. "You're going to have to talk to him later."

"Me?" I asked, startled. Wasn't this 'Man Territory'?

"You're his captain," Bracken murmured. "He may be the werewolves' alpha, but you're his. Besides. You know I don't talk about relationships."

That comment was so unlikely that I almost snorted roast beef up my nose, but Bracken nuzzled my ear. My attention wandered back to where the feeding was finishing up, and my sarcasm stayed my own.

The men were wrapping up the feeding, and the prey stood up and allowed the predators to lick the little puncture wounds on their necks so the holes would close. Because they were all shapeshifters, there would be no scars, but underneath my preternatural, glowing purple vampire mark, my scars stayed mine. Adrian had been a gentle feeder and an ardent lover, and I'd worn those scars with pride and watched sadly as they began to fade.

After letting the blood-doners get some more food we found ourselves gathering naturally around the fire pit in what probably looked like one of those blissful dark-of-night conversations that can last into the wee hours of the glowing embers. Because we'd all worked together before, we all knew it for the strategy meeting it would eventually be.

Like magic (literally) there were lawn chairs ranged in a rough circle around us, but I'd been sleeping for hours, so I stayed standing. Bracken was snug against my back, which was another reason not to sit down, but Nicky took a seat next to me, leaned his cheek against my leg and wrapped his hand around my inner thigh. I ran my fingers through his long-ish, spiky hair as conversation muttered around us like water babble.

Teague was the one who actually pulled the conversation into a focus (if not a *useful* focus) by bringing everybody's attention to the one person who usually didn't accompany us on jobs like this one.

"Hey, Max—what in the fuck is Renny doing here—she's no fighter."

Max scowled—but not at Teague—and rolled his eyes. "Don't ask me, brother," he replied in complete exasperation. "I packed, and then she dropped a bag next to mine and when I would have said something she turned into a cat. I had to drive the damned vamp-mobile—it's not like I could turn cat and ask her!"

"Maybe," I said with meaning, "she didn't want to be left behind."

Teague scowled at me. "I don't like putting them in danger," he growled for the millionth time.

"So I've noticed," I said dryly, and Bracken suppressed a chuckle.

"Well how do you do it?" Teague demanded from Bracken, and I had to smirk at the totally autocratic way he'd gone over my head to the hulking male behind me.

"As though I had a choice," Bracken growled, his hands tightening around me. "You've seen her when she gets left behind!"

Urgh... please... let's not drag *that* story into it. I took pity on the big, inarticulate asshole. "The thing is," I murmured, sticking a foot out to the fire so the sole would heat when I stood on it, "it's not like any of us had a choice."

Max snorted and Phillip and Marcus made 'hurumphing' sounds, and I saw that Kyle, Teague, and Lambent were looking at us with avid eyes. I guess a statement like that was bound to elicit a little curiosity.

I shrugged. "It's just, you know, the bad guys kept coming after me, and I kept walking away."

"That's something of an overstatement," Nicky supplied dryly, leaning his cheek against my leg. I stroked his hair some more, and Bracken's hands too, trying to comfort them.

"Fine," I muttered, "the men kept carrying me away."

Nobody laughed, not even a little. Teague's eyes met Bracken's over my head again.

"Man," he said, shaking his head. "I've only seen her when she's leading. That other thing—that must have been rough."

"What's rough," said Bracken gruffly, "is that I can not count the number of times it's happened."

"Can we change the subject, please?" I asked sharply, but Teague, who never reached for anything, was suddenly a werewolf with a bone.

"No—I'm curious. If it's been such a near thing, why do you keep doing it?"

I shrugged again. "Because I'm the one who can," I said, flushing in the firelight. Wasn't it funny how we were all huddled around the bright orange light, but the darkness and the five billion layers of clothes kept us all drifting in our own little wool-padded worlds?

"So what is it, exactly that you do?"

"Jesus, Teague," I grumbled. "You couldn't have asked me this shit months ago when we started making runs?"

"No," he murmured, looking around at the others and their avid attention—even the guys who'd been there wanted to know what I'd say. "No, this time's about right."

"Okay, fine," I snapped, wanting this conversation to be over. He followed my orders, he ate at my table—all of them, in one way or another had sworn this sort of outrageous, old fashioned, knight-in-shiny-fucking-armor fealty towards me, for no other reason than, what? I was Green's girl? I jumped in the car and said, *Hey, let's go kill something!* and that sounded like a laugh riot? I was the only girl in the car and they were all just too damned chivalrous to the bone?

"I'm a sorceress—I don't know how it happened. Pretty much everybody who settled this area was from Wales and Ireland and Northern England back about a zillion years ago. Somewhere in my family tree, one of Green's people got busy with a peasant, and, hullo, a few shakes of the genetic milkshake later, vio-fucking-la! Here I am."

"Does it run in the family?" Teague asked, perhaps a little fearfully. We knew—all of us—how much that question would mean to him. His body was covered in scars, but unlike my scars, his had all come from someone who was supposed to care for him.

"I doubt it," Nicky answered for me, his voice as dry as he could make it. "Her mother could suck the magic out of a Harry Potter convention."

Bracken, Nicky, and I all snorted, and Renny and Max let out something of a chuckle. "I don't know," Bracken said archly, "we had plenty of magic left over that one morning, didn't we?"

"Yeah," I muttered, "but she tried her damnedest, didn't she?" There was another round of smirking, but Teague was waiting expectantly and the night was wearing on. When this conversation was over, we were going to make plans to put ourselves into some serious mortal danger. Exploring the memory of my mother walking in on me and my three lovers (thank the Goddess we were sleeping by this time!) after our first time together as a collective would probably have to wait.

"Anyway," I asserted, "I...when I came into my power, someone was after Adrian..." well, we all knew how that ended, didn't we? "They kept trying to attack me—hurt him before they killed him, right? And my power was coming out, and I had no idea how to control it, and I kept...you know, killing bad guys, right?"

Bracken grunted behind me, and Max made a little sound as well. Even Nicky, who knew my body and the scars it carried from that time shuddered a little and clutched me closer.

"It wasn't that simple?" Teague asked, eyes bright in the darkness.

"What do you want me to say, brother?" Bracken asked him harshly. "She wasn't even mine to love then, but I got to watch her bleed, didn't I? She'd go out and bleed and Green would fix her up and she'd go out again."

"Or she'd grind herself into the ground," Nicky added forlornly, "Exhaust herself, and get carried back, dying of fever..."

"And then refuse to let us give her life," Max muttered, and I was done.

"And you've all done the same for me, so fuck you all!" I snapped, my voice thick. "We do that for each other, and that's just how we fit. You don't get the gifts I have and just run around wild with them—if you don't use them right, they're just...wildness, waiting to destroy..."

"Wait a minute!" Kyle burst out, and I winced. The kiss of vampires I'd killed had been Kyle's family. His beloved had died because she befriended me on a college track. The sandy-haired vampire had a broad, low forehead and although I'd blooded him and trusted him, I still had a hard time meeting his deep-set, angry eyes.

"What?" I asked, wishing I could go back to the SUV and sleep some more. I hated talking about this shit—I barely spoke about it to Hallow, and Green made me see him because he was supposed to be my shrink! Spilling my guts out, even in the intimacy of the campfire, was an uncomfortable business. But these men followed me, and this subject was important to how they saw me as a leader. Goddess, sometimes this job sucked large.

(For the record? Yes, Green *made* me see Hallow. Female empowerment was all well and good, but if you lived in a faerie hill, you lived by the rules of the leader. Green was my leader who was my equal, but he was *still* my leader. As his *ou'e'eir*, that shit only worked if I set the example. Fucking logic—pissed me off.)

"That's not all you do with your power—we've seen you," Kyle was adding rather sheepishly. "It's not...wildness..."

"Yeah—what exactly is your power?" Teague asked, and this time there was no agenda at all to his curiosity. "I mean, that bubble thing you did the other night was awfully goddamned cool."

Nicky smirked. "Yeah—right up until you knocked Jacky out of his socks."

"Unfortunately," I added dryly, "Jacky wasn't wearing any." There was a ripple of laughter, and Teague flushed, and then I went back to the topic. We tended not to dissect or categorize in Green's Hill—we accepted things as they were—but I'd been living with the bizarre, wonderful, and sometimes terrifying things that erupted from my body for coming on two years now, and I had some theories.

"Energy," I said thoughtfully. "My body converts emotional energy to… kinetic energy, like cholaphyll. And like any energy, there's a couple of uses. Destructive, defensive…"

"Creative…" my stone-and-shadow lover whispered huskily in my ear, and now I flushed.

"Creative," I acknowledged, and then added, "Which can also be destructive, if you don't direct it right. And that's the key, I guess. It took me a while—I'm still learning—but it's all directed by my will."

"Which is pretty fucking indestructible," Bracken said out loud, and I shrugged modestly.

"I get pissed off a lot," I said dryly, and there was another ripple of laughter.

"Yeah," Teague said, and one of the reasons he'd fit right in with us was that he may be curious about my power, but he'd let me be pissed off if I wanted to, "but what do you get out of it? I mean, Jacky and me, we get super-speed and super-hearing and super-strength… what do you get, besides extended life, I mean."

I blinked. "What do you mean, extended life?" I asked blankly, and we all turned that blank look to him, and Teague gaped at me in stark shock.

"But…the werewolves…we age at what? One-quarter? One-third? The normal human rate? Don't you…aren't you like us? Or the elves?" The dismay on his face was eloquent, and I couldn't figure out where it came from.

I shrugged, trying to be casual. "Nope. I'm pretty much like you were, before Katy bit you. Just a really well-armed redneck, who knows a little more than most."

"But then… how old are you? Like twenty-three?"

I sniffed, my dignity a little affronted. "I'll be twenty-two in July."

Teague was oblivious. "Awww…aww fuck." He shook his head in disgust. "Goddammit—I've been telling Jacky he's too young—how am I supposed to keep him away when you're younger than he is?"

This had gone on long enough. "You're not, Teague. You started out as a partnership, you've got to continue on as a partnership and live with it. And you've got to live with it on your own time—because right now, we've got an op to plan."

Everybody stood at attention, which reassured me a little—I was really hoping I didn't lose everybody's confidence by all that confessional shit, and sure enough, we looked good to go. Except...

"Wait a minute, luvie," Lambent called, out, and I almost said, *What the fuck is it now?* except he'd been pretty decent after I stole his fire, as it were, so I just turned long-suffering eyes to him and gestured for him to proceed.

"You didn't answer his question, luv—what do you get from all of this?" Lambent's flame-colored hair crackled around his face in the shadows, and the ambient light that radiated hotly from his lovely, lean elfin features was just bright—and red—enough for him to look mildly demonic against the velvet of the night.

"Unconditional love," I quipped dryly, and although Bracken snorted into the hollow of my shoulder, none of the others were buying it.

"Oh for the love of crap on toast!" I was fucking done with this. "I get to help Green. I get to be useful. I get to have a purpose and do something important with my life! And right now, because I say so, goddammit, I get to have my way and drop *This is your fucked up supernatural life!*—can we just, for the love of my foot up your asses, go out and fight some fucking vampire bears?"

I hadn't meant to be funny, but for some reason *that* had them all laughing, and this time we really did get down to business.

And in this case the business was that I was a liability.

I couldn't see in the dark for shit. I mean, I wasn't night-blind or anything, but compared to everybody else, I might as well be. (Even the Avians had superior night vision, which went so far against nature that I wanted to have a little chat with the Goddess and give her a piece of my habanjero-hot mind.) If I was going to run on the ground, I'd need to keep my little lantern up, and that would probably scare off the bad guys—even *my* vampires didn't want to get too close to it, because it was way too much like the fatal sun for them to be comfortable.

Besides—I was the only one of our little tribe without some sort of jacked-up hyperspeed, and since my flying was still in the elementary stages, well, there was one solution, and it was pretty fucking embarrassing.

"Piggyback?" I asked my beloved unhappily, again, and he chuckled, standing up straight after that extended time of draping over me like an oversized sidhe-coat. I was abruptly aware of how cold I was, but I grit my teeth balefully and turned my ass towards the glowing fire pit.

"It's not like we don't carry you all the time!" he laughed, and I just glowered.

"Not when I'm perfectly healthy," I grumbled, but I decided to just leave it be. We had a plan and an agenda, and that's nothing to fuck with, so piggyback it would have to be.

There would be two teams—Lambent, Mario, Marcus and Max (and don't think we didn't give them shit about the alliteration, either!) with Renny and Kyle bringing up the rear would take the east side of the lake with the campgrounds and the hill-side and the road loop that led to the levy nearby. Phillip, Teague, Nicky, and Bracken would buzz down the road and take the west side of the lake. We'd be passing the hidden cave Teague had investigated before the vampire bear had cut him off from the car at the lake parking lot. The two teams would scatter to sight distance apart and run the land, hoping to catch a scent or a feel or hear a sound that would clue them into something preternatural and wrong.

I, of course, would be along for the ride.

"You're sure you can see?" I asked as he settled my legs around his lean hips. He'd slung a blanket around his back, toga style, to use as a cradle, and even if my death-grip on his shoulders failed, the blanket and his rather amazing sense of balance should have me securely. I kept reminding myself that he was supernaturally strong so I would be okay back there, but ask me how I felt to be putting my entire person at the mercy of supernatural strength, speed and grace—in the dark.

"I can see," he replied mildly, knowing exactly what was on my mind.

"You're not going to trip, are you?" I whined, hating myself.

Bracken's look was full of indignation. "Trip? Sidhe don't trip!"

"The hell you don't!" I argued. "I've seen you trip twice…"

"Those don't count," he responded with dignity, nodding towards Teague who was, by now, a big scary blond wolf. Teague gave a yip, and two distant 'mrowls' resounded through the whooshing quiet of the woods as a reply. Mario and Nicky screeched from overhead, and Kyle, Marcus, and Phillip gave me the all clear between my ears. I nodded to Phillip—or where I thought he was—and he replied *I'm almost behind you, sweetheart—stop trying to see in the dark and just hold on.*

"Why don't they count?" I muttered to Bracken, and his chuckle was lost in the whooshing of the wind as we started our hyperspeed-trot through the underbrush.

My eyes teared up and were totally useless in about two seconds, so I gave in to the inevitable, closed them and rested my cheek on Bracken's back. I asked permission into Phillip's head and was treated to the dizzying sight of my backside as Bracken trotted gracefully through the woodland, and then Phillip did me a solid and looked elsewhere.

It was like being stuck in a real life version of the *Blair Witch Project*. Phillip could see everything—but it was all strangely lighted in his vampire's vision, the branches overhead appearing in an eerie, front-lit negative and the trees in the background turning even darker in an almost foggy ambience.

Goddess, Phillip, is this how the night always looks?

I felt his wolfish, predatory grin in my head. *No, sweetheart, sometimes there's the red heartbeat of prey.* Phillip had a pale oval of a face and a deep black widow's peak—just picturing him saying those words was a cross between incredibly cheesy and chilling to the bone.

Nice, I muttered, and then concentrated on not getting dizzy as I tracked his vision and my own location through the wooded darkness.

The terrain grew terrifyingly steep, as though we were sticking out from the side of a sheer drop horizontally to the ground, and even Bracken and Phillip had to reach down to keep their long bodies from overbalancing. Eventually things leveled off, and I realized we were on the hillside that overlooked the steep and winding road that led in to the campgrounds.

Brother, looking at that road I could only be glad Green put me under. If I had barfed all the way down that, I wouldn't have been able to stand, much less cling to Bracken's bunching shoulders with bony, clutching fingers.

Then something startled us—all of us. We came to such a sudden stop that I think Nicky almost dropped out of the sky, and I was in some danger of being rocketed over Bracken's shoulders.

But stop we did, and I looked through Phillip's eyes, as frustrated as he was that I couldn't see anything. Teague gave a low growl—a very frightening sort of sound in that elemental blackness-- which meant that whatever it was, he could smell it. Bracken gave a very soft grunt.

Reluctantly I pulled out of Phillip's head and peered around the forest floor of dead wood and dust, trying to see.

I still couldn't see, but the three vampire marks at my neck gave a giant throb, and I shivered.

"Vampire." My lips were close enough to touch Bracken's ear, and his body tensed with the urge to make me quiet down. I felt his nod, and sent the thought to Phillip. He agreed, and Teague had obviously recognized the smell.

I aimed a thought to Marcus and Kyle, and got a confirmation that they had turned around and were heading this way, and then I searched the darkness with Phillip's eyes, still disoriented by the cold and white way in which vampires saw the night.

I spotted Teague's blonde wolf, glowing redly with all of that hyperthermic shape-shifter blood. He was all but chasing his tail in an effort to pinpoint the smell that was singing along his nerve-endings. The nervous energy signature that vibrated from him was so very like the man's personality—intense, bright forest green, and shimmering with movement.

His preternatural energy was so bright it almost blinded Phillip and I to the whirling red eyes behind him. But we both saw it in time to scream "Teague behind you!" and then Teague whirled and snapped and the fight was on.

I couldn't fucking follow the action—I wasn't a vampire yet and I didn't want to be—but whatever it was, it was big, Teague was howling and snapping at it, and its *Mreowlls* back sounded exclusively feline.

I swore and threw a light ball above the trees, and the thing snarled and recoiled, but it kept its teeth locked around Teague's ruff. Teague was practically breaking his own neck in an attempt to whip himself around and sink his teeth into the dirty brown animal with the mud-matted fur.

"Stop them!" I hollered to Phillip, and Phillip blurred to the thing and caught it under its compact, wiry body, yanking it away from Teague and holding it out by the scruff of the neck, like a man would hold a dog who'd rolled in shit.

"All right, I give," I muttered, as Bracken slid the blanket out from under my ass and I wriggled my way down his body and around him, "What in the fuck is that again?"

"Watch it, dammit!" Teague called, naked and crouching back against a tree, blood running from a closing wound on his neck. "That thing's teeth are fucking long!"

"Bracken stay clear!" I called and ran closer. A quick thought told me that Marcus and the others were getting closer—we'd been about fifteen minutes out, so we had another ten minutes before they got here. As I got closer, Nicky tapped down next to me and changed and together we approached the big ugly thing in Phillip's grasp: it was snarling with an insane amount of force. If Phillip hadn't had the Goddess' strength as a vampire, he would have been fucked royal, and I made sure I stayed back.

I got close enough to stop and look at it, and the glowing ball came with me. The thing cowered and yowled again and the glowing ball got closer. "Anybody got any ideas?" I asked, at a loss. It *looked* like a young mountain lion—about half the size of a grown one and it was lean, with muscled, massive paws, but still growing. Its teeth were three times the normal size. What would normally be gold fur was covered in mud, twigs, leaves, and what appeared to be, (urgh!) maggots, and from the smell…

"I think its dead," Phillip muttered, a look of revulsion crossing his face as it writhed in his grip. "It's flesh is cold enough to be a brass monkey's nut…"

I stared intently at the poisonously glowing green eyes, looking for a hint of intelligence, a hint of drive—hell, even a hint of the power it had taken to completely annihilate the family of four that had brought us up here in the first place. We'd already figured that the vampire bear wouldn't have done it—there wouldn't have been anything left if it had been that monster, but, judging by this one's size, it wasn't looking like a good bet either.

"It's weird enough to be a brass monkey's nightmare!" I muttered, aware that I probably made no goddamned sense at all. The light got closer, the vampire puma (!!??) screamed, and Phillip put his hand in front of his eyes, saying, "Goddess, Cory, could you put that thing away?" and then a shrill voice jerked us both around, causing Phillip to drop the vampire-critter at my feet.

The thing lunged at me and I did what I do. I scooped it up in a glowing light ball to keep it from getting to my thighs, which is where it was about to leap and probably chew.

It did what a vampire would do inside one of my light balls. It caught fire, disintegrated, and died, and the little voice that had distracted us in the first place screeched, "No!!!! No no no no no no you big ugly troll, you can't kill him he's my friend!!"

We all turned towards the shadows then, and my ball got a little brighter.

"Stop it...it burns!" the voice whimpered, and I dimmed my glow and said, as gently as I could, "Uhm, sweetheart—we hear you, and we're not going to hurt you, but, uhm, could you step out of there so we could see you?"

I dimmed the light some more and we stood in the clearing in silence, and a child stepped into the blank space in the underbrush.

She was small, about eight or nine (eight, if she was who I thought she was). Her hair was probably dark blonde but it was snarled and dirty and full of twigs. She was wearing a ripped and ragged pair of jeans and a sweater that might have been purple once but was now brown was hanging onto her neck by a thread.

She was angry, so her eyes were whirling red, and her fangs were out.

Most of us swore by the Goddess as she stepped into our midst, except Teague who said, "Oh holy fuck!"

The child vampire turned towards him imperiously. "That's not nice—my Daddy said swearing gets you spanked!"

"I'll remember that," muttered Teague before he put his hand in front of his vitals and turned back into a bleeding werewolf in pure embarrassment. There was a hideous, hellific, awkward silence as we all caught our breath and the implications crashed around our ears like freak waves.

CORY

Vampire Queen Dearest

We couldn't convince her to come to our campfire that first night. She'd seen me kill her beloved pet (well, shit!) and I'd scared her with the big fireball, and Teague had been naked, and then a bunch of other men and scary animals came thundering up, and, all in all it scared the hell out of her. She zipped back to the cave like a spider-monkey on speed, I jumped on Bracken's back and did everything but kick his sides, and called Marcus, Phillip, and Kyle with me and made the others stay back.

She really wasn't that far away. My sense of direction in the black of night was for shit, but mostly it was up a hill, down a hill, around a hill and in the side of a hill. I never would have found it during the day, but the vamps assured me that, eventually, they would have found it this particular night.

Judging by the smell, it was probably the cave formerly inhabited by the deceased vampire bear, and judging by the desiccated animal corpses that littered the hills around the entrance, she had been there about a month.

I had so many questions—most of them I wanted to discuss with the vampires while Bracken and Green were listening, but not the little girl.

What was her name again? I asked Green in my head as we neared the cave. I think I shocked the hell out of him—he was eating dinner at the breakfast table and talking animatedly to Grace. When my voice popped into his head he swallowed his linguini badly and she smacked him cheerfully on the back. I laughed a little, kindly, because he didn't have to let me see him be 'human' and then posed the question a little more intelligently.

The little girl from the family that was killed, I specified, *what was her name again?*

Mmmm... he stood up, I think, and went to the computer to look up the article. The four of us looked at each other in the darkness with that head-bobbing thing that you usually do when you're waiting for your computer, and then he said, *Gretchen, why?*

When I told him, the entire world went gray with the force of his anxiety. *Oh, luv,* he hesitated, *this is not going to end well.*

Before I could ask him why, or get details from the vamps, we heard that fearful, angry little voice call out, "Go away!", so I bailed out of Green's head and put my attention where it needed to be for the moment.

"Gretchen?" I asked gently. "Gretchen? Is that your name, honey? I need to know it's you so we can talk like grown-ups here, okay?"

"I'm eight," she said stubbornly, "and you look about fifteen."

"I'm twenty-one," I replied with as much dignity as I could muster.

"You're still not old enough to be my mother."

"Thank Goddess," I snapped, tired of being schooled by an eight year old. "I don't want to be your mother, I just want to get you someplace where you don't have to suck down a poor..." I kicked at the nearest animal corpse, "jackrabbit for food."

"Well what else am I supposed to eat?" she demanded. "It's not like there's any people out here after..." She stopped abruptly, and I had a sudden, horrid, sick suspicion of what, exactly, had killed her family.

"Our werewolves and were-kitties will feed you willingly," I told her now, swallowing, hard, at what damage we may have to fix in the poor child's mind. Green may have been able to do it, I thought queasily—if she'd been an adult. But she wasn't, and the things that usually worked for the hill weren't going to work for her. I swallowed hard and got my head in the game.

"But you have to be gentle," I added, thinking about Nicky and Renny and Max and Teague and all of the people I didn't want to end up looking like the flat satchel of skin-covered bone at my feet. "They hurt easy." Any one of them could pick me up and throw me so far I wouldn't hit ground for a week. But then, so could she.

"Why should I trust you—you hurt my cat."

Goddess. "Kitty was gonna eat me, honey," I said, keeping my voice firm and not guilty at all, nope-no-way-nu-nuh. "I know that's not what you had in mind, but I needed to get him away from me. I didn't realize..." well that was a lie, wasn't it? I *did* realize, I just didn't put it all together in the spur of the moment. "I didn't remember what my power did to vampires right then." Oh crap—that only made me sound flaky. An eight- year-old vampire who'd been living in the woods for a month—it was like doing African tribe dancing on the ledge of a building. Sure, there was some really spectacular footwork but when that was over, the freefall was a sonuvabitch.

"Who says you're not going to do the same to me?" Her voice was echoing out from the little cave, but I could tell she'd moved closer to the mouth of it. This was good and bad, I thought edgily, considering how pissed she was at me right at this moment.

I took a deep breath and crouched down. "Honey, some of my best friends are vampires. You don't see me cooking them to dust, do you?"

"Hey…" her voice was suspicious and we could hear her edge backwards again. "What is that stuff glowing on your neck under your shirt?"

It must have been the complete darkness around us—the moon was still down, and the only light was starlight, filtering down through the trees (which I could now see in silhouette, thank the Goddess). Usually, Adrian's vampire marks weren't visible unless you looked for them—and my neck was bare.

"My…" search for the human word, "my first boyfriend—he loved me very much. He…he marked me. Made me his. Connected me with the rest of the vampires, even though I'm not one."

Sudden, avid curiosity. "I saw that movie!" she said, poking her head out of the cave. "Were you like Bella and everything?"

I shook my head. Adrian and I had been long before *Twilight* had become the rage. "Neither of us were as nice as Bella and Edward," I told her now, honestly. "I was angry, and Adrian was…lost. Together we made one good person and one strong person, and that was different too."

"Did you break up?" she asked curiously, and I shook my head, coming down to face her. Her eyes weren't whirling anymore, and her fangs were only partially out—more in hunger, I would imagine, than anger.

"He died protecting me," I murmured. "I miss him every night."

"I miss my mom and dad," she said nakedly, and I had nothing to say to that.

"I can't bring them back." Oops—so much for honesty. With a huff and a pissy look on her little face, she burrowed back into the cave.

"No one asked you to, now go away!"

I smacked my forehead with my hand and cleared off a spot of underbrush so that I wouldn't sit on anything dead, then plunked my fat ass down and settled in for a little vampire-queen-to-unwilling-subject chat.

"Gretchen, sweetheart," and why do we always feel like we have to use endearments with children? "I don't know what you've been through. I don't know what happened to you. I don't even know if I can say or do anything to make you feel better."

"Then you don't know much do you?" Her voice was clogged and snotty. Wonderful. I made the baby vampire cry.

"You have no idea," I sighed. There was a silence, and after I got tired of hearing the men roll their eyes, I sighed and broke it.

"Look, I'll tell you what I do know." My hands twitched with agitation and I realized that I wanted my knitting. I could knit in the dark, I thought a little desperately. It would definitely make my maternal side a little more visible, that was for damn sure—I mean, at this point, it couldn't hurt.

"What?" Her voice was less muffled—and damn. She had to be scared. It was about time I offered her some fucking comfort.

"I know that you're a vampire, and it's about to get hot and sunny up here, and then you're screwed."

"That's a bad word." but I could tell she enjoyed hearing it.

"It's a bad world," I told her implacably. If anyone knew that, it would have to be the eight year old who had been savagely killed—and then, very possibly, did some savage killing herself. "And you're in it alone right now. You saw all those men with me—you think they're alone? They're big and grown up and scary, and the world would still suck if we didn't all have each other. Now you're scared, and I get that. But we've got a house with rooms that are dark all day..."

"The sunshine hurts me..." she muttered disconsolately, and I didn't want to think about how she'd figured that out. I hadn't had time to look for sunburns on her hands, but I was sure there had been.

"I know it does, honey," I murmured. "We can keep the sunshine away from you. We can give you werewolves and werekitties to feed you, and we can give you new clothes..."

"Can you give me a bath?" Her voice was both forlorn and hopeful—who would have thought a bath would be the turning point?

"We sure can," I told her, with feeling. "A warm one, even."

"Will the kitties become mine?" she asked, and there was something... avaricious in her voice. Covetous. Greedy. I recoiled, Green's warning in the back of my head surfacing for the first time since I'd started this conversation.

"No," I told her firmly. "The kitties are people—they can lose a little more blood more comfortably, but they will only be theirs."

Her disappointment was palpable. It took a great deal of strength and strength of will to haul something back from the dead, even with the traditional near-death blood exchange, and that breath of fear fanned my heart a little warmer. She had made a vampire bear by sheer, childish will. And she wanted another pet.

"I'll have to think about it," she said grandly, and I was surprised to find that I agreed.

"You do that, Gretchen. I'm going to leave a couple of guards at your door—you won't even know they're yours. They'll just keep you safe while you're in there thinking, okay?" And keep us safe when we're sleeping, I thought, that little chill walking over me again.

"Which ones will be there?" And I recognized craftiness when I heard it.

"You'll have to go somewhere to find out," I told her dryly, but inside my head I was telling Kyle, Phillip and Marcus that they were going to have to rotate in shifts with the weres, and that we'd pull the vamp-mobile up to the road so they could get into it as late and as safely possible. And I asked Phillip what he thought the odds were that I could get Gretchen to agree to a blooding before dawn.

"None," he said out loud, making sure I could see his red-glinting eyes in the dark. "And one of us will do it."

My mouth opened, and I was going to argue, but Gretchen spoke up wanting to know what we were talking about.

"We're talking about a way to keep you safe," I told her truthfully, and Phillip nodded his regal head in approval.

Good.

We'll talk about this at the campfire.

Fair enough.

"Gretchen, hon—I'm going to leave now…I'm only human and I'm freezing my ass off. I'm going to leave a were-kitty and her husband here, and a vampire, okay?"

"The were-kitty wasn't the naked man, was he?" Teague's nakedness had really bothered her and I didn't even want to dwell on why that may be.

"No—that was the werewolf. He had to be naked to turn, you know— otherwise he'd be a werewolf in a pair of jeans and a sweater, and that would be silly!"

I heard a reluctant giggle from the cave, and looked at Bracken. He nodded—the others had moved close enough to hear the conversation, so when, as a group, we turned towards camp, everyone knew what was on the agenda for later.

Be careful, I told Kyle silently as he took up a statue's vigil by the cave door. He nodded somberly, and something told me he hadn't needed the extra warning. But… *And keep Renny from going in there out of sheer stubborn perversity!* I added frantically. Renny liked playing 'kitty'—I was hoping she realized that 'kitty' here could end up being very different from what my friend had in mind. Renny bumped my hand with her head, as though she'd heard me, and I scratched her behind the ears in reassurance.

Then I hopped up on Bracken's back and stuck my ass back in the sling and we blurred back through the terrible dark, my eyes streaming in his wind.

We were a somber group of supernatural creatures, gathering about the campfire this time. The pall of discomfort and misery that clung to us made my own personal evisceration earlier that evening look like a show tunes review.

I wiggled out of my sling—I had now officially dubbed it 'elf-trekker'—and moodily dumped a bigger stack of sticks on the embers we'd left behind.

"I'll blood her," I said without passion, looking into the newly caught flame. "Green said this may turn ugly..."

"Which is why it needs to be me," Phillip said from across the fire pit. Marcus cut him an immediate glare.

"Or me!" he protested. "I know kids—I'm better equipped..."

"To get your heart broken," interrupted Phillip again. My eyes widened, but Phillip continued before I could. "You do know kids, Marc—you care about them. I'm a heartless bastard who was planning on getting fixed before forty—I'm the best choice."

"You mean besides the fact that you're not the one who gets to take those risks?" I asked pleasantly.

"No," Marcus contradicted surprisingly. "Jerk-off here," (a smack across Phillip's head punctuated the, er, endearment) "is kind of right. If 'no shame' is the vampire creed, making a vampire child is our one taboo. Nobody in Adrian's hill has done it—the closest any of us have come is Adrian's friend from the mining camps, but she'd come into her adolescence before he brought her over, and I think that's the cut-off line."

I blinked, things slotting neatly into my groping gray matter. "Sexual maturity," I muttered. "You don't want to make vamps before sexual maturity—that brain development shit that we got from Hallow last year..."

"I remember, *chica*," Mario muttered. He'd hated being in that class almost as much as I had. "There are brain chemistry changes-- things grow, things shrink..."

Bracken and I met eyes too. "Vampires are so sexual..." he muttered, and we both shivered. "I bet the changeover fucks large with their little brain pans."

"Shit..." I scrubbed my face with my hands. "Guys... this could end *really* badly—you really don't want a piece of this floating around in your brains if it turns south and craps, you know?"

"Not to bring up the obvious, *Lady Cory*," Phillip emphasized my name and title—he never usually went in for that shit, so he obviously wanted my attention, "but I've got a couple of hundred years to put this in perspective. You don't. Marc and me, we've been vamps for thirty years—we've got some distance from humans. You *are* one, mostly. And you wield a shitload of power—if she fucks with your mind and it bleeds over, we're all fucked. So I'll blood her—and you and I can blood again and make our bond strong, but it's probably not necessary. We've done power exchanges enough times that we're pretty tight that way. You need to listen to me—that's why kings and queens have knights and pawns, right?"

I squinted at him. "I really suck at chess, Phillip," I muttered, in prelude to giving him a flat out 'no'.

"Phillip," Marcus protested again, but Phillip gave one of those fierce gestures that I'd seen Green give me. It was the expression of the person who had the upper hand in the relationship—the expression of the most dominant party, laying down the law. "That's not fair," Marcus said quietly conceding to that look and to nothing else that had been said, and Phillip shrugged.

"I'm an asshole—you know that about me and you stay. Me. Not you." And now I was reminded of Bracken, and I *really* didn't want the dumb asshole taking risks that should be mine.

It was on the tip of my tongue to tell the arrogant vampire that exact thing, but then Green, who must have been listening all along, whispered, *You promised, beloved,* and I swore again.

"Fuck."

Bracken rubbed my neck. "He told you 'no', didn't he?"

"Don't be a smug bastard," I snapped. "It's not at all attractive."

Brack bent forward and rubbed my cheek with his own. "Now we both know that's a lie," he laughed softly, and I stuck my tongue out at him.

"Fine," I grumbled, "if we make it through the night without that cute little urchin trying to make us pets in our sleep, one of you can blood her."

Nicky caught the first thing I said. "Speak for yourself on the sleeping part!" he protested. "If there was ever a night to stay awake until dawn, *this* would be it!"

I sighed. "When we get her to the hill, we're going to have to lock her in the steel room, you guys know that, right?" Marcus and Phillip nodded, and I made a quick trip into Green's mind to ask him if he could have the newly redecorated room (I'd cleansed it to bare steel walls last year—it had needed a little 'softening') newly redecorated again in 'Little Girl Chic' and he agreed.

"So I'm the one who'll blood her, right?" Phillip asked without asking, and I looked from him to Marcus in a quandary. Phillip led—he always led between the two of them, but this time was different. They knew it could end badly—they didn't want their other half to be the one who ended up in the shit.

"You, Phillip," I said after a long pause. I'd been a werewolf's whisker from letting them decide themselves, but that would have been the coward's way out. This way, if something went horribly wrong (don't think about it don't think about it don't think about it) then I could take all their blame.

"Lady Cory!" Marcus protested, and I closed my eyes. When I opened them, the sweet Italian schoolteacher was right up in front of me, having moved with that hellific preternatural speed that was so hard to watch.

"Not the easiest decision I've ever made, Marcus," I rasped, refusing to let myself be intimidated by a friend.

"He's not as tough as he thinks he is!" Marcus protested, and I nodded.

"Which is why he'll need you to put him back together again," I told him, touching his hands with more ease than I'd thought the gesture would entail. "Besides, he's right. He won't see her as a sweet little girl—he'll see her as the monster she might become."

My words rang in the dark quiet, and before I could fight it, a jaw cracking yawn sprung up, threatening to take over my entire face, throat, and neck.

Marcus smiled slightly, and then, because we knew each other, because we'd sat in the dark for months and told each other stories, he leaned forward and kissed my temple. "This could really suck," he said with sincerity, and I had no choice but to nod my head. "We're going to go send Kyle back. Now go to sleep. Take Bracken with you. Make love. The lights alone should be enough to scare her off."

A terrible blush washed my face and neck, hard and hot enough to make the chill spring night steam around us. Bracken wrapped his arm around my waist and Marcus backed away, bowing a little. Bracken looked at Nicky with a raised eyebrow in invitation, and Nicky flushed and shook his head.

"No?" I asked, mostly because I was cold, and falling asleep between two people with high metabolisms was really appealing.

Nicky blushed, much as I had a few minutes before. "Everybody can see… with the way you two glow…"

A hard laugh shook me, because since joining the hill it had seemed as though human squeamishness about sex had completely left Nicky's psychological makeup.

"You'll join us, later?" I asked hopefully. Again, with Nicky it was not so much the sex as it was the compact, human body of a good friend next to me in a strange situation. Bracken was long-limbed enough to practically embrace us both, but Nicky had a way of making me feel not quite so outsized by the world around me. It was a thing I treasured about him.

He stood and cupped the back of my head with his hand and placed a pleasant, mildly passionate kiss on my mouth, tangling his tongue playfully with mine. He pulled back with a peck on the lips and I smiled at him, wondering if it was only the shadows or if there was something hiding in his bird-gold eyes.

"I might even wake you up," he murmured, and I rubbed my cheek against his, reassured.

Bracken's large hands spanned my waist then, with something like relaxed urgency, and together we ventured into the tent.

NICKY

Dark Musings

We sat in quiet after that, watching the fire burn down and listening to the absolute ocean-roaring silence of the night. After meeting that spooky-assed kid, I wasn't sure there would ever be a night quiet I would listen to without the faintest taste of terror.

I glanced briefly at the tent, and saw nothing—they had very possibly just undressed and gone to sleep, but I didn't think so. I had followed them often enough in the last year to know that falling asleep is what she would *expect* them to do, and even what Bracken *planned* to do—but that their highly sexual nature would soon charge their gentle murmurings, and her soft touches on his pale, hairless skin would soon turn hungry, and his large hands on her small body would become urgent. Of the times Bracken and I had arranged for me to be in bed with her, he would wait until she was making unconscious, starving, whimpering noises in the back of her throat until he'd take my hand as it lay on her hip and push, urging me to something more adventurous, more erotic, something she wouldn't mind now that she was completely lost in him and the last of her human inhibitions had fallen asleep, drugged by their rampant sexual chemistry.

I loved that moment. The first few times, I'd believed it was because that meant it was my turn to touch her. Finally, the girl I loved was mine to hold.

But time passed, and my longing for their bed grew, become an ache, and I came to understand that it wasn't that I yearned for her, although I did love the girl I'd met at school, the one who wore jeans and sweatshirts two sizes too large—the girl with the sad eyes and the haunted face, the horrid potty-mouth and the terrible secrets. I loved her, but I didn't yearn for that girl anymore.

No. I yearned for *them*.

And it wasn't that I was in love with Bracken. I'd started to like the guy—hell, I'd even started to see in him what Cory saw in him—but I could never feel the same heart-fever for Bracken that I felt for Cory and for Green.

It was just, I had come to believe, that the light they produced between the two of them--the glow that encompassed her and Green when they made love as well—that light was not a thing a mortal, even a shape-shifting mortal like me, got to touch on a regular basis. The light that flashed off their sweating skin, that sparkled with their urgent, crying moans, the sexual energy that radiated from their heaving forms was, to the sensual people of the Goddess what the light of the divine might be to a Christian. Except, with Christians, it was a matter of hoping the light existed.

With me, it was a matter of slipping into the right bed, invited.

Should sharing a bed with your lovers be a form of worship? Truth was, I didn't give a shit. It felt worshipful to me, and I'd done too much harm following a 'god' who told me that 'worship' should be full of pain—self-inflicted and otherwise—to dismiss that feeling for something more 'divine'. It wasn't the nature of crawling into bed with my gods that bothered me.

It was the nature of the humans (or shapechangers) that seemed to attract me that bothered me.

Last year, I'd spent a week rolling around naked with every species and gender under the Goddess' watchful eye. It had been a helluva week, but it just wasn't in me to sustain that sort of thing. Eventually you want companionship and kindness, and while I got that from Cory—and even from Green and Bracken—there's a difference between your friends and your lovers and your gods. If it wasn't for the sex, Cory and Green would be gods.

If it wasn't for the fact that he'd never look at me twice if we weren't married to the same girl, Bracken would be my choice for a lover, and I was just as lucky that I'd met Eric, because as lovely as it would be to taste (or be tasted) by Bracken some more, Eric adored me and me only, and sometimes a person needed that.

I'd come to accept my sexuality. It had been rough. The first time Green had taken my cock into his mouth and held my hips in his hands I could almost hear my friends at school, my cousins, the people I grew up with, shrieking in my ears about how faggots go to hell.

It hadn't felt like hell then, not Green's mouth, not his tender hands, not the rain of kisses on my face afterwards.

It still didn't.

"Hey Nicky," Mario said softly from the other side of the fire, and I jerked myself from that warm moment in the gray-lit city by the bay into this orange-lit black night, surrounded by pine trees and the smaller roaring of a smallish body of water nearby.

"Yeah?" It had gotten terribly quiet—even my voice sounded like sacrilege. I glanced towards the giant three-room tent that had been set up for us, and saw nothing but a low-grade ambient glow. They were still talking then—I could hear Cory's river-running alto and Bracken's canyon bass. When they sang with Green, it was everything the Bible said about angels and choirs. When they were murmuring jokes to each other, soon to become bedroom talk, it was damned near the same thing.

"You tell her about your folks?"

His voice was soft, and I knew Cory's hearing wasn't hyper-sensitive like mine, or well, really, like any of ours, but that didn't stop me from glancing at the tent again.

"No," I murmured. "I don't know what I want to say to them." Christ on fucking crutches, that was an understatement.

"To your folks or to the family?" Mario asked perceptively, and I shrugged.

"Either one." My folks hadn't come to the wedding. You'd think the fact that mom was married to a giant shape-changing bird would sort of open their mind about certain things, but they hadn't understood. They hadn't understood about being bound to two people, about entering into a family agreement with my lover's lover as well, and they sure as shit didn't understand about willingly entering into a relationship with another man.

Eric, the one lover who was mine and mine alone, who loved me for me and who didn't sit at the table of the gods and would rather share a crust of bread (or a warm rabbit, when he was a coyote and I was a big carnivorous bird) with me anyway, might as well have been the engine grease under my dad's fingernails.

"Are they coming to visit?" Teague asked, and I looked at him and grimaced. He and Jacky had dealt with their own version of this problem around Thanksgiving time—with some pretty dramatic results. If anyone would appreciate my dilemma, he would.

"They're making noises about it," I told him, glad to talk to someone about it. Our conversation gathered Kyle and Lambent as well, probably because even if you could see the world clearly in it, nobody wanted to be alone under the velvet sky if they could help it. Not even vampires, not even elves, certainly not birds and wolves. Over in the tent the song in those murmuring voices changed, went up a notch, and I had to smile. Certainly not human sorceresses who didn't know their own worth.

"Noises," Teague grunted, his eyes darting to the flickering lights behind me.

"Yeah—they want to come visit this summer. I told them it would have to be neutral ground if they didn't want their mind's wiped. They're still bitching about that, but we might decide on a resort or something." My mom had been the most horrified—I could picture her, narrow, vivacious face pouting in hurt, her streaked, blonde hair perfectly coifed.

"Would Green really do that?" Lambent asked, surprised. Lambent had been with us since October—apparently he was used to a lot more bravado and a lot less honest action, because he still had trouble believing Green was really that fucking strong.

"He did it to Grace's daughter," I told him, although from all reports it had been Grace herself who had done the mind-fuck. I could see that. If it came to protecting Green from my parents, I'd wipe John and Terry's mind myself if I had to use a two-by-four to do it.

"I was there," Kyle said unexpectedly, and I glanced at him. "He was planning to do it himself—Grace stepped in first."

"Why?" Lambent asked, speculation in his voice. Everything with Lambent was about power and struggle. It wasn't hard to figure out that he was trying to assess Green's strength in this story as in all things.

"Why'd he plan to wipe Chloe's mind or why'd Grace do it for him?" I asked.

Lambent shrugged. "Why the exile—even an elf can see Grace is summat special...you'd think her kid would be right fuckin' royalty or something." Like Green, when Lambent relaxed his Cockney came out, and when it did, Lambent became less abrasive and more charming.

"Chloe liked to cause trouble," I shrugged. "She talked shit to Cory, tried to make stuff happen. I don't know—I think she was jealous or something. Three times she did something that put us in danger by being a bitch...the third time was..." I blushed and Mario chortled.

"The third time was Cory's mother walking in on her in bed with all the men!" he filled in gleefully, rocking on the metal rim of the fire-pit without fear. "She had no idea..."

"Yeah, yeah," I mumbled. "It was a laugh fucking riot—why don't we *all* try walking in on people while they're doing the wild thing... the whole hill can have that much fun!"

"Come off it, bird boy," Mario chuckled, taking my surliness for exactly what it was worth. "All you were doing was sleeping—I was there, remember?"

"Besides," Lambent said thoughtfully, "not much point in walking in when they light up the sky as it is, is there?" His red-gold hair and matching eyes lit up hellishly in this light, but for once, without the mockery of the challenge, the fire in his soul was as comforting as the literal fire we were hovering over.

We all looked over our shoulders to where Cory and Bracken had truly begun. I didn't try to look through the tent to voyeur—I got a front row view of that on a regular basis. Instead, I looked to the sky to see their colors— Bracken's ochre/pond-shadow lights playing off of Cory's amazing azure and tropical sunrise, the lights resonating with the white-lit tent glow...it was the definition of magic.

"Man, that's pretty," Teague breathed, and I looked at him wryly. Teague didn't seem to be the type to talk much but he was moved, the same as we all were.

"Yes," I murmured, conscious of everything that *wasn't* in my voice. No jealousy, no rancor, no yearning. I had finally found contentment with who I was and my place at the gods' table. It was okay.

"Why didn't you go with them?" Mario asked softly, and I shrugged. The animal, erotic truth was that tonight, the part I looked forward to was slipping in when they were done and tasting Cory's man on her thighs and in her body, listening to her moan as Bracken palmed her breasts and breathed in her ear.

I went with the personal truth instead.

"Because I didn't feel like being a dark place in the light," I said, and Mario 'hmmmmd' in his throat. Both of us kept our eyes on the light ballet as it waltzed its way against the black stage of the night.

CORY

Blood Sunrise

I was fast asleep when Nicky crawled into bed and buried his head between my thighs. I woke up for a shocked, sleepy moment to gasp orgasm into Bracken's chuckling mouth as Nicky lapped at the hidden slippery folds of my sex, and then again as he moved his fingers into position and thrust and played and penetrated.

Bracken's clever fingers worked, plumping at my breasts and pinching my sensitized nipples. My body, charged and humming from our lovemaking earlier burst into a high, keening wail of finality. Nicky scooted up to rub his sticky face on the shoulder of my T-shirt, and Bracken fumbled with the underwear I had forgotten when I'd fallen asleep earlier.

I think I mumbled something like "Take care of you, Nick?" Only to hear him chuckle and thrust the wet front of his boxers against my thigh. Apparently taking care of me *had* taken care of him, and I had just enough consciousness to be grateful before I fell immediately back asleep.

The vampires checked in with me about ten minutes before dawn, and I woke up enough to feel relieved—and to realize how badly I had been sleeping in the first place—and I pretty much passed out after that.

The next day was oddly relaxing.

Bracken rose at the crotch of a slutty dawn (as Nicky called it when we had to leave early for school) and slipped away to walk this new earth— presumably with Lambent, since it was new territory and the rule was (and I'd told the other sidhe this) not to get separated. An hour or so later I heard them murmuring to each other—or rather I heard Bracken's mild, arrogant tones and Lambent's snotty ones back. My stone and shadow beloved could be one of the few people on the hill that didn't get rubbed wrong by the fiery elf—probably because of their basic natures. Stone was generally unmoved by short bursts of fire, and shadow did nothing to feed it. I'd seen them interact—Lambent would flare, Bracken would ignore him, and Lambent would subside.

Goddess, I envied Bracken.

Maybe it's because my power was in sunshine and fire is always pissy because sunshine is brighter, or maybe it's because my mouth could sometimes be classified as a natural disaster, like Hurricane Andrew or something, but the day Lambent and I actually agreed on something and *acted* in concert would be the first day of my adulthood.

So far, it looked like my twenty-first birthday had been a suggestion rather than an actual landmark, and my little temper display with the fire the night before didn't improve my opinion of my own behavior one little tiny ember's worth.

Fuck.

Nicky tried to burrow his way through my chest, and although I'd been blinking and awake for a while now, I realized that the entire reason I wasn't getting up was that I didn't want to get cold.

"Lambent…" I called through the tent, trying not to sound like a weenie but trying to sound humble at the same time.

"Yes, my liege?" came the cheeky answer, and I fought back the 'Fuck off' that the morning seemed to inspire.

"Could you inspire my eternal gratitude and start a fire in the pit before we have to get up?" I asked, trying to be gracious while prone and trying to crawl right into Nicky's warmth on the air mattress as he was trying to crawl into mine.

"Is she serious?" Lambent asked Bracken, sounding stunned. "Was that a real request and not an order?"

"She usually requests," my beloved replied mildly. "She just expects us to do as she asks."

"Well yank my bloody balls…" Lambent replied in wonder.

"I can hear you, you know!" I called back, enjoying the sound of him choking on his tongue. "And I'd rather not touch your privates. I asked nicely, Lambent, and you know I don't have to—but could you please start the fire so the rest of us who want to might at least have a reason to get up

"Right-o." His voice was still cheeky, but there was a muffled 'whump' and then the picnic space outside the tent grew orange and warm. There were sighs and mutters throughout the 'three-room' tent, and a gruff chorus of 'thank-you's. After a few moments during which I felt the shivers leave my bones a bit, I shrugged into my jeans, wiggled my bra on under my shirt (much to Nicky's amusement) and pulled the three layers of fleece and wool that Bracken had stacked neatly in the corner into the sleeping bag and managed to get into those too.

By the time I was ready to get out of the bag and tie my tennis shoes Nicky's laughter had thoroughly awakened the rest of the camp.

"Thanks a lot, bird-boy," I muttered as I ducked out the flap. Nicky just rolled around in the sleeping bag like a dork and I got to listen to the rest of the camp whine about not quite being ready to get up.

"What was so fuckin' funny?" Teague grouched as we stood around that lovely, cheery fire and ate. The breakfast had simply appeared before we got to the table, along with plastic mugs with our names written on them in sharpie. I got warm oatmeal and hot chocolate—one of my favorites—but there was bacon and eggs for the shifters. Nicky kept putting bacon on my plate and I kept giving it back to him. I was comfortable with my weight now—there was no reason to push my luck. If I wasn't careful, my ass could become a national landmark.

"I've just never seen anybody get dressed like that!" Nicky chortled. "She didn't even break the surface of the sleeping bag!"

The others at least broke a smile, and Bracken brought his great big hyper-metabolic body behind me like he did last night, and I got to listen to him chuckle as I leaned into his arms.

"I hate being cold," I grumbled.

"You're not so fond of being hot," Bracken contradicted in my ear and I arched an eyebrow.

"That's you guys," I retorted. It was true—with a few exceptions like Arturo and Lambent, most of the other elves didn't really do well in the heat. Even the high sidhe—like Bracken and Green—who were the most all around powerful both physically and preternaturally, tended to 'wilt' when the mercury cleared ninety. It didn't stop them from going out and hitting the lakes—Clementine, Folsom, and the one glinting pewter sapphire through the dark-green of the trees—but it did mean the elves tended to frequent the night in the summer. It probably added to their mystique—and, I'm sure, cemented Bracken and Adrian's friendship when they'd been a couple.

Sigh. Speaking of doomed vampires, it was probably time to stop bantering and actually come up with a plan.

"So?" Mario asked, making one of those bird-ruffling twitches that the Avians tended towards, and I rolled my eyes. It was like they could read my damned mind, wasn't it?

"Well, first of all, shapeshifters take turns—someone goes and lets Max and Renny come back and eat and sleep. The other two fly or run around looking for animal corpses. One or two happens—the number I saw last night? That needs to be hidden. Bracken and I will hike around the lake on the road. Lambent, run where the wind takes you—we need to make sure there are no more vampire critters, and that all the dead things are hidden. The lake's not that big—between all of us, we should be done by lunch. Then we come back here, spell whoever's on guard duty, and rest up. It's going to be a long-ass fuckin' night."

"I'll take first watch," Teague volunteered. "Let me get a book from the tent."

I nodded, thinking that I didn't want him there at night—seeing Teague naked had really freaked little Gretchen out. He needed to be far in the shadows as we dealt with her this night. I was also thinking that, given how much Teague *didn't* like to sit still, that was a pretty generous offer—we must have been thinking along the same lines for him to make it.

Regretfully, I gulped the rest of my hot chocolate and swallowed what was left of my oatmeal. One more time Nicky handed me a piece of bacon and I absentmindedly finished it, trying to work out who would go where, which really sucked because I wasn't great with math or maps.

Bracken leaned over and picked me up by the middle, making me squeal and shriek and, as I thrashed around helplessly in his ginormous muscular grasp, he chortled, "Give it up!"

"What!"

"Stop trying to give us a map, dammit!"

"How would you know…" I sputtered, still wiggling, and he laughed, full and hearty in my ear, and I loved that sound. It wasn't as rich as Green's laugh, but that was because Bracken was younger—where Green had richness, Bracken had sturdy heart and vigor, and I loved them both.

"Because you only get that look on your face when you're doing something map related… confess…"

"I was…"

"Confess…"

"Put me down!" I gasped with no dignity at all, and he did, mostly because he felt like it, and I humphed and sighed and turned to him with a sheepish grin.

"You all really do know what you're doing, don't you?"

"Absolutely," he grinned back, and then hefted me up again, this time facing him, and kissed me for no reason at all.

By the time we were done, we were alone in the campground and it was too late to give orders anyway.

"You're getting subtler, beloved," I told him with a glance at the sky where

Nicky and Mario were circling and shrieking and dividing the land between them.

"You scared the raisins out of every jackrabbit for forty miles with your squealing," he retorted, "and you think that was subtle?"

I laughed and took his hand and remembered to watch out for his sturdy bare feet as I walked in my shoes. "Were we yelling at each other in front of the whole camp?" I asked him mildly, and he shook his head, his grin conceding that maybe we actually *had* grown up a little in our stormy, take-no-prisoners relationship.

"Then we're getting subtle," I declared, and hand in hand we began trotting towards the paved loop that led to the road around the lake.

The walk was pleasant. We eventually had to stop holding hands—the man *is* more than a foot and a half taller than I am, but I had been running for more than a year, and the three mile trek around the lake was no big deal. We talked—a lot of it was shop, since we worked together at Grace's yarn store, attended the same classes together, and he was there with me through much of the hill business. I often hear humans complain that they need a break from their spouses. I guess I got my breaks in Green's arms, or when Bracken was off doing business on the rare times I'm stuck at home, but mostly, it is not a day unless we spend a great deal of it at each other's sides. He told me once that he would be the most human lover I would have. I guess in this, as in pretty much everything involving my stone and shadow beloved, he was superhuman. I could be saturated in his strength and his temper and in his quiet conversation and still not need to be elsewhere for many, many days at a time.

When we returned, after lots of little side trips into the brush on the side of the road to look for more kills or anything suspicious, it was a little past lunch time. I had to incinerate a couple of desiccated corpses, and I found that, bacon or no bacon, I was ravenous.

There were hot sandwiches waiting for us—mine had meatballs and marinara sauce—and I mentally reminded myself to leave something really heavenly, like pizza and ice cream, in the corner of my room when I returned. If I left the ice cream in an ice chest, the sprites, brownies, gnomes and so-forth who kept invisibly serving us here would get high on the sugar and live well and happy for two days at the least.

The others were back when we arrived, and after sending Mario to go take Teague's spot, I went to my tent and got my knitting and a good hardcover book (the better to sit flat on my lap) and sat down in the peaceful quiet of the woods.

It really was beautiful. The lake smelled fresh, the red dirt was earthen and not powdery like it would be in the summer, and the trees whispered and roared quietly in the breeze overhead. Between my fleecewear and the fire I wasn't too cold, and for a sweet hour or two, while Bracken read a book next to me, I was able to actually relax. I mean, after all, this *was* my spring break and I was hunting—I didn't feel bad about a little real R&R.

The R&R was interrupted when my chin nodded forward and touched my chest, and I ended up curled up in the tent with a two big kitty cats who were napping in that self-satisfied way that only cats have.

When I woke up, it was late afternoon, and the sun was slanting through the pine trees, and the cat whose fur I'd buried my fingers into was now a naked young woman, disentangling herself from me.

"Ewww…" she was laughing, "Cory, would you get off me?"

I groaned. "I don't know… could you turn back into a cat so I can get warm again?"

"No way. I'm hungry and I want a sandwich with*out* dirt on it. Besides, Max has been waiting for you to wake up for half-an-hour so he can change too."

"I've seen him naked you know. It's no big deal," I grumbled, standing up anyway and pussyfooting around the bedding. When Bracken put me to bed like a sleepy infant, he hadn't bothered to take off my shoes and I didn't want to get dirt on the sleeping bag. (This could, perhaps, be why I wasn't really fond of camping as a whole. It was that eternal dance between you and the dirt…and if you stepped wrong, it ended up in your underwear, and that would throw the whole trip in the shitter.)

I had barely cleared the tent door between an indignant Max hollered, "Thanks a lot!"

I shook my head—I didn't know what his problem was, and since Renny was cracking up, I figured it wasn't that severe.

The sun had dipped behind the trees enough that the chill hit the air again, and I danced on my toes a bit in front of the fire. Bracken came up to me with a savory bowl of stew and I ate without objection—once dark hit, we were going to be all business.

One by one the others looked up from what they were doing—talking, reading, or, in Lambent's case, making lovely apparitions dance in the flames—and stood with their own bowls of stew, ready for the pow-wow. I saw that Nicky was missing and realized that he must be the one in front of the cave—good. Even though Nick was a good fighter and fearless in his own way, he looked pretty innocuous. I couldn't say that about any of the other men in the camp.

"Why didn't you do that last night?" I asked Lambent thoughtfully. There was a pack of wolves running in the flames, frolicking as I'd seen Teague, Jack, and Katy doing—I could have stared at it, hypnotized, for hours.

"Not my flames. Not my fire, not my place to play," he said softly, and I nodded.

"I'll keep that in mind—that's pretty. I'd like to see it again."

His face grew ruddier in the firelight, and I looked around. Renny and Max bundled up, neither of them wearing half as much as I was wearing and both of them looking considerably less cold.

"Fuck it," I muttered. "I should just let something bite me."

I'd meant to be funny, but Bracken and Lambent both shuddered.

"That would be bad, beloved," Bracken muttered and I looked at him in surprise. "Your power, a shapechanger's power... just..."

"Don't worry about it, Brack," I soothed. "We saw what that can do—I wouldn't risk it." Last year around this time we'd run into a real nasty—a little bit of elvish power, a new life as a vampire, a lot of people dead and a bitter taste on our tongues. "I wasn't serious anyway—I just," I rolled my eyes, "I was just bitching about the cold."

There was a ripple of laughter, and that was as good a place to start as any.

"Renny, did she eat last night?"

Renny shook her head, her fuzzy brown ponytail bobbing. "No—but she's getting hungry. She's not going to be pretty when she wakes up."

I closed my eyes. Shit. Phillip had told me, on the ride back, that he would try... but winning her trust had been so important. "Fuck," I muttered. "She won't let any of the guys near her."

Renny shrugged. "No worries..."

"The hell it's not!" I shot back. Oh Goddess... she weighed about ninety-eight pounds, soaking wet in fur. "The kid's not Phillip or Marcus—she's a little kid with an ice-cream sundae—she won't care how ugly it gets, she's just going to want more!"

Renny grinned. "Well, kids who chase kitties get scratched. I'm not helpless, Cory!"

I frowned at her. "I didn't say you were. I just..." I looked at Max and made my own helpless gestures, and he shook his head grimly.

"I was hoping you could do it, oh fearless leader," he muttered. Wonderful.

"She's dangerous, Renny," I said levelly. "And if I thought you were helpless, I wouldn't have let you stay with her in the first place. But we're miles away from Green, and I know you guys can get sucked almost dry and still replenish with a beer and some chips, but if I'd be bad as a werecat, you can bet damned sure you'd suck as a were-vampire."

Renny grinned, her lips drawn back from slightly parted teeth, like a cat. "Yes I would suck, but mostly on Max, so it'd be okay."

"It's not funny, beloved!" Max snapped, and he must have been rattled because he wasn't an 'endearments in public' sort of guy.

"It would be if I was nibbling on your neck!" Renny flirted and I gritted my teeth.

"Renny, you've got the guy, stop trying to jolly him into bed," Bracken snapped, and I looked at him gratefully. If I wasn't the only one getting uber-protective, I wasn't the only one she'd be pissed at. Cats hold grudges. But Renny and Bracken always had a soft spot for each other—hopefully he could at least convince her to be careful.

"He's good in bed," she said mildly, and then because even Teague and Mario were looking annoyed, she held up a hand. "Look, she's afraid of the guys. We can all guess why that might be, although no one wants to say it. Cory bleeds out like anyone else—it's just like you were saying last night, Cory. I'm the best one for the job, and the job keeps the family safe. It doesn't only work if you can shoot fire out your ass, you know?"

I looked at her sourly. "If I ever shoot fire out my ass, remind me to fart in your general direction—but yeah. I get it. But you need to know that if she gets ugly, we're taking her out. No one chews on you without showing a little fucking respect, right?"

"Absolutely," she replied mildly, and turned away in that graceful way cats have and picked her way to the table to get more stew.

"Shit," I muttered, and Bracken put his hands on my shoulders in sympathy.

"I'm glad it wasn't my call," he murmured. "Don't worry—I'll stay far away."

"And the hell of it is, you can't," I told him, unafraid to lean into his touch. Bracken's chest against my back was as comforting as a sun-warmed slab of granite to a napping cat, and in the last year and a half, I'd learned to love the feel and the smell of him, that rock-hard core of peace and strength in my stone-and-shadow lover. It was especially important now, when everything else in my head was such a barbed-wire maelstrom.

"I can't?" he asked, surprised, and I shrugged, as unhappy with this solution as I had been with any other.

"Phillip's going to have to blood her, *due'alle,*" I muttered disconsolately, "and you're going to have to help him do it."

"Shit," he echoed, groaning, and I had to agree.

Have you ever taken a gamble and had it pay off? Have you ever felt so fucking sick about how things wrapped up in the end that you had a hard time being all happy-skippy about the shit you did that went right?

Yeah. For starters? If Phillip hadn't blooded little Gretchen first, the damned kid would have ripped my best friend's throat out, and that's the best that can be said of the whole affair.

About five minutes before absolute sunset I once again put my ass in a sling (Brack and I couldn't get enough of that pun) and we went caroming through the damned forest, towards the little girl's cave of horrors. Having learned from the night before, this time I just kept my eyes shut and hoped for the best—it was easier than I'd thought it would be, actually. I'd spent the last two years nearly, learning to trust the people I loved with my wellbeing. Believing that Bracken wouldn't throw us into a tree or off a cliff was sort of like a final in 'Relationships 101', and I found myself wondering what the graduate level project would be.

I didn't have too much time to wonder, because directly at sunset, Phillip, Marcus and Kyle emerged from the bottom compartment of the SUV and zoomed for the cave, much as we were doing, and getting Marcus' mental *She's still here, Nicky's in a tree, and she looks PISSED!!!* Was one item off of my list of reasons to panic. One of my biggest fears would be that, being young, she'd have that same hyperkid ability to just wake up before everybody else in order to make the adults around her miserable. It was good to know that the same things that held true for new adult vampires held true for new child vampires—the newer you were, the more of the night you slept through.

We hadn't wanted to be in the clearing before the vampires were, and we hadn't wanted her to be gone when we got there. It was good to know that at least one thing reacted according to plan.

We slowed our (terrifying) pace before we burst into the area around the cave like some sort of host of avenging angels, and hopefully it was a casual group of people who stepped into the clearing to watch a clearly-baffled Phillip argue with a little girl.

"What if I don't want to go with you?" she was saying, and there was something about her voice that made me absolutely sure she was on her last legs of being ornery.

"Of course you want to go with us!" I laughed, trying to be gentle, but about up to my teeth with this particular argument. "What's not to like? There will be food, clean water, and a room all in pink with all of the toys you could wish for..."

"Don't lie to me!" she screeched suddenly, with enough passion to make us all step back and blink.

"What makes you think we're lying?" I asked carefully into the shocked (and uncomfortable) silence of men gone far beyond their comfort level.

"He lied," she muttered angrily, and I grimaced, pinching the bridge of my nose like that particular gesture (learned from Green) would do me a fucking lot of good.

We'd known it—we'd all known it. Any vampire who would make a child vampire would probably be a child predator all around. We were all—Renny included—warriors. We were the people Green (or I) sent into situations where strength and cunning would be called for. I mean, if Green needed a diplomat, was he really going to send me?

So this kid needed a rape counselor, and she got us. We'd have to do.

"So he promised you ponies, and you got caves and corpses," I said heavily. "It was a sucky deal all around, kid. But we're not going to lie to you, and I can prove it, right?"

"How?" she asked bitterly, her matted, dank hair swinging in front of her face because she wanted to hide behind it.

"You and Phillip," I said, fielding a glare from Marcus with more poise than I felt, "if you taste each other's blood, you'll know if the other one is telling the truth."

"So I'll know if he means it, about a room and a bath?"

"And he'll know if you mean it about wanting to go there," I told her. There was a lot I wasn't telling her—like the fact that Phillip could control her actions to an extent, force her body to do things her mind didn't want to go along with, like, say, keep her from killing her food or keep her in the boundaries of Green's hill. He could also bind her—albeit indirectly—with me. But if we were going to (oh, my churning stomach) let this poor kid live, we'd have to omit a few truths and get her into the damned SUV and on the way home, because another abomination like the vampire bear or the vampire wildcat was something we absolutely could not afford.

But, for all I was leaving out, I was giving her some real truth, and maybe she could hear it in my voice.

Maybe she was reassured that we had been there for her come the dark.

Maybe she was just fucking tired of sleeping on the ground and stinking like blood and unwashed corpse.

Either way, she narrowed her eyes at me carefully.

"Would he have to touch me?"

I shook my head. "No—here—watch. It's like magic."

I took out the little razor sharp pocket-knife I kept in my pocket since I'd been forced to hack through an enemy's vein with a pair of yarn-snippers last year, and touched it gingerly to the fleshy pudge on the back between my thumb and forefinger. This was where our whole plan could fall apart, because if she figured out that I didn't want to actually blood-bond with her, she'd wonder why. She'd have a basic impression of my good will and my own wariness when she tasted my blood—as well as sort of a heartbreaking memory, if things held true—but if I didn't taste her blood first, the bond wouldn't be complete.

With a ginger prick of the knife, I watched a little blood well up and looked at Bracken. Bracken nodded, something like greed in his eyes, and the tiny drops of blood coalesced and lifted themselves off my skin, glowing like rubies in the starlight.

They were easily seen in the dark, and as they flew towards the bemused little girl, her mouth opened slightly, and for a moment there was an expression on her face that was truly childish, and truly enchanted. Bracken played to that—sidhe adore children, and for all his gruffness, he was no exception.

The globules swirled, chased each other, sparkled and played, and when she laughed, their antics grew more complex. After one too many passes near her face, she let out a disconsolate and hungry little sigh, and Bracken stopped playing and popped my blood in her mouth.

This was, perhaps, his most wondrous and frightening ability, and I winked at him as she swallowed, because my heart was suddenly pounding in my chest with how much I loved him. But we had business to do, and even as he took my hand to his mouth and sucked lightly on the wound, making it run a little with his power so he could swallow my blood like the creamy chocolate that goes cold on your tongue, I was watching Gretchen.

Sorceress blood is pretty tasty and pretty filling—hopefully it would be like feeding a starving man hearty bread with some really awesome gravy on top—and she took a gulp and smiled, just a little bit of the wildness easing from her eyes.

"Sunshine…" she murmured in awe. Perhaps she was too young to fathom that this taste of blood was the closest she'd ever get to it again, because the memory of the sun didn't seem to hurt her like it hurt the other vampires I'd blooded. She swallowed and smacked her tongue then, like a wine connoisseur tasting for anise or lavender.

"You like him a lot," she murmured, watching Bracken warily as he finished sucking on my hand and dropped it to my side to heal a little before he touched me again.

"I do," I told her sincerely, "and that's the truth."

She nodded, and then smiled shyly. Her eyes were whirling a little slower, and her fangs were not quite so pronounced, but that shy smile on that predator's face was still pretty damned unnerving.

"Can we?" she asked, and Bracken nodded. "Will you make the blood dance again?"

"Of course," he nodded, bowing slightly. From above us there was a bird sound that I could easily interpret as *Oh, puhleez!* but I didn't dare laugh.

"Bite your own wrist first, little one," Phillip murmured. With his black widow's peak and his eyes whirling red with the prospect of blood and his fangs held up to the inside of his arm, he really did look like a bad Dracula movie come to life, but that was okay too. Fake vampires are all over the media—this little girl wasn't going to be afraid of Phillip, not now, not when the prospect of shelter was so damned close.

Gretchen brought her wrist up to her mouth, and with a little rabbit nibble and scarcely a crunch and a pop, she opened a vein for Bracken to use. Phillip made a sizeable hole in the crease of his arm, and his blood flowed slowly and freely into the air as Bracken did his thing.

Brack held his hands out at both sides, and played with the blood for Gretchen's delight again, but this time, he was extremely careful to make sure Phillip got his share of the blood first.

Phillip made a noise—a hurt noise, with a grunt in it like a blow to the solar plexus—and then kept his face still and stone.

Goddess.

Gretchen's noise on the other hand was considerably happier—Phillip had loved snow-skiing and hot chocolate and steak dinners and plays when he'd been alive, and with the exception of the hot chocolate and steak, he still had a passion for those things now. I'm sure Gretchen was getting a swirl of sophistication and joy, with a solid dose of the contentment Phillip had shown in his life as a vampire at Green's Hill.

She made a happy grunt, in counterpoint to his agonized one, and then sighed, her entire body relaxing into the taste of vampire. Suddenly, her attention sharpened.

"You like *him*!" she protested, looking in horror at Marcus. The two had finally settled down into something approaching sanguinity (sigh—yes, pun intended) regarding their on-again/off-again relationship, with the emphasis on "We're on again asshole, because I apparently can't live without you."

"Yes, I do," Phillip replied his voice almost flat with suppressed emotion. "I love him."

"But that's *wrong!*"

"Jesus!" I muttered before I could stop myself. She glared at me, and I suppressed my complete irritation.

"Not for vampires, Gretchen," I told her sweetly, and, like those explanations tend to do with children, this one worked.

"God hates us anyway," she muttered, kicking the nearest tree with enough preternatural strength to make it tremble.

"Maybe," I conceded, "but you're the Goddess' chosen, so that's good," and then, before we could debate theology anymore—and before she could see what her pre-death memories were doing to the usually stoic Phillip-- I said, "Are you still hungry?"

She nodded her head miserably—like it happens sometimes, a little taste of something totally whets your appetite, and while her eyes weren't whirling anymore and her teeth had receded, her face had become pinched and miserable, like that of a regular starving eight year old.

"Okay," I said, congratulating myself on the fact that no one was dead yet. "You see Renny over there? She was there last night as a big kitty cat?"

The little girl nodded and I took a deep breath.

"She's willing to be your dinner tonight—but it's just like a regular kitty, Gretchen. You've got to be gentle, or she'll scratch you."

Gretchen looked at me, her eyes suddenly crafty. "She was a pretty kitty... does she want to be my pet?"

I caught Renny's eyes, girlfriend's communication kicking in big time. *Are you sure you want in?*

Renny swallowed and nodded, then started taking off her clothes in preparation to change. I shook my head subtly, and Renny caught my hint. It was less easy to think of her as a 'pet' if she was a young woman.

But Gretchen wasn't stupid.

"I want her as a kitty," she said imperiously, and I wanted to smack my head with my hand.

"She's fuzzy as a kitty," I said mildly. "How about you feed from her as a girl?"

"Maybe a kitty would be best, Lady Cory," Phillip said, and I risked a look at him. Oh Goddess, was he green around the gills—whatever was in her head, it was horrible with a capital H and squared to the *nth* power, and he had a good reason for his request or he wouldn't have used my title.

"Okay, Renny—go ahead and change." *Phillip you'd better be right about this.*

She killed her family, Cory.

We knew that...fuck. She'd given him the images, confused, sunk in an abyss of black denial, and because we were linked, I got to share. Ain't telepathy grand? Her mother had screamed when she'd run in, clothes torn, red-eyed, covered in blood. If she hadn't screamed, maybe, maybe, little Gretchen could have reigned in her blood-lust, maybe she could have seen her parents and her brother as family, instead of throbbing heartbeats, food, prey.

Her mother's skin ripping under her teeth had been sweet... and then... then...redness...screams... a confused mélange of shredding, tearing, the bitter, warm, rusty tang of blood...the purple of viscera, the crunch of bones...

I must have made a noise or something, because Bracken's hand was on my elbow and my tiny wound was running freely, dripping on the ground, and Phillip had snapped his mind away from mine in mid image.

That was the last human...

She'd ever talked to, fed from, loved.

I looked at Renny again, thinking that I could stop her, but in the time it had taken me to get the message, Renny had put her clothes back on and dropped to her knees in front of the little girl. Gretchen wiped her mouth with the back of her hand, leaving a clean spot in a month's worth of filth. I opened my mouth to stop them just as Gretchen closed her mouth over Renny's carotid, punched in for the flowing blood, and began to feed.

I breathed deeply through my nose, trying not to spread my panic, and Renny, long accustomed to being dinner, relaxed limply into the feeding, drugged on the passive euphoria of allowing her life force to slip away.

And I started counting silently in my head.

Vampires can't really 'drain' a person. They can help—and a fully grown vampire can ingest about two pints of blood. (Whereas a fully adult person can only ingest one pint, because, hello, if you're not a vampire or some sort of being where blood drinking is a part of sustenance like Bracken, it's really frickin' icky!!!!) A child can probably drink about a pint of blood—and that's a lot, just the way a pint of milkshake is a lot for a human child.

How long did it take for a human child to drink a pint of milkshake?

Kids gorge themselves all the time on cookies and cake and shit that makes them sick... if Gretchen drank too much of Renny (don't think about how helpless Renny's little face looks, peering up from Gretchen's lap, how predatory and strange the little girl with the whirling eyes looks with her fangs plunged into my friend's helpless, white and bloody throat) then she'd probably puke it up in short order, but that would be a fucking waste of something my friend needed to live!

Oh fuck it all, I couldn't do the goddamned math. I pulled a bottle of water out of a pouch on the sling and started to gulp it. When I got mostways down, I thought *make her stop, Phillip. It's gone on too long.*

Phillip's affirmative noise was coupled with some soft words to the little girl. "Gretchen, hon—that's enough. Renny's been more than generous..."

Gretchen growled, the sound of a feral creature, not a human, and gathered her shoulders over Renny's still body like a territorial and wild dog. Renny whimpered, laid still, her breathing growing sluggish and far too quiet.

It was a horrible tableau—all of these adults, all of them with preternatural strength and speed and some of us with supernatural powers, standing in the velvet breath-smoking darkness and watching this rabid brat from hell bleed our friend to death. Nobody wanted to hurt her, nobody wanted to lay hands on her, everybody was very aware that with one jerk of her dank little head, this Disney Channel nightmare could rip Renny's throat out, but if we didn't stop her, and soon, it wouldn't matter.

Make her stop!!! I screamed in our heads, and Phillip replied, *I'm. Trying.*

And he was. He was probably a master vampire, if our kiss worried about such things. Phillip loved power enough to pull the dead back to life with his blood kiss, but his formidable strength of will might not be enough against this braincheesed kid.

He needed my help.

Green! I called, because he was always there when we were out on a call, always listening with part of himself, always just the breath of a summer meadow away, and my shock when he didn't answer stopped my breath in my chest like the frigid fucking vacuum of space.

But Renny was dying and I didn't have time to breathe anyway.

Phillip, can you hold just me?

Swallow. *I don't…*

A sudden flooding of Green, blessed blessed Green, my *ou'e'hm*, my equal, the growing to my sunshine, and I didn't even let Phillip finish that sentence.

Together, Green and I flooded Phillip with power, and he directed us with his will. In the dark, there was a subtle sparkle, like dust motes in a sunlit field, and it engulfed Gretchen, literally prying her jaws apart like a pissed-off crocodile's, and forcing her corpse-stiff arms to relinquish her hold.

"Max take her to Marcus and Lambent," I gritted, knowing that Marcus would use the power the Goddess gave the vampires to close the wounds in Renny's throat before they could bleed out anymore, but most of my will was focused on what Phillip was doing with that fearful collective of my power and Green's.

Gretchen was fighting us. I could hear the echo in Phillips' skull, *She's mine, my kitty, I want her! I hate you, you're not my daddy, you're a…a…a big mean JACKHOLE, that's what you are!* It was an out and out tantrum, as she released the full force of her anger and her self-pity and her sorrow on the people who had offered her redemption.

Phillip was too close to her.

I could see it, could feel it in his head. He'd seen her transition and it was every bit as awful as we'd thought… *pawing limbs, hurtful fingers digging into her private places…don't touch don't touch ow ow ow…mommy mommy mommy daddy daddy somebody…* and he felt for her, he felt for the poor kid he really did and…

And goddammit all to a bucket of fuck she had TRIED TO KILL MY FRIEND!!!

With a yank, Green and I jerked our power from Phillip's control and used it to circle Gretchen like a second skin.

Her mouth opened in shock and indignation as we bound her in power, my angry, deadly-to-vampires sunshine buffered by Green's healing kindness, we wrapped her in it, swaddled her tightly, like the abandoned newborn she was. Together, we trusted Green to keep that bond while I distanced myself enough to talk.

"Guys, I can hold her, but you need to move us to the vamp-mobile. I'll shove her in the bottom and keep her still while Renny, the vamps, and I and fly down the fucking road home, you hear me?"

There would be logistics, I thought hazily. Who drove in what car, how many people could the SUV hold, packing up the shit in the other two cars... and all of it was going to have to resolve itself.

Renny needed Green to heal her, and the vampires needed shelter, and this kid needed a room with pony-puke-pink décor and three feet of steel between her and the rest of the world and we needed these things sometime in the next (*Christ!*) three hours.

I was pretty sure we could make it, but as Bracken threw me on his back and I towed Junior Vampire Barbie behind us with the combined-power-psychic-death-swaddle, I knew we were cutting it close.

I have vague memories of the ride—thank Goddess.

We were crowded—the thing sat eight and there were seven of us, but Bracken's legs alone are the size of two of Renny or me, so I seem to remember bruising my ribs a lot against his kneecaps. My mind was locked on the girl in the hidden compartment underneath the car, keeping her swaddled, because the car wasn't the steel room, and she was a newborn vampire and if I let go of her she would shred through the bottom of the car and then through us and then through the entire population of North Placer County for all we knew. It was absolutely imperative that my mind, my entire will, stay focused on keeping her bound and still—and on giving her light to see by, so she could see that there were pillows and blankets and (Marcus' idea of a joke) a stuffed teddy bear that Grace had knitted for him with vampire fangs and a bunny-victim in his paws.

We hadn't meant for this place to be a prison—she was making it one on her own.

I knew that Renny was breathing and groggy and Max had given her water and beef jerky from Bracken's pack, and I knew that Marcus and Kyle had needed to drag Phillip into the SUV, and that he'd been incoherent with the horrors of a little girl's last worst nightmare and the terrible clash of wills.

I knew that even though my mind was locked in a terrible strife of mental versus physical, my body was still on that fucking winding road. I don't know where Bracken got the waterproof bags, but I spent a good half-hour filling them, and, I'm sure, the entire car spent at least a few brain cells praying that the damned things didn't burst.

By the time we fishtailed through the graveled drive to Green's Hill my body hurt from the bruises, my stomach muscles screamed in agony, and my head was pounding with the effort of keeping her still.

I was dimly aware of the car screeching to a halt in the garage under the hill, and the vampires opening the compartment below us. There was a sudden touch of Phillip's hands on my face as I rested it against Bracken's thigh, and he peered into my eyes, trying to get my attention.

"Cory... Cory..."

I looked at him with vacant eyes, and he shook me gently, and Bracken was saying something urgent to me, but it wasn't until Green spoke directly in my head that I heard what they were saying.

Beloved... let go. She's quite passive now that we've opened the car. Dawn's close, she knows it—let the vampires handle her, yes? Grace will take her down to the room, you can start again tomorrow.

Green?

You heard me, ou'e'eir, *let go.*

It was like unclenching a fist that had been knotted around a rope in the frost for hours. The slow, painful loosening of my will (and Green's) from around Gretchen's body actually hurt, and even as the wisps of power sparkled into the garage's cool dark, the entire wash of it receded from my body, leaving me weak and sick and trembling.

Phillip left my line of vision and then Bracken was hefting me into his arms, and as I came back to the (ouch, shit, ouchie ouchie ouchie) physical world, I was aware that my hand was sopping in sticky blood, even as Bracken cradled it in my lap.

"Aw shit," I mumbled. My little bleeding wound—it hadn't had a chance to close before Bracken grabbed me, and apparently had been dripping all over the floor of the SUV.

"Second longest trip of my fucking life," Bracken swore fervently, and since I knew what the first longest trip had been like, I knew exactly how awful he'd felt.

"That. Really. Sucked." I muttered, and suddenly Green was there, taking me from Brack, closing the wound on my hand with a thought and cradling me against his strong, damp body.

"Why is your hair all wet, Green?" I asked dreamily, and he smiled a little, and I wasn't so far gone that I couldn't see the twist in it, but I wasn't quite strong enough to ask where it twisted.

"Because I got out of the shower, luv—had to make myself sweet for you, didn't I?"

"Renny...?"

"Is fine, luv—really. I gave her a little kiss, and now all she needs is a whole lot of steak, some juice, and a little time with Max and she'll be fine."

"I shouldn't have…"

"No…shush…" Green kissed my temple, and another wave of healing washed through me, this one taking away the muscle cramps that came with puking my guts out for an hour. "It was a good call—a hard call. All of them were hard calls, and if I'd wanted you to do any different, I would have told you…"

"You *did* tell me…"

He laughed then, all the twist gone from his smile, and the final healing washed through me, leaving me with the desire to be clean and the desire to be held by him, and the desire to sleep.

"Quite right," he said now, "I did—and thank you, beloved, for listening."

I was being hustled into his room, into his shower actually, which stood six, and I was in that dreamy, hazy, fugue state that I'd learned accompanied injuries and physical demands. It was a state where even the most basic words deserted me, and all of my attempts to be tough were as crappy and transparent as a dead fly's wings.

"You were gone," I whimpered, as he sat me on the bench in the shower and soaped my hair. My hair wasn't that dirty, but it was his hands on me, being strong and gentle and kind and dependable and all of the things I loved Green for, and I wanted his hands everywhere.

"I was," he murmured, tilting my head back and using the showerhead to rinse. Ahhhhh…it felt so good, I just leaned my head against his naked hip and wrapped my arm around his thigh and hung on. His boy parts (laughable, calling something that big 'boy parts') hung, heavy and saggy from the heat of the shower, surrounded by wet coarse golden hair, and we were comfortable enough with each other for that not to matter. He was beautiful when he was engorged and erect, and lovely and powerful moving inside me, but he was my Green, and in romantic relationships there comes a time when it stops being about sex (although sex is pretty fucking awesome) and goes beyond it.

Many people had seen Green naked and touched his body.

There was a place in his vast, open heart where only I resided, and this was the place I was seeking for refuge tonight.

"Will you tell me why?" I all but begged, and he set the showerhead in its holder and bent that long ways down to kiss my head as it rested against him.

"Yes," he murmured, something in his voice broken. "I wasn't there for you tonight because there was something I didn't want you to know."

"I was scared…"

"It was dangerous," he agreed, and suddenly I could hear the self-blame there and it made me feel worse. Green…Green worked so hard for all of us… it was wrong to hear him angry at himself.

"We were okay…" I found myself comforting, and he gave a masculine laugh/grunt sound and held me to his middle and I wrapped my arms around that slender waist and held on.

"I put you in danger by keeping you in the dark," he murmured. "I'm sorry, beloved…I…I didn't want you to know."

"It's okay…" Oh Goddess… my Green, there was shame in his voice. "Anything," I sniffled, "you know Green, anything. I'll forgive you anything, I'll protect you from anything…just don't do stuff that hurts you anymore…"

Oh there they were… the inevitable fucking tears that always came with aftermath. Anyone who thinks I'm tough should watch me do this, because Green and Bracken have probably seen enough of it to last even Green's eighteen-hundred years.

"Shh shh shh shh…" he comforted, and I was ashamed of how glad I was that he'd put off telling me the Big Bad until tomorrow. I was here in his heart now, and the terror of everything that had happened in Sugarpine was shaking me in his embrace, and tomorrow, tomorrow, when we were clean and dry in the sunlight, would be time enough to air the shadows.

GREEN

True Sunshine

Green slid back in bed with her after he'd walked the earth of his hill in the chill dawn. Bracken (who had crawled in next to Cory in the night) had awakened with him and they'd gone walking together—not speaking, as was the custom of the elves and high sidhe who observed the quiet, strengthening meditation of the walk—but Bracken's recriminating silence spoke volumes. Green had been to the point of blurting out *I'm sorry, you git wank, could you just give me a fucking chance to explain!* when their walk finished and they touched the porch, and Bracken characteristically ruined the dramatic effect of all of that impressive brooding.

"You'd better fucking tell her, leader, or she's going to castrate you with her vicious fucking tongue."

Brack's untraditionally short, black hair was sticking up all over his head, and his drawn in brows and puckered eyes gave him the appearance of a disgruntled porcupine. In spite of himself, his guilt, his worry and his acknowledgement that he'd fucked up, Green had to force back a snork of amusement.

"What's so goddamned funny?" Bracken huffed, and Green just shook his head.

"You're very right, brother," he said, fighting the full-blown grin that was threatening, "but it would be a hell of a way to lose them, you think?"

Bracken growled low in his throat, but it was hard to argue with Green, hard to cross him at all, especially since Brack had practically worshipped him since birth, and since Adrian's death and their helpless attachment to the little human sorceress in their midst, they had become especially close.

And the fact that Green admitted he was wrong really did take the charge out of Brack's impending tantrum, Green could tell.

The tantrum dissipated like a smog cloud over the ocean and Bracken stomped off to his own shower and his empty bed, muttering something unflattering about silver-tongued elves and the fucked-up deadly magic secret poetry of fucking lunatic sex-gods. (This also made Green giggle, but very quietly, and to himself.)

But he wasn't laughing now.

He hadn't needed to shower-- Cory had gotten used to cold, slightly damp feet in her bed in the morning. This morning, she looked so charming, so vulnerable lying mostly on her stomach but a little on her side, with her hands bundled up under her chin clutching the blankets, and her bare shoulder peeking out of his enormously sized white T-shirt. It just seemed imperative that he strip naked to slide into bed with her.

He wanted his body to be as bare as his soul when they were done, and she could choose to do with that what she wished.

"My hair's a disaster," she mumbled, squinting up at him, and he moved closer to her, so he could stroke a bare arm with one attenuated finger.

"The sprites have been at you, luv—you look like you had full hair and make-up for your 'morning-after' scene." Normally, after going to sleep with damp hair, she would wake up to find her reddish, curly hair was as tall on her head as it was long down her back.

She giggled a little and hid her face from him. "I barely do hair and make-up for my 'night-before' scenes," she muttered, and Green laughed, the sound like sunshine.

"You don't need to, beloved," he told her throatily, and then leaned forward to breathe in her ear until she turned her face to him.

"Sure I do," she told him, still shy and pleased with the compliment. "Just so you know that I care enough to do it."

"I wouldn't doubt your love if you cut it short and dyed it black again," he said semi-seriously, and he was rewarded when her out-and-out grin made an appearance, no shyness added.

"If the sprites ever give up on me, I may hold you to that," she warned. "Easiest hair-cut I ever had."

Green laughed again, remembering who she had been and what she had looked like when she first arrived at the hill. But his laughter stilled, and he caught her sombering eyes and nodded, lowering himself off his elbow to lay, side-by-side, just inches from her, their bodies not quite touching, their faces just barely close enough to feel the breath of a hard sigh.

"It's time, isn't it?" he asked regretfully.

"Yes, please."

There was no recrimination in her voice, no anger, no bitterness—but there was expectation. He hadn't been there for her, and all she asked was to know why. *Goddess,* he thought, a real pain squeezing his heart, she was all of him, the throb of blood in his veins.

"Adrian wouldn't have noticed at first," he murmured, almost to himself. "He would have just let it go, until he reached for me. And then he would have been pissed as hell." He and Adrian had very rarely fought—but an instance like this one had been one of their few angry moments.

He'd never told Adrian the truth that spawned that particular argument— Adrian hadn't worried at it the way Cory had. Adrian had complete faith in Green, and Green had tried to live up to that without involving Adrian personally.

Cory wouldn't let him get away with that shit—she never had.

"Adrian was better than I am…" she murmured unhappily, jumping, of course, to the most wrong conclusion she possibly could.

Green reached out and traced the pattern her freckles made across her cheeks. He couldn't put his fingers yet, on the subtle changes wrought by the last two years. There were no lines, no sags, no puffy skin moments—but he knew that they were there. He'd never minded human aging—but he was relieved he didn't see it on her yet. More time for him, mostly. More time for them.

"Adrian was more of a self-centered git," he corrected almost absent-mindedly. "You are right here in the moment with me, luv. You won't let me do this shit…and it scares me, you know, scares the hell out of me. All I want to do is all I've ever wanted to do…"

"Keep us safe," she murmured, so he would know she understood.

"But you've been running out on these 'jobs' since last year," he continued, mindful that she'd moved her hand up to clasp his restless fingers and bring them to the warm beating space between her breasts, "and I can't seem to tell you 'No.' So I need to share this with you too…I…" he sighed, a memory of Adrian suddenly so clear in his mind that he was surprised Cory didn't see him as well. He'd been lying in this bed, almost in her exact position, but his white-blonde hair had been shorter, and his eyes, that clear, autumn-sky blue, had brightened the moonlight that flooded the window.

"So many people here, Green. Maybe you were right—I don't think I can be trusted with all of that." Those stunning eyes had been oh-so anxious, and for the first time in a decade, Green saw the frightened victim he'd raised out of hell in the hold of a ship.

Green's smile had been proportionately soft, proportionately protective.

"Peace, beloved," he'd murmured, lacing their fingers together, remembering the taste of Adrian's skin just moments before, craving the feel of that taut, giving, cool flesh around him again, even now, when their breathing had hardly stilled.

"I'll take care of you, Adrian," Green reassured then, propping up, kissing that lovely, vulnerable shoulder blade, up to the curved hollow of the neck, his hands moving lower to the flesh he'd just violated and loved, rubbing the traces of himself on Adrian's backside into that delicate, ticklish cleft that hid all of Adrian's not-so-secret places.

Adrian gasped, moaned, bared his fangs as he rolled on his back and opened his body up for complete submission to the one person he loved above all others.

"You always take care of me, Green," he'd panted, and Green had taken that invitation and moved lips and fingertips over the sweet, pale, cool body with reverence and passion, even as Adrian clutched his hair and moaned again. "You take such bloody good care of me..."

Cory was gazing patiently into his far-away emerald eyes, and Green forced himself to come back, in spite of the fact that his erection was called to attention by the memory, and by Cory's very warm, very soft, very *human* body next to him.

He remembered that he had a sentence to finish.

"I don't supposed you'd let me make love to you so we could not have this conversation?" he asked out of the wild blue.

Her smile was sad. "Adrian would."

"But not you," he nodded. "I love you for it, you know."

"Love me but don't trust me?" she asked, getting to the heart of the matter.

"Trust you, and don't want you hurt," he replied, not taking offense. He hadn't been there. Two years of promising he would always be there, and he hadn't been there. She could have raged and ranted—two years ago she would have—and he would have taken it, because he had promised her the world but ripped the rug out from under her feet.

She blinked, slowly, her red-brown lashes fanning her cheeks. "So tell me," she said at last, and he did.

Two sentences in, her jaw clenched. Halfway through and she sat up in bed, clutching the sheet protectively to her T-shirted chest. By the time he was done speaking, she'd dropped the sheet and was off the bed, her eyes burning and her fist clenched.

"I'll kill him..." she murmured, the emotion building momentum in her throat.

"Beloved, we need to find out how far this goes..." he interrupted reasonably, but she wasn't feeling reasonable.

"Fuck that. I'll kill him." She started to pace on his floor, her bare feet padding on the hard wood. "You know where he lives, Bracken and I will go and I'll do a mind-whammy to find out where the pictures are, and then Bracken will suck his heart *out of his fucking chest!*"

Green scrambled out of the bed to take her shoulders and calm her down. "Corinne Carol-Anne…" he began, knowing that her full name still had some power for her.

"He touched you!" she growled interrupting the whole of it. "Fuck the logic, fuck the reason, he's slimy and he's demonic and reprehensible and corrosive and *he touched my Green!*" Her brown eyes were burning with fury and Green put his hands on her shoulders to soothe her. She scowled and clamped her hands over his, pulling them to her chest and cuddling them like kittens, stroking their backs like fur.

"No one touches you like that," she murmured brokenly. "You're *Green*… you're all that's good. All that holds us together."

He bent forward and kissed her angry forehead, and she glowered at him. "This is what I do," he murmured. "My body, my gifts—they're all about pleasure, I use them as I can…"

She shook her head and stroked a suddenly wet cheek against the back of his hand. "You're wrong, *ou'e'hm.*"

She was very adept with words. She used his title for a reason. "That may have been what you were given, but that's not how you've used them—all the time you've put into making your home a haven, a sanctuary—it's not about sex anymore, Green. It's not about pleasure. It's about love. He profanes you with his touch. I'm your…your paladin, Green. The tasks I accomplish, the missions I run—that's about keeping our people safe, your dream alive. And I say no." Only the fact that her voice broke on 'no' indicated that she knew she was lecturing him, giving him orders, and that wasn't the way their relationship worked.

"Cory," he tried again, when a tense, wrought silence had weighted the sunshine on their backs, and she interrupted him with a shaken head.

"You just can't," she whispered, still stroking his hands. "You had to do that once to stay alive. I can take care of myself, I can take care of *us*… you can't do this anymore."

"I'm not ashamed of what I do to make you safe," he said with injured dignity, and she stopped looking at his hands and looked him solidly in the eyes.

"Then why wouldn't you tell me?" she asked brokenly, and he grimaced.

"You're human, dearest—in spite of everything, you grew up with words for people who did what I just did…"

She stepped back as though he slapped her, and the look on her face was enough flay his skin. "*bullshit...*" she murmured, then stronger, "Bullshit..." and then as he neared her to touch her hands, to calm down the storm he saw (and heard) breaking, "*BULLSHIT!*"

"Cory..."

"Fuck you, beloved!" she shouted, and he actually flinched, because she fought with Bracken like this, but not with him.

"Corinne Carol-Anne..."

"Kirkpatrick op Crocken Green!" she finished with gritted teeth. "If the Goddess doesn't strike you with cramps, sweat, and barf right now it's because you've completely deluded yourself, Green—I'd hack out my tongue with yarn scissors before I called you that word."

He blanched, because he'd misjudged her, underestimated her the way the world had done so often before she came to the hill. "Shit," he muttered, yanking his hand through his hair and snarling it at the ends.

"Shit is right—you know better than that from me," she accused, "and besides—you *showered*. We got here and you were in the fucking *shower...* there's only one reason you'd do that, Green, and we both know it."

And once again, he'd bollixed things up completely.

"I used to be better at relationships than this," he said almost to himself, feeling completely lost after nearly two millennia of living. "Adrian and I never had this conversation. One-hundred-and-fifty years, and it never even came up..."

She was listening to him ramble with such a terrible, inexplicable look of hurt and anger and bafflement twisting her plainly-pretty face, he wanted to hold her hands, touch her face, anything to help her sort it all out. But she was Cory—his Cory, like he was 'her Green'—she did just fine on her own.

"Say it," she whispered, a sudden serene (almost Green-like, had he known it) kindness suffusing her face with softer colors.

"Say what?" That lost feeling was still there, the horrible one that seemed to hollow out his stomach when he was least ready to fill it. It was the same blood he'd tasted when he'd held Cory at the bottom of a gravel hill, and realized they would both survive Adrian's death, and the same clink he'd heard when his prison door faded shut in Oberon's faerie hill. It was even the same feeling he'd had, if the truth be known, right after he'd escaped, and boarded that fateful ship with a hold full of lime trees giving him strength and protection from the deadly salt ocean, when he'd smelled the fresh spray on the air.

And here she was, his beloved—perhaps the last beloved his heart would have the strength to bear—and her voice promised a path out of this wilderness.

He listened to her with the grip of a drowning man on a rope.

"Tell me why you showered—you were sopping wet…I remember you, there in my head for most of the trip, but there was a…a gap. A tiny gap. I wouldn't have remembered it if you hadn't been dripping wet. Why the shower?"

He closed his eyes. "Ah, Goddess…" He opened them again, and she was still looking at him without flinching, her gaze absolutely relentless.

"Say it, Green!" she demanded in a voice that trembled.

"What's there to say? I didn't want him touching you? I didn't want him on my skin when *I* touched you? Is that such a big surprise?"

She made the first move, suddenly close enough to touch, and her little, rough hands came up to his lovely, narrow face, cupping against his cheeks, stroking his cheekbones with her thumbs.

"If he's not good enough to touch me," she said, her voice as firm about this as he'd ever heard it, "he's not good enough to touch you."

He was going to try to convince her otherwise. He played chess—he was good at it. He knew his role on the board, and he knew what it would take to keep the blackmailer in line until they had all of the evidence tracked down. Stopping what they were doing would only make their lives more difficult.

But then she said, "Are we clear, Green?" and the hurt in her voice was bare, raw, and bleeding, and he could probably bear the difficulties ahead but he couldn't, under any circumstances, bear being the one to hurt her.

"This will make things harder," he warned, bending down because she was standing on tiptoe to press her lips against his. He wanted the absolution in that kiss more than he wanted breath or blood, more than he wanted his heartbeat to echo in his ears.

"Hard I can handle," she told him with a crooked little smile. Her hands came up and rubbed his bare chest, smoothing away imaginary wrinkles, sweeping imaginary dust off his high shoulders. "Something that hurts my Green will not be borne."

"I'm fine, luv," he assured her soberly, and she shook her head, the tears she'd fought back so bravely running again.

"This hurts you," she murmured, and kissed the center of his chest, around his sternum, where her lips met his skin when she stood flat-footed. "It makes you feel soiled. It rankles in your heart." Sometimes, he'd heard her poetry when she was with the men who went with her and Bracken on their 'runs', but mostly, she only wrote voice poems on the pages of their hearts when they were alone.

"Yes," he confessed into the wildness of her hair, afraid of her censure more than he was afraid of the Goddess' punishment on the fey who lied. Cramps and nausea he could live through—and he had. Having his beloved angry with him… in her words, it was not to be borne.

"Then let me cleanse you," she begged, kissing his chest again, moving her hands up his ribs in a sliding whisper of skin on skin.

"Yes," he accepted, bending over her, putting his hands on her arms, fighting the temptation to lift her off the ground and crush her to him, protecting all that was precious in his soul with the barrier of her flesh alone.

"Let me..." she ordered, pulling his head down to meet her in a kiss, and another, and another, using her kisses, her sex, her power, and her love to protect all that was precious in her soul with the power of her flesh alone.

"Yes..." he pleaded, opening his mouth, pulling her with him until he fell backwards onto the bed, carrying her with him. She kissed him more, and kissed him, and touched his skin with her cheek and her tears, held his manhood and stroked it, rubbed her body over his and took him inside of her, touching, touching, cleansing him of the deception, of the pain, of his remorse, of the touch of the interloper on his skin.

"Let me..."

"Always..."

"Oh Goddess...please Green..."

"Anything..." Her hair, hanging in her face, her intent expression as though polishing fine and tender silver with her sex. "For you beloved, anything..."

"I'll do anything, Green..."

"Anything..." he groaned underneath her, lost, helpless, so damned grateful she would lead him to the sanctity of his own skin inside her. His palms on her breasts were reverent, her arched back and climaxing cries sacred. He spasmed and groaned and came inside her, cleansed and new and found in the harbor or her body, the sanctuary of her giving soul.

CORY
The Body Politic

I sat with Jacky, Renny, Max, La Mark, Nicky and Bracken at the campus
picnic table under a glaring May sky. Bracken, who was across from me and
at the other end of the damned table met my eyes miserably, and I wondered
sourly why there weren't any bad guys to kill.

It would be a serious improvement on my mood to kill something right
now.

Allergy season had hit Sacramento—and that's a bad fucking thing.
About twenty years ago, someone with way too much time on their hands
did a survey of cities with the most trees. Sacramento came in first. I don't
know if we're still in the lead but we're up there and while it made for some
nice shade here at the college, the trees in the valley were every *human's* worst
fucking nightmare.

You think I'm kidding? Howzabout take every pollen known to man,
whirl it around like an allergen milkshake in an unholy blender using the
winds off the surrounding farmland, add some serious smog issues because
the city planners were *high* and forgot a couple of fucking freeways back in
the day, throw in a forest fire within two-hundred miles of the valley bowl,
and you know what you get?

You get air that has color, taste, *and* texture. You get an area that is known
for full grown people who have never had allergies in their lives getting off the
plane to their new homes and then getting rushed to the hospital for a mongo-
sized shot of Benedryl and an antihistamine drip. You get a place where even

natives suddenly wake up in their adulthood with red, itchy eyes, sore throats, clogged heads, and body aches when there's not a virus to be found.

You get me, driving us to school about a week earlier, clearing the sphere of Green's influence, and then almost killing us all with a sneezing fit that lasted three miles on a very scary road. (They haven't let me drive since.)

As soon as we could pull over, my eyes and throat swelled like a big fat poisoned toad, and my entire body started to hurt and pretty much everything went to hell after that. When we're on the hill, it's all hunky dory—but as soon as we pull off the hill? I become phlegm-zombie-bitch from hell. I couldn't take anything for it either—after puking blood with the ibuprofen incident, I didn't even want to *fathom* what allergy drugs would do to me, so I stocked up on the aloe Kleenex and suffered in surly, bitchy, irritability because I didn't have a fucking choice.

And to top it off, I had cramps that made a wolverine chewing out my ovaries feel like a Swedish massage.

"Cory?" Jacky said next to me, and I tried to turn my attention to him, because he was tutoring me in political science and until this week, had worked very very hard to be nice to me. He had been working on his own version of public relations since he'd watched us put ourselves on the line for Teague, and it had made our situation here at school easier, that was for damned sure. I didn't want to fuck it up by ignoring him.

"I'b dorry, Jacky—I wandered off." I'd been doing that a lot, and Jack was not the most patient of tutors.

"Of course you wandered off," he muttered. "You can't expect me to take your tests and do your homework for you the way Bracken does—*I'm* not sleeping with you."

"I can kill you from across the table, college-puke," Bracken growled from across the table, and I squinted my itchy eyes and tried to focus on the two of them before Bracken tried to do just that.

"I dake by owb tests, Jacky," I said as succinctly as possible. "I woulbn't axe you to do dat." I should have been angrier, but the truth was, Bracken and I had been trying not to kill Jack all semester. That last passive-aggressive masterpiece was actually almost livable.

"Well that doesn't seem to stop Bracken…"

I rolled my eyes. "Bwacken sdeaks indo by backpack a'd swaps out by hobework—iss not my fault!" Dammit, it wasn't! I told Bracken I could do it, but, Goddess bless it anyway, he needed less sleep than I did at night. I fell asleep in the middle of my English paper, and when I woke up my statistics homework was annotated and rewritten so I could complete it on my own. He was like my own behemoth-sized live-in math tutor, and Jack seemed to think I was violating some sort of 'royal codex' by taking his help.

"No—and it's not your fault that the thing in the basement tried to eat Teague for breakfast, is it?"

"Teague went in there against her express wishes…"

"Orders!"

"Yes, orders," Bracken finished for me. "Please let him take responsibility for his own actions, Jack—Cory does her damnedest to keep us safe, but she can't do everything."

I sighed, gazing sightlessly at my homework. The werefolk had been taking turns feeding Gretchen—always with Lambent or Green or Sweet in attendance, in case she went round the bend and tried what she did with Renny. It hadn't happened again until three nights before—when Teague went down in wolf form instead of Katy. I was about five minutes behind him, and I'd told him—I'd *told* him that we'd find someone besides Katy if he was too nervous to let her do it, but that he shouldn't go down because he freaked Gretchen out. He might have made it work, though—because he's Teague and he's determined--but something horrid and dismal got in the way. I had just gotten down to her pink/fluffy cased steel room and in the middle of her dinner, her eyes had glazed over, whirled red, and she had looked up and smiled into my face around a mouthful of wolf ruff and said I smelled like candy.

I was starting to hate those words.

"Pweaze," I begged now, not wanting to think about the fact that all of the headway we'd made with Jack and his piss-bitchy attitude had gone south in a hurry after I'd had to channel Green's power again to pin Gretchen back against the wall and pry her jaws open so she could drop a dazed and unconscious Teague.

Jacky turned to me, eyebrows raised, and I shrugged, wishing for death or an analgesic or alcohol or *something*.

"Jacky, you do id wadn our fault… pweaze stop taking your wowwy oub ob us—id doebn hep. Ad for da hobework, it doedn't madder—I'b compwetewy wost." The Canadian politics thing and a vote of no confidence. Why would a leader want to call for a vote of no confidence ? I totally didn't get it—I mean, if my guys didn't have confidence in me, I assumed they'd run away and leave me to face the bad things by myself. I looked up to where Bracken was glaring balefully at me from across the table and amended that thought.

He'd step in front of me and get eaten first.

I gave him a lame smile, and then an expression of horror as I saw who was approaching us from behind his right shoulder.

"Sit," I muttered and Bracken's handsome face scrunched up in puzzlement.

"I am sitting," he replied blankly, and I sighed and pulled out another Kleenex just as a cultured, British voice spoke from behind him.

"Good afternoon, Lady Cory, afternoon, all," said Professor Hallow, and Bracken closed his eyes and mouthed "Shit!" at me while I widened my eyes in agreement. That's what I'd said, dammit!

"Good abdernoob, Professor," I tried, and blew another phlemwad into the Kleenex.

"You're sick?" he asked, puzzled—as he should be. People didn't get sick on Green's Hill. The non-humans didn't *get* viruses, and Green could cure anything else.

"Abberdzeez," I tried, and was relieved when Nicky supplied the actual word for me.

Hallow looked a little bemused. "Allergies? Oh my. I forget sometimes..."

"I doh, I doh—my poow widdow fwagile human body. Gween cab heal da sympdoms, but da abberdeez aw till deh." Oh Christ—*I* couldn't understand what I just said. I resisted the urge to bang my forehead against the table.

"Cory," Bracken said hesitantly, "I can't tell your sarcasm from your snot anymore. Maybe we should just give it up and go home..."

"We hab fibals next week!" I protested. "I cab take you awwl oub ob cwass wib fibals!" Auuuuuurrrggghhhh!!!!

Suddenly Hallow wasn't behind Bracken anymore, he was in front of me, and I raised my face up to him and gazed at his handsome sidhe face with bleary eyes. As rotten as I felt—and as itchy as my eyes were—I could almost see him with his glamour on, and he was still damned handsome. To humans he looked to be in his late 40's, with short silver-blonde hair and a clean, to-die-for academician's profile.

To those of us at the table, he looked like a very handsome sidhe, with a hip-length silver braid and unfathomably beautiful triangular features that became his people. To me, right now, he looked like the uncle you'd avoid because he was the only one in the family with high expectations for you and you didn't know how to deal with that.

"You can't take any medicine for this?" he asked kindly, and Nicky and Bracken both gave a heartfelt "No!" Nicky was right next to me, and I leaned against him in comfort. I missed his smell—when my head wasn't clogged with crap, he smelled like vanilla and bird, and I liked it. It was comforting.

"I boff bwood," I tried, and Nicky shook his head, rust-tipped bangs flopping in and out of his eyes.

"'Just let us talk, please?" he begged, and I shrugged and gestured for him to continue.

"She barfs blood," he translated, and Hallow's eyebrows met his hairline and his expression grew... well, hurt, I guess.

"How long has this been going on?" he asked, looking to Bracken, and then *looking* at the distance between us. "And are you and Bracken at odds?" Bracken and I were usually touching—always, we were touching. There had been days when he would hoist me up in his solidly muscled arms and not put me down until schools' end—and even if he wasn't carrying me like a child, he was still touching me. My hair, my shoulders... I'd felt naked for the last two days, because I hadn't had Bracken on my skin.

"No!" I protested, my own voice growing hurt. "We're fibe!" Frustrated and miserable, I put my face in my hands, and Hallow crouched in front of me and took my hands in his, meeting my angry, swollen, unhappy eyes with his own gorgeous turquoise gaze.

"Then why aren't you touching?" he asked quietly, aware that his outburst may have just driven me further into the self-protective shell that his presence grew on my back.

I opened my mouth and closed it again, and Renny, being the only girl at the table, rolled her eyes and chuffed, "Because she's on the rag, Professor, and the last time he touched her when she was riding the pony, she bled out into the john."

I closed my eyes and wished for death. It had happened two days after we'd gotten back from Sugarpine, and it had sucked large.

In retrospect, I should have guessed something because of the way the vampires treated me that night. It started when I was in the steel room with Gretchen, trying to convince her that just because I had killed her pet kitty (!) didn't mean I was a mean bitch, out to spank her.

It hadn't gone well. She's warmed to me since, but on this night she was irritable and pissy, demanding new clothes (the ones we'd gotten her were not frilly enough, apparently. Ick!) and missing her mother and crying for her family. In spite of the fact that Phillip had tasted the clear memory of her killing her loved ones, she seemed to have forgotten that fact. About once a week we told her, gently, that her family was dead, and then she cried, and then, within a couple of days, she'd forget again. It was like Alzheimer's disease in a little kid, and it was baffling and tragic. Sometimes, when we couldn't take the sadness of telling her one more time, we simply told her that they were on a trip and would be back soon.

Two days after she'd arrived at Green's, she still remembered they were dead and how they died, and she had been edgy and restless, pacing and refusing to let me read to her or play dolls—she even ripped a few of them apart, looking puzzled and lost as she did so as though she'd forgotten she had the strength to do it. I was just about to give up and let someone else take a turn, when she stopped still and thrust her nose in the air like the consummate predator she'd been turned into.

Her eyes closed, and a very vulpine smile crossed her narrow, apple-cheeked face, and the look she gave me through suddenly red and whirling eyes made my stomach cramp.

"You smell like candy," she murmured delightedly, her fangs partway extended and her little behind moving like a lion cub about ready to pounce.

I've learned a few things in the last two years—I didn't think twice as I threw a power barrier up between us and sprinted through the door.

When I got outside of the steel safe—complete with titanium lock—and closed the door behind me, leaning on it in relief as I did so, I looked up and realized that every vampire in the hill except Grace was in the common room outside.

They were all looking dreamily at me, their whirling eyes half-closed and their teeth half-extended.

Marcus gave a sweet, psychotic half-smile and said, "You smell like hot chocolate..." and I decided enough was enough.

I put power in my voice—everything I had—and commanded them all to stay downstairs in the lower darkling. And then, without running (and pricking that whole 'predator' thing they've got going) I walked with as much dignity as I could to the top of the stairs.

Grace was waiting for me at the top of the stairs, some serious control in place to keep her eyes from whirling.

"Baby," she said when I got to her, "I think your body has finally caught up to you."

I sent her a blank, puzzled look, and she sighed and looped an arm over my shoulders, steering me towards my bedroom.

"Cory, darlin', you're about to start your period—it's like a vampire delicacy. Usually on the hill we don't run into it but..."

"Oh," I said numbly, thinking immediately that there went all my evening plans with Bracken. Then, "oooooh!" because suddenly I understood why I was wearing eau de tasty as far as the rest of the vampires were concerned, and then... "Oh...ICK!" because I am not without imagination and the word 'delicacy' finally hit me.

Grace chuckled a little, but the sound was strained. "Cory, my girl, don't ever forget that we're not human anymore. Now I'm going to rustle up some supplies for you, and then I'm going to make myself scarce. We'll stay out of the hill or down in the darkling for a couple of days—and maybe next month, we won't be caught so unaware."

"A couple of months…" I said numbly, and she looked at me with surprise. "I never was very regular—two months, sometimes three…"

Grace nodded her head with approval. "Well, that at least should make things easier. Now scoot—I need to send someone shopping."

I wandered back to my room in a daze, and after sitting in fuddled silence and knitting for a half an hour, I realized that I'd felt funky and crampy and tired since I'd left Green's bed that morning, and the light bulb went on. I'd known this was coming—it had just been so damned long, I'd forgotten what it was like.

Bracken came in then, fresh from helping Teague and Jack remodel their refurbished barn/garage/cottage, and as he started stripping, I made a dash for the bathroom so I could be done before he took his shower. It didn't matter—he moved too quickly, and the fact was, the elves had no shame and no disgust over bodily functions. Taking a piss was taking a piss—everyone did it, and it didn't really faze them. Bracken walked in on me once when Adrian was still alive and he was so casual about it, I don't think he even remembered me, freaking out.

So on this day, as I was sitting on the potty, staring stupidly at the stained crotch of my underwear, neither of us even flinched as he brushed my leg on his way to the shower.

And that was when my uterus turned itself inside out in a frantic attempt to get closer to him, because, hello, it was saturated with blood, and that was Bracken's element.

When I came to, Bracken was crouched in the corner of the shower, looking like powdered death from shutting off his power in a helluva hurry, Green was hovering over me, propping me up on the toilet, and everybody in the hill who *wasn't* a vampire was crammed into our tiny bathroom, staring at me as I dumped three days worth of blood in two and a half minutes.

Fun times: remembering them now made my face flush and seemed to have some sort of magnification effect on the goddamned cramps.

Lovely.

Hallow read the wealth of what I was *not* saying as it trotted across my face, and if anything, the look on his face grew more hurt than it had before.

"This is a good thing, right?" he asked, as though struggling to be positive about something. "Your body is functioning correctly, it hasn't done that in a very long time, right?"

"Righb," I murmured, trying to forget the ashen pallor of Bracken's face as Green had healed me and then cleaned me up in front of fifty-gazunga people. Besides cutting himself off from his source of power—which was potentially deadly for him if he did it too long—Brack had felt as though he had done something wrong.

"Tell dat do Bwacken," I added, looking at him now. His neck was drooped over his textbooks, but he was looking at me intently, and I was completely unable to fathom the expression in his dark, pond-shadow eyes, so I turned back to Hallow. "Wad deh sombdig you wandig, Pwofeddor?"

"Isn't your menstrual cycle enough for me to be here, Lady Cory?" he asked, with that inexplicable hurt.

I looked out over our little table with a pained expression. Jacky, Max, La Mark, Renny, and Nicky looked right back with undisguised interest, and I suppressed a groan. Not a one of them hadn't trusted me with his or her life, or worse, the life of a loved one.

"Pwofeddor, cad we nod talk aboub my pewiob wight dow?"

"Why not?" he muttered, seemingly to himself. "Apparently we can't talk about anything, can we?"

Oh Jesus. "Wad I do?" I asked, so exhausted by this conversation that I was on the edge of tears.

Fortunately, Prof Hallow is not nearly as repressed as I am.

"Is this why you missed our last three sessions?" he demanded, and I winced as Bracken and Nicky both said, "*Three sessions!*" practically in tandem and I shook my head.

"Doh!" I'd missed the last three sessions because I didn't want to talk about Green—my period had nothing to do with it.

"Then why in the name of trees in summer didn't you ask me to heal you?!" he demanded, standing to his full height, and I blinked at him stupidly.

"Heal be?"

"Yes—I've done it before, remember?"

"Heal be?" I asked again, feeling dimmer than a dark star.

"You don't remember?" he asked, the hurt and exasperation easing up in his lovely features and his habitual, neutral-friendly 'counselor's expression' resuming its place.

"I do *dow!*" I wailed with some emphasis, and he laughed a little, kindly, and sat back down on his haunches and took my hands.

"Would you like me to heal you, Lady Cory?" he asked, and at the promise of no misery, the tears I'd held back threatened to spill over.

"Da cwamps too?" I asked, hating my weakness, and Bracken let out a hoarse little groan. I hadn't complained about the cramps—he hadn't known.

"The cramps too," Hallow murmured with gentleness. "In fact, Sir Knight," he said to Bracken, my lover/protector, "if you wish, you and your lady and I could take a walk—if we take much care, you two may even hold hands. Would that be acceptable, Lady Cory?"

"Pwease?" I begged pathetically, and Bracken stood up, shoved his books in his backpack and started issuing orders even as Hallow took my hands and kissed my forehead. Jacky got to take our notes, Nicky and La Mark took our backpacks, and he'd get my yarn bag and the SUV keys—we'd all cut our night class and head for home early. (The class was Film as Literature—we'd all seen *Lone Star* already. Since most of the elves had, at some point, gotten busy with a much older/much younger/much separated by time/space/genetics half-sibling, they really didn't get it. In this case, I was doing Bracken's homework for once instead of the other way around.)

Within five minutes, I was walking across campus with Hallow's companionable arm looped around my shoulder and holding Bracken's hand. We were all eating chocolate/vanilla swirls. The ice cream was Bracken's idea—it was hot and I'd been miserable with phlegm and ice cream had been a forbidden treat. That was why he'd packed up his stuff so quickly—so he could run across the campus to the student union and get me a soft serve.

I took a lick of my chocolate/vanilla swirl and looked at our twined hands, enjoying the look of his long, blunt fingers wrapped around mine and feeling like my body was taking it's first full breath in two days. I raised his hand to my lips and kissed the back of it and pressed it against my cheek.

Oh the humiliations I would endure, just to be able to have his skin against mine when I needed it.

"Thank you, Professor," I said quietly and sincerely to Hallow. "This is lovely...thank you." I smiled at him, my heart in my smile, and the oddest expression flirted across his face. It was an odd mix between a child getting praised by his favorite teacher and that baffling hurt that he'd shown earlier. I looked at him in confusion and then looked at Bracken. Bracken's gaze was level and kind. He knew what this was about—I didn't. Wonderful.

I kissed his hand again anyway, because I could, and then asked the obvious question.

"So why were you looking for me?"

"Mmm?" Hallow asked, taking a go at his own ice cream—it was hot, and he looked a little bit droopy and distracted in the heat. Bracken did too, truth be known, but I'd been so immersed in my own misery that I hadn't noticed until now. Part of the tribute to Green's power was that his hill didn't get much warmer than 78 F, even when the foothills *really* started to cook 'round 'bout July and August. Bracken could come to school with me, but it was really a good thing finals were in the last week of May.

"You were looking for me—you know, before you got all mad because I was sick—why were you looking for me?"

"I wasn't angry because you were sick, my Lady," Hallow corrected, "I was angry because you didn't ask for help."

I flushed and looked at Bracken, who managed to look sheepish. "I'm sorry," he muttered, "it should have occurred to me too—but..." Bracken's eyes narrowed, their pond-shadow color seeming to burn, "but if you had visited him when you were supposed to, he might have suggested it himself..."

I was scheduled to see Hallow every two weeks, but Hallow talked about things. And he didn't let me get away with shit. And I wasn't ready to talk about Green.

"I had something on my mind," I murmured unnecessarily, and Bracken rolled his eyes. Of course he knew I had something on my mind—he had known since the morning I'd come from Green's room.

Green and I were solid now. Of course we were--we had been from *Let me,* and *Please.* He hadn't done anything that needed forgiveness—well and truly, I felt that with all my heart, and we had both told the others about Nolan Fields and the danger to our little community that evening. The entire hill knew to watch for the douche-bag photographer, and they knew that we were in danger when we went out. The vampires had been scrupulous about flying out the back way from the hill, and only frequenting places that were owned and operated by Green's people. The shifters had been running the property and the woods only. And the fey? Well, Bracken and Lambent were something of anomalies—most of the fey who could pass for human preferred their earth at their bare feet, and none other. The other fey—the trolls and the brownies and the red caps and others who liked to wander the back woods and unexplored crannies of the foothills—well, we figured Nolan wouldn't have noticed them before, and he probably wouldn't notice them now. Most of the time, they blended in with the homeless and the discarded. People like Nolan Fields wouldn't be looking there if there wasn't a story.

So no—although I had never cleared up the problems in Teague's love life and Nicky was still getting mysterious phone calls and pretending they didn't hurt his heart like knives, there were officially no secrets between Green and me.

But still... there was something. It wasn't a secret. It wasn't—it was more like and unresolved feeling, one without human words to give it wings and get it the fuck off my chest.

"Aren't you supposed to see me when you have something on your mind?" Hallow asked, a long-suffering note in his voice, and Bracken snorted.

"She's stubborn," he said, taking a slurp of his own ice cream.

"And you're not?" I shot back.

"Name it!" he quibbled, smiling a little. "When was the last time I gave you grief?"

"How about the last time I wanted to see Gretchen?" I asked seriously. It had been four days ago—he'd insisted that it was too dangerous, and I'd promised the little girl that I'd be in to read to her that night. It was true—she was getting more and more vague, more and more like a trapped animal. Taking her outside to fly in the garden was getting to be a job for ten or more vampires, because she would test the boundaries we'd set for her with increasing ferocity, until the outing ceased to be fun and started to become a test of wills.

We had managed to get something from her, though, via her blood-link with Phillip. A license plate with a 'mountain on it, and words not numbers except for an eight.' With a little more digging, and some quick sketching, we'd managed to come up with the word "BLUD*E*F8". Bloody Fate. Get it? Fucking pedophiliac vampire. Max was in the process of tracking the plate down in the Sheriff's department—it would take some doing and a visit from one of us who could give a mind-fuck power-whammy though, and we hadn't been able to schedule it in the last week. Besides, Bracken and I were talking about a whole other incident.

"As I recall," I accused, "you ended up by hefting me around the waist and hauling my ass out of the darkling!"

"Phillip told me you smelled like candy!" he retorted, and I blinked and took an absent, clean-up lick of my neglected ice cream.

"I did not know that," I said with dignity and a little sniff. "You could have told me, you know?"

"It's hard," he mumbled dejectedly. His grip slackened on our hands and I tightened them up. We had been able to sleep—Green spooning me and me spooning Bracken—but we all had tasks to do, our jobs outside the hill, and homework and dinner... I was not getting my quota for touching Bracken, and I was not going to squander this precious, cramp-and-allergy-free walk through campus.

"We don't talk when we don't touch," I mumbled, and Hallow gave an amused snort at my side. I rolled my eyes at him. "And we've gotten off the point—why did you come to see me again?"

"Because," Hallow said with a sigh, like he was letting go of something important, "Nolan Fields has been on campus asking for you."

I stopped short, my ice cream cone halfway to my mouth.

"*Fuck!*" Bracken and I both said in tandem, and Hallow shook his head.

"You knew this would happen when you stopped Green's original plan, right?" he chided gently, and I flushed. Bracken and Nicky hadn't known about Green's original way to stop Nolan—but Brack was going to get a crash course in it now.

"This is my fault," I said numbly. "I should..." I stopped that thought.

No I shouldn't have. I'd die before Green humbled himself again—and I could give a rat's ass if he was willing to do it. "I should have known this was coming."

Bracken was looking at me oddly. "That wasn't what you were going to say."

I swallowed. "No, it wasn't. Can we keep Nolan off campus?" I asked Hallow, and he shook his head.

"For the moment," he said cagily. "I've already marked a perimeter with sprites and touch, blood, and song—we'll know when he's here, and I guarantee his cameras won't work. We've already fried a considerable and costly amount of his equipment, so I think he might try another tack. I've taken other measures to keep him away from you, but you need to know he's here."

Unconsciously I leaned more fully into Bracken's embrace, but he took a step away from me and regarded me levelly.

"What?" I asked him, hurt, but I already knew.

"I am tired of secrets." His voice was quiet, but his eyes were literally spitting sparks.

"Glamour, Bracken!" I hissed, and he glared even more sharply.

"Fuck that!" he snarled quietly, but his eyes toned down. "Green was hiding something, and now you're hiding it, and Nicky still hasn't come clean, and the only one without some dark bird fluttering in their chest is me, and I'm sick of it. If you can't tell me, then you need to at least tell Hallow—because this is bullshit. You don't *get* to be lonely at Green's hill—that's not why we had that little ceremony last year, and it's *not* why we band together and share a bed and share comfort when we need it. Your heart is lonely, and you may think you're helping Green by keeping it close inside, but what hurts you hurts him and I won't let you do it anymore!"

I stared at him, feeling a freight train of resentment pile up in my chest as he spoke. *It wasn't fair* I thought desperately, trying to halt that damned derailing locomotive, because Bracken hadn't done a damned thing but be too open and too honest in every emotion he had from anger to lust to keep this feeling in his heart like I had.

"What do you want me to say!" I demanded, and we'd released each other's hands and were confronting each other. Hallow was still at my back, touching my shoulders and unconsciously I shrugged him off, because this was between me and Bracken as so little *was* between us alone, and nobody else got a say.

"I want you to tell us what you've been hiding!"

I took a vicious bite of my ice-cream cone and nursed the cold blob in the roof of my mouth. "Wha' d'you tink," swallow, "I've been hiding!" I burst out, wishing I could talk some other way besides pissed off. "Green knew about this first—how do you think he dealt with it, Bracken? I'll give you three guesses, but since you know as much as I do about my *ou'e'hm,* you'll only need one!"

Then Bracken got one of those looks—I've come to recognize them, they're a hazard of my living situation. It was the "I'm sorry you don't understand this cultural difference but you're really overreacting" sort of look, but I wasn't buying it. Not this time. Not with this.

He reached out a conciliatory hand, and I glared at it. "Beloved…"

In a fit of temper I chucked the rest of the ice-cream at the nearest trash can. I missed, and it splatted against the side.

"No." I relocated my glare and met his eyes. "We don't get to do that—not with this. There is no 'We're fey so we do things differently'—not with this. If it was about sex and about healing and about kindness and binding people to me with power—I get that. You *know* I get that. I get that and I deal and I don't complain and I accept and I love and I enjoy. This isn't *about* that. This is about Green touching something he *loathes.* This is about Green *lowering* himself to protect us. And I'll let Green protect us about anyway he can… but Green doesn't get to humble himself. Not my Green. Not for me, not for fucking any-fucking-body. We've had this discussion before, he and I—he's not a warrior elf. I get that. He's a sexual elf—I get that too and most of the time I'm so damned proud of him that I could almost grow an inch or two. But he's not…*not… NOT,"* and here's where my voice, which had been low and intense and furious, finally started to crack a little, finally started to crumple, leaving my heartbreak raw and bleeding for the both of them to see, "he's not anyone's victim anymore. Not Myst's, not Oberon's. Not this scum-fucker's. I would rather kill this guy with my bare hands than let Green do that to his own heart, and I know you think I'm foolish," oh Christ, here they came. Fucking tears. "and I know you think I'm naïve, but I'm supposed to be his weapon. I will rip this miserable ass-fucker's throat out with my teeth and savage him like a dog rather than let Green hurt himself that way."

It's a good thing Hallow was quicker than Bracken with that hand on my neck. Bracken couldn't let me cry like that for all the world and I would have bled out with the first touch of his hands on my arms, the first crush of his wide chest, engulfing me, welcoming me home.

"Why didn't you say anything," he whispered, his breath so good on my ear that I gave it up and whimpered. "Why just let this sit on your chest, pressing you down…"

"I couldn't have you think… what you thought…" I babbled. "I don't think worse of him. I could never think worse of him. I didn't want you to… you'd be disappointed if I…" So hard to put into words. I was Green's. I was the hill. There were no ugly words in my heart for what Green had done—there was only my conviction that he was too good, too golden, too shining and perfect and beloved to be allowed to do it. Bracken and I—we were too passionate, too quick with our words. And Bracken idolized Green—I would never threaten that or kill that or fuck that up in any way shape or form.

"I didn't have words," I whispered at last. "I still don't. But I told him he couldn't…and he let me. And now this fucker's back, without even Green's power to check him… and I can't even kill him."

Bracken's chest vibrated under my cheek. "Who says you get to do the killing? Your way's too quick."

I whimpered a little laugh for him—of my three lovers, Bracken's way was most like mine. Green would love the enemy into submission. Nicky would fight a bloody fight with his talons, but he wasn't a killer. Bracken and I would leave no bodies, but they'd be dead just the same.

"Your way's messy," I murmured, wishing with all my heart that we could be alone. Bracken and I did the best making up after fights—and although the sex *was* spectacular, it was the closeness that I missed.

"So what are we going to do, professor?" I murmured to Hallow, who hadn't let off his gentle grip on my neck. "We can't have these pictures show up in the tabloids, and we can't have this guy stalking us. Keeping him off campus will work for a little while, and once summer begins we can hole up at the hill for a while, but until then…"

Hallow nodded. "I know, I know… uhm, both of you, may we continue walking for a bit?"

I looked over my shoulder and realized that we had stopped at a nexus between the math, English, and education building, and we were getting more than our share of curious glances. So much for tender moments. We resumed walking, and I began to willfully steer us towards the book store—mostly because beyond that, there was a staircase up the levy and we could walk over the bicycle bridge and it was one of my favorite places on campus.

"We need to know when he's planning to release those pictures," I said after a silence. Bracken and Hallow switched positions, so I was holding Hallow's arm and Bracken had me pressed against his side. Bracken dropped a kiss in my hair and mumbled agreement.

"Do you think we could get someone to mindfuck him?" he asked.

"It can be done," said Hallow as though he'd thought about it a lot, "but it's going to have to be someone he doesn't have his sights on. When humans are as ambitious and as focused as this man, changing their minds with power doesn't always work. It's got to be someone he doesn't expect—I'm afraid, Lady Cory, that he knows you're important. You're the only one who shows up in his photos, and we don't hide the fact that everybody else defers to you.

Anybody in your inner circle is right out as well—he knows you by sight. He calls Bracken "the enforcer" and Nicky "the best friend", and although he's never seen Renny change, he calls her "kitten"—he's not stupid or blind, and he's intuitive or he couldn't be successful at what he's doing. He likes getting to the truth of things. Last year he took a picture of a party leaving early from a funeral, and he thinks he's found gold."

"Truth is overrated," I mumbled, flushing with guilt. Green hadn't told me how susceptible we'd be when he agreed to go sing with me at the funeral of a friend. I knew now—and I cursed my innocence. Not even the most innocent gesture was free from danger—not where my worlds collided.

"You would say that," Hallow snorted, and I looked at him sharply.

"We're going to have to talk, aren't we?" I asked suspiciously, and he gave me an incredibly bland look.

"Why on earth would you want to talk to me, Lady Cory—I'm just some git Green hires out to be your shrink." I could swear a seagull flying overhead plummeted to the ground, killed by the bitterness.

"Aww fuck…" I muttered painfully, "Bracken…" I so didn't want to squander this chance to hold his hand, but apparently I had inflicted more than one wound here, and it was mine to heal.

"I'm gone," he volunteered, bending down and kissing me one passionate, torturously short time. "I'll be at the student union, buying those…female things and some sweats."

Oh shit.

"I've got a blood spot on my ass, don't I?" Fucking menstrual cycle. Oughta be a fucking law.

He made a non-committal noise that translated to *Yes, beloved, the size of Texas,* and vanished (figuratively), to leave Hallow and me to promenade up the bike path like old and good friends.

"You didn't have to do that," Hallow said mildly and I rolled my eyes.

"The fuck I didn't—you think I'm going to ride up the hill with my cut-offs this messed up? Besides, we need more sweats and shorts for the back of the SUV." Sac State sweats were our regulation gear after our clothes got fucked up on a run. Green told me he could tell how badly or how well the whole thing went by how many of us were sporting obnoxious green and yellow.

"My poor feelings aren't that fragile," he told me, trying to make his voice hit the 'amused' octave, but I wasn't buying it.

"Bullshit. What'd I do? You've got to tell me, Hallow, or I can't fix it. I mean I know I'm a pain in the ass, but I'm not a total bitch—I don't hurt people for kicks, or if I can avoid it, but how can I avoid the big pothole in your heart if you won't give me a goddamned flashlight?"

Hallow laughed in spite of himself. "Eloquent," he commended, and was met with another eye roll.

"Again, bullshit. So, are you going to tell me, or are you going to be really petty and show me all the avoidance tricks I've taught you in the last year?" I smiled winningly at him—or as winningly as I knew how to do. I wasn't really a flirt, but I figured at this point Hallow deserved my best effort.

"Heaven forbid," Hallow laughed, and we stopped then on top of the suspension-style bike bridge and leaned up against the side. I liked to watch the river—lazy as it drifted by the campus—wander along beneath us in the shade of the campus-side trees.

"So?"

He sighed, and watched the river with me. "You're very self-sufficient, Lady Cory. Even when you need me, you could probably survive without me."

I blinked. This was a bad thing? "Don't you want me to be able to survive?" I asked, confused. "I mean, my biggest concern is that I'm too much of a weak, human pain in the ass…"

Again, that bitter laugh. "Hardly. One hundred and fifty years I've been waiting for Lord Green to ask me something, do you know that? And when he finally does ask me…when I finally have a chance to put things square between us, the task he gives me is…"

"Insurmountable?" I asked, panicked. One hundred and fifty years? That was a helluva long time to pay back a debt. That was also a suspiciously familiar number, and while I spoke to Hallow, I also tried to do the math and come up with a connection. (My nearest and dearest will assure you that this was much harder for me than it should have been.)

"What do you mean?" he asked, genuinely surprised.

"Oh please, Professor Hallow, don't tell me I'm too fucked up to help—I mean, Green told me to behave and I've been trying, I swear. I know I missed the last couple of weeks, but I just didn't have words for you—I won't miss again, not even in the summer when you come up to the hill. Just don't tell Green I'm a lost-cause psychopath, please?" Oh Jesus, it wasn't fair! He hadn't even told me what I'd done yet to hurt his feelings like this!

Hallow's amused laugh helped put me at ease, even if it did make me feel about twelve years old. "You're not hopeless, my dear," he said, sounding charmed. His hand, which had been resting at my waist, came up to my back, and he patted me fondly. "It's just…" he shook his hair back and stared down the river to where the bend at the horizon cut it off.

"I grew up with Titania and Oberon. You know who they are, yes?"

My eyes narrowed and my teeth gritted. Oh yeah. I knew. "Yes."

He nodded. "You know then—they were not very nice people."

I'd kill them if I ever saw them, legends of the fey or no.

"No," I said simply.

"A very wise sentiment," he said with a little smile. "But still—there is something comforting, in having a monarch. There is something reassuring in the idea that you don't have to worry about whether your world is wrong or right—it is simply as the king would have it. And…" he shrugged a little, embarrassed, "and some of us loved to serve. It didn't matter—much—if we received no praise or if the things we were asked to do were abominations. Serving someone who controls the fate of a people—that can give a great deal of satisfaction."

Click. I knew why that date was important now.

"You knew him," I said, my heart suddenly jumping in my throat like some sort of possessed frog. "He was locked in that horrible place, and you knew him…"

Hallow flushed, and wouldn't meet my eyes. "I did," he murmured. "And I was told to go take my pleasure with him, and I did. But there were no rules against talking, afterward. Or before. Or when we were supposed to be in bed."

I looked sharply at Hallow, trying to decide if I should be angry at him for this, even though it had been two-hundred years ago.

"And I liked him." Hallow gave me a lost smile. "Not like a beloved… you know how that feels, I've seen it in you, and in Bracken—Goddess, I even saw it in Adrian, and for a while I had the same prejudice every one of my kind did about vampires. So I wasn't Green's beloved, but I liked him. He was pleasant to me, when he didn't have a cause to be. He enjoyed my visits—he even covered for me, when we had become so engrossed in talking about literature and science and the way the human world worked that we lost track of time and what we were supposed to be doing."

With a sigh, Hallow continued his perusal of the horizon. The sky was nearly cloudless, an eyeball-searing smoggy-azure blue, and the sun was a punishing white, but tilting, just a little, with the afternoon. Soon, it seemed to promise, soon, the relentless spring heat might cool down, and we could breathe again.

"You loved him," I said, feeling dense. "Not like a lover…you just…loved him. Like a friend."

Hallow nodded, pursing his lips. "Except…the greatness in him. The thing you see in 'your' Green now—I saw that too, and I loved that too. All of my time squandered, serving beings who were… petty, and corrupt… full of shining words and nasty, dirty snakes in their hearts. What they did to Green, tricking him like that, taking him prisoner just because he could please them…it was despicable. The more I spoke to Green, the more I realized that maybe the reason they looked down on him was that he was greater than they were, more noble than they could ever be."

His hand on my back stilled, and he unconsciously put it on the concrete railing in front of him and leaned on it, lost in the past in a way I've seen the older fey do. Just like with Green, I was content now to let the past spill out of him—as with most of the high sidhe, the really, really old beings, he would get to his point when he was ready.

"I was the one who begged Oberon to let us go to the garden. When we got there, and I saw Green's comfort, his happiness there, I knew. I knew exactly what he was planning. But he never told me, and I never had to lie."

No, I thought, looking at the way Hallow's jaw clenched, but he must have walked one hell of a fine line, in that treacherous place. I abruptly decided that I forgave him. No matter how he had started out, he had ended up a friend and an ally.

"Did you get in trouble," I asked, "when he escaped?"

Hallow shrugged. "Not to speak of." Dumb men—Hallow was the last guy I would ever have accused of machismo, but I could make another direct translation. *Not to speak of,* obviously equaled *Torture beyond your wildest dreams.*

I grunted and quirked an eyebrow, and he shrugged and conceded.

"One year of what I endured...it was nothing, compared to the two-hundred years of what your Green endured with a whole heart. If your Green could come here, begin his beautiful hill, and not hold any grudges? I can forget a year of a very long life."

Fair enough, I thought sadly. No wonder he could counsel people, though—was it just an elf thing to be damned well adjusted? "Why didn't you come with him," I asked Hallow instead. The well-adjusted thing would just be rhetorical.

Hallow shrugged, and his face grew remote and cold—an ice-berg gazing at a Caribbean island. "Green is very brave, for our kind of sidhe—do you know that?"

I smiled, feeling a breeze off the river, or maybe just the refreshment of thinking about something beautiful that I loved. "I know he's so incredibly brave," I murmured. "To have lived for so long, and be hurt so often, and to still love us... he's braver than I am, I know it in my bones."

Hallow let out a sardonic laugh. "Don't be too sure of that, my lady," he murmured. "But he is brave. He was brave enough to go out on his own, to found his own hill. I didn't understand that—I didn't get it when this country was founded, and I certainly didn't get it when Green levitated those damned trees through the walls of Oberon's garden. He asked, but I was less afraid of Oberon's wrath than I was of being on my own." Hallow snorted softly.

"It's just as well," he murmured. "If I had been there, he never would have made the deal with Lucian, and then he never would have met Adrian. The world would have been a sadder, less vibrant place, if the two of them had never been."

I couldn't argue, so I said nothing. He slanted me a look then, amused and self-deprecating.

"You're very good at this counseling thing—are you sure you don't want my job?" he asked with a smile.

"Are you kidding? If I had to deal with bitches like me, I'd kill myself. And them."

He laughed outright then and in that neutral way of a sexually driven people, looped a completely sexless arm around my shoulders. "You're not that bad, my lady—and remember, I can't lie."

I laughed then, and leaned against him companionably, thinking that it was going to be a lot harder to ditch out on my therapy sessions after this odd, lazy afternoon.

"So I was too afraid to come with him, but that didn't stop him from sending word." Hallow shook his head, his white-blond hair shaking out of his braid and around his face. "I can't even imagine what he had to do, the strings he had to pull, the people he had to sleep with or kill, to get word to me in Oberon's hill. But he did it, and he offered me a way out and a hill to come to, and I did. He gave me someone worthwhile to follow, someone who didn't run rife with power, someone whom it would be an honor to serve."

He was so passionate, I thought, looking at his remote face. This touched him deeply, hit to the core of who he was, and my shoulders drooped suddenly with how badly I must have let him down.

"And then he had to go and bring me home," I muttered, and the arm around my shoulders tightened considerably.

"I was worried, yes," Hallow conceded. "Especially after Adrian died, and the consequences of his death."

I tried to pull away then, not feeling like I was worth being touched, but his arm tightened around me and kept me there—hot and sweaty but comforted, so it was worth it.

"Are you worried now?" I asked, dreading the answer.

Hallow bent then and took my chin in his fingers—a surprising, tender gesture from a man who had tried very hard to maintain his personal distance from me for more than a year. "Not at all, Little Goddess," he said kindly. "When I do worry, it is about you—your heart is surprisingly fragile, for all that we love you for your strength. Now that I've met you, I will never again worry that you will run roughshod over all of those whom have come to treasure Green."

I smiled then, shyly. "I'm glad," I murmured, grateful for his reassurances, even though I didn't share them. "But why tell me all of this?" I asked then, not wanting the silence between us to become awkward.

Hallow dropped his hand but kept contact with my eyes. "For one thing, you wouldn't trust me unless you knew me. I tried to do the 'human professional thing'—for a year, I've tried. But you wouldn't buy it –I couldn't do my job, dammit, and it was irritating me no end!"

I laughed a little. Well, I had confessed to being a colossal pain in his ass.

"And for another?"

Hallow sighed. "Because I will do anything, my lady, just like you, to keep Green from humbling himself again. This…nuisance can not be allowed to run rampant, exposing us, blackmailing us. Not after all Green has done to make our people united and happy and safe. Don't worry about Nolan Fields for the moment—he will need killing, but I can control him until we find out how to get the rest of the negatives."

I blinked. Hallow was a healing elf—not the sexual kind, but still, the sidhe were sexual creatures. There was only one way he had of controlling somebody for certain.

"No," I mumbled, surprisingly embarrassed.

"I'm sorry?" he asked, feigning surprise. He'd known—he had to have known—that I wouldn't agree to this.

"No," I repeated, my voice stronger this time. Asshole kept calling me "my Lady"—well, he was going to have to live up to it.

"No what?" he asked neutrally.

"You can't, Professor—you can't do it. I wouldn't let Green, I won't let you. Green wouldn't want it and I certainly don't—that's the reason you told me, right? You like authority. You figured I'd be your authority and I'd give it the okay and Green will never have to know. Well bullshit. That's crap. You can't do it. We'll find another way. You want to hurt Green more already? You go and hurt yourself in a way I told him he couldn't. He loves you—you're his friend. It will rip him up to know you did what he wouldn't." I found myself getting mad—dammit, I loved these guys, and I loved that they asked questions first and killed painfully later, but *Jesus,* did they have to sleep with it, even if it was slimy?

Hallow laughed a little—in cacophony. "Have you ever heard the expression, my Lady, 'It's better to beg forgiveness than ask permission'?"

Aww fuck. I buried my face in my hands. I didn't want to see the beautiful day anymore. "Professor…" I whined. Oh, this was so uncool. The tears I had pushed back with my physical misery broke for me now, and his arm tightened on my shoulders.

"You wouldn't let me serve you," he said gently, and then laughed at my tearstained outrage when I glared at him. "No, this isn't your fault, I'm not saying that! It's just..."

"Just what, dammit!" I burst out, at a complete loss for words. *"I might, with bold faced power sweep him from my sight!"* I quoted, because when I was out of words, Shakespeare wasn't, and it was what I'd wanted (and what Arturo and Bracken had wanted) to do with this guy from the first.

"MacBeth was a coward, my Lady," Hallow murmured. "You and Green are anything but."

"Well we've apparently let you do our dirty work for us, just like he did!" I accused, and then he did that thing... my Professor, my shrink, this hundreds-year-old graceful, poised, and self-controlled being did that thing... that dropping-to-one-knee-in-public-before-me thing, and I stared at him in horror and shock.

"You haven't asked, my Lady," said Hallow, very clearly, from his position of *kneeling at my feet,* "why I would choose to live off of Green's Hill when I spent so much time and energy to get here."

"Please tell me," I muttered, at a complete loss.

"Atonement, Lady Cory. Please, I beg of you, allow me to earn my place."

"Green would never make you..."

"Green has forgiven me—you know that. But I need to do this, so I can forgive myself. Please, my Lady?"

Oh Goddess. "Yeah," I muttered, less than graciously. "Okay, Professor... just please, get up. Please." I looked over to where Bracken was walking up the slope of the bridge and thought yearningly of his arms and a quiet place to sob in them.

It wasn't going to happen—but I suddenly thought it would be worth bleeding out in the toilet one more time to hasten the moment when it could.

BRACKEN

The Other Side of Helpless

She cried most of the way home.

I was not sure what happened between the time I left to give Hallow the privacy he so obviously wanted and the time I came back with the extra clothes, but by the time I walked up the bridge, she looked like hell.

She tried to hide it—for all I know, Hallow may have been fooled that she was going to be fine. She saw me and turned to him, a note of pleading in her voice as she said, "What can I possibly say to make you not do this?"

Hallow twisted his mouth. "You could always, 'with bare faced power sweep it from your sight.'"

"Fuck you, Professor," she said sourly, and in response he laughed—and then bowed.

That was when the first tear slipped down her cheek.

He stood and took her arm and walked her to me, so I could actually *touch my wife,* and I wrapped my arm all the way around her disconsolate shoulders.

"What happened?" I murmured into her ear, heedless of the fact that Hallow could hear me, and she shook her head and mouthed 'later', and still silent tears slipped down her cheeks.

Hallow walked us to the SUV in the (blessed) coolness of the parking structure where the others were waiting, and assured us that the allergies wouldn't trouble her anymore as long as she was on campus.

She gave a very polite, very formal bow. "Thank you, Professor," she said, in her most remote, 'royal' voice. "We're privileged to have you serve us."

Hallow gave a very low bow then, surprising those who hadn't seen it on the bicycle bridge, and took her hand in his, kissing the ring that marked her bond with all three of her lovers.

"If you believe nothing else, my Lady, believe that the privilege is all mine."

She nodded then and wiped her face with the back of her hand, beyond words. Nicky, who is neither blind nor stupid, met my eyes in surprise as she crawled into the back of the SUV and into his arms. I shrugged, and looked unhappily at the man who had tried his very best to counsel all of us in our unusual situation.

"I'll give your regards to Green," I said, trying to deal with my bafflement. (Cory has frequently assured me that I don't deal with it well—I am trying to improve.)

"Thank you, Sir Knight," Hallow said with that little twisted smile, "but I would prefer if my Lady does the honors."

I looked to Cory to see what she thought—she was looking away from all of us, out the window of the SUV, sitting shoulder to shoulder with Nicky and trying for all the world to behave as though he wasn't there.

"Whatever you wish, Professor," I said, and he bowed and left.

The SUV was unusually quiet as I negotiated the ins and outs of Sacramento traffic—usually there was chatter and pleasant cacophony. We were not a quiet bunch. I could see in the rearview that Nicky had coaxed her into his arms. She was nodding as he murmured things to her, and I could see her faint smile through the tears she pretended not to notice.

Her eyes when they met mine in the rearview were bleak and troubled.

We hit the I-80/Business loop merge, and I started to swear.

"Mother-fucking-son-of-a-whore-kissing-buggering-git-turd-cock-swilling-pig-sticking-crap-sucking..."

"Bracken..." she said, sitting up a little more, and holding back laughter through her tears.

"Cunt-poking-shit-slurping-manky-fuck-faced-bitch-humping..."

"*Bracken...*" she insisted, and the others were looking at me with a combination of amusement and concern. Jack especially had raised his eyebrows to his hairline and widened his eyes as though taking disbelieving notes.

"Corpse-rutting-cockroach-licking-crab-itching-ass-scratching..."

"BRACKEN!!!"

"BASTARD-CRACK-OF-A-SAILOR'S-BALL-SAC!" I thundered at

her through the car and the shocked laughter of our friends. "What in the blue fuck is wrong?"

And now she giggled through her tears, and Nicky giggled with her. "Jesus, Bracken Brine," she choked, "if you wanted me to choke on my snot you could have just held me upside down!"

I flushed, but continued to flash glares at her (when I could) in the rearview mirror.

"Are you going to tell me what that was all about?" I asked, still furious.

She shook her head and wiped her face, and then, less gracefully, turned her head to the side and wiped her nose on her T-shirt, which was all she had since we'd left the Kleenex in the back compartment with the backpacks.

"When we're alone, tomorrow," she said softly, surprising me.

"Why tomorrow?" I asked, all suspicion. Six weeks. Six weeks she had known about Green and Nolan Fields. Had she told me? Had she even *tried* to put a voice to the pain of that? I know there are things she doesn't understand about the world of my kindred, but did she think I wouldn't understand her pain at Green humbling himself? Green should *never* lower himself. Not our Green. Not the man who sheltered us all in the warmth of his clean and generous heart.

"Because, idiot, I want you to hold me, and you can't do that tonight." Her brows drew together and her lip stuck out, and I could tell I'd irritated her and charmed her at the same time—we do that for each other a lot.

I shook my head and muttered something dire, and she giggled again, wearily, and went back to leaning into Nicky's arms. Nicky caught my eyes in the rearview and shrugged a little, and I was both grateful for him and irritated that he got to hold her and I didn't.

I longed for something to pummel bloody—and everybody in the car knew it too. The quality of silence didn't improve after that, and I bullied my way through rush hour traffic, up the hill and towards home.

Right after we reached the Foresthill bridge she actually spoke, her voice clogged with tears and not allergies. She talked to Jack.

"I'm sorry, Jack," she murmured. He was in the seat bank in the middle. He got up on his knees and turned towards her. With the exception of her, none of us wore seatbelts. The were creatures could endure and re-knit any wound not made with power—if power was a consideration, we had bigger things to worry about than seatbelts.

"'Bout what?" he asked, genuinely surprised.

"I thank Teague all the time—he works really hard. He loves working for us, you know?"

Jack nodded, looking away. He did know, I thought. A year and a half they'd been working together before they'd been bitten—Teague hadn't been doing it for the money, that was for damned sure.

"I never thank you. I should." Her eyes met mine in the rearview again, and they were an inscrutable brown. "His work is your sacrifice. I'm sorry. Thank you."

Jack looked away. "I'm a passive aggressive shit," he said at last. "Our bullshit shouldn't be your headache."

"You're right there," she said with a faint smile. "But I really value your beloveds. I...I've tolerated you for their sake. I should be more grateful to you for who you've given us."

Jacky turned around and faced forward, his face working for a moment and I almost felt sorry for him—leave it to my beloved to figure out why the pissy whiny little bitch had sprung up in the place of the pleasant young man who had first arrived at Green's home.

"I should work to be someone to be grateful for," he said at last, graciously. "I just...I feel like I'm an intrusion—an imposition because of who Teague is to you."

Nicky was the one who actually answered that—with a snort and a grim smile. "Hell, Jacky—we're all accidental impositions. The trick is to make that work for you!"

I'd never thought I'd be so grateful for Nicky, but watching her lean into his comfort as our whole college group just lightened the fuck up, pretty much paid for his upkeep right there.

So things were better just before we got home, but she still darted for Green's room when we got upstairs, and her disappointment rolled through the hill when she found the door locked. She looked to the kitchen automatically, but the sun didn't set for half an hour, and Grace wasn't there, and she almost stamped her foot.

With an exasperated growl, she grabbed her backpack and the sweatshirt looped around it and announced to no one in particular, "I'm going to the fucking garden," and then pounded the granite stairs behind the living room into the Goddess Grove.

Arturo watched her go with eyebrows raised, and then he looked at me and Nicky.

"We don't know," I said shortly, watching as Jacky grabbed a couple of bottles of chocolate milk from the refrigerator and headed outside.

Teague was home today, and Mario too, and we had seen them taking apart some more of the old garage/barn that was still being renovated into Teague, Jack, and Katy's off-campus 'home'. Although most of Teague's uneasiness at being surrounded by people had faded, much of his pride seemed to be tied up in creating a separate space for him and his family, and he worked at it with concentration and attention to detail. I enjoyed working with him on the house, and part of the reason I hadn't actually killed Jack yet was that he was an entirely different, secure, funny person when he was in the company of his beloveds. I actually respected him when we were banging out drywall.

Of course, it's hard to maintain a grudge against a man when you are sweating together in physical labor—a fact for which Cory had professed often enough that she was eternally grateful.

Right now, that physical labor seemed like the best panacea for the ailment of the day.

"I don't know," I repeated to Arturo. "She had a talk with Hallow—and it didn't end well. She said she'd tell me when I could hold her."

Arturo winced, and I made an abrupt decision.

"Hang out there, Jacky," I called, stalling him at the door. "Let me change and I'll come out and help you!"

Nicky met my eyes and looked up the granite staircase. Then he looked at Green's room, and then out the window where the last hour of daylight beckoned with a sweetness to the air that had been smogged out of the valley but that hung thick and promising here in the hills.

"Wait up!" he called, sounding almost desperate. "I'm coming with you!"

We worked in relative silence for an hour, when the last of the daylight disappeared, and we sent Jack and Nicky ahead to the house to shower and tell Katy (who had arrived as we'd worked) that we'd be eating in the were common room tonight.

I helped Teague and Mario put away tools, and he looked at me, then looked at the direction Jack went.

"He still giving you trouble?" he asked reluctantly, and I shrugged. There had been an unspoken rule not to complain to Teague about Jack. Things were complicated enough without that, and we all loved Teague. We all loved Jack, for that matter—he just made things difficult sometimes.

"He'd be more secure if you had bonded," I said without thinking, and then winced as Mario made a sound suspiciously like chicken startled in her nest, and Teague dropped a hammer on the wooden floor with a loud bang.

We all stared at each other in surprised silence, and I wished desperately for Cory, who probably would slap me upside the head first, but she *would* find a way to fix what I'd just done.

"How'd you know that?" Teague asked, his green eyes wide and a fight/flight pulse throbbing in his temple.

"The vampires at Sugarpine," I said numbly. Damn, damn, and damn. I was seventy-seven fucking years old for sweet Goddess sake! "Cory was going to say something to you..."

"Well thank God you said it first!" he burst out. "It would be like talking to a little sister about jacking off!"

I nodded at the analogy, although the incest taboo was a thing my people did not have. "I'm sorry," I muttered. "It's just... he's all about you and Katy. All. If he's uncertain about you, or worried, or he thinks we're taking advantage of you...he's a giant pain in the ass."

"I don't know why I haven't bonded..." Teague muttered. "It's not like I don't *want* to..."

"Whatever reason you haven't bonded," Mario said with a sturdy roll of the eyes, "it ain't cause you're in love with anyone else either."

"It's a power thing," I said, surprising even myself. Something about the way Hallow had looked at Cory, his anger when he thought she was too proud to ask him for help. It wasn't love—at least, not the kind I had for her--and it certainly wasn't attraction.

"You're bonded in service to Green and Cory...you take that seriously. It's probably... just stopping that werewolf thing from happening. You can't bond with them because you have too many other directions to go."

They were both looking at me as though I were brilliant. Cory must be rubbing off. Thank the Goddess—if I kept blurting out shit like that, it would be good to have a follow-up game.

"So," Teague said slowly, "it has nothing to do with sex?"

Mario shrugged. "Don't think so, *poppi*. Think it's all power."

Teague nodded. "Excellent. I need a fucking beer."

And that was Teague.

We all ended up eating in the were-folk common room. Cory was still up in the garden, and I could feel the tingling, right up under my heart, that told me that even if Green wasn't done with his appointment until the morning, she was not alone.

Good. If anyone could make her life simple, even for the span of a conversation, it would be Adrian.

I liked the were-folk common room—it was built and decorated like a human bar—varnished wood tables, dark wood bar, brass fittings, hanging tiffany lamps—the works. Jack and Teague looked very comfortable here—or they would, but something weird happened to their personal space the minute they crossed the threshold.

I wasn't sure if it was because Jack had showered and Teague had not, or because Katy was sitting between them, but suddenly Teague hunched over the table, shoulders forward and aggressive, and Jack leaned back, scooting his chair far enough out from the table and Katy that when he spoke (and he spoke softly, which was out of character) we could barely hear him.

Their dialog was still the same.

"Want more?" Teague asked, shoving his plate of potato skins towards Katy. In the banquet room, in the living room—hell, standing in the ruins of the place that was going to be her home, Teague would have been in the middle, and they both would have been shoulder to shoulder with him—close enough for him to simply gesture. Katy rolled her eyes and ate her grilled chicken salad and pushed the plate towards Jack.

"Not hungry," Jack muttered.

"Eat." It was an order, and Jack grunted and scooted forward just close enough to scoop the food off the plate.

I looked at them curiously—Teague was drinking his beer with a reverence that Cory reserved for steak and steak alone, and Jack was looking at Teague sideways, as though he were something he yearned for, something long denied.

"Stop that," I muttered roughly, shoving a bite of Thai pasta in my mouth in irritation.

The three werewolves looked up at me in surprise.

"Stop what?" Teague said after a swallow of beer.

I glared at him. "Stop acting like gay men in a straight bar," I muttered, shuddering with the horrors that humans inflicted on each other. "You can touch each other. Nobody gives a shit. Nobody gets hurt, nobody bleeds out. Just fucking stop it."

They all looked at me in surprise, and I felt, under the table, Nicky's understanding hand on my thigh.

"It's their space, Brack," he murmured. "Maybe we should let them be."

I nodded and swallowed. There was a noise from the doorway and I looked up in time to see Leah, looking like tears and sex, come through and sit next to the other were-cougars, who all moved around her in a commiserative pack. So Green was done, I thought vaguely. And still, that buzzing in my breastbone, that…feeling… Adrian was here, on the hill, and I was denied my family by stupid human things I had no control over.

Looking at the three of them hurt, and suddenly I had to get out of there.

I pushed my dinner aside and stood up, excusing myself gracelessly, and walked blindly to our room.

I'd been sitting in one of the overstuffed chairs that were grouped around the table and lamp—our homework place, or dinner place if we didn't feel like eating in one of the main rooms—for a couple of moments, looking at the essay question for our missed film class and wondering if anyone would mind if I went into the front room and watched that strange movie again. Then I saw Cory's note, in the margin of the prompt:

Don't stress, due'alle—I've got this one covered.

I might have broken something then, but there was a courtesy knock on the door, and Nicky came in, slamming his cell phone shut as he did so.

He was going to sit in her empty chair, but he looked…miserable. Sad. As alone as I felt.

I took advantage of the odd closeness we'd built upon in the last year and grabbed his hand, yanking him into my lap. He laughed a little as he landed, but he was a small man—almost as small as our beloved—and he fit there, like a child.

It was telling about both of us that he simply leaned his head against my chest and let me comfort him.

"You have a secret," I said after a few moments.

He did me the courtesy of not trying to lie, even though his kind were perfectly capable of it if they needed to. "Yes."

"So does Cory—she said she'll tell me when we can touch. I hate human things." I nuzzled his straight, rusty hair—Cory was right, he did smell good. Like dust and cookies—it was a happy place.

Nicky laughed a little, and patted my chest condescendingly. "You should like this one, big man—it means she's healthy and can have children."

The thought of her body— small and with its fragile mortality—burdened with a child on my size scale terrified me and I said so. "It will kill her! I would rather die!"

Nicky looked troubled. "Believe it or not, that has occurred to me," he murmured. "But I don't think it will stop her."

I recalled myself. "But that has nothing to do with your secret." I didn't want to think about this—an elf's birth control was his will, so mostly, I didn't have to. Besides, I wanted to hear what he said. I wanted the secrets to end. If I couldn't hear hers tonight, Nicky's would do.

It came out surprisingly easy—I think he was just waiting for one of us to ask him while we had been respecting his privacy.

"Mom and dad—they want to visit."

I was surprised—that didn't sound like such a bad thing. "They are welcome!"

"No they're not," he protested. "Not by me, anyway."

I blinked at him. My mother and my father were…essential to my life at the hill, I guess. I may not even see them everyday. I think, according to human standards, I may even have 'out-classed' them. I ate at the leader's table—I had since Adrian and I had been a couple. Even when we had separated, become mostly friends instead of all lovers, I still sat there, listened,

gave my input. Da and Mom may have served differently, but we all still…
served. (Was that the right word for what it was my family did? It didn't feel
like the right word. We loved unconditionally. We did what our skills gave us
to do for the happiness of our home. Was that service? Was it patriotism? Was
it cooperative living? I am not sophisticated enough to answer these questions,
so I don't normally bother asking them.)

"Why wouldn't you welcome your family?" I asked, feeling thick.

Nicky gave a little snort, and rubbed his cheek against my T-shirt. I
wrapped my arms around him feeling…like a brother, perhaps. An older,
often annoyed brother, but a brother. He was my beloved's lover—and
sometimes we touched in bed—but mostly, he was my family, and just like
it was my family's job to serve, it was my job to comfort him and see to his
happiness. For the first time, I understood why Cory was so unhappy with
those questions around the campfire—it was hard to put into words the things
that simply sat beneath our skin.

"My father may sprout wings," Nicky was saying against my chest, "but
he and my mother are both…I think they're everything you loathe about
humans."

I looked at him, surprised. It had not occurred to me that one of the
Goddess folk could be…

"Yes," he said, nodding with a tired smile at the expression on my face.
"They're petty, ignorant, prejudiced, and they base most of their impressions
solely on appearance and gender."

I gaped. "*Your* parents?"

Nicky rubbed my shoulder a little in the same way I nuzzled my hair. "My
parents, big man—you don't know how lucky you are."

"That's why they wouldn't come to the wedding?" I asked carefully—I
had only been told that they hadn't 'approved'—I hadn't been told exactly
why.

"Oh yeah," he murmured. "And why they haven't made it Christmas, and
why I don't want them to come here. I mean…it's bad enough, that they're
embarrassing…and judgmental—but if they came here, Green would probably
have to mindwipe them, and then I'd have to disown them completely, and
that would suck even more!"

I looked at him in sympathy and disbelief. "But…Nicky—surely all they
want is for you to be happy, right? I mean, at worst, we introduce them to
Cory, and downplay how often we all share a bed and… just try to pretend
we're as 'normal' as they want you to be. They're your parents, right?"

"They…" he shook his head. I was not the only one who had difficulty
finding words. "You know, Bracken… the thing is… when I went away to
school, if any one asked me where I sat on the hetero-scale, I would belted out

"A ten, mother-fucker" and then beaten them into the ground. And then...
then Green healed me the first time...and I sort of had to admit that maybe
being, say, a nine on the scale wasn't so bad. And then...the bonding thing
happened, and I woke up and he...we..." Nicky blushed, although Cory and
I had seen him and Green together many times. But we had all been there,
too—the things Green did willingly to your body and his own in order to
bring you pleasure...well, I'm sure in some states these things were illegal.

"You made love to a man. You liked it," I supplied, and he nodded
gratefully.

"And then I made love to Cory...and it was good...I mean it was great...
but I...I started to suspect...and I thought that maybe it was because she
wasn't Green. Because, you know, there's *no* comparison with Green, right?
And then we all went to Texas to get Green, and there was a *lot* of fucking
going on... and we got back, and... you'd think I would have ended up with
Leah, right? Or even Willow... I mean, if I was going to have my own lover,
and I was a nine on the hetero scale..."

"What in the hell is this 'scale' you're talking about?" I asked, annoyed.
Fucking humans and their numbers.

"It's like...a sliding scale. I don't know—my friends and I came up with
it in Junior High..." And now he buried his head in my chest, like a little
kid. I kept up a soothing motion against his outer arm, and for the first time
wondered what Nicky and I had looked like in shape-shifter common room.
Had we had the same awkward, uncomfortable space around us? Or did we
look as though we would cuddle on a chair and commiserate over missing
the focus of our family?

"So maybe adolescence is where you should have left it?" I asked sharply,
and he nodded.

"But you don't—not in bumfuck Montana, you know? Everybody's a ten,
in bumfuck Montana—especially bird people, because we *have* to be—our
survival depends on it. We're like the Goddess' own right-wing-execution
squad. But I didn't come back from Texas a 'ten' on the scale. I came back in
love with Eric, and in love with Green, and still in love with Cory, but even
a little in love with you—that's three men I've loved, Bracken, and only one
woman...and the more I love her, the more I think it wasn't loving her like a
man loves a woman in the first place. It was like a friend loves a friend, or a
subject loves a monarch—but not as a man loves a woman. And maybe that
doesn't matter—maybe I can just tell my parents that she's my wife and leave
it like that. But...but I want them to meet Green. And Eric—and even you.
I want them to know who I am—I'm not a ten on the hetero-scale. I think
I'm barely a four."

He was weeping. Holy Goddess, our Nicky was weeping, and my beloved was not here to comfort him, it was only me. I rocked him for a moment and let him use my shirt as a tissue.

"I love you too," I said awkwardly. "You are my family."

He sniffled. "Dude, you don't *know* how good that makes me feel."

Well of course—since he was planning to give up his own family completely, it would be good to know we were there for him now.

"You should meet them somewhere else," I said thoughtfully. "We've got property, cabins, resort things, all over the state—Green will set up a vacation for you. Cory and I will come."

He was looking at me with a combination of gratitude and inward amusement. "I thought about it," he murmured. "I just...I didn't know how to bring it up."

I looked at him sharply. "Green would have understood," I said.

Nicky's narrow, pretty face didn't hold sadness well, but it did hold it. "Green is so amazing—I didn't want to hurt him, by suggesting he shouldn't come."

"We are not made of glass," I sniffed with dignity. "You and Cory should trust that we can hold your hurt too."

Nicky looked up and took the liberty of smoothing my hair back from my face. I glared at him and he laughed. "We don't want you to hold our hurt," he said fondly. "That's the point."

I rolled my eyes. Two years, Cory had been here at the hill, and I was no closer to understanding her than the day I'd been tussling with Adrian and had seen her through a plexiglass window, wearing an ugly blue smock, counting Cheetohs.

Nicky yawned, and I sighed. It was probably time for bed. My usual gauge for that sort of thing was Cory, because although I didn't need as much sleep as she did, my compulsion for touching her skin brought me to her bed as soon as she was ready. I'm not sure if I would ever tell her how much time I spent, lying awake in the dark, listening to the precious music of her heartbeat.

Fuck. She would obviously not be coming to my bed tonight.

I looked at Nicky, dozing in my arms, and sighed again. "Go get your jammies, little man—you can come sleep with me tonight."

Nicky opened his eyes and for a moment, I thought he was going to refuse for the sake of pride. Then he remembered that he was a grown man who had just spent fifteen minutes pouring his heart out in my arms, and that he apparently didn't have any pride to speak of.

"Do I really need jammies?" he asked, sliding from my lap and stretching. It was a valid question—we both usually slept naked when Cory was in bed with us.

I shrugged and went to my drawer to pick the loosely knit bottoms that she'd gotten me for Christmas in case her mother came over to visit while we were still in bed. It had only happened the once, but there was no telling Cory that.

"Call it a precaution," I murmured.

"Would it matter?" Nicky asked, curious but nothing more. "I mean... we've shared a bed—shared her—for a year now. You and I have, uhm, recently had...well, contact. Would you really...uhm...self-destruct. Melt, thaw and resolve yourself into a goo, if we...uhm...did the thing?"

I looked at him, surprised. We'd planned what he called 'Cory ambushes', came up with sexual techniques and combinations outside of bed so we could push her to her limits on the inside—and he hadn't blushed once. He was blushing furiously now.

"I don't know," I told him simply. I really had no interest in finding out.

"And would you know if we were doing something wrong?" he asked, suddenly wide- awake. "Would you feel pain, get a warning or would it be, like," he put out his arms and pumped his hips suggestively, "hoocha hoocha hoocha, eek, ouch, dead!"

I do not know what my expression was, but it was enough to make him burst into surprised laughter. "Don't bother..." he whooped. "Don't answer that, big man...I'm going to get my pjs now like a good boy." He eyed my crotch with an appreciative roll of the eyes. "Because, you know, heaven forbid that thing have an accident and fall up my ass or anything."

I blinked at him, my lips curving into a bland smile. "Should that ever happen, little man, believe me when I say you'll know that it's coming."

Nicky burst into another whoop of surprised laughter and chuckled his way out the door.

In the morning, long before the alarm went off for school, she surprised us both by clambering over Nicky and into my arms.

I opened my eyes, and she was there, light brown eyes twinkling, sunshine grin in place and her red-auburn hair *amazingly* riotous from sleep. Her breath was minty, and she jumped up and down on me like a small child at Christmas morning.

"I'm done," she giggled, kissing the bemused expression right off my face.

I pulled back and blinked at her, feeling stupid and thick. "Done?"

"Mmmm-hmmm..." she kissed me again and pulled back. "The stupid human bleeding ritual... all gone... Green said I'm done for this round... now shut up and keep kissing me!"

"Oh Christ!" Nicky groaned from my side. "I may as well go shower."

With that he sat up on his knees and snuck his head in to kiss Cory's cheek, so close I could smell his dust and vanilla smell and even his icky morning breath. Cory turned her head for a moment and kissed him back, reaching up and touching his cheek with her hand. They pulled away and there was something dark in her eyes, deepening on his face, and his gaze flickered to mine.

"Later," he muttered. "You and Bracken, you catch up," and then he slid away.

She was going to say something, but she was warm and soft—so soft, I couldn't stop running my hands along her lushening curves.

"Later," I murmured, knotting my hands in her hair and tugging her face back to mine again. She gazed at me with happy, playful eyes. There would be things to say now that we could touch again, but for right this moment...

"Later," she said, the sound rich in her throat. Then she kissed me, and my arms engulfed her, folded her into my heart, and we dropped into a pocket of time.

CORY

Garden Pleasures

Of course I ran for the garden. Adrian was there.

I had to wait until sunset, of course, but that wasn't hard. I had my knitting, my i-pod, and since both my paper and Bracken's paper were already finished, I had a historical romance for a little stress relief. I was driven, but I wasn't stupid. If I didn't get my brain off-topic, it would be like feeding a hamster meth and putting it on a wheel—the damned thing would run until its heart exploded and ran out my ears.

I needed to feel like something smarter than a dead hamster, so I hit the refresh button on my brain and chilled the fuck out.

It worked so well that I have no idea how long Adrian had been sitting at the foot of his marble memorial bench, watching me knit and read and listen to music.

"Bad day, luv," he murmured, and I closed my eyes and let his presence wash through me. If he had been alive, we could have felt each other's emotions, talked easily inside each other's heads...seeing through the other's eyes wouldn't be a wrench like it was with Phillip, but second nature, like taking a breath.

He wasn't alive, but if I closed my eyes I was close enough to smell him... the leather he used to wear, the coppery smell of blood...a light, spice smell, like chamomile or citrus or both—most vampires smelled like that, but Adrian's smell had been special.

"I started my period," I said glumly. He had comforted me the first time round, no embarrassment needed. (Of course, he'd leered and pointed out that he was sorry he didn't get to be there for me. I had called him a pervert and threatened to go back downstairs unless he dropped *that* subject right quick. I mean--and this can't be said too often--uhm, *ewie!!!*)

"My condolences," he said now, dryly but sincerely at the same time. "How's bloody big lummox fuckwit asshole taking it?" Ah, brotherly love.

"He's miserable, like I am," I said with a little smile. "I… I needed you today, beloved." We tried, Green, Bracken and I. We tried with every meeting to pretend as though he was only gone for a moment, for a breath, and that seeing him as a hint of wind on the odd night in the garden was no different than his day death as a vampire.

It wasn't true. None of it. One day, he would come see me in the garden and realize that I'd aged, and he hadn't been there to hold my hand for it. One day, he would come out and I'd be pregnant with Green's child, or holding the baby in my arms, and he wouldn't have been there to feel it grow. One day, he would come into the garden, and only Green would be there to greet him, and Green would have no one but a ghost in the garden who would love him for him, and not for the leader he had become.

Today, realizing that I had grown into the kind of person who would let Hallow sacrifice himself instead of just going to *kill* the motherfucker responsible for this bullshit made me nothing if not painfully aware: *that* day was creeping closer with every tick of the clock. I would *never* live as long as Hallow, to a day when his sacrifice, his atonement, was acceptable—but Green and Adrian had.

So tonight, I couldn't pretend that I was still nineteen, and that I still believed in happy-ever-after. I couldn't pretend that his ghosthood was just a temporary glitch, a new way to live.

My beloved was dead. I needed him, and he wasn't here to hold me, he could only listen to my troubles, like the stove in the faerie tale, and offer his warmth in return for the story.

"I'm sorry I wasn't there for you," Adrian's ghost said wistfully from his post at my feet. "I'm sorry I'm not there for you a lot…"

Oh Goddess. I smiled for him, brilliantly, and met the startling blue of his transparent eyes. "Beloved, you felt my heart ache and came for me now. It will be enough."

"What triggered it, luv?" he asked after a moment when our eyes met and it was only the two of us and the sound of the breeze in the trees. "Why the need?"

I told him, then, about Hallow, about the sacrifice I wouldn't let Green make, about everything but the snot and the cramps, actually, because that would just be whining.

The look he gave me when I was done was eloquent.

"Of course," he protested, holding his face up to a breeze he couldn't feel. "You couldn't let Green do it—after everything else he does for us…"

"But…" I murmured, wanting someone to understand. Bracken might possibly—but he took this royalty shit for granted. Adrian hadn't—Adrian had been there from the beginning, when it had been two guys and a coffin and an ungiving land.

Adrian had loved Green as I had, and he had seen Green when he'd been left the most vulnerable after his escape. Adrian would understand, I thought almost desperately. He would know.

"No one should have to do that," Adrian said now, and I wanted to weep, because he did. He had always been more human than a vampire should have to endure. "Not even for atonement."

I wiped my cheek on my hand, and saw a translucent thumb come up to my cheek. It didn't work—I had to wipe my own tears—but I appreciated the gesture.

"And that's why I needed you, beloved," I murmured.

"And that's why I was here."

I watched then, as he faded away, because I'd called on him a lot in the past weeks, and he couldn't stay long, not really. We lived as we had always lived—on borrowed time.

I was still looking at the place Adrian had been when Green came up into the garden. He walked behind me and wrapped his arms around my shoulders, something about his touch so honest and clean and sexy that I whimpered a little for the act itself, which I missed after the last three days. (Yes, I'm spoiled—but it's where I charge most of my preternatural power…I was like a cell phone on my last bar.)

"Did he help, luv?" Green whispered in my ear, and I squirmed a little more, because something about that dead-sexy British voice, purring against my ear-whorls just totally did it for me.

"Yes…" *but not as much as your touch on my skin.* The things we never said, the lines of exposition we never crossed.

"Care to tell me about your day?"

"No," I muttered, "but I will anyway."

His sigh dusted my ear as well, but he moved around the arm of the bench and situated himself behind me. I leaned against him, warm and solid, but not rough. Not the cold marble of the bench but the earth-solid humanity of my Green.

When we were comfortable, and my head was resting on his chest, our warmth, our love, cocooning us in complete emotional safety—that's when I told him about Hallow.

When I was through, his sigh shook me to the ticklish soles of my cool bare feet.

"He doesn't need to do that," Green mumbled, and I could almost smell the discomfiture as it poured off his body.

"I think I said that," I told him, scowling.

Green's chuckle was weak, but it was there. "So I imagine, beloved. I just don't know how to make it any plainer… what we need to do is kill this cockroach. Stomp him 'til his bones crackle, squash him on the concrete and walk over his twitching legs!"

I guffawed heartily as the indignation in his voice crept up—it took a lot to get Green truly angry, but the results were usually spectacular, and, contrary to his normally even temper, very often unpredictable.

"I'd like to see you do it, beloved," I told him sincerely, "but don't forget that I'm your weapon—I might have something planned for him as well."

Without warning, Green's hands came up behind me, and I found myself hefted up by my underarms and turned deftly in his grasp like a child. Green pulled me close and spoke seriously into my eyes, and only his terrible sincerity kept me from rubbing his cheek with my own like a cat.

"You, *ou'e'eir,* are more than a weapon," he growled, and I nodded seriously, and replied with the assurance grown in nearly two years of the warmth and fine soil of his love.

"And you, *ou'e'hm,* are more than just a sexually-triggered human resources arc-welder."

His lips, lean, sensual, full where it counted, pulled up at the sides out of habit. "That was right brilliant, beloved—did you practice that?"

"Only all day," I told him, flushing. Only since Hallow had told me he was whoring for our safety and I couldn't think of a fucking thing to say.

"Worth the practice." He gave me a playful kiss on the nose, and I dropped my head into his shoulder, taking most of my weight on my knees and giving him the rest.

"What are we going to do?" I asked seriously. "Green…we can't let him do this… I know he feels bad but…"

"He shouldn't," Green muttered bleakly. I looked at him—his emerald eyes were staring off, beyond the ambient light of our holy place, and into the dark beyond the hill. "He was my only friend in a dark place, beloved. I never meant for him to feel…obliged to me, in any way."

I touched his face with my rough little hand, and he rested his cheek in my palm. "I'm so afraid, beloved," I told him frankly. "I'm so afraid of becoming what you escaped in England, of becoming our worst enemy. People…Hallow, just doing this for us… it feels so wrong…"

Green nodded into my hand. "I hear you…and I don't know what to say about it. I've begged Hallow to come take the shelter of our hill for years…if this is what it takes for him to feel as though he's earned it, I don't know that it's fair of us to say no."

I closed my eyes and rested my forehead against his for a moment, and longed for the brief, ephemeral times when Green and I alone could be Green and I alone, without the weight of the hill and half of California cramping at our shoulders.

For a quiet, somber moment, I felt the thickness of the warm May darkness around us, the faint breeze that blew through the lighted Goddess Grove, and Green's breath dusting my face and shifting his chest beneath my palms. His eyes were closed, but his lips found mine anyway, and then my eyes were closed and we kissed gently, without urgency, and kissed again.

We had so much to be grateful for in each other—taking care of our people was really such a small price to pay for that, wasn't it?

We necked like teenagers, kissing languorously, petting sensuously, touching without urgency, until, without warning, things became breathless and urgent and my frustration at not being able to go any farther made me growl in the back of my throat.

Green pulled away, shaking his mussed braid to his back, and panted just a little. "Luv… your people have come up with a wonderful solution for this sort of thing."

"If you say 'blow-job', I'm going for a run," I mumbled, and he laughed softly, placing a rough, glorious kiss at my temple, the corner of my mouth, my throat.

"I was talking about a bottomless shower with bench seats," he replied from the top of the hollow between my breasts.

Brother, I was so there.

Something woke me, early in the morning, and I lay there, head pillowed on Green's shoulder, feeling his hand stroking the satin of my stomach, under his billowy white T-shirt and above the elastic of my cotton panties.

"What time is it?" I mumbled, arching into his touch like a sleepy tabby cat.

"An hour before you usually get up with Bracken," he said back, nuzzling my hair. "Trust me—you'll be happy I woke you…"

"Sure I will…" I muttered, and he laughed and shushed me.

"But first—you and Brack working at Grace's store tonight, luv?"

A Yarning for Crafts. Most of us took our turns supervising Green's businesses. Arturo took Denny's because that's where many of the Hispanic immigrants gravitated, the vampires took the gas stations to keep them safe at night and to supervise the hard-partying were-folk, and I took Grace's craft store, because she'd taught me to knit when I was sick and I loved it there. Bracken took it with me, because he loved me there.

"Yeah," I murmured listlessly. It would suck working there if Brack and I couldn't brush up against each other as we were stocking the aisles or working in the back, but the days were too long now for Grace to go in until later, so we were needed to pick up the slack in the evenings.

"We'll have a late family dinner when you're done, yes?"

I heard him—big pow-wow among the inner circle—the four of us, Aturo, Grace, Marcus, Phillip, Teague, Max, Renny, Lambent, Sweet— elves, vampires, were-creatures, and little ol' me, the mortal cherry on the immortality sundae.

"Yeah," I sighed. Last night had been nice—but we needed to get to business now. Hallow, Gretchen—even Nicky and his not-so-secret little secret. (Okay, I didn't know *all* of it, but I did know his parents had called. What can I say? Were-folk gossiped worse than women in a knitting circle. I'd been waiting for him to come to me, but if he wouldn't, well, I could listen.) "I hear you," I yawned into his waiting silence, "but I still don't know why you woke me up early."

Green chuckled, which was really the world's best alarm clock, and rolled over to his side and engulfed me in his long, lithe, moon-lit pale, satiny body. When he had me cocooned against his chest, safe in the warmth of his body and my breath, he murmured, "Your moon cycle, luv—it's all run. You're no longer bleeding, not even a bit. It's good news, eh?"

I pulled back and shot him a shining grin, fully awake now. "Oh shit, yes it is!" I crowed, almost vibrating from the bed in my glee.

Green laughed. "It is indeed—now wouldn't you like to go tell Bracken?"

I nodded and, conscious of my morning breath, kissed his neck until he laughed, and then scrambled out of bed. "Absolutely," I sang, as I danced to the bathroom, "but first I'm going to brush my teeth!"

Later that night, after Bracken and I had closed the store and driven home (with Bracken nagging me the whole way there about the yarn I took with me. Men! They think that the only yarn a girl needs is the yarn in the projects she's working—how do you plan your next project that way, tell me that!) we sat in various positions in the living room, eating dinner and dessert and whatever Grace had laid out on the big, solid wood coffee table between the couches.

Teague was eyeing most of a chocolate cream pie with the serious covetousness that children usually reserved for toys at Christmas, when Green sighed, grabbed a fork, stuck it in the pie and handed the entire thing to our alpha werewolf, who shoved a largish bite in his mouth in sheer surprise.

The day we could get that man to reach for something besides his lovers would be a moral victory for pretty much the whole damned hill.

When most of the munching had died down, and the pixies had started the cleanup, Green settled down on the arm of the couch next to me and waited politely for everybody's attention. He didn't exactly say 'Report!' but when we all looked at him quietly and he arched an eyebrow our way, that's almost exactly what happened.

I went first, and my news about Nolan Fields wasn't welcome.

"Oh, Christ," Lambent muttered. "You dumb wankers and that urge to work with the human world—all you'd have to do is have Hallow fake a piece of paper for you, and this git wouldn't have the access to you that might sink us all…"

"Fuck you, Lambent," I said with narrowed eyes. "This kind of bullshit is going to put food on your plate and keep the property intact and consolidate our holdings forever and ever more. You wonder why you all aren't still big in the old country? It's because you didn't own your land and dumb assholes moved in and destroyed your hills. Nobody's destroying this place, if I have to learn six languages and get three law degrees, Green's hill is going to be safe."

The others in the hill had either made their peace with my goals or taken them for granted, but Lambent's eyes got really big, like he hadn't thought of that and even Teague blinked twice and looked at me hard. There was something in his eyes like sorrow then, and I didn't want to think about why that might be.

"Anyway," I grumbled, not able to look anybody in the eye for this part, "Hallow's found a way to keep him silent, but the sooner we can… uhm… relieve him of that obligation the better, right?"

There was a digestive silence, then, as this curdled bit of information dropped into place and started everybody's bile working.

I was sandwiched between Green on the arm of the couch and Bracken on my other side, and Bracken took my hand in his and stroked it, even as Green bent and dropped a kiss in my hair. Nicky, who was couched at our feet, leaned back against me and let me run my fingers through his hair.

None of us liked this, but we'd discussed it in the course of the day, and the only solution we could think of was to find Nolan's contacts as soon as possible, so we could kill him dead.

"Anyway," I said, recalling something that Hallow had told me today as the lot of us had been on our way to our political science class (oh Goddess, I could barely look him in the eyes!) "Apparently Nolan's big break is coming sometime in July—we have until then to get this sorted out and locked down. Unfortunately, it's going to be cut pretty damned close—we'll be able to trace all of his contacts about two days before we get a big fat layout in some magazine with more clout than the Enquirer but less moral fiber. Once we know who has the photos, we go in, pull a mindfuck on them, and eliminate every damned picture, and…and…"

Bracken's hand grew a little firmer on my shoulder and I closed my lips over my bared teeth and stopped making maim/kill grimaces with my hands.

"And squash him like the piece of living cat-barf he is," I finished with grim dignity, and I got a nodded chorus of gimmehallelujias and felt a little better.

Renny, who was human and everything for this—she was even dressed in jeans and a shirt that fit, looked at me with slitted green eyes. "My fur balls have more integrity than that," she growled, and Max stroked her back until she relaxed.

From there we moved on to Gretchen—the news wasn't good.

Grace perched comfortably (if not elegantly—that wasn't her style) on Arturo's knee, and gave the grim account of the little girl's deterioration.

"It's like she's got alzheimers," Grace said at last. "Some days, she's perfect, she's eight years old, she thinks her family is coming to get her tomorrow. Some days she remembers what she's done, and she's beyond terrifying and entering the land of 'totally fucking evil'." Grace gave me and Teague a measured look and we both shuddered.

Teague had gone limp in her jaws and trusted me to channel Green and get him the fuck out of there. We had—and then Teague had sprinted for the door with me and I'd thrown up a power shield between Miss Junior Lady Vlad, and we'd both made it out the door—but she'd been… vacant. Distant. Immune to reason, to humanity—her only plan had been to drain Teague dry so she could bring him back over, just like that damned bear and wild cat.

"And we never know when the little girl's going to be there or the nasty force of nature is going to try to take us out. We need a minimum of ten of us to take her outside at night—and we all need a blood tie to her, because otherwise she tries to get away."

We all shuddered. It had been luck only that we had brought her in before she discovered the entire rest of humanity—God, Goddess, and other, the horrors she might have visited upon all of us made Nolan Fields' driving ambition look like a baby's single-minded, innocent quest for a bottle.

In a stomach-dropping silence, the entire room was looking towards me, and I shuddered when I looked back at them.

"Not yet," I murmured, heart breaking. "Maybe we can… I don't know.

If we find the person who did this to her… maybe he knows a way to… to fix what's wrong in her head, right? I mean… we all watch the same crime shows—this can't be the first time he's done this. He must have seen how it turns out. And then we can stop him and… you know."

There was a silence then—a conceding silence, and I was suddenly angry and near tears. They couldn't hold this against me—how can you hold the fact that I didn't want to commit cold-blooded infanticide against me?

"Don't worry about it, Lady Cory," Grace said gently, and I turned unhappy eyes towards her. "We can hang on to her for another month or two—if there's hope, there's hope, right?"

I didn't miss that her hands were as tightly woven with Arturo's as mine were woven with Green's and Bracken's.

"She likes you!" I tried gamely, and Grace shrugged.

"I'm a female, a vampire, and a mom… the deck's stacked in my favor. She asks about you all the time…"

"Yeah, when she forgets that I killed her pet kitty!" I snorted, because I hadn't been down to the 'nursery' for a few days and in spite of the fact that it was NOT my fault, I still felt guilty about the absence.

Grace shrugged, unwilling to concede that this one young member of the hill did not appreciate me as Grace thought she ought. The entire situation should have been amusing—as much time as I spent reading that kid stories and knitting her doll clothes (Blech! One more pony-puke-pink-pint-sized acrylic poncho and I really would vomit!) and Gretchen still stared at me with that same squinty-eyed distrust she'd had from the very beginning. In spite of my best overtures of mature patience (and don't think that wasn't a stretch) I would remain the authority figure to resent, to outwit, to overtly dislike.

I wasn't even twenty-two yet, and already, I was 'the man'. Fucking lovely. Bracken snorted next to me, and I sighed and Green redirected the conversation in the silence.

"To that end, Max—you did some research, what did you come up with?"

Max shook back his dark hair and stood officially, like a cop at report, and I raised a sardonic eyebrow at him. He shrugged, as if to say, *Sue me, it's the paycheck job,* and took a manila folder from a bright-eyed, proud-as-punch Renny.

"There's a couple of places in Cali that put out 'mountains' on the plate," Max said, pulling out pictures of license plates that had been run off from an old printer with a few lines missing. "We've got Lassen county, Shasta county, and up near the Oregon border…"

"Wait a minute, brother," Green murmured quietly, and reached out his hands for the printouts. "Shasta county… like maybe, say, Redding?"

Grace and the other vampires caught their breath (even though they hadn't been breathing), and I blinked, feeling as though a significant puzzle piece was just a big blank in my brain.

"Wha?"

Phillip and Marcus blew out twin breaths they hadn't needed to take and looked at each other, then at me. "We have vampires there—Rafael is the leader up in Redding."

I blinked. Well shit. Feeling like I'd forgotten to do my homework *for my entire life*, I gestured numbly for Marcus to proceed.

"He's not a bad sort," Marcus murmured, running his hands through his curly black hair. "But he's got sort of a…" Marcus grimaced, searched for the perfect word, and his mate found it for him.

"A good-old-boy mentality," Phillip supplied with a slight sneer. "A friend is a friend is a friend… a great trait in a friend, not so great in a leader."

I blinked, and fought the urge to whine *But you guys are my friends…* At one time or another, I'd done something to piss everyone in this room off. Phillip had a point—and it was sharp and jagged and it spilt blood.

"So," Green was saying, oblivious to my uncomfortable self-realization, "he's the type of bugger to shelter a mate—even if he's doing something like this?"

Phillip nodded absolutely, but Marcus shifted and shook his head. "He won't be happy about it," Marcus said thoughtfully. "And he's probably tried measures to make it stop. No—if he knows about it, it's simply gotten out of hand and he doesn't know what to do about it."

"What if he doesn't?" Nicky asked. "Know about it, I mean."

I let out a whistle. "That's bad too."

Everybody looked at me, and I shrugged. "Hey—if someone walked into my turf and told me that one of you needed to be put down, I *might* let them live long enough to hear their reasons why."

There were nods, but then Grace spoke up, my mother-defender with pointy teeth and whirling eyes. "But sweetie, if one of us were doing something like this, you would have put us down before anyone had to tell you it needed to be done."

I scrubbed my face with my hands and fought the clenching in my stomach against the dinner I'd just finished. She was right, but it didn't feel like a good thing.

"So what do we do?" I asked randomly. "I assume Hallow will let us know if Fields steps up his activity—and until we know his contacts and where his computer files and prints have been sent, none of us can kill him, or we'll suddenly be put on the expose' pages. But this other thing… we can run up to Redding on a weekend—hell—right after finals, next week…"

"No," Green interrupted ruminatively. He looked at me and shook his head. "No, luv—not a quickie. You remember the werewolves this winter?"

I blinked and nodded—we'd had sort of a 'royal parlay' that had ended in both triumph and disaster. The original plan, though, had been to do it up right. Pick up from the airport, big dinners (it happened the week after Thanksgiving... we were just sort of going to turn it into a big long party,), a tour of the digs, that sort of thing. It hadn't turned out that way—there'd been blood, death, bruising, and general mayhem that had left us gobsmack in the middle of a giant turf-war over California that was still going off and on. We were lucky to be in a peaceful moment now—but the whole thing had started with us doing the King and Queen thingie as the werewolves arrived.

And suddenly the import of the question hit me.

"Oh *hell* no!" I burst out, and looked around wildly for some support. "Green—you saw what happened in November..."

"All due respect, my Lady, that had nothing to do with you," Teague said with a grimace and I waved him off.

"I suck at it," I muttered, not able to meet anybody's gaze. "I can't do the holy-queen-ship shit—guys—you've seen me!"

"What I've seen, Corinne Carol Anne op Crocken Green," said my beloved, the thunder of my real name vibrating the floorboards and making us all pay attention, "is a child barely of majority by human standards facing down an entire room full of sidhe, some of whom pre-dated the age of Roman emperors. I've seen her overcome the ultimate corruption of greed with a few drops of her blood. I've seen her cleanse the soul of innocents by a simple act of will. You *can* do the royal-queen-ship shit, and you will do it admirably," he paused and gave me a grin to take some of the formality out of his words, "if not in an entirely predictable manner."

I flushed, and looked at my hands like a guilty child. It was the only answer I had, really.

"So," Bracken asked, "when are we going to send out the entourage—and who is going to be in it?"

There was a sudden chorus of "I'm in" from around the room, and I looked at everybody sourly. "Of course you're in," I muttered, rolling my eyes. "I'm going to suck so bad at this, you could probably charge admission."

"Wouldn't miss it for the world, luvie," said Lambent smugly across the room, "but where and when are we going exactly?"

"When?" I turned searching eyes towards Green. "How long will this last, beloved? A week? Two? Three?"

"I don't know," he murmured quietly, seeing where I was going with this.

Finals let us out right up to the first day of June. "And whatever happens, there may have to be some follow up…it could take up a bit of your summer."

"I need…" I swallowed, uncomfortable even though everybody in the room knew why this was so. "*We* need to be here during Litha, and a few days after."

Bracken went still next to me, and Green's breath fanned my temple in the silence.

"Of course," Green murmured, and at my feet, Nicky shifted uncomfortably.

"Did you think we would make you work on our anniversary?" he asked, trademark impudence in place.

I ruffled his hair, and stopped and squeezed his hand when it grasped mine.

"I was worried for a minute," I teased, and, moved our twined hands to his cheek. He hadn't even known Adrian, and he was comforting me. How could you not treasure Nicky?

"As for where," Green said, trying to crisp up the atmosphere, "we own some vacation cabins out at Lake Shasta. We can rent a boat, you all can make a holiday out of it…"

"And we can invite Nicky's parents, so they can come meet Cory and get off his back!" Bracken supplied excitedly, and as I blinked in surprise, Nicky said "Fuck you, brother," and Green covered his eyes with his hands.

"Oh shit," Bracken murmured in complete horror. "I am such a fucking asshole."

Nicky released my hand to bury his face from the rest of the world and I used it to cover my mouth as horrified giggles escaped me.

"Jesus Humphrey Christ, beloved!" I managed to gasp. "You could always shuck his shorts and make him streak around the campus—it would probably have felt better, you know?"

Bracken was hiding his face in his hands. "I know…I know I know I know… Christ, Nicky, I'm sorry."

Nicky's shoulders were shaking with horrified laughter, and I felt a breeze around the room as I bent and wrapped my arms around his shoulders and buried my face in the hollow of his shoulders. When I looked up from behind him, the room had cleared out, and it was only the four of us, the ever-shifting balance of protons and neutrons that made up our little family nucleus.

Nicky's laughter faded, and we were left in the aftermath of Bracken's little emotional bomb.

"When were you going to tell us?" I asked into the silence. "I mean… I'll be honest, Nick—I knew it was your parents, because you can't keep too much of a secret around here, but I didn't know it was about meeting them."

Nicky shook his head and rested it on his knees, and I slid off the couch to sit on the floor next to him. Green did the same on his other side, and I wasn't too surprised when Bracken slid in right behind him and spooned him, sheltering our most fragile proton with the mass of his shoulders. I had found them, sleeping in our bed, pajamas on, cuddling like children this morning—Nicky was ours, all of ours, enough Bracken's for Brack's dumbassed thoughtlessness to hurt.

"I'm fine," Nicky choked unconvincingly. "Really, I'm fine—I just...I'm so embarrassed! You guys—I can't bring them to the hill, to where I live, because they're so dumb and so redneck that Green would have to brainfuck them to let them leave!"

I took his hand and leaned my head on his shoulder. "Honey, they can't be worse than my parents, can they?"

Nicky's look was eloquent, and I had to laugh.

"Okay, okay... well, as much as a dumbshit as Bracken was about it..."

"I'm so sorry, I suck at secrets..." Bracken moaned, and Nicky patted his big hands where they wrapped around his chest.

"... he probably had a good idea. We carry off two things here—we do the visiting royalty gig with the Redding vampires, and we do a meet and greet with your mom and dad. Green won't be there," I tried not to whine, "so they won't get to see our best face,"

"Stop it," Green murmured, and I rolled my eyes and continued.

"But they will get to see us. They can meet me, meet Bracken—see that we're not some sort of... freak-show, that sucked you into our evil clutches, okay?"

Nicky looked at me and grinned shakily. "That's exactly what I was thinking," he said gratefully, and we bumped shoulders in the confines of our little group hug in perfect companionship.

"Uhm, Nick—do you want to invite Eric?" I asked after a moment. He really loved Eric—Eric was his Bracken, his lover for him and only him. I know that I wouldn't have been happy if my parents had never met Bracken (or Nicky for that matter, but especially Green and Bracken.)

Nick looked at me again, this time leaning away from me to where Green was offering a comforting shoulder as well.

"You know I'm more gay than straight?" he said after a quiet moment, and I blinked at the phrasing.

"I guess so, yeah." I mean, it had occurred to me that, given his one choice of a lover had been male that maybe he swung that way more than he thought but, "We really don't, you know, put shit in those words here."

Nicky nodded. "We don't here—but I've had to, talking to mom and dad. I... I don't think I could stand it, if they were as awful to Eric as I think they're going to be to you and Bracken. You guys… you're my leaders, too. I'd fight for you to the death, even if I wasn't sleeping with you, and I think they'd get that. But Eric… he's… he's my beloved, you know? If I still want them in my life after this summer, I'll introduce them to Eric, but…"

"But you want to protect him, because you can't protect us," Green said gently, and Nicky raised their now twined fingers to his lips and kissed them.

"I love you all so much," he said at last, his voice a little choked. "You… my life could have sucked so badly, after we got bound. But it's really wonderful. I want you to know that I love you, even Bracken you loose-lipped asshole, and that I'm so grateful you're willing to do this for me…"

He was getting all choked and misty and I didn't know what to do for him or say for him, so Bracken hugged him tighter and Green stroked his hair, and I sat there and leaned my head on his shoulder, and together, we were the family we'd forged so strongly in the past year and a half.

"We love you too, Nicky," I said softly, and those were the only words in the room for a while.

That night was a group bed night… we just sort of melted from our hug on the floor to mine and Bracken's room, a way to reassure Nicky, to cement our peculiar, many-faceted and strange relationship. Bracken made slow, urgent love to me, and Green and Nicky did a similar thing next to us, and then Nicky and I were rolled together in the center and surrounded by big, strong sidhe men who pattered our backs with kisses and stroked our hair from our faces as we drifted off to sleep.

I saw Nicky's eyes, glistening a little in the moonlight and took his hands between my breasts and kissed his knuckles. "We love you, sweetheart," I said softly, "but I think this sort of thing is a little hard to explain to mom and dad."

Nick's sleepy grin was watery, but sound. "We don't have to explain this," he murmured, back-spooning into Green's lovely warmth. "As long as we know it ourselves, no one has to know this but us."

It was a good way to close out the night—and a very good thing he knew his own mind before the whole thing cymbal-crashed the way it ended up doing. There's a surprising strength and a surprising wisdom in Nicky. I'm so glad he's ours.

BRACKEN

Knight's Restraint

Goddammit. We were *this* fucking close to getting out of school without meeting up with the revolting cockroach responsible for so much angst.

As it was, I barely escaped killing him.

Cory is not allowed alone at school—she's peripherally aware of this, but she has no idea how tightly our day is orchestrated around not even letting her go to the bathroom without Renny in attendance, to make sure she's not ambushed.

The entire reason we continued to let Jack come with us to school was to facilitate this. He was one more person on campus who could take one more class that didn't fit on everybody else's schedule. It was the only reason Cory got to take poly-sci when she seemed to feel she needed it to help Green in the first place, and the only reason Jack got to take poly-sci when he definitely needed it for his degree next spring. I had the feeling that Green and Hallow had done a complicated dance of their own so that our schedules would mesh as well as they did.

So when I'd forgotten my backpack at Hallow's, I sent her ahead to the class with Jack, and ran irritably back towards the row of offices in the crappy old English building across from Douglas Hall.

As I entered the glass doors and rounded the corner to the hallway, I barreled into a squat little man with a comb-over, thick glasses, and a scrubbed-shiny face, pink as a baby's, with jowls and a pudgy chin.

He bounced off my chest and looked up at me in startlement, and then the most abhorrent smile crossed his face.

"I know you," he crooned, and I blinked. We hadn't been told what Fields looked like, but this little man was wrapped in polyester and stinking of sweat and too much cologne. The thought of him touching Green made me want to vomit.

"You know nothing about me," I growled, and made to pass him. He was obviously coming from Hallow's, and since he wasn't in the office and I needed to be, I may as well get what I came for.

"I know what I don't get," he said with a leer, and I knew I'd regret it, but I turned to him anyway.

"What's that?" Ugh... could I not just keep this short?

"Why her? Man...you guys—I don't know what you look like really, but in person, you've got it going on!" He talked excitedly, with his hands making random, useless gestures and his pudgy little face squinching up. His eyes practically disappeared in his squint. "If I looked like you, I'd be screwing some high class women! Why do all of you gather around her like she's some hot-shit queen bee or something! I mean, you should *see* what this professor guy is willing to do to protect her—it's got to be illegal in half the sta..."

He couldn't finish, because my hand was around his throat and his little legs were kicking their shiny shoes against the cinderblock of the old wall of the English building, and his face was turning purple.

I heard a 'meep' behind me and realized that we had company, so I dropped him abruptly, but kept my hand suspended three inches above his heart. I glared power at the perky young woman in the mini-skirt and the bleached hair who had spotted us, and she clapped a hand to her head with a whine—wonderful. Wiped memory and instant migraine, and I couldn't bring myself to feel sorry for her.

"Do you have any other observations to make about my beloved, Mr. Fields?" I asked, wanting an excuse to suck his heart out of his chest with my blood-power alone. "Would you like to call her plain? Perhaps comment on her lack of breeding? By all means, tell me she wasn't worth sacrificing my immortality for. Because right now, I'm holding my temper by a thread...all I need..." I punctuated by tugging at the throbbing in his chest with my power, and I watched as his face turned white and a little trickle of blood came to the corner of his mouth, "all I really desire at this moment," tug, "is an excuse," tug, "to cut," tug, "that," tug, "thread."

I let go of him and stepped back, smiling a little as he fell to his knees and coughed blood onto his short-sleeved, pointy-collared shirt.

"Just..." he coughed, "tell me why her! I'm trying to write a story here and she makes shitty copy. Why her?"

"Because," I said, looking down on him without any pity at all, "she would kill you to spare me the foulness of your sweat. You're a fool if you don't love a woman like that. You're a fool if you think glory or fame will replace her."

I went to turn away and almost ran over Hallow, who was looking at the revolting little cockroach with a pained expression on his face.

"Bracken," he muttered, "you couldn't just walk on past him, could you?"

"He insulted her," I said stonily. "Nobody talks that way about her."

Hallow's eyebrows meet his hairline, and his expression as it centered on the irritating human was all disgust. "Nolan, we tolerate you, do you understand me?"

Nolan Fields' eyes widened as they fell on Hallow, and Hallow's expression was all theatre—I'd seen it in humans who liked to wear leather and chains in bed, and I was not fond of those games at all. "Yes, Professor," he said eagerly, bending his head and averting his eyes.

I fought the urge to make a gagging gesture, because that would spoil the game, and asked politely if I could get my backpack from the office. Hallow rolled his eyes and sneered at the little man who was, for all intents and purposes, groveling at our feet.

"Nolan, I tire of you. Leave us."

The flirty little leer that writhed across Fields' face almost made me gag for real, but he picked up the briefcase I'd made him drop and simpered down the hallway.

Sometimes, my beloved's vernacular bleeds through.

"Gross," I said, with feeling.

"Too nice and yet too true," Hallow quoted, leading the way down the hall to his office, and I grimaced.

"What *is* it with you people and that play?" I asked rhetorically, but I knew. It was all about leadership and what not to do—sort of the anti-handbook for effective faerie hill administration.

Hallow knew I knew, so he didn't even bother to answer as I grabbed my pack (which was weighted down with seven tons of her stuff that she didn't know I snuck out of her pack as the day revolved—she may think she's healthy and strong, and I certainly worried about her less, but she was still fragile and she was still mortal, and I got to carry some of her burdens, it was my privilege to do so, dammit if it wasn't!) and went to walk out the door.

An unsatisfied sound from Hallow stopped me, and I turned.

The elegant looking sidhe seemed to be uncomfortable—and upset.

"She won't look at me," he murmured out of nowhere, looking into outer space somewhere beyond the end of his desk, and I regretted not sucking Nolan Fields' heart out of his chest and into my hand.

"She feels like we failed you," I answered baldly, and it surprised him enough to look up.

"Goddess," he swore softly. "A year and a half, I've tried to be her counselor, and I still don't know her."

I rolled my eyes. Join the club. "She'll kill him for you," I said, knowing—I hoped—how to comfort our people.

It worked. His smile was cold and wolfish and almost gleeful as a child's.

"And that," he said happily, "is what makes it all worth it."

I grabbed my pack and bobbed my head and ran for political science. I was rather amazed that my beloved had such a hard time with this class—she seemed to have mastered the practical exam after all.

CORY
Queen Forward

Litha came and went, a celebration of the most awful hole in our souls, the gaping rip in our chests that would never stop bleeding.

Green and Bracken and I sat up top the hill that night in vigil, the one night Adrian would never be there for us, the excruciating, cathartic reminder that our beloved was really gone and that his ghost was one step removed from an illusion, conjured by our screaming hearts.

And then, like Eid after forty days of Ramadan, the next evening we strung lights across the garden, played faerie music and rock and roll until the canyon rang with it, and partied and made love and celebrated the lives we had, the precious binding that supported our hearts and our hill.

Three days later, we packed up what felt like half the hill and took off for Redding.

It was hot—blazingly, body-meltingly, skin-scorchingly, stick-to-the-upholstery-even-in-the-air-conditioning-can't-move-until-nine-at-night *hot*. The sun was a white-blinding cloud of distortion waves in a sky bleached yellow by its fury, and the entire state quailed and wilted under it's ire.

The elves don't do well in the heat.

Green and I were all charged and amped and shit before we left, so Green was able to keep the temperature on the hill somewhat tolerable for the more delicate fae, but with me gone... well, just like a lot of my power came from Green, a lot of his power was bound up in me. I liked to think that as I got older, he would be able to bind up some of that power in Nicky, so that the hill wouldn't be left completely defenseless should I die, but Green, for all his strength... whatever. I refused to think about *that* now, but I did worry.

"It's a-hundred-and-five in the shade, beloved," I said fretfully, watching as the vampire's SUV was packed during a sweaty midnight. Outside the hill, it was easily ninety-five degrees. Inside the hill, Green kept it to eighty F, but it took a toll. He'd needed to sleep as long as I had since the beginning of June, when the heat had taken over and blanketed nor-cal in a suffocation of sweat and dust.

Without me, he would be taxed to his limit—and there were so many things to maintain. The weather, the secrecy, the geas that made people forget where we were—all of it depended on Green, who, for all his greatness was just one sidhe, a one man umbrella against the broiling fury of a fucked-up Mother Nature.

"Maybe we should postpone, you think?" I didn't want to whine, but I had been dreading this for a month.

"No," he said softly, a smile on his face like he knew what I was doing.

"At least don't let me take everybody... please..."

"You're not taking any of the sidhe," he said quietly. "Only Lambent and Bracken—and Bracken would be going with you anyway. I'll be fine."

"We could leave Teague and the werewolves..." Jacky and Katy were coming, for intricate, convoluted interpersonal reasons that not even Teague could explain. It had something to do with Teague *just about* to maybe let Jacky out of his crystal box and go out on some runs, and Katy not wanting to be left behind while I go "be all ninja bitch and shit!" In short, it had something to do with the fact that Teague still hadn't completely bonded to his new family, and after some awkward conversations with Hallow, I didn't have the heart to tell them that he might never bond completely.

Apparently Green and I were his alphas... he owed his allegiance to us so completely, that it was like being married to his job. It didn't mean he loved his people any less, it just meant that (and it was so infuriatingly typically Teague!) that he needed a higher cause to find himself worthy of them. We—our little collective, Green's hill and its royalty—we were it. And so he still got involuntary hard-ons at inappropriate times (or, really, appropriate times) and no amount of us telling him to talk to them (oh gods, all the shit I'd avoided during high school!) would make it any better.

He had to tell them. They had to believe in him. It was that simple.

And now we all had to put up with their funky/hot/sexy/dysfunctional dynamic in the middle of trying to be a royal entourage.

Lovely.

Add to that, Max and Renny (because she apparently said so, dammit?), Phillip, Marcus, and Kyle, Lambent, Mario and La Mark (who were happy to be in my entourage again), and, of course, Nicky since it was *his* parents we were meeting, and, yeah. We took up three SUV's and a hearse, since the hearse was doubling as a darkling in the middle of the salted frying pan that was Shasta county in the summer.

"I don't need all these people..." I tried again. I was used to going out with one SUV worth of people—if too many wanted to go, they all did rock/scissors/paper or kick-him-in-the-shins until it was down to one vehicle. Now we were taking three SUV's and a hearse? "I mean, *Goddess*, Green—I could pack up the entire cast of Lord of the Rings in less than four cars!"

"You are the Queen of a small sized country," he said quietly, "but it's a dangerous country, and you need to look dangerous. You can't look dangerous without dangerous amounts of pageantry—you know that, luv."

"I know this is fucking ridiculous, that's what I know," I scowled. "You need us here—the weather is our enemy, and we're kiting off to some place where the weather is worse, the people hate me, and there's an entire kiss of vampires who would rather kill me than the pedophile in their midst."

"We don't know that for certain," he said reluctantly, and I pulled in my temper, because he was right. It would probably be best that I walked into a foreign kiss of vampires with an open mind. As my little exercise in menstrual chaos had proved, vampires were predatory creatures, incensed by blood. I was lucky—all of my vampires still behaved human, or at least appeared driven by human motivations and a willingness to keep their vulnerabilities in spite of their strengths. I didn't know what these vampires would be like—and I shouldn't make assumptions until I knew.

But we both knew it was a very real possibility, and that's why I hadn't grumbled about the three vampires in attendance. Grace had wanted to come too—in fact, she'd wanted to come *very* badly, but only Arturo's gentle insistence (and, I suspect, some rather spectacular moves in bed) managed to convince her that the odds of being recognized in the town she'd grown up and died in had been too great.

I was both sorry and glad he'd succeeded—if I ever needed a mother figure, it was going to be when I was facing Nicky's parents.

The very thought made my stomach churn, and Green, who had listened this past month to the things I *didn't* say, knew exactly what my sour expression meant.

"They'll adore you, luv," he murmured, bending down in the thick air of the garage and nuzzling my hair.

I think it's a tribute to how much the man loved me that he didn't bend over with cramps and sweats when he said that.

"They'll call me the whore that seduced their son," I said with pursed lips and then I glared dourly when Green burst out laughing.

"That's unlikely!" he chuckled, and I just shook my head.

"Green, these people are just like *my* parents, except my parents said 'fuck it' and made it to the wedding. This is going to be seven buckets of fugly, and about all I'm confident I can do about it is scrape Nicky back up and put him together at the end."

And there they were, my worst fears, splat out on the pavement between us. I hadn't spoken them aloud since this plan had been conceived, but something in me wouldn't let us go, wouldn't let me leave the hill unless Green knew all of my heart before I left.

He pulled me in quietly, bathed me in his blessing, let me touch is strong chest, bury my nose in the skin of his neck and comforted me with all of that love, all of that lovely confidence that I could do no wrong.

Of course I could—I mean, we both knew I could fuck this up in unfathomable ways—but he believed in me, in my intentions, and *Goddess,* if that wasn't worth giving your soul for, I don't know what is.

"I don't want to go," I said at last, childishly because the time when either of us could make that sort of decision was past.

"I know you don't."

And that was all he could give me, but it was his, so it was enough.

Green had left me a lot in the last year and a half—at least once a month he was gone from the hill for a span of days if not a week. It sucked. Really sucked.

Now I got to see it from his side of things, as we put the last goddamned thing in the last goddamned car …

You can always send the sprites if you forget something, luv.

But not yarn, Green—they won't know which one I'm talking about.

Are you really going to use all that?

Doesn't matter if I use it… what matters is that when my nerves are about to break, I have EXACTLY the project I need!!!

And suddenly I knew—knew even before they loaded me in the passenger seat and I clung to Green trying to be stoic and failing horribly, knew before Green kissed me too soundly to cry, before he kissed Nicky brief and sweet, knew before he shook hands and did the 'man embrace' with Bracken, knew just then, at that conversation, that leaving was worse than staying.

Leaving wasn't just leaving Green, it was leaving home, leaving every reminder of Green, the smell of his clothes, the knowledge of his room just down the hall from mine, the grove we had created with Adrian…

Leaving was leaving everything I loved except the people I took with me.

And Green left without me and Nicky all the time.

Sucked for him—sucked for us all.

I heaved a sigh that threatened to sink the car into the pavement and looked over at Bracken. He was driving, and there was something in his face as we cruised through the night, the silver canyon to our left and the hard face of the filleted hill to our right. His lean mouth was parted slightly, and his lips curved up. His pond-shadow eyes were wide in the starlight, and his face thrust forward eagerly.

Bracken was enjoying this.

I blinked.

"You've never been beyond San Francisco, have you?" I asked curiously, and Bracken, with his great size and great heart, flashed a child's grin at me, all eagerness and excitement.

"No," he said with a smile. "You?"

I had, actually—LA, Oregon, Canada—school trips, camping with parents. It didn't make me a world traveler—in fact, it had mostly made me want to get farther away. Funny, because now a simple trip to Redding felt like exile.

"Didn't Adrian take you to Redding?" I asked with a little smile.

Bracken shook his head. I couldn't be sure in the dim light, but I think he flushed. "You have to understand—when we were...uhm...exclusive, I was barely old enough to be let out of Green's hill. And even when everybody lightened up a little bit… well, Adrian said that if two men walked down the street in Redding touching like we'd touch, they wouldn't need to be non-human to be chased by pitchforks and torches."

I grinned at him. "Sort of like now," I said brightly, and he shrugged.

"Since I'm probably not going to be touching any men in public this time round, I don't think it will be a problem," he stated with a lift of his eyebrows and a quirk of his lips, and I laughed.

"So you're excited to go," I marveled, and his grin lit up the inside of the car.

"It's an adventure," he said simply, and much of my misery fell away.

"We do okay on adventures," I said, thoughtfully. Behind us, Nicky shifted a little from his spot in the middle of the car, so deep in his ipod and his own thoughts that it was unlikely he even knew we were talking. Max and Renny were taking the wayback, and they were having a soft conversation I couldn't hear.

"We do fucking fabulous," my beloved said with a smile.

"And we do fabulous fucking," I told him, because he'd given me a sweet set-up and he wanted to hear me happy.

We crossed the Foresthill bridge then. It's terrifying height and double lane span looked alien and fragile in the moonlight: a green-metal spiderweb, to transport steel scarab beetles. I plugged my i-Pod into the sound system and looked at Bracken. He didn't need music to stay awake at this odd hour, and he was driving.

"Preferences?" I asked, thinking I'd like to hear some old redneck rock, myself.

"VanHalen," replied my beloved, reading my mind as he did so often. I loved his stone-and-shadow eyes in the moonlight—they promised mystery and magic and they always delivered.

I whirled my finger around the controls and settled the thing in its holder just as Eddie's first syncopated notes filled the car.

C'mon baby finish what we started… all right then.

After you passed Sacramento and took the sharp V-turn up the state, much of I-5 looks like some idiot put a ruler between Sacramento and Redding, drew a straight line and said "Og put road THERE!"

Much of the road was a simple straight shot between two points, through big square-cut acres of farmland and horse country and big flat expanses. Nope, not a curve or hardly a hill in sight—straight as a Kansas virgin. Which is why I got to drive.

People haul *ass* on the road to Redding. We stopped for gas about a half-an-hour after Sacramento, and after loading up on quickie-mart-cuisine, (because, you know, you can't get enough Diet Coke and Reese's Peanut Butter Cups EVER!) I parked myself behind the wheel, put the ipod on some Drop Kick Murphys and AC/DC, and took hold of our little convoy for the next two hours.

It wasn't my fault that Bracken picked Coldplay as we were crossing the causeway over the lake.

Lake Shasta sits about sixty miles from Mount Shasta—which is so damned big that you can see it as you drive up that last stretch, giant curves scything through the darkness.

The mountain itself was a brooding, almost frightening presence. There were old Native American myths permeating the region—my least favorite of which was that of a double eruption between Lassen and Shasta, which the natives imagined as two angry gods, hurling fire at each other through the blackness of night. I really hated the idea of them doing that while the terrified natives huddled in the valley in the middle, begging the gods for mercy. Something about all of that raw power, assaulting itself regardless of the cost to the weaker beings around it—well, it pissed me off. Mount Shasta looked like an enemy in the distance—a big seething bad-guy, something I could hate with impunity.

The lake… well, the lake was something special.

I'd say it looked like an amoeba… but amoebas have more cohesion. The lake was the result of a dammed up volcanic valley, and the water filling up the deep crevices of the twisted hills around it took the shape of a branching tree root—a thousand little tree-hair inlets, and none of them had a beach to speak of.

The lake itself was narrow—there wasn't a place on one side where you couldn't see the other. I was pretty sure the water looked green in the sunlight—lots of red dirt underneath to make the color opaque—but at night, coming across the causeway, it looked like black glass—something unholy and primordial. You could hide big slimy dinosaurs in that lake, and no one would know until they thrust their necks out in the moonlight—and then disappeared.

Hearing the chilly music of Coldplay as we crossed that black water and wound our way to the mountain road that led to the lakeside cabins made me suddenly aware that adventures were exciting because they were often dangerous.

The road got skinnier and skinnier, and I was both grateful and frustrated by the dark—on the one hand, it was harder to see, but on the other, the likelihood of meeting someone else on the wrong side of that tiny, twisting road was considerably less at four thirty a.m.. I would have stopped and let Bracken drive but…

"Just keep your eyes on the road and I'll keep my eyes on the dawn," Bracken muttered, one hand on his cell phone. According to the almanac, we had forty-five minutes until sunrise, but when you're in a strange place, and you don't know where the sun will hit or where to put the car…

It was nerve wracking to say the least.

"We should have left earlier," I muttered, but the sun hadn't set until nearly eight-thirty, and we'd wanted the vampires to be well-fed before we left. We were taking enough were-creatures to feed the troops, but so much of interacting with another kiss of vampires depended on being level-headed—nobody wanted a stomach growling for blood to trigger a turf war if we were surprised. Besides—packing took longer than I think even Green anticipated.

Bracken didn't reply to me anyway—his body was on full alert so if I had to stop the car he could run back and take over for the vampires while they safed up in the special floor of the SUV or the hearse.

The line of quaint, well-kept cabins appeared beneath the horizon of a vertigo-dip in the road, and for a moment it looked like the car would just drop off into the lake.

It didn't and I wrestled the damn thing down a slippery gravel hill. The whole convoy of cars skidded to a halt in front of the manager's office, where one of Green's people was waiting for us, cracking her gum and watching late-night TV.

She/he must have been a sylph *planning* to be a 'she' when she bonded, but I didn't think that had happened yet.

It's not everyday you see someone with a boy's flat chest in a tight girl's tank-top and a miniskirt, with barbell-pierced nipples protruding through the thin white ribbing of the tank. She also had thick mascara and heavily gelled hair, long glittery nails, and high heels—at the crotch of dawn, no less.

But for all her spectacular appearance, she smiled happily at us as we pulled up, cracked her gum and introduced herself as Tanya, and then ran to help us unload the gear into the vampires' room. (Yes—they got their own room, even if they wouldn't be sleeping in it. Marcus and Phillip were a couple, for one thing, and for another, nobody likes to actually 'live out of their car'.)

"I hope this is all of you," she said cheerily, "We had an unexpected sign in, yesterday and all of the cabins will be filled." She threw what was easily two-hundred pounds of gear on her slender shoulders and helped us schlep stuff in. The vamp's SUV was first, of course, and then we'd all unload into our own cabin room.

"All?" Uh-oh. Green had told me that we'd be alone.

Tanya dumped the gear in the open door and I walked in with my (considerably smaller) load. Jack and Teague were behind me, each of them with as much as the sylph had, and I rolled my eyes and sighed. Well, considering the effect of cold iron in the hill, lifting weights was right out.

That took care of the vampire's stuff, and Marcus, Phillip, and Kyle rushed in quickly, wanting to take showers, I think, before dawn.

"Be careful, guys!" I called, and they all grunted reassurances as I closed their door.

I trotted back to the SUV and wiped my forehead on my sleeve. In spite of the fact that the sky was barely turning gray it was already around 85 F outside—ugh.

"So this other family…" I asked delicately, and Tanya shrugged.

"A mom, her teenaged son."

"Uh-oh…" My memories of teenaged boys were not fond ones.

Tanya wrinkled her nose. "Kid's a major perv—couldn't get him to stop ogling my bitty-tits, and I think he actually tried to cop a feel of one of the studs…"

"Ouch!"

Tanya flashed a grin. She'd had a little diamond insert put on one of her front teeth—she could pull it off, too. "Felt better than I thought—but not from a teenager." She shivered. "Perv oogies—big time. But other than that, he seems pretty content to swim and boat and listen to his brain-sucker—I don't think he'll give you any trouble."

I shrugged—the only people who thought I was hot were the non-human men who loved me—I was probably safe from 'perv oogies' or any other sort of oogie for that matter. Being plain as a potato had it's advantages.

"I'll warn everybody—we'll try to keep the weird stuff down to a… oh for crissakes!"

Because the packing was over and Renny and Jack had walked down to the little dock with it's six bobbing flat boats, shed their clothes unselfconsciously, and changed into their other forms to jump into the water.

Tanya smirked. "You were saying?"

I sighed and shrugged. "Well, in their defense, it's still mostly dark outside—and we all thought we'd be alone."

From the cabin next to mine, a shadow nosed it's way out of the doorway and trotted to the edge of the lake. Teague. Teague had scars he wouldn't want the world to see—he had changed in his room.

I knew the feeling—and as I watched Bracken strip to his pale, magnificent, naked bottom, I was feeling left out.

"I'll go change and then I'll join them," I told her. "Don't worry—I'll let them know we have to be careful."

Tanya gave me the once-over. "You're not going in naked?"

I tried not to squint at her in horror. "Druther not, no—but you're welcome if you want to jump in with."

The sylph's face lit up for a moment. "Shining ones…"she whispered. "We have so few elves, up here, you understand?"

I nodded. "But don't get too close to Bracken—we've got a geas, sort of."

She shook her head. "I can't get too close to any of them… but there's so few of my kind up here… it would be wonderful to just…" her tongue came out, pink and helpless—and studded-- and she licked her lower lip. "It would be nice to just be."

I nodded and smiled. "Feel free—but… you know that party that's coming tomorrow?"

She nodded.

"They're shifters, but… well, maybe not Green's people."

Tanya nodded. She knew what that meant. "It's all good—I'll have you all for a week. It will be like vacation for me too."

I nodded, satisfied, and trotted off to change.

When I got to the little cabin, squat and painted a cheery green and brown, I finally got a chance to look inside.

It was like a hotel room, but a little more cushy. The bed was huge—

biggest King-sized they had, I reckoned, and maybe even a little bigger. It was covered in a cotton quilt instead of one of those sticky, nylon things, and it appeared to have fine cotton sheets underneath. The walls were rough wood for effect, and the whole cabin was done in rust and olive and crème. Not my favorite colors, so much, but still pleasant and rustic. There was an oaken table with four chairs in the corner with wifi near the plug in outlet and notepaper and pens.

We could plug in the ipod speaker/charger—excellent!

With that, I started rifling through my luggage, looking for my suit—it didn't seem to be on top, but I found what looked like one of Renny's bikinis in the bottom. Too small, I thought with a roll of the eyes, and then I gave it up, shucked my jeans and put on some cotton running shorts and an old tank top over my black sports bra.

It's not like anyone in the water would give a rat's ass anyway.

I got to the bottom of the hill and to the water's edge and, leaving my flip-flops at the water's edge in spite of the rough bottom, stuck a cautious toe in the water…

And jerked it back with a shiver.

"Are you people insane?" I called to the group of bobbing heads—some furry, some just wet—about twenty feet away.

"There's a drop-off!" Nicky called. "You'd better go in all at once!"

"It's fucking freezing!" I called back. "I'm waiting for some sunlight!"

"It gets better," Tanya told me, walking up by my side. She was wearing a one piece cut high at the skinny hips in bright lime green. Man, I loved this chick's style. "And you're not going to want to swim in the height of the sun for too long—complexion like yours, unless you've got a shitload of sunblock, you're going to crisp up like your guys in cabin four."

The vampires. "Nice!" I smirked with rolled eyes, and she laughed.

"Where's your suit?" Bracken asked, coming to the edge of the drop off and standing up. The water came to his stomach, but by the way he was balancing, it looked like one slipped step and he'd fall off the edge.

"I couldn't find it," I muttered. "It looked like Renny's got put in by mistake." Gingerly, I toed my way around the edge of the lake to the dock, which bounced pleasingly underneath my feet. Squinting at the water was useless—I couldn't see the drop-off in the pre-dawn light so I used Bracken as a guide and walked about five feet beyond him, and backed up the width of the dock.

Brack saw me and raised his eyes and grinned. "Going in balls out, huh?"

I grinned back. "Is there any other way?" Besides. Everyone knew it sucked worse going in slow. With that, I took a deep breath and two quick steps and a leap.

The water was *exquisitely* cold, cold enough to stop my breath, to make be gasp and shriek when I struggled my way to the surface, cold enough to make me struggle a little and flail when Bracken came up behind me to make sure I wouldn't drown.

His strong arms came around my shoulders, full of their residual heat, and I calmed down and shivered in his grasp.

"Whew!" I scooted away from him and treaded dark water alone. There was a bump under my arm and Renny thrust her head under my grasp. "You want me to ride you, puss? Are you insane?" She gave the cat equivalent of a chuckle, and Max came around under my other armpit, and the two of them began to churn the water with their padded paws.

Now, tabby cats can actually be very effective swimmers—and full-grown tigers really love the water. Max and Renny were no exception, and they moved so fluidly—like really big platypuses--that pretty soon we were nearly in the middle of the lake.

It was both one of the coolest and one of the creepiest moments of my life.

Being in water is… wonderful. Water—even water that stains your clothes red with iron ore, cleanses your body and your spirit. Water this cold when the day was this warm and promising hells to come, well it practically cascaded under your skin, made it's own little healing spa for your capillaries, bathed everything about you in fresh.

I let my body be pulled through that cold loveliness and closed my eyes, smelling cool red dirt, pine trees, fresh water, clean dust, and then I opened them and saw that flat black water.

And felt panic explode into my throat like a grenade.

For a minute I was too frightened to move, which is good, because it kept me from drowning in the middle of a cold alien lake surrounded by friends. I couldn't see my feet. I was in water with an infinite bottom, any number of horrible things could be beneath me and *I couldn't see my feet.*

I had a scar around my ankle, thick, white, and jagged from one of the horrible things that could grab you when you *couldn't see your feet.*

My companionable arm around the two giant cats on either side of me tightened suddenly, and when Renny whined, I managed to keep my voice reasonably free of skull-frying panic.

"Uhm, Renny…sweetheart…any way you could get me back to where I could touch?"

I couldn't close my eyes on the way back, because if I did, the vision of that bony hand with the rotting flesh stripping away from it clenched behind my eyes. I concentrated instead on the sudden chill as the air dipped to almost eighty degrees, and the darkened green treetops shattered into gold.

"Pretty," I grunted, and then I thanked them for the ride when I felt the slimy/rocky bottom underneath my foot.

The werewolves were playing water tag, Lambent was swimming, seal-like, so far lengthwise down the lake that I could barely see him. La Mark, Mario, Nicky and Bracken were chatting companionably with Tanya and treading water about twenty feet from where my wet feline taxi dropped me off.

I stood gratefully on wobbly knees and padded on tender feet to my flip-flops. When I got there I turned and called to Bracken, hoping I looked normal and calm and everything the lot of them needed me to be when we were in a strange place with strange people and possible enemies facing us down.

"I'm gonna go shower," I called, and tried not to wince when my voice cracked on 'gonna'. "Have everyone meet me in about half an hour."

Bracken looked at me oddly but nodded, and I shivered my way back to the cabin, dripping lake water off my cotton clothes, down my legs and leaving puddles of red-dirt pudding behind me as I walked.

Twenty minutes later I was clean and fresh, unpacking into the rough-hewn dresser and chatting with Green on my charging cell phone. I carefully didn't mention my embarrassing little 'episode', but told him we'd gotten there safely and filled him in on my plans for the day.

"Plans?" he laughed. "I thought you just got there?"

But Bracken and I had talked quietly in the car, and as I filled him in, he seemed more than impressed.

"Napoleon Bonaparte had nothing on you, beloved." His voice smiled, I thought wretchedly. How was it possible for even his voice to smile? But I didn't get sad and mushy on him, because we'd been doing this for a while, and although it never stopped sucking, we got better at putting a bright face on the suckage, because moping just made it suck harder.

I didn't get a chance to answer anyway. Bracken and Nicky came in then, and they would have been sopping wet, but they'd been wandering around naked, and I remembered I had something else to talk to the family about, and I had to ring off.

But first, "Green—do you remember putting the bathing suit we ordered in the suitcase?"

He 'hmmmmm'd evasively. "I remember putting the bathing suit *I* ordered in the suitcase," and even as he said it, a big read flag popped up in my head. However, Bracken was demanding to know where the hell I'd put his cargo shorts as he soaped his hair in the shower. I tamped down on a less than polite—and less than truthful—answer/anatomical description, and sighed. "I've got to go, beloved," I murmured, getting out of Nicky's way as he rooted around the drawers. "Apparently I put everything away all wrong."

"Why didn't you let the sprites do it, beloved?" he asked in long suffering tones, and I flopped limply across the bed. Well, wasn't I becoming quite the control freak?

"My bad," I mumbled. "I'll remember next time. I still have to go—love you lots?"

"Love you forever," he murmured back, and because he was Green, that meant all the comfort I needed.

I still stayed on the bed, partly because I was feeling pensive, and partly because it got me out of the way. Brack hopped out of the shower and Nicky hopped in, and in that weirdly quick way that I'm starting to think has to do with gender more than species, he seemed to be dressed almost instantly. With a little leap and a spring, he landed on the bed next to me, and I smiled a little and rolled into him, because hey, touching him never got old.

"You okay?" he asked, picking up on my mood. I tried and failed to smile brightly, and he frowned and bumped my shoulder with his instead. "What happened out in the water by the way?"

I don't know what I was going to say as I opened my mouth, but it didn't matter, because there was a perfunctory knock at the door and Max and Renny walked in, and I scrambled to sit up on the bed to greet them.

Max had on shorts, but Renny was the way the Goddess likes her children best, and I groaned. "Didn't Tanya tell you?"

Renny looked at me with the even, unblinking gaze of a contemptuous housecat. "So?" she asked. "The civilians are still sleeping." She gave a little wiggle and shimmy. "Besides, I *like* being naked in the mountains.

I sighed—of all the times I hated being a leader the most, dealing with Renny topped the list. She was a leader's nightmare—no one in their right mind tried to train a housecat, no king or president on the planet would place his life in the hands of a creature so fickle it couldn't even decide whether to lick its foot or the end of a twitching tail.

But she was my friend, and I did trust her with my life. Every day.

"Renny," I said firmly, "if that kid comes out of his cabin and sees you, you're going to be dealing with a teenager and a hard-on that won't quit for the rest of his life. If Nicky's parents see you, I'm going to be the skank ho with the skank ho friends, and Nicky's going to have to live with that for the rest of *our* lives. Please, for the sweet love of my foot up your ass, remember to put on some fucking clothes."

Renny stuck her tongue out at me and then opened the nearest drawer and pulled out a pair of my underwear and one of Bracken's T-shirts (that I had been planning to wear!) and got dressed.

Then she promptly turned into a cat (in my clothes!) and curled up into a little ball at the foot of the bed and went to sleep.

I looked at Max helplessly. "It's a good thing you earn your keep," I said sourly, and he eyed his wife with a grimace.

"She... uhm..."

I shook my head. "Yeah. That's all I got too."

And then the werewolves walked in, Katy's musical accent pattering in rapid-fire nag as they did.

"I don' care if you got work to do, Daddy, you don't talk to her, you don't look at her, she just furniture to you..."

I blinked. Jack was a jealous bastard all the time, but Katy?

"Katy," Jack was placating, "she runs around naked all the time at the hill..."

And now Bracken and I both looked at each other and blinked. Katy was jealous of *Renny?*

"Katy, I thought you *liked* Renny!" I protested even as they walked in, and Katy blinked like a sleepwalker.

"I do!" she said, surprised, and to prove it, bent down to scratch the ears of a very puzzled giant pussycat. I think Renny's confusion was the only thing that kept us from the cat/dog match-up to end all wars.

Totally befuddled we all turned to Teague, who turned red to his ears, widened his eyes, and shrugged. That helped. And then the Avians walked in, followed by Tanya, and we officially had a party in the big-kid's room. Oh well, my turn to talk.

I pulled my legs up so I was sitting cross-legged, and outlined the plan.

"You all know Nicky's parents get here tonight, right?" Nods all around. "So the night after tomorrow, we go meet up with the vampires—they don't know we're coming, or at least, they don't know we're all going to descend on Rafael's bar en masse. Today, I want to take Nicky and Bracken and scope out the bar and the surroundings—recon, I guess."

"We're coming with you," Mario said immediately, but Teague was close on his heels.

"Guys," I shook my head, "we're not even getting out of the car, or," I amended with a grunt from Bracken, "we're not getting out of the car after we stop at the store." The units all had mini-fridges—we were stopping for yoghurt, cheese, soda, peanut butter, jelly, fruit... whatever. Grace would probably arrange to have the sprites beam in some dinner, and there was a strip about five miles away with some fast food, but we were on our own for food. I looked at the mass of faces around me and thought we'd probably need two carts. Renny sneezed, and I remembered that most of us were shapeshifters with killer metabolisms. Make that three.

"So anyway, tell me if you want anything special, and we'll get it. But you can't come because while we're out there, I've got a job for all of you."

Ears perked up, and figurative tails waved and twitched. Mario and La Mark shifted where they stood in like hawks on a perch, and Lambent leaned forward on his chair with clasped hands between his knees. I hadn't realized we were itching for action—I'd been enjoying the peace.

I laughed a little, and ran my hands through my hair, stopping to re-do my ponytail when it came out.

"It's not *that* exciting, people—all I really want you to do is take a piss!" That got me a few raised eyebrows, and I laughed some more and elaborated.

The thing was, after the attack of the vampire critters from hell, I didn't want to deal with anything else 'wild kingdom' style in our area—not by accident and not by design. Besides that, we had been dealing with frequent threats from the were community in Southern California since Thanksgiving. Teague, Bracken and I had somewhat put those threats to rest, but you never knew when shit like that would pop up, so mostly, I wanted more recon.

More specifically, I wanted recon with urine markers all around our half of the lake. I figured the causeway would be a good cut-off line—the lake on our side of the freeway was ours, and the other side of the lake belonged to all of the other wild animals *without* day jobs.

It would take all five of the furry people a couple of hours—even running with Goddess speed, and it would take Mario and La Mark up in the sky and coordinating with Lambent, in a flat boat in the lake, to get it done. For one thing, when the critters were run out, they needed to be able to hop in the water and have some place to rest. They needed to avoid the shore line—because there was a gazillion miles of it, with a gazillion little tiny root-hair like inlets—and concentrate on a rough half circle around the lake itself, and they needed to avoid actual humans. There were caves on the other side of the lake, and hiking trails and a gazunga things that could go wrong and...

"Beloved?" Bracken called me to myself with a little smile before I could truly go off into the stratosphere with my fears. He was right—I would have to trust them to do their jobs.

"In short, people," I finished with, "if I'm a satellite up in the heavens, I want to see a mass exodus of bob-cats, bear-cats, and pole-cats scratching their pits on the way out of Dodge, you got me?" Everyone nodded. "If you don't think you can finish, though, don't push it. We'll be here for a week, minimum, and it's supposed to get to be a bajillion degrees today..."

"Is that real math, Cory, or did you just make that up to make us feel sweatier?"

I stopped in the middle of my nagging, and blinked at Mario, who was looking at me with a quirked mouth and guileless brown eyes.

"Don't look now, people, I think Mario just made a funny," I retorted dryly, and I didn't let him dissuade me from one final nag. "And don't forget we've got civilians in the last cabin… and after tonight, we're going to have Nicky's parents…"

"Who are probably worse than civilians," Nicky warned, saying his first piece of the day. I nodded in concession—if Nicky said they were going to suck, I'd believe him. People hadn't believed me about my mother until she'd barged her way into our bedroom. Did I mention it was awkward? Well let me mention it again.

"So whether you're done or not, we want to wrap this up in a couple of hours. By the time you get back, we should be back with the food and the skinny on the vampires, and we can have lunch here before we nap." None of us had slept the night before—with the weight of the heat, even the elves would be tired by the time we were done, so I got no arguments about the nap.

Everybody stood up to go, and I managed to snag Renny before she padded out next to Max (who had stripped and changed form so easily it was hard to remember when he'd been the highly uptight cop out to make my life miserable two years ago!) and made her take off my clothes before she pissed all over them and/or dragged them through sixty stages of brushfire hell.

"What's wrong with you?" I asked in exasperation. "You haven't been this feline since San Francisco!"

Renny blinked, much as Katy had, and wrinkled her nose, even as she shucked my T-shirt and panties. "There's a smell here," she said dreamily. "A wild smell." And then she was a giant cat again, and following her mate out the door.

I stared after her for a moment with an open mouth. If anyone would know about a 'wild smell' it would be Renny, who was more in touch with her wildness than most real cats. The question was, what kind of smell? Real? Imagined? Organic? Magic? Unfortunately for me, the thing that made Renny so in touch with the smell, also made her the least articulate person on the planet. If she said there was a smell, I'd believe her—but I wouldn't get her to name a flower from flatulence without a *lot* of effort.

I looked up at Bracken. "Did you hear that, baby? There's a wild smell out there."

"Well," said Bracken, returning my bemusement, "considering that we just told a bunch of human-sized wild animals to go piss in the woods, I think it's about to get a lot more pungent."

I laughed, but I could tell we were both a little unsettled. It didn't matter—we still had shit to do, and the temperature was climbing with every breath.

Redding is not a large town. It was larger than Loomis or Penryn or Ophir (which mostly consist of one 'historic main street' apiece, built along the railroad with various shops grown up around it) and it seemed to cover a lot of hot, windblown territory, but mostly, it looked to be a bunch of car dealerships, some hotels, and a *really* big Wal-Mart.

I know I wasn't seeing the best of the town at all. I understand that it has a museum, and in our wanderings we even caught glimpse of a lovely park and some riverfront businesses that looked a little too swank for me, in my shorts, T-shirt, and flip-flops. I hoped, at some point in time, to visit Turtle Bay, and the arboretum—and even, to get a better look at that really cool sundial thing that seemed to cross the Sacramento river off of hwy 273—but that wasn't what we were looking for, and it wasn't what we saw this time out. So Redding may have been a 'bustling metropolis' of 70,000 people (or so the sign said), but my first impression of heat and wind and of brown space out beyond the manicured green spaces of the homes on the little residential streets could never be fully re-imagined.

As in most small towns (and most big ones, for that matter) if you wandered the backside of the business streets, you would find the not-so-swank places.

These were the sorts of places vampires and shapeshifters loved.

It didn't take long to find it. It was actually behind a small cluster of residential streets, backed up against the hill that surrounded Whiskeytown Lake.

"Caves, you think?" I asked Bracken as we looked at the squat, dusty brick building—I knew from experience that such buildings often seemed much bigger on the inside than the outside. This one proclaimed itself *Rafe's Place,* and even through the filtered air of the SUV, Nicky and Bracken had lifted their very astute noses and breathed in *vampire.*

Nicky made a bird's sound—a sort of affirmative squawk—and I looked behind me with amused eyes. Nicky blushed and stammered, "That was supposed to be a 'yes'—I can smell something... probably underground. There're caves across the lake from us, I think it's just what happens in volcanic hills."

Bracken and I nodded—it would make sense, especially in a place with such brutal sun in the summer. Underground would be the best choice for a darkling—and the brick building with one dusty green Dodge sedan parked in front of it would be a most unexpected doorway into vampire-land.

"Hey look," Nicky pointed, "they've got karaoke the night after tomorrow!" He was laughing as he said it, but Brack's eyes narrowed.

"Hey—Nicky—run inside and get us a playlist, would you?"

"Why? Who's singing?"

Bracken looked at me and I flushed. "Oh Bracken, no…"

Brack shook his head. "It's all about making an entrance, beloved. You practice a song, ham it up on stage, mark all the rest of us as your flunkies— you'll have Rafael's attention and you won't have to…negotiate…quite as much, right?"

I shrugged, but it was clear that while I'd been worrying about Nicky's parents and naked werewolves in public, Bracken had been fretting about more important things. And the good Goddess knew that 'negotiating' was never my strongpoint. Nicky took my silence for yes and in a whoosh of oven-heated air was in and out of the car in a heartbeat, a little packet of papers ruffling in his hands on the way back.

I studied the packet on the way to Wal-Mart, and the song I should do was the topic of hot debate as we loaded up three carts with everything super hungry shape-shifters could possibly want—including *several* packets of cookies and a couple of cases of chocolate milk for Teague and beer for Teague and Max, neither of whom would have asked for such a thing even with a gun pointed to their heads.

We were almost to the checkout when I trotted off and came back with a basic green one-piece swimsuit with the cool bicycle-short bottom and a high back and neck.

Bracken eyed it with distaste. "What in the fuck is that?"

I winced. "I think we forgot the one Green ordered for me."

Bracken shook his head. "It's in there."

I rolled my eyes. "Well, we're getting this one in case you're wrong, okay oh mighty domestic god?"

"We'll get it, but you're not wearing it unless I get to rip it off your body!"

I shook my head. "I wouldn't try it—elastic doesn't rip for shit," and I thought that was the end of the matter.

By the time we returned, it was nearing one o'clock and more than one-hundred degrees F. Bracken took one step outside of the SUV and literally staggered—I sent him inside the air-conditioned cabin without argument, and started to unload. The urinators (as we'd started calling them in the car) were there to greet us and help with the groceries—and to share some unsettling news.

"There's bodies out there," Teague said bluntly, taking the bag of cookies from me without even looking inside to protest. I handed a flat of chocolate milk to Jacky who blinked and mouthed 'Thank you' when Teague wasn't looking, and I remembered—once again—why we liked Jacky and how he could be a stand-up guy and not a pissy little bitch.

"Whose territory?" I asked, and Teague jerked his chin at himself. Okay—so across the lake and under the caves—good to know.

"It was a kid," he said roughly, and I grimaced. Okay--bad to know. "And parents."

Oh Goddess—so there was another family out there just like Gretchen's. Which meant…

"There's probably more of Gretchen," I muttered, and Teague followed me and nodded.

"Whoever does this… he's still out there. These were two months old, at most."

I blinked. "Were they out in the open? Is there any way someone else can come find them? I don't know… put them to rest or something?"

Teague shrugged. "They looked like they'd been buried, but not well—someone tried to cover them up—but it was a rush job."

"Like, say, a vampire in May?" I asked sourly, and Teague nodded again, rubbing his hand through his short-cut dark-blonde hair.

"Well," I sighed, "we'll have to arrange to have someone find them… and maybe tomorrow, we'll have Jacky go into town and look up the library, maybe find out who they are. We can keep an eye out for the baby vampire, you think?"

Teague frowned and I followed him into his cabin with another bag of groceries. "Why Jacky?"

"Cause he's good at it, Teague!" I told him with a laugh. "I mean, he wants to help too, you think?"

Teague nodded, shrugged, and I blew out a breath in exasperation. The first time I'd ever seen Teague, exhausted, worried to the death about Jacky, should have clued me in, but somehow, I thought he'd learn to let his boy fly a little.

"It's the library, Teague—what's going to happen at the damned library?"

Well, famous last words, really—but there were other worries that day, so they didn't bite me in the ass until later.

NICKY

Grooming

Bracken was really beat by the time we got back—and frankly, it was a little scary seeing him so limp when usually he was a terrifying ball of vitality.

Cory thought so too.

"Cold shower, cold swim?" she asked brusquely, coming into the air-conditioned room and rooting through the bags we'd left on the floor.

"Gawds..." I groaned, looking at Brack on the far end of the bed, "cool nap!"

Cory blinked. And yawned-- and I had to laugh. Sometimes I could actually watch her brain remember that she wasn't superwoman, and this time, I could almost see exhaustion drop from the heavens onto her shoulders.

"Okay," she yawned again. "Cool nap. But first, Bracken... where the hell is that swimsuit I bought at Wal-Mart?"

I watched curiously as he looked at her sideways from those big, round eyes. "I left it in the cart when we unloaded," he said sleepily. "On purpose."

Cory abruptly stopped her rooting, and I snickered so hard I woke myself up a little. I'd seen him do it, actually—he'd made eye contact with me, picked the damned thing out of the bag with his thumb and forefinger, and wadded it into a corner of the plastic cart. Getting between the two of them was like getting between two boulders rolling down two different mountains towards each other. It was better, really, just to run like hell, hold your arms over your head, and see what the fallout would be.

"Bracken!" Abruptly she started rooting through the drawers, and came out with two little amber colored scraps of material. "This is the only suit in my suitcase—what am I supposed to wear in front of Nicky's parents?"

Bracken pushed himself up on an elbow and scowled. "That will do fine," he muttered, and then flopped back onto the bed with a sigh. Cory stopped and blinked, and then got one of those 'Cory's busy, call back later' expressions that meant she was talking with Green.

She came back to herself with big eyes and a little bit of fury.

"You *bastards!*" she shrieked. "You did this on purpose! How *could* you?"

Bracken sat up in bed now, and some of his tiredness fell away. "You're not a nun, you're not fat, and you're not wearing a uni-tard to go swimming in this heat," he said unequivocally.

"But..." she stuttered, "Brack, I picked out the suit I *liked!* Why couldn't we have had this discussion then?"

Brack blinked and scowled some more, his eyes already at half-mast. "Because you're exhausting, beloved, and you bitch a lot less when you know you don't have a choice."

She scowled back, but I could tell she was having difficulty staying angry at him when he so obviously felt like crap. Then she spoke, and she was close enough to tears for this to be about more than a swimming suit.

"Bracken Brine," she muttered, shaking her head, "not wearing a bikini doesn't have anything to do with being fat—although my hips are getting to have their own zip-code, thank you very much."

"Well what then?" I asked curiously, hoping that a little interference might calm the storm I saw coming.

She shook her head and wiped a hand across her face, grimacing when it came back smeared in mascara. "You guys... you see me naked all the time... don't tell me all you see is the size of my boobs and my tattoo?"

I blinked in confusion, because that's all I did see. Boobs—squishy and good. Tattoo—bright and exotic. All of it—the softness of her freckled skin, the cinnamon color of her nipples and private hair—sweet, pretty, fun and erotic. I was completely lost by the tears and the shyness and the entire scene, and was about to say so.

Then I saw that Bracken had come off the bed in irritation and there was a smell of wildflowers in the air, and now I wanted to crawl under the bed. This, I thought in complete loss, was why Bracken and Green got to be her beloveds, and why I had needed to find someone else I was more suited for. They had the strength to match her strength—and to comfort her vulnerability. I could only follow and I was miserable at leading her away from the darkness of herself.

Bracken embraced her, buried his face in the sweet hollow of her neck, and then stood and looked firm and stoic, the way he did best. "They're scars of honor," he said, the anger in his voice tempered by gentleness. "You don't get to hide them from anybody. You got those scars defending us—defending yourself. We've had this conversation before—why are you dragging it back now?"

I caught Cory's embarrassed look at me, and the lightbulb went on and I wanted to die.

"Goddess—Cory!" And now I stood up and went to do some of the comforting because this was my fault too. Her shoulder looked like a grenade had exploded through it, and there was a thick band of tissue across her chest and stomach from the charred end of some bastard's bone. There were various cuts along her upper arms and upper body, and a thick band of something white and jagged at her ankle. I didn't see these things when she was with us—how could you see these things, when she was in your arms?

"She didn't want my parents to see them," I muttered, and Bracken grunted, his look at me challenging and irrefutable.

"Too. Fucking. Bad."

"I agree," I returned mildly—I couldn't even be mad at him for being mad at me, because I should have seen.

Cory sniffled and shook us off. "We're *not* having a happy family moment over this," she sniffed. "We are absolutely not." She grabbed our arms and gave us a push back towards the bed and started rooting in her yarn bag, coming up in triumph with a little pair of scissors before she cast a look of complete disgust at us, still fighting tears.

"Now what are you doing?" Bracken demanded, and her nose-wrinkle was almost an entire rant.

"Something I didn't think I'd have to do when I was going to wear the one piece suit with the briefs," she snapped. "I'm going to have to go..." she made a vague hand gesture around her upper thighs/lower abdomen, "*groom*," she finished, leaving Bracken and I blinking at each other in the dimness of the room after she'd shut of the light.

"Groom what?" he asked blankly, obviously fighting sleep.

"Groom her pubes," I told him, not sure how I knew this, unless it was from watching reruns of *Sex in the City*. "They're sort of... I don't know... bushy. Apparently that's bad."

Bracken glared at me before his eyes closed. "I hate the entire human race," he grumbled, his voice trailing off. "With one tiny exception..."

I had to laugh at that, but when Cory came out of the bathroom fifteen minutes later, I had fallen into thoughtfulness. She scowled at me—one of those expressions that said she was wrestling with her humanity and her femininity, and had come out somehow on bottom, and I returned the expression with a smile.

She really cared for me, I thought with a funny little quirk in my chest. She worried about my parents—she cared how they thought of her. Everything else she had to worry about, and I somehow ranked, and I'd been too blind to see it.

With a sigh she crawled into bed between the two of us, Bracken's hand coming around her middle with the same possessiveness he always showed. I'd almost come to treasure that feeling—I could have fucked her life up so badly, if Bracken hadn't simply asserted that their love would be.

She turned to him and touched his face, and he hardly stirred. Even for a sidhe, his skin was pale and his breathing quick—it would take a ten-mile sprint to wind Bracken, except here, where the heat was in the teens and your skin stuck to your skin, and the air seemed to sear your lungs.

"Does it get this hot in Montana?" she asked me, her eyes sleepy and worried.

I blinked. "Sometimes...it's... wet heat, mostly, and not for four or five months, like it can get here."

"Mmmm..." She didn't seem to be ready for sleep yet, so I took her hands in mine and kissed them.

"Thank you," I told her, "for doing this for me. It's hard for you—I know it. You're...anxious, and nervous..."

"And psychotically insecure," she supplied dryly, rolling her eyes, and I grinned at her softly. She really must care for me, I marveled, and in spite of the fact that I think I loved men better than women, I never doubted that I loved her best of all.

"And psychotically insecure," I nodded, just to make her laugh, which she did. "Don't worry about the scars, Cory. If my parents can't love you, then fuck'em..."

"Nicky!"

"They don't deserve to follow you, much less have you as their family." There, I'd said it. I guessed with most humans there was—or should be—a time when a husband or wife declared an allegiance: spouse or family. I'd chosen my spouses, and they were my family now. It wasn't everybody's family, but whether my parents wanted it to be or not, it was mine now.

She nodded, and chewed her lower lip, her dark eyes luminous in the dim light. "Thank you, Nicky—that means a lot," she said sincerely. "I just hope I can live up to it."

"I just hope I can live up to you," I told her, meaning it. She grinned.

"Maybe it will all hinge on how well I groomed my pubes," she predicted direly, and I laughed and kissed her freckled nose.

"Maybe I should check that for you," I told her, and now she laughed, the sound rich and deep. "Would you like me to do that?"

"Oh of course," she murmured, and my hands found her skin easily, pulling at her shorts and rubbing under her shirt. We kissed, and there was no thundering pulse, no sensory overload, but it wasn't bad.

We laughed when we made love—or giggled was more like it. I had seen her with Bracken, been with her and Green, and she was breathless in their arms, eyes wide, smile ready, but also in awe that they should touch her, and they returned the sentiment. It felt like that when I was with Eric—every touch was perfect and awesome—and I loved that feeling. But with us it was all giggling, like kids playing doctor, and I had learned to enjoy this too.

I liked the taste of her, in the center of her sex, and when we were naked I knelt between her thighs and she covered her face with her arms.

"How bad is it?" she mumbled, and I laughed.

"Like your privates were attacked by a miniature lawn-mower, steered by a blind gardener!" I told her truthfully, petting feebly at the patchy cinnamon hair. Then I licked the pink, tender flesh anyway, laughing as she wriggled. "And you're giving me rugburn!" I complained when I came up for air.

"I'd think that was something you were used to!" she teased, and I waggled my eyebrows at her and pounced, driving myself inside her body as deeply as I could go. She gasped, and so did I, and the giggling stopped for a few moments until the climax washed over us both like waves on a lakeshore—a small lake shore, not Lake Michigan or anything, but still pleasant.

She licked the sweat on my collarbone when we were done, and I rolled away, gasping, because we were slick with sweat and I wanted to lay naked under the fan to cool off. Cory pulled on the T-shirt I'd taken off, and shimmied into her underwear, and then checked on Bracken again.

He had watched with hooded eyes as we made love, and his color seemed to be better—sometimes, I think for the sidhe just *being* around sex made them better, but in this case, he was smiling, so maybe our giggling had cheered him up a little too.

"You make love like sprites," he commented sleepily. "Now nap like them."

Cory grinned at him, relieved, and nuzzled his cheek. As hot as it was, it was never too hot for them to touch. Then she yawned and reached out to brush my hand with her own, and I stroked her wrist with my thumb, and that's the last thing I remember for a while.

About an hour later I woke as she shimmied out of bed, whispering, "I've got to practice," and I listened to her change, barely remembering what it was she needed to practice. I only felt a little bad before I fell asleep again.

I came to an hour later, and I heard my parents' voices outside.

I blinked.

They were talking to Cory.

I sat up in bed.

There was my mom's trilling soprano, "Oh, honey, you're such a sweetheart to help with the bags—John, honey, could you make sure this nice girl gets a tip? I only wish my son could have settled down with someone nice like you!"

"Oh *fuck!*"

Bracken, as used to emergencies as the rest of us, sat bolt upright in bed himself and looked at me in alarm.

"My parents are here!" I scrambled out of bed and started rooting for my cargo shorts... oh fuck oh fuck... Cory had thrown them somewhere...

"So what?" Bracken asked blearily, standing into his flip-flops on wobbly knees.

"They're talking to Cory..." Oh crap—there they were, and my turquoise cotton boxers with them, only... oh Goddess... I smelled like sex... I smelled like *her*... oh fuck...

"So..."

"Brack, they think she's the *help!*"

"The fuck they do!" he shouted, suddenly completely awake, and then he stared at me, hard. "You—go shower. You look like sex. I'll go talk to them."

I was going to argue, but he was right. We had done nothing wrong—I had made love to my wife, and it wouldn't help if I acted like that needed to be defended.

"Give me three minutes," I told him seriously, and he returned a sour grimace, smoothing his wild black hair back and looking fabulous anyway.

"I'll hold you to that—don't forget your shorts."

CORY

Lasting Impressions

You know those girls who can wander around in butt-floss bikinis with their asses hanging out, getting tan while they paint their toenails?

Pretty, aren't they? Confident. Their hair always looks fabulous, with some sort of awesome hair product that streaks it and keeps it from frizzing and probably conditions it all at the same time? You know those women?

I don't. I wish I did. For the sake of the men, I wish I could be one, but I'm not. So, while everyone else was sleeping, and I was wandering around the blistering hot dock vamping to Allanah Miles' *Black Velvet,* I wore Bracken's T-shirt over that little bitty bikini and a little cotton sun-visor, and I hoped I'd smeared enough sunblock over my face to keep it from bursting like a hot-dog in the heat.

I also hoped you couldn't see my pubic hair at the crotch, and wished Renny was awake so I could ask her if *she* could see it. (Although, on second thought, I should probably ask Katy, because Renny had no problem lying about something like that if it meant she could watch me spaz out later.)

After a half-hour, hearing my own voice echoing among the lonely trees got old. When I finished the song for the zillionth time, I heard a round of applause and looked up to see the young man from the cabin at the end looking at me from a rock in the shade by the cabins. He had a wild mop of dark hair, a sun-burnt nose, spots, braces, and searing blue eyes.

He also had a grin through the braces that made me respond, and I rolled my eyes and gave a little bow and a wave. He waved back and returned his attention to the electronic whatsit in his hands, so I turned to the lake.

I was starting to think about it as a nemesis. It was a hundred-bajillion degrees outside, and here I was, mere feet from something that would cool me off. Something I enjoyed. Something I had used before with comfort and ease.

Something that now seemed to terrify me with the thought of black immensity beneath my feet.

I scowled. Oh fuck *this!* With care I shed my flip-flops on top of the dock, and put my i-Pod on top of them. I debated shucking my T-shirt, but the thought of wearing it wet when I got out was immensely appealing, like an air conditioner on my back.

Gingerly, I put my hands on the edge of the floating dock and put my feet into the water, gasping a little as I slid to the middle of my thigh before I touched bottom. I looked down and wiggled my pale toes, kicking up some of the red dirt that permeated everything here—including our toenails and the cracks of our skin after we'd gone swimming. I could still see my feet, I thought happily, so I backed away from the dock and started inching towards my right, towards open water.

My foot slipped off of the underwater ledge, and I almost shrieked. I held it together, teetering on the brink, and reminded myself under my breath that I'd been swimming in lakes since I was three years old. Unfortunately, my dumbassed traitor-brain kept up a clip video of everything that could possibly go wrong, complete with Wes Craven soundtrack and Oscar-winning make-up and special effects.

I sucked in a breath and deliberately tread water, battling the billowing shirt under the surface, and very aware that my visual knowledge of my body turned into a big pale blank somewhere around my knees.

Fuck this. Fuck this fuck this oh *fuck this!* I was the fucking Vampire Queen of fucking Northern California, I could vaporize giant bad things from fifty-feet away, I could negotiate peace treaties with werewolves that I decided not to kill, and I could, for the love of chickenshit on the sidewalk, get over this dumb-fucking-ass-kicking baseless goddamned phobia.

I started to shiver, and it wasn't because of the water (which was more refreshing than cold at this point) and still I kept treading water. With a sharp series of breaths I turned away from the docks and dove under the water, kicking horizontal to the shoreline and concentrating on the sweet feel of all that coolness on my head and not on the fact that I still couldn't see under the murky, red/green watercolor tint of the lake. (My eyes were stinging like a sonovabitch from trying to look, though!)

I came up and took a deep breath, and swiveled my head frantically around to get my bearings. From behind me, I heard that damned kid cackling like a serial killer, and I resisted the urge to flip him off.

Even *I* knew I looked like a fool, and as much as I didn't care about how I looked to this random stranger, I'd suddenly had enough. This little exercise in overcoming my fears was over, and I was ready to go wake everybody up now, thank-you-very-much-the-end.

I hadn't brought a towel, so I pretty much let myself drip for a couple of minutes before mooching back up towards the cabins.

The big red Pontiac crested the rise and dipped towards the driveway in front of the cabins just as I got there myself, and I blinked. There was a couple in the front—middle-aged, average people, who could have been my parents or Nicky's parents or even Renny's or Max's for that matter, and, in the back, there was a young woman. Why would Nicky's parents bring a girl with them? He didn't have a sister.

My first thought was irritation—oh, shit, do we have *another* civilian to deal with?

I didn't have time or space for a second thought, because at that moment, Nicky's mom got out of the car.

She was extraordinarily pretty, with a tiny, feminine nose, a little pointed chin, and Nicky's high cheekbones. Her hazel eyes were wide and guileless, and she'd dyed her hair the color of strawberries and sunflowers. I walked forward to introduce myself, and she smiled perkily and waved, and then opened the back door of the car to let the young woman out, and together, the two of them started talking so quickly, I literally couldn't get a word in edgewise.

"Well hi there, did they send you out to help with the bags? That's just so nice, you never can get good service these days, isn't that right, Annette?"

Annette nodded in complete agreement because no, she wouldn't ass-kiss at *all,* and said, "That's right, Mrs. Kestrel. Remember that that waitress at the IHOP? Wasn't she a complete bitch! I was actually worried that everybody in California might be that way!"

Oh. Goddess. "We're not," I replied with a hesitant little smile, and tried for *Let me introduce myself,* but what I got out was, "Let me…"

"Oh, yes, absolutely," said Nicky's mom, "and you both call me Terry, now. Annette, I swear I've been trying to get you to do that since we left Montana!" And before I could ask why, in particular, Annette had been *with* her since they left Montana, Terry, in that completely familiar way that some people have with strangers took it upon herself to tell me.

"We're meeting my son here—he got caught in one of those, you know, shotgun weddings?" Terry Kestrel leaned in to me and winked. "We brought Annette here to see if maybe he's got a reason to come home."

I looked deliberately at Annette—lots of blonde hair, a wasp waist in bottle-cap shorts, and a front-buttoned halter-top showcasing melons that would win first prize at the county fair. I sighed, and turned my attention back to Terry, who had wandered opposite her husband and was working with him to take the luggage shell off the top of the sedan.

Mr. Kestrel was a fit looking man in his early fifties, with lots of graying hair that might have been Nicky's rust-color at one time. He was dressed in American Dad—khaki shorts, Burkinstocks with socks, and a Hawaiian shirt. In true, American Dad fashion, he seemed completely oblivious to the machinations of the women around him.

"I don't know if there's another room for Annette," I said practically. "Where would you like her bags?"

"Oh she can stay in our room," Terry chimed with a wink for her prospective daughter-in-law. "Hopefully, she'll be staying somewhere else very soon!"

Annette giggled and pulled some bags from the back of the car that she dropped at my feet, and Teague sauntered out of his cabin just in time to watch me bend over in bemused horror to pick them up.

"I'll get them, Lady," he muttered, eyeing the newcomers with intense distaste. "Who the fuck is that?"

"Nicky's parents," I said, waving to Tanya as she came out of the caretaker's cabin and dangled a key at me.

"Who's with 'em?" He hefted the bags easily over his shoulders and Tanya came up and took the other two at my feet. I held out my hand for a bag and they both looked at me in horror, so I took the key and walked towards the one cabin *not* on the end and *not* occupied by my people.

"That would be Annette," I said sourly, opening the door so they could dump the bags. "She's a hopeful for Nicky's new daughter-in-law."

Teague was so surprised he dropped the suitcase off his shoulder. It hit the floor and burst open, shirts and underwear dumping in its wake.

"You're shitting me."

I gave my most neutral shrug. "I shit you not," I said, turning on the air conditioning—it was ninety in the room, and it could use the head start.

"Why'd they tell you?" Tanya asked, horrified.

"They think I'm the help," I said, unable to gauge my own expression. Teague and Tanya gaped at me, and together we walked out of the room, leaving Mr. Kestrel's underwear strewn over the carpet.

When we got out to the car, there were more bags waiting for us, and Terry and Annette were panting in the shade.

"Jonathan went in that cabin to register," Terry fluttered her hand, and Tanya muttered, "Shit!" and trotted off to go take care of business, but not before glaring at Annette's wide-eyed gaping at her pierced nipples, lip, nose, and eyebrow.

Annette looked to me as though to share in on the joke, but maybe she caught sight of my own double row of six-plus piercings along my ears. They were fine gold hoops with little charms now, but at one point in time, they'd been skulls, daggers, and Blue Oyster Cult crosses. Either way, she flushed, and then smiled winningly at Teague.

"Oh my—looks like you got yourself a man too!" she trilled, and Teague and I looked at each other blankly.

"No," I said with a shake of my head, "he's a friend," and Annette's smile turned condescending.

"Oh honey, well don't worry—you're still young. A little hair, a little make-up, and no one will even look at your figure—you'll have a man in no time."

Beside me I heard Teague suck in his breath in horror, and let out an honest-to-Goddess werewolf growl. I hissed at him, alarmed, and Annette continued on, in happy oblivion. "Anyways, everyone knows that it's the personality that counts. As long as you let a man know he's the king of the roost, you can make a good man happy!"

Teague growl turned to a guffaw, and I let out my breath with a little relief. "What's wrong with you?" I hissed, scowling, but Teague's look was fixed on Annette in fierce, werewolf hatred.

"Did you hear what she…"

"Every. Word." I gritted through a smile. If I could deal with this, then he had better be able to—Goddess knew what would happen if Teague lost his temper. Any of us, for that matter—there were just too many personalities here in this little place for us to come unglued!

"C'mon, brother," I said in a regular tone, "let's get these to the cabin."

"Lady, forgive me," Teague muttered, "but you don't carry anybody's bags."

"Damned straight," said Max quietly behind me, who had just followed Renny out of their cabin. Well good—at least I didn't have to wake everybody up!

Max was human, but Renny was cat, and as the guys took the bags she came up underneath my hand and rubbed her head there, while I fondled her ears. I think it comforted us both.

Terry frowned, the expression doing nothing to make her one bit less attractive, and looked at me with more dripping pity. "Oh, darlin'—I'm so sorry—is that your name? And is there something wrong with…" a sudden gasp, "Oh no—you're not pregnant, are you darlin'? What, with no husband and all?"

Katy padded up to me, obviously ready to go swimming human style this time, and she sucked in her breath much as Teague and Max had done. "No!" we both answered loudly, and I heard the werewolf in her voice too.

I put a hand on her shoulder—the hand with the intricately wrought ring that matched Bracken's, Nicky's, and Green's-- and answered evenly, "No to both—no, I'm not pregnant, and no, 'Lady' isn't my name..."

Annette looked puzzled, her blue eyes big and wide, "Well then why did they call you that?"

I swallowed and heard another door open—oh, goody—Mario and La Mark were up. Was everybody in the entire fucking entourage going to witness this little bit of humiliation *besides* Nicky? I swallowed again and fought the urge to screech Nicky's name over everyone's head.

"It's more like a title," I said, literally petting Katy's arm in an effort to smooth her hackles.

"Oh-oh!" trilled Terry, "You're like the head manager—you know, the 'Lady of the Cabins', right?" Teague and Max were back, and Jack took his place behind Katy, and holy shit and pass the salt, Jacky snarled first, and I had to put an end to this crap.

"Look," I said, in my down-to-business voice, "Mrs. Kestrel, do you know whose place you're staying in?"

Terry blinked. "Well yes—it belongs to my son's," beat, "employer." I saw the blush and sharpened my gaze.

"He's not your son's employer, and I know you know that," I said, my voice getting hard, and Terry cleared her throat and looked sideways at Annette, apology in her voice.

"Well, yes, my son *did* fall in with some bad people, but we're here to take him home now..." she faltered, because not even Mrs. Kestrel could miss the mass growl behind me. I should shut them down, I thought—I should. But I didn't want to.

"Your son *did* fall into a bad crowd," Mario said behind me, his voice shaking, "but Green saved him from that. Don't you dare blame Green for Nicky's mistakes."

Terry nodded, and pasted a condescending smile on, for all the world as though her son hadn't been introduced to Green as the fucker who'd mindraped me and left me for dead. "Well, be that as it may, it's time for your nasty Mr. Green to yank his clutches out of my son and let him come home to me. I know he still has... obligations..." more blush, "but that wife of his is messing around like some... some rank whoring bitch, you know, and it's time for Nicky to give her up and come... come..."

I swallowed and turned around and faced my people—to a one, they had already initiated the shapeshifter's change. Ordinarily, this is something quick, painless, like changing clothes... but my guys, they wanted to kill someone, and their human halves were keeping them from doing it. There were half-grown snouts, and ears in mutant positions midway up the head, slitted eyes, and claws twisting on the end of human arms—this had gone far enough.

"You." I said deliberately, "All. Need. To. Chill." I took a deep breath and motioned everybody to follow me, and was relieved when they met my eyes and did just that. Another breath and they released some of their anger. Another breath, and most of their changes had reversed, and they were left, glowering at the two women over my shoulder, and I needed to put an end to this conversation once and for all.

"Mrs. Kestrel," I said, turning back around, "how much does this one know about your world?"

Terry blinked. "I'm sure I don't know..."

Oh Goddess—she was going to make me do this, wasn't she? "Stop dicking around, Terry—does she know the Kestrel family secret or not? I need to know how much of her brain we're going to have to wipe or if we should just send her home now."

Annette gasped and held her hand up to her throat, and Terry patted her arm reassuringly. "Now sweetie, don't you worry—we've told you everything, haven't we?"

Annette brightened like a child. "Oh yes—I know all about the bird thing..."

Wonderful. What idiot told her that? "Well does she know he's not the only bird in the sky?"

Terry blinked, and Annette blinked, and I filled in the silence with fantasies of smacking them both until their noses bled.

"You do realize," I said slowly, my voice getting harder as I went, "that we have a very eclectic population here, don't you?"

Annette smiled that clueless smile that I was starting to loathe and then opened her mouth one more time. "Oh, that's okay," she said brightly, looking specifically at certain members of our party, "we have blacks and Mexicans in Montana too—I can live with that!"

"Like we'd let you, *punto!*" Katy snarled, and Jack and Teague both grabbed her arms and pulled her behind me before she could attack, and I was just about to ask both women if they could find another way to be offensive so we could just out and out kill them, when suddenly the light bulb went on. Annette looked to Renny with a wreath of smiles. "Oh my god! Is this a magic animal, like Nicky?" She bent down to scratch a fuzzy brown tortoiseshell head and Renny actually cat-spit at her, backing up with her feet splayed and her hair standing out all over her body.

I jumped between them. "Bitch, you touch my friend and she'll take your fingertip off at your armpit! Now listen, both of you—because I'm not saying this again!"

They both gasped, and it was as though they suddenly *saw* the lot of us—and they realized that we were all more than we looked.

"You are on Green's land, by Green's invitation—you insult the master of these lands again, and I will make my apologies to your son and make sure you are banned in every preternatural community outside of Montana for the rest of your life. That's almost every state in the union and all of Europe, Mrs. Kestrel—I'd think long and hard about that, do we understand each other?"

I nodded my head deliberately, hoping they would nod back, and when they did, I buried my hands into Renny's ruff and took another deep breath.

"Now look—I'm afraid we got off on the wrong foot. You haven't let me introduce myself, I'm…"

And because I was apparently running a bona fide Circus of the Fucking Damned, two things happened right then. The first was Nicky's father, running up and panting in the heat, apparently fresh from a little chat with Tanya who probably ripped his nipples off with outrage, and the second was Bracken, my knight protector, barreling out of our cabin on unsteady legs to plant himself between me and the horrible monsters from the depths of his worst nightmares about Cory-eating humans that needed to be smushed like bugs.

"Beloved," Bracken muttered, casting a venomous glance over his shoulder, "you should have woke us up!"

"I probably would have," I told him truthfully, "but… well things got sort of out of hand really quickly."

Bracken looked over his shoulder again and growled. "How are they treating you?"

I swallowed and smiled grimly. "We're having a misunderstanding right now, but we're about to clear that u…"

"We're so," pant pant, "very sorry," pant pant, "Lady Cory," said Jonathan Kestrel, trying hard to do a proper bow in the heat. "We had no idea who you were."

Mario and La Mark's door opened then, and Lambent-- ignoring the meeting of the worlds--came blurring by. (Literally--all the human eye could see was a light-flame-colored-whoosh, like a special effect.) Screaming like any kid jumping in the lake on a day like this, he zoomed down the hill, across the pier, and up the side of the small floating bait-shop on the end, his momentum taking him nearly twenty feet into the air and well clear of the end of the dock. With a gleeful whoop, he hovered in the air for a moment and then plunged into the center of the lake.

I watched him deliberately—we all did, welcome for the distraction, because the process of recognition working its way across Terry Kestrel's face was truly painful.

"My goodness," she said to no one in particular, "was that one of your people too? Have we met everybody, because that sure is a lot!"

I forced myself to look at her and gave a brief, unfriendly smile, moving Bracken to the side so I could face her as I did so. "You won't meet the vampires until dark," I told them, feeling for Bracken's hand. It was there, hard and sure, and my heartbeat slowed just a little more. This was *not* mortal peril—I should remember that.

Terry nodded, and Annette, incapable of staying silent to save her life, said, "I don't understand—he called you 'Lady Cory'—does that mean you're…" she trailed off, looking horrified, and I stepped forward and bowed, unwilling to extend my hand.

"That would make me Cory Green," I introduced, begrudging them even that much of my name, "but you would know me as the 'rank whoring bitch' who is married to Nicky."

To make things perfect, Nicky came rushing out of our room just in time to hear that last line, and the debacle was complete.

BRACKEN

Knight's Unyielding Position

"Jesus, Mom," Nicky said, reading the situation accurately at a glance, "you've been here, what? Ten minutes? You couldn't be here ten minutes without pissing off my entire family?"

"Oh, honey," Terry said, turning around to her son with a conciliatory air, "you're exaggerating."

"Sure he is," Max muttered under his breath, "Lambent seems happy and the vampires aren't up yet!"

The humor rippling through the werefolk was a relief—their tension had been hotter than the horrendous air, and I felt Cory relax next to me. Thank the Goddess—it wasn't that I wanted these people to live any longer than necessary, but I didn't want Cory to be responsible for killing them, either. That was no way to run a family.

Knowing this it seemed, she turned around and flashed a grateful smile to the mass of hyperbolic bodies behind us. "Guys, if you, uhm, want to go swimming with Lambent, Brack and I will be there in a few minutes, okay?"

She did that thing with her head, where she nods it trying to get people to agree with her. A lot of times it worked, and it seemed to this time, until—as a unified whole—the men all dropped their swim trunks and deliberately stepped out them. Katy's eyes widened, and then she sighed. She wasn't nearly as free with her body as Renny, but Teague—who didn't like showing his scars any more than Cory did—was as bare as everybody else. Even the Avians were naked when they didn't have to be and, well, it was a show of solidarity.

With a little moan that only I could hear, her pretty blue bikini hit the dust, and all of the werefolk turned deliberately to the Kestrels and their unwelcome guest.

And then they changed.

The big-titted human woman next to Nicky's mother let out a breathless half-shriek, and the werecreatures flowed around our knees. Jack and Katy trotted to the far side of the car and Max and Renny took the side near us, and four tires steamed under a solid yellow stream of urine. They all did that "fuck you in the cat litter" thing with their back paws, and trotted away with pleased expressions on their various animal faces, until Jack and Katy turned back towards Teague.

Teague was pissing on the big-titted woman's feet as she squealed and tried to sit on top of the heated car, and Cory and I could do nothing but step back and—in Cory's case—cover her shocked laughter with her hand.

Teague kicked his feet at her and then joined his mates. Just as Nicky's mom gave a sigh of relief there was a terrific thundering splat on the car's hood, and then another on the roof, as Mario and La Mark did their part to make their displeasure known. Both women shrieked and moaned as they were spattered with the worst bird bomb of all time, and Cory and I simply took another step back and looked at them at a complete loss for something to say.

Cory tried. "They're very protective."

Terry looked woefully at her car and her companion's sodden, stinking sandals. "I can see that," she replied, and then, with a glimmer of self awareness, she looked Cory in the eye. "You do not know how much I would give to be able to go back and do that last ten minutes over again and start fresh."

Cory let out what might have been a laugh. "I'm sure you would," she said quietly. "And we will get a chance to talk later."

Her eyes wandered down to the water. Everybody else was in—most of them human, having changed in the water itself, except for Mario and La Mark. They were hovering about fifteen feet above the glossy surface, and then, almost in tandem, they changed into humans, and their whoops of excitement could be heard up where we were as they plunged into the cold lake.

Cory's lips twitched, and she looked up at Nicky's parents, just a hint of apology in her voice this time. "Right now, I think I'd better go keep them company—they were very self-controlled." She pulled at my hand, saying, "We should bring their clothes down, you think?" and I shook my head.

"Tanya will get them," and she seemed to be happy with that.

Together we gathered around Nicky, who stood miserable and upset, and she took his hands in hers, then leaned over and gave him a sweet, lingering kiss on the corner of his mouth. "How about you join us in a few minutes, sweetie," she ordered, her eyes troubled, and he met her gaze with a truly unhappy look and nodded.

"I have a few things to say here," he told her, and she nodded in return.

"Just make sure one of them is, 'I'm happy you made it okay,'" she said, and his shoulders shook in a laugh that contained no humor at all.

"I'll try, darlin'—I really will." And then he kissed her, as he'd kissed her in bed this afternoon, and not even his sun-blind parents could miss that they honestly cared for each other. They parted and I ruffled his hair with my free hand, and together we started for the shore, but not before she turned and added one last cherry to what apparently had been a giant shit sundae of a meeting.

"Mr. Kestrel, we're really sorry about your luggage—Teague totally dropped that bag on accident, and we weren't sure if you'd want us touching your things."

As we walked away we heard Nicky, as angry as we'd ever heard him, saying, "Annette, I'm not sure what the hell you're doing here, but you may want to go shower—and I'd leave those shoes at the door before you go in. Dad, I bet if you ask Tanya, she's got a hose somewhere..."

I could hear their unhappy replies, but by now we were far enough away that Cory couldn't, and I opted not to give a ripe flying shit.

Since everybody in the lake was naked, I was on my way to dropping my own trunks when Cory rolled her eyes in the direction of the hill.

Crap—there was the civilian, and he'd just seen all of the werepeople, doing their changing thing. The kid raised an ironic eyebrow at me, and I shrugged. Lambent and I would probably have to do a mindwipe on the kid and his mother anyway, but I'd keep the shorts on so he didn't get too 'damaged'. Humans and nakedness—another thing I would never get.

With a sigh I hopped on the dock and ran to the end, stopping a few feet short of the floating bait shop and running off and plunging into the blessed coolness that was Lake Shasta.

Goddess, I loved it in the water. There was enough stirred up powdered red dirt in it to feel as though I was not just walking the earth, as I did almost daily anyway, but *rolling* in it, drawing power from the iron and from the organic, peaceful heart of the Goddess herself. Besides the fact that it was a relief from the thrice-damned heat, it was like a rolling, massaging energy bath as well, and I was suddenly glad for the shorts. My erection was big enough for Cory to sit on like a park-bench, if she'd been so inclined.

But Cory wasn't in the water. She was sitting on the edge of the dock, her oversized T-shirt tucked under her bottom and her feet dangling in the water where they could touch. I squinted at her against the glare, and she smiled back from under her sun visor. Her ponytail was wet, hanging in a snarled point over the back of the visor, and her white T-shirt hung stretched out and still a little transparent with damp—she'd been swimming already.

Why wasn't she in the water now?

"Get in!" I glared at her, and her lips twitched.

"Bossy, ain't you?"

"Your face is turning red from the heat—why aren't you getting in?"

She stuck her tongue out at me. "I think the T-shirt is stuck under my butt—I'm not sure how to get unstuck, and if I just hop up from here, I'll fall face forward. That'll be fun!"

I ignored her bright sarcasm. The sound of our people playing in the deeps of the crooked lake faded behind me, and for a moment I could only hear her heartbeat.

It was accelerating.

I knew it! Dammit, I knew this morning that there was something wrong. Damn humans and their casual ability to throw lies into the wind. She was getting good at it—between the human ability to lie and what she was picking up from the sidhe about bending truth, she was becoming almost opaque, but not to me.

"Stop lying and get in the water," I said darkly, and she made a face. Her heartbeat got threadier as she stuck out her tongue and laughed at me.

"Don't be an asshole," she murmured. "I'm happy here."

"Bullshit. It's a… a… a *gazunga* degrees out there… it's not comfortable, and you love the water!" She did—I'd seen her playing in Clementine, although that was almost unfairly called a lake. It was more an extra wide spot in a lazy river—most of the time, even Cory could still touch bottom.

"I like the water at home," she murmured, and I squinted at her. An evasion. Like I said, she was getting sidhe-slippery when she wanted to be.

"What's wrong with the water here?" I thought it felt glorious.

She swallowed, and gave me that false-sun of a smile. "Nothing—here, I'll jump in."

This morning when she'd jumped in, there had been a wealth of childish glee in her movements. Now, she stood and squared her jaw, like she did for any op we'd run, and ran the short width of the dock with a concentrated scowl. When she was in the air, prepared to hit the water, her face was twisted into the same expression a human might wear at the dentist's office, and she plunked heavily into the lake.

Her rise to the surface was a grim struggle of tightened muscles and shivering self-control. She flung water from her face and hair and proceeded to tread water next to me with a face so tight and jaw so clenched, it looked like her snarl of battle.

"You've gone swimming before!" I exclaimed, appalled, and she closed her eyes, breathlessly, and then opened them, rolling them almost wildly. Her heart was pounding a tympani in her temple, and I'd had enough of this shit.

It was so deliciously easy to maneuver behind her and catch her midriff with my hand. She gasped and I pulled her back against me, trapping her thrashing legs with my own, and maintaining a lazy, balanced paddling with my other hand.

"Bracken..." she choked, and I leaned down and whispered in her ear, knowing it was a sure way of getting her attention.

"Now I've got you, *due'ane,* do you hear me?" She let out her breath and nodded, and I continued on. "I need you to calm down, and remember that you could probably kill every fish in the lake, plus us, with your fear alone."

"Do you think I don't know..."

"And then remember that you won't."

"Why aren't you sinking?" she asked in a stony little voice. That was my beloved... practical to the bone.

"Because I'm a sidhe... our blood and our bones aren't iron and stone..."

"Honey and sunlight are your blood and bone," she supplied, pulling the rhyme from her busy mind, and I laughed appreciatively, keeping my mouth and my breath in the hollow of her neck. Her body was cool against mine in the water, and I remembered her, lying on the bed playfully, accepting Nicky's touch, and the urge came again to make her tremble and scream.

"That's right," I murmured, letting my hand rise and fall with her stomach. "Now that we're singing nursery rhymes, I want you to tell me a story about why you're so frightened."

"I can't see my feet," she said baldly, as though that would mean something to me.

"So..."

She shook in my arms, but not the way I wanted her to. "You remember, don't you? The last time I couldn't see my feet?"

"Ahhhh..." Oh yes. Oh, Goddess... I remember. "Green had to put me under," I told her humorlessly.

"I didn't know that," she said, her body still vibrating like one of those little dogs with the big eyes.

"Mmmmhm," I told her bleakly. "I told him I'd never move on Adrian's girl... but seeing you hurt, seeing you be so amazingly brave...oh, it hurt to know I'd never know you."

"Mmmm…" she was using the memory to fight the fear, I could feel it in her, she was leaning her body back on me, and her muscles were loosening, becoming liquid, delicious and refreshing around me. "You would have known me," she said, surprising me. I'd said the words before, to the phantom of our lover in the garden, but I never knew if she'd believed them or if she'd even thought them possible.

"I pray everyday that's true," I murmured, and she shivered again, convulsively, in my arms, and then the last of the adrenaline seemed to bleed out of her and into the water around her.

"I can't swim like this for the next week," she said on a breath of laughter, and my hearing broadened, and I realized that the others had drifted off, leaving us here, in the shadow of the bait shop—privacy when there should have been none. It was a gift, and I was grateful.

But she was right—it was a gift. She would need to be able to relax. There was nothing to do out here—which wasn't a bad thing. We weren't a frantic people as a whole. We were happy with activity—swimming, studying, building, reading, running, being a part of Green's businesses, these were our day-to-day and they were good ways to spend our time. But it was hellishly hot here in this alien place, in this amoeba shaped bowl of a valley looking over the scorched green of hardy trees and red earth. If she couldn't swim it would actually become a weakness.

There was a sudden breath of wildflowers, and she sighed, relaxing a little more in my arms. The scent was gone, and she spoke.

"Green says I should be able to feel out with my power," she murmured. "Want to try it?"

"Promise not to boil me like rice?" I was kidding, of course. I had great faith in her.

"Promise." There was a subtle glow there, around us—I was pretty sure that none of the others could see it or even feel it's tingle where they were.

"Can you feel anything?" I asked, burying my nose in her wet hair. It smelled very animal, and I found I liked that too. Would there be a way to get her alone on this trip? Not that I minded Nicky's presence and participation, but… oh, Goddess, did she come undone in my arms when we were alone.

"I can feel that there's not a suicidal vampire down there," she laughed, "But other than that…well, I'm not going to be catching any fish with my prodigious mind, either." Her body regained some of its normal tension—not the relaxation of sedated panic, and not the initial panic, either.

"Why do you think he did it?" I asked, because now that she had brought it up, it was something that had always bothered me. "To hide down there, staying awake in the day, hoping one of our people would come by?"

"Mmm…" Cory thought carefully before she answered. "Crispin wasn't letting them feed—I don't know why. Maybe because Sezan was just...just crazy and controlling...I've wanted to ask Kyle forever, but..." Her shudder was purely sympathetic.

"Yeah—not a subject we want to bring up." Speaking of suicidal vampires—if we hadn't brought Kyle into our kiss after his beloved had died, he would have greeted the flesh-scorching dawn with maniacal delight. Some memories shouldn't be resurrected—but we did it on a regular basis to keep our people safe from the same things. I'd have to think about that. Slowly. Like a giant tractor with gear problems. But I'd think.

"Anyway," she shifted away from me naturally, so she could look in my eyes while she treaded water on her own. A puzzle. A puzzle would keep her occupied, keep her mind off of what could be lurking under her feet. I respected irrational fears and phobias—they were what had kept my people living in solidarity for many millennia before my birth.

"Anyway?"

"Yeah… maybe it was just that. Maybe…maybe he hurt, watching his kiss become twisted and horrible. He'd been told I was the enemy—maybe it was worth it to let his flesh rot and risk being flambéd like dessert in order to take us out. Maybe it was worse living when your code for living was insane…"

Oh Goddess… I knew what she was talking about, and her fear made me cold, when I'd finally been comfortable for the first time in a month.

"So," I muttered, remembering that cursed play, "if Banquo had lived are you saying he'd kill himself rather than serve?"

She shook her head, an appreciative smile on her face, even as her arms paddled and her legs tread. "I'm saying he'd do what MacBeth asked him too… he'd just die in the doing."

"You're not…" I muttered grimly, and she looked honestly surprised, and the lake was my gloriously cool and nourishing friend once again.

"No!" she laughed. "Not even. It's just something to think about…hey Nicky!" She looked up, shading her eyes even under the mint-green visor. "Hop in, yeah?"

Nicky smiled, a weary, harried smile, and nodded. If anyone looked like he needed a dip in the lake, it was Nicky.

"Shit yeah!" Instead of hopping, though, he changed abruptly into a bird, and flew out to about where Mario and La Mark had gone, and then shifted back, whooping happily as his body arrowed into the green blankness of the lake.

"Shit," Cory laughed next to me, and I had to concur. "Please tell me he's got another set of trunks in his suitcase!"

I hoped so, because the pair he'd been wearing when he'd stood over the dock and talked to us was most *definitely* gone when he'd turned back into a young man and plunged into the water. So was the casual button-up shirt he'd been wearing. Judging by the hysterical laughter of the rest of our people, we weren't the only ones to notice.

Cory laughed again. "And I thought *I* was stressed!" With that she extended her body and started a no-nonsense freestyle to the center of the party, and I joined her. The middle of a cool lake was as good a spot to have a parlay as any other in a place like this, and I had the feeling that at least here, we wouldn't have to worry about civilians overhearing.

Her face was taut and controlled by the time we reached the others, and I wondered how odd we looked, gathered around her and listening to her talk like a tiny general. I looked around and tried to fathom if anyone else guessed that she was tamping down on her new anxiety of the water, but I couldn't do it. I was finely attuned to my beloved, but was not as good at gauging everybody else.

"Okay." she smiled gamely and kept up the pretense that she was enjoying this little swim. "Here's what we know."

Within five minutes Max and Renny were scheduled to take the cave tour on the other side of the lake the next day—and to get lost on the trail and find the remains that Teague had spotted earlier. She had also covered our meeting with the vampires the next night, and, blushing as much as she could for someone whose face was pale in the chill of the water, how she planned to make an entrance.

"You *do* realize this could end up being the single most humiliating moment of my life!" she muttered at me, and Nicky and I met gazes.

"What we did in San Francisco was a lot bigger," Nicky murmured, and Max and Renny had to agree.

Cory shook her head. "Yeah—that was the whole lot of us singing. This is me, doing the ass-wiggling slut-bitch thing, and… well… guys, I don't know how much theatre is in me!"

Katy was chewing her lip. "It will help, Mommy, if you can get the mens into your damage path, you know?"

I watched Cory translate that for a moment, and then a slow smile flowed across her tightened face. "Yes. *Exactly.* Guys—how hard would it be to wear something… I don't know, cutaway or removable over your tats? Cover your marks so I can come by in the song and pull them off?"

She looked at me and I held up my wrist, with that twined vine of oak and lime traveling around my arm from wrist to elbow. "I think we've got something at home that can do it," I said thoughtfully, then looked out at everybody else. Teague held up his wrist, with the impressive stylized oak tree, and the others showed an assortment of bicep, wrist, or forearm tats that could be easily costumed—even La Mark's was a day-glow nest of limes on the front of his cocoa-colored shoulder. The only exceptions were Max and Jacky.

"No can-do," Max sighed, and he did one of those things that puppies did, when chasing their own tails, except he did it in the water and ended up on his back in a full roll. "Mine's on my back," he sputtered when he came up, his eyes crossing more than usual.

Renny looked sideways at her husband and burst into a peal of giggles so passionate that she actually dunked herself and came up sputtering. In a heartbeat, she was a cat again, but she was sneezing through wrinkled whiskers, and Max and I were laughing hard enough that *we* were having trouble staying afloat.

Cory let out an honest laugh, the deep chuckle calming things down a bit. "You're still not excused, Max—you can wear a sport coat over a backless tank, and we'll put Renny, wearing something backless next to you. Her tat won't be so noticeable until everyone else's is revealed. What about you, Jacky? Nothing we can see in public?"

"NO!" Jacky and Teague both shouted in tandem, and they were suddenly the focus of the entire group's attention, and now Katy was the one laughing.

"No, Lady," she shook her head between guffaws—she was having trouble staying afloat, and her two lovers were doing their best not to look at each other. "I don't think the world is ready to see all of Jacky's shit, just flappin' in the breeze!"

Cory blinked. "Oh yeah," she muttered, "I'd forgotten that!"

We all looked at her, and she shrugged, the water rippling over her shoulders. "He stood right over my head buck naked during the vampire bear attack." She let out a prodigious yawn and covered her mouth with a pruny hand, speaking through the yawn. "I was thinking about other things, but, yeah," she grinned up at Jack, "you actually *are* excused, Jacky. That's just a little TMI." Jack blinked, as though he was surprised it had been that easy, but before he could say anything, she yawned again and I shook my head.

"Did you nap at all?" I asked, and she managed to look sheepish. "And you're getting cold—here, let's get you out of the water." I looked at Max, who nodded, and in a minute he was a cat just like Renny and together they moved under her arms, in spite of her awkward attempts to bat them away and keep her head above water.

They ignored her, and we left everybody else out to play as Nicky and I followed to make sure she got to the room okay. She stopped where she reached a place she could stand, and turned to holler, "Dinner at dusk, at the picnic tables behind the cabin!" and when everybody waved, she nodded and let me take her arm back.

"I need to be up before dusk," she grumbled, and I agreed. "And I'm sorry, Nicky, but we're not going to invite your parents for dinner—not tonight."

"Can I still eat with you?" he asked mournfully, snagging a towel that he'd found at the shoreline and wrapping it around his waist. She took his hand in her free hand and leaned her head on his shoulder.

"I can't imagine a thing you could do that would make you unwelcome at your family's table," she murmured, and he kissed the top of her wet, frizzy head and looked at me.

"She's really tired," he murmured. "I should have made her nap."

"Contrary to all evidence, I *am* a grown-up," Cory sniffed, and then she stubbed her toe on a rock hard enough to start it bleeding. "Oh fuck it all anyway!" she snapped in exasperation, and then we all looked up in time to catch Nicky's parents coming out of their cabin with their eyes open in horror.

There was a shocked silence, and Cory turned a green smile to Nicky. "Swearing's not so big in your house, is it?"

Nicky shook his hair out of his eyes ruefully. "Not so much, no!"

"Fuck…" she hissed, even as I swung her up into my arms, heedless of the blood running from her toe. "Bracken, I'm not helpless!"

"No but you're mine," I murmured quietly, "and I get few enough to chances to care for you. Besides, you can blame this on me and miss out on the social awkwardness you were about to walk into!"

"Arrogant bastard," she muttered, and I didn't argue.

"Owwieee!" said Mr. Kestrel on the approach. "That looks like a bad stub—did you do that all by yourself?"

"Bracken's making it worse than it is," she murmured, watching the blood drip steadily into the dust, "but if Nicky helps me dress it, it'll be okay."

The skinny young woman emerged from their room in time to hear this.

"Well here we were, thinking you were the help," she said with a forced laugh, "and it looks like the whole world really does fall all over you when you stub your toe."

Cory smiled sourly. "Only my corner of it. Now if you'll excuse us—I'm bleeding and it's icky."

"Uhm," Nicky's mother interrupted apologetically, "I was wondering what you all were doing for food tonight? We thought there'd be… something nearby?"

Cory nodded. "There're some restaurants about fifteen minutes from here—you can eat there. We brought some food in today from Redding, snacks and things." She glanced at Nicky with her own apology. "If Nicky wants, he can share his with you."

Nicky shook his head. "You'd better bring your own," he said shortly, and Cory gave him an appreciative smile.

"So what—you all are eating some super special weird people food, now?" Annette (I think Cory said that was her name) asked, her lips curled off her teeth like a ferret's.

I wanted to snarl in her face, but Cory answered first, and I was so proud of her in that moment it made me tolerate the repulsive woman's presence for far longer than we should have. "My people take breaking bread very seriously," she said clearly, "and I will not ask them to eat with someone they do not trust." Another smile, this one sincerely apologetic, "And now, we really do have to get in and take care of this... darn it, Bracken, you've made me all dizzy."

As I charged through the door to grab a towel and deposit her on the big bed, I heard Nicky's father say miserably, "Well, dear, I can't say you didn't earn that for us," but I wasn't waiting for Terry Kestrel's reply.

Nicky did a fair job with the bandage, and by the time she'd showered to wash the lake out of her hair and put on a T-shirt to settle down under our watchful eyes, the bleeding had stopped and I could lay next to her and hold her. We turned off the lights and left on the ceiling fan, and the paneled room was cool and restful.

"She's going to be awesome in front of the vampires!" Nicky enthused quietly in the cool dark, even as she slept.

I grinned at him. "Yeah, but she's going to be a basket case until it's over. You may want to go outside and take a 'Cory break' or she'll make you crazy."

Nicky nodded and sighed. "No more'n my folks."

I could only shrug in commiseration. "Well, do what you can, brother. You know I feel for you."

Nicky bent over the bed and kissed her cheek in the quiet. "You all do," he murmured. "It may be the only thing that gets me through this while talking to them at all."

"Nick," I said as he started to leave, figuring he'd need to know this. He stopped at the door and turned around. "She's scared of the water. She'll go out there, because she doesn't want anyone to know, but keep an eye out for her."

Nicky blinked. He'd been out with us to Clementine and Sugarpine before, so I could see his confusion.

"It's because she can't see her feet," I elaborated, and nodded towards the scar on her ankle. "Something grabbed her when she couldn't see."

Nicky's eyes widened, and he nodded at the scar too. "I always wondered. What was it?"

I grimaced. "A suicidal vampire in the middle of the afternoon," I muttered, and his eyes widened. He stood there for a moment, like there was something else to say, and then shook his head.

"Of course *you're* telling the story," he said after a moment in disgust. "I'll have to ask her for it later—she does a better job."

I snorted. "She flew out of the water, yanked off his arm, the damned thing combusted around her ankle and she fell back in. Arturo went in and yanked off it's head, same thing happened, but Arturo didn't almost die of pain and shock." I rolled my eyes. "Green healed her. It sucked. I almost lost my fucking mind. So did Adrian. Green yawed off to the wild-fucking-blue to get a bead on what in the hell was going on, and in the end it fucked us anyway. What else did you want to know?"

Nicky blinked, and a slow grin warmed his pretty features. "Bracken, I truly love you…I'm not sure which box you'd put it in if we were human, but you are a fucking treasure."

"Fuck off," I muttered, and he laughed his way out of the room.

I lay there watching as the long-tree shadows lengthened and tasting the melancholy of late afternoon in a place where the sun and the stars were that much closer to your face when you peered at the sky.

The heat outside was horrible, deadening, life-sucking, unless you were submerged in the blissful water… but that muddy water—so worth it! I looked at my beloved—her cheek was pillowed on the back of one hand, so she faced me, and her other arm was crooked behind her back. If she'd been sleeping in jeans, it would have been tucked into her back pocket.

I felt a sudden whisper of our fragility here—she depended on Nicky and I for life-force, and Nicky was distracted and I was…weak. I was weak with the heat for most things. It was only her—she was the one who needed to be strong for us, when we had always tried so hard to protect her, even from herself.

I gave a sigh, and settled down in a position that mirrored hers, so I could watch her sleep. Perhaps Green would have gotten on his laptop, and Nicky may have picked up a book. I might even do these things later, but not now. I was the only one who got to do this. It was my right and my privilege.

CORY

Research

The sun pounded brutally down on my back, over my shoulders, and in my face. There was no escaping it, and no reprieve, and my lungs seared with every breath.

Fucking Redding.

It was wrong, I was sure, to base all of my assumptions on a town on the fact that the sun seemed to want to wipe it out with bad vibes alone, but there you had it. My animal self had felt the sun and decided that any solar wave that could cook food without benefit of a microwave sucked ass. It wasn't fair, but neither was the feeling that my brain was poaching in my skull like an egg in a sauce pan.

On either side of me, Jack and La Mark stood, throwing out their own animal heat, and I fought the urge to shake them off my shoulders like a dog would shake water. They were our best students and our best researchers, and their help would be invaluable.

Besides, it was damned nice of them to leave the lake, where everybody seemed to be having such a swimming time, and come here with me to the Redding branch of the Shasta County Public Library.

The building was modern, with some aluminum bars shading the west-facing horizontal entrance, and inside, besides the quiet and the carpeting and the wooden tables and suppressed hush that you can find in most libraries, there was the most important thing of all.

Air conditioning.

With a big sigh I blessed the innovations of my own species—we could be a pain in the ass sometimes, but dammit, could we build a machine.

With the weight of the heat off my brain, I spoke for the first time since we'd parked a block down and walked, trying to formulate a plan.

"I looked them up online," I murmured, "and they've got a newspaper database here. How about La Mark and I take the newspaper database, and Jack, you chat up the locals and see if there's any buzz about missing family, right?"

Jack grunted, and then looked at me with his mouth quirked in puzzlement. "Because my people skills have proven soooo useful to date?"

I grimaced. "Oh Goddess, you're right... we should have brought Katy."

Jacky shook his head. "Katy has no subtlety—and Teague was always the best interrogator when we went out on runs... which was why it was a good thing Green always did the groundwork first."

I grunted and rubbed the bridge of my nose. "Damned straight. La Mark, how about you?"

La Mark looked around at the mostly white population in the library. "My lady, I haven't seen another black man in three days. I think you're probably our best bet here."

I let out a sound that was suspiciously like a whine. "I'm not good with my own species," I complained. "Haven't we had a demonstration of that already?" I turned accusing eyes at La Mark. "You've seen that, right? Remember last year? Chloe, Max's sister—any of this ringing the 'run-away' bell?"

La Mark shook his head and tried not to laugh. "Now *that's* who you should have brought with you. Max. He would be able to ask those questions..."

"Just like a cop!" Jacky supplied for me.

I nodded at La Mark. "It's true—he is a cop. He's the only guy I know who could manage to live at the hill and be a cop at the same time." Besides, Max and Renny were out with Teague, 'finding' the bodies that we'd discovered yesterday. I hope they got a good look at the caves—just for the hell of it, actually, because the idea was so damned cool.

"Okay okay," I finally said in answer to their unvoiced conclusion, "I'll do it. Cory and her native species shall engage... it's gonna suck."

And with that we went up to the desk to figure out what we had to sign to use their search engines.

Three hours later—after offending one librarian by accidentally suggesting that Redding was chock-full of serial killers and completely titillating another, who apparently watched too many crime shows, we had a disturbing set of facts and an overwhelming urge to get back to the quiet of the cabins on the lake. It was the closest thing we had to home right now, and after being bumped by strangers all day in an unfamiliar place I could see all of us—even Jacky, who had taken a while to get comfortable at the hill—itching to be someplace home.

And the news itself was bad.

"Three families in the last two years?" I asked again. We had each found one, and it was staggering. That didn't count families in other parts of the state. Anywhere a vampire could drive in a night, that was this predator's hunting ground—I wasn't naïve enough to think we were the only ones who'd come up with the special compartment in the bottom of the hearse or the SUV.

"If he's got a small plane," La Mark theorized over my shoulder, "that could be a hell of a lot of territory.

Oh fuck. What kind of moron was I to not even think about planes?

"Way to go, bird-boy," I muttered. "There goes my good night's sleep!"

Jacky grunted. "And that's only the kids with families."

Now that I *had* thought of. "I'm thinking that's part of his...you know, glitch." The word was 'pathology', but it sounded like I knew what I was talking about and I didn't. "I think he likes to take kids," because there had been boys as well "from their families." I swallowed. "And these are the families that got press. There are probably some poorer families out there that didn't."

"You know what else this means," Jacky cautioned, and I nodded grimly.

It meant that there were more 'Gretchens' out there.

"Maybe they died with the sunrise," La Mark postulated hopefully, and I nodded just to do something. Some of them might have, but all of them?

"No," I murmured, finding myself unable to lie, not about this. "Not all of them. Some of them are probably in the kiss. Tomorrow night we're going to have to keep our eyes open."

So we were feeling pretty grim and stern as we left the library, so much so that I almost didn't recognize our 'civilian' when he passed us near the entrance. He nodded and smiled, though, and as I was doing the automatic return nod and smile, his face clicked.

"Hey!" I tried to add some brightness to my tone. It would be lonely, spending all that time at the cabins without friends.

"You have no idea what my name is, do you?" he asked cheekily, and I felt La Mark and Jack chafe at my side and ignored them.

"Not a clue," I told him dryly. "But you know I look like a giant dorkfish in the lake and that I'm clumsier than a drunken prom queen on fm-heels, so I figure you rate a 'hey!'"

That earned me a near-blinding flash of some seriously impressive hardware. "I'm Sam," he said, running his tongue across a spacer. He didn't offer to shake hands, maybe because he was still a kid, but he did look at me expectantly.

"I'm Cory Kirk…" I stopped, and I heard the guys on either side of me suck in their breaths. I'd almost spilled part of my name to him—the part I didn't hardly give *anybody*. For one thing, in my world it could be dangerous—names were power, and one of the few things I had in my puny mortal favor was that my name was so damned long, it was hard to know enough of it to control me.

"Cory Kirk?" The boy asked slyly. "Like 'Captain Kirk', except 'Cory Kirk'?"

I nodded, and figured that it was probably a better 'half-name' than my full name. "Pretty much!" I nodded brightly. "Did you get so bored you decided to read books?"

The boy shook his head. "Libraries rent video games too, you know."

I blinked. "I did not know that," I told him bemusedly, "and now I do. You have a good day then—we'll probably see you around."

The boy nodded, and there was something sage and wise about it, as though he was a very youthful king, or a very old and mischievous god. "I'm sure you'll be wary of me, 'Captain Cory'." He smirked, which took some of the mystery away, but I was squinting after him as he entered the library and the guys urged me back into the glare.

And I almost ran into two small boys that I know.

"Gavin? Graeme?" Shit-a-fuckin'-fire, I really was running the 'Circus of the Damned', wasn't I?

"Are we in a bad Nick sitcom?" La Mark muttered behind me, and before I could tell him that he watched way too much television in the Avian's aerie, I found myself the recipient of two enthusiastic hugs.

"Hey guys!" I said to Grace's grandchildren, and they peppered me with questions.

"Hey Lady Cory, what are you doing here? We're still coming in August, right? Mama said that's when we're doing 'Camp Green', so we'll be there. We're still coming, right? Where's Bracken? Is Green here? What about Nicky? Grandma's not here, is she? Did you bring Arturo? What about the sprites? We miss the sprites—we never had to fold our clothes!"

I didn't have a chance to answer even one question before Graeme, the youngest, and the one with the clearest, most direct reasoning, stopped short. "You're not supposed to be here, right? We're not supposed to… uh-oh."

Yeah. 'Uh-oh' was little-kid-speak for 'Oh fuck!'.

"Do we know you?" asked a thin-faced, lanky, freckled woman who looked like a bitter, sour version of the vampire we all loved so well.

I smiled winningly, and for once hoped that I could act like a human and not a complete freak.

"We're counselors from 'Camp Green'," I told her truthfully. "We just came up on a group camping trip—the boys saw us and said hi, that's all."

Chloe eyed me distastefully, some vestige of her wiped memory telling her that I was undesirable around her children.

"You're not the only counselor, I trust," she said after a moment, and I smiled widely.

"No, ma'am, there's a lot of us." Damned straight there was—those two boys spent two weeks on Green's hill being spoiled silly by every creature whose existence was doubted by man.

The boys weren't stupid—they backed away chastely, trying to look more 'publicly appropriate' as their mother shepherded them away. They gave me one last glimpse behind their shoulders, when mom wasn't looking, and I waved and winked and treasured their secret grins as they walked inside the library with their mother.

As the door closed behind them, we stood at the crosswalk ready to get back to the cabin with every fiber of our beings. I shook my head in wonderment and said, "Okay, La Mark, since you're the expert on bad sitcoms, what's going to happen to us now?"

The light changed while he was still thinking about it, and we started across the street where we were almost killed by a Dodge Caravan barreling through the intersection before he could answer.

I saw it in slow motion—the forty-something man behind the wheel, looking panicked, stepping on his brakes fruitlessly, and I knew, knew without thinking, that the three of us could *not* get out of his way fast enough. The panic-shield of power I threw up around us stayed intact, even as we dashed for safety, and it clanged like the gong-of-the-damned as the car clipped it and careened into the intersection where it smacked a green Chrysler in the rear quarter panel, and the two vehicles spun, hit again front to front, and ground to a halt.

Jacky, La Mark and I stared at the smoking, folded vehicles in absolute horror.

"Are you shitting me?" I asked no one in particular, and then I started to struggle as the two men each grabbed my arm and started hauling me off down the block.

"Guys… guys… what if someone was hurt…" It was my first reaction. It was who I was for my people—we took care of our own, didn't we? Except the panicked guy behind the wheel of the car didn't count. Did he?

"And what if someone notices that the car should have taken Jacky out but didn't?" La Mark hissed in my ear, fighting me away from the scene.

"Or a cop wants us to give a statement!" Jacky muttered from my other side. "Who the hell are we, Lady, and what are we doing here?"

"We *have* driver's licenses!" I snapped, hauling out of their hard grips and turning around to go back and take care of business.

The two drivers—our guy of the Caravan and the young kid driving the Chrysler—had both wobbled out and were tottering over their totaled vehicles in a stunned way as an ambulance passed in front of us, quicker on the scene than I would have thought.

It was well in hand, and this time when the guys seized my arms and hustled me into the car, I didn't resist at all. La Mark copped the wheel and drove straight out, and we sat with shell-shocked faces and a complete inability to come up with one single coherent thing to say for the forty-five minute drive to the turn-out to the lake.

Of course, this meant that La Mark was driving when we hit the winding portion of the road on the way to the cabin. I broke the stunned silence with the inevitable.

"Oh Christ, La Mark, pull over. I've gotta hurl."

Ugh. It doesn't get any better doing that, you know? It certainly doesn't get any better when it's a hundred-gazillion degrees Flamingheit and your skin sticks to your skin and your sweat's running down your pits and in the crease of your body as you bend over to spew. Between that and the merciless, bloodless, bitter motherfucker of a sun, my head was starting to throb in time with the heat distortion coming off the road. The guys were sweet about it, but I felt like Bracken had looked yesterday as we pulled up in front of the cabins.

Bracken took one look at my face as he opened the door and swore. "Why didn't you drive?"

I shook my head and took another swig from the water bottle Jack had given me. "Do you want the long version or can you live with 'It didn't come up when we were loading the car'?"

"The long version can wait. Come inside, shower, get out of the fucking sun…"

I started to giggle, having gone completely round the bend. "If the sun was fucking, it would be a hell of a lot cooler!"

"Why's that, genius?" Bracken asked, swinging me into his arms because he liked to do that when he was feeling all big and manly.

"Because then all we'd see is his moon!"

Behind me I heard Jacky and La Mark grumble, "Oh Jesus!" and "Now *I've* gotta hurl!" and then Bracken had me inside the cabin and into the blessed, blessed coolth and the shower was running and they ceased to matter much at all.

Fifteen minutes later, I was lying on our bed in a pair of gym-shorts and one of Bracken's T-shirts, watching Katy paint Renny's claws some bizarre shade of purple.

Renny was obviously fighting the urge to sneeze because her whiskers were drawn back from her long teeth and her pink cat's tongue kept coming out and licking her nostrils, trying to get the sharp odors of acrylic polish and acetate out of them.

I watched them, because the logic of painting a were-cat's toes when odds were good the polish would go away when she changed to human was a lot easier to fathom than pretty much anything else that had gone on that day.

"Why are you doing this again?" I asked, hoping this time it would make sense.

"Because," Katy said, shaking her hands and looking at Renny to do the same with her paw, "when we go from peoples to animals, the polish isn't wide enough... it's just like a little dot, you know? Somewhere on the back of the claw? It gets caught on something, that's it, adios, goodbye, no more manicures, all gone. But this way, we go from creatures to peoples..."

"And it's going to be all over your hand... you'll look like you dipped your fingertips in a vat of it," I postulated grimly, and Katy rolled her eyes.

"Look who's being all pessimistic and shit. You jump into the face of danger with a 'we can do it!' and you get all shitty about a little nail polish?"

I had to laugh. "Okay, okay...you finish Big Game Mani/Pedi and I won't ask Renny what happened across the lake again."

Renny growled—I gathered it had been bad. Teague was off on a run as wolf, working out his puzzlement and bad feeling, and Mario was flying with him, just for safety. Max had been in for a moment, checking on her the way my guys checked on me, and when he saw she was happy (weird, but happy) he'd nodded grimly and walked away with a 'We'll talk later'. Oh yay! More good news! But not now. Now, we got a few minutes peace, and I was enjoying the girl stuff—or rather watching the girls do girl stuff. I was mostly enjoying laying down out of the sun and allowing my skin to cool, even though Bracken hovered protectively near me and Nicky kept giving concerned glances from the other side of the bed.

Ah, peace.

And then there was a knock on the door, followed by a quick open—you know, the kind that you expect from friends?

It was Annette and Terry, and as Terry poked her head in our room with a "Hello, everyone decent?" Renny let out an honest to Goddess mountain-lion scream that had both women jumping back into the dust.

Terry made a quick recovery. "I'll take that as a 'Yes'!" she burbled, and I shot a quick stare at Renny who looked innocently back.

"You shouldn't," I said mildly. "Our were-folk are pretty comfortable in their own skin."

Renny snorted and Katy suppressed a giggle, and then Katy sat back on her haunches. "There you go mommy, let it dry okay?"

Renny rolled her slitted golden-eyes at the five crescent-daggers-of-death, painted a gorgeous, glittery purple, placed both paws delicately in front of her, and then rocked back on her ass and shot her back leg up so she could give her privates a thorough—and thoroughly feline—washing.

Annette gasped. "Why's she doing that?"

Renny looked up at me with half-closed eyes and her pink tongue partially protruding from her mouth, and then resumed business.

I rolled my eyes. "Same reason dogs do it—cause they can. Can I help you ladies?"

"We were just wondering if you and Nicky wanted to go boating with us this afternoon," Terry said quickly, probably because it looked like Annette was going to open her mouth again in a minute.

"No," Bracken said implacably next to me. His hand moved to the small of my back gently, and even if we hadn't had business to deal with this afternoon, I wouldn't have had the heart to countermand him.

"Not today, Mom," Nicky said, standing and moving towards the door. "We've got some stuff to do today. Will tomorrow be okay?"

"Business?" Annette sounded stunned. "What business do you people do?"

"It's complicated," I muttered, not wanting to bring up the vampires. The guys had awakened the night before as we'd been eating, and as they'd moved into a darkened corner of tree and shadow with their own dinners, Annette had exclaimed loudly enough to carry over the lake, "Oh my *God*, what are those two guys *doing* over there!"

She'd managed to make Marcus so uncomfortable the he hadn't been able to bring himself to feed from Mario until much later, after the dumbshit civilians had gone to bed. Conversing with these people about anything of substance was like tap-dancing on a bed of knives.

"Oh," Terry was clearly disappointed, and I felt bad. But since I also still felt like crap, it wasn't bad enough to go out in the sun again until twilight softened the glare, if not the heat. "Well, would you all be up to sitting with us to eat tonight?"

Renny looked up from her kitty-crotch and hissed, and there was a suspicious warbling growl coming from Katy's throat as she carefully stashed her nail polish in a special little box she'd brought with her when I'd been in the shower. Apparently cats and dogs really can agree—especially when they have a common enemy.

I looked ruefully at Nicky's mom and sighed. "Probably not a good idea just yet," I apologized, "but Nicky, Brack and I can come over and keep you company after we've eaten."

"You're just going to let them…" Annette flailed messily for a word, "*control* who you eat dinner with?"

It was a patent attempt at manipulation, and I couldn't help but regard her distastefully. I had been immune to that bullshit in high school, and I hadn't changed in *that* regard at all.

"They trust me to take care of them," I said levelly. "I won't break bread with someone they don't trust." My headache thundered back, and I looked tiredly at Nicky's mother. "Can I help you with anything else, Mrs. Kestrel?" I asked with a pointed smile, and Terry sent an annoyed glance at her travelling companion.

"No, hon, we're good. Unless…" her eyes shifted helplessly to the flats of bottled water we'd bought in town, and I could finish the sentence for her.

"Nicky, do you want to carry one of those flats to your mom's cabin for her?"

Terry let out a sigh of relief—apparently they had gone shopping the night before without tasting the tap water. "Thank you, hon—I can have Mr. Kestrel give you some money…"

"No worries, Mrs. Kestrel," I told her, swallowing the offense. "We may be choosy about breaking bread, but the fey are big on gifts."

"Is that 'fey', like 'fairies'?" Annette asked. I was just going to ignore her, but Bracken had enough.

Looking at Terry Kestrel quizzically, he said, "She was a better alternative for your son? *Really?*"

Terry gave a weak smile and backed out of the door with a "Thank you all, see you later tonight!" I guess there wasn't anything else to say.

As soon as the door shut, Bracken put his hand on my shoulder firmly and led me to the bed, a cool washcloth in hand. Then he turned off the lights (which didn't stop the manicure session, since everyone's vision was spectacularly better than mine, especially in the dark) and forced me to lay down in the relative quiet of the room, where I stayed until my head stopped thundering at me and I could fall asleep.

Two hours later, as we pow-wowed in my room, I rather wished I had stayed that way.

"Okay," I muttered, rubbing my temples, "let me get this straight."

It had been such a simple plan. Max and Renny would take the ferry across the lake and take the guided tour of the caves like the tourist couple they'd always wanted to be. Teague would trot along in the foliage beneath them and guide them to the bodies, so that they could stray from the trail and 'accidentally' stumble upon them. Renny had been looking forward to letting out an ear-curdling scream and (her words) girling-all-out for the benefit of the trail guides.

The plan had worked too—except they'd been stopped by the guide as they'd gone off the trail, and Renny, who usually walked in her girl-self with the grace of the cat form in which she spent most of her time, had one of those dumbshit-cat-falling-off-the-television moments and literally *tumbled down the hill*.

And Teague—Teague, who was level headed, never panicked, and hated being naked in public?

Teague *changed form to catch her and keep her from falling into the nasty decomposed bodies.*

And Max. Max, who was used to the entire fucking world seeing his wife naked, but who, until just this exact moment hadn't truly given a ripe shit because Renny was Renny, and if she chose a mate, it was for life, had lost his temper, and screamed, *Don't touch her you horny bastard!* Drawing the entire tour group's attention to the naked man in the brush.

Teague had given Max an anguished look, turned back into a werewolf and gone hauling ass into the forest, Renny had remembered what in the fuck they were there to do in the first place, kicked some leaves and started squealing, and Max had been so embarrassed that he'd hidden behind a tree, stripped, and turned into a cat to go find a wolf and apologize.

Leaving Renny alone, to explain to a very puzzled guide why he should call the cops but not mention the naked man and the missing husband.

By the time Jack, La Mark, and I had returned, Max had managed to make peace with Teague, but Teague had been so unsettled that he figured being a wolf would keep him out of trouble, and Max had been in his cabin, sulking with beer and wondering if three or four more apologies to Renny would make up for the fact that he'd left her alone to deal with the authorities when that had been the whole reason I'd picked *him* to go.

I listened to the story with the same horrified fascination you would use while watching—wait for it—a car crash. Immediately after the car almost hit you.

"Merciful Goddess, indifferent God, what an unholy goatfuck."

La Mark snorted. "Makes our trip almost normal," he muttered, and Jack nodded, having to agree.

I groaned in frustration and looked around for something to kick. "There is nothing normal about this," I snapped, and Bracken spoke up in agreement.

"It feels... wonky," he said, his eyebrows scrunched together. "It feels... us. It feels preternatural and... not exactly planned, but... prompted somehow."

"Could it be the moon?" Nicky asked, and since Avians weren't driven by the tides he looked around at the people who would know.

"No," Teague said shortly, and Jack kicked his foot and prompted him to continue. "No, because the moon was full five days ago. It's still pretty bright in the sky, but it's waning—it doesn't...thunder in our blood."

I turned to Katy then. "Katy, what were you thinking yesterday, when you yelled at Renny?"

Katy shrugged. "I was thinking she's always naked! But that don't usually bother me none—it was like, my top ten things to say about the thing? I picked number fifteen."

Max nodded excitedly. "Me too! Dammit—I had a thousand things to worry about—Teague catching Renny? Last goddamned thing on my mind— and there it was, the first thing out of my mouth." He looked unhappily at Teague. "Can I say one more time that I am *soooooo* fucking sorry?"

Teague shrugged. The two had always gotten along, and right now I held my breath that this moment wouldn't hurt them. "No worries," he said simply, and I let out my breath on a sigh. If Teague said it, it must be truth.

I stood up to pace, barely noticing when everybody on the floor backed up and gave me a path.

"So something's dicking with us—not in a normal way, just... just dicking with us. The shit we say, accidental bullshit—I'm fully prepared to blame seventy-five percent of what went down yesterday with Nicky's parents to this whatever-the-fuck-it-is..."

"You're being generous," Nicky grumbled. "My mother gets fifty-percent of the blame at least."

I shook my head. "No... it was the timing of everything, Nick. It was..." I whirled around and looked at La Mark. "It was sit-com perfect. That thing with Teague and Max—it was like a sit-com."

"Yeah, but that car coming at us wasn't so goddamned funny!" Jacky said seriously, and Teague—who had just come back from his run—looked at Jacky in sudden panic.

"Car?" he asked, and I shrugged it off.

"It barely clipped my shield. If I hadn't been so...off-kilter from meeting the boys..."

Bracken—who hadn't heard the whole story either—broke in, "Boys? As in Gavin and Graeme? They were there today?"

I sighed and flopped down on the bed, staring moodily at the ceiling fan. Jesus did I wish I could take a fucking Motrin for my goddamned head. "Did I mention sit-com timing, Bracken Brine? Yeah—first we ran into the civilian in the end cabin, then we ran into the boys, and then a big fucking Grand

Caravan driven by a really freaked out suburban dad almost tanked into us and took out a Chrysler four-door instead."

Lambent, who had spent the last two days frolicking in the lake like a fish of fire, let out a low whistle. "Sounds like a party—and you people say *I'm* the source of chaos in this outfit."

I turned my head on the quilt to glare at him. "Well lucky us it hasn't hit you yet, or we'd all be crispy-fried vulture-vomit by now, wouldn't we?"

Lambent had the nerve to grin. "Now luv—I wouldn't crispy-fry you—I like my birds par-boiled."

I had to laugh. "Well, this partridge would prefer to keep her feathers on, thank you." I propped myself up on my elbows and wished desperately for Green. I'd been trying so hard not to get his attention unless it was by phone—the heat was hurting him just like it hurt Bracken, and I didn't want to tap his strength from this distance. It was hard for him to spread his presence, but this time, when I scented mustard flowers and tall grass in a cool spring, I raised my face to it, and smiled. My headache even faded. Just that much, I thought clearly, so he could hear me if he was still here, just that much gave me strength.

I think you're right on the money, beloved. I don't know what it is, but I think you're right.

"Whatever it is," I said, trying not to yearn after that lovely moment, "its trademark is chaos. I'll have to ask Marcus if he's brought his laptop with him—we both have some stuff in our files, and we can do some research from here. There's got to be something we can find out. And until then…" I sat up completely and looked around the room, making sure I had everybody's eyes.

"Until then, I think the key is to not take offense. Goddess knows when this weird 'talking thing' is going to take over and bite us in the ass. We all have to be totally willing to forgive and forget. If the last thing on our minds is the thing that comes shooting out or our mouths, there's a reason it was the last thing on our minds. So be careful about what you say, but be very ready to blow it off if the person you're talking to has a lapse, right?"

There were nods all around, and I suddenly felt less freaked out.

"We're good people—we like each other. If we can just keep that in mind, we can make it through tomorrow night and do what we came out to do."

I sighed then, and met my accidental lover's eyes. "I'm just sorry we're going to be dealing with this… random chaos generator with your parents here, Nick. It could make things a little bit awkward—and I don't think you can explain it to them, either."

Nicky shrugged. "I still say fifty percent of yesterday was my mother."

I looked at him, and made sure our gazes stuck. "And I still say I'm sorry."

Nicky nodded. "You take on too much. Next thing you know, you'll be apologizing for..."

"Don't even say her name," Bracken snapped adamantly and there was a chorus of nods from the group.

"She's not a demon..." I said, trying to keep my humor.

"Says you!" Renny piped up, and I had to laugh. Okay, okay—Annette was the devil—we had all agreed, and so-be-it.

Nicky rolled his eyes. "Yeah, but the good news is, if you say her name backwards and offer to get her off, she'll disappear!"

We all looked at him. "Awk-ward," Max muttered, and I had to agree.

"Please tell me that was the chaos thing," I begged, and Nicky shrugged. "Probably—but that is why we broke up. She kept begging to get married, to... you know... 'consummate the relationship'. I told her that I wasn't that serious, but I could..." Finally—*finally*—he flushed. "And she told me I was trying to cheapen our relationship, and dropped me before prom."

"Un. Believe. Able." I could barely look at him I was so embarrassed— and appalled.

"Moving right along..." Bracken said, trying for innocence, and I had to laugh.

"Absolutely. Okay—good news, right? Focus on good news."

"The good news is the bodies have been reported," Teague muttered. He had a beer in his hands.

"Good news!" I crowed, pumping my fist in the air, and to my amusement—and relief—the room full of people followed with pumped fists and a chanted, "Good news!"

La Mark spoke up. "Good news is, we didn't get pancaked!"

And the chorus again, "Good news!"

"Good news is, I kept Teague off the Most Wanted list," Renny said dryly, and we all pumped our fists in the air and shouted, "Good news!"

"Good news is, Lambent hasn't set anything on fire yet!" cracked Mario, and we followed it up with "Good news!"

"Good news is I *never* have to sleep with the demon prom queen!" Nicky hooted—oh yeah—"Good news!"

"Good news is Cory performs tomorrow night!" Bracken threw in smugly, and I groaned and covered my face with the bed-pillow, but that didn't stop the delighted chant of "Good news!" from echoing yet again.

And so on. We managed to celebrate the research we'd accomplished, the lake outside that everybody loved, the fact that our vampires would arise tonight, and each other. By the time we broke up to go out and swim in the deepening shadows of evening, my headache was gone and I thought that maybe, just maybe, we'd survive this little vacation alive.

BRACKEN

Little Deaths

Watching the vampires almost killed her figuratively, and the abominable big-titted human almost killed her for real.

Of the two, I definitely preferred the vampires.

Dinner was much the same as it had been the night before. About fifteen minutes before the vampires awoke, when the woods surrounding the lake grew thick and deep with shadows, a feast appeared, complete with a tablecloth on two of the picnic tables behind the cabins. The tables were illuminated by strings of lights in the surrounding trees, with one large lantern per table, including the one at which Nicky's parents and their unwanted guest sat.

Phillip, Marcus, and Kyle awakened quietly when we were all eating, and Cory stiffened next to me for a moment, until we heard splashing down at the lake. She'd been keeping a quiet eye on Phillip for the last month. Gretchen's deteriorating condition didn't seem to be bothering him—until you saw how haggard Marcus was from caring for him. But that's not why Cory was concerned now.

"Did they remember their trunks?" I asked her and she shook her head.

"No, but they will by the time they come up to eat!" She dug into her plate then—Lambent and I were eating vegetarian baked beans and salad, and she and the shape-shifters got some sort of sausage. Whatever it was, it must have been very tasty to carnivores, because they seemed to be enjoying themselves. I watched, though, as she stopped very deliberately after one serving.

"All done?" I asked, carefully.

"All weirded out by wandering around in a bikini," she answered, although she'd changed back into shorts and a T-shirt after we'd gone swimming and had yet to actually wear the thing without a T-shirt over it. I glared at her, but at that moment, Nicky's mother came up and asked us if we wanted to sit with them for dessert.

We'd been expecting the invite, and we got up without ceremony to sit at their table—and honestly, it felt less awkward than sitting in a happy group while they sat alone, exiled by their own thoughtlessness.

They had bought some kind of chocolate creme pie from a store, and I thought wistfully of whatever it was that Grace had sent over via the sprites, but dug in anyway. They'd better save some for me over at the next table. I was halfway through when I realized Nicky's mother had asked me a question.

I swallowed and then swallowed again—it had been a big bite. "What do I do at school?" I asked, feeling dumb.

"Yes, hon," Terry said, bemused. "What classes do you take?"

I stared at her in the lamplight, wondering whether she was being dense on purpose. "I take whatever classes Cory takes," I said through another bite.

Nicky's father answered. "Well, son, that's nice for kissy face and all, but it's no way to decide on a living."

I blinked and Nicky laughed. "You should see your face right now, Bracken!" he chortled. "It's like they asked you how to split the atom!"

I grimaced at him. "Well, what's your major, bird-boy?" I asked, and he flushed.

"See—I'm right, aren't I! You just take more classes you're interested in because you can!"

"Why can't you?" Asked Jonathan Kestrel, and I could actually *hear* Cory roll her eyes in the semi-dark.

"Don't say it," I warned. "Don't even think it. I could give a f...damn about the human piece of paper. That's your job. My job is to..."

She held out her hand. "Yes, beloved," her voice gentle with humor, "I know what your job is—I've made my peace with it. I just don't think you ever put it into words before."

"I don't get it," Terry asked, genuinely puzzled. "What's his job? Why's he going to school and not worrying about a degree?"

"He's there to keep me safe, Mrs. Kestrel," Cory said bluntly. "It's the only reason he ever agreed to go to school in the first place. When Nicky and I first met in San Francisco...well, we were under attack and didn't know it."

"That was my fault," Nicky said quietly.

"You were coerced," she reassured. "Anyway, he assures me he enjoys it now,"

"I do." It was only the truth.

"And I don't think I could have passed physics or poly-sci without him,"

"You could have." I believed that—it just would have taken her a little longer.

"But the whole reason Bracken started coming to school in the first place was to keep me safe." She flashed me a smile that was just for me. "And so far it's worked."

"Unless you've gone haring off without us," I grumbled, and she grinned back at me.

"That was one time!"

"Yeah," Nicky added, "but you almost got killed!"

"Which is why," she reasoned with a quick nod at his family, "it was only one time!"

"I don't understand," Terry murmured. "I don't understand any of it. You all talk like soldiers—how dangerous can your lives be?"

Cory grew abruptly sober. "It depends on how you look at it," she murmured. "The three of us can wield a tremendous amount of power—yes, even your son. There are things out there that will prey on that. We're also part of the leadership of one of the biggest collectives of supernatural creatures in the area..."

"Continent," I corrected, and she raised her eyebrows and flushed. She didn't like to think of it like that.

"Okay—fine. Whatever," she continued. "Green's hill wields a lot of power. And because we have that power, we're obligated to keep it in check—nobody likes the power police, Mrs. Kestrel. They're pretty much everybody's asshole. So we tend to travel in groups, and we take our family very seriously."

"You've got magic powers?" asked Annette from the other side of the table. "Bullshit! You've *got* to show me your magic, honey—I'm dying to see it!"

Cory turned a miserable and cold glance at the woman. "Usually people who are dying to see what I can do, Annette, end up dead. I don't do demos."

There would have been an awkward pause then, but the vampires came up at that moment—dripping into dry clothes, as it were. Marcus—usually the best 'public face'—led them as they came up to talk to us.

"Evening, Cory, evening Nicky's folks," he said with a charming smile. The Kestrel's and their guest gave a blank, frightened stare back. The night before had been that much of a disaster.

"Heya, Marcus," Cory smiled against the strain. "Good swim?"

Marcus' answering smile was dreamy. Everyone loved the lake. "Awesome—we should have Green make one of those in our backyard."

"We have one, genius—its called Sugarpine," she quipped. When Marcus' surprised laugh had subsided she added, "Hey, do me a favor?"

"Anything O Mighty Queen!" Accompanied by the requisite bow.

"Oh Goddess…" I could smell her blush—even with the teasing. "Anyway, could you feed from the Avians tonight?" She gave Nicky an apologetic glance. "If that's all right with you, Nicky?"

Nicky shrugged. "Me and Marcus are always good for a party, sure."

Cory nodded. "We'll fill you in later, but there's…" she gave a furtive glance at the civilians, and flushed more, realizing she had been indiscreet. "Let's just say that personal dynamics are a little wonky—no one's fault, but thank you. This'll make it easier."

Marcus gave a nod and Nicky stood up to go find a *very* quiet corner with the others. He turned to us and waggled his eyebrows lasciviously. "Back in a flash!"

Marcus snorted. "I'm better than that and you know it. C'mon, breakfast."

The banter between the three vampires and the three Avians continued as they disappeared—far beyond Annette's censorious and prying eyes.

"Well I just don't see why they'd do that," Annette sniffed in disgust, and Cory and I looked at each other with bittersweet memories of the same vampire vibrating between us.

He'd bitten me in bed, in the yellow light of his yellow room, his profile so thrown into light and shadow that it seemed the shadows had grown cold breath to nip at my carotid.

It was a sensitive place anyway, but with his cool, hard body printed against mine, with his erection pushing insistently at my hip, my neck was suddenly every hot spot on my sidhe-sensitive body, from the ticklish underside of my head under the foreskin to the crown of the dark place only Adrian, Andres and Green had ever invaded.

And just as I'd had this thought, I gasped, groaned in need, begging for Adrian's teeth to invade me, and he'd pulled sex from that vulnerable place under my jaw just like he promised to pull come from my cock, as he ground against me and fed…

Cory and I blinked at each other slowly, coming awake from our own sex-saturated memories, and Cory turned an unrepentantly sultry face to our bemused audience.

"There are perks," she murmured throatily, and then she cleared her throat and tried to sound all business. "The vampires protect us—and they're formidable. And the bite… can be nice."

Suddenly Nicky's father, who had been quiet for much of the last two days, squinted his eyes at Cory and sucked in a breath.

"You've been marked!" he murmured in horrified fascination. "More than once! You have a harem of husbands and you've been marked by a vampire? Wasn't one good enough for you?"

Just that quickly, the pleasant memories of pleasure and comfort were replaced by the memory of pain.

"Your son fell in love with me when I was recovering from Adrian's death," she said tautly. "Nicky asked me to dinner, mind-raped me and threw me against a concrete car-port pole." Her voice wavered and grew strong, and I knew she was struggling to summarize a long, complicated happening into a few words.

"And that's just the beginning." She swallowed. It was true—we usually boiled the entire happening down to "bad shit stories"—it was hard to resurrect them now. "But it doesn't matter, because we still love him. We care for him. We treasure him. If you can't respect me or my choices because you don't understand that sometimes the Goddess is a fickle Bitch and we do what we can to survive Her, you should at least respect the fact that for all the reasons we had to despise Nicky, we chose to love him forever instead."

The silence then transcended 'awkward' and breached 'painful'. She stood up on watery knees and fumbled for my shoulder. I dropped my fork and stopped eating their goddamned pie.

"Excuse me," she murmured tensely. "I'm done with dessert."

I watched her stalk blindly into the dark of the surrounding woods, knowing she couldn't see to –literally—save her life, and turned to the people who should have been a joyous part of our family.

"We love Nicky," I said after a moment, remembering the trusting way he had simply sat in my arms and accepted my comfort. "He's going to stay with us—he's happy with us. But you are under no obligation to stay in his life. Remember that, when you try to hurt her."

And with that I turned around to catch her before she gave herself a concussion by walking into a tree.

I found her, trying to step on moonlit patches of path between dark lengths of black-shadow. Teague had been right--the moon was still bright, even though it wasn't full. I came up to her side and took her hand, then walked along the clearest ways, knowing she would trust me to take her where she couldn't see.

"Maybe it was the… the chaos thing or whatever," I consoled her, although it seemed unlikely. Those words had been hers—and they were the words she *should* have said, and not the words she shouldn't have.

"I doubt it," she grunted, gasping as I took her around the waist and moved her over the pit she was about to fall in.

"Me too," I was forced to agree.

"I'm getting worse at this," she lamented after a couple of moments of walking towards nowhere.

I caught a branch that was about to whap her in the face and said, "At walking in the dark? Damned straight!"

"No, genius, at talking to my own goddamned species," she snapped back, and I steered her away from a big patch of poison oak before I replied.

"You're getting better at not taking shit," I corrected, and was rewarded by her unladylike snort.

"I'm pretty sure I never took shit!" she threw back, and I had to concede.

"You never took shit from strangers, but humans you know? You try too hard."

I heard her let out her breath slowly between her teeth. Her expression in the dark glow of the moon was almost amused. "That's part of being human, Bracken Brine: compromise."

"When you're queen of every-fucking-thing, to compromise is to take shit. It's not an option." It seemed basic. I could *swear* we were talking the same language. What part of *She takes shit from no one* was my beloved not getting?

"I *should* be able to take shit from these people," she said softly, almost to herself. "I mean, they're not the enemy, I don't have anything to prove. I should just be able to suck it up, eat their crap, and know it's good for Nicky, you know?"

"Nicky wouldn't ask you to do that." She hadn't been there—Nicky had thrown in his lot with us in a way I admired. I could only thank the Goddess that I had never been asked to make such a choice.

I heard her sigh in the slight breeze, and wondered if she was sweating like I was. The sun was down, but the temperature was still in the mid-eighties. Maybe it was cooler down by the lake-edge but before I could veer her that way, there was another rustling and I looked up to see Nicky coming towards us. The vampires really *had* gone deep for their feeding!

"I wouldn't go that way." Nicky waved in the general direction of where he'd come from. His face was flushed pleasantly, and he not-so-subtly adjusted himself in his shorts. From far off we heard Kyle whooping as he dove into the lake much as the Avians had. Another whoop followed him, and I frowned.

"It sounds like they're swimming—what's over there we shouldn't see?"

Nicky laughed, looking away in embarrassment. "Nevermind. What are you guys doing out here anyway?"

Cory walked up and kissed his cheek. "I'm sorry, Nick—I fucked things up again. They…they…"

"They hurt her feelings and all but called her a vampire's whore," I told the truth sourly, "and she defended herself."

Nicky scrubbed his face with his hands. "Oh Goddess… Cory, I'm so sorry. I… I'll ask them to leave. I thought we could do both these things at once, but my folks… they're just…"

She shook her head. "They love you, Nicky—they're doing their best. I'll apologize in the morning…"

"The hell you will!" he shot back. "There's no reason for you to apologize. They may think they're mom & pop America, but they're not. My dad turns into a bird and my mom has been married to him for thirty years, and if they can't accept that the world is bigger than their big charade of being normal, that's their fault."

Cory shook her head. "But your happiness here is more important than my pride. If they're not insulting our people, I should be able to smile and take it. Losing my temper isn't going to help."

And Nicky did us all proud. "You *are* our people, Cory. You're our leader. You don't take anyone's shit. Not even the in-laws. No—you keep on losing your temper. They're going to have to accept you or lose me. I may not like it, but dammit if we haven't worked for a year-and-a-fucking-half to have them fuck with you and our relationship. No. You swallow nothing. You are my lover and my queen, and you take shit from no one."

She laughed a little, and wrapped her arms around his shoulders and kissed him full on the mouth to make him stop his rant.

"Except, sweetie, I apparently can still take lectures from my lovers." She was laughing as she said it.

"Damned straight. Here—go into the woods, be alone with Bracken." He smiled up at me and I raised my eyebrows in appreciation. My thoughts exactly! "I'll stay up with my folks and try to talk some sense into them—but you don't worry. Keep us safe from the bad vampires and safe from whatever the chaos generator turns out to be, but don't worry about Terry and Jonathan Kestrel. I've got them covered."

"What about Annette?" I asked, having grim thoughts about using my grim power.

Nicky and Cory both made a purely human face of sour distaste. "I'm sure she'll find a way to completely fuck up her own life," Nicky muttered, and he and Cory met eyes and nodded in complete agreement.

"Well, if she doesn't, I'm sure one of us will do it for her," I grumbled, and Cory laughed and took my hand in hers.

"Remember we love you," she murmured, to Nicky, and I took the lead again and pulled her deeper into the dark.

We were a few steps in when I heard it. The sound of a man, aroused beyond endurance, the gasp and groan and plea in his voice... and a feral growl of his beloved tormenter, moving in to finish the dance.

I was immediately hard.

I stopped and put my hand over Cory's mouth, and she trusted me enough, could feel the tension in my body, to know that I wasn't afraid. Her eyes darted nervously in the dark, looking for my expression and I leaned close enough for her to see my wicked smile.

I picked her up around the middle, and her body was fit and tight. She simply held herself stiff and still until I got to a rise which looked down into a little dip of shadows. I could see them right away, but Cory had to wait patiently, blinking in the moonlight, until she saw them, across the clearing, moving brightly pale against the black-purple shadows of night.

Marcus and Phillip hadn't gone for a post-feeding swim after all.

Phillip was the one making the groans. His back was to a tree, his leather jacket around his bare back to keep the splinters out of his skin. His head was thrown back and his dark hair falling sideways from his widow's peak. His eyes were closed, but his mouth was half open as he groaned again, his fangs partially extended, his breath coming in pants because that's what a body did during sex, whether it needed oxygen or not.

Marcus was on his knees in front of him, one hand wrapped securely around the base of Phillip's engorged cock, one hand out of sight, between Phillip's parted thighs, cupping his testicles, moving, and I could imagine busy fingers, lubricated in saliva or blood, invading and twisting, plunging and tormenting, drawing out the groaning sounds from Phillip's tortured throat. Marcus pulled his head back and opened his mouth, preparing to sheath Phillip to the back of his gag-less throat. But first, his tongue came out, pointed wickedly, and he teased the head of that purpling, slickened cock with it, until Phillip made little begging noises that might have been "Please, oh Goddess, please..."

Cory's eyes adjusted and she caught her breath. Marcus turned his head, and his whirling red eyes caught sight of us, watching with shock, with arousal, pure voyeurism, surprised and breathless.

The scent of the sudden flood of slickness between Cory's thighs overpowered the scent of pine and earth and water for a sweet second, and Marcus' lips drew back from his fangs in a feral, sexy smile. He wanted us to watch, and watch we did as he turned his attention back to Phillip, extended and exposed in the night air. Marcus widened his mouth again and he wrapped his lips around his pointed teeth and slid his mouth around Phillip tightly and wetly, and his other hand kept up that teasing, insidious rhythm.

Phillip groaned again, more loudly this time, and his hands knotted in his lover's hair, working, trying hard to force Marcus' head to move, faster. Marcus chuckled: the sound tormented Phillip even further.

Cory choked on a whimper I could feel against my hand, and then her own wicked tongue came out and traced a wet pattern against the inside of my palm.

Slowly I sank to the floor of the woods, leaned back against a handy tree and balanced Cory on my lap. The thrust of my erection ground against her ass and settled into the little fabric valley between her cleft.

Phillip was about to come.

His hands in Marcus' hair were clenching and unclenching, and Marcus made a sound of pure animal hunger as his lover started thrusting in his throat without inhibition, with a frenzy that Marcus matched with every slurp of his taut, welcoming mouth. Phillip gave a hoarse, muffled scream and stood, jerking his body as Marcus kept suction and swallowed loudly enough for us to hear across the clearing.

There was a breath, a rest, as Phillip tousled Marcus' hair, and then Marcus pulled away and looked up into his beloved's eyes., panting in arousal. He didn't have to say a word, probably didn't even have to think it, because they had been sharing a bed for twenty years and although Phillip was the bloodless leader in public, it was obvious who led when they were skin to skin.

Before we could even blink, Phillip was on his hands and knees on the forest floor, his body open, stretched by Marcus' busy fingers, glistening in invitation.

Marcus lost no time in shucking his shorts and taking Phillip up on that.

Cory whimpered again and quivered, releasing another flood of damp that I could feel through my shorts. I wanted her. I wanted her hard, bent over, face against the wall, wailing for my come. I wanted her helpless against my sex, whimpering and mindless, all of that will bent on taking me, raw and huge, inside her slickened tightened, madly convulsing body.

But first I wanted us both to see the end of this.

Marcus' own erection was fully sheathed in his lover's body and he was making furious, conquering noises, feral growls of domination and pleasure, of the ruthless taking of sex from someone who would give and give and give.

Phillip was pleading for Marcus to take.

The sound of their hips slapping together filled the clearing, and after a few uncomfortable, terrible, arousing moments, Marcus gave his own roar and reached out to grab Phillip's hair. He hauled Phillip upright and without ceremony or finesse gave a howl and buried his fangs into Phillip's throat.

Phillip keened, and his body jerked and he spattered a few remaining drops on the leaf mold in front of him, and both of them growled and heaved frantically, in a terrible frenzy. Marcus howled again and shuddered, his hips jerking, buried inside his beloved and pouring himself into Phillip's cold, spasming body.

Silence electrified the shadowed clearing, and then there was a low, tender chuckle, and Phillip turned his head to bump noses with his lover. There was no more violence, no more crazy-sexy-aggression in their touch anymore— there was gentleness and humor, and it was time for us to go.

I stood with Cory in my arms and blurred away in the dark so quickly that I don't think even Marcus saw us go. I didn't stop until we got to the back of the cabins, where I dropped Cory's feet to the ground of the rise at the cabin's foundation and whirled her towards the wall.

She stood patiently, chest heaving, feet splayed, while I ran my hands up her inner thighs, feeling the moisture that pooled there as she'd watched. I thrust my fingers under her panties and drew intricate slippery patterns against the stubble on her mound as she stood.

She let out a keening whine, "Please, Bracken, please…" but I needed to talk to her, heighten her, bring her to the place where she came just from my cock inside her.

I stood behind her, the slope of the hill making my height just perfect, and cupped her breast from behind with one of my hands and grated in her ear.

"You liked that."

"So did you…aahhhhh…" because I'd penetrated her with my fingers again and was using her moisture to play with all of the sensitive places between her thighs.

"Of course I did…" play, lubricate, penetrate, stretch… "the question is, what part did you enjoy imagining me in?"

"Auggghhhh…" because now she was being penetrated in two places, and she flexed her knees to drive my fingers deeper. I wouldn't let her, and she whimpered again. "The *bottom,*" she snarled viciously, "I want you on the bottom, I want you receiving, I want to see you fucked into the… *aaaaaaaahhhhhhhhh….*"

I tore our shorts down so quickly I might have been using the Goddess' speed, and I thrust into her heedless of her tiny size or her vulnerability. I knew that tonight, as furious as she was for it, she'd be matching me stroke for stroke.

CORY

Briefly

Bracken surged into my body and I bit my arm so I wouldn't scream. *Ahhhh....*
Goddess...

He wasn't being gentle tonight, because he'd driven me to violence with
his passion and his throbbing words, and he knew I'd fight back with the
same weapon. I couldn't move, could barely stay standing as my toes scrabbled
for purchase on the top of the incline, so I was at his mercy, and he held me
pinned to the wall with his hands on my hips and his driving, thrusting body
inside my own.

And the bastard wouldn't stop whispering in my ear.

"You want to see me fucked..."

"Oh Goddess..." pound pound pound... a hand at my hip disappeared,
worked its way between our bodies, and a finger penetrated me again. The
dark deliciousness of the way he wanted to be taken made me whimper.

"Say it..."

"Yes, you bastard...I want to see you fucked into the fucking gr..." Two
fingers, and I saw stars in the back of my eyes and the orgasm was bursting
at my skin again.

"Oh fuck..." I muttered desperately, but we'd done this before.

"Purple," he muttered and drove himself into me again.

I muffled another scream on my arm (I'd have bruises tomorrow) and
thought purple with olive trim and yellow stars to match the silver ones
dancing across my vision and he growled into my neck and bit me, hard

enough to leave a mark and then I was coming, bursting, flying through the warm summer darkness, and Bracken was right there with me, warm and liquid in my body as we shuddered violently in climax.

It took a while for our breathing to settle down.

I was still panting a little as Bracken pulled up my shorts and buttoned them around my waist, and then helped me down the hill so we could take the long way around the cabins. We slipped into our cabin, heedless of the party that seemed to be going on down by the water, and merged into the darkness, kissing, licking, giggling throatily, our bodies still humming and still ready.

And when we were bare in the starlight streaming from the high windows, we did it again.

Nicky slipped inside shortly after that, and after scenting the air, he slid off his wet trunks, dried off, and slid into bed next to me naked and ready, and the three of us tumbled again, my body so rapaciously tender that by the end of the night their every touch made me quiver and shriek and gasp. We fell asleep when the moon had set, nude and sticky and not caring, not even a little, that the whole world would know.

Shortly before dawn, the vampires came knocking at the door, and I greeted them in one of Bracken's T-shirts down to my knees and nothing else, sliding outside into the chilly black of deep pre-dawn.

"Mornin'," I yawned, trying not to blush when Marcus met my eyes with his very ordinary brown gaze. I failed, and he grinned and blushed too and I rolled my eyes and tried to pretend like we hadn't just watched him naked, pounding Phillip into the forest floor.

"We didn't get to talk last night..." Phillip inquired delicately, and I nodded. Not nice to leave the vampires out of the loop when you're off getting laid—must remember to pow-wow with them *before* the sex and not after.

"We'll have a dress rehearsal tonight, before we leave," I told them, "and be in the cars by ten-thirty. Wear something that can be taken off or moved so I can see your tats—it's part of the show." Fortunately, the vampires were all about the arms. "If you need something, try and contact someone back at the hill before you go to bed. Did you guys talk to anyone about the... the... the..." I moved my hands vaguely.

"Random chaos generator?" Kyle asked dryly, and I nodded.

"Yeah—that. You guys all know about that?"

Marcus *must* have fed well from Nicky because I was pretty sure I could see him blushing again in the dark. "Uhm, no offense Cory, but I think we all sort of lived it last night."

Oh my Goddess, he was right.

"I hadn't even thought," I muttered, stunned, and Phillip and Marcus exchanged heated and flustered glances, and I guess they *had* taken time out to talk about our bizarre encounter in the woods the night before. Well, shit. We still had to work together, right?

"I guess I should have," I said briskly after a truly uncomfortable moment. "The key is, just give your people a break, you know? Uhm," blush, "the sex is fine, if its consensual—we all live with that sort of heat anyway—we can deal. But... you know... don't rip anyone's head off if you can help it—remember self-control, right? We're all pretty decent at that by now anyway."

The guys all nodded, and then Kyle—who spoke about as often as Teague—said, "Uhm... that civilian chick with the big boobs and bigger mouth... are you *sure* we can't kill her?"

I blinked and swallowed, and realized that there was a tiny part of me on the verge of blurting out, *Sure, just make sure you hide the body, would you?* I had even opened my lips on the 'shhhh' sound when I clamped down on my unruly thoughts and shook my head.

"Sadly, no," I grated. "Don't worry—she's one of those cases where just being allowed to live is its own punishment."

There was scattered laughter, and then I yawned hugely—we'd been up *late* and here it was early and...

Marcus and Phillip were both kissing my cheek and saying goodnight, and Kyle gave a short little bow and did the same thing, and I crawled back between my men. Bracken spooned up behind me, and sleep came quickly.

An hour later there was another pounding at the door.

"Awww shit..." and why was I the only one waking up? Fuck it. I stumbled to the door to open it on Tanya's bemused and exasperated expression in the cold gray dawn.

"What the hell?" I mumbled.

"What in the fuck did you do to my cabins?" she demanded, half amused and half appalled.

I squinted against the light and tried to focus on the outside of the rooms instead of the inside, and I could see now in the dawn what I couldn't when the vampires had woken me up. My eyes widened, and I was a little more awake. *Purple*, Bracken had said. Well, it was purple. With olive trim and yellow stars. As ordered.

"Uhm..." I managed, but she cut me off.

"And my tree!" She gestured behind me and I stumbled onto the gravel in my bare feet to turn around.

"Tree?" And there it was, behind the cabin, probably right behind Bracken and I when we'd first gotten busy, purple, with olive colored pine-needles and bright yellow pine cones.

"And the Kestrels' car!"

"Green will pay for that..." Because sure as shit's afire, Nicky's parents' sedan was purple with olive trim and yellow stars scattered across the hood.

"And if you were going to redecorate, why for the love of the Goddess couldn't you have made all the cabins the same?"

"What the fuck?"

The cabin at the end, where the teenaged civilian had been staying unobtrusively with his mother, was decorated in the same colors, but at negative values. Instead of purple walls, there was bright sunshine yellow, and instead of olive trim there was purple, and the scattering of stars on the front was that understated green.

"You didn't mean to do that?" she asked, her eyebrow rings rising with her amused expression.

"Which part?" I mumbled, my face flaming in embarrassment.

"Any of it."

"Well, I was expecting some of it..." I muttered and tried to rub my face into an expression that showed I had my shit together. It wasn't working. I needed soda and oatmeal first.

"What did you do?" she asked, laughing in earnest now.

"I got laid," I told her frankly, feeling a sleep-deprivation headache coming on. "Look," I yawned, "I'll call Green and he'll pay for the repairs..."

"Don't bother." Whatever irritation she'd experienced at the beginning had completely receded now. "I sort of like it... even that random one at the end. Besides, if I'm lucky, I'll get to listen to you explain how this happened to the in-laws. That'll be peachy." She gave me a grin and flashed her tongue stud at me, and I stuck my tongue back out and wished I'd gotten one of those when I'd been into piercings.

"Wench," I muttered affectionately, and Tanya waggled her eyebrows.

"Go back to sleep—I just wanted to make sure I wasn't going to start looking like a sprite or a niskie in my sleep."

"Fat chance," I muttered, "but I'll keep it in mind the next time I get laid."

"So this afternoon then?" Tanya laughed, turning to leave.

"It's a hard life," I told her philosophically.

This time the knock came as I crawled back between Bracken and Nicky, but I was done. I elbowed Nicky awake, and as he was climbing out of bed and stumbling for the door, pulling on his boxers as he went, I mumbled, "Tell them Green will pay for it," before I snuggled back into Bracken.

The last thing I heard was Nicky laughing, "Jesus, Cory—purple?" before his mother's shrill shock took over the conversation. But he was still chuckling as he closed the door behind him to deal with her and sweet silence took over the cabin once again.

Needless to say, our excursion into the lake on the flat boats was even more awkward than it had promised to be already.

I sat on the boat as Nicky's dad piloted and Nicky stood by him, making standard human conversation about how the boat worked and how much horsepower and what speeds and stuff it could do. (To me, the answer to all that stuff was usually 'magic'. It was as good an answer as any.) The air—however hot it was—felt good on my face. I'm always fascinated to see the boat's prow (or flattened edge, in this case) cut through the water, and even though our top speed was about fifteen miles an hour, I liked sitting on my knees in the front and looking below me, trying to see if I could fathom anything under the opaque green of the flashing surface.

I'd brought one of my knitting projects (socks) and the waterproof bag was looped securely around my wrist, the top cinched closed until I was ready to open it. For the moment I was content to watch the land whiz by in a flash of green trees and red earth. We could also see the occasional boat of people who had nothing to do with us, and I enjoyed looking at them and wondering who was out there and what they thought.

The rest of my entourage (ulg!) was in the boat behind me, and every now and then we'd slow down and motor into some inlet or another, and I could hear them laughing and chatting excitedly over the lowered engine noise. Bracken was with them I thought unhappily, and I wished heartily that I was too.

With a sigh I sat sideways on the seat with my legs in front of me, and pulled out my knitting. It was a plain sock, and I was working the leg, so it was a lot of knitting around and around and around, which was just perfect for something like this—especially with the magic loop method, where I didn't have to worry about all the little pointy needles.

Nicky's mother, who hadn't said much to me since she'd greeted my shy apology about the car with a stony silence, came to sit in the jump seat next to me, and—obviously—to have a little chat.

"What are you working on?" she asked brightly. Blessed knitting—always a conversation builder.

"A sock," I replied politely, showing it to her.

"You make your own socks?" she asked, surprised. A lot of people were surprised about socks—people just don't get how cool they are to make.

"Actually it's Nicky's," I told her smiling shyly. "He tends to lose a lot of his in trans."

Mrs. Kestrel made one of those little surprised 'mother-moue's and gave a little laugh. "Yes—he did that when he was a little boy."

I grinned at her. "I really freak out on him when he loses the hand-made ones."

She nodded, grinning back. "But you still make them."

"Oh yeah." I looked at my knitting for a second and decided to work another inch before I started the heel.

"I'm surprised you're not making socks for Bracken," she said into the relative silence of engine noise and wind.

It was a pointed question, we both knew it, but it was civilly asked, so I answered back nicely. "I just made him a pair—but the elves hate sh...stuff on their feet, so I think Bracken's going to stick with sweaters."

"Have you made Nicky a sweater?" Another pointed question. I looked to where Nicky and his father were discussing engines, and wondered if men talking about mechanics and women talking about crafts had been code for neutral family prying since time began.

"I made him a vest last winter," I said, liking the way his rusty hair ruffled in the wind like a bird's feathers. He was tanning (the were-creature fast-healing thing kept him from burning) and his freckles were coming out making him look like a little kid.

"And this year he got a knit hoodie," I finished. I was faster this year—knitting him something that would last a season or two, maybe, before the colors lost their appeal didn't piss me off like it might have the year before.

"And Bracken?"

I was tired of this conversation, and I never get tired of talking about knitting. "I knit them all sweaters, Mrs. Kestrel." I noticed there was no more pretense about 'Call me Terry'. "I knit them all sweaters and socks and hats, and when I'm not knitting for them I'm knitting for Renny or Max or Mario or La Mark or any of the other people you've met. I like to knit for people I care about. Is that wrong?"

Terry looked away to her son in his tank-top and khakies, and I could almost feel her eyes fall on his arm tattoo—green lime leaves and dark green oak-leaves, in a diamond surrounding Nicky as a bird. Somewhen in time—I don't even remember—a little bit of Bracken's trademark blood had started falling from the leaves.

On the peak of the diamond there was a coyote, that he'd had specially done for Eric—I remembered when he'd asked to go do that. I thought it was lovely.

But most parents aren't really fond of tattoos, and her eyes narrowed unappreciatively.

"I see you've found a way to mark everyone who comes under your 'protection'," she said with an edge to her voice.

"Do you think I don't have a mark on my body for him?" I asked, but I was damned if I was taking off my T-shirt in that tiny bikini to show her my back.

She cocked an eyebrow. "Do you? You won't even wear his ring—he's wearing yours."

Nicky had showed me the ring—a plain band of white gold and one of silver, twisted solidly together—that his grandfather had given it to his grandmother, moons and moons ago. Nicky had inherited it and was supposed to give it to the love of his life. He'd showed it to me right before he'd caught a flight to Austin.

"Eric's wearing that ring," I said now. "These rings," I flashed the one on my finger that couched the symbol of all of us—lime tree, oak tree, sword, blood, stone and bird—even as I spoke. "These rings are important. They mean something different."

She didn't hear me. "What do you mean, 'Eric's wearing that ring'—that ring was meant for his *wife!*"

Oh shit. Another can of fucking worms. They were lying around our conversation like landmines.

"Eric's the love of his life," I said mildly. "It meant a lot to all of us that Nicky gave him that ring."

"Aren't you even a little bit jealous?" she asked, appalled. "Doesn't it bother you at *all* that my son doesn't really love you? That you are so wrong for him that he'd rather sleep with another man?"

Ouch. Just fucking ouch. My face flattened, and my stitches grew tight and angry. "Your son loves me enough to die for me," I said quietly. "And if I were you, I'd be more bothered by the fact that you don't know Nicky at all."

Very carefully I put my knitting back in the little bag and cinched it tight and around my wrist again, then pulled up on my knees to lean over the railing and look woefully at the water. I'd jump out, I thought mournfully, I'd jump out and into that big puddle of unfathomable fear, if I thought for a moment it would get me on that other boat.

There was a rustle next to me and Annette—tan and resplendent in a peach colored bikini top and bottle-cap shorts—came to lean over the railing next to me. I didn't even look up at her—I was hoping that by *acting* alone, I might actually get *left* alone.

"My, you just do keep on making friends and influencing people, don't you?" she asked snidely, and my lips came back from my teeth in a snarl she couldn't see.

"Better than pissing off strangers and alienating entire countries," I returned mildly, and I heard her process that for a minute. (Literally—I could swear there were gears turning. It was painful.)

"What country?" she finally asked.

"Mine," I murmured.

"Oh that's just silly—we're all Americans here…"

"Not me," I returned, caught up in some sort of dreamy, sleep-deprived seque. "I belong to the Preternatural Sub-States of Northern California."

She didn't really know what to do with that, so she resorted to mockery. It could be the one thing we would ever have in common. "Well, your country has crappy taste in color."

I wrinkled my nose, still staring at that peaceful refractory of sun off water. "You wanted a demo."

She sniffed. "How do I know you didn't just all…"

I laughed and closed my eyes, hypnotized by the feel of sun on the back of my neck and that unfathomable water. "Drop our vacation plans and paint the cabins while you were sleeping just to fuck with you? Sorry, Annette, you're not that important to us."

"Well then how did you do it?" The question was reluctant. She truly didn't want to believe that there was anything different about us. Her hands—perfectly manicured and tipped with peach nail polish—slid into my peripheral vision, and the seat cushion next to me shifted under her weight.

I laughed a little. "That's what happens with really *good* sex," I said with an almost friendly smile, "Or at least it does when you're us."

The hands disappeared from my view and the physical space between us widened considerably. "That's just nasty." Her voice dripped contempt, and I had a sudden wish for Green. Sex was never nasty around Green.

"It's too bad you think that way," I murmured. "Maybe you haven't found the right person." I was bored with this conversation, somnolent, my lack of sleep the night before and the heat of the mid-morning sun catching up that way.

"I," she sniffed with complete disdain, "am a virgin."

I eyed her with only a little surprise. "I doubt that," I said thoughtfully. "The vampires would have told me."

Her expression was almost worth enduring her presence. She started to sputter, and before she could give voice to the thought of "How in the hell would they know that?" I put her out of her misery.

"Smell and power," I said, holding up a forestalling hand. "There's power released in the first blood shed in human sexual maturity. It has its own smell." I shrugged. The vampires hadn't known I'd been a virgin—or Adrian hadn't. Adrian—Goddess love him—hadn't been the most responsible vampire in the universe either. By all accounts our first lovemaking, in the hill, without Green's presence, had been terrifying to all parties involved.

Except me. I'd thought it was lovely.

Anyway, our vampires—*all* of our vampires—had been schooled since that night. If she'd smelled of any sort of power, they would have known.

No matter how repulsive someone is personality-wise, vampires are always evaluating a food source.

"My hymen is intact," Annette was saying now, and I rolled my eyes.

"That doesn't mean you've never come in your pants," I said crudely, "or that a man's never scratched your back while you were giving him a blow job. Sex means an awful lot to our people—it's not just confined to the one thing that can get you pregnant."

Her mouth opened and closed fruitlessly, and I shrugged, realizing that I may not have been as politic as the situation called for. Maybe I should have apologized, maybe I should have given her a way to save face. But she was dealing with forces that took this sort of thing very seriously, and she was using a child's ignorance in place of innocence. 'I may have seen a penis, I may have touched a penis, I may even have achieved orgasm, but because these things didn't happen in specific order, I still have no actual *knowledge* of a penis.' When you lived with the Goddess' people, it was the kind of thinking that could get you killed.

"You're disgusting!" she finally burst out, and I was surprised at the force with which I wanted Green.

"And you're a lousy ambassador for the human race," I retorted, and then turned my back on her.

I felt a shift of weight on my other side and could smell the sun-warmed vanilla-and-animal that was Nicky. I closed my eyes and sat up on my knees, tilting my face up to meet the sun under my visor. Nicky's hand came up to massage my neck, and he leaned over and whispered, "How much would you pay me to let you go play on the other boat?"

"I'm out of currency," I muttered, loving that hand on the back of my neck. "I'm already making you socks for life."

"My mother's hella jealous about that you know."

I looked sideways at him and enjoyed his immature smirk. "That's good to know," I said quietly. Then I looked at him *really* and realized the smirk was hiding white lines of stress around shiny brown eyes.

I took his hand—the one rubbing my neck—and kissed it. "What's up?"

He shook his head and leaned in so he could talk softly into my ear. "I just came out to my parents. Again."

I looked over my shoulder and saw his mother, wiping her face again, the back of her hand black with mascara. His father was staring straight and morbidly ahead, all attention on the boat's meandering course around the inlets of the little amoeba-lake. The same compressed lines of grief Nicky had were lining his mouth, and, probably, the brown eyes hidden by his sunglasses.

I kissed him on the mouth, gently. "Looks rough," I said, rubbing his cheek with mine, and he nodded.

"Can I stay here with you for a minute and stare at the lake?" he asked sincerely, and I nodded. Distraction now—help Nicky cope when we were in private.

"Come here," I said, leaning over the rail far enough for things to get dangerous. "I think if you look close enough, you can see fish."

Nicky let out an honest chuckle. "You can't see fish in the lakes at home..."

"Yes you can!"

"Not from a boat! What makes you think you can see them now?" He spoke lightly, but he punctuated the question with another of those tender touches at the small of my back through my T-shirt.

I looked at him and grinned, so very glad when he grinned back. "Force of my formidable will!" I intoned dramatically, and was rewarded by his laugh.

Together we dangled our torsos over the rail, holding our free hands out and reaching for the peace and the coolness in the center of that dark lake. We also ignored—and had been ignoring—Annette's ostracized presence on my other side.

We shouldn't have.

I had antagonized an enemy, showed her disrespect, disdained the things she held sacred. In retrospect I had it coming, but at the time I felt nothing but contentment as my accidental lover and I leaned over the railing to find the relative peace and safety in the lake that we were looking for in our own hearts.

The two hands on my ass, lifting me up and shoving me hard were a complete surprise, and that was nothing to the shock of the green-black snow-fed water as it closed over my head.

NICKY

Life as Bird Boy

You know how some people hate the kid's table at Thanksgiving? I had loved it. Me and my cousins, getting together, cutting up, throwing mashed potatoes, telling embarrassing stories about our parents—good times.

Getting to sit with the adults had been overrated.

I could hear the boat with our people on it—they were laughing. I had never realized how much we all laughed together as much as I did now, fending off my mother, dealing with my father, and watching the dejected slump of Cory's shoulders as she leaned over the side of the boat and wished she was anywhere but here.

"She doesn't have anything better to do with her time than knit?" My mother's voice was suspiciously shrill. She'd tried crafting, I remembered. She'd never been able to sit with one project long enough to finish. We had an entire closet full of yarn, paper, scrapbooking punchers, funky scissors, fimo clay, beads, and quilting fabric—and not one single scarf, scrapbook, necklace, or blanket to show for it.

"She has lots of shit to do with her time, mom," (work, go to school, archive the Goddess folk, go out and kick ass) "but knitting is what she *gets* to do in between."

Maybe because I had grown up assuming I'd live a mortal lifetime, I understood the drive to create something that might be around for a year or two. Bracken and Green thought the knitting was magical. I thought it was mortal. All of us respected the hell out of it.

"Like a mini-vacation in a plastic bag? Isn't that a little common for the queen of Green's Hill?" Mom's lips were drawn back from her teeth, and since we were in the prow of a boat and the wind was pretty fierce, it was just luck she didn't catch a bug.

I winced at what she said anyway. I'd been the one to give Mom that title. It was the closest I could get to who Cory was to us.

"She hates it when we call her that," I said, wishing I didn't have to shout it and shifting in my seat so the wind didn't hit my eyes quite so brutally. They were tearing up. "She hates it when we call her 'Lady', she hates all of it—but when shit goes down, she's the first one out there, you know?"

Mom shook her head and looked at Dad, who was stoically steering the boat. Dad didn't talk much, but he tended to see things nobody else did—like last night, apparently, when he'd noticed the vampire marks. Great timing, that—I had to wonder if he'd waited until I'd walked away to say anything.

"Okay, fine." Mom was still talking. "I get it. Best president you ever had—great. But why *live there.* You don't have to. She's already made it very clear you only need to visit..." Mom blushed and lifted her hands to refasten the clip holding her hair. Good. It was an unworthy thought—Cory and Green as life-force booty call?

"I dare you to finish that sentence," I said quietly, and with so much force Mom jerked back in her seat.

"Dominic, honey," she said, placating me, "I just want you to be happy. I'd like to know my grandchildren, you know?" I was reminded, again, that I was an only child. I looked up and saw Annette approaching Cory and I sighed. I'd tried to tell them this before, but maybe they would hear it now, when we were face to face.

"Cory's your only chance for a grandkid, mom," I said, and I was kind of glad I had to talk above the engine noise now, because it meant I couldn't mumble, I had to say it loud and proud. "She's the only girl I'd ever want to sleep with. If it wasn't for her, I'd like men exclusively. I'm gay, mom." It was a confining word—but humans didn't have a better one so it was the one I went with. "She's the best thing to ever happen to me—if it wasn't for her I wouldn't have met Green and I never would have been able to love Eric. I will *never* love Annette—or anyone like her. You shouldn't have brought her—it was cruel to everybody."

There was a hiccup in the engine, and I realized Dad's hand had choked on the throttle and then put the pressure back on. I looked at him, tried to look past the sunglasses and the bird's nest gray hair. *Please, Daddy...please look at me? Please?*

Then I looked at Mom, and she was crying. Fucking wonderful.

"I'm sorry," I said, not actually feeling sorry, because maybe there's just enough asshole in me to not care that this hurt them. "I didn't mean to upset you, but you're not getting the message."

Mom nodded, and wiped her face with the back of her hand. Her make-up washed away, and although she didn't look old, she looked vulnerable, and I stood up, keeping my balance on the shifting floor of the flatboat, and moved in to kiss her cheek. She nodded and gave me a game smile—suddenly I could feel the sun a little, and I realized how cold I'd been. Yeah, it's easy to talk big, but everyone wants his mommy too keep loving him, right?

I took another step back and Dad said, "Son?"

I turned to him hopefully, but the sunglasses and the habitual squint against the wind weren't giving me anything in terms of expression.

"Does it really have to be her?"

Oh Jesus. Ouch. Just fucking ouch. "Why don't you like her?"

"I like her fine," Dad said, actually looking at me. "I'm not lying—I see what you see, son. She's strong and I can tell you've got something together… and I'm damned grateful she didn't let you die. But… she's dangerous. That job you're going to do tonight—you make it sound like nothing, but I know better. It's got vampires in it, and there's a reason you brought all those people and it sure as shit wasn't to meet your folks."

Dad took off his sunglasses and met my eyes. "I could give a crap if you're queer, Nicky. I just want you to live."

Easiest answer I'd had to give them yet. "I'd rather die by her side, fighting for Green's hill, than live in peace, sleeping next to Eric forever."

After that, even her smell was comforting. Her kisses on the cheek, the mouth, the way she leaned her cheek on my shoulder—it all helped to ease the ache in my chest left by that fractured conversation.

We spoke distractedly, and she turned the full force of her smile on me—and I felt deep in my soul the rightness of my world.

I didn't notice Annette at all—I had forgotten her completely. She even spoke once or twice—a shrill attempt to get my attention—and all I wanted was to touch Cory and be soothed.

I was so shocked at the violence in her, the sudden force from behind, Cory's pissed-off shriek as she hit the water, that for a moment, all I could do was stare at Annette in a dreamy sort of surprise.

Her mouth was drawn back in a snarl, those carefully pretty features twisted beyond something human, and her breathless cackle was shrill and chilling.

Then the dreamy moment was over, and I was a bird, the wind from the boat catching under my wings as I used my bird's sight—specifically designed by God to find things in a big fucking lake—to find our girl.

I didn't see her for a moment, but I did see Bracken's clean dive from fifty-yards away as he swam with preternatural speed to where he'd seen her disappear.

And then she was feet from smacking into me, screeching with a warrior's yell on the crest of a waterspout she had obviously created with her furious, panicked power when she found herself in the cold darkness. I saw her face as the spout crested, and in spite of the reflexive scream, she was a study in self-control. The moment her self-awareness conquered her fear and she let herself fall back into the water before she attracted any more attention was painful—and beautiful. Her jaw was clenched in absolute determination to keep herself together and her lips were drawn back in a snarl of retribution. She controlled her fall, held her arms at her sides and closed her eyes in sheer concentration, and let herself plunge again into this thing that suddenly scared her.

I marked where she fell and hovered a few feet away, my wings flapping madly against the stiff, hot breeze, and then I changed (remembering to keep my shorts on this time) and let myself fall like she had into the chilly green madness.

The water closed over me in a whoosh of quiet noise, and my hands and feet flailed to push me to the surface—I gasped when I broke water, because even prepared, the chill was something frightening. The sun was overbright when it hit my closed eyes, and I cleared my eyes with my fingers and looked for her. Thank the Goddess, Bracken had gotten there first.

He was behind her, his large hands splayed over her stomach, and, I assumed, his knee under her bottom, keeping her afloat as she bent her will and her fist and her power in the direction of my parent's boat.

Dad had killed the motor, but the boat was still sailing bloggily on inertia, and Mom was leaning over the railing, casting stunned looks over her shoulder at Annette. Annette was holding her hands over her mouth, her eyes sparkling with an evil glee—right up until Cory raised her hand, focused her power, and ripped that bitch-heifer out of the front of the boat, then threw her across the water like a screaming skipping stone.

Cory's outraged yell of triumph echoed off the surrounding hills and bounced off the water, even louder than Annette's helpless shrieking as sheer momentum carried her over half the lake.

Our people in the nearby boat let out a tremendous cheer, and I looked at Cory with a shocked laugh.

"Bitch..." she muttered, "bitch bitch bitch bitch...*fucking* bitch..."

"Uhm, Cory?" I tried, seeing that Annette was heading for one of the big two-story boats with the wet bars and the slides off the top.

"Bitch-cunt-whore-heifer-trash-fucking-shitbag..."

"Cory?" I ventured again, a little more panicked.

"Beloved…" Bracken cautioned, and she snapped "Fine!" and held up her hand again, even as she tread water, then squeezed her fist tight.

Annette's body whooped up an invisible power-slide, like a kid's at a water park and sailed over the boat. She was splayed crazily, with no dignity whatsoever, and she all but belly-flopped back into the lake with a splat we could hear even from where we sat.

I gave a kick up so my torso cleared the waterline and pointed at the bitch's flopping, floundering body with meaningful energy, while looking at my Dad. He nodded and the boat's motor revved again and they puttered off to go clean up their mess. When I turned back to Cory, she was taking deep, angry breaths as she kept her head clear of the lake. Bracken was behind her, chuckling into the chilled hollow of her neck and ear, and she sent him a disgusted look.

"So much for taking shit for the team," he chortled, and her pissed-off snarl eased up as she fought the urge to chuckle with him.

"Cory," I sputtered, "I'm so…"

She shook the wet hair out of her eyes and smiled at me, the lines at her mouth telling me she was still fighting panic but getting better at it.. Her lashes were spiked around her murky-brown eyes and her hair was half out of its ponytail and plastered down her neck. She was so beautiful. "Don't say it, *ou'e'alle* you don't have any reason to be sorry."

I blinked, and not just to clear water from my eyes. Cory and I rarely used our titles, although she and Bracken used them as terms of affection frequently. It was loosely used to a lover who owed his allegiance—I was not her equal. I would never be.

But sputtering laughter in the cold lake under the bright, hard sunshine, she told me very plainly that she never doubted me, and that she trusted me with her life.

I wanted a quiet moment with her and Bracken, and swore I'd take one, to tell them both that I'd die for them.

It was the best and the least I could do.

"My pleasure, *ou'e'anne*," I murmured, and I loved the word as it touched her ear.

CORY

Black Velvet

And after all of that, the bitch still insisted on coming with us to the damned vampire bar. It's a damned good thing I'd had a few hours to cool off, or I might have killed her—literally and for good and forever—just for suggesting it.

But I *did* have a few hours to cool off, and damned good hours at that.

After our boat picked us up—precariously balanced with far too many people on it, but we didn't care—we puttered around until we found a deep inlet, one with a narrow neck so none of the passing boats could see us. Lambent asked permission and set a geas on it—a sort of 'vague feeling' or 'repelling spell' to keep the other campers away. Everybody stripped naked (Renny & Lambent, mostly) or shape-shifted or did a combination of the both, and either jumped in the water or took turn sunning on the boat and generally hung out as a big, rowdy, happy group. Bracken had brought an i-Pod and a speaker jack, and we plugged it into the boat and played that puppy as loud as we wanted, and I sat in the shade and knitted with Katy and Renny, pleased that my waterproof bag had kept the water out in its little adventure. (The fact that the yarn was double bagged in a zip-loc helped too.)

Green visited my mind as I sat—he'd been there when the water closed over my head, his presence keeping me from panicking completely—and although we did little more than bump telepathic noses, that soothed me too.

When it got too hot, I put the knitting down and Bracken came to my side and helped me in the water—and no judgments were passed as I took deep breaths and clung to his hand, and the splashing and horseplay toned down, even when I sighted a spot on land and took off in determined strokes to a place where I could feel—however fleeting—slippery mud under my toes. Bracken kept pace evenly beside me, and every now and then would go upright and extend his feet or go under to tell me how much farther I had to go.

I felt accomplished—absurd, because I'd been swimming in lakes since I was very small—but the feeling stayed with me nonetheless. I'd conquered a fucking fear, no matter how irrational. Go me!

When we returned to the boat it was time to go back to the cabins and rest—and then rehearse. The i-Pod jack came in handy then too—I practiced matching my voice, my pacing, and my blocking to the music, positioning people randomly and then moving seductively around the men to 'strip' off their breakaway clothing and reveal their marks.

I could do it when the music was on, but when Bracken killed the sound to tell us to take a break for crap's sake, I was right in the middle of tiptoeing my fingers up Jacky's chest and crooning, *Mississippi, in the middle of a dry spell...* The music died and we looked at each other blankly, and then personal space reasserted itself and we almost killed ourselves trying to get away. We heard a bizarre snorking sound and together we looked down, and there was Teague, sitting on his ass in the dust, cracking up as though he'd never laughed before.

I blinked.

"I don't think I've ever heard him laugh like that before," I muttered, and Jack and Katy looked at me in complete bemusement.

"Man, it must be that random thing," Katy said, "cause I ain't never seen it either."

"Two years," Jack said, shaking his head with affection as another round of laughter shook his beloved. "Maybe chaos isn't such a horrible thing after all."

That made *me* laugh, and then Annette walked up and shit all over our mood.

"You all practicing for a show or something?" she asked brightly, ignoring the wall of icy hostility radiating at her from the eleven of us.

"Go back to your cabin, Annette," Nicky said seriously, and she tried another sunshine-and-sugar smile.

"Now you aren't going to hold that against me today—it was a joke—you know, like the way you were laughing just now?"

I turned towards her with a hint of laughter in my own eyes—the nasty, corrosive kind of laughter that reminds you that everyone can be fucking evil.

"Yeah, Annette—it was hella funny watching you skim across that lake. Did you want another demo? Because I think if I tried that here you'd have some serious road-rash before you hit the water."

She blanched, and I amped that evil smile up a little, willing her to go away. Instead she tried a game smile, and ignored me.

"I was just thinking," she said, trying to make eye contact with Max and Jack, "that maybe I could come with you tonight when you go to meet the vampires. It sounds like fun." Max bent down and scratched Renny behind the ears, and Jack deliberately helped Teague up—and then hauled that bandy little Irish body into his own long embrace, just to squick her out.

Teague went, though, and I wondered if he'd been afraid of the force of his own laughter, because there was that almost shivering air around his body that spoke of a man who needed comfort. Jack whispered in his ear, and the two of them became their own island, a bubble in time, and I turned back to our enemy, daring her to say anything.

"You can't even look at *our* vampires!" I was a stunned—not just by her boldness, but by her stupidity.

"Well if I'm going to be a part of Nicky's life, maybe I should be!"

I blinked at her slowly, and Nicky started to laugh—loud and long and as violently as Teague had. He walked up to her, slowly, still chuckling, and bent a tender head towards her while she watched with enchanted eyes. He didn't touch her, he just leaned into her space, and she smiled sunnily up at him, as though he was about to answer all her 'maidenly' prayers.

"I'd sooner fuck a garbage pit," he said succinctly, and she took a step backwards.

"You don't mean that," she said stubbornly, and he nodded, looking at me with sincere exasperation.

"You can bet your bubble-ass I do," he muttered and then walked past her, meaningfully headed for his parent's cabin.

I looked at her as she stood alone, her face a study in naked hurt, and I tried not to let any of my pity leak through. I loved Nicky, but that had been harsh. I shook my head. Forget my pride. I'd pulled back—I could have hurt her—*really* hurt her—but I hadn't. Those were the boundaries on Green's Hill—but they weren't the boundaries here, and they certainly weren't the boundaries in a kiss of vampires that was sheltering a predator.

"You're so mean," she said, sounding like a lost second grader. "He can't like you better when you're plain and mean—you'll see. If we could only get someplace with normal people, he'd see you're not much at all."

"Vampires," I said carefully, talking to the child she apparently was, "aren't normal people. What I did to you was playing. It was nothing. It was swatting at a fly. What the people we're going to see will do to you will be for real. I can't offer you protection." I looked around at the people I cared for, the people who had 'handled me' all afternoon to make me happy because they knew I'd put it on the line for them, and my face and my voice hardened and my power leaked into it.

"I *will* not offer you protection. I can't stop you from following us tonight, but you can't ride with us. When you walk into that bar, it's going to be naked and alone. Nobody here will look out for you. You've been protected here. You've been associated with Nicky—but you are no longer a part of his family. He's made that clear. My people will *not* put themselves out to keep you alive. We have real business here, and we can't afford to let you fuck it up."

I stopped speaking and an honest-to-Goddess chill breeze swept over us, and I realized my power had leaked into my words. Oh crap—it was a binding. I'd lost control of my power and it had become a binding. I looked around with almost wild eyes, and my people—all of them—were looking back with bemused, besotted expressions on their faces.

They wouldn't help Annette pick up her fork, much less look sideways at her to save her life. I had actually *bound* them from any action to help her.

I looked at Bracken, who was squinting with a pained expression and I knew I was right. "Oh shit."

Don't let it bother you, beloved.

But Green, I... I just bound them to let her die in traffic or some shit like that...

And I said leave it be. If she suffers from her childishness, she suffers. This way you don't have to worry that any of our people will endanger themselves making that decision. You've made it for them. Well done.

If it had been anyone other than Green, I was pretty sure the 'well done' would have drowned me in sarcasm sauce. But he meant it, and my stomach roiled in misery. Another plate in my armor, another chink in my humanity.

It didn't matter. It was done. Nicky had felt it in his parents' room as he hauled his mother back and told her angrily to talk some sense into Annette and clean up this mess, and even his parents had asked what the breeze had meant.

Tanya—who had been watching us rehearse—said it felt like her first clear breath since the bitch had driven up.

So, since there was very little we could do about it, we ignored it, and tended to our business. We took a break, took another swim, and practiced until sunset. The vampires woke up and we had dinner with a fervent prayer watched on skeptically by Nicky's parents and their intruder. They still were not invited to eat—and Grace had really outdone herself with tri-tip and salad tonight for me and the shape-shifters, while the elves got pasta with garlic-pesto sauce. I couldn't even make myself feel guilty.

Phillip eyed them nastily as he and Marcus walked towards us, hand in hand. Of course, Phillip's mood had been unpredictable at best lately—Gretchen had been seeping through on a more and more corrosive basis. Last night, as they'd woken up, I'd gotten a flash in my head from him. She'd been frenzied, screaming, and bound by three other vampires as she tried to fly off into the dark night sky. No wonder he and Marcus had gone straight from feeding to having happy romping sex in the forest. It was probably Marcus' one weapon to keep his lover even keeled when his mind-link with the little baby monster made his own head a personal hell.

"So," Phillip asked briskly, while we both pretended I didn't get glimpses into his head showing everything *wasn't* all right, "what's the agenda for the night?"

We powwowed with the vampires and eventually acted out the dress rehearsal—and then went to shower, where Bracken and I had a little 'wardrobe dispute' in the privacy of our cabin.

You'd think I'd get used to walking into my room to see that the clothes laid out on the bed weren't the ones I was planning to wear.

"What the hell is that?" I asked, staring curiously at the green lame` halter nightmare Bracken had apparently pulled out of his lemon-scented ass. I picked it up gingerly and tried not to tangle the gold chains (!!!) that held it together.

"*That* is what you're wearing tonight." Bastard looked *way* too pleased with himself.

"What am I wearing under it?" I asked. "I don't see any leggings..." My eyes widened. "No."

Bracken didn't even bother to ask *No what?* He just came up behind me and grabbed my ass. "It'll cover you just fine—you've even groomed. If you wear black underwear, you'll be fine."

I looked at him, mortified, "Groomed?"

This puzzled him. "Groomed—isn't that what you told us you were doing when you shaved your..."

I stopped him with a hand over his mouth. "Yes. That was grooming. And no—I'm not wearing this without a skirt... or pants... or a goddamned circus tent!"

Bracken raised his eyebrows, perfectly aware that in matters of clothing, costuming, and make-up, he generally came out the winner. It wasn't even that I was weak, dammit—it was that he got his taste from Green, and screw-it-all if the elves weren't whip-spiffy dressers from the get-go.

About that time Nicky wandered in from his own shower and gave a low whistle at the thing hanging from my fingers. "Swwweeeeettt!!" he whistled. "That'll show off your tattoo *and* your legs!" I stuck my tongue out sourly at him.

"My legs are squat and average," I said truthfully—we all knew it for a fact. How I had lucked into a culture that thought *I* was attractive was one of the big mysteries of life, and I was done with examining it too deeply.

Nicky shook his head. "With all that running you do? Your legs are *toned!*"

I shook my head, remembering why I had ever dated Nicky in the first place. But still—the gauzy, chain-y thing in my fingers was not one bit more appealing. I looked at Bracken again, who was looking smugly back, the smirk he wore when we were waltzing this number customarily in place, and his grim, pond-shadow eyes twinkling.

"Where did you get this?" I asked carefully, and his smirk widened to a full out blinding grin.

"Green sent it with the sprites while you were in the shower," he all-but crowed.

I didn't have to even smell the wild-flowers and the sweetness to know that I'd lost. But it was lovely to feel Green's touch on my face anyway.

There was a gold-colored wrap that came with the gauze/chain/halter nightmare—it had been hand-knitted, it buttoned at the shoulder so I could drop it at the appropriate time, and was made with some weirdo rayon/linen mix so it didn't schwack to my skin in the heat. What it did do, however, was hide the mark on my back until we were ready for the world to know who I was—the big-assed triple-diamond tattoo I sported was pretty distinctive, and it would ruin my chance to see how Rafael operated on his home turf if everyone knew the boss (ha!) was in the place before I was ready.

I also got gold strappy sandals. Oh yay.

Bracken did my hair—something up off my neck, thank the Goddess-- and all in all I was grumpy, uncomfortable and ready to rip something apart by the time we emerged from our room and met the others by the cars.

But it was all good.

We gathered together by the SUV's and commented on how everybody cleaned up well, even though I'd seen most of the guys' outfits at the dress run-through, and they returned the favor. Lambent, Bracken, Nicky and I were going with the vampires—that way we'd smell good and vampy by the time we walked in. I hoped that a bite on the wrist and eau de-undead would let us clear the bouncer I knew would be at the door, because I really didn't want to have to pull the 'I'm your queen' card before the right moment. I assumed shape-shifters would be welcome in any vampire bar—yum, right?—so I had no worries about people in the other SUV getting in to our destination.

Teague was driving and he came up to me as we were loading up, holding up his iPod which was loaded just like mine.

"Bleed it out?" he asked hopefully, and I grinned. I don't know what I looked like, but his grin back was ferocious and bloodthirsty and nobody had better fuck with us because we were bad-fucking-business.

"Bleed it out!" I answered back, and we bashed closed fists together and got ready to roll.

I don't know when we had started the tradition of listening to head-banging music on the way to our ass-kicking runs—I think I just started co-opting the stereo and playing stuff that got me pumped. It didn't matter, because when Teague joined us in November, the tradition was locked in stone, and now we even had a couple of playlists, culled from iPods full of every metal, rock, or alternative cd produced in the last twenty years.

Without a doubt, the vampire's favorite was Adrian's favorite—*Linkin' Park*—and their hands-down, love-it-forever, rhythm-pumped-in-their-veins, favorite kick-ass song was *Bleed It Out*. We'd built a four -hour playlist around that song, and on nights like this, it felt *good* to thunder that shit through our veins.

We drove out of the campground with music blasting loud enough to shake the windows. Knowing that Annette was driving determinedly behind us, the guys let me drive—we left her in the dust before we hit the freeway. I knew she'd find us eventually—she'd heard us talking enough to figure out where we were going, but she'd have to use Google and her palm-pilot to get there so away we went into the wild blue.

Redding was a different town at night.

The sun-bleached bustle of the day was replaced by the heavy lassitude of an entire town too hot to sleep. The pump and buzz of air-conditioners rode the air, and even at eleven at night there were entire families on their lawns, trying to catch a breeze as it limped down the mountains and onto the lower plain that was the city proper.

There was a sense here—you couldn't see it on the suburban streets, but there was always a knowledge that beyond the boundaries of the city there was… less humanity, maybe, than there was in Sacramento or any of those suburbs. It was an island of people, surrounded by flat, scoured farmland and brutal mountains. The houses in the suburbs seemed to huddle, even in the heat.

The squat brick building that housed Rafael's club didn't look any bigger or more imposing at night—but it did seem to be overflowing with people, a lot of them big, tattooed, and riding motorcycles. We parked the SUV's in the overflow parking lot, and the guys turned to me expectantly.

Time to eat!

"Are you guys going to be civilized about this," I asked, turning to the back of the car, "or are you going to bicker like five-year olds?"

Sorceress and elf blood were both real delicacies—although I understand that elf-blood was pretty damned intoxicating, especially on an empty stomach. Shapeshifter blood was more sustaining—and tasty—than human blood, but our guys had a steady diet of shapeshifter, and not a lot of sorceress or elf. (There was only one of me, and the elves tended to shy away from blood exchanges—I think Green and Bracken had been the only two elves ever to make year-long habits of being lunch.) Any way you looked at it, more than one kind of fun was on the menu tonight.

Marcus answered, but he was looking a little shy. "Uhm, we were actually sort of hoping... we could, you know. Sample. I know it's an imposition..."

I slanted a look at Bracken, and Nicky. They rolled their eyes and shrugged—why not? Lambent sneered and tried to look bored, but he was obviously hiding a curiosity under that flame-haired nonchalance. Once upon a time, he'd refused a vampire's bite, but now he'd seen the shapeshifters getting fed from all week. He wanted to know what the shouting (and ooh-ing and aah-ing) was all about.

"Sure," I said with a good humored smile, "but could you start with Nicky first?" He didn't get as woozy with blood-loss as I would, and Bracken and Lambent would make them drunk on an empty stomach.

After some shifting in our seats, Kyle bit Nicky first, and I watched with a growing excitement—the brief exchanges for the blooding were ceremonial in nature—they came nowhere near the excitement of a true feeding. As Kyle bit Nicky's wrist and worked his throat and I heard Nicky's discreet little sigh, I tried to remember the last time a vampire had fed from me.

Only one name came to me, and it had been more than a year and a half ago.

"Andres," Bracken murmured in my ear, and I turned to him, flushing. Andres had wanted us both—what he had gotten was a true taste of my blood to fill a contract with Green and a shared bite between Bracken and myself that still made me hot to think about. Andres was what Bracken had in mind whenever he thought of stepping outside our little circle—and maybe the only person I would consider taking into my bed who was not wearing our ring.

"Andres might be helpful with this situation," I murmured, trying to cover the fact that the slight, suave vampire still held a fascination for me. Nobody would hold it against me—I knew that. But just because I *could* do something—even with full approval of my lovers—didn't mean I *should...* right?

Kyle swallowed and then looked at me expectantly, and I held out my wrist. There was that pressure, and then the pain, and then it faded, replaced by the endorphins or whatever the Goddess put in vampire spit. That sweet numbness cruised up my bloodstream like a cocaine fish, giving me a buzz and a slightly dirty feeling, and as Kyle sucked and swallowed and sucked and swallowed, I started to feel like a party girl doing lines in the car before going clubbing.

It was something that I'd never been.

My head tilted back and I sighed and relaxed, and then Kyle released me and Phillip took his place. Next to me, Bracken made a soft grunt and then a long, drawn out sigh, and my nervousness about tonight's little performance drained away with my surplus red-matter. Perform in a bar with a gazunga people watching me? No big deal. I was queen of the flying vampires, duchess of euphoria, countess of kink.

I could do anything, as long as these guys kept pumping Goddess juice into me as they fed.

I don't know how high I would have gotten if Marcus hadn't broken my concentration.

"Uhm, Lady Cory?"

I half-opened bemused eyes at him, and he smiled a little through his feeding face. The expression was sardonic, as though he knew how good I felt.

"May I..." he stammered and blushed (again, odd in that face!) and Phillip released my wrist. I sat up a little, adjusted my obscenely short skirt, and tried to remember who and where I was.

"What do you need?" I asked reflexively. That's what I did, wasn't it? I met people's needs?

"May I feed from your neck?" he finally stated baldly, and I smiled and blushed. "Bracken can hold your hand...it's just..." he stopped stammering and met my eyes. His eyes weren't whirling red, yet—they were still brown and liquid, and I remembered his little crush from last year. "This is an honor we don't get much. I was hoping I could do it right."

Next to me, Bracken traced his fingers ever so subtly down my bare arm. Why not? It was getting hot in the SUV anyway, now the motor and the a/c were off.

We slid outside of the car, and I winced when my back stuck to the leather—it really *had* been getting hot in there and we hadn't noticed. Bracken grabbed my hand and Marcus advanced on me—he wasn't that much taller than me, and he wasn't that much broader, but for a moment, in the shadows, I remembered why people were afraid of vampires. Then the erstwhile schoolteacher smiled, and even with fangs there was something so gentle, so game in his liquid brown eyes that it was the most natural thing in the world to tilt my head back, feel his breath on my neck, and surrender.

Bracken and Nicky were getting fed from too, but as I sank into Marcus' gentle hug, I didn't think they were having nearly as much fun.

It was pleasant—and over quickly, since we were, in essence, just topping off the tank—but it reminded me of what I didn't have in a vampire feeding anymore. Bracken's pressure on my hand became my lifeline, my anchor to emotion, to love, to anything but this sort of detached pleasure that I felt in the arms of a man that I cared about, but did not love.

Bracken's warm hand squeezed mine, and Marcus broke off from the feeding and smiled shyly. I kissed his cheek like the brother he was, and stepped back.

I was still riding the vein-wave, so I felt a bit of disembodied happiness, but the euphoria had disappeared. I was reminded of all the reasons I couldn't succumb to that sort of high—there were too many people who could not afford to have me suffer the same fate as my beloved.

It was with a sense of grim anticipation that I adjusted my little shawl on my back and put on the party-girl face I'd started out with, then grabbed Bracken and Nicky's hands and ran for the door.

The two bouncers were were-creatures—they must have been, because they *weren't* vampires, but our pass in was to hold up our punctured wrists to let them smell the vamp whose bite vouched for us.

We got some funny looks—we'd left my vampires near the car for a late entrance, partly so they could bite the others as they arrived, and partly because they knew some of the people here and didn't want to tip anyone off. It didn't matter-- it was clear that while the species was recognizable, the individuals were unfamiliar: strange vamps were in town—now they knew.

Either way, it got us in, and no one stopped Bracken and Lambent for being elves, and I trotted down the short flight of stairs with the confidence of a girl out to have fun dancing for the night.

The club was—as we thought—unpredictably large inside. Once you got to the bottom of the stairs, the building stretched out far enough into the hill to make the dance floor large and the speakers not overwhelming to the stage. It was dark but not smoky, and I guess that made sense too. Nobody here had addictions like nicotine—they'd all been cleared out of the blood at the change.

But that didn't stop the crowd from looking… well, out of my league as a college student, that was for damned sure.

They were rough—many of the vamps had tattoos from before they died, and so did the shifters. A lot of them were big, beefy, and bald or short and scrawny with tree-roots for muscles and braking cable for sinews. The women were weed-thin or cheeseburger-plump (my leaning before sorcery started burning all my calories) with deeply lined faces—even the ones who had been turned in their twenties.

I didn't need to look at the room with power in my eyes to see that these people had grown up together, turned together, and shared blood often and only in the tight little circle that claimed tables with the arrogance of long familiarity.

They were like us in a way, I thought, trying hard not to be intimidated. The cast-out and cast-off, the aliens in their homeland, the underground members of a secret society.

I watched as a beefy vampire who had been in his sixties when he turned and sported long, grizzled hair and only his fangs for teeth, walked by a female shapechanger and casually backhanded her.

The woman landed on her ass and bumped her head on a chair going down, but in spite of the clatter, the rest of the bar ignored them. The guy glared contempt at the girl as she stared stupidly back—she obviously didn't know what she'd done wrong.

"I told you, bitch," the guy grinned nastily, "you need to eat with the other dogs." He jerked his chin in the direction of a table in the shadows, and I raised my eyebrows. Apparently there was a shape-changer pecking order, and she'd violated it. Sucks to be her!

"Rafael isn't going to like that." I turned at the grumble and saw a *very* young man standing behind the bar—or at least he'd been young when he'd been turned. Fifteen, maybe? Just beyond the age when we'd probably have to worry about him turning into the feral creature in our basement—but I wouldn't have wanted to make that call!

"Happen a lot around here?' I asked casually, and the kid grinned at me, white teeth in a brown face—he must have had one hell of a tan when he went over. His hair was buzzed cut, and he appeared to be standing on a platform behind the bar—I estimated he wasn't much taller than I was.

"Not when Rafael's out. He keeps trying to make us civilized, you know?" The kid-vampire dropped his voice and jerked his head towards the big, grizzled, toothless vampire who was heading our way. "Guys like that, they want to make like being a vampire is just like being in their old riding gang… Rafael wants it to be better. Says the guy who made him wanted it to be better, he's just passing on the favor."

I nodded. Change was hard—Rafael was working towards it. I could respect that: Green had needed to do a similar thing with the elves when I'd first come to the hill.

"So what can I get you?" the young vamp asked, and I grimaced at the number of female shape-shifters who were eyeing Bracken before I replied.

"Diet coke," I murmured, and nodded to Nicky. Max and Renny had just walked in—Max looked like a cop, even in his jeans and sport coat (over a backless tank-top, of course), but Renny, like all cats, seemed right in her element. Nicky saw them and nodded back at me, then made his way towards the karaoke moderator to drop off our request. A young shapeshifter with a very nice tenor was just finishing up Blind Faith's "Can't Find My Way Home" and I could only hope I hit all my notes as well as he did.

"Are you shitting me?" the bartending vamp asked, jerking my attention back to him. "Diet coke? You come into a dive like this and ask for a diet coke and it's likely to get you killed!"

My mouth pulled up on the side in a crooked grin. "And losing focus in a place like this is going to do the same thing. I'll take a diet soda, please."

I couldn't think of him as anything other than a kid—he probably ate kittens for breakfast, but that grin made him fifteen forever. "I'm not serving that," he said flatly, his front two teeth still showing in a partial smile. "You want to stay here, you have to order a real drink."

I eyeballed the interior of the bar again. Lambent had taken up a dark corner, where he sort of glowed ominously, and the werewolves had just entered. I had to look at the werewolves twice to recognize them—their appearance wasn't any different, but the guys had developed what I could only term 'heterosexual space' as they walked into the bar with Katy between them. It was possible, looking at them, that you might guess they were both Katy's lovers. You would never in a million years guess that they spent every night in each other's arms. It was probably self-protective—and it definitely served them well here—but it made me a little sad. They still had shit to get over, before those three would rest easily on Green's Hill.

"Kid," I said cheekily, "what's your name?"

"Walter," he replied dryly, "and I'm probably older than you."

"Not by much, Walter." I estimated he'd been turned maybe ten years ago. "Anyway, I'll tell you what—you make rum and diet coke, don't you?"

"Yeah." One side of his mouth pulled up as he wondered where I was going with this.

"Well how about you make me a rum and diet coke, without the rum."

"Doohhh!!!" the kid chortled, amused that he'd been so easily caught. Next to me, Bracken choked back on a snicker and I eyed my beloved with sour amusement. He was wearing his redneck glamour, which meant he had a short-cut mullet and saturnine lines around his forehead and cheeks, but no fewer than four women had licked their lips and widened their eyes in his general direction. Cute—one more woman did that, and I was going to rip her lungs out through her nostrils, geas of death or no.

One of the women saw my glower and grew quickly sober, so I checked back on the scowl a notch or two—I forgot, sometimes, that I had plenty of practice looking like a badass before I had the muscle to back it up.

Turning back to Walter, I raised my eyebrows. "So, darling, can we do that?"

Walter smirked and filled a tall collins-glass with ice and soda from the soda gun. "Don't see why not—but it's gonna cost you the same as a rum & coke."

Mario and La Mark walked in, looking like buddies, and, thanks to Mario, like nobody's meat. The vampires were waiting to hear me announced—Nicky nodded to me and held up ten fingers. Ten minutes—sounded good.

I turned back to Walter, who had missed the by-play. "Tell you what, Walter," I purred. "If your boss doesn't offer to pay for my drinks by the end of the night, I'll pay you double what we order and you can pocket the rest."

Bracken choked back another guffaw and we smirked at each other for a moment. Neither of us had forgotten the danger, and we certainly didn't think the evening was a wrap—but if we couldn't get Rafael to spring for a virgin rum & coke, we were doing it wrong.

I wiped out the first soda, and tapped the bar for a refill, and Bracken leaned over to whisper, "If you're not careful, you're going to give yourself the hiccups!" That got a burst of semi-hysterical giggles from me, which was probably a bad idea.

Cocking his head at my laughter, Toothless the Badassed Woman Beater stalked over to me like he was going to pick his fangs with my bones. I sneered back and turned my head. His eyes narrowed and I realized what a complete dumbass I was. Oh Jesus, I had just shamed the bar's resident prick—I could probably take him, Bracken *definitely* could, but the point was, we didn't *want* to take him. Revealing ourselves in a barfight would not be nearly as powerful as revealing ourselves when we damned well pleased—with the bar behind us and beneath us, so to speak.

So I didn't back down when Toothless got to me, but I didn't pin him to the ceiling with power and let Bracken eviscerate him either.

"What you doing here, little girl?" the guy growled, and I beamed up to him with my heart—and my power—in my smile.

"I was going to sing tonight," I said disingenuously. "Would you like to hear me?"

The guy laughed without breathing—and, without laughing, really. It was a dry-gravel growl of a sound. "You might not live that long—you're not in a Starbucks, sweetheart, and your pretty little girlfriend isn't going to protect you, either..."

The guy put his hand on my arm, and Bracken said, "I'm not?" with a pleasant smile, even as he grabbed the guy's wrist with enough veiled granite-and-tree-root strength to break even a vampire's bone.

Well shit. He was wearing a sleeveless denim jacket and nothing else, and I could see that the guy had one of our marks—a tree that was half-oak and half-lime on his chest, that bore skulls as fruit. Nice—and we could use it to compel his actions—but if we did that, we'd be letting the entire world know *exactly* who we were, and it was just a little too early for what we had planned. We were going to have to do this dirty and old school. My heart was pumping in my throat and I got a notch more buzzed as adrenaline flooded my senses.

The guy's eyes swung to Bracken and I cleared my throat and touched his chin, and stared into his eyes. He tried to spell me—most vampires and all of the elves could do it, but this guy wasn't very good at it. Green had been telling me for nearly two years that I was strong enough so that if I really wanted to resist him and Bracken, I could.

This night I learned that he was right.

Toothless' eyes whirled, and I raised my eyebrows, still keeping it cute. "Jeepers, mister—those are some really red eyes, would you like some Visine for those?"

Our guy scowled, and Bracken's grip tightened, and a little bit of blood began to leak from Toothless Badass' skin where Bracken called it, and for the first time it registered that maybe we *weren't* fuzzy plump little bunnies ready to be stew.

Not a bright guy, really.

"Tell you what's gonna happen, Chuckles," I simpered. "You're going to go back in that corner and watch me perform, and you're even going to clap when I do it. And if you try to raise a hand to me—or to anybody who wears my mark or who's defenseless against you, your brains are going to gel, putrify, and run out of your nose. Do we have a deal?"

I put a lot of power in my voice—but it was subtle. People looked up from their drinks, the guy on the stage singing Kenny Rogers stuttered, and Walter our young vampire friend tripped behind the bar and thunked down on his knees—but nobody looked at me and Toothless Badass or my frightening sidhe lover who was sealing this power with vampire blood.

The guy nodded then, and Bracken released him. He moved backwards to the shadows—behind, even, the shapeshifter table he'd so disdained earlier. Bracken wiped his hand on a bar napkin and carefully threw it behind the counter. There were enough couples in the shadows sharing a vampire snack that the blood didn't attract too much attention—but it's never a good idea to just be wandering around with blood on your hands. Brack grimaced and looked at his hand again, then jerked a thumb towards the men's room, and I nodded.

I'd stay right here until either my name was called or he got back.

As he disappeared behind the swinging door, a midsized, lean, Hispanic vampire who had probably died in his early thirties rounded the hallway, as though he was coming out of the back offices. He was dressed snappily in black jeans and a red mandarin collared silk shirt—and he was looking around the room sniffing, probably for the preternatural power release I'd just engineered.

I looked away before he could see me watching him, and at that moment, Nicky fought his way through the crowd. The guy doing Kenny Rogers was belting out the last lines of *Lucille,* and Nicky leaned in close to talk to me.

"The paper had some sort of geas on it for a true name. I used 'Corinne Kirk'—you think that's okay?"

I grinned. "Perfect." Sometimes it helped to have six names.

We sat in silence for a moment, and I scanned the crowd again for my guys. We'd done tricky things with gauntlets, Hawaiian shirts and artistically ripped sleeves, so not everybody was wearing a sport-coat like Max, which was good because it would have looked like a mob uniform in the ninety degree heat that still saturated the air. I risked a glance at Rafael and saw him, still sniffing, trying to put a marker on the change that rent the atmosphere.

That he couldn't was a score for us.

Bracken came out of the bathroom, casually edging an inch or two away from the head vampire as he spotted me and came over. He got to me, and without turning around, flickered his eyes. I shook my head silently. The glamour had held, and our guy hadn't so much as blinked funny as my six foot eight inch non-human lover came a cat's whisker from running him over.

It was a near thing—I stood between Bracken and Nicky, trying to look strong (so as not to alert the vampire-predator-radar) and yet unobtrusive, and I saw Rafael make note of the number of new people in the bar—many of them shapeshifters. But he hadn't yet made me.

There was a commotion outside, and I winced. Oh Goddess—Annette had found us. But she wasn't screaming my name to try to get past the bouncers, she was screaming Nicky's, and although the three of us couldn't hide our wince—of distaste, of disgust, of sheer exasperation—Nicky was a common enough name. I could tell it was killing him not to respond, but he didn't, and there was a sudden *eep* sound, and a silence.

A second later, Kyle walked in stoically, and although the deep-browed, sandy- haired vampire didn't flash a single tell I could tell he was resisting the impulse to look my way and nod his head.

I took pity on him and initiated contact. *Is she totally gone?*

No. The disgust in that one mental word could have smothered a cheeseburger in onions.

? Now I had to resist the urge to wave my arms around, and at that moment, three things happened.

The first was that my name was called for the next song, and I stepped forward and waved with Bracken and Nicky in my wake as they put themselves into position.

The second was that Marcus and Phillip entered, a furious and chastened Annette between them. Her nice up-do was down around her shoulders, her black stockings had a run in them, and one of her false-eyelashes was starting to come off, and I had to try *really* hard not to glare furiously at Phillip as I ran by them and pretended we didn't know each other for just five more minutes.

What in the hell? I asked, while grinning and weaving through the tables.

She threatened to scream your name loud enough to make ashes stir up and become a vampire. Your geas won't let us spell her for her own damned good or ours.

When this is over, stuff her in someone's trunk, I ordered harshly, because the third thing was happening at that moment, and I needed to get up on stage.

Rafael scented the air as soon as Marcus and Phillip entered, and as I conversed with Phillip, I saw Marcus make eye-contact with him. One quick glance behind me as I dodged a table and made it to the steps to the stage showed him mouthing 'Corinne Kirk…Corinne Kirk…' to himself, even as his eyes widened with recognition for the two vampires who walked in. Their marks were still hidden, but they were well known to be Adrian's vampires.

I got up on stage, grabbed the wireless mike, and stood there, trying not to pant, as the spotlight found me and the opening riff of the song began.

Mississippi, in the middle of a dry spell…

I've always had this theory about what it takes to get people to pay attention to you when you get up on stage. It comes down to a bone-deep belief that what you have to say, do, or perform is so pure, so perfect, and so necessary to human existence that people HAVE to listen.

This is why a lot of crazy people get lemmings to follow them off cliffs and into the abyss of human evil—if a speaker believes what he's saying/doing/performing with THAT much passion, it MUST be true, right?

Now personally, I know I can sing okay, and I can hit the notes and my voice is alright—but I'm not Jimmy Hendrix or that lovely woman who blew everybody's socks off on the British talent show—I'm ordinary, and I'd never make it pro. But there was a rogue pedophile making child-monsters, and a real chance for all out war. I was new, I was *mortal,* and I had to show that I knew what I was doing, that I had power and I had people and I could get a room to follow me. There was a real chance of looking ridiculous here—and a real good reason why it couldn't happen. Goddammit, I *had* to make an entrance here, I *had* to get the crowd on my side, in a very necessary, what-I-am-doing-is-for-the-greater-fucking-good so listen dammit! sort of way.

It's probably the only time or place in my life in which I have had the confidence to pull off the throaty-voiced slink-fest that followed.

Rafael's eyes grew oh-shit big, and he met Marcus smug look with an oh-you-gotta-be-*shitting*-me roll, and I launched into *Black Velvet* like I was possessed with the spirit of Alannah Myles even as she lived.

It went pretty damned good, if I say so myself.

We'd blocked it loosely, so I could compensate for distance and tempo, but essentially, as I belted out the sultry, seductive song, I moved from table to table, exposing my people for who they were.

I yanked Teague's gauntlet off first, and he flexed his oak & lime covered wrist, then I daintily placed Katy's tattooed ankle in his lap. For Jack, I simply walked my fingers up his shirt and looked suggestively into his sardonic blue eyes. He shook his head and I gave him Katy's hand and then moved on. I stripped Max's sport jacket, showing his skin under the backless tank, and then Renny's scarf, showing the inkscape of her lower back. After Mario and La Mark's Hawaiian shirts came off, revealing wreaths around their upper arms and shoulders, I moved to Kyle—who got an old shirt ripped to expose his bicep. Phillip and Marcus lost their leather jackets, and then linked hands to show the same continuing design. Lambent needed his wife-beater ripped off his body so we could see the lime tree and oak tree twining on his chest and throat, and then I had the last slow verse left to get to Bracken and Nicky.

Nicky was on the stage and he dropped his Hawaiian shirt himself, then fell to one knee. I tugged Bracken's gauntlet slowly, stretching it out with the 'pleeeeeeeeeaaaze' at the end of the song, and stood while Nicky flexed his bicep around my thigh and rested his cheek against my hip. When I was done, Bracken flashed his tat with a nod of his head, and then undid the clasp at my neck. I angled my back to the audience and looked at them over my shoulder, so I could see the same dawning realization ripple through the crowd that had flickered in individuals at the exposure of every mark.

When my tattoo was there, in the spotlight, distinctive and irrevocable, with Bracken's tattooed wrist spanning my waist, the music died, and all of Rafael's people who knew anything, knew who I was.

There was a stunned, uncomfortable silence, and then Rafael inclined his head regally towards me and began clapping. His people followed uncertainly, and when the applause reached its peak, he stopped, held his fist to his heart, and bowed.

There was some iron in the backs of many of the vampires, and a lot of water in the spines of the shapeshifters, but to a one, all of his people followed his lead.

I bowed back the same way, and to a one—and with a lot more enthusiasm—my people turned towards Rafael and followed my lead.

"Thank you for you hospitality, Rafael," I murmured into the microphone when we had straightened. "Whose got next?"

The young deejay—a brown-haired shapeshifter, at my guess-- took the microphone from my hand and rolled his eyes. That was going to be a tough act to follow and we all knew it.

"I think we'll put on some music and take a break now, Lady Cory," he said gamely, and I smiled. Bracken took my hand and led me from the stage.

Up close, Rafael had stand-out cheekbones, full lips, and killer green eyes—he was, in fact, a poster boy for South American loveliness—probably by way of Brazil--and even I was not immune as he took my extended hand and raised it to his lips. I rolled my eyes—show-off.

"Thank you so much for the show, my Lady," he said smoothly. "I can see why Andres calls you 'Little Goddess'."

I flushed, and pulled back my hand, and Bracken laughed a little. "'Cory's' fine," I murmured. "Thank you for the show of solidarity—I know it couldn't have been easy."

He inclined his head in acknowledgement. "Here I was, all secure in being the king of my little castle…" there was a self-mocking note to his voice, but also something deadly serious.

"You still are," I said sincerely. "We just need… a little help. A little information, that's all."

He inclined his head—still not entirely at ease. "Well, in that case, let me buy you a drink. Walter?"

Walter popped up from behind the bar, his lips pursed in good-natured acknowledgement of the fact that he'd been had. "Yes sir," he muttered.

"Anything the Lady Cory and her people want, on the house." Rafael made a grand gesture and I nodded my head thanks.

"Walter," I smirked, "I'll have another virgin rum and diet coke, thank you."

Walter shook his head in mock irritation, and then popped up with an irrepressible grin, dimples, fangs, and all. He must have been a fun kid, and I wondered what had happened to bring him here.

Bracken ordered a Shirley Temple (the elves and sugar—it may be the only thing that got them giddy, but they had to drink a *lot* of it!), and Rafael snagged a waitress and told her to take care of all of my people—I guess there could be no doubt as to which ones were mine.

I took a hearty swig of my soda and followed it up with the inevitable hiccup, and Bracken laughed. We exchanged a quiet glance of support—we'd pulled off our entrance, and now the really hard shit was up on the table. I looked up from my stone-and-shadow beloved and saw that Rafael was unbuttoning his sleeve and rolling it up his arm. There on his wrist, subdued against his caramel colored skin, was his own mark—Green's lime tree, my oak tree, and Adrian's rose, twining around them both.

My smile was genuinely warm this time. Anyone who had Adrian's rose had to have either known Adrian or loved his memory, and it was good to know where Rafael stood. I nodded.

"We miss him," I said quietly, and Rafael extended a fang and punctured his wrist right above his tat.

"To Adrian," he said in toast, and I blinked, and was relieved when I felt Bracken tracing a delicate finger on the skin of my wrist as he opened a capillary or two so we could do this civilized.

"To Adrian," I murmured, and offered him my wrist in turn.

I tasted first—I didn't drink, mostly I just extended my tongue like a cat and lapped up the black blood as it welled up slowly. I closed my eyes and smiled. Spice and beans—mom's cooking—his dog, a golden retriever, swimming at Whiskeytown on warm, sunny days, ice-cream, the taste of a pretty girl's smile, dusty old books that he had loved to read, had lived his life by... I don't know what Rafael had died of, but his life had been sweet and peaceful, nestled in this notch between the foothills and the windswept plain of Nor-Cal.

I told him about his life, while he breathed in the scent of my blood, and then tasted from my wrist, a good solid pull before releasing it. He didn't fall to his knees, but he did fumble to sit on a nearby stool, weaving as he put his hand against the bar. As a vampire queen, it was pretty much my best trick, and it was all in the taste of my blood.

"Sunshine," he muttered. "Ah, Goddess...sweet, sweet, sunshine..." he closed his eyes in pain, and I watched him pinch the bridge of his nose as though that would stop the crimson trickle of vampire tears from running down his nose. When he looked up, his face was nostalgic and bleak with yearning for what he could no longer have.

"Bless you, my lady," he said huskily. "There is not much I wouldn't do for the taste of your blood, willingly given, on the tip of my tongue."

I smiled weakly—I'd given a lot this night, and I didn't want to show how woozy I was. "Let's wait until I eat a little protein," I said chirpily, and Rafael smiled.

"Of course—Walter? Some appetizers?" And it was generous of him, but as Walter bustled away, I knew that this was my cue to get down to business.

Or it would have been, had not that bitch-faced-agent-of-fucking-chaos not stomped up in her poor broken heels and screeched in my face.

"*You,*" she hissed through smeared coral lipstick, "are *so* disgusting..."

I glared at her and shoved a wad of power-field in her mouth. She grunted for a moment or two and then glared at me impotently, tears starting in her eyes.

"A friend of yours?" Rafael asked, pointedly, and I cursed the girl all over again.

"Not even a little tiny bit," I said, iron creeping into my voice. "In fact, we were just going to go stuff her into the trunk of her car, right Phillip?"

Phillip nodded, then popped his fangs out and put on his feeding face, leering into Annette's eyes until she started to cry. I sighed—he wasn't usually the type to go out of his way to be nasty. One more sign that Gretchen's time in his head was getting to him.

"Marcus?" I said delicately, and Marcus tapped Phillip gently on the shoulder, the touch doing much to tone down Phillip's irritation and make him back away. Marcus bumped him gently, shoulder to shoulder, and Phillip nodded. Together they grabbed the girl's arms, hauling her off towards the night.

"Would you like one of us to go get her?" Rafael asked smoothly, and because his blood was still tanging on my tongue, I knew what he was really asking.

"No," I said regretfully. "We've been bound with power from helping her, but Nicky's parents would be really pissed if we... uhm... lost her while she was here." I shrugged, trying to be philosophical. "Well, you know, some in-laws bring ugly furniture, Nicky's parents brought...*that.*"

Apparently Annette heard me as she was being hauled away, snarling Nicky's name through a mouthful of Cory-flavored nothing, because her eyes got big and real hatred poured off her form. It didn't deter Marcus and Phillip in the least.

Nicky, who was on Bracken's other side, snorted, "My parents should kiss your bloody feet, Cory—I'd throw her to that Toothless guy who tried to whammy you."

Rafael blinked, and mouthed "Toothless..." before turning and searching through the shadows. He saw Toothless Badass, standing in the shadows, staring blankly ahead, and turned to me in exasperation.

"What did you do to my enforcer?" he asked, his words compressing into a hard Hispanic accent in his excitement.

"Oh," I tried to make my smile apologetic. "Not much... we just told him to leave us alone, and..." how should I put this?

"And that if he ever hurt one of our people or anybody helpless again, his brains would liquefy and run out his nose," Bracken supplied dryly. I used the threat when I'd mind-whammied Jack's parents this last winter—I'd liked it so much, I saved it for people who really pissed me off. We were all pretty sure it wouldn't work, but it really did scare the shit out of people.

Rafael grimaced again. "That was the power I felt..." he glared at me. "Did anybody ever tell you that it's bad form to ruin a master vampire's enforcer without his permission?"

I glared back. "Did anybody ever tell *you* that it's bad form to have an enforcer who backhands people just because they can?"

Ouch! That one got him where he lived. Well, score one for me, and score another for Rafael—he hadn't liked his enforcer's tactics either. Well, maybe we could help each other then.

Still, there was face to be saved. "I don't see you walking into Andres' territory and mind-fucking *his* enforcers," he grumbled, and Bracken and Nicky both guffawed as I flushed.

"What?" he asked warily.

"That's because she killed him instead," Bracken said with grim relish. "Haven't you wondered why you haven't spoken to Robert in a year and a half?"

"He was going to eat us," I mumbled. Great. So much for mutual sharing and simpatico. I was a vampire slaying bitch from hell. Aces!

Rafael looked at me with a sudden understanding—he'd tasted my blood, he knew it was true. "I see," he murmured, nodding. "I'd wondered why he was no longer Andres' contact—you don't like to ask."

"So," I tried brightly, "are we all scary now?"

Rafael looked back, his eyes painfully sober as he licked the wound at his wrist closed. "You are terrifying, Little Goddess, don't you ever doubt it."

Oh Jesus. "Are we too scary to chat with?"

Rafael shook his head. "No, no—in fact, I think you're too scary not to."

Walter arrived with the appetizers and I gave them both a 'Thank you' and a game grin and dug in.

Phase one, complete!

BRACKEN

Queen Takes Rook

Sometimes, I wish she could see herself through my eyes.

She had seen tonight's performance as something she must do in order to achieve a desired effect. There had been no vanity in it, no awareness that the entire room had followed her, mesmerized, as she'd slunk around the room and lay claim by touch, blood, and song to every soul there who owed her fealty.

But I had seen. Our people would lie down and die for her.

There were people in Rafael's care who would die to kill her.

And the look on the bitchy little human's face, as the entire room silently bowed in homage to my beloved, warned that she would slaughter worlds to shed a drop of my beloved's blood.

My *due'ane* didn't care that she had the world at her feet and assassins at her back. She didn't wield that power like a cosmic mace over the heads of these people who were not hers.

All she wanted was to find a cure, a cause, an action to take that would stop the abomination of child vampires from continuing.

And Rafael was being deliberately obtuse.

Cory ate some fried cheese and passed the plate to me and Nicky. We ate—partly to replace the blood the vampires had taken, and partly to show Rafael that we trusted him. I saw that appetizers were being delivered around the room, and blessed Rafael's tact that got fried zucchini delivered to Lambent instead of those miserable chicken wings that Cory and Nicky were eating now that I had the (mmmm...) cheese. Nicky was cracking the bones and sucking the marrow moodily, and I thought he probably enjoyed wild game in his bird form very much. Did his parents know that about him?

I turned to my beloved, who was leaning over the bar and trying not to make it too obvious that she was afraid her breasts would spill out of the front of her mini-dress. They wouldn't—Nicky and I had put double-sided tape on the sides and they were still not that big, but I took her little capelet and fastened it at the neck around her shoulders anyway. She flashed me a truly grateful look, and I resisted the urge to touch her face.

She needed to be Green's *ou'e'eir,* Adrian's chosen successor tonight, not the sweet woman who yielded to me in bed.

And now she turned to Rafael and became who she was meant to be.

"So," she said, taking a dainty sip of her soda and pitching her voice throatily under the music from the stage, "Rafael, you'll never in a hundred years guess what we are keeping in our basement right now."

"'A dragon with five legs?'" he quipped.

"I might also be keeping a dragon with five legs in my house," she quoted with an arch of her eyebrows, "but no one has ever seen it."

Rafael's eyes widened. "*The Crucible,*" he said with a genteel smile. "I didn't know you liked literature, Lady Cory."

Cory wrinkled her nose, and I suppressed a grimace. Sore subject.

"One of my degrees is going to be in English lit," she said with a twist to her mouth. "Apparently I like it more than I suspected."

"One?" Rafael asked, impressed, and Cory waved him off.

"Actually, Rafael, I'm less concerned with my next year in school than I am with the poppet in my basement."

Rafael's expression became as closed as a virgin's knees.

"You're young, Lady, but not quite young enough for dolls."

Cory narrowed her eyes and I saw her fighting against taking a look at me. She didn't have to—we both saw it.

"Well," she said, pulling her lips inward in that playful grimace that usually meant her mind was working double-time, "since this doll can rip people apart and create undead wildlife, I'd say she's more my speed than your average Raggedy Ann, you think?"

The sound of a harsh breath from a body that didn't need to breathe can transcend the music of a crowded bar. Several vampires looked our way— either they heard Rafael's gasp, or he just had a flash of panic that escaped his control. When he met Cory's eyes this time, his face had become carved and gaunt in a moment.

"That's a *very* dangerous toy, my Lady," Rafael muttered unhappily. "That kind of toy can be deadly if you're not careful."

Cory's jaw clenched. "It's not like I went out and bought that puppy on my own, Lord Vampire," she retorted. "All we had to do was follow her pets back to her lair *before* tourist season in the foothills, and we discovered someone had left a mutant third-grade-Barbie doll right on our doorstep. Now who would build that sort of toy, Rafael? And how would a conscientious toy collector *fix* such a thing so we don't have to lock it in the basement anymore? Do you have *any* ideas?"

Rafael scrubbed his face with his hands and looked woefully at the closing wound on his wrist. He could lie to her all he wanted—and he very likely would—but she would know. She would know and would be within her rights to sweep his house clean with a sonic-bleach-broom.

"Cory," he said at last, turning to look her square in the eyes, "there are some things that are broken that cannot be fixed. It's my understanding that the... basic flaw in the design is so massive, that this particular toy is one of them..."

"*Dammit,* Lord Vampire!" Ah gods... her temper. Well, this was her barbecue. "We're not talking about a fucking toy here, we're talking about a little girl, and all she was doing was camping with her family and now..."

"I *know!*" he all but shouted, and now his voice was loud enough that the music stopped and there was a sudden hostile turning of over a hundred supernatural people, as they became instantly aggressive towards Cory and everyone with her mark.

Jack and Teague stood up immediately, going back to back as easy as breathing. Katy still sat, protected, between them. Lambent's glow went sungold with anticipation, and the two Avians were nearly on their chairs, they were so ready to fight. Marcus and Phillip had returned and they had gone back to back with Kyle already, and Max stood easily, his hand at the silver-shot loaded guns at his belt.

Renny changed into a giant tabby cat in a puddle of miniskirt and a black tank top that still fit over her fur. Well, we hadn't exactly brought her along for her fighting skills.

In fact, the entire room went on alert—but not Cory. Not Rafael. And, by example, not Nicky and not me.

Because I was touching her thigh with my hand, and Nicky was bumping my shoulder, we could both feel her revving enough power to blow up the building—but nobody else could.

"I know," the master vampire repeated in a beleaguered voice. "It's not a toy—it... *she*... was never meant to be a toy. But...but the last 'toymaker' I knew of, he...he promised that he had stopped."

Cory sighed, and her field relaxed as well. Some of the threat must have left the air, since the two leaders were still talking quietly, their backs to the facing armies, because the music started again and people began to stand down. I looked around and gave everybody the nod. Renny was a girl again, and with a quick pull of her mini-skirt, she was even dressed. This was still civilized—this was still a favor between friends.

"Well he's lied, Rafael," Cory said softly. "And not just about this one—we found bodies out at Lake Shasta—they've been reported already, and they're not the only family in the last four months since we've found Gretchen."

"Mother of God," Rafael swore—and his horror was genuine. He'd had no idea, and it hurt him, badly.

Cory paused, very deliberately, and let the import of his words sink in before she asked this next question. "Would you like us to put this toymaker out of business for you?"

Rafael looked at her, and I could see an almost wild inclination to say "Yes!" light up his eyes. I'd seen Cory look the same way—the terrible hope that someone, some *grown-up* could come along and do the hard task and make everything okay. Cory always squashed that light, that yielding—not once had she ever given us the hard job because she didn't want to do it herself.

And Rafael had been loved by Adrian—I had never met the man, he was from a time after Adrian and I had been exclusive—but Adrian had spoken highly of him. Redding was a rough crowd, Adrian had said time and again. Rafael was the sort of gentleman that a kiss like this one needed. Adrian had known people—he had known how to judge the best and the worst in them.

Adrian had been the first of us to look at Cory and see someone extraordinary.

He had not chosen wrong in his lieutenant.

"That is very kind of you to offer," Rafael said now, carefully, "and I shall be happy to take you up on it if things become…" he grimaced, "difficult. But our toymaker is a… solitary worker. I think an invitation from family would be the best way to bring him in."

Cory nodded, and met my eyes. "Tomorrow?" she mouthed, and I held up two fingers. That settled, she turned back to the man we had decided to trust.

"Two days, Lord Vampire," she said formally. "We'll be back in two days, if that's all right with you?"

Rafael nodded, and flashed some relieved fangs. "Two days should be sufficient," he murmured. "If for nothing else, than to let you know the matter has been properly investigated."

Cory pursed her lips—this was Rafael, giving his people a way out and a way to stall. "Rafael, you seem like a good guy—a guy who wants to do his best for his people, right?"

The man nodded, and I realized that all traces of the handsome, insouciant club owner had been burned away by the heat of this painful conversation. He looked sharp and haggard and weary.

Well, good. This had happened on his watch—and it wasn't a picnic for us either.

"Yes," he said heavily—Cory wasn't trying to be opaque.

"Well, then, you need to do more than prove that you 'investigated the matter'—do you understand me? I get it—you took a friend's promise for fact. That's fair—and you don't want to betray a friend to the big-bad-bitch in town—I understand that. This is one of your people and you want to protect him. I get that too. But he signed on for this life. Gretchen, the kid in our basement, was raped, killed, and resurrected without a say in the matter. Do you know what happens to their minds, Rafael?"

Her voice started to break a little, in passion, in pain—we didn't talk about Gretchen much, but she weighed heavy on our minds.

"She forgets that she killed her parents, and she asks us about them, every day. And we've started to lie to her—we've started to tell her that they're coming soon, you know? Because it just seems kinder that way. She's started to imagine conversations with her brother... 'What happened to your doll, Gretchen? I thought you liked her?' and she'll start yelling for Marvin because she's *sure* she saw him come in and break the damned thing."

Cory swallowed, and I put my hand on the small of her back. I didn't go visit, and Cory never shared. Wasn't it funny, the sorts of pain that could build up in our beloveds when we weren't looking? Nicky's pain, Cory's pain... they knew it would hurt us, so they kept it to themselves. I wasn't good at that. I figured Cory knew about all there was to know about the secret workings of my mind. I was as mysterious as a boulder in the sun.

There was a brief, heavenly smell of mustard flowers in the rain, and Cory took a deep shuddery breath and kept going. Bless Green—he really would have felt her misery from two-hundred miles away.

"Anyway," she murmured, dashing her hand in front of her eyes, "I respect you, Rafael. I like you. And I don't want your kiss—they're yours. But you had better not underestimate the havoc I'll wreak--or the bodies I'll leave in my wake--to make sure that there is *never* another vampire like Gretchen. Have I made myself perfectly clear?"

Rafael nodded, and stood. If he hadn't been vampire-pale already, I think her anger would have drained him of color completely.

"I understand, my Lady," he said quietly, and then he put his fist to his heart and bowed. "I would be honored if your people would stay and enjoy their evening, however, when two a.m. comes…"

"We're mice and pumpkins—I understand." She hopped up from her stool and bowed back. "Thank you, Rafael. I'll see you the night after tomorrow."

He nodded and left, and the deejay, sensing that karaoke night was over, put in a power-ballad for slow dancing.

She put up no resistance as I led her to the floor.

When we got there, Max and Renny were on the floor already, and Jacky and Katy as well. Marcus and Phillip had each politely asked local shapeshifters, and so had Mario. Lambent moved out of the crowd to the back corner of the dance floor, Kyle had shifted to the opposite corner, and La Mark took an empty table towards the front center. Nicky joined him there with an extra soda in his hand to share.

It was smoothly done, and completely natural—we wanted to dance, so our people covered for us—and I knew Cory noticed.

I also knew it bothered her.

"They didn't need to do that," she murmured against my chest. REO Speedwagon blared *I Can't Fight This Feeling* and I slid my hand under her capelet to touch the skin on her back.

"They wanted to—it makes us look impressive."

She grunted. "I'm tired of theatre." There was a trembling in her limbs, an adrenaline bleed, that showed me alone what her interview had taken from her. "I want to go back to the cabin and just sit and look at the stars and maybe talk to Green on the phone."

"Maybe go swimming?" I asked dreamily, and that brought a laugh from her.

"You're really going to miss that lake, aren't you?" In that moment everything disappeared for her but my face in her vision and the feel of my body under hers. *I'd die for this,* I thought hazily. It was truth.

"You have no idea," I said through a tight throat, and she leaned her head low on my chest, and for a moment I felt the weight of everything we had done this night, resting on me because I could hold it.

"Junkie," she murmured, and I laughed, mostly so she could hear the rumble of my voice.

We danced for a little while more, even when the tempo went up and even when it went more country than rock. There was an impromptu two-step lesson to Chris Isaak's *Diddly Daddy* that had the three women in the party being whirled from man to man, and enough laughter among all of us to lure more of Rafael's people onto the dance floor.

After that there was another slow song, and as Jack left the dance floor, his shoulder brushed up against Teague. There was enough softness in the touch, that even as Teague held onto Katy, their sham of 'heterosexual space' completely dissolved. I thought that maybe it was time to go.

Cory noticed it too, and nodded at me from Nicky's loose embrace. When the song wound down, I stood and everyone gathered together, and we left as a group. Many of Rafael's people wished us a noisy goodbye as we left, and there were smiles and waves and a couple of bows. There were also silent wishes of death—and we could feel those too.

The humid darkness outside was different from the stifling darkness inside. The stars arced above us in a magic canopy of wishes, and although we stayed on alert, there was a relief of tension that flooded out of us. I didn't have to look to know that while one of Teague's arms was draped around Katy's shoulders, his other hand was locked firmly in Jacky's. Phillip and Marcus were side by side—their hands weren't linked, but their shoulders bumped often. Lambent's glow softened, and the heat radiating from his body eased back as he relaxed, and Renny gave up all pretense of being a girl and became a giant cat in a tank top again. Max grunted softly and bent down to pick up her mini-skirt and pretty sandals before catching up.

"That went well," Cory said loud enough to be addressing all of us. "Good job, guys."

"What's going to happen?" Kyle asked, the only one to break the silence. The deep-browed vampire was usually pretty taciturn—I think seeing himself surrounded by members of a group made him suddenly wish he was tighter with us.

"What's going to happen?" Cory blew out a breath and we exchanged bleak looks. "What's going to happen is that in two days, we're going to meet with Rafael again, and he's going to try to stall, because this guy's a friend and he feels like shit about having to kill a friend."

"Wonderful, Mommy!" Katie protested. "Then why we just get all dolled up and pretty for show?"

Cory smiled and turned around to grin at Katy, who was wearing a glossy plum-colored mini-dress with little cut-outs at her hips and back. "Well you look pretty spectacular, and the guys got to dance with you—I mean, isn't that reason enough?"

Katy rolled her eyes and blushed, especially when Teague let out a suppressed snork of laughter. "You know what I mean!"

Cory nodded, and I finished the thought for her. "Yeah, we do." I kissed Cory's knuckles. "But there's a… a rhythm to these things. Meet nice, shake hands, and then…"

"Let them betray you," Nicky said darkly.

Cory snickered, but nobody else did. "It's funny because it's true," she said into the stony silence, and there was a universal grunt. Every damned one of us had seen personally that it was true.

"What do we do then?" Katy asked, wide-eyed, and Cory looked behind her and smiled.

"Then you and Renny stay home," she said, some steel in her voice.

"And Jacky," Teague rasped, and Jacky made a cross between a grunt and a growl, and then we all moaned and he subsided. Whether they liked it or not, the entire hill knew how Jacky's last important run had turned out, and the lover's bargain, sealed in desperation, that kept him from runs now.

"Why?" Katy asked, even though she knew the truth.

"Because," Cory replied sweetly, "after they betray us, then we kick some ass. Now whose trunk is whatserface locked in?"

"Nicky's parents' car," Marcus grunted.

"Aww shit—someone's got to drive that back." We all looked at the car—bright purple with yellow stars and olive fenders and hood.

"Ohhh!" Renny was suddenly half-naked girl and talking excitedly. "I'll drive it! Can I drive it?" She looked at us, naked from the waist down, with her eyes wide and happy. "Oh, Cory—do you think Green would let me *have* it?"

I looked around at a dozen expressions just like mine—hands clapped over mouths while bright eyes peered over, keeping our amusement to ourselves.

We needn't have bothered—Renny, being Renny, was oblivious to everybody but Cory and Max, and they both could laugh all they wanted, because she was secure in their love.

"You want that car?" Cory asked, looking helplessly at Max. "Why didn't you say anything this morning?"

Renny shook her head and smiled shyly. "I've been looking at it all day." She grabbed Max's hand. "Isn't it beautiful?"

Max looked at Renny, the girl who was more cat than girl, and who had cemented the stoic cop into our midst more surely than his curiosity or his stolid sense of right. Her flyaway hair had escaped its pretty clip, and her bare bottom peeked beguilingly from under the long tank-top, but her eyes were childishly bright and her smile was as winsome as a kitten humping a ball of yarn.

"Gorgeous," he said roughly, daring the rest of us with our eyes to say anything. Our smirks faded, but our amusement remained.

Cory laughed fondly. "Fine, Renny-cat—if Green says it's yours, it's yours. But first check to make sure our ugly furniture is still there."

She was there, a kerchief in her mouth instead of Cory's power-wad, glaring at us with poisonous eyes.

I didn't want my beloved to deal with this shit anymore. She was busy making the world safe from monsters—the least I could do was make her safe from the world.

I stepped in front of Cory before she could say a word, and hauled the girl out of the trunk by the armpits. Marcus had apparently used her own black pantyhose to tie her arms behind her back, and her broken shoes made a clatter as they fell back into the car. If she had looked roughed-up in the club, she looked worse now, and the little black dress that showed off her boobs was now almost ripped off of them. Her falsely blonde hair was a tangled mess falling around her face, and the raw hatred and contemptuous sneer that ravaged her features took away the illusion of prettiness that fine bone structure and full lips had once given.

The girl made to struggle, to scream, and I clamped my hand over her mouth instead.

"Look here, human," I said and something about the timbre of my voice made her eyes grow wide and the screams die in her throat. "You were not invited. We don't like you. Cory here has been fending off offers to kill you for three days. We take that shit seriously, human, so you should get down and lick the dust off her toes."

She looked outraged and I thought briefly about flicking her on the head like a child. I sighed—I was stronger than humans. I'd probably crack her skull.

"We don't want you to do that, but we would like you to not scream or to make life miserable for Max and Renny, right? So we're going to let you sit in the back of the car instead of the trunk. But if you fuck with them, or even don't fucking shut the fuck up, Max here can turn into a giant cat and eat your throat. Or if he doesn't feel like doing that, he's got a giant fucking unregistered gun in the holster under that jacket. Either way, you'll eventually be quiet, do you hear me, human?"

Even under the best of times I can be a grumpy fucker, and Cory has told me that when I'm in a bad mood, I am positively terrifying. I lost control of the pitch of my voice with that last sentence. I must have—she gave a whimper, and there was a trickling splat into the mud, and then the unmistakable smell of urine.

"Oh Jesus, Bracken—we're going to have to live with that all the way back to the cabin?" Max whined, and Renny made a little whimper. Her new car—she'd been so excited.

Mario broke into an out-and-out guffaw though. "Keep your shirt on, cop, we've still got sweats in the SUV—I'll be back in a second."

It worked out—between the sweats (uncomfortable in the heat) and the towel and the wool blanket we made her sit on, the car was saved, and the nasty little human got let out of the trunk, and Renny's new car (on loan, of course, to the Kestrels until we bought them a new one) was kept clean during the ride back.

The vampires rode back with us—there had been some talk of them staying as we drove up, but given the way Rafael had left things, it had seemed impolitic, at best, and out and out defiance at the worst. They hid their disappointment, and I felt bad—of course we were their family, but we weren't their brethren—sometimes there's a distinct difference. They would have liked to have gotten to know the others in the club, at the very least.

Marcus was driving, and we left the windows down for much of the ride, the night air getting moist and bearable in the low eighties. Cory's *Bleed it Out* sound track had a winding down counterpart, and the moody strains of Springsteen's *Secret Garden* haunted the back seat as Cory snuggled in with me, and Nicky and Kyle kept up a desultory conversation in the mid-seat.

"Did you see the werewolves?" she murmured, and I grunted an affirmative in her ear.

"Do me a favor," she said quietly. "After we go sit and you have your swim, let me hang outside and knit for a while. I think Teague may want to talk."

I didn't ask her how she knew this. Most people when they came to the hill looked to Green—but not Teague. Maybe it was the way Cory had been there to talk with when Jack had first been injured, or maybe it went deeper. The two of them had spent the first part of their lives so absolutely certain that neither of them mattered, only to find that their lives mattered a great deal, to many. Teague would talk to her when he would talk to nobody else, not even his mates.

At that moment Nicky popped his head over the seat.

"Hey—what should I tell my folks about Annette?" he asked, and Cory gave a groan and snuggled into my chest.

"Can you get them to put her on the first plane back to Montana before I have to kill her?" she asked while playing with the edge of my shirt's button band.

Nicky snarked, and her body went still. It was, perhaps, the first time she realized she wasn't joking about the subject.

She looked up and I saw Nicky flinch from whatever was in her face. I heard the pain vibrating from her. "You get that, right Nick? You understand that if she gets one of my people hurt with all that poison, I will kill her. Between the crowd in that bar tonight and the funky chaos thing, we're not fucking around here. Tell your parents that—I'm pretty sure they're not going to warm to me at this point, so be totally brutally honest with them. If she gets one of my people hurt because she's too fucking clueless to piss behind a goddamned tree, then I will kill her. See if you can get her on a plane—for everybody's sake."

Nicky nodded, and then did something he wouldn't have dared to do, even a year ago. He leaned way over the seat and kissed her cheek as she lay in my arms, then sat back on his knees.

"Lady Cory, whatever you need to do," he said with more affection in his formality than I've heard in some people's endearments.

When we got back to the cabins, not everybody was ready to go sleep (or make love—as the werewolves and were-kitties obviously ran inside to do). A spirited card game started at the picnic benches, under the two bright kerosene lamps suspended from trees. Lambent was unashamedly winning, but from the occasional shocked groans I could tell that La Mark was doing well for himself, and that Tanya (who had come out to greet us as we drove up) was amazingly good at hiding her cards. And that Mario was showing some interest in where the sylph might *hide* those cards if they truly disappeared.

Cory disappeared for a moment to shower. Her bravery of earlier notwithstanding, she certainly wasn't ready to be in the lake at night, and nobody wanted the stink of the club on them for long. I hadn't been in the water for more than a few heartbeats before she came back out with a little camp seat and an electric lamp, and, of course, her knitting.

She sat quietly, thoughtfully, and knit without hardly looking at her stitches. (It looked to be a hat—in the dark brown-purple she always used with me. I loved that color.) She was so deep into her own thoughts that she almost didn't look up when Nicky and his parents came out to speak with her, and when she did look up, she shook her head and looked back down again.

Quietly, I tread water into the shadows of the dock to listen.

"You can't make us take her back," Mrs. Kestrel was saying shrilly. She pulled the belt of her flowered wrapper tighter around her body, although it was warm enough still that Cory was wearing shorts and a T-shirt.

"No, I can't," Cory said softly, still looking at her hands. I saw her eyes flash in the moonlight, and she fixed Terry Kestrel with the same hard look she'd fixed Nicky with. "But you should. You should *want* to. She spent most our time locked in the trunk of a car..."

"While Cory asked the nice vampires not to kill her as a personal favor!" Nicky broke in, his voice hard.

"Kill her!" Terry's hands fluttered, her robe temporarily forgotten. In silhouette she appeared... out of place. Ridiculous. Our people were at home during vampires' hours—she was wrapping her shoulders against the darkness.

"She's offensive—and she doesn't understand what we are." Cory sighed and stood, stretching muscles and shaking the mark of the camp chair off her skin. "I pitched her across the lake today—she thinks I was kidding. If Nicky hadn't spoken up, I would have let her smack into a boat head first, and we'd be having a very different conversation."

There was a silence, and Nicky's mother didn't even refute the possibility that Cory would have let the nasty little baggage die.

"What if we don't?" Terry asked, when the stars refused to speak for her. "What if we don't send her home? Are you going to punish us? Mind-wipe us? What?"

Cory snorted. "I'm going to call you responsible for the consequences. And why you'd want that on your head I'll never know."

The woman's body posture stiffened, and she leaned forward. I couldn't see the lines of her face—but I think the darkness was merciful, because the voice was an ugly snarl. "You're just afraid she's going to take my boy back, that's all. All this talk about 'keeping her safe'—you just don't want any competition."

Cory's laugh was surprised and truly amused. "Mrs. Kestrel, you are either too blind or too ignorant to see that competition is the last fucking thing I'm afraid of. Go to bed and live with your own pettiness. And let us know if you want to buy a new car now, or if you want to fly back and buy one when you get home."

And with that she sat down, picked up her knitting, and broke out her iPod, making it clear with a crank of the volume that the audience was well and truly over.

I wondered if she knew how very royal she had been—right down to the dismissal at the end.

Nicky bent down to kiss her cheek and said, "I'm going to walk her up…"

"And call Eric?" Cory's voice was hopeful, and Nicky's answering laugh was affirmative. Good. He needed to hear his lover's voice. I was certain that Cory had called Green while I'd been swimming as well.

There was a movement from the shadows of the woods after Nicky and his mom disappeared under the carport towards the cabins, and I stiffened as I made out the form of the boy who was in the odd-colored cabin.

I was going to warn Cory about him, but she looked up and waved openly. "Heya, Sam!"

The kid looked surprised, and waved back, and then disappeared to whatever late night wandering he was inclined towards. Given the fact that he was a teenager and he might find any combination of our people fucking in the woods on any given night, it was probably like the best scavenger hunt of all times, if you weren't afraid of the dark.

I shifted in the water, and her voice drifted through the warm darkness, like a cool breath of air on my cheek. "You ready to go in?"

I grunted. The water was so chill and alive, wrapping itself around my limbs... "Not yet," I murmured.

"I want you," she said simply, but her voice was so empty and tired, I was pretty sure she wasn't trying to be seductive. "You're...essential to me, beloved."

Ah gods...

"You speak poetry in the darkness," I surprised myself by saying. The stars were shattered glass above us, the night sky so black around them you could almost touch it like you could touch the air. Even her weary poetry was profound under such a sky.

"You are my poetry. You and Green..." her voice trailed off, and her needles clicked again. "I don't think Teague's coming..."

"Shhh..."

Because I'd heard his cabin door close, even from far above us.

"Are you just going to hide out there and listen?" She was amused, and I snorted gently.

"I think he expects me to by now." Considering how many of their conversations I'd overheard while looking for Cory when she had crept out of bed to knit or to worry or to watch television with Grace, it was not an understatement.

"Shhh..."

Her needles clicked quietly as the werewolf approached the dock.

TEAGUE

Knight's Dilemma

How did she do that? It was as though she had some sort of 'Teague sense' that told her that he was awake and in need. Not sexual need—thankyoujesus NO! Because wouldn't that just fucking complicate shit to all gettout? No—just need. Mostly, just need to talk to someone he *wasn't* sleeping with, to make sure he was treating the two people he *was* sleeping with right.

She'd said once that he would want to hang around Green's hill to see how successful relationships worked. She'd said that maybe he'd want to look at Green, look at Grace and Arturo, look at Bracken's parents—they'd be good examples. They would show him how it was done.

He was not sure he would ever tell her that his best example was her.

She looked up as he walked by and smiled. She looked exhausted, and he wondered at how much the evening's performance had taken out of her. She had hidden it well, but only because he knew her when she was kicking ass, his werewolf sense of smell had picked up the adrenaline even when she was practicing.

Performing tonight had been difficult. He never would have guessed to see her sing.

"You look tired," he muttered as he sank to sit, legs crossed, next to her chair on the dock.

"Shhh…" she murmured with a smile so faint, wolf's eyes could barely see it in the dark. "Bracken might hear you."

Teague grimaced. "Is he out here?"

"Somewhere, yeah." She gestured grandly to the glittering silver-black expanse of lake in front of them.

He felt a little better—odds were, Bracken would still hear, but he was fairly sure Cory would edit out the parts where he was a total bone-fuck loser.

They sat in silence for a moment, and Teague realized there was never total silence out in the woods. Insect noises, the whooshing of the dam out in the distance—even the occasional car, invisible on the causeway beyond the trees—all of it was there, a counterpoint to the background of this alien wilderness. Teague had smelled bears when he'd done recon—they cut the were-creatures a wide berth, but he'd forgotten about them, until this very moment.

There was a ripple and a splash, about fifty yards away, and they both watched as Bracken, sleek as an otter, pushed mightily out of the water, did a flip under the perfect moon, and incised cleanly back from where he'd come.

Cory gasped and laughed a little, covering her mouth with her hand. "Arrogant bastard," she muttered, but it was clear she was delighted. A human couldn't have done the move with strength alone, and Bracken's nude body had been so very beautiful as it had hovered between the silver moon and black lake, before the impossibly graceful roll.

"He likes the water," she said into the silence when they'd recovered. "I think it's the only thing that makes the heat bearable for him in the day."

Teague had seen this too—and her obvious worry, at the height of the sun, when her normally strong, hale lover became lethargic and weak.

"How do you deal with the worry," Teague asked bluntly, and not for the first time.

"You remember the strength," Cory answered automatically. "But that's not what you want to talk about."

"No?"

"No—you want to talk about why you haven't bonded yet."

Teague sucked wind in through his teeth—she was right, but she was so casual about it. "It's not funny," he muttered. "In fact, it's damned embarrassing."

"I wasn't laughing, not even a little tiny bit." She turned her tired, wide-boned face towards him, her dark-hazel-brown eyes fathomless and kind.

"It's not your problem."

"You're my friend," she retorted. "And I can be just as much as a terse, laconic asshole as you can, so let's just cut the shit, shall we?"

"I thought it was shoot the shit and cut the crap," he said mildly, and she laughed.

"Anything besides talk about yourself, right Teague?"

"You wrote the instruction book, my lady, I just follow it."

"Fuck you," she laughed again. "Or, better yet, grab your balls in one hand, your wanker in another and man-the-fuck-up."

Teague sighed. It was fun—they could probably go back and forth for hours—but she was also right. "Okay—why haven't I bonded?" he asked, although, given his conversation with Bracken in May, he was sure she already knew.

She sighed, and her knitting stilled, and one hand came out to run through her drying hair—which immediately erupted into a cluster of curls as a result.

"You know, the old knights of the Round Table, Teague?"

"Urm." He'd heard of them.

"Well, most of them weren't just dedicated to fighting at Arthur's side, right? Most of them were dedicated to fighting to protect the Queen."

"Mmmhm." It was a different sound altogether, and she flashed him an arid grin, glinting in the starlight, to let him know she heard the difference.

"So Lancelot—when he and Gwenyfar got it on, well—he'd violated sort of a horrible code..."

"I'm not..."

"I've already got a Lancelot, Sparky. Cool you're jets."

"Thank God." Beat, beat. "Bracken?"

"Yup." There was a pause, and then she relented. "When... when Bracken was *courting*, I guess is the word," she laughed as though there were no words for her and Bracken, "Green told me that Arthur and Gwenyfar and Lancelot could have made it work, if they hadn't been living with a bunch of people who told them it couldn't. All Green's people knew it could—we've been blessed."

"So... it didn't matter."

"That he violated the code? That he fell in love with me the minute his brother showed me to him and said 'she's mine'? No. But you're not Lancelot, Teague. You're... I don't know. Gawain. Tristan. Galahad. One of the others. Maybe Gawain—he made honor hurt too. You have lovers—and you'd die for them. But the thing that makes you think you're worthy of your lovers is that you serve your Queen. So that whole werewolf mating thing... it's not going to work for you. I don't know. Your sense of yourself is wrapped up in being our Alpha. And I don't think it's a bad thing—not for you. But..."

She peered at him in the darkness, squinting, because her vision was ordinary and mortal, like so very much about her. He could feel her, searching for the right words—the entire reason she'd stopped, he figured, was because she'd been going too smoothly, talking too much like a Queen, and not enough like a college kid, and she'd forgotten for a second that she was still pretending to be just a college kid. When he didn't roll his eyes, or snort, or even laugh, but simply regarded her steadily back, she felt safe enough to continue.

"You need to believe in yourself enough to convince Jack and Katy that it doesn't matter."

Teague snorted. "Jacky won't buy it."

"Bullshit."

Teague looked at her. "I'm sorry, have you met Jacky yet?"

"He'll believe it if you will," she insisted, looking at the night sky. Suddenly, she stood, stretching, and moved to the end of the pier, bouncing on her toes at the edge. She reached her arms over her head and grunted a little as the muscles gave, and then turned and felt the mild roll of the dock under her feet with the motion.

"What? I'm just supposed to say 'I'm broken. This is just one more thing you have to put up with because I'm… flawed. Fucked up. Too much damage to repair?" The disgust in Teague's voice was hard to hear.

"We're all broken, Teague," Cory told him, her voice gentle in the dark. "You think I'm not broken? You think Green isn't?" Only the hesitation in her voice before she said his name told Teague how hard the three-day distance had been on her.

"Bracken seems just fine," he said, trying to be funny. Her snort told him that he'd fallen flat.

"You think Bracken isn't broken? He could have lived forever, Teague. He could have had anyone—anytime, anywhere. Elves, sidhe—they're like exposed sex nerves, you know? A walking clitoris with a hormone chaser. A true binding—like the one we have? Never happens—one couple in every twenty years, if that—I talk to the old sidhe. They tell me. Do you think he'd have needed a binding with just me… do you think my health would be so dependent on him, on Green, or that Green would need me quite so bad, if Adrian hadn't hauled off and gotten killed and broke us all?"

"You're dealing," Teague said numbly, wanting to stick his head in the lake and keep it there until he passed out.

"Of course we deal—we're pretty fucking happy, actually. But we're still broken. You should know that better than anybody—our being broken almost got you and Jacky killed this winter, remember?"

Ah, Goddess. "You got there in time," he muttered, not knowing what else to say. He'd been the one dumb enough to let Jacky come.

"Yeah, but we're still fucked up. We're not perfect--we're not even whole. All we really have is our faith that we're all trying—Nicky too. So you get boners when you don't want to? Welcome to the human race, werewolf. Didn't you ever spring wood as a mere mortal?"

Teague flushed, his body warming the cooling night, and Cory closed her eyes tight. "Your thing with Jacky surprised the hell out of you, didn't it?" she asked perceptively.

"Nunghan..." he replied coherently, and she laughed a little.

"Yeah, I wouldn't know what that feels like, to be attracted to someone when you think it's wrong... you know, like my boyfriend's old lover or something," she said dryly, and he just shook his head and looked away.

"You're a real smartass, anyone ever tell you that?" His voice came out as a bass growl, and she laughed, the sound tired but whole, for all her talk of being broken.

"No, Teague, you're the first," she said with a totally straight face, and he rolled his eyes. Suddenly her stretch was done, and she came towards him earnestly, not touching him (because Jacky would smell it and lose his everloving mind), but getting close enough for him to see the expression around her fathomless eyes.

"Green sleeps with anything that moves—it's part of his job. They're all beautiful, too—even the freaking vampires and shapechanges. It's like some sort of fucking law. And I am plain. My face is plain, my body is plain—I am ordinary, and half the time, I'm fighting a losing battle against being a real bitch. But I have not doubted his love for a moment, not even a nano-second. If Adrian had lived, one night—maybe not in the first year, but definitely in the years that followed—he would have needed to spend a full moon night in the room they won't even let me in, because they think I'm still too innocent to know about it. And I wouldn't have doubted his love, either, not even a nano-second. Bracken would have joined us eventually, and I would have watched all of them stay young and beautiful while I got old and gray and wrinkly—leaving them behind as perfect and as lovely as when I'd first stumbled into their lives. I wouldn't have doubted their love then, not even for a minute. They wouldn't let me doubt it, and you learn to take some things on faith. You were broken, Teague, and you fixed yourself. There's no shame in that. But you're treating it like there is—like you're ashamed, like you've done something wrong. That's why Jacky thinks you're doing it on purpose. You just need to tell him you're not. He's passive aggressive, and I can see how this would have gotten out of hand, but..." her mouth quirked, and when she spoke next, he heard Katy's unmistakable accent in her voice. "It's not like you talk too much, right *Papi?*"

Teague found he was smiling fondly. "I guess I'm not the only one to come talk to you, am I?"

Cory flushed and backed away. Teague had reminded her that she was more than a friend—she was an authority figure, and she really didn't like that.

Tough.

"Thank you, Lady Cory," Teague said, taking her hands in his. He kissed them—a courtly, old-fashioned gesture, that of a knight to his queen—and then he bowed. He knew he was making her as uncomfortable as hell, and he couldn't help smiling about it anyway. She was wonderful—not wonderful like his mates were wonderful, just… just like a real queen—and a real friend.

"Go!" she laughed, and he shook his head.

"I'll go for a swim first—that way Jacky won't get too worked up when he smells you on me. Besides—you and I both know Bracken will jump up here as soon as I get in the water, right Bracken?"

There was a splash and the dock rocked subtly under Bracken's weight.

"She's getting tired, wolfman," he warned. His voice was friendly, but he was also serious, and Teague could see that too.

"Thanks for letting her stay up late with me," he said sincerely, and Bracken gave a bow. Even though the young sidhe had probably never seen a real court, that long, muscular body looked like it was made for executing grand and courtly gestures.

"Our pleasure, Teague. Go swimming. Go enjoy your lovers. You have done nothing wrong." He turned to Cory. "And you, beloved, you're so tired you're making the fish yawn!"

She giggled, just like a little kid, and Bracken wrapped his arms around her, dripping lake-water and all. She didn't complain, just murmured low in her throat and let him lead her away, leaning almost drunkenly on him, probably from sheer exhaustion.

Teague watched them go thoughtfully.

They didn't look broken. She didn't seem broken.

Maybe surviving was the ability to take your damage and make it work for you. That thought cheered him—he had plenty of damage to make work for him. Suddenly the swim sounded lovely, his werewolf metabolism making up for the vague chill of air that had dropped to the low eighties, in spite of the smallness of the hour.

With one memorable exception, Teague didn't do naked in public, so he was wearing his shorts and T-shirt when he made a clean slice into the water. There was something pure in the darkness, something cleansing in the red dirt that scoured his skin with the wet. The thought wasn't coherent, but it was pervasive as he stroked as far and as fast as he could. Maybe it would scour him of his damage. Maybe it would make his skin clean and good enough for Jacky and Katy to touch.

He pushed his muscles a little farther, and a little farther, and when he turned around, he was out in the middle of the lake, the cabins small in the starlight, two heartbeats in them almost red in his vision, calling him, chanting that home is where they were.

His body was loose and happy enough, he decided. He enjoyed every stroke of the swim home.

ARTURO

Bishop Panics

Green's Hill was missing its joy when Cory was gone, there was no doubt about it.

Green hid it well, but without his beloved, he was a pale shadow, stalking the halls of his merry home and looking grimly determined not to let anyone feel sorry for him because this time, Cory was gone and he was left behind.

"You are making me crazy," Arturo snapped at last. It was the night after Cory's grand entrance to Rafael's kiss, and they were *supposed* to be doing accounts—Arturo's least favorite chore, but one Green wanted out of the way before Cory returned. He had plans for that moment which had nothing to do with sales figures and property deeds, and the more he had done now, the less he had to worry about when she was back. The two of them worked very hard to make sure they had time that was theirs and not the entire hill's—Arturo, who knew what he knew about royalty, would do everything he could to help.

But Green had just re-worked the same figure six times—dammit, the man had to get out into the fresh air and remember how to think and breathe again.

"Sorry, Arturo," Green muttered contritely, pinching the bridge of his nose. "I'm just..."

"Distracted, brother—yes, I've figured that out." Arturo rolled his eyes. "Look—Grace, she wants me tonight—what can I say the woman's insatiable..."

"Egotistical bastard," Grace snapped from the small kitchen that sat adjacent Green's front room.

"Don't deny it, woman—you know you want me!"

"You're good in bed—what am I supposed to do, turn that down?" Grace came in with two plates of pasta covered in pecan-cilantro pesto, which she knew Green particularly liked.

"You could quit hounding me for it," Arturo said mildly, just to hear her snort. The fact that she stuck her tongue out at him was a definite plus.

"Oh please—*Bite me, Grace, let me feel your hot fangs sinking into my flesh!*" Grace mimicked, and Arturo flushed—he admitted he had grown a taste for the passion of his vampire's bite, but he didn't think he sounded *that* needy.

But Green laughed at their antics, and Arturo thought he'd gladly hear Grace spill any other embarrassing thing he had to say out for their leader, just to see that wide grin split his clean-featured, narrow-jawed anime perfect face.

"Seriously, brother," Arturo said as he was digging into the pasta, "you need to get out and talk to her."

"I talked to her after her meet with Rafael! Hell, I was with her this morning," Green said mildly, as though that meant he didn't miss her in the flesh.

Arturo snorted. "Doesn't matter. She won't be back for real until at least another couple days—we'll get this done by then, I have no worries."

"On this, you shouldn't," Green agreed. "The thing I'm truly worried about, all I can *do* is wait."

He was talking about Nolan Fields. They knew when he was releasing his photos, and they were pretty sure they knew most of the locales—but they couldn't take steps to erase the pictures until right near the release date—otherwise, he'd know how to hunt down others. No, it was best to discredit him so completely, he didn't want to *try* to blackmail their people again. Of course, Arturo planned to kill the vermin before the thought even occurred to him.

Green might not approve, but he'd definitely forgive, and after months of living in this sort of submission, Arturo could live with a little disapproval.

Green was chewing thoughtfully, the expression on his face wistful. This was one of Cory's favorite dishes too—of course, she preferred hers with chicken. Arturo and Grace met eyes, and Grace nodded. If Arturo said it again he'd sound like a nagging wife, but if Grace said it she'd sound like a concerned friend—it wasn't fair, but there it was.

"Are you done?" Grace asked abruptly, sinking down next to him with loose-limbed ease, and Green looked at his plate and shrugged.

"I usually go for seconds of this…"

Grace snorted and bumped Green's shoulder with her own. "It doesn't matter—I'll leave it out for you. Look, leader, I'm telling you this as someone who loves you. Go. Outside. You're moping and it's pissing me off. Even worse, it's depressing me. Get the hell out of the house—let her into your head and enjoy the freaking ride. Anything but just missing her—you keep doing this and the garden will turn brown and the foothills look like shit as it is. Get the fuck out of here. I'm begging you. We'll be fine without you, please?"

Green was laughing before she was done, the sound of his chuckling echoing through the empty living room like chimes. Not only was Cory gone, but her entourage had emptied the front room of the people who usually stayed for her company—yet another thing that made the house lonely. He swallowed deliberately, wiped his mouth, stood, leaned over to kiss Grace on the cheek.

"It's good that you chose Arturo, sweet, because I can't think of another man on the planet who is good enough for you. I'm going, I'm going—I won't be long, it's still hot out, but I'll leave the hill without my moping, will that suffice?"

Grace's smile was gentle and maternal. "Since we don't have the option of complete and total happiness, that will have to do."

"Enjoy yourself, brother!" Arturo called as Green disappeared down the hall to change, and he chuckled as Green's hand came up in a laughing salute. Arturo smiled happily as he went back to his pasta.

"Well done, beloved," he said with his mouth full.

Grace shrugged. "I have a finite skill set—it's good when it comes in handy."

And Arturo laughed so hard he almost spit pasta out his nose. "Woman," he choked when he'd recovered, "what exactly is it you think you can't do? 'Finite skill set' my painted ass!"

Grace rolled her eyes. "Can I? Please?"

Arturo grinned at her. "You, woman, can do anything you please with me—I await your command."

Grace blushed, but her wicked brown eyes met his. "Okay, for starters, you can get naked."

Oh yes—there was not much this woman couldn't do.

Arturo was always fascinated by her skin. It was vampire pale, with freckles all over—but mostly on her shoulders, where she had burned as a human and the skin had never repaired. He especially loved her skin when it was exposed and slicking up against his, when he could touch as much of it as possible, when he could make it pucker and slicken and tremble.

Their first time was always quick, and then there was a breath, and a slow, easy time, when he swore he saw her fingers shaking with tenderness and want.

He was reasonably certain that moment would never get old.

They were taking their breath after their first round of lovemaking, laughing and playful, when the lights in the house flickered and turned a brilliant blue, and a keening wail that sounded like the very molecules of air shrieking in pain pierced their eardrums.

"What in the blue fuck?" While Arturo was still scrambling up in bed, Grace had fast-forwarded into her T-shirt and a pair of jeans.

"It's Cory's perimeter system," she gasped. "Someone's out there... shit!"

Because the lights had returned to normal and the noise stopped.

"It warned them off?" Arturo said hopefully, still following his beloved out of bed and into some clothes. He was unprepared for Grace to still be on full panic.

"Don't you get it!" she yelled, pounding down the hall as though she knew he'd follow. "Green's not *on* the fucking hill!"

Oh shit. Oh shit oh shit oh shit oh shit... *Green.*

"Call the vampires!" Arturo called, fishing his cell phone out of his pants and wondering at the odds Green would get the call before whatever it was got Green. "Get them out there, get the weres on perimeter..."

Arturo thought about whom he would call from his own people, and realized with a faint shock that he was barely close with any of the sidhe or fey. When had that happened? When had his entire being become about those who had been or were still mortal? With the exception of Bracken and his...

"Crocken!" he roared. "Blissa! Get the fey! Get the sidhe! Goddammit! Everybody out on the perimeter fucking now fucking now fucking *YESTERDAY* do you hear me?"

He was pounding down the stairs in his bare feet, glad he still had keys in his pocket for his blue Cadillac and wondering whom to get to ride with him. He saw black shadows lifting from the hill like hurtling planets from a nova sun, and gave thanks for the vampires, and then saw bright bodies doing the same from every window and every landing and even the crown of the hill. His own people, off to find their leader. Thank the Goddess.

He was scrambling to the car when a were-puma passed him, and then a young vampire who was not particularly adept at flying, and then one of Teague's young werewolves—not a fighter, but still a finder, and as he unlocked the car they all streamed in and changed, some of them struggling back into the clothes they'd been wearing when the alarm had first gone off.

He had barely turned the ignition when his cell phone rang.

It was Nicky, distraught and panicked with Cory in the background, her voice fractured and raw.

They knew where he was.

CORY

Queen's Defense

After our little meet-and-greet with Rafael, I slept past the cool part of the morning and woke sweating in sympathy to the heat outside. The sun was roaring in through the outside skylight, rough-textured with ferocity, and framing a laser-like square around my thighs. Bracken was next to me, pale and limp, his breathing shallow, his body sodden with the same sympathy sweat. Nicky was moving around in the shower—avoiding his parents, if the row they'd been having as we'd neared the cabins was any indication.

After the still moment of establishing where I was and who I was with, I was suddenly missing Green with so much force it stopped my breath.

Ah gods... I closed my eyes and I could smell him, taste him, feel that lovely yellow curtain of hair, protecting me from the world, from the weight of our people, all of them looking to me for something I felt so inadequate to give.

Kyle had been sitting—just sitting—under the soda-light above the cabins, looking into the night sky.

I'd had his blood—I knew he was looking, somewhere, for some proof his beloved, my friend, was out there in the universe.

I stumbled. Bracken caught me, and as we walked by I reached out and grasped the vampire's shoulder and squeezed. He captured my hand and squeezed back.

"I like it out here," he murmured, staring at the stars. "It's so quiet. I could live here."

Oh Goddess. I'd known—I'd known since we'd taken him in. Our kiss had too many bad memories for him. He loved me, he loved us, but he needed some place where the vastness of the sky could soak up some of his pain.

"*I'll try to make it safe for you to stay.*"

Sounded like a simple promise, right?

I felt so foolish and lost. My little entourage, my kingdom of lucky thirteen—I couldn't barely keep them even.

How did Green do it?

Practice, and you.

His voice in my head was so welcome I felt tears slide weakly down my eyes and into my hair. *Simple formula, beloved.* I stretched out the word in my mind, as though spending more time thinking it would put him there within touch.

This was always hard. I had gotten better at dealing with it in the last year and a half, but not being able to touch Green, trace my thumb along that clean, narrow jaw, and breathe in his peace and his passion was never going to be easy.

It's not a simple formula? I could almost hear the wryness in his tone. I closed my eyes and he drifted in front of me, pushed up on his elbow, his green-pale skin translucent in the sunshine, his yellow hair swishing down over us like a satin-stranded curtain.

It's hard to have a + b + c = x when 'a' is in another part of the state, I whined.

Try being 'a', he complained forlornly, and I found a small smile in my head. Green could do that for me. When we'd talked on the phone both before and after Bracken and I had returned to the cabin, so much of it had been business. Here, lying in bed and talking like this, it was all silly stuff—our hearts, speaking to each other.

I lay there and glowed with Green for a few moments, but eventually he had to go, and he left me in a hot, sweaty funk with Bracken, who was not much better. Finally I swore and rolled out of bed and kicked Bracken out too.

"C'mon, dammit—let's go get in your precious water before you melt into goo!"

"The water scares you," he said, but there was no heat behind it—no real emotion, really, and given how tempestuous Bracken usually is, I was spurred into action.

"Move it, damn you!" I snapped, truly alarmed. "Up. Get. Up. Get. The. Fuck. Up. C'mon—into your trunks, we're going swimming!"

I thought the walk to the water in the hundred plus degree heat was going to be the death of both of us, but I bitched at him until he snapped back at me and still we held hands as we walked into the water. I could feel the rush through his body as soon as it hit his mid-thighs, which was about my waist-line, and two more steps and we hit the drop-off.

I was ready for it this time, so treading water was no big deal—especially when I was looking at Bracken for signs of improvement.

He'd perked up like a dying plant with in a rainstorm, and I blew out a sigh of relief.

He stared at me with sober eyes. "You were really worried," he said softly.

"I don't get to worry about you?" I asked, although he knew I did. Like I'd told Teague, we were broken that way.

But the words haunted me throughout the day. Worried—would we ever stop worrying about each other? It didn't seem so, and by the time the sun disappeared behind the volcanic hills in a harsh smudge of tarnished peach and purple, I thought that maybe this was a good thing.

I didn't realize how much we needed each other as a group until Bracken and I looked up from to the purple sky of the day's closing. We had all spent the day scattered—swimming, playing cards, napping, eating, running through the woods wearing fur, flying—whatever it was we did best. But the sunset ended, and here we were, my whole little kingdom away from home, gathered together reverently watching as the first of the stars glimmered on the black water.

Nicky was on my other side, leaning on me after a day spent fighting with his parents, and I stroked his arm softly. This, I thought incoherently. This was why Green and I worked so hard. This breath of peace from people who looked to us for guidance.

We stayed together after that—the vampires fed, of course, and then we all played cards together under the lanterns. Nicky's parents asked to join us, and we let them, although they kept a careful distance from me, and that was fine. The young man, Sam, did the same, and I asked him where his mom was. He smiled that charming teenager smile and said she was sleeping, and I made a mental note to ask Tanya to make sure she wasn't dead. It wasn't that I didn't trust the kid... I just didn't trust his smile. But we let him play, and the giant round of Uno/Trivial Pursuit that Renny and Max had made up the night before continued with a whole lot of laughter.

Annette tried to join, and we all pretended she didn't exist, even Sam-the-teenager, although he cast her dark, speculative looks that had too much adult in them for my comfort.

We played and ate, and for a moment Rafael's vampires were forgotten, the domestic quarrels were tabled, and it felt like a real vacation—something I had not actually had since I was young enough to be Sam, awkward and uncertain, and enjoying the profanity and ribald laughter of the adults who let me hang around.

I stood up and moved restively away, letting Bracken take my place at the table, and wandered outside the illuminated circle that marked the game area. Turning towards the lake, I leaned against a convenient tree and watched the glimmer of the stars off the pewter/obsidian water, and thought of Green.

In a roll of sun-warmed wildflowers and clean earth, I was there, inside his head and he was welcoming me in. I could feel the wind in my face and hear the roar of Adrian's motorcycle—not Green's monster cycle, I thought, Adrian's, which meant he was feeling nostalgic. The foothills smelled different than Redding and Lake Shasta—not as many cows, more people, maybe, hidden in the crevices of the hilltops, more ozone from the city, seeping into the stratosphere. There was manzanita around Lake Shasta—it gave a creosote air, sharp and acrid and tangy, that Green's senses didn't have, and he had more rose bushes, blooming on hidden yards behind mysterious driveways.

Either way, it was different—and I settled contentedly into his mind and enjoyed the stately, passionate kindness that was my Green. I had never questioned the ability that gave us access to each other's minds—it had happened so naturally, so wonderfully, as easy as thinking about your boyfriend and knowing the phone about to ring is him on the other end. Tonight it was a comfort, and I looked at the world with my beloved's kind eyes as he roared through the humid, warm dark with me on his shoulder.

And maybe what happened next happened because I was relaxed and happy in his mind. Maybe it happened because he missed me, and his concentration was not what it should have been. Maybe the heat had sapped him more than either of us knew.

And maybe we were just not prepared for the utter snake-shit, lizard-barf, amoeba-puke lowness of our enemy, and that was both our faults, because the enemy took us unaware.

A whirling pressure smacked into his/our body, torquing Green's shoulder and shoving him to the ground. In a black-rubber squeal of tire and concrete, the bike slid sideways from underneath him and he went sliding... ah, *Goddess* sliding, his leathers disintegrating and then his skin, scoured away by the ragged blacktop, and then the thing attacked again.

We got a clear picture of her, fangs extended, sneer in place, as she scooped a struggling Green up in her arms. I don't know how high she would have carried him, or how far she would have dropped him, because there are some things even Green wouldn't have survived, but he fought—oh, Goddess my gentle lover fought, kicking out at her, making her scream, and finally, a bit of his bare skin came in contact with her cheek and I could feel the resistance of flesh as he pulled our mark of power to the surface. It cut through her skin like wire, and she screamed and her grip on his tall, struggling body loosened. He threw his palm forward into her nose, cracking it, slamming it back into her brain—a death blow to a mortal, and as it was, it sent her spinning into the ether and Green plunging onto the steeply descending hillside to the canyon below.

It was a long way down. Oh, Goddess, it was a long way down, and it wasn't until he took a breath and prepared to take the fall on his legs that it occurred to me that of all the skills my beloved had, flying was not one of them.

Love you. And then he hit the ground with a crunch of bones, and rolled down the hill at a terrifying speed, rocks and earth and sky spiraling past our consciousness as we tried to control the fall.

The tree came as a complete surprise, and my head exploded into pain as everything went black.

Abruptly I was in my own head, surrounded by my people, screaming his name until my throat bled and the hills echoed with my sobs.

Bracken grabbed my shoulders and shook me deliberately, twice, until I took a deep ragged breath and then another. I gazed sightlessly into his frantic pond-shadow eyes and said, very clearly, "We need to call Arturo."

I don't remember much after the phone call, where I gibbered landmarks to Nicky while he translated over the phone. I remember grabbing car keys and hitting the car door with the force of my hurtle, and then having Bracken pick me up by the waist and haul me out of the driver's seat so Max could drive.

"Get out of my fucking way…" I screamed, and he used his considerable mass to pin me to the car and yell back at me.

"You're too busy panicking, and I'm too busy keeping you from bolting out the window, dammit—let him drive!" He was roaring at me, his face twisted with anxiety and the same panic I felt… Green. Oh Goddess, neither of us could survive…

"I am NOT panicking!" I retorted with something less than a sob, and to prove it I turned to Nicky, who was getting ready to get in the car with us, and actually slowed down to think.

"Nicky, Nicky honey… no." I took his both his hands in mine—we were both shaking, and the shaking stilled, and my breathing calmed down a notch. Okay. This was not panicking. I could do this. "Nicky, you have to stay here."

"Because of my parents? Fuck that!" he snarled, and someday I might spare a moment of regret for the fact that they were outside in the crowd of us to hear that, but not now. The betrayal on his face ripped me open and I shook my head against it.

"Think Nicky. It's just like when he was in Texas. One of us needs to go to him and the other needs to keep things running. I need you to keep things running. The bad guy is still out there. Green... Green's an elf. He can heal about anything—and I'll make it happen faster, but he can do it. We..." My voice warbled, cracked, shattered...Oh Goddess. Oh Goddess. The alternative to what I was saying was unthinkable.

My words next were as clear as individual stones, plopped into a still pool. "Nicky, if this doesn't turn out well, I'm coming back here to murder the fucking world, and I'll need you for that too, do you hear?"

Nicky took a deep breath, and let it out, shuddering. The betrayal eased on his face—he understood. He'd always been reluctant to acknowledge that he had a place in the leadership ranking—that people would look to him if me or Green or Brack or Arturo weren't there—but it was sinking in abruptly and painfully now.

"You and Teague are in charge," I said rationally, so hard, so hard to do when my insides were being dragged naked over gravel and broken glass. "Keep people to the cabins, keep them safe, nobody outside without a vampire nearby, not even Lambent to swim, dammit. We need one shifter changed at all times to smell intruders... and... and..."

And that was it. That was the limit of my ability to be rational—my breaths were coming faster and faster and my face felt cold and white and black spots were dancing in front of my eyes that had nothing to do with the suddenly feral night. Nicky's hands were warm on my face, and his lips on mine helped to soothe some of my panic.

"Call us," he said roughly, "the minute you hear anything. I will always love you."

"I love you too," I whimpered, and then Bracken, who knew me, who knew my limits, pushed me into the car before I could lose what was left of my composure. I had led our people enough to keep them from panicking— that was enough for now. Renny came hauling ass out of our cabin with an armload of shit, and threw herself in the passenger's seat, and then we were on our way.

We were on the causeway, the lake heaving on either side of us like a prehistoric monster, when a there was a sudden physical pain in my head, splitting enough to make me scream. While I was gasping in shock, holding my hand over my eye and trying not to whine in reaction, my cell phone buzzed, and I was so shocky that Bracken had to fish it out of my pocket and answer it.

It was Arturo. Green had been found. The minute I heard the news, the pain receded—Green's pain, to tell me my world wouldn't end, my heart would still beat in my chest, the sun wouldn't implode into a blood-ravaged quantum singularity, and that every vampire in Redding might not have to die with their spines ripped through their throats and my sunshine ripping the viscera from every orifice in their bodies.

As my temple stopped throbbing, I became aware of my own whimpers, and then of Bracken's arms, strong and secure, keeping me anchored to the world. If anyone could make me feel safe right now, it was the rough, sound half to my heart.

I fell apart then, in the back of the SUV, as I have not allowed myself to come apart in quite some time. Green was fine. My Green was fine. Bracken rocked me and crooned, his voice lovely and passionate—a thing that seemed to surprise people about him, but not me. Never me. I may have bawled for the entire trip back home, but after my ripping sobs had been reduced to keening wails, I felt Bracken's whisper soft touch on my mind, begging me to let him put me under.

I did, trusting him with all of my soul, and I didn't wake up until I felt the tingle of my own magic on the perimeter of home—Bracken was still singing softly to me, and my head didn't hurt a little teeny bit, not even at all.

I skidded out of the car while it was still moving, fell to my knees and heard Max swear as he slammed on the brakes. Bracken was right behind me, hauling me up by the elbow, and we ran across the yard.

Green was there, naked and covered in a cotton throw, stretched out where his body could touch the earth of his hill to heal. He was in a puddle of light streaming from the front window, and surrounded by a circle of sidhe. His brethren had parted, though, to let the vampires and weres in who wanted to touch him, to give to him to aid in his healing. Some brought a cloth to clean his blood, some brought pillows or blankets or talismans—there was a teddy bear from Leah the were-puma and a Saint Christopher's medal from Ellis, one of the young vampires, and a hundred of other small, precious things, all within easy touch.

This is our love, Green, this is everything you've given us, take it, heal, it's yours.

Someone—probably Grace—had brought out the first sweater I'd made him, the one that had been unraveled to save my life and knitted up again. His head rested on it, the fractures in his skull obvious by the swelling and the discoloration, and he was stroking his cheek against my sweater like a child.

I don't even remember running to his side.

I just knelt for a moment, stroking his chest, and at the first contact of our skin his eyes flew open and his breath grew deeper. I felt the draw from my body, like a vampire taking blood except more vital than that, and I opened my heart and my mind and I gave.

His head wounds eased, the lumps going down, the skin returning to its usual pale green, and his eyes sharpened in their clarity. I realized his pupils had been small, in spite of the darkness, and thought with a shudder how close his body had probably been to irreparably damaged. The thought almost stopped my breath—almost stopped the flood of my power and life force, and his hand came out to grasp my own.

"I'm fine, beloved," he murmured. "I'll live."

I bent over him and rubbed his cheek with mine. "That's a promise, dammit. I'll hold you to it."

He laughed a little, and his arms—snapping back into place in a crunch of healing bones even as we spoke—wrapped around me and pulled me to him until I sprawled over him, feeling his ribs knitting beneath my breasts.

"Oh Goddess," I groaned, allowing relief to shudder through me, allowing the last barrier between Green and all the healing power of my heart to dissolve. "Beloved, you can't scare me like that. You can't. That wasn't fair. That wasn't..."

I couldn't speak anymore. I could just lay there, in his arms, and joyfully let him bleed out all of my strength and all of my power, because without my healing, sunshine, daylight lover, I would have no strength, I would have no power, and the heart I used to sustain Bracken, to hold on to Nicky, to lead our people, would be nothing but blackened dust.

When he finally spoke, the myriad people who surrounded us had drifted away. He was going to be all right, they could see it, they could feel it, and although there were probably dozens of eyes watching us from the wrap-around window, they loved him enough to give us our privacy.

So only Bracken remained, sitting quietly cross-legged near the willow tree that marked the tiny Goddess Grove—it had been the hill's place of worship before Green and Adrian and I had turned sex into song. And Bracken, being Bracken, let out a hearty laugh at Green's next words.

"Not so much fun when it's someone else doing the dying, now is it!"

"You bastard," I muttered, since I was safe in his arms and he was well. "You're strong enough to play this part... I'm not."

"Shh shh shh..." because my voice had cracked and he was now comforting me instead of the other way around. Bracken came over and slid down next to him and put his hand on my back, soothing me too, and I felt weak with relief and strong with it at the same time.

There was nothing else to say for a while after that. We simply lay there, under the stars, under a wide, smiling, waning moon, and listened to Green's steady breathing.

My human needs started to weigh on me. It was almost as hot here, without Green's power to keep the hill cool, as it was in Redding, and we were starting to sweat enough to stick to each other. I might have clenched my bladder one too many times, because Green laughed and shifted and I rolled off of him and into Bracken's body. As Green rolled away and stood up, naked under the starlight, he was no longer drawing from my strength, and I realized how woozy I was. Bracken helped me stand up, and I wiggled under Green's arm and Bracken took his other side. We hadn't taken more than three steps when Arturo was there, big, sturdy Arturo who hadn't been feeding Green his strength because his bond with Green didn't work that way, and he swept my beloved into his arms and carried him up the steps to the house the way most of the men always carried me.

For once, I wished I was the one being carried—it was so much easier to be strong and brave when it was only your own health and well-being at stake. Beside me, Bracken wavered for a moment, and I realized that Bracken had been shoring me up as I'd been feeding Green—Green's closeness to death assailed me all over again and I wrapped my arm harder around Bracken's waist and fought the urge to break down like I had in the back of the car. Then I listened to Green whining about being well enough to walk on his own and some of my weakness bled away too.

It was good to know he was almost as shitty a patient as I was.

"Honestly, Arturo," he grumbled, "you'd think I was a child…"

"You're not a child," Arturo growled. "You're recovering. Let us take care of you."

Green was actually taller than Arturo—if it hadn't been for the preternatural strength ratios, it would have been ludicrous for the smaller sidhe to even try what he was doing, but the set of his shoulders and the grim purpose of his stride told us that for once, Arturo was going to get his way.

"I was not as close to death's door as everyone seems to think," Green said mildly, and Arturo's reply was thick with emotion.

"Any vicinity is too close, leader. You…you are not allowed in the same room with that door, ever again, are we understood?" Arturo—steady, dependable Arturo—stilled the cracking in his own voice, and I forced myself to put one foot in front of the other. Oh Goddess—he was so much to so many of us. Arturo wouldn't have made it, I thought in pained wonder, if Green had died.

I had Arturo put him in the shower, and after a quick phone call to Nicky, because we couldn't just leave him hanging, Bracken and I undressed and joined Green. We cleansed the blood from his healed skin, and the blood-covered gravel that stuck to his back and his hip even as it had been pushed out of his flesh. My hands were shaking, and my breath was harsh, but I made myself be strong for him—all the times he had been strong for me, and now it was my turn to pony up and I'd be fucked three times sideways if I let him down.

Eventually we all slid into bed, Bracken on one side and me on the other, feeding Green strength with our bare flesh and the power of our love. I sang softly, without being asked, because I knew Green loved my voice, and I would do anything, anything, to give something pleasant to this horrible, terrifying night, and as Bracken sang a lovely counterpoint, we all drifted to sleep.

When I woke up, Green was sleeping peacefully, looking as radiant and whole as he had in my vision the morning before. Bracken was gone somewhere, and I was *starving.*

I was also damned if I'd leave Green alone.

It sat up in bed and dragged the sheet over my breasts, because I was alone and there was nobody to chide me for being human and young and a little bit shy, and pushed my hair back, trying to decide what to do next.

"I won't melt, thaw, and resolve myself into a dew if you go use the bathroom and get a T-shirt, beloved." Green's voice was sleepy and satisfied, and I frowned at him to see one clear, emerald eye was regarding me with some amusement.

"You're quoting Shakespeare, you must be better," I snarked back, so relieved I almost took him up on the going to the bathroom part a little early. I made it to the potty, though, and came out of the bathroom with clean teeth, an empty bladder, and wearing one of his oversized T-shirts. .

Bracken opened the door as I was crawling back into bed—he had a ginormous tray of food, piled with everything from spiced oatmeal to toast to really big cookies. There was even a banana cream pie—Green's favorite.

I blinked. "Seven guesses to how Grace worked out *her* anxiety before dawn."

Green smiled a little and sat up, letting Bracken place the tray around his legs. "That's okay, luv, I only need one." He patted the bed next to him and I had a sudden vision of him as he had looked the night before. Black nausea swept me and I sat down a little too quickly.

"I'll keep you company," I murmured, but all my hunger had fled.

"You'll eat," Bracken said shortly, his tone so autocratic that I raised my eyebrows at him. He glared right back and continued to dish food—oatmeal, which he was mixing with cinnamon, sugar, and walnuts.

"We all need to eat," he continued, shoving the bowl at me. "You know that—power requires energy—you need to keep yours up."

Old argument— he always won. I rolled my eyes, took a bite of my oatmeal, and felt much better. We ate in silence for a moment, and Arturo knocked on the door and peeked his head in.

"We all good in here? Nobody throwing up or dying?" He tried to keep his voice light, but it was clear that last night had shaken solid Arturo's foundations.

"We're good, brother," Green murmured. "Come in and have something to eat."

Arturo's best smile split his face, showing off his silver capped teeth and notching up the sun just a little. I suddenly wondered how many breakfasts he and Green had eaten together—I'd seen them, sometimes, when I was home in the mornings, and it had seemed a comfortable ritual. Funny, how much small things mean to us, especially when something threatens to take them away.

So Arturo joined us, and we ate in what felt like companionable silence until the strain of NOT talking shop wore on Green's last nerves.

"Okay—spit it out. What are you all thinking?" He had just swallowed what he thought was his last bit of toast until I buttered another piece and spread it thick with blackberry jam for him. He looked at the toast mildly and I shrugged.

"Don't look at me like that—I learned how to nursemaid from Bracken."

Bracken managed a smug glare and I stuck my tongue out at him.

"That's not what you were thinking," Green reproved, and I would have rolled my eyes, but he'd asked twice so I was sort of obliged to answer.

"Okay. Fine. I was thinking that I know what she looks like, I know where she lives, and that tonight, I probably need to go rip out her heart and set it on fire." It sounded horrible—bloodthirsty, political, bitchy, and not in keeping with healing Green at all. But I'd forgotten what so many people tend to forget about Green.

He was not above revenge, and anything that threatened him threatened me.

He grinned with a touch of evil in it and chucked me under the chin. "Now what makes you think that's not suitable meal conversation?" he asked drolly, and Bracken interrupted what might have been a sweet little moment between us.

"And what makes you think you can yank her heart out of her chest?" he asked with a growl, and I stopped. He was right—I could move shit and push myself off the ground and do force-fields and lasers and shit, but ripping hearts out of bodies was right out of my skill set. Bracken replied to my grimace of disappointment with a smile of carnivorous joy. "I'll rip her heart out, beloved. You can set it on fire."

I perked up immediately. "Oh baby, you do give me the best shit to do!"

Arturo listened to the by-play and nodded in satisfaction. "You two should have breakfast with us more often—this beats going over accounts any day."

We could have chatted like that for hours—I know I could have, I was just so happy to be home, to be in Green's bed, to know he was okay. But he yawned, once, twice, and before I could even wipe his mouth, Arturo and Bracken had cleaned up breakfast and left the room. (Bracken took time to put on some jeans, not that anybody but me was relieved.)

Once the door closed behind them, Green rolled to his side and propped his head up in his hand, grinning at me slyly and tracing the outline of my breast through my T-shirt.

"I thought they'd never leave," he murmured, flicking my nipple through the fabric until I yelped and moaned.

"I thought you were supposed to be recovering," I told him breathlessly. I was rolling over on my back as I said it, the better to give him access to both breasts.

He lowered his head, suckled my nipple through the fabric, and then raised up to kiss me, deeply, thoroughly, and with so much passion I might not ever doubt that he was here, with me, and not gone, helplessly, hopelessly, vanished from my life forever.

He pulled back, that lovely, wicked grin spreading warmth and anticipation through me. "I'm a sexual creature, luv. This *is* recovery…"

I chuckled lowly, and then I gasped, and then I moaned, and then I screamed… and then we slept.

We spent the day like that—sleeping, making love, eating, always touching each other, by turns tender, voracious, and teasing.

I snuck away for a few moments, to check on Bracken (who was sleeping in our room, in our bed, as though not having to worry about his feet sticking over the edge made him *very* happy) and to grab a snack.

Arturo caught me standing in front of the refrigerator in my T-shirt with my mouth full of chocolate cream pie.

"Cory?" he said hesitantly, and I turned, sheepishly, holding the tin and a fork, and no dignity whatsoever.

"Wha' canh ah…" chew, swallow, "do for you, Arturo?"

He smiled then, looking suddenly weary, and gestured to the table. "Sit down and finish, for one."

I grinned at him and he reached out and thumbed some whipped-cream off my nose, and we both laughed. Uncle Arturo—I missed him too. I made myself comfortable and dug into the pie in earnest.

"It's about that Nolan fucker, isn't it?" I asked between bites, and he nodded.

"Hallow says he's got the story ready to publish—he's apparently fanatical about keeping as much to himself as possible until he's good to go, which works in our favor. He'll gather everything, write it all up, add the pictures he wants, and put it in his master file with all of the extra notes—but he'll have made back-ups. Computer files, e-mails to himself, to his editor—we'll need to get a hold of his computer and magnetize the drive and then get into his e-mail…"

"We've got people who can hack," I said, thinking about Jack and La Mark. "As long as we catch him before his editor sends it in."

Arturo nodded. "Five days. His deadline's in five days."

I thought carefully. "Well, we're going to have to give Rafael two more nights—so that's three days. I'll be back in four, and we can run in, shake him by the scruff of the neck, and run out."

Arturo nodded. "You know, Little Goddess—you don't have to do all of these things yourself. You put a team together and I'll take care of it." Arturo grinned savagely. "In fact, I'd sort of enjoy it."

I grinned at him. "Me too," I told him mildly. "But I get you. You're right. I don't need my finger in every…" I laughed, and took a final swipe at the tin with my finger to get every last bit of decadent chocolate-cream goodness, "pie."

Arturo laughed, went to the refrigerator and pulled out another one. "Yes, Corinne Carol-Anne, but this one has caramel in it—are you sure you don't want a bite?"

Well hell yeah! We shared some more pie and some more planning before the ache in my chest told me I'd been away from Green too long and I pattered back down the hall.

Bracken slid into bed towards the late afternoon, more to hold me, to reestablish our normalcy, than anything else--and also to charge me up, feed me power, for what we were going to have to do when we got back to Redding.

The fact that he got to pull me back together in the car when we left was probably an added bonus. How could I leave Green? The image of how we'd found him the night before drifted constantly behind my eyes, until he had to hold my face between his long hands and breathe "Peace, beloved."

I stopped my silent sniveling, and we shared one last sweet goodbye kiss, before he belted me in and shut the door. With a rev of the engine and a sedate crunch of gravel, the SUV left home in a melancholy, aching silence.

Eventually, though, Max started the *Bleed it Out* playlist, Renny handed me my knitting (which she'd brought from the cabin as we'd left) and Bracken rolled down the windows, letting the humid summer cleanse the melancholy and fill us with electricity. We had serious, bloody work to do tonight—I could miss Green when I was sure I'd kept him safe.

We were an hour and a half out of Redding when the sun went down and I called Nicky.

"What's news?" he asked, and I gave him the plan—it was pretty simple, all things considered. There were no prisoners, there was no forgiveness. No one hurt Green and lived.

"Right," Nicky said decisively, "what time should we be there?"

My heart stuttered in my chest. "Nicky…" I stammered. "Nicky…uhm… you know what we're doing tonight? I'm thinking Marcus and Phillip…"

"Not Kyle?"

"No." Kyle wanted to live here—I didn't want him a part of anything that would make that difficult. "But maybe Teague and Mario…"

"Not Lambent?"

"We need some fighters back at the ranch, Nicky," I said, sure of this at least. "I don't want our people unprotected." I grimaced at Max and Renny. "If I had my way, I'd send Renny back to you before we got there, but I don't see how that'll happen…"

"Wait a minute," Nicky interrupted, outrage in his voice. "What do you mean 'back to me'? Why in the name of pissed off fucking birds would I not be there?"

I swallowed, and looked sideways at Bracken. He was leaning so that the wind from the window hit his face, his mouth open so he could taste the dry dust and the moisture and the smell of cows and mulch and growing things in what was more desert flatness than anything else.

"We're going to be doing terrible things tonight, Nicky," I said softly. "Do you really want to face your parents with blood on your hands?"

There was a silence and I couldn't tell what kind. Was he accepting? Was he angry? Did he understand, at least, why I was trying to spare him?

"I'll be there, *ou'e'ane*," he said at last, quietly. "I love you and our *ou'e'hm*."

I swallowed. Wasn't it weird how a word you didn't have in your own language came to mean shit you would never think of?

"We love you too, *ou'e'alle*. Meet you at the lion's den—wait for us, Brack and I will go in first."

I rang off and put the phone in my pocket and then leaned back against Bracken and picked up my knitting to ease the nervousness that wanted to vibrate me across the seat.

"He's coming, isn't he?" Bracken asked against my ear.

"I wish he wouldn't." I gazed sightlessly at my sock, and my fingers kept doing their happy little dance to make it grow.

"I know you do—but he's a good fighter—and it looks good if he's there."

I scowled at my stone-and-shadow beloved, which he probably didn't deserve but, well, he was there. "I don't give a shit how it looks—I didn't want him to have to tell his parents he was going out to murder someone tonight!"

Bracken looked at me mildly. "I don't see why he'd have to do that, Corinne Carol-Anne—I thought that was our job."

I blinked at him. He was right of course. I thought of Green, laying in a pool of light, naked on his own earth, his skull misshapen, his limbs shattered, blood coating his skin, and my rage threatened to boil up and consume me.

"How silly of me," I rasped through crimson vision. "You're right—Nicky will get to watch."

Max cranked up the music and I knit furiously on.

There were clouds over the plains as we drove—they'd turned a sullen pink at sunset, and as we approached the sprawling huddle of Redding, they seemed to spread out like a Bela Lugosi cloak to muffle the stars. The cloud cover gave a weight and heft to the heat as we got out of the car, but that didn't stop me from tucking the two guns Max gave me into the back of my cut-off jeans, and throwing a denim jacket on to cover them up. I patted down my ass and applied that special salt-water/aloe/sidhe-magic gel stuff that I kept in a Purell bottle in my purse. A cold iron burn on an elf was no joke, and I was damned if Bracken was ever going to get so much as a singe again because he wanted to hold my hand or help me with my gun.

Marcus, Phillip, Teague and Nicky got out of the SUV, and Nicky managed not to rush too badly to hug me breathless.

"Here," I murmured, lifting up my chin, because he's a bird in his other life and he could stick his nose into the hollow of my neck and breathe in Green—his health, his warmth, his want—all in that last kiss and embrace before we left.

Nicky's nose bumped against my shoulder, and he groaned and shook in my arms. "He's okay," he whispered.

"He's fine," I whispered back. Nicky didn't need to know how badly Green had been hurt, how long it would have taken him to heal if I hadn't been there. I couldn't do much for Nicky, but some things I could spare him.

"How are you?" Nicky asked, stepping back and taking stock.

"I'm ready to kill someone," I calmly and there was a low bass rumble from the men surrounding me. I'd just made their day.

"Renny?" I asked, just to make sure—she was, after all, a cat, and they weren't known for their 'see-spot' obedience.

"I got it," she said with a little bit of bitterness. "I'm good in a fight, you know!"

"You're brave in a fight, sweet," I murmured, stroking her hair back from her face. "But you're small, and nothing we're trying to kill is mortal. Please, Renny-cat? I don't want to worry about you, not tonight."

Renny's lips curled back to reveal her teeth, still a little pointed from so much time in her cat form. I opened my mouth to get all stern, and Max gently elbowed me out of the way. Renny knew what that meant—she would obey Max, her mate, as she would not obey me, and her disdainful sniff told us all plainly that this time, at least, she would mind.

"Nevermind, I got it. Assholes. Stay in the fucking car. I'm good" She rolled her eyes and looked away in purely feline dismissal.

"You in car, yes," Max said, his narrow, stoic face tough with worry. "Fucking is optional, and hopefully later."

She hissed at him. "Fucking is a dream of the past," she growled, and Max narrowed his eyes and kissed her, hard. When he backed away, the cut on his lip was bleeding even as it closed, but we had all seen Renny respond after she bit him, and it was hard to look sullen when your face was all dreamy and shmushed.

"We'll be back in a minute," Max said with a smile on his bleeding mouth, "in fact, you may want to keep the motor running."

"Wait a minute, Max," Bracken called, as everybody started forward, "I didn't get mine yet."

His handsome, scowling, stone-and-shadow face neared mine, the murky green-brown of his eyes intense. I took a moment, and the humid night faded, and our grim task faded, and I breathed in and smelled a hard boulder in the sun, with the soft darkness of earth and growing things beneath. It was an honest, strong and brave smell, the kind of smell that anchored your feet into the earth and brought you peace.

"I'm not going to bite you," I said mildly, willing to fall into his eyes and draw the strength to fly.

"Right now," he added, his hard lips curving up wickedly.

I nodded, caught the soft chuff of his breath on my face and closed my eyes as his lips descended. The kiss was quick, hard, and lingered just long enough for him to capture my lips gently with his teeth as he pulled away.

"For Green?" I asked, treasuring Bracken's shoulders under my reaching hands.

"For all of us."

We turned then, separate but together, and stalked to the front of our group and headed for the entrance.

The bouncers knew us, and, even more, seemed to know we meant business. They didn't try to stop us—instead, they held the door. We stepped inside the red-lit club, still pounding with music, and I scanned the crowd with hard, angry eyes.

She wasn't hard to spot. In other circumstances, she could have been me.

She was short and squat, just as I had before I came into my power and started burning calories like a fusion reactor. Her hair was dirty blonde at the roots, and bright blonde at the ends, and she probably went through a pound of Depp in a day, and the resemblance didn't stop there. She'd had piercings before she died and she'd kept them—skulls, crosses, that whacko symbol from Blue Oyster Cult—and a lip ring and an eyebrow ring and a nose ring—and no chin and acne scars and a look in her eyes like the world fucking owed her and she was going to rip out exact change through the balls.

She also had a bleeding lime tree ripping its way through the flesh of her cheek. It was growing, spreading like a rash, every line shredding skin and flesh, like a decorative wire pressing its way through blood-dripping clay. She touched the mark nervously as we watched, and winced, and then wiped her hand on the napkin at her table.

I bumped my shoulder against Brack's bicep and we met eyes, then I looked in her direction.

He nodded as though he didn't see any resemblance at all, then put his hand on my shoulder to stop me—I'd raised my hand and was about to announce our presence in a big way.

Our friend, Toothless Badass, was leaning near her, putting his hand on her shoulder with enough pressure to crumple her sleeveless button-up denim shirt into her shoulder. Blood from his own mark was ripping its way up his arm.

I hadn't seen another vampire—but this guy tended to backhand the newbies until they pleased him. And since he wasn't going to try to attack something he thought was defenseless...it added up. Toothless Badass obviously had his own part to play. I met Brack's eyes and he nodded. Both of them, unless they could give us a reason otherwise.

I squared my feet and clenched my diaphragm and pitched my voice loud enough to carry over the music and the chatter—loud enough to carry to the back room, and bring Rafael out to see what was doing.

"Yo, Bitch and the Baddass!" I cried, and my grin might as well have had fangs. They looked up at me immediately—they knew who they were and they knew why I was there and without more than a twitch of my hand and a charge of my will, I slammed them back against the wall, both of them, suspended about three feet above the floor, their eyes bulging with the pressure of the power-field I'd used to imprison them in front of most of the population of Redding's underworld.

The music stopped abruptly and one of the bouncers hit the lights, and when I called out next, I didn't have to shout quite so loud to be heard.

"Rafael! Rafael, you get your ass out here, because we have housecleaning to do."

Rafael was pissed off as he rounded the corner out of his office—narrowed eyes, fangs bared in a scowl, a roar of protest on his lips—and then he saw the two people slammed up against the wall. His eyes widened, and his hand flew automatically to his own cheek in sympathy for the dripping infection that was forming on the girl's dead flesh. I held my hand up, keeping them pinned, and his eyes flew to mine.

He swallowed—a very careful, human gesture in a man who had been dead for nearly fifty years—and, making eye contact with his people, inclined his head stiffly in my direction.

"And what can I do for you, Lady Cory?"

There was a mass intake of breath—he'd conceded control of these people, and now all of them knew it.

"Don't bow to her, Rafael!" the girl shrieked. "She's weak! We killed her lover, that pansy-assed faggot barely put up a fight…"

My people and I laughed harshly, a sound as ugly as twisted chrome and breaking glass, and Rafael winced.

"You think you killed him?" I asked, derision coating my throat and pulling my snarl back until I was all teeth. "You think any of you would be alive if he was dead?"

I'd unconsciously increased the pressure of the power shield around them, and Toothless Badass could barely force air out to speak. "You're all talk," he hissed. "Look at you—just a kid with a gun—probably shoot yourself in the head if you tried to kill us…" He tried a laugh but I constricted his throat and the sound stopped.

I looked at Rafael and shook my head, as though sad. "You didn't tell them, Rafael?" I asked, as though in disbelief. I knew. We both knew. But Rafael and my people were the only ones here that did.

"I… I thought it best kept private, my lady," he said with a ghastly attempt at sheepishness.

"Tell us what?" the girl gasped—she was starting to look afraid. Good. I'd been in Green's head and the fear that he'd never see me again had washed my body in cold, aching sweat and barbed wire pain. I needed to see fear dripping off her body like gore.

"Tell you all what happens when I lose a lover, sweetheart." I showed my teeth. "Marcus, do you remember the last time someone killed somebody I loved?"

"Until God comes back to kick our asses, my Lady," Marcus said softly.

"Do you remember, Phillip? Max? You were there."

"Til death and beyond, Lady Cory," they said, hard voices in tandem. To my right I saw Teague close his eyes as though this hurt him. Well, it hurt us all.

"And you, beloved?" I turned to Bracken. "What do you remember about that night?"

"You almost killed me, beloved." Bracken looked positively gleeful for this horrible fact—a thing I never understood. "You almost killed us all."

I nodded my head sagely, meeting the eyes of the two vampires pinned against the wall. They were starting to look very, very uneasy.

"I did," I told them conversationally, moving laterally, so I was looking at them squarely from the same distance back. "I almost killed a lot of our people—but I didn't. Would you like to know who I did kill?"

Their eyes were bulging against my power shield, but the girl was nodding in spite of herself. I looked at Toothless, my eyes wide and quizzical. "And you, Badass? Would you like to know who I did kill?"

He nodded reluctantly.

"Why don't you tell them, Rafael, since, you have to admit, it's a story they might have wanted to know before they tried to kill Green last night."

"Tell them?" Rafael sounded lost, looking at the proof of their treachery and their complete confusion, and knowing they were doomed.

"Tell them," I said, my fanged, bloody smile in place, "who I killed, the last time someone carried out a threat on someone I loved."

Rafael looked away from Badass and Goth-girl, and stared blindly out to the room filled with his people. "Everybody," he said clearly. "You killed everybody who wasn't you. All the vampires in Folsom. All of them. Over a hundred vampires, their shapeshifters, the people who came with Sezan... all of them. We tried to count it once... it came to nearly two-hundred of us. You killed two hundred people with your grief..." his voice trailed off and his gaze finally fastened on me, as though I was his worst nightmare come to life.

"Two hundred people," I repeated—and for the first time I wasn't ashamed of this fact. Hell—I was thrilled. "I killed two-hundred people with my grief..." I shook my head. "Well, aren't you all glad they didn't succeed in killing Green, so I didn't have to grieve again?" It was a smile like death rictus, but it was a smile. It didn't seem to bring the people in Rafael's club any comfort.

Badass and Goth-girl were looking at me now as though they both saw me for the first time—and I was finally damned scary. Goth-girl started to babble.

"I'm sorry, Lady Cory... Jimmy said it'd be easy, said it'd be protecting our family... I didn't know about you... I never would have tried to hurt him if I'd known who you were..."

My gaze grew colder. "So what you're saying is that you only try to kill those you think are weak and helpless? Well doesn't that make you a prize? Tell me, sweetheart—how weak and helpless was he?"

She swallowed. "He wasn't," she whispered. "He fought like a son-of-a-bitch. My face hasn't stopped bleeding."

"Do you know why?" I asked, my voice deceptive and mild. I looked around at the stone-cold-sober dance club, and saw a lot of alarmed, whirling eyes staring back at me blankly.

"That thing on her face is our mark. *Our mark.* You all swore blood loyalty to Rafael, and Rafael swore it to us. We hold your marker, people—you betray us, you betray the people who hold your life and death in their hands, and that mark will rip you apart slowly. Eventually, it'll kill you. I've seen it happen—it's an awful, painful death. But you don't have to worry—these two aren't going to be suffering much longer."

"You *fucking* twat," Jimmy Badass shrieked, and I crushed him with power again until he couldn't speak anymore.

The time had come.

"Rafael," I said softly, "what are their names?"

"Jimmy Reynolds and Missy Camden," Rafael replied promptly, but his voice was still lost. I looked at him until he met my eyes, and he seemed to square his shoulders and stand up straighter. "They're all yours, Lady Cory—we take our blood oaths seriously here."

Missy Camden had begun to blubber, bloody tears dribbling off her quivering lip. "I'm sorry..." she mewled, "I didn't know...if I'd known who you were we never would have...I swear we wouldn't have..."

She almost got to me—not because I believed her, or even because she was just like me, but because she was so pathetic. How can you kill something that small, no matter how mean? But my beloved was there with his bloodlust, and he hadn't been squashing the shit out of them for the last ten minutes.

"I throw, you catch?" he growled, delight in every syllable, and I found I wanted to please that bloodlust more than I wanted to reward that meanness.

"Batter-up," I hissed back.

Ribs crunched like crackers as he ripped their hearts out of their chests, and the squelching sound was like hauling a boot out of a puddle of sucking mud. The black-red blood spattered across half the club, but Bracken and

I caught the brunt of it because we were standing right in front of the two shocked vampires, about fifteen feet back. I caught the hearts with my power, and they hovered, suspended between us, beating blackly with the slow old blood of the undead.

I looked at the girl, pity in my eyes for the inevitable consequences of treachery.

"I'm sorry," I said uselessly.

"Go to hell…" she snarled, blood gushing from her lips as she spoke.

"You first."

The hearts conflagrated hotly, blazing with sunshine, and the vampires all moaned and covered their eyes. The blood hadn't blackened before the bodies caught too, and I reinforced my shields and made sure the burn was quick and clean and merciful.

Before I could breathe three times, in and out quickly, pumped by adrenaline, the two traitors and their remains were reduced to ash, and the club was permeated—not with the stench of burning flesh but of the more subtle scent of graveyard ash, fluttering in the wind of a strong, hot sun.

I was shaking with reaction, and ready to just turn away and stalk out of the club on the horse I rode in on, trailing my people behind me, but Rafael interrupted, reminding me that I was not only myself, I was my people, and I was trying to avoid a war.

"My lady," he said humbly, not meeting my eyes, "I gave Jimmy the order to… to deal with that problem we discussed before. I'm afraid the message might not have gotten through."

I understood now—Jimmy assumed if he took out Green, they wouldn't have to police their own. Rafael hadn't suspected the treachery.

"Two more days," I said through a raw and constricted throat. I couldn't even look at Rafael--I had to gaze sideway. Nicky, Teague and Mario looked grim and angry from the corner of my eye. "But after that, Rafael, I'm done. I'm amped, I'm pissed, and I'm a hair trigger away from wreaking fucking carnage on this place because I can. This needs to be taken care of, and it needs to…FUCK!"

Someone—I never learned his name afterwards—decided my people were fair game. He was lunging—a silver knife in his hand—and Teague was a heartbeat away from his ultimate sacrifice of service before I caught the guy—dark haired, shapeshifter, young—and destroyed him in a blast of sunshine fury.

The complete, appalled silence was broken by Teague, looking at near death with wide, inscrutable eyes. He bowed at the waist. "Appreciate it, my Lady."

"Anytime," I rasped, and turned back to Rafael, done with talking and done with threats.

"Two. Days." And then, because I was a hair's breadth from going nuclear, a darkened shadow from becoming the very thing I loathed and feared about myself, the thing I was still trying to atone for after two years of self control, I threw my head back and screamed. It was human scream, barely, but it was human and not a sunshine scream. Anything, anything, to bleed away the terrible surge of power and raw red wrath that was pulsing through my body in scorching, scathing molten-Valkyrie waves.

My people joined in—all of them—heads back, eyes meeting the eyes of every vampire in the place, faces caught in terrible snarls, grotesque, furious alter-forms of the familiar, beloved men I trusted my life with and the scream went on and on and on until every head in the place was bowed in grief and penance and fear.

The last echoes died down and we walked out, a bleak, despairing silence in our wake.

BRACKEN

Pieces Moving Beyond the Board

After the adrenaline pumped ride to the club, the ride home was tense, dysphoric, and depressing. Nobody liked what we'd had to do, nobody liked who we had to be--especially not Cory, who had pulled the trigger herself.

She moved restlessly on the seat next to me, leaning back against my shoulder and staring out the tinted window to the purple canopy beyond. The sky was vast here--long stretches of unbroken canvas before clay lumps of hills, like children under blankets of earth--and I wondered if that sense of space oppressed her.

I knew I missed home as much as she missed Green, but I would not have missed seeing her snarling violent poetry of justice for the world.

I had known how she would feel, even as we'd made the plan over breakfast this morning. I knew about the self-loathing, I knew about the regret. I knew that the part of her who was sweet and warm in my life, was wailing, dying, in the throes of what she had just done.

I knew the part of her that would fight to the death to keep me alive was still screaming that awesome, awful, primal howl.

I knew she would fight within herself until her heart was shredded and bruised, trying to reckon on the forces of love, the forces of power, and the forces of revenge that had created the havoc we'd just wrought, but I did not know which side would win.

Nicky drove back with us—he sat with Mario in the middle seat, as she leaned stiffly on top of me in the back. The mood in the car was tense with unspent rage, and Max continued to play the hard, pounding sounds of Adrian's playlist until Cory spoke up from the back.

"Job's done, Max," she murmured just loud enough to carry. "Maybe we should wind down now."

"Don't know if I can," Max replied, and the set of his shoulders said it was true. "Don't know if any of us can."

Renny made a tentative movement next to him, as though to soothe the top of his hand as it was on the wheel, but something in his voice, the vibrating set of his jaw, discouraged her from it. She turned away then, and gazed silently into the night. If she'd been a cat, her tail would have twitched.

Cory let out a shaky breath. "You're right—I'm going to need to swim or something... something..."

"Swim at night?" Nicky asked from the middle seat, and her smile was almost close to normal.

"If I can't do it with this much adrenaline pumping me up, I'll never be able to do it."

Nicky grinned, the type of grin that reminded us that carnivorous birds were fierce predators. "Then let's go. Swimsuits optional, adrenaline a must!"

"Required," she muttered next to me. "For me, swimsuits are required."

"Me too, *mija*," said Mario from Nicky's side, and Max added his grunt of assent. I would wear a swimsuit for her, I thought as I touched a strand of her hair and rubbed it softly. A part of me I'd never kept hidden started whispering that being inside of her while we were inside that black electric water would be like bursting into star fragments in the center of a supernova, but I could let that pass. She almost needed to be by herself right now—but only if I was with her.

Sadly enough, even that was not to be.

As we drove up to the cabins, Marcus, Phillip and Teague in our wake, the headlights picked out the figures of Kyle, one hand clamped uncomfortably around Annette, and of Lambent, who was gazing disgustedly at our young civilian.

Young Sam didn't look in the least repentant, and Annette looked decidedly mussed. She also looked furious at Kyle for detaining her.

Cory and I met appalled glances, and Nicky put his face in his hands.

"I am *sooooo* not in the mood for this shit," Cory muttered grimly as she slid out of the car, but when she spoke to the youngster in Lambent's care, her tone was decidedly lighter. "Heya, Sam—good night?"

"Awesome night, Lady Cory!" he said with a grin. He still had braces on—a human thing, and one that made him look particularly young.

"Lambent, did you discover this fine young lad in the dark woods alone?" she asked, and Sam rolled his eyes.

"Discovered? Right, luvie. Alone? Sadly. Not." Lambent looked in Annette's direction and physically recoiled, as though the flesh of his face was actually crawling back his skull to get away from her.

"So, Annette," Cory said sweetly, "how's that virginity thing working out for you?"

I had to hand it to the ignorant big-titted human—she had just enough of a complete lack of self-awareness to scrounge up some dignity.

"Everyone knows that kind of sex still makes you a virgin," Annette retorted snottily, and everybody there—including Sam—widened their eyes and looked at her twice.

"Really?" Cory blinked and shook her head. "Do you still feel like a virgin, Sam?"

Sam's look was smug. "Well, if I was one before, I don't think I'm one now!"

Annette's sideways brush-off had enough contempt in it to make even a horny teenager feel used. "That's not *really* how you do it, you know."

Sam's eyes grew a little unfocussed, and his smile was uncomfortable and totally adult. "Well, I could say the same to you," he murmured, and Cory, Lambent, and I all did a yawning, ear-popping gesture as some sort of power fluctuated around us.

"Oh. Fuck." Cory gazed at the casual young man who had been in the periphery of our vision for the last week. "It's *you*. The fucked-up colors on the house, the jealousy, the life in a Judd Apatow movie… it's you!"

Everybody but Annette was looking at the kid in awe and a little bit of fear—he was shifting uneasily, his hands in his pockets, his shoulders hunched over his chest.

"Sweetheart, what *are* you…and more to the point—what did you do?"

The kid shrugged. "I tried to take it back. She was being a bitch, saying it didn't count. I just wanted to take it back."

Oh and *now* Annette was paying attention. "You can't *do* that!" Her face twisted, and between the running mascara and the visceral hatred, she was uglier than toe fungus on a human. "I put *out* for you!"

"You used me," he said simply. "And you got something—but I don't think it's what you wanted."

The boy was not full grown yet—she was taller than he was, and she marched over to him, her flip-flops slapping against her heels and grabbed him by the arm, shaking him hard. "You make it right you little fucker! I let you touch me and you fucking *owe* me! Ouuuuchhh!!!"

We were all strong men, trained not to take advantage of the weak—there were really only three people in our group who would have felt comfortable touching the woman physically, and the one who got there first had claws.

Renny pulled back claws, which were dripping red over the top of some sort of purple paint and licked them daintily while Annette screamed and hopped up and down on a shredded calf. Cory snapped her head like a dreamer awakened and started giving orders.

"Sam, darlin', I want to talk to you later—don't worry, you're not in trouble, and I'm not mad, but you and me…"

"We gotta talk—I understand, Lady Cory."

"Oh don't you call her 'Lady'," Annette hissed, still nursing her bleeding calf. "I'm about sick to death of it--all these people kow-towing to you, 'Lady Cory'—when all you are is just a white-trash whore, with your three husbands and your disgusting vampires. Nicky will see through you in a hot second, you just wait and see!"

Cory looked at Annette and blinked. After what she had been forced to do this night to protect her people, to avenge her Green, the other woman's vitriol didn't phase her in the least.

"I'm not the one getting ass-fucked by minors in the woods, now am I?" Cory asked, and the rest of us smirked. That was our girl. With an exasperated sniff, she turned and gestured to Annette in the same way I would gesture towards a rock or a tree. "Nicky--I thought your parents were going to take care of this?" She let her words come up in a question, and Nicky shrugged.

"I don't know what to tell you, *ou'e'ane*--they don't seem to be taking it seriously."

Cory sighed with frustration and looked down at her blood-spotted denim jacket, and then at me. We both had blood on our faces, spattered across our clothes, and our expressions were even grimmer than our accessorizing. With another sigh and a scrubbing motion of her hand across her face, she strode across the drive to Nicky's parents cabin and pounded on their door. Without being asked, I took Annette's arm in a cruel grip and hauled her, limping, bitching, and protesting the whole way.

Nicky's mother opened the door and looked decidedly shocked by her chosen daughter-in-law's appearance.

"Is this yours?" Cory asked shortly, indicating the squealing heifer I was dragging by the upper arm.

"You know very well she's with us," Nicky's mother said guardedly, and Cory nodded once, the hard, decided movement of a warrior.

"The last two people who threatened my family are dead, Terry," Cory snapped, and I took my cue and shoved Annette through the door so hard she fell to her knees when she hit the carpet inside. "You might want to make an effort to keep your trash in your room."

With that she turned around and Nicky took her hand and I wrapped my arm around her waist and together, in the stride we'd developed in the last year and a half, we made our way back to the circle. Where we really wanted to go was our own cabin so Cory and I could bathe, but the conversation with the kid could not be put off.

Lambent spoke up as we got there and I noticed that everyone else had emerged from their cabins. La Mark was talking quietly to Mario and Tanya was on his other arm, listening. The vampires had parked and were keeping an eye on Sam and Max was scratching Renny happily behind the ears, just to hear her purr. The werewolves were out, checking Teague's body anxiously: Jacky was sheltering Teague's face with his height and his wide chest and Teague was making "I'm fine, leave me the fuck alone, we've got bigger shit to shovel" noises. As we approached everyone formed a loose circle, with Sam roughly in the middle, and Cory went to join him.

Sam looked around apprehensively, and she shrugged. "You're not on trial—we're just curious, that's all." She looked up and found Lambent over her shoulder. "You felt the power surge? That's what sent you out into the woods?"

Lambent shrugged. "Every boy has the right to shag something he'd shouldn't—but yeah. They were lit up like a Christmas tree when I rounded the corner, and she was shouting as they did it. He's not likely to take whatever he did back—not all of it. It was too firmly buried in her arse, if you know what I mean."

Cory shook her head and scrubbed her eyes. "Sadly I do—and where's the toilet brush for your brain when *that* image comes around, that's what I want to know!"

"So I'm in trouble because she screamed 'Fuck me, Nicky'?" Sam asked and next to me, Nicky gave a little wiggle of revulsion.

"Ewwwww!!! Oh *Christ,* I could have lived my whole life without knowing that!"

I patted his shoulder. "Join the club."

Cory tried not to smirk, but it had been a long-assed day. "Sam—have you heard of touch, blood, and song?"

The kid looked completely non-plussed, and Cory sighed and scrubbed her hands over her face again. "It's sort of how we exchange power, except you don't really need the blood and the song, you know?" She looked at him meaningfully, and his eyes widened. Oh yeah, he got it *now.* Cory sighed—he was so young, and there was a lot he knew that he hadn't told, but a lot he obviously didn't know that he needed to be told. Doing it all tonight was *possible,* but it probably wouldn't do any of us any good.

"Look—kid," she said at last, "your mom's not going anywhere tonight, is she?"

Hs shook his head slowly, and there was something terribly sad in the motion—a story here, I thought.

"Bracken and I are covered in blood—and man, I've got to get it off of me, or I'm gonna start screaming. You just got laid and got your heart broke…"

"I didn't really love her," he supplied helpfully, and Cory and I met eyes and tried not to grin.

"Well did you get your ego stomped?" she asked, straight-faced, and he nodded and conceded that yes, maybe there had been some pain involved.

"Did you give her power and then try to get it back?" The kid nodded again, and the grim lines around Cory's eyes eased up a bit.

"Would you like to continue this conversation later—hell, even later tonight—after you've had time to think it over and I've had time to fucking wash?"

The kid grinned, braces flashing in the soda-light, and nodded. "Yes, my Lady…"

"Oh gees…" she whined, and the kid looked surprised.

"Everyone else calls you Lady… you are the queen, right? I mean, you're a shit's sight better than *that* heifer."

We could all hear Annette shrieking through the walls of Nicky's parent's cabin. Cory closed her eyes.

"Yeah, whatever," she said softly. "Either way—give us an hour…"

Sam yawned, shrugged, looked sheepish. "How about in the morning? I promise…" He closed his eyes, thought for a minute, and brightened. Then he turned his head and spit on his palm. "Touch, blood, and song, right?"

Cory cocked her head. "I thought you didn't know about that?"

The kid shrugged. "I'm not stupid—if it wasn't blood when we were…" he blushed, "well, you know, then spit's probably as good, right? So, touch blood and song—here, shake my hand."

Cory spit on her hand first, and they met in the middle of the circle and shook hands like shipping magnates. "You promise you'll be here?" she said softly. "There's a lot to talk about."

"I promise, Lady Cory," he said solemnly, as only a teenager could. There was a brief glow of light around their hands, and she stepped back.

"I'll meet you by the lake around nine," she said softly. "'Night, young Sam."

"'Night, Lady Cory." He walked quietly out of the circle, which collapsed on itself as people started demanding details and reassurance and news on Green.

"He's fine!" Cory said after the furor died down. "He's fine—nothing's bleeding anymore, nothing's broken, and I think if that bitch hadn't blindsided him like a coward, he could have taken her."

"How'd you take her out, mommy?" Katy asked, her snarl as close to wolf as Katy got in human form.

The bunch of us got quiet, and Cory quirked her eyebrows enigmatically. "Bracken threw and I caught," she said softly, and there was a moment of silence, and then Lambent started swearing.

"Goddammit, my lady—all I ask—all I have *ever* asked is to be of service to you. Are you telling me you're so mad for your own violence you couldn't let me do that? Is my only job her going to be catching dumbarsed cows getting buggered in the woods?"

The shock on her face showed that she hadn't even thought of asking him, and only her hand on my arm stopped me from rounding in on the arrogant bastard and taking out his lungs.

"This one was ours," she said at last, so lowly that only our preternatural hearing would register her voice. "Me and Bracken... this one threatened our Green. That's why Nicky got to come. He's ours. Believe me, Lambent, the next time someone gets their ass cooked to ashes, you can share in the fun."

Lambent blinked, and looked mildly ashamed. "Of course, luvie," he said thickly. "I... I just want to help."

Cory looked up at him, a keen speculation in her eyes. "You think you didn't help? Folks, do you realize we've got walking talking proof that this funky bullshit here isn't just us? My *Goddess,* Lambent—if that's not help, I don't know what you want to deliver!"

There was a generalized chuckle, and Renny curled up at Max's feet and started purring.

A wearied sigh went out through us, and Cory suddenly leaned fully on me. "Anybody up for that swim we were talking about? Because if not, I'm going for a shower and going to bed. If nothing else is going to shit on us from above, I want a clear head when I talk to Sam tomorrow."

She went on the swim for me, I was sure—her body was boneless, her heart almost too weary for the fear she'd been fighting all week. For once—maybe it was the dark—she forsook the now-silt-stained white T-shirt hanging over the cabin's shower, and simply wore her swimsuit and her flip-flops, discarding the shoes at the lake's edge.

She padded into the lake quietly, and when the water was up to her waist, she dove in, forcing her arms to haul water and her feet to kick by an act of effort alone. I tread water and watched her, looking beside me when I saw Jacky at my elbow.

"He said she saved his life tonight," Jacky said quietly. "Everybody else says it's true. I get so used to thinking of him as invincible—it always surprises me when he says that she does that."

I raised my eyebrows. Jack had been in good form this trip—no pointed remarks about how she was using Teague, no complaints when she took him out on this run. Something had happened—maybe something permanent—to make his attitude less irritating, at the very least.

"Why would you ever think differently?" I asked, completely out of patience.

Jack shrugged. "You've got to understand—the only people who ever saw him for who he really was were me and Katy. It took a while for me to think you didn't see him for what you could use."

I tilted my face up to the stars, and wished a little for the sun. "You want to see a user, you look at... at..." Oh Goddess, none of us could even say her name! "That *thing* screeching out her lungs in the cabin up there." We could *still* hear her. In fact, I think there was a general consensus that we would all stay in the water until she'd worn herself down.

"I know," Jack said quietly. "Just like I know that you wanted him there tonight not so much as muscle as... as representation. I'm starting to get it now. It's... it's like the politics of keeping us safe, you know?"

I let out a little puff of air, and watched her startle at the sound her foot made as it broke the water. Her hair had come loose and was in her face, hampering her attempts to breathe, and her expression while fighting her fear of the water was nearly as fierce as it had been when yanking the half-life from the vampires we'd killed.

"Do you know why she's out there?" I asked, my jaw setting almost angrily.

Jack shook his head, still treading water. "No—she's terrified. We can all see it."

"That's why she's out there. She's got all of us to worry about—she can't afford weakness, and that's a weakness." I swallowed hard against the lump in my throat. Damn. It was so unfair—we would only have a mortal life span together, and I was pretty sure it would take an eternity for her to cease to amaze me.

Jacky snorted, and nodded towards Teague, who was literally doing laps across the entire lake. Yes, he would know about someone who drove himself to be worthy—and what a damned hard thing it was to live with.

"They're so damned much alike," he murmured, and I looked at him and smiled.

"Too much alike for you to worry about her like that."

Jacky grunted. "So he tells me."

"Believe him—I've seen them together, when they talk. You know who they remind me of?"

"No idea."

"Green and Arturo."

I remembered this morning (was it really only this morning?) Arturo—who had never desired a man, not in three-thousand years of living—and his desperate happiness to sit on Green's bed and assure himself that Green was safe, was well.

"I hadn't thought of that," Jacky said quietly. Cory gave a muffled shriek, as an imaginary hand grasped her mortal ankle, and I didn't even nod in Jacky's direction before I took off towards her. She knew the drill now, and I positioned myself behind her and pulled her back up against my front.

She was shaking.

"We're done with this," I said gruffly. "We're going back to the cabin to call Green, and then you're going to bed."

She nodded, her trembling abating just enough for her to turn around and start hauling herself back to shore. Abruptly, there was a wet, furry presence between us, and she must have been tired because she took Jack's offer and looped her arm around him so he could tow her to where she could touch.

"Thanks, Jack," she said quietly, trying to stand. Her knees were wobbly, and I picked her up before she could fall down.

"I'm fine," she said mildly, but she laid her head against my chest anyway.

"Of course you are. Nicky!" I called out to the water where he was still swimming, "Could you get her flip-flops?"

"I hear you, mighty hunter!" He was not that far out in the lake, and his voice barely echoed off the shiny black water.

"I'm still dripping wet," she mumbled. Her hand had risen up and was petting my chest as she spoke. She rarely did this anymore, tired herself out beyond exhaustion. I was glad the days when I did this all the time were gone, but I still treasured the moments when she needed me physically. I knew she needed me emotionally, but there was something satisfying in holding her like this.

"I'll undress you," I told her, ignoring the gravel under my feet.

"It's only a little bikini."

It looked charming, even in the dark. Her bare skin, pale and freckled, was smooth and sweet and innocent over tarnished gold. She might look appealing with a tan, but in the moonlight, her paleness gleamed with all she was to me.

"Then that'll make it easier," I murmured.

"Mmmm…" I think she meant to keep complaining, sparking the banter we had raised to an art form, but I was warm and she was sleepy, and she felt safe in my arms as she perhaps felt safe nowhere else in this alien place. This was who I was to her—the lover she could lean on, the lover who would shelter her in my clasp. I did not do politics and the only words I've ever known are the words we've spoken to each other.

I took her to the cabin and put her in one of my T-shirts, then undressed myself, throwing our wet things in the small bathroom. (Although I'm given to understand that it is bigger than most bathrooms of it's sort, the shower could barely fit two people.) She muttered something about calling Green as I was in the bathroom, but I could smell the wildflower scent even as she said it—he'd come and kissed her goodnight.

I slid into bed next to her, and remembered how she'd looked in battle, fierce and feral, power burning a halo around her body, her dark eyes narrow and flat and sparking with fury, her lips drawn back in a snarl of revenge.

She'd been beautiful.

Tonight, softened by moonlight and sleep, her gold lashes fanning her cheeks and her expressive mouth relaxed like a child's, she was helpless in my arms and relying on me for protection.

She was just as beautiful.

CORY

All the Players on the Board

Nicky slid in, cool and welcome, and I muttered something about setting the alarm. I'd told the kid nine—I didn't need touch, blood, and song to help me keep that promise.

Mornings camping always feel too early until the sun arrows through the dusty green tops of the trees like the light of Zeus. Since our little spit of land was mostly night people, it was even lonelier, especially since we faced west and our area would be in shadow until at least eleven o'clock. (This did not necessarily mean that it would be cooler come noon—the shadows just made the heat closer and more personal.)

Still, it was in the seventies when I flip-flopped out of the cabin, and that warranted a hoodie over my cut-offs and T-shirt, and I dropped my knitting in one pocket and a bottle of water and my iPod in the other. Hey—a girl had to be prepared.

The lake was so still and clear in the angled light that the surrounding hills were reflected clearly in its surface, and the trees over my shoulder were long deep shadows against the blue sky in the water.

Sam was there ahead of me—more, I think, because he was young than because I was late. He was dressed in cargo shorts and a white T-shirt that might be big on Bracken, and doing that thing that boys do—finding shit at the edge of the shore to hurl across the lake. He skipped a stone for more ripples than I could count, which impressed the hell out of me—I'd never been able to do that.

Just watching him there, he looked like what we had all assumed he was: a kid. A civilian. Nice enough to accept us for what we were, but still... waiting... to be someone to really pay attention to.

If we hadn't been guided by Green's principles, he could have had us all at each other's throats in a matter of hours.

This was a *very* dangerous young man.

"Morning," I murmured. I brought a peace offering: an entire box of Hostess chocolate cupcakes--just what every growing boy needs, right? I held up the box and the kid brightened, and I shuffled around the iPod and water in my pocket and came up with two small bottles of milk that we'd been keeping with our supplies. That brought out a grin and I nodded him towards the dock so I could dangle my feet in the water because I wanted to.

As we were making ourselves comfortable, I heard dog noises. When I looked up, there was a splash and Teague was paddling through the water, towards the little inlet behind the cabins. The wolf was wearing shorts, his tail poking out through the legs, and I wondered what he was up to until he shifted in the middle of the water and became a human man, floundering to fix his clothes for a moment and then continuing his workout in the lake. Teague wore a T-shirt, same as me, out in the water, and it wasn't for his Irish-pale skin.

Well, weren't we a sorry piece of damage, right?

Sam tore off a wrapper and tucked it into the box, then devoured his first cupcake in one gulp. He looked at me for permission, and when I nodded, he ate two more in quick succession, and my stomach got twitchy just *looking* at all that sugar for breakfast, but then, I wasn't a fifteen-year-old boy.

I decided to drink my milk instead—there would be oatmeal waiting for me up at the front, and I'd save the sugar for a slice of the pie we kept in the mini-fridge at all times.

He finally slowed down, and was nibbling at his sixth cupcake in a desultory fashion, when he spoke up.

"I don't know what I am."

I looked at him, wisely and (for once) silent.

"Weird shit just happens around me. Sometimes good, lot of times bad. I feel a... a tingle..." he put his hands in that little dent between his sternum and his stomach, "right here. And sometimes it guides me, and I'll go somewhere and then the shit that happens is usually good. If I ignore it, then it's usually..." he swallowed, and his voice cracked, and a terrible look of guilt and sorrow made his features look pinched and young. "Bad," he whispered. "If I ignore it, the shit that happens is bad."

"Does it always guide you?" I asked, curious.

Sam shook his head. "Nope. Seventy-five percent of the time, it just. Fucking. Happens."

I looked at him in dawning horror—and terrible sympathy. "Oh. My. Fucking. God." The implications—it was scarcely a gift, more like a curse. It was staggering and horrible—the kid wasn't a sorcerer, or anything that could direct his will... he was a plague, a potential natural disaster, an agent of chaos. Hello—wait a second. That was ringing some bells...

"Sam—who is your father?"

If anything his expression got bleaker, the color and animation washing away from his face and leaving a blade of a nose and acne spots against white skin.

"My... my stepfather di...was killed about six months ago. I have no idea who my real father was."

I had to breathe deep with this one, and remember I was a human first and a big bad sorceress second—at least I hoped that was the case.

"I'm sorry about your stepfather—how'd it happen?" Because although it clearly hurt him horribly, I think he was also dying to get it off his chest.

Sam shook his head and for a moment I thought he wouldn't tell me, no matter how painful the infection bursting from his heart. "I... I had a tingle. I tried to tell him to drive another way, and he laughed it off. He was a good guy, you know?" Sam kicked water at no one in particular, and we both watched as the droplets glittered in the sun, and then spread dark ripples over that happy mountain sky in the heart of the lake. The kid shuddered, and kept talking.

"Good to my mom, nice to me. Liked to watch basketball—we'd sit on the couch during the games and eat popcorn and drink sodas and talk during the commercials. He...he loved us. But...if we'd gone the way I told him, we would have been in traffic for two hours watching a parade. But he went his way, and caught a golf-ball in the ear from a shooting range we couldn't even see on the other side of the freeway. It...it was freaky. They said it caught a wind gust or something, but... all I know is one minute he was telling me not to be so superstitious and the next minute there was glass everywhere and he was dead."

Aw Christ. What a fucking disaster. Awkwardly I put my hand on his shoulder, but I wasn't hurt or surprised when he flinched away.

"It's not your fault," I said inanely. It wasn't—not by intention, anyway. Not judging by the pain that was shining in his black-fringed blue eyes.

"No... I'm just a walking...earthquake, or hurricane or something, waiting to happen—but it's not my *fault*. I'm just, you know, fucking chaos! And my mom... whoever my real dad was, he didn't stick around, and now I kill the world's nicest husband? I'm surprised she can even look at me. And she does, she keeps telling me she loves me, but she just... she just stays in her room and...drinks..."

Oh Jesus. "Sam—Sam, why are you here?"

The kid wiped his face with the back of his hand and we both pretended he didn't. "I got a tingle," he said gruffly. "We've both... both learned not to ignore those, right?"

A tingle. The son of chaos and man, walking around with a tingle, right into our arms. Spiffy.

I swallowed. "Chaos doesn't always have to be bad, kid," I said after a moment. I was desperate, I guess, to lighten shit up, to make this kid feel better.

"Yeah, give me one example." He was angry and affronted, and I didn't blame him.

"The Christmas before last," I said, because it was the best example I could think of. "I mean... it should have been a shitty Christmas, right? I... we...we'd lost Adrian—he was my boyfriend... Green's too. Brack's best friend. He was just, you know, loved by a lot of people. I... I was really sick. But Green—he wanted the whole thing done up right. There were lights around the house and the gardens, and a million presents. It..." Now *I* was getting teary. Fuck. "It took us half the day to sort them out, because the front room was so full with them that you couldn't walk through it, and about a thousand people live in the hill... it was a mess, you know? But...all the little people at the hill—you know, sprites, fairies, nixies, pixies—those guys?"

"They're real?"

"You've seen werewolves, elves, vampires and a chick who can shoot out of water—you really going to draw the line?"

The kid laughed a little through his misery. "No."

"Well, they all wanted to give me a gift—but they're like, anywhere from two inches to a foot tall, so it's got to be something small but special. So they all gave me seeds. Thousands of seeds—all of them with a teeny-tiny bows on them out of gold thread."

Sam nodded. "That does sound like happy chaos," he said thickly.

I nodded, sniffling a little. "But wait, it gets better! Because the thing is, they planted them, as soon as the snow melted, and there were all these fairies—and you haven't seen them, but they're like a thousand different colors, and shapes—and some of them look like tiny animals and some of them look like tiny bugs, but they're human-shaped... anyway, they all have their *one* seed. But that seed's for me, and it's for Green, and they love us, right? So they're zooming in about a gajillion different directions—man, they're all *over* the yard—and they're all looking for *their* spot, and it's total chaos..."

"Do they ever fight?" he asked, looking for the tarnish in the silver lining.

"Of course—but they never get violent, they just argue and bicker, and then go their own ways—like us, you know, but on a small scale. And eventually, it all gets planted, and it's the foothills, right? And there's all sorts of flowers—wildflowers, poppies, tulips, daisies, frickin' chrysanthemums— and most of them—not all, mind you, but most of them—all bloom in a span of about two weeks. And for the last two springs, that means that every morning, for two weeks in a row, just as soon as the vampires go to bed and the sun comes out, they absolutely *have* to have my attention. So they buzz over my bed in a little cloud of perfect flying little magic rainbow people, and then they drag me outside, and then they all fly over to their flower, and jump up and down and sing and beg me to come see *their* flower, and I have to stand in the middle of the yard, right? Because I don't want to step on anyone *else's* flower, and it's this incredibly sweet chorus of them, and me and Green saying, "*It's beautiful! Yes, it's lovely! That's perfect! Thank you! Yours is wonderful! Thank you!*" until they all forget why we're there and fly away!"

Sam was laughing by now, honest, full-hearted kid laughter, his shoulders shaking, his head tilted back, as happy as any teenager ever was—except he kept having to wipe his cheeks with the back of his hands. Not the scrubbing the whole hand over his face, like a grown man, but the other way, like a little kid.

"Chaos isn't always bad, Sam," I said at last, when his laughter had died down a little. "I think... I think your thing is, you're the child of... of chaos and man. There's not a lot of you—maybe that makes your mom pretty special."

Sam nodded, sober suddenly, even if he was no longer crying. "She's pretty. And she's really nice. She used to make such a big deal about how lucky she was, to have me and my stepdad."

I nodded. "So sometimes Chaos is beautiful—and your mom caught his eye. And then there was you. And you have an... an affinity, I guess for it. It's your magic superpower, if you learn how to use it. You just need to learn how to use it."

"Sometimes?" he asked, still bitter. "You just gave me one example—and it was a hell of an example, my lady, but no offense, you're like one person in a million. How is that going to help me in my life?"

"Sam, I may be one of the few mortals to ever really see a fairy, but I'm not the only one to ever see wildflowers! They're everywhere! And they're still chaos. Have you ever been in one of those baby wards? A mom will come in to get her baby, and suddenly they're all making noises and pooping and gurgling or crying or some of them sleeping right on through that other madness. That happens every day! A box full of kittens, two kids playing with a crate full of toys," my hands made helpless gestures to the world around me, "stars, clouds, raindrops, freckles, snowflakes—it's all chaos, Sam! None of it is predictable. You told me you didn't like the bad tingle—well that means you're probably not a bad person. You have a good heart. There's a good way to live with this just like there's a good way to live with…"

"My stepdad!" He stood up now, angry. It was like he had to paint all of the evil in him in excruciating detail, so I'd know how hopeless it was. "There's a good way to live with that?"

"You think you're the only one who's fucked up like that?" I asked, irritated because, dammit, I *was* going to have to bring this funky bullshit up *again*. Goddessdammitalltofuck, why couldn't I just write a self-help book—*I Became a Mass Murderer and Kept My Soul Intact*—and publish that fucker and get it over with? "You think you're the only one whose power got away from you?"

"It wasn't just *him!*" Sam shot back angrily. He was jumping up and down on the dock by now and as the thing bobbed up and down in the water, I looked up to the floating bait shop apprehensively. How freaked out did he have to be to break something serious and send us both plunging into the lake in the sucking vortex of that thing? Fear can be an ugly ride sometimes, can't it?

"Who else?" I asked. "I mean, I snapped and I actually killed people. Your stepdad… that wasn't even in your control!"

"Well when I'm pissed, I can make it happen, okay?" His agitation stopped, and I drew a quiet sigh of relief—it was like he reminded himself that becoming pissed was a bad thing.

"Handy," I said neutrally. "How'd you find that out?"

The kid shrugged, trying to be casual. "I… I was flirting with this girl, right?

I nodded. He was fifteen. I'd mostly hated boys when I was fifteen, mostly because they were walking hormones and I'd been invisible.

"So she… she laughs at me, in front of my friends, and I'm pissed, and we're walking into a rally, and the tingle just builds in my stomach, right? And I feed it, right? And then… then suddenly, on the floor of the gym, there's just… you know. Stupid school bullshit going on, and that tingle just builds and I just feed it, because I'm pissed…"

I closed my eyes. Shit. This had hit the news about a year back. Someplace south, like Bakersfield. "You started a riot…" I muttered. "Kids started swinging at each other—like two people died."

"Four," Sam muttered disconsolate. "Four. I didn't know a damned one.

No one I had a grudge against, no one I'd miss. Just four random-assed people, dead because I...I got pissed."

"It wasn't your fault," I said, trying to reason. I mean, technically you could make an argument for it—the kid had been pissed. But he hadn't known—it didn't help the dead people, but he didn't deserve to torture himself with it either. "In order to actually assume responsibility for that, sport, you had to know you'd kill someone. It's all very well to be a pissed-off kid and *think* you want to murder the world, but unless you *know* you can murder the world, wishing for it isn't murder."

"And how would you know?" he asked, and I was tired of answering this question.

"How do you think she knows?" Teague asked, appearing like magic, hopping out of the water so fluidly, I was actually surprised he had his trunks on.

I gave a little shriek and Sam actually jumped, and Teague gave a grim, hard smile and rolled his eyes.

"Jesus, brother!" I said breathlessly. "You sure do know how to make an entrance."

"I know a lot about regret, Lady," he said gruffly, slicking his dark hair out of his eyes, "and I know how much you don't want to open that vein." He was standing there, scars and all, to defend me—Goddess bless him.

"Thanks, Teague," I told him, moved. "But I'll bleed over Sam if I need to—it's all good."

"Never good to bleed like that," he muttered, shaking his head, and then he sliced cleanly back into the water quicker than I could breathe, barely leaving a splash. He must have been listening to us, even as he swam, just to make sure I was okay.

The kid laughed a little. "He's not even sleeping with you, is he?"

I shook my head. "No—his dance card's full. But those of us on the hill—we watch each other's backs, you know?"

The kid nodded. "I get that. For a while, I thought... you know. That Annette was one of you."

Aha—lightbulb on. I'd been wondering what Sam had seen in Annette—apparently, he'd thought he'd seen us.

"She was supposed to be Nicky's 'real wife', you know?" I still didn't know how to say this. The idea was ludicrous—but it was also hurtful on a superficial level I wasn't sure I should be hurt on. Didn't seem to matter. I was anyway.

"Nicky's mom's a bitch," Sam said, and I wondered at the interactions I *hadn't* seen between them. Well, shit. I couldn't be everywhere, and I sure couldn't be Green.

"She hasn't been nice to *me* yet," I said with a small smile. I went to go for my sock—we'd been out here long enough, and I was getting twitchy without something to do with my hands, but I stopped my hands and I sighed. It would be hot soon, and we hadn't even taken on the subject.

"Sam—about Annette..."

"You need to know what I did for her." He nodded, and I wondered if we should go back, talk about his guilt some more, but Teague, for all his good intentions, had broken that moment.

"I really do."

"I have no idea..." he laughed grimly and shook his head. "I mean, she... she started hitting on me, telling me that I looked special, like the rest of... how'd she put it? 'Nicky's in-laws'. I told her I had some... talent, you know? And she got all... little girl—she wanted some talent too. I told her I could probably give her some and then she hinted that she'd..." he blushed.

"She'd put out if you would?" I supplied, and he shrugged.

"And when we were doing it, I felt the tingle...and I sort of..." again, that blush.

"Pointed and shot."

The full blush took over his entire body, down to his knobby knees peering out from under his cargo shorts. "A-yup." He looked entirely embarrassed, but at least I'd figured out what was so alluring about her that he'd been willing to fuck her behind a tree. For a little while, she'd wanted the thing he feared most about himself—what's not to like?

She'd spent the night shrieking obscenities about me from her cabin because she'd been caught. I imagined that whatever 'little girl' appeal she'd had the night before had flaked and crumbled, like bad varnish, in the intervening hours.

"Well see," I murmured. "You do know about touch, blood, and song."

"That was probably more fun than blood," he told me dryly, and I found myself liking him immensely.

"Until the end," I reminded him, keeping my voice gentle.

"She seemed nicer than that." The sun had moved as we spoke, and we were no longer in the shade of the surrounding hills. Sam turned his face up to the sunlight and closed his eyes. I knew that feeling—that maybe you could fly away into the big blue, and these awful things that hurt you wouldn't hurt you anymore.

Sweet, sweet Goddess—please give this kid a break—if any kid needed a clear light through the confusion, it would seem to be this kid, the mixed up, well-intentioned, insanely dangerous son of Chaos and man.

I sighed. This conversation had gone on long enough as it was.

"Sam," I said, keeping my voice pitched low. Even with Teague now doing laps in the distance (and probably still listening), there was still the illusion that we were alone. We were night people and a loud voice right now felt almost obscene. "She wasn't real, boy--I know you want to think the girl in your bed likes you, but really, all she wanted was what she thought you could give."

The kid nodded. "Lady Cory, I knew she didn't love me--or even like me. I mean--I'm a kid and she's a grown-up. I figured we were using each other, and that was okay."

"But..." I urged him on—we both needed him to complete the thought.

"But that she despised me so much? That's... that's wrong. I mean, lust is okay, right?"

"If it's sensual and consensual," I replied neutrally. It was the hill's creed. We lived by it.

"So why's she so obsessed with our sex not being real?"

I shrugged. "She's got this idea of purity... she's trying to keep herself 'pure' for a guy who doesn't really exist."

"Aren't you sleeping with him?" the kid asked, justifiably confused.

I laughed a little, and sat back down on the dock. Experimentally I poked a toe in the frigid lake. I shuddered--you really did have to be a werecreature or an elf or something to swim here in the morning, didn't you? Out in the distance Teague was hauling his bantam Irish body through the water with the sleekness of a river otter. He seemed to prove my point.

"Her idea of what should be perfect isn't real," I amended in the thoughtful quiet. "It's chimerical--it's like a unicorn or a griffon or something. Just because you can imagine it doesn't mean it exists."

"Well then," said Sam logically, "I shouldn't exist either--and neither should you."

I shrugged. "Well, just because you can imagine it doesn't mean it DOESN'T exist, either. In our case, we're alive in breathing—but our superpowers cause us as much pain as joy. In Nicky's case, his mom wants him to be happy, but he wouldn't touch that heifer with an electric cattle prod and a hazmat suit. There's always a disconnect between your dreams and reality, Sam. In Annette's case, it's like the disconnect between *Greenday* and that kid banging on his tennishoe with a pencil. Never the freakin' twain shall meet, if you know what I mean."

"Yeah, well I wish I'd never met her freakin' twain, if you know what *I* mean," the kid grumbled, and I didn't blame him in the least.

I laughed. "Well, the real question is, now that you've freaked her in the twain, what can she do with it?"

The kid shook his head. "I'm sorry, Lady—I don't know. I honestly don't. I've never done anything like that, and even when I have a little bit of control… well it's a crapshoot, mostly. But if she's like me, that…tingle…it will let her know when she can do something with it. And…if she's as… just plain pissed nasty as she seemed last night…"

"It will be a nasty thing she does with the power—we both know that, Sam."

He sighed and stood and stretched, and looked unhappily at the phone attached to a lanyard around his neck. We had been out there for some time—I half expected Bracken to come out looking for me in a minute.

"I've got to go check on my mom, Lady…" He didn't sound happy about it—I wasn't either. This conversation only felt half done.

"Why you gotta call me that?" I asked, almost out of habit. Still, I stood and stretched next to him—we'd shifted about in the course of the conversation, but still, I thought I'd carry the imprint of the rough, slip-proof plastic on my ass for the rest of the day.

He looked at me seriously "You know, some teachers, they *demand* you call them by their names, or they give themselves a nickname and they make you call them that. But some teachers, you *have to*—it's just respect, you know? You're Lady Cory…"

"I'm maybe six years older than you!"

"You're Lady Cory. That guy out there," a gesture to Teague, "I think the whole reason he came out and swam for freaking ever was to protect you. What kind of asshole am I, I can't see that?"

I shrugged, hating this truth a lot right now. "Yeah. Well, a title isn't necessary, Sam. I just want to keep us all safe. And with that in mind, can you tell me *anything* about how to counter what that bitch might do to us?"

Sam thought for a second, and shivered. He shivered again, and before I could ask him, *"Tingle?"* he gave my hoodie a little downward zip and pressed his hand against my bare shoulder.

"What in the *fuck*…" Tingle, he'd called it. Tingle my fat white-trash ass. This was a fucking bee-sting swelling of power, it was a spider-bite, a poison-oak reaction, and I could tell by Sam's wide eyes and sudden *"Ouch!"* that he hadn't been expecting it either.

He yanked his hand from my shoulder and shook it like it hurt, and I glared at him. "What in the fuck?" I repeated dumbly. I zipped my sweater down a little more and checked out the place where his hand had been. I expected it to be red and swollen, but it wasn't. It was pale still, like the rest of me, since I'd been swimming with SPF 50+cotton shirt, but underneath it, contained in the outline of the handprint there were… stars. Tiny purple stars, like a tattoo, but sitting translucently under my skin.

"Sam?" I asked, feeling out with my power. They weren't… binding. Not in the way our mark was on the people who followed Green and I. They were almost... hovering. "What did you do?"

"I felt a tingle," he said a little numbly. "I wanted to help you... make up for what I did... I just... followed it, that's all."

Green? I thought a little desperately, and as usual, Green reassured me.

Protection, beloved. It's protection. Thank the nice boy, Corinne Carol-Anne. The sons of man and chaos are...unpredictable, at best.

"It's okay, Sam," I said out loud, because Sam was truly starting to look upset, and Goddess knew we didn't want this kid upset. "It's okay—I think its protection. Whatever she's doing, she won't be able to do it to me, that's all."

"That's all?" he asked, hopefully, and I nodded.

"Go back and check your mom, sweetheart," I said gently. "Tell her you love her—believe she loves you back. This... this is a great gift, and I'm grateful, right?"

The kid nodded, dashing his hand across his eyes "Lady... we're going to have to go. I'm... I'm getting a tingle that says home. I've had it since last night, and I was just putting it off until we talked... I can't..."

"You can't ignore them," I said, nodding. "I get it. Look, Sam—do me a favor. Before you go, stop and get my phone number, and my cell, and the hill's phone number. If you ever have trouble, a problem, a thing you can't resolve... you wanted to be with Annette because you wanted someone who'd have your back, right? Well, we've got your back. Fuck her..." I blushed and rolled my eyes. "Or not," I finished lamely, and he actually laughed.

"I got you... I'm sorry. I'd like to talk more...I just...I told her we were going and I've been out here forever and..."

"And you can't ignore shit like that, I got you."

He trotted up the road to the cabins, and I blinked once and then twice, trying to put our entire conversation into context and failing.

I'd need to talk it over with Bracken, I thought. And Green. And Nicky, and Teague and Max and Mario and...

I watched that angular, half-grown figure ambling away, and suddenly he looked so alone it made my chest ache. Poor Sam. I hoped really hard he'd get those phone numbers. Oh Goddess—if anyone needed someone at his back with good intentions, it was the son of man and chaos, now wasn't it?

I went back to the cabin to change—we had plans to go hiking before it got *really* hot, but Sam stopped by for our numbers before I had a chance to show Bracken and Nicky the handprint of stars on my shoulder.

Just as well. After the kid had taken the paper and made a show of entering the info into his cell phone and then bobbed his head nervously away, I did show them. They almost crapped live baby chickens.

"You let him WHAT?" Bracken roared, and I scowled at him.

"I didn't *let* him… he just did. He was a nice kid, and he wasn't grabbing anything important—it happened."

Bracken blinked and then squinted, mouthing the words, "Anything important?" as though they were heavily accented Latin. And then he figured out what I was talking about and got *really* pissed.

"You are important, Corinne Carol Ann! I could give a *shit* if he groped your boobs!"

Oh Jees… not *this* again! "I'm *fine!*" I pulled my hoodie sideways to show them the mark. "See—even Green agrees that it's not binding—it's just protection, right?"

I didn't say it was wise, Corinne Carol-Anne—I just said it was a protective spell.

"Oh for the love of crap!" I glared at Nicky. *"You're* not going to use my given name too, are you?"

"Would it help you see that it was a stupid thing to do?" he answered, scowling right back.

"You all suck when you gang up on me!" I snapped. "Hey!" Because argument or not, Bracken was looming and fondling, his touch warm and feathery on my shoulder. My mouth went dry and I remembered that we (I) had been too tired and too heartsick to make love the night before, and that this was sort of a rare occurrence for me.

"It's pretty," he grunted, and I tried to keep my glare in place. He could be really adorable when he was pissed off.

"There's something weird about your touch…" I mumbled, suddenly ramping at a thousand miles an hour. I'm a fast starter, I'll admit it, but his hand, on the skin covered with those stars… it was like I could *feel* how he felt about me on my skin. There's some part of touch that's always elemental—a touch is a touch. It's why some people end up having affairs with people they hate—the person's touch is skillful and the results *feel* so good that the body gets fooled into thinking the heart's involved.

This was like the exact opposite. It was *Bracken's* touch that was making me hot. Like I could feel his soul through his skin.

"Wait a second…" I muttered, before my eyes closed and my knees buckled and I came right there from the feel of Bracken's love on the front of my shoulder. "Nicky…dude… touch that spot."

Nicky's touch was good…whoo boy, was it good. But it wasn't Bracken's. It was… it was a high school boyfriend's touch, or a good movie buddy. It was how we'd always felt about each other, and circumstances had forced more. The more was nice, but it wasn't vital and overwhelming, like Bracken's touch was, and like I suspected Green's touch would be.

"Okay, okay… hey… someone go get Max or Mario or La Mark…"

"Why?" Bracken asked, using his hip to muscle Nicky out of the way and touch that spot in fascination again.

"Because I want someone who doesn't feel that way about me to touch me… I want to see what it feels like…" With an effort I backed up and broke away from Bracken, who blinked at me with slow, dreamy shadow-colored eyes and a smile that made me wet all over again. Oh yeah—we had some unfinished business. We *always* had unfinished business, and my smile must have been dreamy as well.

We didn't even notice that Nicky had left the room until he came back, practically hopping up and down to see what the little experiment would turn up. He had the entire camp at his heels, and the look I shot him was eloquent.

"What—you couldn't go across the lake and get some stray hikers to feel me up?"

He grinned unrepentantly at me as the room filled up. "We'll leave to let you have your thing with Bracken in a minute—I just want to see what this is, because right now, it's looking hella cool."

And it was. Mario's touch felt like a bird's—sweet, but asexual. Max's touch felt like a gun—but I was comfortable with guns, so it was reassuring. Renny's touch felt like her whiskers and a cold feline nose. She rubbed the spot with her thumb and it felt like her tongue, when she'd tried to exfoliate my shins with it. Katy's touch felt like a silk scarf, and Jacky's… I frowned. Jack's felt like wolf fur, or a cold, wet canine nose. I looked at him carefully—I'd been expecting teeth. In fact, I was half-braced for some sort of pain.

"You like me?" I asked baldly, and he flushed.

"You've grown on me," he said neutrally. "You keep keeping him alive, I might even love you like he does someday."

I smiled so hard my eyes watered, and I don't think he was prepared for the hug I launched at him. Oh *Goddess,* it felt good.

"You've hated me for months," I sniffled, "and you didn't have to like me, you know, but it *hurt.*"

"Oh Jesus," he muttered, his narrow face crumpled in embarrassment, "I'm sorry. I… I was just… you know. I wanted me and Katy to be all he needed…"

Teague came walking in at that moment, still drying off from his prolonged swim and curious as to why our room was bursting with people.

"All who needed? he grunted, and Katy twined her arm around his waist.

"We're all touching Cory's mystery spot, *pappi.* The boy gave it to her— seems he wasn't so much a civilian after all."

Teague scowled when he saw the handprint of stars on my shoulder. "He put his hand on you? When in the hell did that happen?"

I winked at him, trying to get him to put his back down. "When you were on the other side of the lake—I think it was for protection. It's... it's sort of helping to sort out the chaos right now, you know?"

"Well, that would fit right in with who he is," Nicky said thoughtfully, and then I had to explain to everybody who the kid was again.

The whole time, Teague was looking at me with a wrinkle between his eyes and his pouty lower lip thrust forward. "Let me touch it, will ya?"

I wasn't sure if that was such a good idea—but I certainly wasn't going to say that now that Jacky didn't hate my guts anymore, either.

Teague's skin was rough and chill from the swim, but that's not what I felt against the star handprint. What I felt on the little place of magic was... touch. It was a father's touch, or a brother's or an uncle's, and there was love—so much love. But it wasn't sexual love, not even a little. He thought I was beautiful—sexy even—but... I had an old fashioned vision, Teague, in a frock coat, asking me in a Scarlett O'Hara dress to dance. My suitors were waiting behind me, and I couldn't wait to get back to them, but this man was a guardian and a family friend, and I loved him too.

I wrinkled my mouth. "You're too complex to describe," I said thoughtfully. But he wasn't going to make me come in my pants as he stood—not the way Bracken almost did, and that was a great relief to both of us, I'm sure. "It's like my Dad, dressing a wounded knee." It was the best analogy I could think of, and it seemed to please Teague immensely, because he bowed slightly and backed away, leaving the room full of innocent speculation about the nature of the thing itself.

It wasn't until later that I realized that the most reassuring thing about the exchange was that I hadn't seen a wolf at all. Teague's wolf was reserved for Teague's mates—and that's exactly as it should be.

"It's a chaos filter," I said after a moment, when the 'ooh' factor had worn off and nobody knew what to say but they all wanted to check out this new anomaly I was cursed with anyway. "I think that's what it does... it takes away all the... extraneous, weird-making shit about other people, and you see exactly who they are to you."

"So," Katy said thoughtfully, "it's like, you know who wants you for you and who just fucks anything that moves, right?"

"Right," I muttered, a little taken back by the analogy. Katy blushed, and I remembered her past and felt like a moron, but somebody else spoke up.

"Or," Bracken said with emphasis, "it might tell you who's being motivated by how they really feel, or who's being motivated by whatever that big-titted human bitch is carrying around inside of her."

I grinned at Bracken, none of my desire for his skin on mine dissipated. "Yahtzee!" I cried, putting my finger on my nose and pointing at him with the other hand. "That's why he did it!" I was excited now, jumping up and down and looking at everybody.

"Don't you see? He said he wanted to help me, and then he followed his 'chaos tingle'—this was the one way his power worked!"

"Awesome," Max said dryly. "But I'd like it better if it made her explode as we drove away."

"If she's going to explode," Mario added with some deep disgust, "I'd rather she do it where we can watch!"

And that made us all laugh, and people left to go find whatever they had planned that morning—some of them were going across the lake to hike the caves, some of them were going out on the boat, and Bracken and I were going to touch and touch and touch, because our smoky, painful desire for each other had only grown more intense as he'd had to watch every man in our little group come up and touch my bared skin.

Nicky filed out discreetly with the rest of the crowd, murmuring that he'd be back in an hour.

He was back in two, and we were barely done.

And after that, it was barely twelve o'clock, and it was too late for Bracken to hike, and we had nothing to do.

I understand that some people live for this—the ability to hang out quietly for days on end. And maybe if I had a zillion kids and a full time job and a house that *wasn't* self-cleaning, I might appreciate another day with nothing to do, but as it was, in the summer, my life was in a pretty sweet balance between a side job I loved and responsibilities that challenged me, and enough leisure time with the people I loved to balance the whole rest of my life.

I missed my job, I missed my home, and I missed my Green.

Right now, I missed something to do. I wasn't used to being bored—it made me itchy.

"I can't even go to the yarn stores like I'd planned," I grumbled to Bracken, pulling the sheet up to my breasts as he dressed. They'd been on my to-do list, but we'd left the preternatural community so rattled, I didn't even want to try to walk down the streets of this alien city for no reason at all except yarn. What really sucked was that my itchy, unfocussed dissatisfaction with what we'd done last night might have been assuaged—or at lease less onerous—with some honest work. Right now, my mind was too pumped up with shit I didn't want to think about to even read.

"I wouldn't even mind going to the outlet stores with Renny and Katy to shop," I said at last, admiring his fine, long, hairless body, even in a wife-beater and pair of cut-offs, "but that's probably not such a good idea either."

Bracken nodded wanly—now that we were no longer making love, his skin had grown clammy and I'd seen the fine tremors in his hands even as he put on his clothes.

I sighed and flopped backwards, looking at my pale, heat-exhausted beloved who smiled back and stroked my cheek in sympathy. He really couldn't be out in the heat—even in the air-conditioned car, taking him that far from the lake would be a cruelty.

"You want to go swimming?" I asked gamely, and Bracken's limpid gaze of sheer gratitude was enough to get me in the water. His gentle nagging was enough to get me far out into the depths and back without my heart bursting from panic.

But we couldn't stay in the cool forever—not even a T-shirt and SPF rating of 'Flannel Shirt' was enough to keep me from burning after too long in that brutal sun. Eventually we came back to find that Renny and Katy had taken over our cabin—and, apparently, bribed our little flitting buddies to bring some more yarn from home.

The table and chairs by the bed looked like a wool&dyeworks had gone out of business and exploded over our stuff, and as Bracken crashed on the bed to recover from the scant walk from the lake to the cabin, I went and showered and came back out to chat and knit. We managed to set my laptop up with a dvd of *The Princess Bride* and sat and chattered and knit and quoted the movie until late afternoon, and it was perfect. Their funny, sarcastic chatter—and our helpless devotion to the silly, sentimental, lovely movie—turned out to be like diaper ointment for my chafing mental ass. I spent a few hours in peace, with no emotional demands whatsoever, and I felt like I could breathe again.

We didn't know what Mrs. Kestrel and Annette were doing, and we didn't care.

In fact, we could have been perfectly content to do that up until the evening when we all would meet for dinner, but the sound of a strange—and large and powerful—car crunching up the gravel of the cabin driveway interrupted our next movie (*The Italian Job*) and we set down our knitting and wandered outside to see who it was.

It was a stretch limo—no shit. The back was so completely blacked out, and so completely dark, that there was a limited number of people who would actually want to ride in it, and all of them had been dead for quite a bit.

But the identity of the occupant was sealed by the identity of the driver. He was medium height, brown hair, blue eyes, average looking and slicker than lube on a chrome anal probe. He looked like a lawyer because he was one, and he didn't look anything like the alpha werewolf of San Francisco because he looked exactly like a lawyer.

"Orson!" I said in surprise, and he flashed me a grin heavy on canines, and got out of the car, wilting like an old cabbage in the heat. My heart started pounding in my chest like a kid who got called by the teacher for fighting in class, and I had no balance at all to order it down.

"Lady Cory," he said with a bow, brushing his khakis straight like someone used to wearing a suit.

"Holy Goddess, Orson—what in the hell is Andres doing here?" I was dismayed and embarrassed—but judging by Nicky's delight and Bracken's dreamy-eyed speculation, I was the only one.

BRACKEN

Wants and Needs

Andres was the last man I'd kissed on the mouth.

Before my bonding with Cory—which I wouldn't take back, even if I could—I had (in Cory's words) slept with anything that moved, male, female, or anything in between.

I'd enjoyed men in my bed, and Andres had been a particularly aggressive lover—a thing a person wouldn't know lurked underneath his urbane exterior.

It was a thing Cory knew.

One blood exchange, one frenzied kiss, and Cory and I had been left hanging with that chapter of our lives unexplored. Judging by the expression on her face, she was not nearly as excited as I was to have that book re-opened.

"So," she said, her forehead wrinkled and an unexpectedly wounded look in her murky eyes, "why are you here? Did, uhm," she swallowed, "did Green send for you?"

Orson's eyes widened—he was obviously surprised. "No, Little Goddess—this was, in fact, Rafael's idea. He… he seemed to feel as though a neutral party here to enforce your ruling would make it easier for people to obey.

"In other words, he thought Andres presence might stop an all out war," I said thoughtfully, and Cory's eyebrows went up.

"Dammit—that's not fair! One guy. One gnarly pedophile—that's all we want. Does this really have to be an international incident?" The pleasant, happy glow that had brightened her pretty-plain features when we'd been alone together dimmed abruptly. Her freckled forehead seemed to have developed a permanent scrunch, and her full lips were pulled in and pursed.

It hit me then, how much pressure she had put on herself—and how uncertain she was that our actions the night before were the right ones.

"We couldn't have let them live," I muttered quietly, and if anything, her expression hardened to galvanized steel.

"I know that," she muttered. "I know it."

Orson was the alpha of the San Francisco area because he was known for being ruthless in the boardroom—a shark of a businessman, yes, but not a gladiator who shed actual blood. So he was almost scintillated when he said, "Okay, I give, who'd you kill?"

"Rafael's enforcer," she grumbled. "And the ..." her face worked, and she turned and spat, having no words for this particular person, "who attacked Green."

"*Punta,*" Katy said from behind us. "Sometimes it just sounds nastier when you say it in Spanish."

Cory turned around and grinned at her friend over her shoulder. I had heard the three of them, chattering as they'd knit and I'd napped. It had been comforting, like the constant sounds of people in and out at home. It was too quiet here—beyond the occasional ocean sound of the distant cars on the causeway, there wasn't even any breeze to stir the pine trees overhead. Even the boats out on the water had a void, echoing, alien sound.

Her look at Katy was almost nostalgic for the familial comfort, and my heart ached—all of that quiet, and there was still something weighing terribly on her. Even in this godless heat, I could see the waves of tension that had begun their slow burn from her body as Orson pulled up.

Her grin stretched tautly over her cheeks and she tried for courtesy over her worry. "Well, Orson—you're in luck. The last cabin on the end..."

"The one with the reverse paint job?"

Her grin relaxed a fraction. "Yeah, that's the one. That one opened up this morning. Let me talk to Tanya, and we'll see if we can get it fixed up for you."

Orson nodded gratefully. "Here—let me park this monster in the shade, and then..." he looked around furtively. "Lady, who else is here?"

And that grin cranked tight a few notches more. "Most of the cabins are filled with family," she said meaningfully. "The one that isn't has people who know about family—but be careful. They're Nicky's parents and a guest. The parents don't really approve of us... and the guest..."

"Is an evil bitch who wants to fuck us over," Renny supplied—probably so Cory didn't have to use her diplomacy up on a person we all disliked so intensely.

Orson remembered Renny—we could tell by the way he raised his eyebrows and nodded. There was something indulgent in that nod—it was like a big bull-mastiff watching a kitten struggle up the stairs to greet it. Lots of people had a soft spot for Renny.

"Good," the young lawyer said. "I'd *really* love to get furry and go swimming in that lake!"

He went to move the car, and Cory turned to Katy. "Darlin'—where's your mates?"

Katy tilted her head and made an "ooooohhh…" sound. She knew exactly why the question. "I think they're on a dog run around the lake—I'll go find them and warn them, right?"

Cory nodded. "Make sure they know that Orson's not a threat—and physically, he's not really a fighter. I think Teague could take him in a hot second, so that means…" She trailed off and let Katy fill in the blanks.

"That means there's no need to fight—I gotchu, Lady Cory. Damned werewolves," she pronounced it 'woofs', "always trying to prove whose teeth is sharpest and whose dick is biggest."

Katy trotted off, black hair shiny and blue in the hard sun, and Cory and I both looked at each other with chagrin at an embarrassing memory when we'd seen more of her mates than anybody had wanted. "Teague's," Cory muttered. "Teague's is biggest."

In spite of the discomfort, I had to grin. By human criteria, Cory was probably right. "Very probably," I told her, just to watch her blush, "but let's go tell Tanya we've got some more guests."

Tanya, as it turned out, knew, and after we'd left Orson with the key and helped him take his luggage in, I grabbed Cory's hand and steered her towards the lake so we could walk in the shallows and talk.

"Spill," I ordered, as she tread out to where the water was at her ankles and let her foot bob up with her floatable shoe.

"Spill what?" She cast me an oblique look from under her brow, and adjusted her visor so I couldn't see her eyes. I knew that look and I knew why she was masking her expression and I didn't give a royal fuck if she didn't want to talk about her feelings. We had too much going on and too much at stake for her bottle up that considerable passion now.

"Why are you so upset that Andres is here. You *like* Andres—we both do!"

It was hard to see her flush, not in the heat, not when her skin was getting a rather bright pink patina as it was, but I could hear her heartbeat speed up and I knew. I admit—I felt a little disappointment. I had hoped...after that kiss...

But she had never asked for this. She had never asked for three possessive lovers, three people who depended so heavily on her that her tiniest flaw felt as though it could topple our whole kingdom.

"One more lover would be difficult," I said softly, wading out to where the water was at my knees and the look she sent me was so grateful, so shining, that I thought it was worth it. I could give up the dream of Andres, if it meant she could look at me as though I were her hero.

"I thought," she said softly, "at first, when Orson got out of the car, that Green asked him to come." Her voice grew thick, and she looked almost directly at the sun, so she could blame her watery eyes on that. "I thought, you know, that we...that I couldn't do this. That I'd fucked up too badly for this to work. And for a minute," she smiled and wiped her cheek, and then walked out a little further into the water so she could splash it up on her arms and on her face.

"For a minute?" I prompted, and she shrugged, and kept laving water on her freckled flesh.

"For a minute, I was really glad. I..." her mouth twisted, and she looked at me eyes-on. "I don't regret what we did last night, not even a little. I feel absolutely no pity, no remorse, no nothing—they fucked with Green and I'd kill them again. I'd kill them, bring them back from the dead and fucking kill them twice, and I'd do the same for anyone who fucked with any of us. But the scary thing is, I *can* do that. And, you know, a gun can blame the guy who pulls the trigger, but the guy who pulls the trigger needs to know how to use the fucking gun."

Ah... ah gods. This is when she needed Green. I simply followed where she led. I had one answer to this problem, and it was what moved moved towards her through the water, pulled her face into the shade of my shoulder, and gave her my body as protection from her own self-doubt.

"You are not a gun. You are a girl—a young one—and you're leading us to safety. Everyone fucks up. Everyone feels things they'd rather not!"

"People hate their in-laws and feel guilty, Bracken," Cory said against my shirt. "They usually don't kill and feel a moral victory."

I ran my hands from her shoulders, down her back, to her bottom again, feeling the soft cotton of my own T-shirt under my hands, and the firm flesh of her strong, runner's body under the shirt. Her wide hips were definitely narrower than they had been a week ago. "They don't usually save people's lives with their touch, either," I told her. These were things she knew. How is it that never matters, when our hearts are tied to the rack of our conscience?

She tilted her face up, the shade of her visor keeping her freckles from standing out in stark relief. She'd spent the morning out in the lake, just for me. Goddess, she was beautiful—how could the world not see that she was brighter than the fierce sun on our backs, and stronger than the red earth at our feet?

"How can you love me?" she asked seriously. "I'm not a nice person."

I laughed a little, and tracked her cheekbone with my thumb. "*I* am a dreadful person," I told her seriously. "I am selfish. I am self-centered. I am violent. I am possessive. And I would rather fuck you blind and into the mattress on any given day as opposed to apply myself to politics the way you do. But you continue to love me. Sometimes you should just accept things as they are given to you—there can be no changing them. It's like the fucking godsforsaken heat in this godless brick-oven nightmare of a soup-bowl. It's just a force of nature and you find a way to live with it."

She was laughing, honestly laughing, by the time I was done, and I felt as though I had won something tremendous, like a lifetime of free movies or a potpourri box of her favorite sock yarn.

"You *are* a force of nature," she said softly. "I'm so grateful to be in your damage path."

I kissed her then, in the sun and the water, standing on the earth, and I felt the power of that mark on her shoulder throb through us both, as it had been doing when I was inside her.

"Two things," I said, as I pulled back from the kiss.

"Mmm?"

"One, let's get out of the sun, or you're going to look like broiled lobster—and I think you should stay inside the cabin until the sun goes down too."

She started immediately towards the front, telling me that she'd been as uncomfortable as I was, but willing to bear it for me.

"And the second?" she asked.

"I think you should make love to Nicky as soon as possible—that mark on your shoulder is catching."

She giggled a little. "Sex as inoculation—brilliant! I'm sure Nicky would love to bend over and take his shots!"

I shook my head at the unlikely image. "Unfortunately, neither of us can give him *that* sort of injection," I muttered, and she looked at me with enough astuteness to make me squirm.

"You could—but you two…"

I shrugged. "We don't really click like that. Maybe, someday, but for now…mostly, our relationship revolves around you, and Green, and the hill."

"mmmm…" It was a quiet sound—speculative, wondering, and I was about to ask her what she was thinking when we rounded the corner up to the string of cabins and ran smack dab into Terry and Annette.

I would have just ignored them, but Cory nodded her head and gave a neutral, "Afternoon," as a greeting.

The women regarded her icily, without even a greeting, and Cory looked at me sideways and smirked.

And then we felt it—a clumsy push of will, like a toddler's attempt to push an older sibling in a wrestling match. We looked at each other, and Cory rubbed her shoulder—which was undoubtedly tingling—and before Cory could react I'd grabbed Annette by the armpits and shoved up against the door to Tanya's office, oblivious to Terry's startled shriek.

"Is that all you've got?" I growled contemptuously. "You let yourself be assfucked in the woods by a child for *that?*"

"I...I... I don't know what you're talking about..."

The dawning horror on Terry Kestrel's face should have told her that it wasn't a very convincing lie.

"What did you hope to do with that?" Cory asked, coming up to peer under my arms into the tanned woman's face. From this close, her make-up was obvious and running with sweat. I could smell the hairspray on her blonde hair, and the chemicals used to make it blonde, and I could smell the corruption of magic coursing sluggishly through her veins.

"You murdering slut..." Annette spat. "Now I've got tricks too!"

Cory and I met incredulous glances, and Cory looked over her shoulder at Terry. Terry was looking decidedly embarrassed—and she should be. She'd thrown in her lot with this person—she'd chosen her loyalty for this... this...

"Yes, Annette," Cory said calmly. "You molested a child and now you have his magic power. Aren't you proud of yourself? And you want to know the fun part? The *really* fun part?" Her voice was wicked and evil, and I remembered our conversation. We weren't always good people—and sometimes, that was a whole lot of unholy fun.

"The fun part," Cory continued, "is that the kid gave us a defense for his power—and I didn't even have to get on my hands and knees for it. I just had to be human. The next time you call me a 'murdering slut', remember that I'm *still* more human than you are."

"That little bastard..." Annette growled, and I remembered the look and the boy's face when she'd turned on him the night before. I shook her—hard—until her head smacked against the door to Tanya's office. Tanya came out from her little stool and counter and peered through the window at us. When she saw Annette's feet kicking against the door, she nodded, gave me the 'thumbs up' and went back to her business.

"Would you like to know what my magic power is?" I asked, feeling really evil. I gave a pull—just a little one—and watched blood gush out of her nose and onto her bright white shirt and matching tan shorts.

Annette screamed and I dropped her, bleeding into the dust. Cory was grimacing and pinching the bridge of her nose, and I shrugged. *I'd* had fun.

Cory crouched into the dust then, and put her finger on Annette's forehead so as not to expose herself to the blood. I didn't blame her—humans carried diseases in their blood that Cory could catch.

"What's your endgame, Annette?" Cory asked gently. "Think about that, the next time you take that evil little tingle and go shoving it at someone. What's your final product? You want Nicky? I'd say 'over my dead body', but he'd still hate you, and all that effort would be for shit. You want me dead? Just remember, I could have killed you personally more than once—you come at me with intent, and I won't hold back. You want to kill someone else here, just to be a fucking bitch? Well, even if you did succeed—there is not a person in my family who wouldn't kill to avenge someone else here. Not one. It's not a 'Sweet Annette vs. the evil bitch alone' scenario, darlin'—you take on one of us, and the rest of us will take you back. There is not one of us who hasn't killed, sweetheart. Not one."

Cory nodded, and pushed at her finger on Annette's forehead to make the woman's head bob. Annette was still cupping her nose, although the blood had stopped and was now getting sticky on her hands and clothes.

"You understand me, don't you?" And they nodded, because Cory said they should.

Annette's pretty blue eyes (it was a contact—I'd seen it up close) were so bright with hatred that they were almost supernaturally glowing, but Cory's grim, flat stare kept that unfocused fury dimmed. Annette had no choice but to submit when they were face to face. Now everyone knew it.

Cory dropped her hand and stood to look Terry Kestrel in the eyes.

"You should get your visiting done with Nicky, Mrs. Kestrel—we have business tomorrow night, and after that, we're leaving."

"But you said we'd have another week..." Terry looked truly surprised, but I wasn't. I'd seen this weighing on Cory's shoulders for most of the afternoon.

Cory shrugged. "We're not doing anything productive here, and we," she jerked her chin to indicate all of our people, "have lives waiting for us back home. Once we're done policing the vampires, I'll have Green set you and your husband up with a ticket home, and we'll give you two a ride to the airport."

"But Annette..." Terry's voice trailed off before she could finish that thought and Cory didn't even spare a shrug to justify the question. No, we would not be paying the girl's fare or giving her a ride to the airport. It was not going to happen.

Cory continued as though Terry hadn't spoken. "Green will buy you the car of your choice when you get home—sky's the limit. Feel free to take advantage of his hospitality in this matter just as you have here. I'm sorry for the inconvenience."

And with that she grabbed my hand and pulled me away from them, Terry Kestrel standing open mouthed, staring after us, and Annette weeping and bleeding in the dust at her feet.

It wasn't over—Cory knew it, I knew it—the girl wouldn't be ready to stop until someone was dead.

We just had no doubt as to whom it would be.

CORY

Queen's Gifts

We were sitting at dinner when the vampires awakened, and Andres was at my elbow before I even had time to feel nervous, and then I couldn't feel nervous because, well, he was Andres.

Andres is beautiful. He started out beautiful—a Roman nose, limpid, sloe brown eyes, curly blue-black hair, skin the color of a latte, lots of steamed milk—then that vampire thing kicked in and he took all of that natural human beauty and amped it up a few thousand notches, and he was pretty much a wood-erecting-panty-wetter on anybody's block party.

He could also charm the rattles off a snake, and Goddess knows why, he had a hard spot for me, and very likely a soft spot for Bracken.

And did I mention the charm? Yeah. It bears repeating.

"Good evening, Little Goddess," he said sweetly, almost magically there in my ear, and I squealed and hugged him without thinking. Andres had been a good friend when I'd needed one, and had given up what would have probably been a spectacular evening in bed in favor of letting Bracken and I find our own balance together—and he'd been one of the willing bodies to give me strength and save my life when I was close enough to death to drag Green, Bracken, *and* Nicky down with me.

All in all a good guy to have at your back—even if I wasn't going to sleep with him, the squeal and the hug were the least I could do.

"Heya Andres!" I'd been in the middle of eating—some sort of braised meat and vegetables prepared so fancy I didn't have a name. You could tell

Grace was missing the lot of us because dinner just kept getting more and more impressive and hard to pronounce.

"Here, don't let me keep you from dining," he said suavely. He barely had to tap Nicky on the shoulder before Nicky scooted down the picnic bench so Andres could straddle the seat facing me.

And there I was, sandwiched between my beloved Bracken, man-god extraordinaire, and Andres, any girl's dream of sex, blood, and bisexuality. My body lit up like a lightning storm on a mountain, and I wondered if the entire table could smell my arousal. Nicky snickered for no reason whatsoever—I figured he could, at the very least.

"You're looking damned good, Andres," I said, figuring honesty was my strength as nothing else was. "But I have to say—I was surprised to see Orson drive up." I took a bite of meat and chewed, inviting a detailed reply. Andres—who knew more about manners and nuance than I would live to see—took his cue.

"Rafael's doing, not yours," Andres assured me quickly. He could have been lying, but the words still eased something sore. "He was a little… frightened, I think, after your last visit."

"He was pissing in his girl-panties," Kyle snorted, and I looked up, surprised. I hadn't realized my guys were at the table yet—and then I realized they weren't, it was only Andres and Kyle. A quick mental query and then I was blushing—okay, I guess I could brief Marcus and Phillip about Annette's freaky power sometime later. Anything, anything, to give Phillip a little bit of peace.

Andres smiled slightly at Kyle and nodded in acknowledgement. "That he was, Little Goddess—I don't know what sort of theatre you and Bracken were aiming for, but you lot pulled off 'stone-cold-killer' to a 'T'."

I swallowed—hard and painfully—and took a sip of the ice tea at my plate. "It wasn't theatre, Andres," I said softly, meeting his eyes so he would know me. "Rafael's people ambushed Green, trying to get us to leave it alone. Did he tell you what we want?"

Andres shook his head. "No—all I heard before dawn hit was that Rafael needed to fulfill his duty to you, and parts of his kiss wanted to stop him."

I nodded—it sounded sufficiently diplomatic, and completely the truth. It was also so much an understatement as to be a complete lie.

"A pedophile, Andres. There is someone in his kiss that turns little kids into vampires in the worst fucking way—and just deserts them. Leaves them to slaughter their families."

Andres' eyes were wide, and his skin was taut against his high cheekbones. "Holy Goddess," he muttered, and then spat over his shoulder. The background chatter of us at the table had disappeared as we all recalled *exactly* why we were there. "You know this how?" he asked, upset.

"We have one of the children—she survived—hell, she was converting wildlife when we found her. She's..." I met Kyle's eyes. It wasn't pretty—there was a reason Marcus had Phillip off on a corner of the woods and was fucking him silly right now, and it had very little to do with sex and an awful lot to do with actual healing. "She's not doing well," I finished lamely.

Andres put a hand on my shoulder and I covered it with my own. "You know where this is probably going," he said softly.

I looked at Bracken, who raised his eyebrows and pursed his lips softly. We knew. We had always known how this might end up, but it had been worth the chance to not have to do it cold-bloodedly, while she looked at us with some hope for salvation.

"Yeah," I said, sounding tired even to myself. "We know."

Andres nodded a couple of times and squeezed my shoulder. "So, you traced the pedophile to Redding, and came and asked Rafael for him, and..."

"And the next night they took a shot at Green. Except I was in his head and I saw who did it, and her buddy gave himself away when we walked in, and I took them out."

"We," Bracken said mildly. "We took them out."

I flashed him a supremely grateful look. "We. We took them out."

Andres grinned, and I could feel his eyes collide and connect with Bracken's over my shoulder, and I warmed to the sweep of Bracken's heat as it flushed across his skin. Suddenly what my lover wanted seemed ever so much more important than what I wanted, and I had a desperate need to talk to Andres alone.

"And that's when Rafael called me—interesting, you know. He extended his hospitality to me for the dawn."

I raised my eyebrows. "And you came here first..."

He nodded and extended a fang. "I thought it would be... politic, for me to strengthen my bond with Green's people first. And, of course, to blood with my Queen."

Oh shit. I dropped my fork, and my stomach roiled with such ferocity I thought I might throw up right there and then. Blood with me? He'd bitten me before—yes. And it had been *spectacular,* but for me to take his blood in return? It would make him... well, mine. As it was, we were bound by his honor, but once we'd blooded... well, theoretically, I would have the same control over Andres that Phillip had held over Gretchen. Andres was more than a hundred and seventy years old—he was a leader of his entire kiss, and they were bigger than mine.

"Andres..." I muttered, and took a hasty gulp of my tea because my voice sounded like an engine with sand in the oil tank. "Andres? Seriously, what in the hell?"

"You. My queen. Basically the queen of every vampire in the northern half of the state. You're not stupid Lady Cory, and you heard me right. It's something I would have done a year and a half ago, if I'd thought you were up to it at the time."

He had a little half smile on his face as he said it, and all I could do was shake my head at him. "Why? Why would you do that?"

He shrugged, such an elegant, insouciant gesture, I suddenly heard Shakespeare in my head... *to throw away the dearest thing he owned as though it were a careless trifle...*

"You love being a leader..." I finished weakly.

"I love being a leader of *my* people," he said softly. "My little family, in my little corner of the earth. What you did here—come up to police our kind—I have no wish to do that. And yet that is exactly what you did. You didn't ask for my help—which would hurt me dearly if I didn't know how important it was to you to do your job well—and you've shown no weakness. If I didn't know any better, Little Goddess, I'd swear you had fangs."

"I'm mortal..." I rasped. "You will be alive long after I'm gone—what will happen then?"

Andres shrugged again, and this time even I could see the age and the melancholy in it. "I happen to believe as Green—I have great faith such a thing will not come to pass. And if it does, then we will deal with it when it does. Life is uncertain—even for the deathless, my lady. What is some uncertainty about the future, when there is the possibility of peace?"

"So you want to bite me tonight?" My voice hit dog-whistle pitch on the last syllable. For the unholy love of gilded crap—how could we... and the bite! The thought of the bite made me shudder sensually, when that was the last desire on my mind. Oh Goddess, was my mind screwed on crooked—here we were, talking about a job I would hold for my entire *lifetime,* and the first thing I could think of was the sexual intensity of Andres' bite. My skin felt like I was spilling spirit out the top, bubbling over with sexual saturation.

"Tonight?" It didn't come out any easier this time.

"It would be logical," Andres said with mild amusement. I looked at Bracken, but if he'd been a cat, his mouth would have been half open and he would have been tasting the possibilities on a savoring tongue—he didn't sense my panic or my dismay, the smug bastard, all he was thinking about was getting...

Oh Goddess. I remembered his excitement when we'd seen Marcus and

Phillip—I knew exactly what he was thinking about getting, and... and he gave me so much. How could I deny him this?

"Why logical?" I swallowed, stalling for time. I looked around the table, trying to find a reason not to do this, and all I saw was the usual claustrophobic ring of faces, staring back at me with unabashed interest. Even Kyle and Teague, who had been shy of the sort of kindred theatre that was performed so often at the hill were watching me avidly, to see if I was going to get the ultra-super-special-get-down-and-dirty tonight, and I didn't have the ground to stand on to so much as stick my tongue out at them and tell them to mind their own business. I was their queen, and, fuck-it-all, I guess I *was* their business.

"In all likelihood I'm going into a trap tonight—but I doubt a fatal one."

I blinked. I had to admit, the thought had occurred to me, but I'd assumed Andres had a contingency plan. I just hadn't realized I was it!

"I'm the best you can do?" I had to ask it. "You've been the king of San Francisco for a hundred years, and a college student on sorcery-steroids is your back-up? Come *on* Andres—I *know* you've got better hoo-doo up your sleeve than *me!*"

Andres didn't even chuckle. He simply put a steadying finger under my chin and tilted my head up to meet his gaze. "You and your people," he said softly, "are better than *anything* I could have planned. Look at them." We both looked at the avid, fierce faces around us. "Kill or die, my lady. They would kill or die for you—and you for them, I don't have a single doubt. You have *no* idea how formidable and terrifying that makes you. And I have every trust in you—you will not abuse them. You would sooner... sleep with that big-titted human bitch who screamed and ran away when I walked down here than violate their faith. And if you go rogue..."

Oh Goddess... okay. I could buy into this. "You'll stop me?" I asked hopefully. He laughed and shook his head. "Not possible. I was going to say, if you go rogue, damned if I don't eat my own tongue!"

I felt ill again, and scrubbed my face with my hand. I looked at Bracken, but he was still in I'm-gonna-get-laid-land, and he wasn't really picking up on my I'm-not-worthy vibe. I had to laugh, but at the same time, I felt so adrift... I was so used to him, being there, being in tune with me an...

It's a logical step, beloved.

Oh, thank the Goddess. Green was here.

I don't think I'm ready, Green—it would make me his boss and I'm feeling like my pants are too damned big as it is.

All the better to fit another lover in, you think?

NO!

Well then, why not blood with him—he's offering you unlimited back up, and a pretty decent guarantee that the next time you try to police your kiss, a master vampire will give up his own mother rather than piss you off!

This conversation was starting to piss me off as it was—dammit, did nobody see that I was not all that? Annette had just called me...

If you complete that thought I will drive up in that appalling heat and spank you myself. And there was no arguing with that beloved, infuriating, calm voice of reason in my head, so my next thought was as far from reason as I ever got.

I'm a baby! I don't want to be in charge of him!

The next sound in my head was hard to translate, and I have no idea what my expression was, but suddenly the weird attention of every person at the table shifted to an amused silence. Of all people, Teague broke the silence.

"What in the hell did he say to you?"

"I don't want to talk about it."

"Seriously, Mommy—whatever it was, you look like you swallowed a bug."

I looked at Katy and managed a blink and a sour smile. "It tasted worse." I turned to Andres. "Sir Vampire, my night vision sucks, but if you and Bracken want to steer, I bet Tanya would let us take out one of the flat-boats before you leave for Redding, you think?"

Nicky made an "ooooooh" face over Andres shoulder at me, and I could pretty much feel Bracken's full-body grin on my other side.

"Don't get all excited," I grumbled, "it's a boat ride. I need some fucking air."

"Well then," Bracken said, bright and undeterred, "maybe you should go change into something that will let you appreciate all that 'fucking air'."

I would have said 'Fuck me!', but I think he thought that was what was going to happen. Funny, actually, since I wasn't the one who was going to get nailed to the boat floor, but I didn't want to tell him that in front of Goddess and everybody and the goddamned picnic table, now did I? As it was, I stood and let Bracken drag me to our cabin where I was pretty sure he was going to make me wear that goddamned bikini.

Which he did. It turned out, there was a pretty cool fancy wrap that went over it. Awesome.

But as he was setting the wrap around my shoulders and fussing with my sun-streaked, curly nightmare hair, I took his hands in mine and told him to stop.

"I'm not doing this, beloved," I said softly. "I can't." I could taste the disappointment in the expression on his face, so I reached up and smoothed my thumb over that lean, chiseled, pouting mouth.

"But that doesn't mean you can't," I told him, cupping his cheek. In response he closed his eyes and leaned into my touch.

"I could spend eternity," he murmured, "with only your touch on my skin."

"I know you could." I held up my other hand, holding his face in my hands literally as I knew—I *knew*—without a doubt, without a question, that I held his heart figuratively. "I know you could—which is why you shouldn't have to. You deserve…everything, Bracken Brine. I would give you a thousand lovers if I could, just to have you look at me the way you do. I don't have to—I know it—but I would if I could. I can't—so the least I can do is give you Andres."

He bent and kissed me then, which is what I'd been craving because you never seem as close to a lover as you do when his mouth is hot on yours, and his hands are skimming your body. He pulled back, and without any more fussing grabbed a couple of towels and a spare blanket under one arm, then took my hand as we left the cabin.

"So," he asked, as we walked back down to the table to get Andres, "what did Green say?"

I grimaced. "I told him I was a baby and I couldn't handle Andres."

Bracken grunted. "That's a laugh."

Green's golden laughter—even more like church bells in my head than when it was actual sound waves in the air—still echoed in my cranium. "Yeah… that's sort of what he said too."

And now Bracken's laughter, straight from his belly and shaking his broad shoulders, rang through the night as well.

At least I'd made them happy, I guess.

Bracken went down to the water with Tanya to gas up the boat and fix up some lights on the prow—like I said, he didn't need them, but other boaters might want to know where we were. Odds were good we'd go to a secluded cove and 'park', and don't think *that* idea didn't make me wiggle like a worm on a hook, but all I could really think was that the sky was bright as a diamond razor overhead, and the blackness of the water as it reflected the stars was alien and lovely.

I *wanted* to go out on the boat. Everything that happened on it, well, I'd probably enjoy it, but mostly? I just wanted to be out with the pine-scented wind on my face, and Bracken by my side. The idea of it felt like freedom, felt like vampire flight above the dark world, felt like setting your burdens on the ground and soaring into the black velvet sky… oh *Goddess,* did I want to lay down some worries and fly.

Andres and I waited on the bank, and I took in his moonlit profile as the breeze ruffled his hair. He was so beautiful—and so not for me.

He grinned at me, appearing to be suddenly younger—I knew he'd been in his twenties when he turned, and it occurred to me that by the time I was ready to actually make love to this very pretty man, I would probably look too old for him, but I didn't think that would stop him one bit. And even if it would have, I don't think I could change where I was... where my *heart* was, at this very moment, and forcing it wouldn't do any of us any good.

"I can't," I said softly, and his brows lowered in puzzlement, even as he reached out and took my hand.

"Can't?" He stroked the soft space between my fingers with the pad of my thumb, and I caught my breath.

"The bite... I think I can do the blooding, Andres. I think I can—I mean, I have my doubts, but Green and Bracken..." I shook my head and looked out to where Bracken and his uber-confidence were making short work of attaching running lights to the outside of the boat. "They think I can do anything... and I keep surprising myself by living up to that, you know?"

Andres smiled kindly... ah, Goddess, that's what I remembered most about Andres. The sexiness—well, that seemed to dim, mostly so it could just assault me every time I looked at him again. But the kindness—just like in Green, it's what made the sexiness a deadly serious lethal quality that could level a girl at the knees. Or between them, I guess.

"I think you can do anything as well, Little Goddess—are you telling me I just caught you on a good day?"

I laughed shortly. The day Andres and I had met had been in the top five worst days of my life. It might even have been number three. Of course it was in the top three best days of my life as well.

"I think you caught me at an amazing time," I told him softly. "Everything—possibilities, my heart—seemed to be wide open—which is why I could catch the best and the worst of things, you know?"

Andres nodded, and put his arm platonically around my shoulders—I think he knew where I was going with this. "I do know, Corinne Carol-Anne. And now?"

I shrugged in the steel circle of his cool embrace. "Now...my heart is full, Andres. I know Bracken...he can...he can share his body with someone he merely likes, and that is all it is. Sharing his body. But me... Nicky and I love each other as friends. We like each other enough that making love is a pleasure and not a chore. And... I think that's as close as I can get to an affair, you know? I think..."

Oh Goddess... his eyes were so brown... and they were so hurt. I couldn't hurt this man. The very idea was horrible. But... all of the worries I was prepared to leave on the shore came back and settled on my chest, making my breaths shudder in and out of my chest. It was all so muddled...

In an act of desperation, I bared my shoulder and placed his hand on the mark there that I could still feel, but that you couldn't see in the dark.

His eyes went round, and his mouth made a little "ooh" and I had to catch my breath.

He wanted me. Purely and simply—he wanted my power and my flesh. He liked me—sincerely and without prejudice, and that alone was an incredible mindfuck—but he had admired me since that horrible night, when he saw me face down his enforcer, saw me kiss Bracken, make the two of us one, saw me save lives using desperation and a fading power.

"You could love me?" he said in surprise.

I flushed and looked away. Compared to how he felt about me, it sounded melodramatic and overwrought, but it was very nearly the truth.

"Not as much as Green, not as much as Bracken," he murmured softly, exploring the ideas even as he said them. "Not even close. But you could. And that would complicate things—and your feelings are complex beyond complex right now."

He shuddered, and I backed away and covered my shoulder nervously with the wrap again. Andres reached out and grasped my chin, looking me in the eyes.

"Don't look away, Little Goddess—I understand. More than you think— I've been balancing people in my bed and people under my rule for nearly a hundred years. Your heart is… full. Your life is full. There's no need to explore someone else's flesh, no matter how tempting. You are happy." His lips twisted in a smile so bittersweet it stung. "You are *very* happy with the people who love you. You would not upset that balance for all the potential in the world."

"But," I said softly, flushing at how accurately he had read me in that one touch, "a night in your flesh wouldn't upset Bracken's balance at all."

Andres smiled wickedly then and oh! *Goddess* did my switch flip. Not enough to change my mind—but those white teeth in that pretty light-chocolate skin…mmmmm…

"As I recall Bracken's preferences, I think I shall be spending the night in *his* flesh."

I laughed then, giddy with arousal and with Andres and with the thought of my lover, pleasured and cared for in a way I could not see to.

"Damn, brother if anyone was worth messing with my equilibrium here, I swear to the Goddess, it would be you."

Bracken jumped off the boat and onto the dock then, and gave us a wave. We walked down the embankment and over to the dock, holding hands like friends.

And oh, the wind in my face as we motored through the liquid dark was heaven. I leaned out over the side of the boat and watched the running lights in the velvet matte blackness of the water, feeling the humid air on my skin. The temp was down to a tolerable eighty-five degrees and the sliver of waning moon was bright. In a few days, it would start waxing again, and I was glad we wouldn't be here long enough to see it full. *I* wouldn't want to be obligated to turn furry in this foreign place—I would feel too vulnerable, too at the mercy of the other lycanthropes to spend my full moon comfortably. I certainly didn't want to saddle my friends with that burden.

But it was lovely here—especially on this night, with Bracken and Andres talking companionably in the center of the boat where Bracken was steering—even though I knew we all missed Green's with an aching pit in our stomachs.

It was my job to get us home.

I turned towards the men and smiled a little. Andres was standing, his hand on Bracken's shoulder as they leaned their heads together and spoke softly so I couldn't hear. They both looked out at me though, with enough heat that I flushed and looked away. In the lights from the tiny open-air cabin I could see that sweet-chocolate colored hand brush the bare whiteness of Bracken's neck, and I shivered. Blood pooled to the slippery flesh between my thighs, and the whole works grew swollen, achy, and hungry.

I wanted to see this. I wanted to see Bracken, at Andres' mercy, eyes glazed, body thundering in time to Andres' thrusts. I wanted to hold him as he came apart in my arms. Bracken, who was always my rock, the aggressor, the constant state of arousal or sexual empathy in my bed—I wanted to see him lose himself while being fucked into the floor.

It wasn't yet ten o'clock—there were still lanterns out in various places around the lake, where hardy campers had hiked or boated in. We chose an inlet far away from the lantern lights, covered by the tall trees, and smelling like green and red darkness. Bracken killed the motor and dropped the weight that served as an anchor, and then moved towards where I sat.

His body was warm as he pulled my knees on either side of him, leaving the thin crotch of my bikini the sole barrier between his hardened stomach and my sex, and he grinned unabashedly as I strained towards him.

"I know what you're thinking," he purred, and I flushed. Without any noise or any breeze even, Andres was sitting right next to me, stroking my face and pulling my hair back as I leaned forward and nuzzled Bracken's chest, left bare by his opened button-down shirt.

"I'm thinking that it's dark," I muttered, as Andres nuzzled below my ear, and traced my jaw line with his tongue, "which is prob...ab...ly... a good... ah crap..." because now he was nuzzling my ear proper, and all my guys knew that just totally did it for me, and...

"Oh, Jesus, Bracken..." He'd stripped off my bikini bottoms. "This wasn't supposed to... to...involve me...." Oh Goddess—not only was I mostly *naked* in front of both of them but, his fingers worked busily at his fly and he was... oh Goddess...

"You were thinking," Andres murmured as I tried to catch my breath, "that we would leave you out of the sex completely."

"So. Wrong." Bracken grunted, checking with his fingers to see if I was as swollen, wet, and ready as he suspected I was, and... and... Oh *Goddess*... He sheathed his body inside of mine quickly and carefully, and I let out a breathless shriek and took a deep breath and...and... it stuttered to a halt in my chest.

Andres had punctured his thumb with his own incisor, and he thrust it, dripping into my mouth. I closed my eyes and groaned, surrounded by the last memory he'd held onto as a human, the memory of him making love to a plain woman in an empty field, under the brutal South American sun. I saw her face—lovely and perfect in his eyes—and felt the slickness of her quim around my cock and... and...

"*Christ...*" because Bracken moved back, almost out and then thrust forward hard, once, and... and...

And Andres' mouth closed over my vein, his hot tongue tasted my skin, and his teeth, oh Goddess, his teeth...

A completely unexpected orgasm ripped through me, so potent and so powerful that I couldn't contain the sunshine scream streaming from my mouth.

I turned my head from Andres—the last sane thought I had!-- and poured that fire into the night, thinking sun-warmed wild-flowers, thinking hot, dusky skin and sex, not thinking at all as Bracken started to thrust inside me with all the force he would allow and Andress suckled from my neck with that potent, skin-buzzing euphoria that a vampire bite—especially *this* bite--could give.

Andres groaned then, grinding hard against my hip and I felt him shudder and spend, the wetness in his trousers seeping against my skin as Bracken kept thrusting, and I tried not to lose my fucking mind beneath him.

I failed.

Another orgasm shredded my nerve endings, and another, and another, until I lunged up and clenched Bracken to me, biting his shoulder in mindless howling pleasure. I tasted salt and then blood, and Bracken groaned--loud enough to shake the boat in the water--and came, triggering my final aftershock and leaving me, shaking, gasping, and trying to assimilate the complete sensual surprise of the last ten minutes.

We collapsed backwards, Bracken on top of me, facing Andres who was lapping at my neck to close the wounds. I could feel a trickle of blood running down my shoulder and Bracken stopped it before it got to the chaos-filter (because who knew what *that* would do!) and began to lick the rivulet across my collarbone and up to my neck.

His tongue tickled and titillated, and I was about to giggle when he stopped lapping like an enthusiastic kitten, and with a little turn of my head, I could see that he was licking up Andres' chin, and then into his mouth and then...

I came again, Bracken's body still clenched inside me, bucking to come alive for more, just when the two of them met mouths and kissed.

I gasped when Bracken's hips started to pound again, just as fast and just as furiously as they had before, and thought *No no no no no...Bracken was supposed to...*

But then Andres broke off the kiss, and as I looked up into Bracken's ultimate expression of arousal, something made his entire body *STOP,* and he stayed, cock inside me quivering, just *vibrating* with the need to move and the painful, come-shattering need to stay absofuckinglutely where he was.

He groaned, hard and painfully, into the hollow of my throat, and I risked a look over his shoulder.

I could barely see the top of Andres' head, moving rhythmically, doing something...something delicious and *dirty* to Bracken's backside... and Bracken was growling obscenities into my skin.

"Goddess..." he spat, and I laughed—I had to—my stone-and-shadow lover was so damned powerful, so titanic in breadth, and between Andres and his treacherous tongue and my slick, throbbing sex, Bracken was...

Helpless. Happy. At our mercy, and grateful for it. Beautiful in his submission. Oh Goddess...I shrieked a little and came around his cock again, and if anything it seemed to grow larger with the constriction of my body around its length and width.

He swore again, and Andres rose above his back, fingers busy between them, and I moaned, knowing what Andres was doing, and Bracken moaned and cried out because it was actually *happening* to him, and it was as dark and earthy and *good* as I remembered. Andres grunted, thrust, and sighed, and Bracken groaned *"Goddess!"* just as Andres started moving at vampire speed. There was a brutal, savage edge to Andres' pumping that made Bracken's eyes roll back and his head and his erection fist inside of me as he grunted more desire into the hollow of my ear.

I'd hoped that Bracken would get fucked into the ground—I hadn't planned on him getting fucked into *me... and oh holy shit and gods and goddesses...* it was so much better than I'd hoped.

Andres kept moving, thrusting, pounding, *fucking,* and Bracken cried mercy into my hair as I nuzzled his shoulder, his neck, his chest...but I couldn't

be gentle. I *couldn't* be gentle, and I found I was nipping, crying, scratching…
and he was howling, begging for more…and more…

And then he was coming again, shattering, undone by the twin assault of
me at his front and Andres at his backside and we were demanding everything
from him he could give.

But Andres was high, riding the sunshine of my bite, living the sex he had
been dreaming of for a year and a half, and he too was quivery and ready, an
open nerve, ready to explode, and he screamed shrilly as Bracken tightened
around him. Andres came too, plunging his teeth into Bracken's carotid for
form. Bracken roared and Andres took a vicious pull, his eyes whirling, every
line of his taut, brown body screaming sex and fulfillment as he collapsed on
top of Bracken, who had collapsed on top of me.

Andes licked lazily at Bracken's neck, closing his neck wounds as we lay
there, panting. For several hazy moments I waited for the darkness at the edge
of my vision began to recede.

"Ohhhoohhhhh…" I managed—and it was hard, because Bracken was
heavy, and with Andres pressed up against him, he wasn't holding his weight.
"That was *not* what I expected."

Andres chuckled, the sound sexy enough to make me spasm again, and
Bracken groaned. "Sometimes good surprises can be the things that keep us
going through the bad ones, Little Goddess."

I tried to chuckle and didn't have enough air in my lungs. "Bracken…" I
wheezed, and he shifted and then looked over his shoulder with a grunt.

"Brother? If you could….?"

Andres chuckled again, and there was an audible *pop* as his body pulled
out of Bracken's, and dammit if I didn't clench some more.

"Would you *stop* that?" Bracken begged and I giggled, and our bodies
did all sorts of interesting things while still locked together and he groaned
into my shoulder. Andres stood, and I got a look at him naked, his sex still
partially erect and reasonably impressive. It was his lean chest and shoulders
though which would have attracted me, and I had a moment to think that
someday, maybe, I would get to explore that masculine beauty. He turned to
me and caught me admiring him, and in spite of the, uhm, wantonness of my
current position with Bracken wedged securely between my naked thighs, it
was his wicked smile that made me blush.

"We will have other chances," he reassured softly, "when your flesh and
your spirit might not feel quite so full." And in spite of my beloved's solid
weight between us, I could be enchanted by the promise. Andres' grin grew
even wider, and then he gave Bracken a solid *thwack* on the tightly muscled
flank. "Come *on* brother—I would like to go swimming, and I simply can't

walk away from you two when you're still like that! Not when I've had one of you and want you both!"

Bracken laughed, but he pulled out too, because experience had taught us that when I was as sexually high as I was right now, I could rev all night.

Andres planned to be in Redding when the bar closed—he didn't have all night.

I shivered as Brack pulled up my bikini bottoms (I was dripping right through them—it was a good thing I was going swimming) and then stood to pull up his own swimming trunks.

I stopped him, mesmerized as always by the beauty of his body, and ran my hands up the insides of his thighs, and it was his turn to shiver. I stuck out my tongue and tasted him, after spending inside me, and then tasted again, and then engulfed him in my mouth while he hissed and knotted his fingers in my hair. I pulled back and gave his little head a chaste kiss before pulling up his trunks and tying the lace in the front, and he kept his hand knotted in my hair, and his fingers cupping the back of my head and massaging my scalp. We met eyes and smiled dizzily, and then he helped me to my feet. As I was standing, I looked up and caught Andres watching us thoughtfully, and I blushed.

"You two are very sweet," he said softly, pulling his boxer shorts from his khakis and sliding them on while standing. He gave a little hop when they came over his hips, and I had to smile. "I can see why your heart is full of him."

"Not just him," I murmured truthfully, nuzzling Brack's hand on my shoulder. Andres conceded with a nod of his head.

"Between Bracken and Green, Little Goddess, I'm grateful your heart is big enough to even consider me."

He turned then before things could get awkward and opened the gate on the boat's railing, which guarded the ladder into the water. He must have been able to see easily, because his dive was clean and fearless into the sparkling, unfathomable dark.

Bracken moved into the gap next, the better to leap in and then let me make my painstaking way down the ladder like the phobic freak I felt like. I stopped him though, and stood at the opening nervously, my hands on either side of the gate.

"So," I said randomly, "that…that thing we just did… you and Andres planned that?"

"Uhm—yes?" Bracken clearly had no idea what I was about.

"You and Nicky do that—have strategy meetings… I, uhm, like the outcome."

Bracken's hand, warm in the faint breeze, came up to my shoulder, and he bent and spoke closely, making our words personal. "I'm glad to hear that, beloved—what are you doing?"

I swallowed and remembered my earlier high, trying to get that buzz through my veins to push out the fear. I was faintly surprised that it worked.

"I'm planning to be strong," I said, and then, rushing on the same breath, "one-two-three-*jump!*"

The water was fresh and exhilarating as it closed over my head, and there was no panic in me as I hauled my way to the surface. I broke for air, scraped the water from my eyes, and looked around our tiny corner of the lake.

The running lights from the boat and the fragmented moon gave me just enough light to see Andres, frolicking like a child towards the wider mouth of our little inlet, and then Bracken broke the water next to me. The surface of the lake was covered with floating mustard flowers, poppies, and lupins, all left over from my sunshine scream.

"How you doing?" he asked with a pleased grin.

"I'll let you know when I panic," I told him, smiling back. But I probably wouldn't panic. I could feel it in my marrow, because—at least for tonight—with sex and blood and joy thundering through my veins, I could do anything.

NICKY

Flying

My folks weren't really talking to me—or apparently to each other—but we were all still awake, playing games out on the picnic table with the other shapeshifters, when the three of them came back from their boat ride.

I expected the sex and sensuality to be obvious, rolling off them like waves of Ripple wine, but it wasn't. *I* could tell that something had happened beyond a vampire bite, but while Cory and Bracken moved together with their usual skinless sexual grace, Andres didn't quite... fit.

I could see them holding hands from the distance, as they watched Bracken situate the boat, and it occurred to me that maybe she hadn't slept with him after all, and I wondered what in the hell was wrong with her. *I* would have taken him up on that offer in a hot minute.

But then, we loved her precisely because she did the things we wouldn't or couldn't do.

I would have spared the girl who had attacked Green—not from mercy, or because I truly felt she deserved it, but because of weakness. I couldn't bear to have those pathetic whimpers on my conscience, and that was the end of it.

I would have, Goddess help me but I would have, killed the little vampire girl that first day, as she slept, without even trying to find a cure or the culprit, because I *am* that much of a coward.

I would have kept clinging to every strength I had, whether it meant eternal binding or not, just to try to keep myself alive, that horrible night when we'd been tied together by bonds too complicated to name. But if she'd done that, I never would have bonded to Green, and then I never would have had the courage to love Eric, and, all things considered, it was a damned good thing I wasn't in charge now, wasn't it?

I'd called Eric, as they'd left, and we'd joked a bit about Andres and how damned cute the guy really was, and then we'd rung off, and I'd fought the urge to cry. I missed him. The thought of him, alone with his law textbooks and his spreadsheets in that big, tan apartment made my chest ache.

And dammit, I missed Green too—and I wondered at the strength Cory had to leave him when he'd been hurt, but I shouldn't have.

I think we'd already covered that she was a better person than I was.

The three of them came up to us, and Andres gave a little bow and escaped to change—I think he was wearing his underwear for form. She came around the table, completely mindless of my parents' disapproving gaze, and bent down and nuzzled my cheek.

"Who's winning?" she asked throatily, and I looked sideways at her and smiled.

"Renny."

We both looked at Renny who, although a girl (in a T-shirt and nothing else) was sitting as daintily as a tortoiseshell shorthair and smiling smugly. Katy gave a disgusted shake of her head.

"You don't even know she's got Uno, dammit—suddenly she'll just walk away from the table and we see she ain't got no cards!"

Teague snorted, and Katy rounded on him. "And you're second for damned near the same reason. I'm tired of you people that don't talk none playing games with us—it's like a superpower or something!"

Mario grinned at her, throwing down a card with studied insouciance. "That's okay, mommy, you and me, we're like their arch-rivals!" Tanya—who had been sitting close to him for most of the night in a shy, tentative way—hid a laugh behind her hand, and that was his undoing.

Max chuffed, "Then you'd better learn not to monologue, Captain Obvious, because you've only got one card left—now draw!"

Mario's good-natured groan echoed through the hills, but he flashed a magic grin at Tanya and kissed her on the cheek. "*Chica,* you're good luck and bad, you know what I mean?"

She grinned pertly. "Yup. I *am* bad—you know what *I* mean?"

His throaty, good-natured laughter echoed too, and I wondered idly what everyone else made of the lot of us, staying up late every night and sleeping past noon. Then Cory rubbed her cheek against mine, and I found I didn't care.

"Want to join us?" I croaked, turning my nose to her neck and trying not to scent her skin too obviously. Andres had bitten her—I could smell that, and in spite of the lake water cooling her limbs I could smell Bracken inside her, mostly because I knew that smell as comfortably as my own.

She looked behind us, and she and Bracken probably spoke volumes with their eyes. "Why not?" she murmured after a moment.

I made a pleased sound in my throat—they could probably be alone, I thought muzzily. I had no doubt about it. But this would be our last night together before shit went down and went down hard. This was the reason we called her 'Lady Cory'—a real queen wouldn't go nuzzle her beloved on the night before a battle, a real queen would stay and play Uno with the troops.

As Bracken rounded up a towel for her to sit on and another one to throw over her shoulders, I figured I knew what made her a real queen. And then she proved to me what made her a real lover.

My parents saw her sitting down and getting comfy, and they stood up and made awkward noises to leave, and she met my eyes meaningfully and nodded her head in that direction.

"What?" I asked grumpily. I hadn't been particularly nice to them—none of us had. As far as we were concerned, they were the reason Annette was here, the reason she'd had a chance to fuck with that poor kid, and a ginormous thorn in Cory's side when a thorn in her side was the last thing she needed.

"They're leaving tomorrow—so are we." Her voice was soft and meaningful, and I shrugged. So? She sighed, the sound suspiciously frustrated. "So go talk to them—it might be your last chance in…" she swallowed and shook her head. We'd all been in the thick of it. Nobody liked to talk about it like soldiers, but there was a reason she worked so hard to have our backs. Tomorrow night promised to be… interesting.

"Please?" she asked at last, after an awkward silence that permeated the entire table. "Please, just go talk?"

I rolled my eyes and sighed, then stood up. "Bracken can take my hand," I muttered, and stood up and left.

It was weird how still the night was in the mountains—as soon as the light disappeared behind me, the voices at the table became distant and disembodied. I hurried to catch up with my parents, thinking that the gray light of the waning moon did a good job of making things look melancholy and lonely.

"Mom, Dad!" I called, and they turned to me warily. Well, part of that was their fault, wasn't it? I wouldn't have to yell if they wouldn't have to judge, right?

"If you're going to apologize," Mom sniffed, "it's too late. I already told you, Annette spent all day in the cabin, crying her eyes out."

I shook my head, feeling my temper rise again. What is it about family? "Mom, if she keeps threatening us, we'll kill her. If crying keeps her out of trouble, let her snivel her way through life right? I didn't come to talk about her anyway."

"Then what?" Mom snapped, and I sighed.

"I..." Oh Goddess. My anger and my love bottled up hopelessly in my chest. *I love you both... please don't leave angry* vied with *I'm sorry you two fucked this up beyond repair,* and I couldn't bring myself to say either thing.

"I hope you have a safe trip," I finished miserably, shaking my head. Bad idea. This had been a BAD idea. I turned to go and my dad made a frustrated grunt.

"Nicky..."

I turned back around, and he shrugged, his almost delicate features crinkling in discomfort. "You guys don't have to pay for the car," he said at last and Mom rounded in on him in outrage.

"The hell they don't!"

"We don't mind!" I said at exactly the same moment. I glared at her. "Green *has* money," I said irritably. "We don't mind spending it..."

"Well if he has so much money why can't you pay to send poor Annette home?" Mom asked in frustration, and I felt my face harden, much like Cory's did before she killed.

"Because Annette isn't family. She's not a friend. And Cory has done plenty keeping people from killing her as it is."

Mom gave an angry laugh, and I just shook my head. "Did you see Cory last night, Mom?"

"She just *shoved* Annette in the cabin..."

"No—did you *see* her?"

Mom blinked. "She was a mess," she sniffed, and I shook my head.

"She was covered in blood, Ma—vampire blood. Because she went out to get revenge on people who tried to kill our lover. And I went with her knowing exactly what she was going to do, and you know what? My only regret is that I didn't get to make a kill, and that's the Goddess' honest truth. Dad and me—we're not human. And the thing we are—it's a predator, and predators don't have any use for rabbits who think they're birds. When I say Cory has kept her alive—I'm serious. Every person who's offered to kill her has been serious. And after what she did to that boy, I'd be first in line. You keep telling me the people I'm with are 'evil' because of the sex—well I've got to tell you, not once have I been covered in spunk and dropped like a used condom, and that's what she did to that kid!"

Oh God. I just used the word 'spunk' when talking to my mother. I was going to hell and I didn't even believe in the place.

"That's disgusting!" she snarled, and I was already in it, hell or no hell.

"*That's* what's been sniveling in your room!" I snarled back. I looked up at Dad and shook my head. "Dad—I'm sorry. I... I wanted to see you guys. I wanted you to know I was happy—truly, truly happy. The people I'm with—they're good, good people. They don't live in the human world, but they'll kill or die for me, and I love them."

"You said they killed people!" Mom shrilled, and I shook my head, grabbed her shoulders, and kissed her on the cheek.

"I love you Mom. You want to help Annette, put her on a bus." And then, convinced that this was Cory's worst idea *ever*, I turned away.

I was unprepared for my father's hand on my shoulder, and that resonant voice—the one that used to put me to sleep as a child, listening to him talk quietly to my mom at the end of the day—saying, "Son—I haven't gone flying yet up here. You want to come with me?"

I don't know how bright my eyes were, but I know my smile was my very best. "Absolutely—there are some air currents over the dam, Dad—it's better than cliff diving!" I'd forgotten—or stopped caring—that we weren't supposed to tell my mom about jumping off the butte near our house as a human, and changing in mid-air. It didn't matter.

Dad gave a grin and left my mom standing, uncertain and miserable, to walk up with me shoulder to shoulder as I made my way to our cabin. I needed to leave my sandals on the mat. No sense in tempting fate, right?

We stood together, my dad and I, and looked up into the sky.

"It's a smaller sky here," Dad said, and he was right—Montana sky was as big as the ocean, as big as a god.

"There's more trees," I pointed out. I liked the trees—places to play, places to perch, and they hid game. They also hid predators, and those were fun too.

"You like the trees?" Dad asked, and I had to admit that I did.

"Trees are complicated," I told him. "Complicated can get crazy—it can make you tired—but it's always interesting."

Dad chuckled, and I watched as he stretched his back, listening to the crackle of a middle-aged spine. Anton, Montana had fewer than fifty thousand people in it. I once tried to do the math, and I figured that maybe two-percent of us were Avians, and until I'd left home, I'd never met another species of the Goddess' get. Dad had married a town girl because that's what our people did. There were rumors throughout Anton that we existed—it wouldn't be much of a stretch for one of the girls in our town to realize she was in love with one of us. I'd heard the talk in the high school—we were a source of rumor, speculation, and glamour, much like vampires, except, in Anton, people knew we were real.

Mom had probably felt like she won the lottery when Dad had shown interest. Dad had probably never imagined a larger world where a girl like

Mom wasn't his only choice. I would never be middle-aged like my father—I would always be as young as I was now, as young as Green, and together, we would watch Cory grow old and beyond us.

I tilted back my head and let the slight breeze off the lake ruffle my hair. I stretched out my arms and with a faint pulling sensation, my feathers spilled out of my flesh. My bones hollowed, my mass became sinew, muscle, stretched skin.

As a human I've stood, arms extended, in a windy alley or on a wind-scoured plain and I've thought of other humans, who couldn't just let the wind take their feathers and lift into the ether. I don't do that often, because it breaks my heart.

Tonight, Dad and I let a breeze pick us up and surfed the wind, climbing for the boundless indigo, plummeting from the windless height like stones to extend our wings again and soar from the ground at the last moment. We sighted fish from above the lake, and arrowed down, shrieking in challenge to our prey—who could not hear us, or did not care.

It didn't matter—we had fed already. We lifted out of the water and released the flopping victims to continue on their fishy ways.

A human son may have talked sports or boats some more. A human child may have talked movies or cars. But Dad and I are not human. Together we flew at night, under stars that did not judge and we played tag with the wind and flirted with gravity, and we made our peace.

It was just as well we had found some equilibrium, because the next evening, after the vampires awakened and fed, Mom came knocking at my door as I was packing.

She had Annette in her wake, with fresh hair spray, a fresh outfit, and a freshly painted smile.

Mom smiled at me tentatively, and when I raised my eyebrows at her, she pasted a smile just like Annette's on her face. "Now honey, Annette just wants to make some amends, that's all."

I grunted (a thing I've been picking up from Bracken) and looked at the suitcases. I was trying to pack for Cory and looking for something small to put a change of clothes in—if we all survived the night, we'd all want some spares that *weren't* Sac State gold and green.

"Now Nicky," Annette said sweetly. In high school, that's what had attracted me to her—she had always sounded so sweet. Of course, when you're in high school, you tend to confuse 'sweet' with 'genuinely good'. Annette was neither—but she could fake 'sweet'.

"You want to apologize, you track down that kid you fucked and dumped and apologize to him," I grated, refusing to even look at her. "I could give a shit what you do with your own asshole, but that kid was a friend of mine."

I'd shocked them both—badly—and I didn't care. Damn Mom. The night before I'd come in after my flight with my father feeling good. We hunted well together, our body language communed all the simple things that human words fucked up. Cory had rolled out of Bracken's embrace—they always slept tangled—and hugged me before he reclaimed her, and I'd thought that my life was good. And then Mom had to try and pull this shit again.

"Dominic Kestrel…" Mom tried, her voice burdened with tremulous indignation, and I spared her a look.

"Mom, I'm not going to marry her. I'm not going to fuck her. I'm not going to like her. I'm not even going to forgive her. You want to get mad at me and leave, please do. I would have *liked* to have spent some time with you—but you've been so…weirdly obsessed with this dumb bitch being a ticket to a normal life that you can't even see that I love the abnormal life I've got. If you really loved me, if you really wanted me to be happy, you'd just fucking drop this. If you had any judgment whatsoever, you'd drop *her.*"

Mom swallowed, and dashed her eyes with the back of her hand, and then shrugged helplessly and walked out. Just walked out, leaving Annette to stand there, glaring at me, that poisonous snarl that she'd been aiming at Cory all week finally out in the open between us.

"I'm not a dumb bitch," she fumed. "I'm not—I'm a good Christian girl, and you're being stupid and stubborn."

I looked sideways at her, and then walked around her to get Bracken's clothes and pack those. Bracken was swimming—his last chance to charge his energy with the earthen electricity that the lake offered—and I was pretty sure Cory was meeting with Renny, Katy and Jacky. They had to be there at the battle—they had to. We weren't just going to leave them somewhere, unprotected, while the people they loved went to war. But there were ways to minimize the danger to them—she'd talked about them with me, with Bracken, and with Green, Max, and Teague, and she was giving a third or fifth run-through to make sure the three of them didn't dart into the open, or shoot off their mouths or do anything to put them in the sort of danger their teeth and claws couldn't get them out of.

Losses were unacceptable—we knew that now.

"But at least I'm not fucking strangers in the woods," I said cattily—mostly, I just wanted to hear her admit it. Not once had she admitted she'd done anything wrong. She wasn't going to now, either.

"I was *trying* to get closer to you!"

I blinked, and then laughed. "Honey—you could actually *be* an Avian, and I still wouldn't want to touch you. You could be a *male* Avian, and I wouldn't want to touch you. Banging that kid to get whatever warped version of his nightmare power isn't going to get you anything but an STD, if he hasn't been careful."

"You just wait and see!" Annette sniffed. "I got more from that little bastard than he even thought to give me! And your precious Cory—that bitch slept with that vampire last night—you can't tell me she didn't! It's not like she's pure, and it's not like she's even nice—and you're going to see what a total cunt she is in about five minutes, and then, if you're nice to me and be sorry, I just *might* take you back."

I ignored the part about Cory sleeping with Andres—for one thing, I knew she hadn't and for another, I wouldn't care if (or rather I wish that) she had. But the threat...I narrowed my eyes at the girl who had dropped me because I wouldn't sleep with her, and who apparently thought I was the one that got away.

"What did you do?" I asked, disturbed.

Annette smiled smugly. "I just tried to get along, that's all." Her smile amped up a notch, and I took a good look at her false blue eyes, and wondered how I had never noticed that they were as deep as a bucket of crazy.

"Oh, Goddess... Annette—what did you *do?*"

"Just tried to make sure you ended up with someone who really cares about you, that's all." She smiled that empty, insane smile again and I shook my head, trying not to panic.

"When did you get the idea that I'm the one? Why can't you just move on?" My voice shrilled—loud enough to catch the attention of anyone around. There was something bad happening, and I needed to keep Annette busy enough to trap and question without her knowing.

There was a terrified wildflower flutter across my face and I kept my expression as neutral as I could as I waited for Annette's answer. Her eyes were hooded, and I wondered what sort of endorphins she'd released when she'd taken whatever gambit she had—she looked both crazy *and* drugged, and Goddess if I could figure out what her move had been.

"You're my ticket out, Nicky," she murmured, walking her manicured fingers up my shirt. "Everyone wanted one of you—and I almost had you. All those dumb fucks going away to college—they didn't know about you. They thought you were a myth. But I knew..." she shook her head and turned her closed eyes towards a warped future only she could see. "I knew, you see... if I could just have you, have an Avian, I'd have my ticket out... I'd be queen forever, just like your mama."

I stared at her in outrage. "You want to sleep with me because studying was too hard?" I was *so* not making this connection, and for the first time, Annette showed some frustration at my complete obtuseness.

"I want to sleep with you, because you're royalty," she said slowly. "And if I'm your wife, I'll be the closest thing Anton, Montana ever had to a queen!"

There was a ruckus then, which snapped me out of my horrified fascination with Miss Queen Crazypants, and made me turn my head to listen. Katy and Renny were in their forms, howling their whiskers off, and I couldn't hear Cory's voice at all.

Shit. Annette put her hand on my arm with a meaningful look and smile, and she looked stunned when I shook her off—apparently whatever mojo she'd used to inspire this little turn of events hadn't followed her into my room, for which I could only be grateful.

Casting Annette's fate to whatever hells I could think of, I went shouting out the door, screaming Bracken's name and heading three doors down to see what in the fuck was going on. I had barely cleared my door when, in an explosion of drywall and wood, Marcus the vampire came shooting out of the ceiling of the cabin in a cannonball trajectory that would carry him smack dab into the darkened, oil-black waters of the lake.

The expression on his face was etched behind my eyes in surreal clarity— he looked like a sleeper awakening from a dream or a drug addict coming down from a high.

The glow of Cory's power surrounded him, propelling him out towards the lake, and Cory—looking pissed off but in control—was wrapped firmly in his arms.

Annette watched them go, arching spectacularly over the lake and then plunging deep into the depths, and made a sound of impatience.

"Do you think she'll survive that?" she asked unhappily. As streaks of black lightning that could only be Phillip and Kyle arced overhead towards the two of them, I felt my own unholy, insane smile twitch at the corner of my lips.

"Oh you can count on it."

Annette's eyes widened, and for the first time she looked afraid.

CORY

Bloody Moves

The thought of Renny, Katy, and Jack in the fight made me a little ill. Not so much because I didn't think they could fight, because I knew that they had all been in the thick of it and done well. It was the 'dispassion' thing that they didn't have going for them.

Renny fought after Mitch had died and she'd been kidnapped—she'd been brutal and mindless and really scary, but that doesn't make for someone who can make an informed decision in battle conditions.

Katy killed the guy who put her in a silver cage and whacked off to her pain. If you can't kill *that* fucker, you really didn't earn your right to be a werewolf.

Jack had launched himself at a group of werewolves who had lured our people into a gunfight—he'd done it to protect Teague, and he'd even fought well, but it had been one of the stupidest moves I'd ever seen. I got his reasoning—brother, if anyone understood it, *I* did--but getting Jack to see it from Teague's perspective sucked.

"I'm not just going to skulk in the shadows while he goes out and gets killed!" Jack fumed, and my patience for this was almost at an end.

"I'm not asking you too!" I shot back. "I'm saying have his back—not his flank, not his front. Guys, your men are our best fighters—but not when they're worried about *you*. Go out there—kick ass, I know you can, but *don't* make your guy so worried about you that he gets himself hurt, do you hear me?"

"Fine," Jack sneered. "You go ahead and plan the battles and we'll hang in the back like stupid cattle who freak out at wolves."

Andres had awakened in my head at dusk, telling me that he and Rafael were being 'tended to' inside the bar, along with the 75% of the kiss and the shapeshifters who were still loyal to Rafael. Trap? Traps were, by nature, subtle. This was a medieval battlefield, complete with captive kings.

My temper, frayed by anxiety, finally snapped with impatience.

"Are you saying my beloved was stupid, Jack?" I shouted, and it showed how freaked out I was that this place, right here, was where I went. "Are you saying Adrian was 'cattle' as he came flying out of nowhere to save my ass? Because all he'd had to do was… was fucking stop and think, give just a little bit of planning, and he'd be here right now, right? Hell—he wouldn't be here right now, because none of this would be fucking happening if he were still around. Because Adrian wasn't just respected, right? Adrian was *loved*. But he saw Green and Bracken and me being threatened and his brain just shut down, and now I'm fighting vampire wars from the fucking ground!"

Jack had blanched at my first sentence, but as I rounded at him and pressed him back against the bed with the force of my frustration, he flushed with shame.

"I'm sorry," he muttered into the sudden silence in the room. "I didn't mean to imply…"

"Of course you didn't," I sniffed, passing the back of my hand over my eyes. "I went there because that's where I go. But you need to know—you need to know what sort of devastation you'll leave behind if you freak out and fuck up. Teague and Max are *warriors*, people. If they'd been born a thousand years ago they would have gone out with swords in their hands and taken over countries. You guys are fierce—but you're not… clear, in a battle. There's a heartbeat between 'think' and 'do', and you just blaze on past it. Max and Teague think in it—it's what makes the difference in them. I need you to give them that heartbeat—fight, fine. But stay out of their way."

We all drew a shuddery breath, and I flopped down on the bed and scrubbed my face with my hands, then looked up at all of them and smiled shakily. They smiled back the same way.

"This is as close to nerves as I get before a job," I apologized. "I…the others, we've worked like this before… we're getting damned good at it. You guys…I just worry about you, that's all."

There was an awkward silence, and I was actually pretty relieved when Marcus walked in. Phillip had been on edge and bitchy since they'd awakened. Marcus had been keeping him on keel as he had been all month, and I wanted some reassurance that brother wasn't just going to fucking lose it on us when we hit the bad shit. (Of course, given Phillip's ability to kick bloody ass, that might not be such a bad thing. I just didn't want to be there when we ran out of enemies.)

"Hey, Marcus—you guys all fed and packed?"

Marcus' eyes were whirling oddly--each eye out of sync, and a slightly different color. His mouth—which was usually compressed in a little Italian cupie-bow, was open and slack, and I tilted my head and squinted at him, wondering what the hell was wrong with him.

"I fed," he murmured. "I fed? Yeah...I must have fed." He shook his head—hard and fast enough to blur in my vision like an elf running in hyperspeed—and I stood up warily and exchanged glances with the others. I jerked my eyes towards the door, and was rewarded with three adamant glares. Well, I'd known they were brave, but I had to say my opinion about their clear thinking hadn't changed a teeny, tiny bit.

"Who'd you feed from, Marcus?" I asked softly, but we knew—we all knew.

"Annette?" he murmured. "Well, isn't she the last person I'd want to eat..."

Of course. There we had it—the reason he was creeping us all the fuck out.

"What did Annette ask you to do, sweetie?" I asked gently, standing up and putting my hand on his. His claws extended, flexed, retracted, and extended again. I tried to slip inside his head, but there was nothing going on there—whatever had been done to him, his own consciousness had checked out to be replaced by the chaos-puppeteer's.

But, I thought slowly, we'd been given a weapon to fight that sort of thing, hadn't we?

Moving quickly so he wouldn't resist, I took his hand and thrust it under the loose neck of my T-shirt, and onto my shoulder, to the chaos-filter that young Sam had given me. Abruptly, I was assaulted by twin images. Both of them featured Annette, looking in through an open ceiling, laughing in childish glee, and the first picture showed me, flat on my back on the bed with my throat torn open.

The other featured me in the same position, naked, with Marcus on top of me.

Wonderful. She'd asked him to kill me—but with Green's people, 'fight it' could turn to 'fuck it' on a dime.

I pulled Marcus' hand out of my shirt, and looked at Renny and mouthed 'Get Brack' at her. Finally, *finally* she took the hint, turned kitty and darted out of the room through open door. I met Katy's eyes and mouthed 'Phillip' at her, and she took the hint too.

It didn't matter. Marcus was so intent on me-- his drives so conflicted and so all- consuming--he didn't even flinch as Katy changed too and zipped out of the room.

I tried reason.

"Marcus, hon—remember, you got rid of all this? It was a crush, that was all—we all get crushes, but you didn't really want to follow through, right?" Of course not. This last month we'd all seen that he was all that held his beloved together. I'd never been more than a fascination for him. Maybe just that—the memory of a crush—was enough to flip the direction of his want.

His eyes were still whirling, but now they were in sync, and the image his mind was blasting on all frequencies resolved itself to a single frame. O—kay...I'd apparently shifted his drive to the single-minded merge to mate. Of course, if Marcus fucked me, Bracken would die horribly, and then I would die of a broken heart, and then Green would go the same way, and really, kill me or do me, we were all fucked now weren't we?

"You smell delicious," he murmured, and I exchanged rolled eyes with Jack. Jack started to advance, his arms outstretched, and I shook my head firmly. Marcus was a vampire—our people tended to forget this, but vampires were stronger than the werefolks, and this was *not* our sweet, scholarly vampire who sat and did research with me in the garden. *This* Marcus might rip Jack's throat out and turn back to rape me as Jack bled to death. Shit.

"I smell off-limits," I replied firmly, and pulled enough power into my body to light up the entire town. Marcus moved closer, and I sorted through any response that may keep me from frying him into powder if he got close enough to be a threat. Oh, Goddess—anything but that, because it wouldn't be one death, but two. Phillip would not survive the death of his lover. Not now, not when Marcus was the only thing keeping his grip on sanity tight. Unlike, say, Marcus'.

He hadn't replied, and I tried an awful grin. "Dude, you know who smells really good right now? Annette. Annette probably has sirloin boobs and chocolate spinal fluid—why don't you go snack on her?"

Marcus didn't say anything, but his eyes stopped whirling and started a laser-straight, murky red glow. He got close enough to touch, and I put a hand firmly on his chest and shoved him back, only to be met with the cold, unyielding force of reanimated flesh. Oh Goddess, please don't let it come down to brute force.

"Marcus," I said dangerously, "you need to get back. You need to think about this—what will Phillip think?"

Those slowly glowing eyes closed, and his smile became childishly sweet. "Phillip loves me," he murmured. I met Jack's eyes hopefully and nodded.

"Phillip needs to talk to you!" he said urgently, and my eyes bugged.

Dammit—did he not *know* that Marcus could check that lie out in his head?

"I'm not supposed to talk to Phillip before I ki...fuck her." The sweet look was gone, and he was advancing on me like he had a purpose—but his movements were stiff. Auuughhhh... *fuck* Annette and her dumbfuck grudges—she must have held a whole lot of hate to push her random chaos will on Marcus like this, and he was fighting it. He had to be fighting it, if he'd changed the drive from death to sex.

"Jack, go get Teague," I said directly. Marcus was on me, chest to chest, and I was a moment from falling back on the bed, my mind scrambling for a way to get out of this without killing the guy. What would it take to snap him out of it? Pain? Water? Phillip hauling him back and having the bitch-slapping festival of all time?

"Teague would kill me if I left!" Jack replied, and I glared at him from around Marcus' shoulder.

"Teague will kill *me* if you get hurt, and you might, because I've got a plan--now go!"

"A plan," Marcus repeated blankly, and I let myself fall back on the bed, with Marcus on top of me. His arms came out automatically, clasping my shoulders, dragging me next to his compact body like a lover—which is the *last* thing we would be, one way or another.

"*This* is a plan?" Jack yelped, and I gathered my power, closed my eyes, and hoped I remembered something about directionality and learning how to fly.

"It is now," I replied grimly, just as Marcus lowered his head to my neck and I shot us through the ceiling.

Water, I'd thought—well, so happens there was a big fucking lake not a hundred yards away, if only I could control our arc.

Marcus took the brunt of the impact through the ceiling, but a few fragments still got through and I could give a shit. He clutched me tighter in surprise as we went arcing together up, up, over, the wind howling through my hair and Marcus' puzzlement looping through my head, the sky with open arms to receive us and...

I dropped us right solid square in the middle of that big black lake, and the first time I panicked was when the water closed over my head, and Marcus' cold skin and bones tightened around me like wet sailor's rope.

Fuck.

BRACKEN

Knight in Darkness

I was almost in the middle of the lake when Renny and Katy came howling down the shoreline, so agitated that I was halfway to them before Marcus and Cory came shooting out of the cabin roof.

Renny stopped her yowling, and Lambent, Teague, Max and I simply tread water in shock as we watched their trajectory and splashdown—Cory was pushing against Marcus even as they hit water.

I was swimming back towards them before the others even had time to say "Holy Fuck."

There were still ripples from their plunge when I got there and started diving down—I could see the glow and the bubbles from Cory's power, growing dimmer and dimmer as Marcus' dead weight dragged her deeper and deeper, and I kicked—hard and furiously—to reach her. Oh Goddess... she'd been so brave, trying to fight this demon—whatever had driven her here, she must have been so desperate.

The glow grew closer, and I tried to force the earth in the water to breathe through my skin because my lungs were bursting, screaming at my chest for oxygen, but I wouldn't go back up without her...until a hand seized my foot and literally threw me up out of the water.

I splashed back down and furiously rounded on Phillip and Lambent who were shouting at me even as I made ready to dive back down.

"Listen to him!" Lambent screamed, seizing me around the waist before I could physically brawl with Phillip in the middle of the damned lake, and

Phillip turned a frantic, pale face towards me and yelled, "Marcus has her! You'll need me to grab him to get her out!"

I nodded tersely and calmed down to as close to icy as I could manage. Then I hauled in a lungful of air, and pumping hard with my legs, I used the Goddess' own speed to get me right back down, Phillip a darkening torpedo at my side.

Fuck they were deep. I could move preternaturally fast—but I was still slowed by the water, and no matter how hard I kicked, it looked as though the azure/orange glow that marked the two of them was going deeper and deeper. I almost despaired until I got close enough to see her flailing in Marcus' grasp, and I realized she wasn't going deeper. She was getting weaker. Oh *fuck* despair—it was time for some good old-fashioned *panic,* and it was a good thing Phillip grabbed his lover or I might have ripped Marcus' arms off, just to get Cory to the surface.

As it was, as soon as the two vampires made contact, Marcus turned instinctively into Phillip's arms, and the two of them sank together, lost in a lover's comfort communion, and I grabbed Cory under the arms and started to kick for all I was worth.

I was going fast enough that our feet cleared the surface of the water when we broke through, and the feeling of her chest, exploding in inhalation as we cleared, was the one thing that let me breathe.

We fell back to the water and I kept hold of her, in spite of Teague and Max's offers to tow her back to safety.

She gasped a couple of times and then shook her head hard, cleared the water out of her eyes, and took a deep breath.

"Let them, Bracken Brine," she said when she could, her breath cold and ragged against my cheek. "We've got to get back up there before Phillip does!"

"Why?" I demanded. I could only see her face in profile, but I recognized the set of her jaw, and the struggle she was pitching against herself to speak.

"Annette—he's going to kill her!" She tried to take her own weight but I seized her around the middle and kept her pinned against my body.

"Fucking let him," I ground. "Whatever she did, she deserves it!"

She let out what might have been a laugh. "No shit, Bracken Brine—I just need to clear away the bystanders before he does."

Oh. Well then. Max and Teague paddled closer, their four feet churning efficiently under the surface, and I helped her loop her arms around them. Between my preternatural speed and her shapeshifting escorts, we hauled ass to the shoreline, giving Renny and Katy a reassuring pat even as we stood up. I ignored Cory's protests then and picked her up to *blur* up the incline to meet in the driveway in front of the cabins.

Terry Kestrel was standing in front of the walking dead-woman, weeping. "Now, Nicky—I'm sure she didn't mean it..."

"Nicky, move her," Cory commanded as her feet hit the ground and I let go. Nicky executed a full bow, and then did what his leader requested. He picked up his mother bodily and forced her to the outer edge of the circle, and when she opened her mouth to protest, her own husband clapped his hand over it.

Max, Katy, and Teague had changed form (Katy's T-shirt was wet and askew, but still on) and Kyle had flown back as soon as we surfaced. All of us were there, surrounding Annette with implacable, indifferent faces. Jack and Katy were on either side of Teague, clutching his hands. Renny sat, panting and hissing, next to Max, who fondled her ears reassuringly. Mario and La Mark stood near Nicky and his parents—Avian solidarity, and something we all appreciated. Even Tanya was there, standing next to Mario, her face sober but her loyalty absolutely unquestionable.

Annette finally—*finally*—had the grace to look afraid.

"Now...you're not going to hurt me..." she tried with a ghastly smile, and Cory looked at me and we exchanged a grim laugh. Corinne Carol-Anne Kirkpatrick op Crocken Green looked like shit warmed over. She had minor cuts on the sides of her face and her arms from the wooden roof of the cabin, and my touch had started the blood running sloppily with the water. Her hair was lank around her face, she'd had make-up on and it had run into her red-rimmed eyes, and her bloody white T and basketball shorts clung to her body. Still, if Annette couldn't see the grim warrior in my beloved's face, she truly had never deserved to draw breath in the first place.

"Don't worry—I won't hurt you," Cory said with a flat smile, and Annette smiled greenly back.

"Thank you," she babbled. "You know, I really didn't think it would work, and I'm sooo glad you're okay and..."

"Phillip will." The words were a bare-knuckled rap on a raw wood floor.

Annette blanched. "I...I'm sorry?"

"You attempted to murder Marcus..."

"I did not! I told him to kill you!" There was a restive movement among our audience, and Terry stopped fighting and turned a stricken glance to her husband. Oh yes—Annette wasn't the only one who finally opened her eyes.

"Yes, Annette," Cory said slowly, as though teaching a parrot to speak. "You told Marcus to kill me. Marcus didn't want to... but you'd bound him with your blood—he had to do something, so he was going to rape me instead." Her voice rose on the word *rape,* and I could tell how distasteful it was to think of a friend that way. "Except, Annette, do you know what would have happened if he'd succeeded?"

Annette tried a game smile. "You would have liked it?"

I wasn't even aware I'd blurred until my hand cracked across her face. Her neck snapped sideways and she fell to her knees, her face exploding in a bruise. I'd probably shattered her cheekbone and her eardrum, and as I stood there, looking at my hand, Cory said softly, "Baby, you're going to need to move—if we don't finish this before Phillip gets here, he'll go through you."

She walked up to my side and took my hand gently, leading me back and away from the... the...*thing* that had wrought so much chaos from the force of her petty human malice alone.

"Bracken would have died!" Cory cried through gritted teeth, her hand clutching mine, and her carefully constructed warrior's face crumbling underneath what we all knew to be her greatest fear. "Bracken would have died—and the entire power structure that keeps this part of the world from falling into chaos would have fucking disintegrated, and all because you wanted to get laid!"

"I'b sorry..." Annette moaned through a broken nose, and it wasn't until Cory started patting my arm rhythmically that I realized I was shaking. "I'b thorry...pwease don' let him kill me..."

Cory shook her head then and wiped her bloody face with the back of her hand. "You almost made me kill a friend, you rabid bitch—Phillip is going to kill you for threatening his beloved..."

Annette looked up, all of her beauty destroyed by blood and purpling skin. "Pweeeaasseeee..." she moaned, and Cory shook her head again. Behind us, I could hear Marcus and Phillip sloshing their way to shore. I risked a glance back, and Phillip was still checking his lover's body for damage, and Marcus was still touching Phillip's face in apology, in reassurance. They hadn't looked up here yet, and Marcus hadn't explained what had happened (and hell, *I* didn't even have the whole story, although I had a pretty good goddamned idea) but it was coming. And Cory was right. Phillip was coming. He'd been living with a diseased mind for four months and the only thing holding him together was the man Annette had almost made Cory kill. He'd be a rampaging thunderstrike of bloody retribution, and there wasn't a thing we could do about it.

"I can't stop him," Cory told her, echoing my own thoughts. "I mean, I could. I'm his leader, and he'd listen..."

"Den whhyyyyyyy..."

Cory shrugged, but it wasn't nearly as casual as she'd like us to believe. "I passed a binding, remember? I could break my own binding—but it would make me weak, and you know something, sweetheart? We're going to take out a bad guy—a real bad guy. A motherfucker who's so hellifically evil he makes you look like a cuddly bunny who shits rainbows out your ass—he's a real goddamned monster. And the fact is," I clutched her hand because now *she* was the one shaking, "I can't protect you and kill him. I can't do both. And when it comes right down to it, your life isn't worth it."

"I'b *thorrrrrryyyy...*" the thing on the ground wailed, and Cory looked at us all sadly.

"I really wish I could be," she told us all softly. But she wasn't—and I, for one, was gloriously proud.

"What'll we tell her parents?" Terry Kestrel asked at last, her voice small and miserable. Annette heard the note of defeat in it, of turning, and buried her face in her hands.

"Tell them she got on the bus," Cory muttered, tugging my arm and making a larger opening in the circle for Phillip to speed through. "We don't know where she got off."

Behind us, Phillip let out a roar that echoed off the hills and lake, and prompted a few ribald hollers from the handful of lone campfires that dotted the surrounding trees. Before the echoes of the roar had truly faded, all of us in the circle felt the howling whoosh of Phillip's passage, but he was moving so quickly we could only see a dark blur as it charged the mewling victim on the ground.

Annette didn't even have time to scream as the blurring fury that was Marcus' lover ripped off her head with a sound like shattered wood, and then Phillip stood in front of us. Her head was under his arm like a football and he was slurping on the spinal fluid that spilled from the gleaming white fascia at the base of what had once been a human being's neck. We all flinched—I hadn't known that was a vampire delicacy, but I guess now we all did.

When he was done, he raised his blood drenched face to the heavens, his black widow's peak smeared back by gore, and roared again and again and again, until the were-creatures shrieked in sympathy, human forms or not, and Kyle was practically levitating with the force of his hissing.

In the midst of this, Marcus came trudging wearily up the hill, passing through the same place Phillip had. Even as Phillip howled, Marcus tugged gently at the head of our enemy, and let it fall to the ground, then he enfolded his tall, cold lover in his arms and started whispering to him gently, until Phillip broke and wept in Marcus' arms. Silence descended, and the two of them made their way back through the circle—presumably back towards the lake to get rid of their bloodied clothes.

As they passed us, Marcus pulled at Phillip's hand until they were both facing Cory, and together they bowed formally.

"Thanks for not killing me," Marcus muttered, shaking his head and avoiding our eyes.

"Brother," she said, moving forward and catching his chin—a curiously adult gesture from a woman who was probably forty years the vampire's junior, and several inches shorter. "I think we have enough problems without panicking and killing our friends, you think?"

Marcus met her eyes and managed a shaky smile. "Damned straight." His smile grew stronger and she dropped her hand and moved back against me. "Besides—we've got a whole new chapter to add—I mean hell, we finally know about the sons of chaos and man, now don't we?"

Cory's grin grew a little wider, and she turned to Phillip—I think to apologize, which would have choked us all—and fortunately Phillip beat her to it.

"Thank you, my Lady," he said formally.

None of us had to ask 'for what?'. "It was only right you should get to make it," she murmured, and Phillip bowed again. The two of them started off towards the lake again, and she called out, "Not too long!" And then she looked back at the circle. "That goes for all of us—we've got just enough time to clean up from this goatfuck, and then we've got things to do. Battle stations people—Rafael and Andres are waiting on us!"

She'd told us that just as the vampires awakened, but it was good that she reminded us now. A collective awareness shuddered through our little circle, and then all of us—me included—bowed low to her, and she forced herself to accept it with a little nod. Everybody started moving away, but she called one person back.

"Lambent?"

The tall fire-elf turned towards her, his orange eyebrows raised. "I thought this was your clambake, luv—you want me in on this?" He jerked his head at the human remains lying discarded on the driveway gravel.

"You've got the control, brother," she told him frankly. "It needs to burn hot, clean, and not even the blood can remain. Turn it to obsidian if you have to, but do your damnedest not to burn down Lake Shasta, right?"

Lambent smiled slightly. "A job with some finesse—right after my own heart, luvie. My pleasure, but first…" he held his hands palms up, asking for permission to touch her. She squinted at him and he rolled his eyes.

"I'm going to heal your boo-boos, luvie—with that bloke on your arm you're turning into vampire bait."

"Doh!" Cory smacked her forehead with her palm, and winced as she hit maybe the largest cut on her forehead. "It hadn't really registered. Jesus, Bracken," she looked up at me, the blood running into her eyes actually thick enough without the water to notice, "why didn't you tell me?"

I grunted. "You were busy."

Lambent clucked impatiently, and I took a step back from her while he touched her face gently, and gave her a kiss on the forehead. Her cuts closed immediately—no scarring whatsoever, and my estimation of the fire elf rose up a notch. She wouldn't have complained even a little, but I knew scars would have bothered her.

"Thank you, Lambent," she said softly as he wiped the remaining blood off her face with the towel draped over his bare shoulders. "That's nice of you."

Lambent grimaced. "I'm never nice, luvie," he said with a roll of the eyes, and then he made shooing motions. "Now scoot—it's going to make a right stink here, and we've got enough to do."

So we did. I wrapped my arm around her shoulders and she leaned into me and let out tiny tremors of adrenaline and sorrow that only I could feel. Together we walked back to deal with our real business, Mr. and Mrs. Kestrel's error in judgment burning clean and hot into ashes behind us.

CORY

Queen's Legion

We gave Nicky's parents a few terse instructions about dropping the car off in long-term parking, and then calling Arturo so he could give them their reservation number for the tickets on hold at the counter.

"We'll pick up the car on the way home," I said, with a sideways look at Nicky. He seemed okay. Fine, in fact. He hadn't been lying when he said he had no love for Annette—I had known that from the beginning, but still. It's hard to know, sometimes, how much you will care about someone until you see her headless and writhing in front of you.

"That's fine," said Jonathan quietly, looking at his son standing at my elbow. "We appreciate the plane tickets and the new car..."

Terry gave an angry sniff next to him, and I glared at her. "Do you have something to add to that, Mrs. Kestrel?"

"We would have appreciated it if you didn't kill Annette!"

"And I would have appreciated it if you'd believed me when I said she was a danger to herself and others. I'm not going to risk an all out war and a rampant pedophile for a dumbassed woman who pissed off the wrong vampire when trying to kill me! You want to blame someone? Blame Annette. If you find that distasteful, blame yourself. But I'm done with it—I have no remorse for someone who destroys herself with her own evil!"

"Listen to you! Who *talks* like that?" She was openly crying, and I had no pity left.

"*I* do!" I snarled. "I'm the queen of my people, and that means being who they need me to be. Right now, they need me to be a goddamned silver-tongued diplomat, and in about an hour, they're going to need me to be a bloodless fucking killing machine. And the people who love me—who *really* love me, they just need me to be me."

"And my son?" she asked fiercely. "What does he need you to be?"

I stopped myself with a furious shiver, feeling Bracken's heat seeping through my shoulder. Then I looked at Nicky. I let my face relax, and a smile tighten across my cheeks. "Kindness," I said softly. "Nicky needs kindness." He smiled at me, sincerely and loyally, and I grinned back. "And a plane ticket to see Eric just as soon as possible."

He grinned at that and nodded enthusiastically, and he leaned in and kissed me softly—kindly—on the lips. I turned to his parents then, pretty sure that I would have to be content with Nicky's good opinion.

I was surprised when his father spoke up. "Thank you, Lady, for caring for him…"

"Jonathan!" Terry protested, but he ignored her.

"My son could have had a horrible—and a short—life. You and Green, you've made it comfortable and happy—and something to be proud of. Thank you." He bowed low then, and I returned the bow with a little nod of my own, and ignored Nicky's mother with her jaw swinging like a baby-seat from a tree.

"But," he added, and I was all attention. It was the closest thing I'd ever gotten to acceptance and I wasn't going to shit on it.

"Yes sir?"

Jonathan Kestrel looked at his son with worry. "Keep him alive, if you can? You're off to do something dangerous—don't think I don't know that. Please… just try not to get him killed."

My face tightened another notch and I nodded soberly. "It's an absolute fucking priority, Mr. Kestrel. Please believe that's true."

They left—Nicky giving them both brief hugs before coming to help us finish cleaning up. The vampires managed to throw a quick patch on the roof so the room didn't fill with dust while Tanya was scaring up a contractor, and in a very quick moment, we were ready to go.

I took a moment to say goodbye to the sylph—she'd been a real part of our family for this last week, and I would miss her.

"Damn, girl—it's going to be dull around here without you!" Her tongue flickered out, tongue-stud and all, and she cast a surreptitious look behind me at Mario. They'd become good friends, and I'd wondered… okay, actually I'd hoped like a yenta, but I knew better than to meddle.

"Well, you're welcome at Green's any time—and for as long as you like. You know that, right?" She actually looked pleased—hell, she even flushed.

Wow—I had Renny, and Katy—I was apparently a sylph away from a slumber party, at the tender age of twenty-two. Would wonders never cease?

"I may take you up on that," she said softly. "I just need to find a replacement…"

I grinned. "I'll tell Green—he might even have someone in mind."

She sobered then. "I wish I could go with you—I'm pretty handy with a knife."

I just bet she was. "I'd rather you be here—waiting for our call. You're sure we got someone nearby for serious shit?"

Tanya nodded, and gave me her cell and the cell number of a shapeshifter—one of Green's, who had access to a medivac copter and an ambulance. Usually Green handled our medical emergencies—and Lambent wasn't bad in a pinch—but with all the shapeshifters, the odds of a non-fatal debilitating wound were significantly raised. And I didn't even want to think about what would happen if I got hurt—so mostly, I just didn't. Anyway, it was good to have someone standing by.

"So," she said awkwardly when the business was done, "uhm, Mario—you, uhm, think he'll be happy to see me again if I come out?"

I looked at her levelly. "You'll have to ask him—you know his wife died a year and a half ago…he, uhm, waited a long time for her." Seventy years, Nicky told me once. But Mario had been flirting pretty hard—and he wasn't the kind of guy who did anything he didn't mean. "But, you know, you've got his cell number and he's got yours—you can learn a lot about someone by how often they call." When I'd been away at school, Green had called me once a day, and we'd talked for a half an hour or more. But then, I already knew I'd love him forever.

We hugged then, and I went out to the cars where my people were waiting for me.

"We know the game plan?" I said needlessly as I walked out, and to a one they smiled.

"We park out of sight," Nicky told me grimly, and I nodded.

"Avians high and outside," La Mark said smartly.

"Vampires fanned out behind you all imposing like," Kyle supplied next, winking at Phillip and Marcus.

"Me, Max, and Teague at your back," Lambent said next, looking pleased.

"And the little women skulking in the shadows to kill fleeing rats." But Jacky was laughing grimly as he said it.

I laughed a little, feeling as good about this run as I was going to get, and I slanted a glance at my beloved. "And you?" I said with a smile.

"Is there any other place for me to be?" Bracken asked mildly, and I took his hand and kissed his knuckles.

"At my side it is," I told him softly, and then I looked out at our people. "All right, brothers and sisters," I looked at Teague and Marcus, who would be driving, "You guys tired of that set yet?"

They shook their heads adamantly. "Bleed it out, Lady Cory," Teague said, and Marcus echoed with, "Bleed it out."

Bleed it out dig it deeper just to throw it away…

And away we rode.

My body was still flooded with adrenaline from my little dip in the lake, and I was so on edge. Bracken kept his large, warm hand on the back of my neck like he was anchoring me to my seat.

"Calm down," he whispered into my ear, and dammitall, he knew that made me horny—which was the *last* thing I needed right now. But, I had to admit, it made a pleasant distraction from the horrible, claustrophobic feeling of being pressed in by water on all sides with a corpse clutching me to its chest.

I shuddered. It would have been one thing if Marcus had been conscious, but his whole brain had been one dead blank of 'reboot' until Phillip had grabbed him around the waist. Bracken knew I'd been terrified—the farthest he'd gotten from me in the last hour was waiting outside of the manager's hut while I said 'bye' to Tanya. When I spoke to Nicky's parents, his arm bumping my shoulder had been the only thing to keep me from screaming.

"All this prep," I said, almost to myself, "and one selfish, spoiled bitch-whore-human could have fucked this all to hell."

I felt Bracken shudder. "You've always known," he said, wrapping his arm securely around my waist. "You've always known that chaos can fuck us more than any force on the planet. You, fighting the water all week—that was order. It was hard, and miserable, and it hurt me to watch—but it was order. What we're doing here, it's keeping order. We're the good guys, beloved. You have to believe that."

Linkin' Park was playing again—*What I've Done.* How appropriate—but then, music had always been our friend.

"I was so scared," I confessed quietly—Goddess knew, and maybe Bracken and Green too, how hard that was for me to say.

I leaned back into the warm security that was my beloved, and Green's comforting scent blanketed me and Bracken held me tight.

You were right, beloved, Green murmured in my head, *all you have to be for us is who you are.*

You were there? I hadn't felt him—I knew he 'lurked', and I knew it was hard for him, energy he didn't have—but I never knew what he heard or didn't.

I was trying not to freak the hell out. I could hear his dry laughter, as he imitated me.

I'm sorry—I didn't mean to…

All you have to be for me is who you are.

Oh Goddess—such simple words, such terrible faith.

I only want to be my best for you.

And this, beloved, is who you are.

I could smell him—wildflowers, earth, sunlight, sex, Green. Bracken was behind me, my foundation, my rock. I had fought the water, and won. I had resisted being the worst version of myself in the face of the worst version of my kind.

Bracken was right—as random as we were, we were order, and when the bad guys were running wild, it was our job to fight them.

It was the first time I ever got pumped up for a fight by finding peace.

We parked in front of a 7/11 about a block from the bar, and I sent Marcus inside to mindfuck the night clerk into watching our cars. Having once been that night clerk, I felt a little bit bad about this, but not much—if the guy wasn't meant for this world, we had no right to drag him in with a weird-ass memory. Honestly, he was better off with a headache.

"I wasn't the first vamp to do that," Marcus muttered, and then I felt a little worse, but it didn't matter. We had a plan and promises to keep, and away we rolled.

There was no party at the bar tonight—no motorcycles lined up, no loud noises, no flashing lights. Instead, there were around fifteen vampires and shapechangers, lined up like pawns, ready to make the first move.

Oh Goddess. I so sucked at chess.

"There's got to be more than this," I murmured. Above us and behind the bar I heard Nicky, shrieking in three sharp bursts—three guards that way. Mario gave an odd sound, and I risked a look up and saw… well, they weren't really big bats, but judging by the way they left my guys alone, I think the three vampires up there still thought the Avians were really big birds.

"Three in the trees," I muttered, sotto voice. Everyone behind me could hear, and I was so proud that nobody else looked up.

La Mark gave a long shriek to my left, and I knew that there were enough guys back there to give us some serious trouble when things got rough. Okay, so I still sucked at chess, but at least I knew where my pieces were.

"Hiya, gentlemen!" I smiled gamely at the guy who came out to meet us. I was wearing a pair of baggy jeans and one of Bracken's T-shirts—and I was sweating in them too—but it meant I had room for more than one gun in the back of my pants. "We thought we'd go in and talk to Rafael!"

"Rafael is busy right now." The vampire was tall, and apparently bought his wardrobe at Virile Vamps and Varlets—black leather trench coat, knee-high biker boots, and a silver-studded leather belt over black jeans—and no shirt. I think he dyed his long hair and beard black, too, but I could see beyond them to the raggedly thin face with the pocked skin. I looked at the rest of the men, and they obviously shopped at VVV too. Jesus—those of us who were carrying guns had jeans. Those of us who didn't wore whatever the fuck they wanted—is there anything more annoying than a vampire in a glee club uniform?

"Rafael is being held captive in his own bar by his own people because you assholes are too busy being 'bad' to do the right thing," I said equably—goddammit, we all knew where this was going, and I was tired of fucking around! "By the way, do you guys have, like, a *store* or something? Because those ensembles are real fuckin' cute." I looked sideways to Phillip, the most 'vampy' of our vamps. "Dude—you want me to find out where they shop? I don't think you've got anything like this guy's shoes."

You bitch, Phillip thought, *don't make me crack up!*

"No, Lady," he said out loud. "I get my suits at Brooks Brothers, and my shoes special made."

"Special made?" I asked, sizing up the other guys—they were all armed with silver, which explained the gauntlets, but as far as I could tell, we were the only ones with guns. Good—because although math wasn't my strong suit, if we counted Jacky, Katy, & Renny, running silent in the shadows, we were possibly outnumbered by more than three to one.

"His feet are proportionately large," Marcus deadpanned. I cracked a vicious smile.

"See—our shoes aren't as pretty, but there's nothing wrong with the size of our dicks."

"You may wish you had a dick, little girl," our snazzy dresser snarled in my face, "but you should probably leave before someone teaches you what a real twat is for."

"Wait a minute," I said with a playful smile—I was charging like a power-plant, but my range was limited by the people at my back. I could probably take the six guys in front of me out of action, and then the battle was on. "You're not the baby-raping pedophile, are you? Because that could explain your obsession with where to put your little dick."

That stopped him. That stopped everybody. The nasty collection of knives and maces that had been up in battle position were lowered for a moment, and the joker I was facing growled, "What in the fuck are you talking about?"

"The guy? The guy Rafael was supposed to turn over to me? The one your whole kiss is ready to die for? Isn't anybody curious as to why we want to talk to him?"

"Don't listen to her, Soto—man, she'll say anything to take over our turf!" Beside me, Bracken grunted, and I shifted my shoulder back to touch his—this could be our scumbag.

"Trey, you know what he's like!" Soto looked honestly dismayed—and not shocked. We touched shoulders again—nope. Not our scumbag. Rafael had pretty much told us—this guy had promised to stop and then fucked up—and now we knew he had apparently hid inside while the rest of us were doing the bleeding.

"I could give a flying pig-fuck about this craptacular piece of real estate," I spat— I was sweating down my back and I had red dust in all my crevices and I *totally* meant that. Someday—in the winter-- I might learn to like Redding, and even take a trip to see the big-assed volcano that had loomed over us the whole trip, but right now it was the sphincter of the universe and I couldn't wait until it shit us out and flushed us home.

"All I want," I continued, "is to blood with the motherfucker who's been making baby vamps and setting them loose on their families..."

"You blood with your kiss?" Soto sounded shocked. "How is that even possible?"

"Does it matter? I want the baby vamps to stop—do you people *know* what happens to kids when they get brought over?"

There was an awkward silence and some shuffling. Apparently, they did, and it was sweet that they felt bad and all, but I didn't stop the huge electric power ball from sizzling in my chest. For a moment, it almost escaped me. For a moment I remembered that I could kill them all, and the people in the building behind them, and me and my lovers and the people we cared for would be all okay.

But Andres was in there, and Orson, and Rafael who had only tried to do right by his people, and that budding moment of being a mass-murdering fuckhead died aborning—for the moment at least. I still kept the power-charge though—I certainly wasn't going to trust their remorse *now*. Trey, bless him, rewarded my skepticism in a big way.

"Well that's our problem, bitch—you got no say in how we handle our problems!"

I blinked. "I'm your queen, motherfucker—I'm the *ultimate* resolution to your problems. Now you can hand over your baby-raping buddy, and we can call this good, or this can go down a whole other way and a lot of people can get hurt..."

Apparently that speech wasn't going to fly—Soto's hand shot out to grab my throat, and that's when the battle went down.

He'd barely made skin contact when I called his mark, and in addition to the other battle ruckus, there was the sound of his scream as the lines of the twisting vine amalgam of leaves and limes ripped its way through the skin on his arm, his bared chest, his face, As he fell to his knees and howled in pain, I took all that power shrieking at my skin, held my arms wide, and slammed as many guys as I could grab hold of up against the wall of the bar, hard enough to crumple their skulls. They fell to the ground, leaving red smears behind them—down for the count but not out, I was pretty sure.

And then the fun really started.

Two shapeshifters jumped Bracken—one from behind--and fell to the ground without their hearts, leaving my lover dripping in gore and laughing gleefully, daring anyone else to come try him. We were immediately surrounded by vampires with knives, and we stood back to back as I pulled powerballs from my anger and sent them spitting lightning at whoever got too close. I only had to do that a couple of times before they became wary of me and started throwing their knives. One big-assed machete came about two inches from Brack's shoulder before I slammed down my shield and shouted, "Shoot these fuckers *now!*"

"Jesus," one guy screamed as Max and Teague broke out the hardware, "that bird took my knife!"

"But don't hit Nicky!" I hollered, and Brack and I kept up our back-to-back circle warily, watching as the knives bounced off the shield like toothpicks off a tin balloon.

Bam! Teague had bought the pump-action shotgun, loaded with silver, and the badass in front of me blinked in surprise as his chest peeled back like an onion to reveal his black, fragmented heart. He pitched forward, leaving his blood to spatter on my hissing shield. Max double tapped his victims—one from each gun—and I blessed the time the three of us spent at the shooting range together. And still, in spite of the threats from the outside, the majority of bad guys were facing us, hurling their fucking knives at us or rushing the shield like, I don't know, it was showing signs of weakening.

It wasn't.

"We could do this all night, fuckers!" Bracken taunted. "Why don't you just let us in the goddamned bar!"

"Careful, beloved," I murmured. "You're starting to sound like me."

"Osmosis—fuck, that one was right at my face."

Outside our circle I could hear various howls, yowls, and growls as the enemies who strayed too near the shadows got picked off by Jack, Katy, and Renny—or got fried to a crisp by Lambent. As strategies went, it was pretty awesome—I just wish I could take some credit for the enemy's stupidity because I hadn't planned on it at all.

A knife went over our heads and Kyle managed to dodge it—while the guy he was hand-to-handing didn't, and as the bad guy's head rolled like a soccer ball, Kyle let out a whoop and a howl of triumph that got him suddenly besieged by combatants. Max and Phillip flew in low and took out two a piece, smacking them headfirst into the bar—where they may have sustained too much damage to get up again. Ever.

"Ya know, Brack—I don't like being left out of the action," I muttered, realizing how helpless I felt when it came to protecting anybody else but the two of us.

"You got anything in mind?"

"Yeah…" I did. "When I give the signal, start ripping hearts."

"Heh-heh-heh…" My *Goddess* that was an evil laugh. "What's the signal?"

I started clenching against my ginormous power dump, and the leftover energy electric-cockroach-crawled over my skin. Good. My shield felt hard and brittle—so I went with that, tightened my stomach, squat-thrust with the mind-muscle that was controlling the power itself, and exploded my shield into powershards that went whipping through anyone standing within fifteen feet of the shield. Men went down clutching at nothing in their chests while their flesh split open and ripped itself in the power-fragment, and Bracken screamed vicious joy into the night and our entire world turned red as all of that available blood went splatting towards us.

"Blargh!" But I had one of my guns in my hand as I said it and I managed to pick off a vampire running for Renny before I even cleared the blood from my eyes.

Bracken howled again, and I backhanded another round of knives out of the air, taking out two guys just because they were still where they stood when they threw them. There was a sudden scream from above us, and a vampire I didn't know came plummeting out of the air in a dive designed to take me out, but I did another backhanded power-swat and in an explosion of cinderblock he went shooping right through the wall of the bar instead. I heard a crash and a scream, and I wondered if maybe that alone wouldn't give the captives in the bar some incentive to fight back.

And like my wishes were commands, Andres stepped into the hole in the bar, two big-assed machetes in his hands.

"Bout time, my Lady!" he called, and started advancing through the bad guys using those machetes like a pro. He carved a way through them, leaving bleeding, reeling and twice-dead vampires in his wake until he took his place back to back with Bracken and I.

"We got here as soon as we could," I gasped, admiring his fighting style. Hell, there was nothing wrong with 'fucking deadly' as a technique, right?

"Well, it's good to know you didn't stop for a quickie on the way!" he snapped, and I risked a glance at him.

Healing silver burns on his neck gave me a clue as to how they had managed to keep him still while we'd been fighting outside.

"Naw, sweetie," I sent a powerball through a fucker who'd been aiming his gun at us and he looked in puzzlement at the smoking hole through his torso before he fell. "We save the quickies for after the battle."

Andres reached out and slashed off the arm of the guy coming at him with a knife. "So, all that wait was to make an entrance?"

"Entertainment," I gritted, sighting another fucker going for our people in the trees. "Anything to get your attention. Fuck." This one was mammoth— the guy must have weighed three-fifty, on the inside, and when he morphed into a bear getting ready to ride Jack's ass without a saddle, I screamed "Teague, open here!"

Teague was about twenty feet away, but he swung around and without panicking locked and loaded to defend his beloved, and together, while Brack and Andres kept our backs clear, we started blasting silver into that big fucking brown bear.

We didn't stop it completely, but it stood on its hind legs and turned instinctively towards us to leave Jack alone, and we continued to blow through ammo.

"On your left!" Teague called, and I turned to take out the vampire coming from me, and oh, shit, I was out. Teague fired two more rounds as that huge-assed were-thing screamed at us and died, and I reached behind me for the other gun, and fuck-it-all, I was too slow. The vamp charged me, so hyper-quick I didn't even have time to throw up a shield, although I did catch him in the face with a round from the Glock—but the damage was done. He may have been twice dead, but he was still hauling ass with enough velocity to knock me out of the circle and change the dynamic of the fight.

The sudden pressure on my chest knocked my wind out, and the quick trip and sudden stop to my back finished the job. I scrambled to my feet before I could breathe while Brack and Andres were still back-to-back. I was alone and now that Jack was out of danger, Teague's attention was focused on me.

It gave the vampire swooping down on him just enough leeway to grab him under the arms and start hauling him up before anybody could get off a shot.

Jacky stood up, a naked, vulnerable young man, and Katy sat on her haunches and howled, and even though we had been winning, the entire battle stalled as I looked to the sky and screamed Teague's name.

And then Soto, who had recovered from the skull-pulping I'd given him, blurred behind me, wrapped an arm around my chest and held a knife to my throat, then pushed me forward, away from the bar, towards the middle of the parking lot, leaving Bracken and Andres, bereft and alone at my back.

"You see that, bitch!" Soto growled. He shook his head, and blood from the emerging mark on his face added to the dripping mess on my body. "You think you can just come into our nest and take one of our own? You want to know what it feels like, to watch one of your own die for no other reason than someone wants it? That could be arranged."

"Teague's got a soldier's honor," I said, my anger boiling in my chest and my mind darting between possibilities. "Your guy leaves the helpless to kill and die." They were going to drop him—I knew it. I could save him—I could—but the knife at my throat...

Green? I asked.

His voice in my head was so close to panic, but not over the edge.

I don't know. Please, don't try it...

It's Teague, Green. Teague, who was so like Adrian. Teague, who deserved a happy ending.

"I could give a shit!" Soto spat, and I growled.

"Of course you could, you honorless pussy. If you had any balls at all we could have worked this out like men." *Green, I can't see them anymore... the fall will kill him. Tell me you can do this from far away.*

Dammit, beloved, don't make me test this now!

Green, it's TEAGUE!

"Let's see how much honor you've got when your manwhore's guts are splattered at your feet."

What an asshole. I ignored him—he was twice dead already. "Bracken—when I give the signal, you know what to do." *BELOVED, NO!*

"What's the signal?" Bracken asked breathlessly, even as Soto jerked my head back. I was still carrying my gun—these vamps weren't used to humans in a vamp-fight. They weren't used to guns.

"What's happening up there?" I asked, not answering Bracken. I was pretty sure he'd know what the signal was, but I used speaking to disguise the jerk of my shoulder as I positioned the gun downwards, towards Soto's thigh. I heard Jacky whine, and a shout from above us, and I knew they'd dropped Teague, even though I couldn't see his body flailing helplessly through the darkness yet. I couldn't move too soon, I couldn't, but Jack didn't think I was moving at all and he screamed and fell to his knees, hugging Katy's neck as she howled.

"Don't worry, Jacky," I promised desperately, wondering how much time I really had, "I'm going to make this right."

I trust you, Green.

"How you gonna do that, bitch?" Soto rasped.

Corinne Carol- Anne, I'm not the Goddess…luv, please.

I said "Like this," *I love you, Green,* and I pulled the fucking trigger and jerked against the knife as Green screamed *Goddammit NO!* in my head.

I was bleeding—I was bleeding a *lot* and I could feel Green, smell him, as he worked frantically from inside my body to bind up the nick in my jugular. It would have been a lot deeper if I hadn't shot the fucker first, and I trusted Bracken and Andres behind me to take care of him as I stepped forward into the night and reached all my power up to catch Teague.

O shit… there he was…I felt him hit my shield, and my vision was blurring, going black, and it was hard to tell how black because the sky was black but I was slowing Teague down. I could see him now, at the treetop level, good, good, and dammit, he was still too high up. The fall would still hurt but I didn't think it would be lethal and I had to stay awake and I was cold, honestly cold for the first time in a week and a…

I didn't even feel my body hit the ground.

BRACKEN

Knight's Gambit

Holy Goddess, *that* was her fucking signal?

The gun fired and she jerked through the damned knife, bleeding enough to make a vampire sick, and I did the only thing I thought I *could* do—I blurred towards them and reached through Soto's spine and tore his heart out before he could move again. Andres yelled, "Green's people, *down!*" and I felt my power—fierce and fed with our fury already—answer my blood with a banshee scream, as I aimed my hand at the chest of every enemy close enough to count and pulled the blood from their bodies. I was *very* careful not to aim anywhere near Cory, and fortunately Marcus, Phillip and Kyle were in her space, with Lambent beside them to keep her safe as she aimed her attention at the sky. We really had been winning before they scooped Teague up, and the few people left to fight after I dropped the five or so backing Soto up were now kneeling, their hands over their heads, begging for mercy.

I would have killed them just because, but I was too busy watching Cory wobble on her feet as she tried to catch a falling werewolf.

"She's got him," Jacky breathed, and that was true—his descent had slowed, but I could hear her heartbeat, and it was thready and uncertain as her blood pumped out and goddammit I couldn't even move to catch her. In a blur of bloody feathers, Nicky was suddenly there, behind her, and we all watched as Teague came down slowly... slowly... he was maybe thirty yards up—what was that, four stories? A werewolf could survive that, right?

Without warning, my beloved simply crumpled to the ground. Teague hit hard with a crackling shatter of bones a fraction of a second later.

Nicky and Andres were at her side and Lambent was at Teague's before the dust even settled from their respective falls, and I heard Lambent order Jack and Katy back, but that was from the dim place in my mind that gave a shit.

She was dying—Green had done his best, her wound was mostly closed but not enough and she was still bleeding and dammit…

She needs blood, Green said in my head, and I could hear his panic and I shared it.

Human blood…

Any blood! He roared. *You're a master of the stuff, Bracken Brine, MAKE it fit!*

I was barely sane as I ran my finger over my wrist and broke skin and vein, and even less sane as I ordered Andres and Nicky out of the way. Blood…her heartbeat was slowing, I needed to feed it to make it run.

"Bracken?" Nicky stammered, appalled. "Bracken—you're not human…"

"Neither is she!" I snapped. With a scalpel will I pumped the blood from my veins to hers, through three feet of black space and that appalling wound in her neck, and listened I listened, listened, as her heartbeat stuttered… slowed…stalled…and…

and…

and…

and…

started racing like a sprinter's at the line.

Lambent said, "Mario, call Tanya, dammit—we need a cast to make this heal right," and then my beloved sat up so abruptly she whacked Nicky's chin with her head and knocked him unconscious, screaming like a horror-show heroine as she did.

CORY

Check Mate

Adrian was sooooo pissed at me.

"I'm sorry, beloved," I said sheepishly, reaching out to touch that fine, white hair as it floated around his face.

He grabbed my hand, our flesh real and human and warm. "You're not supposed to be here!" he growled. "You can't just go and leave them—you know that!"

"I had to," I said softly, trying not to cry. Adrian never yelled at me. He looked so good, here, wherever we were. It was dark, and we stood in a silver pool of light, and as angry as he was, his arms were wrapped around my hips and I leaned into him with something like hunger.

"Why—because he reminded you of me?" So much bitterness. I cupped his face in my hands, pulled his lips down on mine...who knew how long this would last?

He tasted sweet...coppery...like blood and mint and bubblegum and I wasn't sure whose tears slicked across our skin as the kiss broke off.

"There's more than that," I whispered, now that I could remember the sweet instead of the bitter. He cupped my face in turn, and his thumbs stroked the tears away—I guess they were mine.

"We don't have long," he prompted, and a part of me was happy—I wasn't dead for real.

I nodded. "I can't leave them behind."

"I know it…" His eyes were so blue. "Now tell me… tell me, and I can make Green understand."

"They just keep offering their lives for me, beloved." I put my ear against his chest, heard his heart beat. It was stuttering, slowing, stalling…

"And?" I felt his lips brush my hair, and I shivered in his arms.

"And there's not a damned reason for them to do it, unless I'm going to put it out on the line for them." The shivers got worse. The cold was starting to burn in my veins.

"And that's what royalty's for," he murmured, putting me at arm's length and stepping away. *Please, beloved—please understand. Green and Bracken were born to royalty, they're beautiful and gifted and proud. You would know… you were mortal once, and afraid of your power.*

"But my…" oh Goddess, it hurt, but I wanted to say this first, "but my loyalty back…it keeps me sane…honest…in…in…in…" oh Goddess, "in check…" Oh Goddess it hurt. "Love you, A'…" It burned. It froze. Oh shit… oh shit… oh shit…

"Love you back…"

Fuck fuck fuck fuck fuck fuck…

"HWUUUUAAAAAHHHHGGGGGHHHHHHHH!!!!" I didn't even feel the impact of my skull on Nicky's jaw. I was sitting up, trying to breathe, and Bracken was crouched down, his hands on my shoulders, calming me down.

"It hurts…it hurts it hurts it hurts it hurts… *FUCK it FUCKING HURTS.*" Every nerve, every capillary, every dendrite, every atom, every quantum particle in my body was being dragged across a molten cheese-grater in an acid bath. I gasped for breath some more, and finally heard Green… his voice, his smell, his presence soothing me enough to slow the adrenaline dump from the pain.

It's Bracken's blood, beloved. You have to let him touch you…

Bracken's blood? Why would I have Bracken's blood in me?

Because you DIDN'T HAVE ENOUGH OF YOUR OWN TO POWER YOUR OWN HEART! His thunder in my head made me whine and clap my hands over my ears.

I'm sorry I'm sorry I'm sorry I'm sorry… I was crying. Oh Goddess, I hadn't cried since Hallow's confession…

"Cory!" Bracken's sharp voice cracked across my pain.

"Bracken it hurts…" I wept, and he nodded, and stood, holding my shoulders and pulling me with him and then he…he was using his power—I could feel it. It was zinging through my pores, soothing my nerve endings, aligning the shark-toothed ragged edges of whatever was pumping me full of pain.

My breathing slowed down, and the adrenaline dump eased back. I started to bounce on my feet, so hopped-up on elf blood that standing still wasn't an option, and I tried to remember what in the fuck I was doing.

I was almost there, when pain seared across my back. *"Fuck... the guns,* oh, goddammit, *the guns..."* Phillip's touch was impersonal and cool, and the empty gun in the back of my jeans was gone in a moment—along with a nice layer of my skin as well. It was all I could do not to curl in a ball and snivel like an infant at the gun-shaped second degree burn on my back, but I had a feeling the more fuss I made about my pain, the more my lovers would want to strangle me with their bare hands.

"How's Teague?" I said after a moment, nodding my head to keep Bracken with me.

Brack shook his head and looked like he was a cat's whisker from smacking me. "I don't know," he said, gritting his teeth, and at our feet, Nicky groaned.

I bent down to help him up, saying, "Jesus, Nicky—what happened to you?"

Nicky rubbed his jaw and laughed. "You did, you dork—I survive a parking lot full of homicidal monsters and I get knocked out by my wife who was damned near dead!"

"I'm sorry," I said again, not able to meet either of their eyes. "Thanks, Bracken," I murmured—my voice was shaky from pain, from adrenaline, from whatever hyper-elf-steroid was thumping through my body in time to my heart but I didn't want to think about it or it would get worse. I turned towards Teague before we could get all hot and emotional in the middle of a completely different situation.

Bracken stopped me, his eyes finding mine in the dark, and I realized that, among other things, my night vision was significantly improved. Fucking groovy—where was that handy little gift when I was peering into the dark to see if Teague was falling to his death?

"We'll talk later," he promised grimly, the hurt on his face making my blood shred my nervous system all over again.

"I know it," I told him with a quiet smile, and then I moved to crouch by Teague.

The bones in his legs were broken through his flesh like white, glistening, blood-covered shrapnel—and every time one sucked back into his flesh to heal, his entire body clenched in pain.

"Oh Jesus," I breathed. "Teague—I'm so sorry...I should have held on longer...I'm so sorry..."

His snapped femur cracked/squelched it's way back into his body, and my entire nervous system sang empathetic agony. When I opened my eyes, darkness swam in front of them, and Bracken's hand came down on my shoulder to steady me.

"You saved his life," Jack said, kneeling at his side. "You...you damned near killed yourself to save his life."

"My job, goddammit," Teague gritted and while Katy licked his face, I took his other hand and tried not to weep all over this nice man who didn't need my bullshit right now.

"Yeah," I muttered gruffly, "but if I can't put myself out for you, why would you want to throw yourself under my bus?" I didn't let him answer—didn't want to hear the answer. I looked up at Lambent, who was busy wrapping Teague's legs in bandages made from what looked to be Jacky's ripped jeans.

"Did you call Tanya?"

"Do I look helpless, luvie?" he asked sharply, and Teague's eyes met mine in a moment of sympathy. "The chopper's on it's way—we might even have some knickers for our lanky friend here. But I think once we get his legs cased in some plaster, being a werewolf will take care of the rest."

Teague groaned, and Jacky let out a bit of a sob. "Pain, Lambent?" I asked, and Teague shook his head no and Jacky barked out *"Yes!"*

Ah. I held his hand to my chest and tried to command him like a queen worth dying for. "Teague—your job is done here. You'll only hurt them if you don't let Lambent help you."

"I... I don't like being out of my mind, Lady Cory," he murmured. Of course he didn't. His father had done some heinous fucking things to him when out of his mind, and Teague had some *bad* experiences with his first werewolf changes.

"You won't be out of it," I said softly. "You'll be safely inside it. Lambent will put you under until the pain doesn't make your vision red, that's all." He groaned again, and Katy howled into the night.

"C'mon, Teague—for all of us, brother, you've got to let us take care of you."

"I don't want to be helpless for you..." he grunted, and I looked at his lovers, whimpering and miserable.

"Then be helpless for them," I whispered. "Let us heal you, and then go someplace far away, just with them. I know you can do that, right? Be helpless for them? Let them take care of you?"

"Where would I go?" he asked, and I heard another squelch/crackle and cringed.

"Where do you want to go? Green can set you up anywhere he's got territory, you know that."

Teague's mind wandered—away from the bloody night, away from the pain. He was gazing wonderingly into Jacky's face, seemingly mindless of the tears dropping onto his cheeks from his lover's eyes.

"I've never seen the ocean," he said weakly, and Green spoke up, *Monterey it is.* His thick anger coated my inner ear, and I tried not to cringe.

"Then that's where you'll wake up," I said to Teague, and looked at Jacky to see if he'd heard. He was clutching Katy to his side and Teague's hand to his face, but he caught my eyes and nodded.

Please talk to Adrian, beloved. I didn't know how that worked—Adrian here, for me, Adrian there, for Green—it was, best I could tell, magic. But Adrian...he had understood. Please, Goddess, let one of them understand.

I looked at Lambent, and Teague put up no resistance this time when Lambent caught his eyes and put him gently under. His eyes fluttered shut, and Katy curled up near his head, and Jack kissed his hand gratefully, their bodies relaxing as Teague's pain went softly away. I leaned over and kissed his forehead, then patted Jacky's hand before I reluctantly stood. The motion made my skin hurt all over again, and the urge to move, to fly through the bar in a rage was pushing at my chest.

"I don't know about you all," I said sourly, my voice pitched across the parking lot, "but I've about had enough of this shit. Anyone else want a fucking drink?"

There was a scatter of laughter from my people—but Nicky and Bracken were still looking at me like I'd kicked their puppies. I looked at them and tried to smile, and shivered with the shock and the power of the blood running through my veins instead.

"Come on, guys," I murmured, "you can be mad at me later—let's take care of this now."

They stood, one on either side of me, and Bracken put his hand in the small of my back like a gentleman. I quivered and jerked under his touch—dammit, that burn from the gun still hurt--and then I looked down at Lambent.

"Lambent, after the copter gets here, you want to join us?" We could hear it, in the distance, and I blessed Tanya and her contact twice and three times over.

"Nice of you to think of me, luvie—I wouldn't miss it."

I looked at him deliberately, thinking about missing children and the fierceness of Rafael's family, defending the man who destroyed them so utterly. "Be sure that you don't," I cautioned. "I have the feeling we'll need you."

"You need me now," he muttered, watching me try not to jerk away from Bracken's touch. With a sigh he put his hand on my calf, and I could feel the healing travel to that burn, taking away the sting. I put my hand on his shoulder and murmured a quiet thanks, and then I heard Max reload, and then Phillip doing the same while using my gun. Renny trotted up to us from out of the shadows, her whiskers dripping in other people's blood, and Mario and La Mark landed—shirtless and shoeless, and dripping in blood themselves, but none of it was their own.

"Let's get that drink," I rallied, and they nodded with me. Cannyagimme-hallelujia-amen.

I could tell by the posture of everybody in the bar that until we walked in, dripping blood and gore literally from our fingertips, no one was sure who won.

There were very few enemies in the club, actually—six, maybe, there with semi-automatics (doubtless loaded with silver) and bad-assed attitudes, and when we stalked in, Andres in our midst, the expression on their faces was almost comical. I was still in antsy elf-blood-meth-amped-fucking pain and it would have taken a real goddamned miracle to get me to laugh at anything.

"I'm gonna count to two," I snapped. "At the end of two, any motherfucker with so much as a Swiss army knife is going down. One…"

Two guns turned my way and snicked.

It was a near fucking thing, actually. I was angry, I was half out of my mind. I'd been so good—they'd made an attempt on Green, on my people, on me. For a split second…half a pumped-up heartbeat… I tasted how really goddamned easy it would be to take out this whole shit-hole and just start over. Everyone who wasn't *us*… I could level them. I really could.

I settled for the people who'd just decided to fuck with me. I didn't even have to hold out my hands—I looked out at the enemy and incinerated the two guys with the guns where they stood, the fire pulsing outward with my heartbeat, causing the people near them to flinch from the heat, and the dying vampires to scream horribly.

"Two." There was a numb clatter as their guns hit the floor, safeties thankfully on.

Well good. People would live tonight.

"Rafael?"

Rafael glared at the ashes of the vampire who had been holding the gun on him, and then stood up and walked over. "Anything you wish, my lady."

I nodded. "Could you show me who started this bullshit?"

"Goddamn you, Rafael!" I turned my head towards the scream, and saw a vampire, sitting with his hands dangling between his knees, the picture of defeat.

I didn't even have to ask—that was our guy.

I walked right up to him and said, "You don't look like a monster."

He'd been in his thirties when he turned, with that prematurely silver hair that hits some men when they were blonde as children. It was longish, falling from his crown, and when he turned his miserable glare at me, I could see that his eyes were lightish blue. And his face? Long around the jaw, round around the brow, but nothing special. Ordinary. Average. On a good day, he was probably handsome—but not today. Today, he was haggard, meek, and helpless.

Today he was defeated.

"I'm not a monster," he said through those weak-colored eyes. "I'm a coward."

"You'll get no arguments from me," I said with a bitter laugh. I reached out a gore covered hand and wiped the front of it on his shirt, and then the back of it on his sleeve, and then the other hand, front and back on his face, so viciously obsessed with my task that I didn't even cringe when I touched his cold flesh.

"Stop!" he cried out, revolted by the sticky mess as it glommed onto his clothes. "Why are you doing this?"

"Because you had some brave sons-of-bitches out there tonight, just dying for you. Being all honorable and shit and not wanting to turn over a family member to a stranger—and what have you done for them?"

He looked away, leaving my own handprint facing me.

"WHAT HAVE YOU DONE FOR THEM!!!" I shouted, thinking of Teague, falling to the ground, and what I would and almost did give up to know that my friends didn't have to die for me.

"I…" he looked at me helplessly. "I never asked them to," he whispered, and I fought against screaming pain and anger in an emotional vomit of sound.

"You didn't step forward either." My voice was choked, and I wanted to kill him—badly—but I needed to do this right. "Now you need to pay."

"So kill me already!" he gritted, and I could have wept all over again—he wanted to die. I could tell by his voice—he was aching for death. He was just too afraid to step up.

"No—too easy." I used my hopped up elf-blood to hoist him up sitting in a power sling, over the heads of the assembly, as easy as Brack putting a kid on his shoulders. He hovered there for a minute, and I shouted at him, "Now tell them what this is about!"

"I said kill me, bitch!" he cried back, and I turned to Bracken who growled and held out his hand—and apparently pulled—gently--at his skin, until he screamed.

"Now TELL THEM!"

"Fine! Fine!" He started to weep, the blood of his tears pattering down on the faces of the people in the room. "The little ones…they're… they're so beautiful…" he moaned. "So pure… and they smile at me…and…and I have to…I just have to… and their flesh is so sweet…" He sniffled, and it was awful. "But I'm a vampire—I…I can't control it…and I feed…but I feel just so bad. I think…you know…if they rise again in the dark, they'll be okay…"

"Be okay?" I said through a raspy throat. "BE OKAY? Do you know what happens to them? Do you have any idea what you've done?"

"No…" his entire ordinary man's face crumpled, and he began to mewl like an infant. "No…no no no no no no…"

He was lying.

"Where are they?" I asked, my voice breaking, and I was aware that the eyes of all my people suddenly bulged with horror.

"Oh Goddess…" Rafael rasped beside me. "Lady, are you sure?"

I whirled our monster around towards me, still levitating, and brought him down and eye level with me. "Where are they?" I asked, my voice pitching dangerously up, and he raised his hands to his bleeding eyes and sobbed some more.

Jesus.

"Bracken, I need to blood him."

Bracken looked at me in horror. "No."

"I need to find out where they are…"

"No."

I looked at him in appeal. "This needs to end, and it needs to end tonight, beloved…I won't lose myself in this guy's mind—you know I won't. I've proved that…"

I flinched from the hard anger in Bracken's face. "No." His shaking hand came out and jerked my chin back, so I had to look at him. "You will not do this. You think you have to tell me what drives you, but you're wrong. I know *exactly* what drives you—but you can only sacrifice so much of yourself before there's not enough to lead…"

"We have to know…" I said, my voice shaking.

I had turned away from our monster, my power fluctuations making his 'chair shield' bob lightly with my emotions, and I turned suddenly when Rafael stepped between us with a bleeding wrist.

"Dwight," he said softly.

"I can't let you do it, Rafael," he moaned.

"You have to, Dwight—you're done for. I'd kill you myself, brother—you should have told me the urges were back."

Dwight moaned again. "I didn't want to let you down, Rafael…"

"Well look at us, brother," Rafael said sadly. "Our people are dead because you wouldn't step up…because I had to call you in. Look at them, Dwight."

He grasped the man's chin, much like Bracken had grasped mine, and made him look at the lot of us—the blood-dripping, snarling, feral lot of us.

"They came here in peace—they came here looking to protect people—and look what you made them do. That girl—she's planning to blood with you and then kill you…" Rafael's voice shook. "She knows how it feels, brother—she knows the hole it's going to leave in her soul—and all because you won't do what you need to do—what you needed to do since the very beginning…"

"I had to…" Dwight sobbed. "I had to go back and get them, Rafael. Once I knew they weren't dead…"

Oh Jesus… sweet Goddess… I shook again, caught in the throes of both horror and the elf-blood, and I wanted mightily to fall to my knees and sick-up everything I'd eaten all week. He knew they weren't dead because their families were. I didn't even want to think about where he'd been keeping them.

"Well then," Rafael said softly, holding his wrist in front of what appeared to be a beloved friend, a confidant, "it's time you let us bring them to the light, isn't it?"

"Not from me, you won't," Dwight snarled, unreasonable and feral in his final moments, and Rafael thrust his blood into his enemy's mouth and sank his fangs into the upper part of Dwight's arm, which was closest, and after a suck and a swallow, fell to his knees and groaned.

"Do you know where they are?" I rasped, choking back my own nausea, and Rafael nodded.

"He's got helpers," he rasped, "people who didn't fight, but who helped him keep the secret…"

"Don't you hurt them!" Dwight screamed, finally, *finally,* showing some loyalty to people who had put themselves out for him.

"Dwight, my friend, this is no longer your concern," Rafael said formally, and then, nodding to me, "Little Goddess, would you please?"

Awesome—all my battle rage had faded in the wake of my horror and nausea. We were doing this cold-blooded style, with a formal execution.

I swung Dwight around to look at me. "Any last words, sir?" I asked—not being ironic at all.

"I'm not a monster," he said, his voice cracking, breaking, putting a lie to the last thing he'd ever believe.

"Tell your victims that in hell."

I stepped back and let loose, the flame as erratic with him as it had been with the other vampires, burning hot and clean one minute and crackling weakly the next. Fucking elf-blood, playing havoc with my wiring, my emotions, my equilibrium. I grunted in the midst of his screams and concentrated hard, and he was suddenly ash, no more suffering, no more debate, just one dead pedophile with a whole big blood-sodden mess to clean up.

"Rafael," I said clearly, wondering how long my knees were going to last. "We need to know."

Rafael nodded, and looked at me sorrowfully, the shock of the whole evening written cleanly on his face. But he was a master vampire—his love for his people may have blinded him, but he hadn't been made a leader for his weakness.

"Here, Little Goddess," he murmured, holding out his wrist, "let's find them together."

It was sort of like a medieval social pyramid... the king ruled the vassals who ruled their own vassals who ruled their serfs—but the king ruled them all. Vampires tended to sex and blood with the other people they dealt with— vampires, shape-shifters, whatever. I was the king, Rafael was my vassal, and he had control over his vassal's vassals... we just had to follow the blood down the pyramid.

I could do that.

"Accomplices first," I said, looking up and nodding to Lambent as he walked in. He nodded back, and I knew that Teague would be all right, and that we still had work to do.

"Right, Little Goddess," Rafael said grimly, and offered me his bleeding wrist. I offered him my wrist—which was covered with other people's blood, and he licked it off grimly before we each settled to our task.

It would be comforting to say it was as clean as one of those movies, where computer files and images whisked and whooshed their way in front of my eyes and then were picked or discarded by Rafael's sense of who his people were, but it was more complicated than that. It was taking over two-hundred blood trails and following them all simultaneously, abandoning the ones that came to dead ends, and when we were done, we were left with a scant handful of young vampires—young when they were made and not long in the making—who had been beguiled into helping a monster hide his face from a world of monsters.

With a careful flexing of my erratic, hopped up will, I pulled at the marks of the four people who had been most complicit, and I could tell by their gasps and whimpers that as careful as I was being, the cutting of their marks through their flesh was still painful.

"Front and center," I barked, suppressing another shiver. Goddess, I felt like I had when Arturo first touched me—like my flesh was clawing and crawling to escape my skin. I managed to bottle it though, to shove it into a shivering, roiling, screaming boil in my chest, and I looked out at the frightened vampire young—the true innocents—who were looking at me with helpless eyes.

Oh Goddess—I knew one of them.

"Hey, Walter," I said a little sadly.

The small vampire gave me a tired smile. "Bet you want that rum now, hah, Lady Cory."

I swallowed, hard, and graced him with a laugh. "Maybe later—you wouldn't believe what's thumping through my veins right now." I sighed, and realized that Rafael was looking at me without expression. Oh Goddess—he expected me to kill them. I looked at them again, and then at Walter.

"Why?" I asked simply, and Walter looked away and shrugged.

"I...I thought they were like me," he whispered. "I got hit in a hunting accident—my Dad knew about Rafael, he brought me here. Dwight—he just said that they were young. I..." he looked at the two young men and the young woman standing up with him in front of us—young. They'd been in their teens when they'd been brought over, and I guessed Walter was the oldest of them in vampire years. "We...we thought they were accidents. We didn't...I don't understand what happened to them. We gave them blood...we treated them decent...and they just... just..."

I had seen them in the pit of Rafael's mind, locked in iron cages somewhere in the bottom of the cave network that housed *Rafe's Place*.

"Disintegrated," I said softly, picturing Gretchen, prowling in her shredded pink room like a rabid bobcat.

"Yeah," Walter said softly. "Until you came asking for Dwight, I didn't know... and then... all the others got mad..."

He looked me in the eyes then, his solid brown gaze as clear an open as Sam's had been, expecting me to condemn him for being human.

Even the son of chaos, even vampires, were still human.

"What happened to them?" he asked quietly, and I looked at him and the others, figuring that no matter how this came about, they had the right to know.

"You guys remember when you were turned?" They nodded. "You remember what you wanted?"

If it was possible, they would have blushed. "Sex and blood," Walter said directly, and I nodded.

"Sex and blood—except their bodies aren't wetwired for sex yet... so all they want... all they crave..."

Walter closed his eyes. "Is blood..." he murmured.

"Yeah." I shivered—hard, and harder, and then Bracken came near enough to put his hand on my shoulder and I managed to get my treacherous body under control.

"They're all hunger," I said at last, through chattering teeth. "No love, no comfort—their hunger just eats the person they didn't even have a chance to become."

Walter's jaw clenched, and he shook his head. "I'm sorry, Lady," he turned, "Rafael—I..." he looked over at his accomplices, "we didn't know."

I closed my eyes, anchoring my shaking with Bracken's warm hand, pressing angry comfort through my skin. "Lord Vampire," I said formally, "these are your people. I think you would know best how to deal with their crimes."

Rafael's eyes flashed with something like hope. "I think," he said slowly, watching my eyes, keeping our link active so that we could behave in accord, "that they will suffer when the children they've blooded with die."

I closed my eyes and swallowed hard. "They will," I said neutrally—Goddess, this had to be his decision or I would never get out of this fucking town.

"And I also think," Rafael continued, "that I have felt enough of my people die tonight."

Oh thank you, sweet Goddess, thank you thank you thank you. "I would imagine you're right," I told him softly, and another tremor hit me hard enough to knock me into Bracken. His hand moved from my shoulder to around my waist.

"Lambent?" And the fire elf was right there, looking at me and shaking my head.

"You need food," he murmured softly, "and water, to replace the blood you lost so you can start burning Bracken's."

Oh—good. Necessary to know that my body wasn't being taken over by supernatural-glow-in-the-dark-mutant-nuclear-magic-cockroaches, which is pretty much what it felt like.

"If I eat right now I'll puke on your shoes," I told him truthfully, "and there's a job to do first. Walter—could you lead the way?"

Rafael nodded, and we met sober eyes. He looked out at the assembly, and at the remainder of my people who were standing at the doorway like blood-dripping ass-kicking angels of death. "I think we should show our guests and rescuers some hospitality, people, you think?"

"How 'bout a garden hose!" Max asked loudly, picking at a crust of blood on his face with his fingernails, and there was an uneasy ripple of laughter.

"I think we can get you some showers in the employee locker room," Rafael replied, grateful, I think, for something to do.

I turned to Nicky, and he nodded. "I'll get us all some spare clothes," he murmured and moved towards the door to get our shit from the car. I didn't even have to call Kyle to walk him out—we weren't *that* relaxed. Then Bracken, Lambent and I caught up with young Walter.

The hallway behind the room wound steeply down as soon as it cleared the building part of the club. It was close and claustrophobic, and as my body kept up an almost rhythmic shuddering, I couldn't help wish it was large enough for Bracken to do his he-man thing and just take me in his arms. Weakness, I thought on a tremor. I needed to pull up my big-girl panties and get this done.

My vision had started to go dark before we got to the bottom, dimly lit with electric cage lights, and tucked behind what looked to be a wine cellar. Rafael shook his head and laughed bitterly.

"It's perfect," he muttered. "We send our youngest workers down here—it's the shit job, the cutting-your-teeth task—who else would come down here to help him but his easiest targets."

"Now you tell me," Walter laughed bitterly, and I managed to spare him a sympathetic look before I had to wrap my hands around my arms and shake hard in my own embrace.

Bracken swore, and went to lift me up, but I held out my hand. I used it to grab hold of his arm and stand swaying on my feet, but I needed to be standing for this.

We rounded a corner, and there they were.

There were four of them, and they'd been children once—and human.

Now they were crouched in their own filth, snarling at us through lank and snarled hair. I couldn't tell genders, and their ages could have been anywhere from six to twelve. Their ribs were their most pronounced feature, and their eyes were red—permanently—and their bodies appeared to be set on perpetual 'feed'. Two of them were trying to chew through the bars of their iron cages with broken teeth, and the other two were shredding the flesh on their wrists with their teeth, rending it and gnashing it and screaming in pain even as it healed again. There was a healthy scattering of bones and animal corpses on the bottom of the floor. They obviously hadn't been enough.

"Sweet Goddess…"

I'm not sure which one of us said it, but I looked at Walter, and his eyes were closed in pain. "I think Dwight had the only control on them—they must have felt him die."

I started to call for Lambent, but I heard a suspicious noise and saw the blood dripping from Walter's eyes.

"I used to come down and play with them," he muttered. "They had names." He swallowed—one of those supremely human gestures that made me think of Adrian. He crouched down then, and looked into the cages—not close enough for the creatures inside to get him. He wasn't foolish, only broken-hearted.

"Hey, Steven," he murmured, "Hey Trisha. Austen. Cathy." He turned to each child, knowing them. The whispered sound of his voice calmed them down.

"These nice people are here to make it better, okay?" There was some grunting, and I bit back an un-queenly moan. Ouch. Just fucking ouch.

Walter looked up at us then, pretending he wasn't weeping blood. "It's not going to hurt, right?"

Bracken's arm clamped me to his side, and I clung to him like the child I wasn't. "It's why Lambent's here," I told Walter honestly, and looked at the fire elf with considerable pleading in my eyes.

Lambent nodded his head gravely, and I reached out and touched his hand.

"I'm not…stable," I told him, although any idiot could figure that out. "It needs to be fast and clean, Master Elf. I'm trusting you with everything."

Lambent nodded again, and then bowed. "I'm honored, my Lady," he said with complete sincerity. And then he nodded us all out of the room.

I watched, as long as I could, from far up in the confines of that awful hallway, while Walter and Rafael blurred at hyperspeed at my urging. Lambent stood in the middle of the room and mustered his will, and then he began to glow, so white-blue hot that we had to cover our eyes. The poor creatures that had once been human children shrieked in fear—but only once—and in less than a heartbeat, the room was a nova sun.

And that was it—an outburst of pure energy, unbearable heat, terrible light, stopped cleanly at the beginning of the hall, and then it was gone. Even the heat dissipated with the flame—not even the cool of the dank corridor was disturbed. When I felt the elf draw near us again, I opened my eyes, my vision going trippy in the dark, and I could barely make out the black iron bars, gleaming red with heat, and even the bones and the animal corpses and the dirt on the sides of the rock walls had been burned into nothing.

"Thank you," I told him weakly, and then my vision went completely dark.

The hallway was too narrow for Bracken to scoop me up like a blushing bride, so when I came to, he was holding me five-year-old style, with my arms around his neck and my legs wrapped around his waist and his hands linked underneath my bottom.

"Sorry," I grumbled. "You're still mad at me."

"Yes," he murmured. "Still mad. I might be less mad after you eat and can stand up again, but we'll see."

"I couldn't let him die, beloved." He had crusted blood all over his chest, and the thought of eating when we both looked like escapees from a charnel house turned my stomach. "And I want a shower."

"The shower," he said with emphasis, "is the best idea you've had all night."

"I don't know," I retorted, sparking out of weakness for a moment. "I thought drawing everybody's fire while our guys picked them off around the shield bubble worked well."

"That wasn't an idea, that was bloody damned good luck." He grunted then, hoisting me higher as my limp body tried to slide down.

"So was coming back to you, when I had Adrian in my arms." My voice was dreamy, quiet, because my teeth were chattering when I tried to speak, and I thought I was passing out again, but Bracken stopped so short I heard another grunt and a muttered curse word as Lambent ran right up his ass.

"In your arms?" he echoed blankly, his voice a little broken. "What did he say?"

"Same thing I told him." I kissed Bracken's neck then, in spite of the nastiness on his skin. Underneath it was Bracken, my stone and shadow lover, the rock who anchored me to the earth.

"What was that?" Bracken asked, his voice finally gentle, his footsteps pattering lightly again in the long, dank, winding black corridor.

"I couldn't leave you and Green." My eyes were closed because my body was shivering so violently that my vision wouldn't stay still. "I knew that, you know. I never planned to leave you. I just needed to step up, that's all."

"Fuck, Cory," he grated. "You're going to kill me slowly, you know that?"

I whimpered against his chest and shivered some more, but it was not quite as bad. I'd been thinking about being violently sick but that managed to recede. I was glad. Bracken's anger—which usually burnt quick and hot, just like Lambent's fire—was all flamed out anyway. It might not stay that way if I barfed all over him.

BRACKEN

Forgiving the Queen

By the time I got her into the tiny cubicle shower in the club's back room, her tremors were so bad they were nearly convulsions, and I was so irritated, I thought the heat of my ire alone would warm her.

She'd almost died—and not for us, her lovers. For a friend—for a soldier, one who expected a certain amount of risk when he went into the field. Goddess damn her and her nobility and her inability to draw the line at where she should stop caring for others and start caring for herself—and for us.

My anger might have whipped itself up to a fury all over again, but it was quiet in the little white cubicle, and when her slick, bare skin touched mine, my power wrapped her up, spoke to her blood, and while she clung to me, her body stopped rejecting mine and her breathing evened out and she relaxed.

"Better?" I asked after a moment, and she made an affirmative noise against my chest.

"Are we going home now?" I asked wistfully, and she turned water-spiked lashes and a game smile up to me.

"Oh Goddess, yes. But we need to leave the vampires here..." her attention wandered a little, and then she shook herself and looked at me again.

"And I think we should send Nicky to Austin for a week."

I blinked, and used both hands to scoop her hair back from her face. There was a bottle of shampoo on the floor, and with a little maneuvering I picked it up and started to soap her hair and her back and shoulders, turning her around so she could lean back on me as I did it.

"Why?" I asked, when my task was done and she was facing me again. It took her so long to answer that the water had run cold, and I turned it off and held her again, and asked one more time.

"Why are we sending Nicky away?"

She dragged her palm across her cheek, and tried hard not to look at me. "Because I'm going home to do something really awful, Bracken Brine. And then you and Green are going to have to put me back together again. And I don't want him to have to see it. He can take it—I know he can. But this week has sucked for him—so totally and so completely, I don't even think there's a word for it. I want him to have someone put *him* back together again. I don't want him to be worried about me."

I grunted then, and wrapped my arms around her body because the shivers had started again, and they still had nothing to do with the tepid air that surrounded us. Her face was still turned away, as though I would be repelled by her weakness, and true forgiveness flooded my chest. I tilted her head up and kissed her, tasting the salt that had mingled with the water from the shower.

Her body, slick skin, bony hips and all, convulsed against mine, and I realized I was flooding her with my blood call—and that it was finally, finally working.

The kiss went on, and she started to return it with interest, with passion even, and then I broke it off and leaned my forehead against hers.

"We'll never get back before dawn at this rate," I panted, wanting her badly.

She swallowed and nodded. There would be a time for this—a time when it was as necessary to her as breathing—but we had less than four hours to get back home, with a stop in between included, and a quickie in the shower would have to wait.

"It's never quick with us," she murmured, and I found myself laughing softly in agreement. Quietly we dressed, and went out to face the others.

"Okay," she said briskly as we came out into the club proper and the others gathered around us. "Uhm, Kyle, Marcus, Phillip—you're staying here tonight, coming back tomorrow. Max, Renny, Nicky—you're with us, which leaves Mario and La Mark in the other SUV—which is fair enough, because that means you guys can go straight to the Aerie if you like…"

"We want to come to the hill, if you don't mind," Mario said softly. "I have some things I want to ask Green."

She had a secret smile on her lips as she nodded yes to that, and then

Phillip, working on delayed shock, said, "Wait a minute—Cory, we can make it back tonight. There's no reason for us to stay…"

"There's two," she lied, and I looked at her, trying to figure out why. "We need you guys to watch over the kiss, help Rafael out and protect Andres…"

Andres and Orson snorted next to me, and I met Andres' eyes. He shrugged, his lips quirking up. I'd seen him—seen them both--in the fight, and as mild as he appeared, he was as fierce in battle as he was in bed. *That* thought shocked a little heat between us, and his smile turned smug and knowing, and I turned back to my beloved.

"Many thanks, Little Goddess," Rafael said smoothly. Apparently *he* knew what this was about, but Phillip, Marcus, and Kyle were still in the dark.

"What's the other reason?" Kyle demanded without preamble. "Because I'll tell you right now, I'm not staying."

Cory blinked and laughed a little. "Changed your mind about that?"

Kyle rolled his eyes, and I wondered at Cory's ability to make friends with taciturn assholes. "I like my room," he said with dignity. "I'm getting better at chess."

She laughed a little. "Makes one of us. Okay, that reason's shot to shit, but you guys are still staying…"

It may have been the emphasis on 'that', but the lightbulb went on over Phillip's head.

His face grew carefully blank, neutral like white paper, and he said "I'll do it," without really meeting her eyes.

"No you won't," she told him smartly, and Marcus put his hand on the back of his beloved's neck, and met Cory's eyes, and suddenly things clicked into place for me.

I'm going home to do something really awful, Bracken Brine.

The connection of the blood bond weakened with distance—it never truly diminished, but Cory had only been able to communicate with the vampires she'd blooded *in Redding* while she'd been in Redding. It would make a difference—a big difference—in how much pain Phillip would endure when dawn came.

"It's not your job," Phillip said now, that careful, blank look still there.

"The hell it isn't," she told him back, searching for his eyes. She found Marcus' eyes instead.

"Thank you," Marcus said with the calm of the grave. "We'd love to stay here for another night."

"Marcus!" Phillip showed his first trace of emotion, and it cut deep, but his lover shook his head almost angrily.

"Take what she's offering, beloved. Take it, and be grateful, and know that it wouldn't help and would only hurt you worse if it was you."

Phillip glared at Cory, and she returned the glare mutinously—but her hand was locked in mine, and she was drawing strength from me as sure as we were both standing.

"One condition," he snapped crisply, and she gave him a look that said, *Thrill me with your condition!* And he replied to the look, "Don't blood her."

"I wasn't going to," Cory answered innocently, and I could tell by the very tone of her voice that she'd been thinking about it, and she practically doubled over with the force of her convulsion. "God*dammit* Bracken Brine, I *said* I wasn't going to do it!"

I glared at her. "What are you *talking* about!"

"You're mad at me—that's why your blood is screwing with me so badly... it won't settle down in my skin unless you just calm the fuck down!" She raised a shaking hand to my face, trying to soothe, and I realized that she was right, and all my anger turned inward, and her knees went slack and I had to hold her up.

"This *isn't* an improvement," she growled, thumping me on the shoulder, but I didn't know what she wanted me to do about it so I just rolled my eyes at her.

"You were thinking about it," I snarled, and she rolled her eyes back.

"Of course I was—do you think I want Phillip to suffer if I can take that away?"

"It won't, Little Goddess," Andres said gently, and she smiled at him with weary gratitude.

"I know." A sad little shrug, an apologetic glance at Phillip. "And if I can't make you feel better, Phillip, it's just martyrdom, and that's stupid. Don't worry," and now her attention was *wholly* on her friend, her lieutenant, the imposing, severe looking vampire who was stoically refusing to cry in his lover's embrace. "I won't make this any harder than it has to be. You have to share headspace with me too—how awful would that be, if it was bouncing around both our heads like a rubber-ball on hormones?"

"Yeah," Phillip's voice grated, "that would be pretty awful."

She smiled, and the expression was beyond tired. "So now that *that's* out in the open and messy, I really think we should go home."

And that was it. She gave Rafael a bow, and shook his hand, and then went to do the same to Andres. Andres smiled evilly at her, his handsome, Latin features heating as his teeth glinted, and with a wink at me he kissed her, hard and passionately on the mouth. She retreated from the kiss heated and flushing, and looked at me reprovingly.

"Until next time, Little Goddess," Andres said smoothly, and my beloved blushed again.

"Of course, Lord Vampire," she said with dignity, and Nicky guffawed and she glared at him. "You all think entirely too much of yourselves," she sniffed, but the moment had...promise... for others like the one on the boat, in the dark of a country night.

But not now. Now, we were headed home, and there was grim work to be done.

NICKY

Off The Board

Bracken must have forgiven her, because somewhere after Andersen and before Wheatland, she fell asleep.

Max was driving and Renny was next to him, and I was in the middle. I looked over the seat to Bracken in the back and nodded at her. "Will she be okay?"

"No," Brack replied distantly. "Not even close."

I let out a shocked laugh. "Bracken!"

"You know what she's going to have to do, right?"

I did know. I knew, and frankly, the idea made me queasy. I couldn't do it—not cold-bloodedly, not after we'd known the little blood-sucking grade-school psychopath and tried to make her one of our own.

"Yeah," I said gruffly, looking away.

"You won't need to be there," he said softly—and without judgment. I looked at him in the dark, but his face was set on that beautiful, remote expression that said he was done confiding in me. Bracken had a big heart—it was just good to remember that most of it was filled with our wife.

"It will be good to be home," I said, for the sake of some way to respond.

"Wouldn't you like to see Eric instead?" he asked, and I blinked.

"Well, yeah…" Even I was not prepared for the break in my voice, and I stopped speaking for a moment to get myself under control. I wanted so badly to pour my heart out to my beloved—so many things I needed to tell him, so many observations, emotions, stupid jokes, had been burning in my chest. I couldn't say these things to Cory, to Bracken, or even to Green. I understood them—even Cory's little stunt, saving Teague, risking herself, I got that. I was pissed at her, same as everyone else, but I got it. You just didn't take the sort of faithfulness people showed her for granted—or at least, Cory never did. And you certainly didn't let it fall out of the sky at your feet if you could do something to stop it—even if you took a chance with your own life.

Cory never really understood that she was bigger and more to us than a little college student with a smart mouth—but she did understand that the things we were willing to do for her were sacred. Sometimes, sacred things must be paid for in blood—anyone who's ever been to Sunday school knows that.

But now, Bracken had asked me a question, and I needed to try to answer it again without sounding like a total pussy. "Yeah," I said casually. "I'd love to see Eric—you know that, but we weren't planning on it until next month."

"Mmmm…" he murmured, and kept his eyes outside at the stars, which stayed still in the sky even as we blurred on the road beneath them.

So I should have seen it coming when we took the off-ramp to the airport to let Max and Renny off at the bright yellow car with the purple and olive trim, but I didn't. Cory had awakened by that time, and she hopped in the passenger seat as Bracken sat down to drive, but instead of taking the loop back to the freeway, he took us to the terminal instead.

Cory hopped out and opened the door and pulled me out, then went to the back and got my bags.

"You have your iPod in your pocket, right? And that book you were reading?"

I nodded dumbly, completely gobsmacked, and then I took my suitcase from her because it was bigger than she was and she started giving me instructions before I could even figure out what I was doing.

"And if you go to the computer sign-in desk and give them your ID and your credit card, they should have your tickets—they're open ended round trip, so come home anytime, and give Eric our love…"

"Wait a minute!" I barked, and she turned to me, her expression mild and hopeful. "You're sending me away?" Oh Goddess…a sudden hole opened up where I thought my heart was, and then her blank, mild expression melted, replaced by something old and sorrowful and tired.

This was how a queen looked, I realized with shock. This was the face she had been showing to Bracken in the back of the car, while I sat by myself and listened to music and thought about how unconcerned I was that my old girlfriend got her head ripped off and what assholes my parents were.

"You…" she smiled again, and the expression did nothing to lighten the mood. "I love you so much, Nicky. I love you exactly as a friend should love a friend, or a wife should love a husband. I'm so proud of you—and I'm so grateful. The way you stood up for me—and kept standing up for me—damn, honey. I felt like the queen of Redding, you know?"

I knew where this was going, and it hurt, but... but the next week was going to be hard. It was going to be horrible and rough, and she and Bracken and Green would be at odds and fighting, and making up and making love, and the whole thing would be painful and emotional and... well, I guess I'd already figured I wasn't good at making the hard decisions. Or facing the hard emotions.

This, I thought hazily, was why Erik and I got to sit at the kid's table. We were willing to let our leaders do the hard living for us. Sitting out the pain suited us—and we suited each other.

I took her hand in mine and kissed it tenderly. "I do know," I said softly, and she gave me a blinding smile.

"You deserve to be the only bucket of angst in the room, Nicky. This week has sucked for you—I want you to have someone who will cater exclusively to making you feel better. Eric will do that. Bracken, Green and I... we've got..."

"Issues," I supplied, and she launched herself at me, and hugged me so tight I almost couldn't breathe.

"Goddess, I love you, husband," she murmured, and I kissed her on the mouth—hard and passionate and heated, but I backed off before it got too close. Because that's where we were—we loved each other, but we would never be emotionally raw together. Not like her and Bracken. Not like her and Green. These were truths I'd known for a year and a half—but now, looking at the weight that seemed to make her smaller, for the first time I was grateful for them.

I was not strong enough to help her through the next part. And she was strong enough to send me to my lover, and make sure that I was treasured and cherished and cared for.

She kissed me again and gave me one of those game, painful smiles, and then I turned her towards the door to the small terminal and gave her a little push. She trotted away, looking barely legal in her denim shorts and girl's white T-shirt, and I wondered idly how many people thought we were deeply in love the way any normal human couple would be.

I was deeply in love with her—but we would never be normal, and the closest I would ever have to human was the were-coyote who was apparently waiting for me in Texas.

The closest she would ever have to human was the man-god brooding about her in the car. It was complicated and difficult, and I was tired of complicated and difficult, and she'd given me exactly what I needed, before I even knew I needed it.

And I was still hurt, more than a little, that she wouldn't insist that I be there for her, as she eviscerated herself out of love for our world and duty to our people.

Goddess, what a mess.

So yeah--I used to love the kids' table at holidays. Now I knew why.

CORY

Meeting the Dawn

Green was waiting outside for us in the coolness of the hill. Until we pulled along the graveled drive and I saw him standing, beautiful and strong and worried, I had managed to keep my unbounded joy at seeing him again tight and secret in my chest.

As it was, Bracken had to stop short to let me scramble out of the SUV and into his arms.

"You're okay?" I asked, meaning at least six different things. I'm ashamed to say that the first one was *You're not mad at me?* There had been a silence in my head on his end from the moment of magnesium brightness in the dank wine cellar.

"No," he murmured into my hair. "No, I'm not okay. Luv…Goddess… luv—the things you do…"

But that was all—my articulate, cultured Green got no further than that as he held me and held me and held me, and I squeezed him back with all the strength in my fragile, mortal body.

He stepped back first and held his hand up to my throat and made a little keening noise, closing his eyes so tightly shut that silver tears leaked out the corners. I followed his hand and felt…

"Another scar," I muttered, and he narrowed his eyes at me and shook his head and held me all over again.

"I can feel Bracken's anger in my blood," I muttered after a few moments, and that was odd enough to break the moment.

"Really?" he asked, with raised eyebrows. "What in the holy blue fuck?"

I managed a weak grin. "It's cold," I murmured. "Or maybe it's hot, and it makes me cold like a fever does. But when he's mad, when he's thinking pissed-off thoughts—I feel it." I tried to smile about this, but the fact was, I was frightened. Bracken and I—we thrived on our own friction. He grew frustrated at me frequently—I didn't know how I would deal with his anger surging through my blood at the drop of a hat.

Green frowned, which meant this thought had occurred to him as well, and he pat my shoulders lightly. "Well hopefully it's not permanent. It could add one more challenge to an already challenging situation, couldn't it, beloved?"

I leaned my head on his chest again and sighed. "And, uhm…speaking of challenging…" It was the lamest segue of all time.

"You don't have to do this, luv," he murmured, but I looked at him, and I don't know what he could see in the light of the lowering moon, but it was something he knew to look for in the first place.

He laughed a little, and I held my hand to his face. "What am I saying?" It was an honest question, asked almost to himself. "Of course you do. What I should be saying is 'You don't have to do this alone.'"

Bracken emerged from the garage then, and I looked at the sky—it was a breath away from growing lighter. "What do we have, about twenty minutes?"

Green nodded. "About that—I warned Grace. She's ready."

Which translated, I saw, to "Grace has been sobbing her heart out on Arturo's shoulder, but she'll woman up and be stoic Grace for us when we walk into the nursery." It wasn't hard to figure out—Arturo's shoulder was sopped through with the brine-blood tears of his beloved.

We stood at the steel vault door for a moment, looking inside at the destruction. About a month ago, Gretchen had given up all pretense at doing anything with the books but ripping them up, so they'd been removed unless we went in with one. Many of the toys had been broken—anything resembling a humanoid had been beheaded. She'd spent psychotic hours with the Legos though—building wall after plastic wall, until her room was lined with multi-colored prison walls, better than tapestries against the chill steel.

When we got there, she was sitting on Grace's lap, her whirling eyes tracking aimlessly at the colors of her lego walls. Grace was singing to her—some hopelessly sad Bruce Springsteen song about Independence Day—and Gretchen was humming tunelessly along.

Green, Bracken, and I could only watch sadly until the song was done.

"It's good you're doing this now," Arturo said softly—Gretchen was beyond hearing anyway. "She almost killed Leah today—I had to tackle her and pry her jaws open. There's barely enough left of her to say goodbye to—and that would be a shame."

As reassurances go it wasn't bad, and I smiled a little for Arturo's peace of mind. Then I remembered one of the other reasons I'd been driven to come home this night when my heart and my mind and my body would have been so much happier with rest.

Carefully I looked to see if Green was paying attention to me, but he had spent a great deal of time with Gretchen himself—he was busy saying his own goodbyes.

"Arturo—I'm...I'm probably going to sleep late. You, uhm, wouldn't want to wake me up tomorrow, would you? Around one or two—Brack and I can take care of that other thing if you want."

Arturo grimaced. "That's a rather full day after a helluva night, Corinne Carol-Anne—are you sure you can't wait another day?"

I looked at Gretchen, who had spent two months in this pink prison cell while her brain rotted between her ears and there was nothing she could do about it. I swallowed.

"I'm done putting things off and hoping they get better," I said through a dry throat, and he nodded sagely, his copper-lightning eyes searching my face for signs of hope I guess. Whatever it was he was searching for, I don't think he found it.

He put a hard hand on my shoulder and squeezed, and then walked into the little room and gently detached his beloved from the little girl I was about to kill.

"Heya, Gretchen."

She looked up at me, those unfocused eyes suddenly trying to fix themselves on my face. "I know you," she murmured, and then her expression turned to a scowl. "You said my mom and dad were coming." Well, at least she forgot I killed her cat—but I didn't mention that.

Instead, I looked right at her and thanked the Goddess I wasn't an elf. "Your parents *are* coming," I said softly. "In fact, I've come to take you up to meet them."

"Here, honey," Grace said, her voice as natural as it had been a week ago, as she was helping me pack, "here's your sweater. Make sure your mama sees it—she'll think it's awful pretty."

Grace had knit that sweater herself, a blinding shade of purple and blue, but I didn't guess anyone here was going to need it. The smaller members of the hill propagated like lemmings—but they were Barbie Doll small. The were-creatures could only have babies with their same species. You'd be surprised how very often that mating pair *didn't* happen on Green's hill. The sylphs had their own enclave, like the Avians, away from the sexually charged atmosphere of the hill, and, all in all, nothing human sized had given birth since... well probably since Bracken.

Besides, I don't think Grace could have stood to put the damned thing away after we left the room.

Grace bent down and gave the little girl a kiss on the cheek, and Gretchen leaned into it, just a little. She looked at me with flat, unfriendly eyes, and I was grateful. It would be worse if she loved me, trusted me. I was glad—so glad—that I'd chosen to do this.

I was really the only one who could do it cleanly.

I took one hand—not small, but not adult sized either-- and Green took the other. Gretchen smiled happily into Green's eyes and my heart dropped. Green had loved her—as much as she would let anyone. Green wouldn't be spared. No—I had it easy. Green would suffer more, and for us both.

Together, with Bracken behind us, we walked up to the house proper, and then up the granite stairs behind the living room to the trap door leading to the Goddess Grove. The sky was just edging towards gray, and we picked the eastern-most crown of the hill. This is where the cross-country running trail came out, and it was shy a couple of trees.

"Let's sit here, Gretchen," Green said, and I followed suit—we weren't too close to any of the vegetation, which was a blessing. I planned to do this with a heavy power shield between us, and it was easier not to worry about the trees.

Gretchen sat, and I was surprised when she laid her head on my shoulder. With a little scoot, her head fell sideways to my lap, and I smoothed her hair back from her face. Grace had put it up in a ponytail, so there was very little muss, but I know I like it when Green does that to me, so I did it for her.

"My parents are coming?" she asked dreamily, and I looked to where the sky was turning red under the gray.

"Yeah, sweetheart," I said with a clear voice. "Just look through the trees—you'll see them as soon as the sun touches down." Because when the sun touched down on the trees, it would touch down on us. Gretchen had known that, squatting in a cave and running on instinct. Three months ago, she'd been able to keep herself alive.

Today, with only the promise that she'd see the same family she'd ripped to ribbons, she forgot what she knew to live, and lay quietly in my lap, waiting for golden, sunshiny death.

The tingle of my shield as it edged our skin didn't even bother her. She just stared at the trees and murmured to herself. "Do you think Marvin will bring me a doll? He used to spend his allowance on dolls when I was mad at him. Mom always gave him extra so he could buy cars for himself."

"I wouldn't be surprised," I murmured. The tingle of my shield tickled the webbing between my fingers, but I never felt less like laughing.

"I want to hug my mom," she said quietly. "And I bet my daddy has a scratchy beard."

"You'll have to see," Green said, and our eyes met, and it suddenly didn't matter who had been closer to her, this pain was all ours, all on the surface, all in our skin and our bones.

"I'll tell them you were nice to me," she said, and then the top of the trees turned gold.

I drew power, and then some more, to insulate us from the searing heat of her conflagration, and behind me I heard Bracken, swearing softly, praying that we would be all right in the heat and the magnesium light of a vampire meeting the dawn.

In a heartbeat, maybe less, we *were* all right—we were just fine, in fact-- and the soul-wind of her passing blew the ashes out over the hillside, leaving Green and I sitting side by side, glowing in my shield, neither of us touched by either the flame or the ash.

My power bled out of me like tears, and I heard someone take a great gasping sob. My chest tightened to the point of pain, and I realized that it was me.

ARTURO

Bishop Danced

Arturo looked at the clock on the wall above the television cabinet, and then jittered nervously around the front room.

It was after one o'clock in the afternoon, and he knew without checking that Green's door was still locked. Cory, Bracken, and Green were all in there, and whether they were sleeping, making love, or ripping the sheets to shreds in a psychotic fugue, the last thing he wanted to do was disturb them.

Lambent sauntered in and eyed him sardonically. "What, mate—you've got nothing to do? Isn't that, like, against your superpower or something?"

"You're a complete asshole—did anyone ever tell you that?" Arturo asked sourly, and then watched as the minute hand clicked over again.

"Frequently—our Little Goddess being one of the most vocal. Seriously—what's got your knickers in a twist?"

Arturo sighed and flopped down into the love seat, scrubbing his face with his hands. "If you must know, you limey bastard, she was going to go kill someone today—but I really don't think she's up to it. And even if she was up to it, I don't know if it's even right to ask her to go do it—but it needs to be done."

Lambent's eyebrows hit his fiery hair, and his ruddy face went even redder in amusement—and something else, something almost reassuring for Arturo to see. "Sweet mother of morning—it's like watching the family cat stand up and order breakfast. I've never seen you this…flapped!"

Arturo blinked. "Flapped?"

"Yeah, mate—usually you're completely unflappable!"

Arturo's copper-lightning scowl was dark enough to make even Lambent back up a step. "Do you have *any* idea what she went through last night?"

And suddenly Lambent was all serious, and all on his side. "Yeah," he muttered, giving a furtive glance down the hallway. "Maybe even better than you."

"Care to explain that?" Arturo kept his dark hair at shoulder length— today it was in a queue—or it *had been*—because now he ran his hands through his hair and snapped the queue band across the room.

"There were...kids...feral vampires... abominations of the Goddess— whatever the fuck you care to call them, brother. Four of them, locked in Rafael's wine cellar."

Arturo's entire attention was now locked on the slight-figured fire-elf as he looked hesitantly to see if he could come back into the room. "Goddess..." he breathed. "God----dess... was this before or after she almost killed herself?" Jack had called from the summer rental cottage where the werewolves had been flown after Teague had been tended to. Teague would be fine in a week or so—if his mates didn't throttle him for being the world's worst patient— and Jack could barely mention Cory's name without cracking his voice all over the face of the stupid planet.

"That was after." Lambent shuddered, then gave up the flame-in-the-wind impersonation and flopped down on the love seat next to Arturo. "Bracken's blood—it wasn't sitting well with her at the time. She wasn't sure she could do it clean, so she asked me."

Arturo gave a hard shiver next to him. "Fucking wonderful," he grated. "And then she came here and... and..."

"And sentenced another child to death. Yup, guvnor—that would put a crimp in any girl's social whirl, you know what I mean? So who's she supposed to kill?"

The damned clock was not moving any faster. "Nolan Fields," he said glumly, and Max walked through the hallway then in a pair of cut-off sweats and a T-shirt just in time to hear the name.

"That bastard who's trying to blackmail the hill? What about him?" Max prodded restlessly at the contents of the refrigerator mumbling, "Banana, chocolate, there we go... caramel..." while he waited for the answer.

Renny came in behind him, wearing one of his T-shirts and not much else, and said, "Chocolate."

"But you said caramel! What about Nolan Fields?"

"The caramel was for you," she replied, taking the chocolate cream pie out of his hands, "and wasn't Cory supposed to kill him today?"

Arturo watched them both and tried—once again!—to get his head around the fact that Copfuck Max himself was now eating pie and in on the family's secrets. What a difference two years made. "Yeah," he muttered in response to Renny's question. "She was."

Max spoke through a mouthful of pie. "That's asking a bit much—even for Cory." The two of them had been in the living room with Arturo as Green had carried her into his bedroom. She'd been sobbing so hard Green had needed to bespell her just so she could breathe.

"We could do it for her," Renny said blithely, eating her own pie and trying to get the whipped cream off the edges of her mouth with her tongue, like a cat. Max sighed and got the dollop off her nose. She gazed at him with a cat's fascinated adoration, and his slightly-crossed blue eyes gave her the same regard, like an addled Siamese.

Lambent and Arturo exchanged ironic glances, and then Renny's words sank in.

"We could," Arturo said thoughtfully. Before Cory came along, he'd been the enforcer, actually, along with Bracken when some extra muscle was needed. Cory was deadlier, just by the nature of her power—and by her ability to come up with a plan and act on it for better or for worse. (Sometimes for worse, but she was young yet.) But that didn't mean Arturo couldn't handle a simple take down, especially if...

"We could what?" Mario asked, La Mark hard on his heels. La Mark was dressed nattily in slacks and a cerulean button-down dress shirt—and he was looking *supremely* glad to be back. He was a self-confessed cosmopolitan bird—of all Cory's entourage, he'd been the least happy to be camping by the lake.

"We could kill the cockroach turd who's trying to blackmail Green!" Lambent said gleefully, and Mario said, "Without Cory?"

There was a silence then, and everybody met eyes.

"Last night sucked large," La Mark muttered into the silence.

"Anyone hear from the werewolves?" Mario asked tentatively, and Arturo filled them in.

"Renny's right," Max said after they all relaxed—just a little—in relief. "I mean, she's awesome and all, but, well, we're all pretty deadly."

"And it would be really wonderful," Renny said quietly, "if we just didn't have to bother her with this today."

"Too right!" said Lambent with enthusiasm, and Mario and La Mark both said, "I'm in!" and Arturo found himself looking up at five hopeful sets of eyes. Well, he thought with a shrug, why not?

The magic that locked Green's door when he was busy was not particularly powerful, but that didn't mean that Arturo broke through it lightly. First he listened with his power—a thing he *never* did, simply because not doing such a thing meant giving the inhabitants of the hill as much privacy as possible. This time, he deemed the intrusion worth it—especially when all he heard was Cory and Bracken's even breathing of sleep, and the click-clack of Green's laptop as he did business while sitting in bed to watch them.

Green looked surprised to see Arturo, and then dismayed when he realized what time it was. Arturo shook his head and pointed to Cory, and then made vague gestures that Green, bless him, interpreted just right. He aimed a green-eyed gaze at his beloved, and then spoke up normally.

"She's under, and so's Brack—what's so important you need them asleep?"

"I'm going to go…take care of some tricky business, leader. I'm hoping she doesn't need to wake up until it's finished."

Green's eyes widened, and his busy, clever brain ran through all he knew Arturo hadn't said. Then he smiled, widely and a little evilly. "That sounds like a lovely idea, mate. Maybe, if she's not up by then, wake us when you're through?"

Arturo nodded and for the first time since the lot of them had arrived that morning, he flashed the silver caps on his teeth, which were the trademark of his most beautiful smile. "You can count on it, brother. I'll be sure to let you know when we're done."

"Who's we?" Green's expression was thoughtful—weighing strengths, perhaps. Perhaps just judging the weight of his beloved's anger should any of 'we' get hurt.

"All of us in the living room just now," Arturo said blandly, and Green sent him a droll look.

"I'm not going to keep Renny out of the fight you know—Corinne Carol-Anne wouldn't do it, and I'm at least as wise as she is."

Arturo shrugged. "People forget she's not helpless," he supplied, and Green nodded.

"Well, she isn't. And you know who else isn't helpless—and who might want a piece of this?"

Arturo's white grin was breathtaking. "Hallow."

Green answered with grim joy of his own. "Give him a call, brother—I think he'll be glad to be there."

In fact, Hallow was waiting for them.

Arturo drove one of the black SUV's—he would have preferred the Cadillac, but he wanted something as anonymous as possible. As he pulled up to the curb in the shabby, decaying suburb in Citrus Heights, he thought that maybe the Cadillac might have been a better choice. There was certainly more than one classic blue or purple Caddy on Sayonara Street—but Arturo's was still better maintained.

Hallow was standing by his understated white Lexus, wearing pale khakis and a simple white linen shirt and sunglasses in the bright, heavy heat of mid-July. The Lexus was attached to a small U-haul, and Arturo blinked. He'd known—had always known—that the tall, reserved sidhe had been waiting for a chance at some sort of redemption in order to come back to Green's hill. Until he saw Hallow leaning against his car and sending the curious gang members cool glances that made them scuttle away like beetles, Arturo truly had no idea how much going back to Green's mattered to him.

The smile Hallow turned towards him was actually warm and enthusiastic, and he had looks for the shapeshifters that would almost be described as 'tender'. Renny, mindless of the gravity of the occasion, pattered up to the man who heard her deepest secrets every week and hugged him around the waist—which was about as high as she could reach without it getting awkward.

"What's our plan, Arturo?" he asked, and Arturo looked around the neighborhood and grimaced.

"Well, I'm a cat's whisker from having Renny and La Mark change so they can guard the cars," Arturo said dubiously, and while they screeched in protest, Lambent rolled his eyes.

"Right, luvies, move away from the car, Uncle Lambent's going to make it all better for you." With that, Lambent put his hand on the Lexus and concentrated. In a moment, everyone who knew what power looked like could see the sizzling blue field around Hallow's car, and then surrounding the SUV when Lambent moved on to that.

"Now don't touch them until I beep the magic alarm, duckies, I'd hate to see you all crunchy on the sidewalk, right?" The fire-elf sashayed back

"Thank you, Lambent," Arturo muttered, trying not to scowl, and Hallow chuckled grimly.

"The Lady Cory puts up with that shite?" he asked, bemused, and Lambent flushed, the expression making him almost glow in the heat.

"The Lady Cory does *not, Papi,*" Mario muttered dryly, and Lambent flushed even deeper.

Hallow laughed, and pushed his sunglasses up his nose with a smooth little nudge. "I'm glad to hear it—there's much to love in our Little Goddess, is there not?"

There were various murmurs then, but nobody really needed to answer that out loud. It was why they were all there.

Nolan Field's house was actually in better shape than a lot of houses in the neighborhood—the yellow-colored siding was relatively new, the sidewalk was cracked but there were no weeds growing through it, and the lawn was watered, even if it was uneven. It was mostly a squat, one story, two-bedroom ranch house, with very little on the outside to indicate the level of loathsomeness of the creature who inhabited it.

They didn't bother to knock—Arturo turned the knob and the door opened because he asked it to, and before Mr. Fields could stand up from the computer desk that dominated the small living room, there were seven supernatural creatures in it, each of them with a story of his or her own.

The squat, sweaty, balding little man only had eyes for one of them.

"Hallow..." he said dreamily. "This is a surprise...do I ...do we... can I have another session?"

Arturo's stomach turned, and he met Lambent's eyes while avoiding Hallow's. For this alone, the man needed to die. It was, in fact, quite fitting that there were three of the Goddess' shining ones in the group to send him on his way—no one treated the sidhe like this. *No one* shared their bed without profound gratitude and reverence.

That Nolan Fields was too ignorant to know what he had been given ranked as one of his most criminal of sins. That he knew of the existence of the shining ones and used it to harm them was the thundering, indelible stamp of death on his sentence of transgressions.

"Nolan," Hallow said sweetly, "we need to know about your story. You told me that it would be ready to send tomorrow."

Nolan Fields nodded eagerly, and stepped forward on the beige carpet to shake Hallow's hand. Hallow didn't extend his hand to be shaken, and Fields looked uncomfortably around his sparsely decorated room for some way to impress his lover-by-blackmail. There were no pictures to inspire him, though, and much of the room was beige—except the couches, which were sort of a lime/olive green. There was a giant plasma screen television that was on without sound, and piles of books in every corner—most of them tell-alls or true-crime interviews. Well, the man did his research.

"Oh you should see it, Mr. Hallow," he said, not letting the chilly greeting dampen his enthusiasm for long. "It's gonna be a great piece! I made you guys look real good, and I gave that Cory chick a prime layout—but I gotta tell you. It was *hard* to make her look good. That woman does *not* photograph well—looks like a turn-of-the-century farmwife in every shot. Couldn't you pick someone else as your poster girl?" He leered at Renny. "This one here— she'd look *great!*"

Renny was suddenly a kitty in a mini-skirt, hissing at the man while her husband—now furry and tangled in his jeans, T-shirt, and gun-harness— yowled in her face to hold her back.

"Or not," Fields finished weakly.

Lambent looked at the man quizzically, as though examining an exotic and repulsive intestinal parasite under a microscope. He cocked his head at Hallow.

"You say he doesn't do the mindfuck?"

"No," murmured Hallow grimly. "He's entirely too focused for that."

"Excellent," Lambent replied with a truly evil grin. "There's something here I want to try—I saw our Little Goddess do it with Rafael...I think I can do something of the sort here."

Arturo pulled back from his own distasteful examination of their victim. "You mean... trace his bloodline? Except..."

"Except instead of his blood-sharing, it will be his work," Lambent completed the thought. "Our vampire queen can traces a person's thoughts through the blood exchanges—if this one is so focused on his work that it's all he cares about... well, humans call it blood, sweat, and tears—but really, when you think about it, it's..."

"Touch, blood, and song!" Hallow filled in, delighted. "Of course—that should work..."

"What will work?" Fields asked with wide-eyes. The happy expressions of discovery on the faces of the elves closed down to the sober faces of men with jobs to do.

"Mario," Arturo asked, "is there any way you and La Mark could hold it still for a minute? And Max?" Max turned his muzzle Arturo's way. "We'll need you—swat that pussy one and come back to us, will you?"

Renny let out an indignant growl, but Arturo winked at her, so she sat back on her haunches and started cleaning her paws indifferently. Max flattened his ears at her and then changed—and then yowled, because his gun harness had gotten tangled around his crotch while he was a jumbo-sized tabby cat.

"I love it when they do that," the reporter breathed, completely blind to the danger he was in. "Do you think there's any way to get them to do that for the camera?"

"I'll stick my gun up your ass and pull the trigger first," Max rumbled, and Hallow gave him a mild expression.

"Don't get attached to your prey, Max—you've been a cat long enough to know that."

"Sorry, sir," Max said contritely, and Arturo broke in before they could go on.

"Okay—La Mark, Mario, you hold him down. Max, we need your gun because I don't think he'll respond to another threat. Hallow..."

"I've got my own plan when this is done, Arturo," the taller sidhe replied. "Lambent, you can do this with just Arturo's help, right?"

Lambent shrugged, and they all took that as their signal to begin.

"Wait a minute!" the squat human replied, and as the two Avians seized his arms, Mario braced his heavy thigh behind the little man's ass to keep him standing in place. Nolan grunted and looked alarmed, and Arturo thought that maybe, just maybe, the man's mortal peril was sinking in.

"You can't do this! I'm a member of the press—I've got rights!"

"You trespassed in our country," Arturo answered, wanting the man to know what he'd done in human terms before they took him out preternaturally. "You forfeited your rights when you made hostile moves against us."

"Hostile! Hallow—back me up here. When have I been hostile?"

Hallow cast the man a glance of such totally cold contempt that the sweat on Fields' brow literally dried before their eyes. "Blackmail is an act of hostility," he said icily. "Threatening to expose an innocent people who only wish to remain hidden—that's a hostile, aggressive act. And doing it against a kingdom you didn't understand…"

"But I *like* you guys!" Fields' protested, and now Hallow shivered.

"Yes—I've felt what you pass for *like*. You've threatened people I care for. You need a stronger word to defend your actions. Lambent?"

"Ready when you are," the fire elf shrugged.

Fields' started struggling harder, and then he heard the unmistakable click of a .45 releasing the safety.

"Jesus, that's a big gun," he breathed, and then, a little more indignantly, "But aren't you a cop?"

"Cop is a job," Max said mildly. "Goddess-get is who I *am*—and that's what you threatened, here. You threatened my wife, my king, my queen—talk to me about conflicts when I feel them."

Arturo looked hard at Max in surprise, and then grinned. Suddenly having Max here seemed as natural as having Renny. "Now just relax, Mr. Fields—Lambent won't make this hurt." Of course what Hallow had in mind, Arturo had no idea.

"Mmmm…" Lambent seized the man's pudgy, stubbled cheeks and stared directly into his eyes.

"You can't mess with my head," Fields told him smugly. "Hallow was right about…hey…you can't do that… how did you know… *no, dammit, not my work!*"

There were two crackle-pop-puff sounds in rapid succession, and the big hard- drive unit on the computer desk suddenly emitted sparks and shorted out. The screen went completely blank and a faint tinge of smoke drifted lazily up, stirred by the ceiling fan but not enough to hit the fire alarm unit that hung over the short hallway behind them.

The backpack by the kitchen table was emitting the same sort of smoke, but Lambent was still glaring into Fields' eyes while the reporter whimpered in horror.

"No...you can't do that. That's my editor's desk... he'll kill me... my photo processor... no... they'll never speak to me again... please... please... this is my life's work... this story will make my career..."

Lambent's eye twitched, and then he closed both of them, and then he pulled back and nodded decisively to Arturo and Hallow. "Not anymore," he said crisply.

Fields let out a moan and sank to his knees, and Mario and La Mark released him and let him fall further onto his hands.

"Why?" he whimpered. "Why would you do that? All that work... people need to know about you..."

"People *do* know," Arturo said in surprise. "They write poems and songs about us. They write frightening novels and happy romances. They write things that breathe joy into their tired souls. They do not," his voice grew harsh, and the glass-topped coffee table cracked under its sharpness, "*ever* write exposes` that confuse facts with truth." He looked at Hallow then. "Are you ready?"

Hallow nodded. "Oh yes—long since." Gracefully, Hallow sank to a crouch in front of the shabby, sweating, horrid little man who had plagued them for so long. He spent a moment taking care that his white-blond braid didn't brush the ground, and then took Nolan Fields' chin between his fingers and looked deeply into his myopic brown eyes.

"What are you going to do to me?" Lasciviousness twisted Nolan's voice, but Hallow had dealt with that—he was the only one in the room who didn't recoil.

"The question is, Nolan, what are you going to do to yourself?"

"I... I don't understand..."

Hallow tilted his head a little, but kept up that searching, soulful gaze. "The eyes are supposed to be the mirror of your soul—you've heard that?"

"Bullshit and poetry..." The pudgy, unkempt face twisted, his mouth sinking so far into his jowls that it almost disappeared.

"Sometimes, yes. Now look into my eyes, Nolan...what do you see?"

The grimace disappeared, replaced by bemusement, and Nolan drew his head up to take a closer look into Hallow's eyes. "They're...blue... crystal blue... like deep ice..." he murmured.

"Mmmm... interesting you should say that. We all have our gifts here, Mr. Fields...did I ever tell you that?"

"No." Fields' voice was oddly passive now, and the were-creatures stood far enough away to be safe and respectful, and close enough to see what was going to happen to him.

"Well it's true... I tend to see into people's souls. What I'm doing now is letting you take a look at what I see..."

"But..." Nolan Fields mumbled, "I don't see anything... it's an open window into a white sky... you could just fall...and fall...and fall..." he stopped talking, and went completely, totally still. He whimpered, once, and then his eyes lost their focus into Hallow's and seemed to turn inwards. He sat on all fours like that for about a minute, his soul falling into its own emptiness. His body finally realized that the thing that powered it was mechanical only and sputtered to a halt, the engine ground together by the sand of a vacant life.

The squat body plunked sideways, and Nolan Fields continued to stare vacantly into space. His eyes began to run with blood, and the twin red rivers of blood from his nose trickled sideways and mixed with the drool in the corner of his mouth. It all formed a little puddle on the dirty beige carpet. His body began to twitch—not violently, really, but in defeat: his animal vessel acknowledging that whatever intellectual or divine impulses directing it were well and truly gone.

Hallow stood and spat on that jerking corpse, and then spun on his heel and walked out of the crappy little house, his long white-blonde braid whipping around behind him. Without another word, Green's people followed him out.

When they got outside they waited for a moment while Lambent stepped over the twitching teenager on the ground and deactivated the car security system. Arturo made a noise and gestured to the boy, who was wearing a Chicago Bulls jersey over a red shirt, with a matching mint-condition baseball hat. Lambent looked at the boy and shrugged.

"He'll be alright, guvnor—it wouldn't have hurt him this badly if he hadn't had a gun in the back of his pants. Give it fifteen minutes—he'll get right back up."

That seemed to be it, until Renny scampered over to Hallow and changed into a girl again, giving her clothes a cursory yank in deference to all the people on their lawns, staring at the drooling car thief. Hallow looked at them all too, and sighed and waved his hands, and everybody looked blank for a moment and then looked somewhere else. So much for witnesses.

"Professor," she said urgently, "what would happen if you looked at one of *us* that way?"

Hallow smiled at her gently—all the sidhe were gentle with Renny. "With you, little one, all you would see would be a lovely tabby cat, with her handsome mate licking her ear. And lots of love—you'd see that, even in my eyes."

Renny grinned at him, and then turned a troubled look to Max. Max looked just as troubled, and, as he did sometimes, asked his wife's question for her.

"What do you suppose Cory would see?"

There was a restless movement then from all those who had seen her in battle the night before, who knew the terrible cost her fierceness had exacted in the light of a harsh dawn.

Hallow smiled his tender smile at all of them. "No worries, people," he said softly. "She'd see everything you see—only she would see the love in her actions too, and she'd be just as beautiful to herself as she is to you."

Mario's face split a grin then. "Then maybe you should go bump that big lump of man out of your way, Hallow, and give her a soulgaze—girlfriend's hurting, that's for damn sure."

Hallow's smile faded. "Green's children," he said softly, gathering them around him with his voice alone, "if she can not find that comfort from her lovers, then there's no one on the planet who can give it."

Arturo's face fell sadly with everyone else's, but he knew he was not the only one cheered by Hallow's next words.

"Come on, people—can you imagine a day when Green couldn't heal that girl's soul? Especially not with Bracken to help!"

Arturo firmly believed that Green could do anything. "Absolutely," he said now, his voice full of faith, and it was that faith that was awakened in the hearts of everyone in their little party as they jumped into their cars and headed home.

CORY

Changing the Board

I have no idea what time it was when I woke up, but I did know that Bracken wasn't on my other side.

"Where's Brack?" I asked through a yawn, and Green closed his laptop and placed it on the end table, all in one practiced motion.

"I imagine he's scaring up some food," he murmured, lowering himself next to me and tucking my mussy hair behind my ear. "Would you like me to call him for you?"

Green's beautiful, triangular, elfin face was only inches from mine, his hair cascading behind him and over his shoulder. I held up my hand and ran a thumb over his perfect cheekbone, living for his smile.

"No," I whispered. "I'm perfectly happy right now."

He feathered a kiss on my temple, and I closed my eyes to savor it. "Are you still mad at me?" I asked when I'd caught my breath.

"Yes," he murmured, rubbing his cheek on mine. "And so's Brack—I sent him out because you were shivering in your sleep."

"I had to," I murmured, wrapping my arms and legs around his body and *willing* him to give up all distance between us. "Didn't Adrian explain? Can't you see? If people are going to follow me, there has to be some give…"

His arms came around me, and he hugged me convulsively, crushing me to his lean muscle, warming me in his gentle anger. "I refuse to give *you*," he rasped in my ear. "You may take that risk as often as it pays off—and I will never be in a forgiving mood when you do."

I nodded, and what I had to say next was so very painful that I couldn't say it into his depthless green eyes. I had to whisper it into his shoulder.

"Beloved, my dedication to you and Bracken is not reason enough to lead people into what may be their deaths." He made a sound of frustration, and I tried to make myself clearer. "Don't you get it? People will follow anyone who believes what they're doing is necessary. We... we're going around being the fucking conscience of the entire community... we *have* to think we're necessary. But if it's not necessary enough to die for, then it's not necessary enough to get other people to give up their lives." It was hard—so hard—to put words to this. I had to keep trying.

"I can't defend my own survival with other people's deaths... because if I do, I'm no better than... that thing we killed last night."

His hug tightened and then he pulled back and looked seriously into my plain brown eyes, and for the first time made me feel bad about the saving Teague's life.

"That's bullshit, beloved..."

"We don't know that!"

"I know that—I know that you can't risk death every time you go out and lay down the law. We can't do that. We can't live that way. And you, beloved, need to face the fact that you may not live to lead others to victory and salvation if you don't choose your risks very, very carefully. And you'll certainly be the death of me if that happens."

He looked so worried—so worried and hurt, when he hadn't looked worried and hurt when he'd been lying, broken, in a puddle of light on his own earth.

I swallowed and felt tears start. "I had faith in you," I said, trying to smile, but my expression twisted into tears instead. I buried my face into his chest. "I had faith in you," I repeated, and then I sobbed and hiccupped, and then I repeated it again, and again, and then Green was kissing me through our tears.

I returned his kiss—if anyone knew how to make love through pain, through anger, through distress, it was the two of us who had comforted each other with our flesh the morning we woke up and knew Adrian was lost.

Maybe because we were at odds—maybe because this issue would *never* be resolved, and maybe because I had been home once in seven days and the circumstances were extraordinary—but every touch of his hands on my skin was glorious.

His palm, skating on my upper arm made my breath catch, and his kiss on my collarbone made it quicken. His kisses between my breasts to my navel made me groan, and I arched my hips to let him slide my underwear down and off, and then spread my legs in invitation.

Just the touch of his tongue on the center of my sex made me shiver, scream, see black, come. When he continued, I had to knot my hands in his lovely yellow hair to hold on to reality, and still, he tasted me and reality was jerked away, leaving me screaming in climax.

He slid up my body, sheathed himself inside me, and framed my face with his hands as I bucked underneath him, begging him for complete possession, begging him to move, to claim, to take... oh Goddess, beloved, take me, take all of me, the things that scare you, the things that anger you, take me, give me everything, leave nothing back...

"Don't leave me..." he whispered harshly, and I continued to buck underneath him.

"I can't promise..."

"I don't care!" he growled, pulling back and driving his body home inside mine with enough force to satisfy... but I wanted more than satisfaction. I wanted everything—even if it meant pain.

"I can't promise..." I almost sobbed, and then he moved slowly... so slowly, it was almost *almost* worse than not having him inside me at all.

"Don't leave me!"

"Give me!" I snarled in return, moving as hard and as fast as I could from underneath him, and it would have been a perfect impasse, we could have stayed that way forever, locked in wanting, locked in the pain of not having, except... except that Green's hand, which had been on top of my scar-less shoulder, skirting the little star-freckled handprint on the right front of my chest, moved, covered the handprint, and the wave of longing, of need, and of sheer stinking want rolled over both of us, and I knew...I'd known in my head, but now I knew in every atom of my body, immediately, like the certainty of oxygen in my quivering cells, the truth... it was the difference between seeing a picture of a lake under the moon and drowning in cold black water at night.

Oh, how Green wanted me too. There was a desperation, an emotional violence to the need with which Green wanted to take me...he wanted me enough to forgive me, and he was frustrated enough, angry enough, to pound me into the mattress with giving.

I wanted him enough to love it—and to demand more.

"Give me..." I begged, making high-pitched sex-sounds, "give me, give me..."

"Don't leave me!" he ordered, but he'd lost, he'd conceded, and I begged him for more...I reached...demanded... broke and wept and pleaded... *give me, give me, give me... Goddess, Green, I'll give you anything, immortality, my heart, my soul, anything, just give me back...*

He roared as he thrust, the sound probably cracking the foundations of the hill, and then raised his head, his body trembling in climax and howled. I bucked underneath him, feeling his spend pulsing inside me, and knew that something... something irrevocable had happened.

I wrapped my arms around him, stroked his sweating shoulders, whispered into the sacred space between us.

Thank you...thank you... I'll give you anything... I'll stay for you. I promise I'll stay. I promise... as long as I can... until dust and beyond... I'll live for you, Green. I'll live.

I don't know what he thought... he didn't speak, but hot droplets of salt water spattered on my chest until I clutched him closer and he turned his head and wept.

We wouldn't shower immediately—not after that. He rolled to his side, taking me with him, and we simply stared into each other's faces and stroked hands until our breathing relaxed.

"I will love you forever," I murmured, and he stroked the hair off of my forehead.

"I will hold you to that." His face was grim and his voice was sober—he touched my handprint of chaos as he said it, and I knew in my bones that it was a solemn vow, and not a sweet or a kind offering of love at all. Green would make me live if he had to crack the foundations of the world.

In that moment I had every faith that he could.

I must have dozed off after that, but the part of me that didn't want my days and nights completely reversed spurred me out of bed. Green's side was still warm, but he was out somewhere, so I put on a pair of sleep shorts and knotted them on the side, and then threw on Bracken's T-shirt--which was lying by the side of the bed--and made my way out to the living room for something to eat.

I was *starving*.

I pattered out into the living room and Green looked up from putting sandwiches together and smiled tiredly at me. I walked up behind him and wrapped my arms around his waist.

"Thank you," I murmured, thinking about how exhausting I must be to make him look like that.

"My pleasure," he told me, dropping a kiss on my head. There was something wrong—something I didn't understand, but at that moment I looked at the clock and forgot all about what was bothering Green.

"Holy shit! It's four-thirty!" I danced back in agitation. "*Dammit*, where the hell is Arturo? He was supposed to wake me up!"

"Calm down, Corinne Carol-Anne, I'm sure he had his reasons."

My head snapped up and I narrowed my eyes at Green, wondering what he very smoothly just *didn't* tell me. "Where is he?" I asked suspiciously, and Bracken walked into the kitchen in time to ask, "Where is who?"

My quest for Arturo faded, and I looked at Bracken tentatively. I wasn't shivering—either the effects of my impromptu blood donation had faded or, maybe… for the first time I acknowledged how frightened I was that we would be cold with each other forever over this.

Green had just proved how molten his passion ran… but Brack and I were always hot. We were thrown into each other's company constantly—we were more than husband and wife, we were co-workers too. If he got too angry at me for us to function in the same room…

I shivered—and this time the glacial cold was all in my imagination.

"Hey…" I said uncertainly, and he walked right up to me and cupped my cheek.

"Hey yourself," he murmured. "Jumped off any cliffs lately? Slit your wrists for sport?"

I scowled up at him and huffed, and he laughed.

"You're so easy, *due'ane*. I could get a rise out of you from looking at you crossways."

I rolled my eyes. "And I can get a rise out of you from shaving my legs…"

Green turned to us then, a quizzical expression on his face. "But it wasn't your legs that you shaved!" he exclaimed, and I had forgotten about my run-in with the razor for the benefit of that damned bikini, and then *I* was off and running about making assumptions about women's swimwear, and suddenly…

Suddenly we weren't worried about being mad any more. We were us—Bracken wrapped his arms around my waist, I brushed Green's hand while taking the PB&J from him, and we were… easy. We were the happy family that kept me sane.

So Arturo's timing was pretty damned fortuitous when he came thumping into the front room with his smug entourage behind him. I turned an indignant face to him, still upset in a good-natured way about sleeping until nearly five in the afternoon.

"Where have you been?" I demanded, although I was still smiling. "We were going somewhere today!"

Arturo grinned at me, something wicked and gleeful in his expression. "We've already gone," he said with dignity, and I felt my jaw drop.

"You went?" I found myself stammering. "Wi…wi…without me?"

"We didn't want to bother you," Renny said smugly, walking between me and Green to get to the refrigerator. Bracken made a 'hmmm' noise behind me, and I could tell he was as flummoxed as I was.

"So...uhm... where's Nolan Fields?" I asked, not even sure I wanted the answer.

"Dead in his living room, luvie," Lambent reported smugly. "Isn't that what you had planned?"

Well, I really didn't know *what* I had planned and for a moment I thought about getting mad at them. They'd *killed* someone to...

"Why did you do that?" I asked, still completely blind inside.

"We didn't want to bother you, Corinne Carol-Anne." And for the first time I realized that Hallow was here. Hallow was here, and, judging by the luggage and boxes in everybody's arms, he was here to stay.

I blinked at him. "But, uhm... that's my job, isn't it?"

"No." That was all—just 'No'—but he smiled kindly at me, and I went with my first instinct to move around the counter and gave him a brief hug.

"I'm glad you're here," I said softly, meaning it. "Welcome home, Professor."

"Thank you for making it my home, Lady Cory," Hallow replied, and I realized that whatever this had been... for Hallow's sake, I was going to have to not make a big deal over it. It was done. He was free. His loathsome obligation was over, and he had... his face wore a subtle look of power used, of the smug, angry satisfaction in knowing that he had righted something terribly wrong. Oh yes—whatever had happened, Hallow had exacted some measure of retribution--I would bank my life on it.

But I didn't have to at the moment, now did I?

I looked at everybody else, hiding shy and secret smiles—they were like cats who had just left a big ugly dead gopher on my doorstep. *Do you like it, mom? Are you proud? We did good, mom, didn't we?* Renny cemented the impression by sticking her human nose in the air in a completely cat-like gesture of smugness.

"So, uhm," I asked, looking down at my feet, "if going to kill the bad guys isn't my job... what... uhm... what *is* my job?" I was sort of serious. How did I earn my keep around here if I wasn't the head gopher killer?

Bracken laughed before anyone could answer. He wrapped his arms around my waist and hugged, lifting me into the air squealing. "Making love to me!" he asserted and I laughed some more and struggled to get out of his arms—but not too hard.

He put me down as everyone laughed, and I looked at my friends—my people—out from the shelter of his arms.

"Thank you," I said, and their sigh of relief eased my heart considerably. *Oh yay! Mom likes our dead gopher! We've done good!* I swallowed hard, and smiled at them all. "Thank you—this means..." and oh. Oh it did. They did this for me—when my heart was so sore, so burdened, they took this on themselves because they could.

I swallowed, hard, and tried a game smile. "This means the world to me."

It was all I could say—it was simple, and it was the truth.

There was a lot to do that night to keep me occupied.

We moved Hallow into a room in the sidhe quarters that Green had apparently prepared many, many years before. I wasn't allowed to do much of the box-schlepping or unpacking, but I was allowed to sit on the bed next to Green as Hallow stroked the hand-planed bureau, appreciating the aged and mellow oak under his fingers. The bedstead was made of the same wood, and the walls were paneled with it. The room itself was back near the darkling and the staircase that led to the sidhe apartments. It was, in essence, near the core of the house, one of the first rooms finished as Green and Adrian's preternatural legacy sprawled to take over the hill.

"You've had this ready for me for quite some time, haven't you, brother?"

Green nodded, the look on his face poignant, welcoming. "Since I knew you'd received the invitation and left your home." I stroked the back of his hand softly—this wasn't my conversation.

Hallow turned to us then, his narrow, aesthetic, academician's face radiant with a powerful joy. "It's high time then," he said with understatement and shiny blue eyes. "I'll just make myself at home."

We left him quietly, still rubbing the bureau with his fingertips, and I turned my face up to Green tentatively. Something... something had changed between us, since I had rampantly demanded from him in our bed. I did not know what it was—I didn't know if it was good or bad, or if he was angry or sad with me, and I was uncertain.

"That was lovely, wasn't it?"

He cupped my face with his fingertips, almost with the same reverence Hallow had used with the symbols of his homecoming.

"Lovely," he murmured thickly. "That is a good word, *ou'e'eir*, but it doesn't quite carry the right amount of pain to it."

I blinked. "Please..." Please what? He didn't sound angry. I put my hand on his chest then, giving all I knew to give. "Please don't hurt inside."

He nodded, and his eyes never left mine. "You made a promise to me. Do you remember?"

Don't leave me.

"Yes."

"I'll hold you to that. My heart will be fine, beloved, if you remember that what matters isn't the nature of the promise, just that you will keep it."

The message was clear. Nobody loses control the way I had. Not without a price.

I thought about that all night. I thought about it when the vampires pulled in around midnight with Kyle at the helm, and Andres and Orson in the limo behind them. Marcus and Phillip had stayed in the vampire compartment for the entire trip. They'd told Kyle it was because they wanted privacy, but I saw the compartment in the following days as it was being repaired, and thought that maybe privacy was the least of it.

Of anybody on the planet, I should know that grief could turn violent.

Andres came in and visited for an hour before he and Orson started back for the city. I was glad to see him—very glad—but the strain of that morning, of the tension with Green, of my confusion with the thing with Nolan Fields—it all must have shown on my face.

Before he left he took me aside, separating me from Green and Bracken fairly smoothly—they had formed some sort of compact not to let me beyond their touch since Hallow and the others had returned.

"You're not looking well, Little Goddess," Andres said softly, tilting my chin up to look into those soothing brown eyes. "And you keep shivering."

"Bracken's still mad at me," I said huskily. "And Green… Green has a space in him…" I shook my head. Of all things, I didn't want the person I'd become to be worthy of them to get between us.

Andres nodded. "Is there a thing you would have done differently, Corinne Carol-Anne?"

I looked at him in surprise, and blinked slowly. "No," I said after a moment. I couldn't think of a single thing I hadn't agonized over. I couldn't think of a single decision I hadn't made the commitment to honor in some way, shape, or form, long in advance of the time it had to be made.

Andres smiled, the beauty of it still shocking. "Then you are the person they love—they simply need to learn to live with you as you have made yourself."

"What if I'm not…" my voice faltered. Oh Goddess. And wasn't *this* my biggest fear.

But Andres wouldn't even let me voice it. "Enough, Little Goddess. How could they not love you? It was their love that was the making of you? Go." He kissed my cheek like a brother. "Sit with them, be with your people. Have peace. I have faith we will have other moments—your Bracken will certainly see to it."

He shooed me away, and shortly after that they left. Once again, a few words from Andres had put my world into some semblance of order—it was like his superpower or something.

Marcus tiptoed down the hall from the darkling about an hour after Andres and Orson left, specifically to catch me knitting in the common room.

Green had been next to me, watching *Lethal Weapon 4* (because I guess we all have our comfort movies) and he rubbed my knee and stood up discreetly to let Marcus take his place.

It hit me then, that I had done the same thing for him, on many occasions, and I felt a horrible, keening sorrow in my chest that I took pains to mask from Marcus. He had enough on his mind.

"How's he doing?" I asked, hoping the answer was better than I thought.

Marcus shrugged, turning away. "Better than if he'd been here," he told me.

I shrugged. It helped, but not much.

"Better than we'd be if we saw you going through it," he said more firmly, making sure I met his eyes.

I inclined my head. "You called it, brother—he's not the hard-ass he wants us to think he is. Is there anything I can do to help?'

Marcus looked up with hopeful eyes. "Could you... he's fed for real, but, Cory... would you mind being dessert?"

Not even a little bit.

Bracken followed me into their room—I don't know how he heard, but Green had disappeared and suddenly Bracken was at my heels. I was reassured that he was there—he was still a little angry, but nothing between us had changed like it had between me and Green.

Phillip didn't need much of my blood. A brief sting at my wrist, a slight pull, a swallow, and he fell to his knees, resting his head on the bed. His face, which had been taut and controlled as we walked in, stretched so tightly along his high cheekbones and chin that it looked like his skull would split through his skin, was suddenly slack and peaceful under the onslaught of scarlet tears.

Marcus' relief was profound as he moved in to shelter his sobbing lover, and as Bracken and I backed discreetly out (much as Green had earlier) I murmured, "I don't think he'd cried."

Bracken nodded, then swept me up rather breathlessly in his arms. "Balance beloved—you know that. Something's got to give, even if it's a vampire's broken heart."

And oh, how those words haunted me, even as Bracken kissed me with love, and forgiveness, and then passion.

They haunted me as I lay, pinned under Bracken's weight, feeling him still trembling inside of me, and wondered... wondered at the thing that had changed between me and Green.

Because now, smoothing Bracken's shoulders, knowing Green's hand was gentling the tender curve of his back, I felt it changing between me and Bracken too.

GREEN

Bowing to the Will of the Queen

Voyeurism was not a sin to the sidhe, and Green loved to watch his beloved make love—especially to as beautiful a sidhe as Bracken Brine Granite op Crocken.

Sometimes they bickered, even as he was inside her, dragging his body over every tender, sensitized place in her body, and sometimes she looked at Bracken with a variation of the same, big-eyed, worshipful gaze that she turned up at Green. There was something wilder in the gaze she turned at Bracken, and something serene and peaceful in the look that she gave Green, but the heart of the look, the adoration, the awe, the need—that was still the same.

Tonight, she was worshipful—and just as just as demanding, just as in need of being filled as she had been with Green.

Her legs were wrapped around Bracken's hips and he was struggling to be careful—if anyone knew how large and unwieldy his amazing body was, it was Bracken—but she wasn't letting him.

"Gaaaauuughhh…" he panted, "you're killing me…"

"Then *fuck* me, dammit!" she begged.

"I *won't* hurt you…"

"You hurt me by holding back!"

Green closed his eyes then, and then opened them because he had to. He had to see the moment when Bracken gave in, see the moment when he gave… *everything*.

Brack looked surprised as his hips started pumping at nearly supernatural speed and his pulse started to pound in his temple. He was gasping for air like an Olympic swimmer, and every muscle in his body was straining... straining to give her everything... every last bit of will, of soul... anything in his spirit that could assuage the ache of what she'd done, of what she now knew she was.

Green was relieved—he was glad to know he wasn't the only one to be shocked that here he was, an ages old sidhe, sacrificing his will to a very young, very willful human woman—who had no idea what it was she had just done.

Bracken groaned and came, and in the aftermath he still held himself up, above her, looking into her eyes for some proof, some assurance that what had just happened had not been his imagination, some reaction from his *due'ane* that everything he'd spent into her body hadn't been for sport.

The look she turned back up to him in the moonlight was the same wild, worshipful look that Green had seen her turn towards him a thousand times, and Green put his hand on the small of Bracken's back to comfort his brother, give him the reassurance that she didn't know how to give.

The touch worked, and Bracken collapsed on her and whuffled in her ear, just to make her laugh. They shared quiet whispers in the dark for a while, and Green closed his eyes and let their contentment wash over him, along with the scent of their lovemaking and the animal warmth of their happiness.

Goddess knew, that contentment wouldn't last long.

Green knew the moment she fell asleep—Bracken asked her about the ache in her chest after Gretchen's death, and in the long space of time it took her to formulate an answer, her eyes closed, and her breathing evened out, and then she was out.

That was the moment Green opened his eyes and put his hand under the supersized T-shirt she was wearing. His fingers skated the slickness of her thighs, the still quivering flesh of her mound, and then splayed, palm down, on the softness of her abdomen, right above her womb.

"Brack..." he whispered, and nodded to his hand, indicating with a nod that Bracken should do the same.

"What?" Brack looked back at him with those liquid-dark, unfathomable shadow-colored eyes, and then...

Bracken wasn't always quick, but he was nothing if not dependable.

"Fuck!" The oath was vicious and Green frowned at him.

"Don't get angry, brother, or she'll get cold," she was already beginning to shiver, "and wake up or we'll miss it."

Bracken closed his eyes, obviously mastering his emotions, and met Green's wise, calm gaze and nodded. "She's so small," he muttered, sliding his hand under her shirt until it rested next to and a little on top of Green's. "How will she carry…"

His eyes closed, as he felt it, the tiny life already dividing, a little magic bundle of cells and will and predestination, becoming… simply *becoming* under the flesh that was under his hand.

And then… oh… Green shivered with the delicious, powerful, cosmically amazing tingle of what happened next, and he was happy to find that this time was just as magical, just as sacred to him as when it had happened with his own seed earlier that afternoon.

Bracken's breath caught, and he threw back his head until his pale face was shining in the moonlight streaming through the window, and when the shiver passed through his body he let out his breath on a sob.

"Twins," he murmured, meeting Green's eyes again briefly before resting the agonized joy of his gaze on their beloved's face. She looked so serene in sleep, so much like a child herself—not at all like a woman who threatened to crack their world to the core, simply by taking her lovers into her body.

"How on earth will she carry our children?" Bracken whispered, mostly to himself but a little to Green.

"She overpowered our wills, brother," Green told him, interlacing their fingers as they still sat, feeling the miracle of creation under their fingertips. "That's our birth control right there, and she just… just asked us to abandon it…"

"I know how we knocked her up, Green," Bracken replied in an impatient hiss. "That's not what I was asking."

Green's hand tightened on Bracken's—his little brother, the last human sized child who had been raised at the hill, and his partner in keeping their beloved happy, healthy, and alive. "And I'm telling you, Bracken Brine. You know how she got my will to break?"

Brack shook his head.

"She promised me she would live."

Bracken's bright eyes met Green's and he lowered his cheek to Cory's T-shirt to wipe the tears off. "So, by the sheer force of her will then, right?"

Green nodded and moved his hand so he could stroke Bracken's hair. Bracken lowered his head onto Cory's stomach and wept there, much as Green had, in elation, in fear, in conflict. Green knew… oh Goddess, he knew the scalding thrill heaving its way through Bracken's tightened chest and throat right now. It had burned through Green as well.

"Her will is pretty formidable," Green whispered. "There's our hope, mate—have some faith in that."

"I guess if I need something to believe in…"

Green said it with him.

"It's her."

CORY

A Brand New Game

You can miss a lot when you're gone for a week.

Two weeks after…after our return from Redding, I sat in the living room looking at Leah the were-panther in silent horror, wondering why in the fuck she hadn't chosen to go to Green or Teague about this.

Okay, scratch that. Why she hadn't chosen to go to Green or Katy.

The werewolves were back and happily ensconced in their little house out in the yard—Green had seen that it got finished while they were away, and they had been happy to see it.

Of course they had been happy to see *us* after Teague called us in a panic because he was stuck in their little beach side cottage while Jack and Katy were off about to get the shit kicked out of them. Fortunately, Green knew more than one sylph with a helicopter, or that whole getting-my-throat-slit-for-a-friend would have been pretty fucking meaningless on the whole, and Jack's complete and total devotion to me and Green had become a little frightening ever since.

But seriously—Teague was an alpha, Katy was a woman… why would Leah think I was such good candidate for true-were-creature-confessions, the piss-your-leader-off version?

"Leah… you're pregnant?" I still don't see how that worked.

"Yeah—it's Timmy's…or maybe Danny's… you know, the two Avians who've wanted each other for, like, ever?"

I nodded blankly. Yeah, I knew. Green had been trying to fix them up with a sylph—one who wanted to be independent and who wanted to be a woman when she chose her gender in mating—to see if maybe a three-way binding would keep them from self-destructing when they bound to each other.

"I thought they were going to wait…"

"But they didn't *click* with any of those people!" Leah explained patiently, and I just looked at her with my mouth opening and closing like a fish.

"But there's no guarantee that you can carry their child!" I protested, because that was the crux of it, wasn't it?

"But see!" Leah crowed. "That's the beauty of it! Human women carry Avian children all the time—but they're still shapechangers. With any luck, I'll be able to carry their baby to term! And the next one too! And they can fuck each other's brains out, and I'll…" Her voice dropped. Leah was… well, in a hill full of creatures who thrived on sex and had no shame, she was one of the few who actually stood out for promiscuity. None of us judged her—sex was a lot of things to Leah, but a gift of undying, monogamous love was not among them.

"I'll have a home," she said at last, looking at me. "I'll have people who don't want me for sex, but who care about me. I can fuck anything that moves," her lips twisted up, "and I *have,* but…but now I'll have a little family inside my big one, you see?"

My indignation toned itself down a little. I guess of all of us, I was the *last* person to complain about someone who needed an unconventional family. But still…

"Oh Goddess, Leah," I groaned and flopped backwards on the couch. I wasn't feeling well. In my entire life I had never been the bizarre combination of queasy, exhausted and *starving* as I had been in the last week. I was so tired that I actually *fell asleep* on the helicopter on the way to Monterey to save Jack and Katy's asses. I'd never been in a helicopter—I mean, you'd think the novelty value alone would have kept me on my toes, right?

With an effort I pulled my mind off of a nap and put it where it belonged—on someone else's problems.

"The key word here is luck," I said, feeling like the world's biggest hypocrite. "You're placing everything—including Danny and Timmy's lives—on the luck of the Goddess." I sat up and put a comforting hand on her knee. "That's an awful responsibility, Leah, for someone who doesn't know whose bed she's going to wake up in tomorrow."

The Goddess was going to strike me down through the roof for saying this, I just knew it. Somewhere in the hill, I was sure I could hear Nicky (who had enjoyed his week at Eric's very much but who had been glad to get back in time for the kick-werewolf-ass action in Monterey) laughing his tail-feathers off.

"Well yeah, Lady Cory," Leah said, trying to look happy in spite of her hurt, "but isn't that just faith? You of all people should know that sometimes, faith's all you got."

I thought of Green and Bracken, who had been especially attentive in the last two weeks, and of Nicky, who had given up his family to be near us. I'd had faith in all of them—and they'd put up with my shit and my insecurities, and, especially, forgiven me for my risks, and my faith in our family had been rewarded.

I smiled gamely at Leah and reached out to hug her. "Congratulations, sweetheart," I said huskily, the weight of all the things that could go wrong with this event weighing heavily behind my eyes. "Make sure you see Green and Grace—they might be able to help things go well, right?"

Leah laughed, her bright brown eyes sparkling. I had to admit, pregnancy made her look fantastic—her long, dark hair was especially glossy and her oval-shaped, olive toned face was soft and glowing. "Thank you, Lady Cory—it's so good to know you're not mad."

How could I be mad? If this whole thing went south, how much would my saying "I told you this was fucked up" actually help things? I figured the deck was stacked against them enough—Leah needed to know the unconditional love of the hill was still with her.

"Never," I told her honestly, and she laughed and ran off—I would imagine to tell Danny and Timmy that they could move into the hill if they wanted. Now that they had bonded, they could (like Leah) fuck anything that moved and it wouldn't change their balance.

Of course, the only lover they'd ever really wanted was each other.

I sighed and thought about catching her to tell her that maybe we could give them the werewolves' old room, but it seemed like too much effort for the moment. I'd catch her later, I guess, but that didn't stop my complete envy over her spring and vitality. I seriously thought about curling up on the couch for yet another nap.

In my defense, I *had* been up late the night before. Not to feed Phillip—he seemed to be doing okay now. He and Marcus had a playmate of sorts, out at Clementine, a woman, and something about her seemed to be soothing their hearts. The other night I'd heard him tell Marcus to either grow breasts and lactate or to cut the cord and let him be, so I think he was at least to the point where he wanted to act like it was all good. We'd let him. We'd been there.

So Phillip wasn't the reason I was up, and neither was Tanya, who had moved in with the Avians but who still visited us when she could. She and

Mario hadn't made anything permanent (at least her boobs were still as small as mine) but... but the way they looked at each other seemed to be a lock.

No, this particular sleep hangover had been Sam, who had called to let us know that his mother had gone into rehab—and that he needed a place to stay. I'd spent two hours on the phone, arranging transportation and schooling and finding a spare room for the kid. We'd promised—and like Green said, it wasn't the massive measure of the promise, it was just how it was kept.

Of course that, and the fact that Grace's grandsons were here and insisted that every morning started at dawn didn't really help either. But I loved them—they were normalcy and sweetness and excitement. And Bracken and Green were nothing short of breathtaking when they were dealing with the boys. I loved watching that. Someday, they would make wonderful fathers.

This thought was interrupted when Bracken and Green came into the living room, shoulder to shoulder, from the hallway Leah had just disappeared into.

Something about their twin sober expressions and the similarity of their gait told me two things. One was that they'd been waiting for Leah to come out, and the other was that they had something they wanted to talk to me about.

"Where are the boys?" I asked, sitting up and trying to look healthy. I hadn't complained about the tiredness and the queasiness—I was still trying to make up for the night I saved Teague's life. Bracken's anger could still make me shiver, and reminding them that I was human wouldn't get me any points.

"Outside, playing with Arturo," Green informed me. For a moment they stood there, together, looking down at me studiously and I started to grow uneasy.

"What?" I asked, smiling at them tentatively. "Seriously—what did I do now?" I'd been very very careful in the last two weeks—I hadn't even ripped Bracken's face off when he'd stood in front of me during the Monterey op. I had, in fact, tried very very hard to never ever ever make them sorry they loved me, not even for a second, not even a little bit.

Because that thing that had changed, whatever it was, still scared me.

Green laughed a little and looked tired at the same time. Bracken scowled at me, but he, too, looked weary. They were elves—they needed no sleep and pretty much spontaneously regenerated any energy they lost. It occurred to me to wonder about whatever in the hell could make the two of them look exhausted. Together they sat down on the couch, one on either side of me, and put their hands on my thighs.

"Guys," I said, worried by now. "Seriously—what is it? You're starting to scare me. I mean… I've been good, right? I haven't taken any risks, I haven't gotten weepy about the shit I've had to do?" I had, in fact, been the model of emotional health, for someone who had spent a whole lot of time watching old *Supernatural* episodes and weeping copiously for no reason at all.

I looked at them helplessly. "I've been good…"

My voice trailed off, and Green took my chin in his hands.

"Yes, *ou'e'eir*, my *Anyaen.*"

Oh no… *Anyaen*…he never used that word… it was the one endearment he was afraid to use in front of Bracken because it was so… so all encompassing, and neither of us could be exclusive.

"*Anyaen?*" I squeaked. Oh Goddess… we were too far bound to have some sort of preternatural divorce, no matter *how* mad at me Bracken might be.

"Don't panic, beloved," Green said with a smile. "We just have some news for you, that's all."

"News…" I blinked, not panicking as he suggested. "Uhm… does it have anything to do with…" Oh. Crap. How do I say this? "I, uhm. You know. I lost control…" I blushed. "After we got back from Redding. Did…" more blushing, "did that bother you? I'm sorry. It was sort of an…" I quailed, because of all things, *this* seemed to be lightening the mood. "It was an emotional time," I finished in a small voice, and both of them smiled together, and rolled their eyes.

"Bracken?" I asked as a last resort.

Bracken snorted, the sound so normal and so a part of Bracken that I was reassured in spite of myself. Brack wouldn't sound like that if it really was something dire, right?

"I still don't see how she doesn't know," Bracken muttered to Green, shaking his head and stroking my thigh. Both actions were supremely gentle.

Green smiled—his kind, amazing smile, and replied, "The same way she's panicking about our love. She knows so much about the world, but not so very much about the magic going on in herself."

"Magic?" I said, calming down a little. I could deal with magic, and they both obviously still loved me, so this was something that we could handle together, right?

"Yes, beloved," Green murmured, putting his hand over my stomach. Bracken echoed the gesture, and their hands, warm, strong, and protective, cupped something inside of me I had not known was growing.

"Magic," Bracken finished for him, and then, together, they managed to tilt the universe on its axis and turn the world upside down on my head.